THE LYLE OFFICIAL ANTIQUES REVIEW 1990

THE

LYLE

OFFICIAL

ANTIQUES

REVIEW 1990

A PERIGEE BOOK

Perigee Books
are published by
The Putnam Publishing Group
200 Madison Avenue
New York, NY 10016

Printed in the United States of America
1 2 3 4 5 6 7 8 9 10

Introduction

This year over 100,000 Antique Dealers and Collectors will make full and profitable use of their Lyle Official Antiques Review. They know that only in this one volume will they find the widest possible variety of goods — illustrated, described and given a current market value to assist them to BUY RIGHT AND SELL RIGHT throughout the year of issue.

They know, too, that by building a collection of these immensely valuable volumes year by year, they will equip themselves with an unparalleled reference library of facts, figures and illustrations which, properly used, cannot fail to help them keep one step ahead of the market.

In its twenty years of publication, Lyle has gone from strength to strength and has become without doubt the pre-eminent book of reference for the antique trade throughout the world. Each of its fact filled pages are packed with precisely the kind of profitable information the professional Dealer needs — including descriptions, illustrations and values of thousands and thousands of individual items carefully selected to give a representative picture of the current market in antiques and collectibles — and remember all values are prices actually paid, based on accurate sales records in the twelve months prior to publication from the best established and most highly respected auction houses and retail outlets in Europe and America.

This is THE book for the Professional Antiques Dealer. 'The Lyle Book' — we've even heard it called 'The Dealer's Bible'.

Compiled and published afresh each year, the Lyle Official Antiques Review is the most comprehensive up-to-date antiques price guide available. THIS COULD BE YOUR WISEST INVESTMENT OF THE YEAR!

ANTHONY CURTIS

CONTENTS

11

Acknowledgements

Abbotts Auction Rooms, The Auction Rooms, Campsea Ashe, Woodbridge, Suffolk. 0728 746 323
Anderson & Garland, Anderson House, Market Street, Newcastle-upon-Tyne NE1 6XA. 091-232 6278
Bagshaws, 17 High Street, Uttoxeter. 0889 562811
Banks & Silvers, Fine Art Dept., 66 Foregate Street, Worcester. 0905 723686
Bearnes, Rainbow, Avenue Road, Torquay, Devon TQ2 5TG. 0803 296277
Biddle & Webb, Ladywood Middleway, Birmingham, B16 0PP. 021-455 8042
Blackhorse Agencies, 18 Guy Street, Leamington Spa. 0926 27988
Boardman, Fine Art Auctioneers, Station Road Corner, Haverhill, Suffolk CB9 0EY. 0440 84414
Bonhams, Montpelier Galleries, Montpelier Street, Knightsbridge, London SW7 1HH. 01-584 9161
Bonhams of Chelsea, 65-69 Lots Road, London SW10 0RN. 01-351 7111
Michael J. Bowman, 6 Haccombe House, near Netherton, Newton Abbott, Devon TQ12 4SJ. 0626 872890
Bracketts, 27-29 High Street, Tunbridge Wells, Kent TN1 1UU. 0892 33733
British Antique Exporters, 206 London Road, Burgess Hill, West Sussex RH15 9RX. 04446 245577
R. Brocklesbury, 8 Whites Road, Bitterne, Southampton SO2 7NQ.
Brogden & Co., 38 & 39 Silver Street, Lincoln LN2 1EM. 0522 531321
Graham Brierley/Brian Bates, 10 Madeley Street, Tunstall. 035 262403 and 0782 680667
Wm. H. Brown, Westgate Hall, Grantham, Lincolnshire NG31 6LT. 0476 68861
Lawrence Butler Fine Arts Salerooms, Marine Walk, Hythe, Kent CT21 5AJ. 0303 66022
Cantabrian Antiques, 16 Park Street, Linton, North Devon. 0598 53282
Capes Dunn & Co., The Auction Galleries, 38 Charles Street, Manchester M1 7DB. 061-273 1911
Chancellors Hollingsworth, 31 High Street, Ascot, Berkshire SL5 7HG. 0990 872588
H. C. Chapman & Son, The Auction Mart, North Street, Scarborough YO11 1DL. 0723 372424
Christie's, Cornelis Schuytstraat 57, 1071 JG, Amsterdam, Netherlands. (3120) 664 0899
Christie's (International) S.A., 8 Place de la Taconnerie, 1204 Geneva, Switzerland. (4122) 282544
Christie's (Hong Kong) Ltd., 3607 Edinburgh Tower, 15 Queens Road, Hong Kong. (5) 215 396
Christie's, 8 King Street, St James's, London SW1Y 6QT. 01-839 1611
Christie's (Monaco) S.A.M., Park Palace, 98000 Monte Carlo, Monaco. (3393) 25 19 33
Christie's, 502 Park Avenue, new York, NY 10022, USA. (212) 546 1000
Christie's, 219 East 67th Street, New York, NY 10021, USA. (212) 606 0400
Christie's Scotland, 164-166 Bath Street, Glasgow G2 4TG. 041-332 8134
Christie's South Kensington Ltd., 85 Old Brompton Road, London SW7 3LD. 01-581 7611
Chrystals Auctions, The Mart, Bowring Road, Ramsay, Isle of Man. 0624 73986
A. J. Cobern, The Grosvenor Salerooms, 93b Eastbank Street, Southport PR8 1DG. 0704 500515
Coles, Knapp & Kennedy, Georgian Rooms, Ross-on-Wye, Herefordshire HR9 5HL. 0989 63553
Bruce D. Collins, Fine Arts Gallery, Box 113, Denmark, Maine, USA. (207) 452 2197
Cooper Hirst, Goldlay House, Parkway, Chelmsford, Essex CM2 7PR. 0245 258141
Cooper & Tanner, 44a Commercial Road, Shepton Mallet, Somerset. 0749 2607/2624·
County Group, 102 High Street, Tenterden, Kent TN30 6AU. 05806 2083
The Crested China Co., The Station House, Driffield, East Yorkshire YO25 7PY. 0377 47042
Dacre, Son & Hartley, 1-5 The Grove, Ilkley, West Yorkshire LS29 8HS. 0943 816363
Dee & Atkinson, The Exchange Saleroom, Driffield, North Humberside, YO25 7LJ. 0373 43151
Dowell Lloyd & Co. Ltd., 118 Putney Bridge Road, Putney, London SW15 2NQ. 01-788 7777
Dreweatt Neate, Donnington Priory, Donnington, Newbury, Berkshire RG13 2JE. 0635 31234
Du Mouchelles Art Galleries Co., 409 E. Jefferson Avenue, Detroit, Michigan 48226, USA. (313) 963 0248
Hy Duke & Son, Fine Art Salerooms, Weymouth Avenue, Dorchester DT1 1DG. 0305 65080
Robt. C. Eldred Co. Inc., Route 6a (PO Box 796), East Dennis, MA 02641, USA. (508) 385 3116
Peter Eley, Western House, 98-100 High Street, Sidmouth, Devon EX10 8EF. 03955 2552/3
R. H. Ellis & Sons, 44/46 High Street, Worthing, West Sussex NB11 1LL. 0903 38999
Graham H. Evans, Auction Sales Centre, The Market Place, Kilgetty, Dyfed SA68 0UG. 0834 811151
Fellows & Sons, Bedford House, 88 Hagley Road, Edgbaston, Birmingham. 021-454 1261
John D. Fleming & Co., 8 Fore Street, Dulverton, Somerset.
John Francis, S.O.F.A.A., Chartered Surveyors, Curiosity Sale Rooms, King Street, Carmarthen. 0267 233456
Galerie Moderne, 3 Rue du Parnasse, Bruxelles, Belgium. (02) 513 9010
Geering & Colyer, 22/26 High Street, Tunbridge Wells, Kent TN1 1XA. 0892 515300
Geering & Colyer (Black Horse Agencies), Highgate, Hawkhurst, Kent TD18 4AD. 0580 753463

Glendinning's, Blenstock House, 7 Blenheim Street, New Bond Street, London W1Y 9LD. 01-629 6602
Goss & Crested China Co., 62 Murray Road, Horndean, Hampshire PO8 9JL. 0705 597440
Graves, Son & Pilcher, 71 Church Road, Hove, East Sussex BN3 2GL. 0273 735 266
W. R. J. Greenslade & Co., 13 Hammet Street, Taunton, Somerset TA1 1RN. 0823 277121
Habsburg Feldman SA, 202 rue du Grand-Lancy, 1213 Onex-Geneve, Switzerland.
Halifax Property Service, 53 High Street, Tenterden, Kent. 05806 2241
Halifax Property Services — St John Vaughan with John Hogbin, 53 High Street, Tenterden, Kent. 05806 3200
Hamptons Fine Art, 93 High Street, Godalming, Surrey. 048 68 23567
Giles Haywood, The Auction House, St John's Road, Stourbridge, West Midlands DY8 1EW. 0384 370891
Heatheringtons Nationwide, The Amersham Auction Rooms, 125 Station Road, Amersham, Bucks. 0494 729292
Andrew Hilditch & Son Ltd., 19 The Square, Sandbach, Cheshire CW11 0AT. 0270 762048
Hobbs & Chambers, 'At the Sign of the Bell', Market Place, Cirencester, Gloucestershire. 0285 4736
Hobbs Parker, Romney House, Ashford Market, Ashford, Kent TN23 1PG. 0233 22222
Jacobs & Hunt, Lavant Street, Petersfield, Hampshire GU32 3EF. 0730 62744/5
G. A. Key, Aylsham Salerooms, Palmers Lane, Aylsham, Norfolk NR11 6EH. 0263 733195
King & Chasemore, (Nationwide Anglia) West Street, Midhurst, West Sussex GU29 9NG. 073081 2456/7/8
Lalonde Fine Art (Prudential Bristol), 71 Oakfield Road, Clifton, Bristol, Avon BS8 2BE. 0272 73402
Lambert & Foster (County Group), The Auction Sale Rooms, 102 High Street, Tenterden. 05806 3233/3921
W. H. Lane & Son, Fine Art Auctioneer & Valuers, 64 Morrab Road, Penzance, Cornwall. 0736 61447
Langlois Ltd., Westaway Rooms, Don Street, St Helier, Jersey, Channel Islands. (0534) 22441
Lawrence Fine Art, South Street, Crewkerne, Somerset TA18 8AB. 0460 73041
Lawrence's, Fine Art Auctioneers, Norfolk House, 80 High Street, Bletchingley, Surrey. 0883 843323
David Lay, The Penzance Auction House, Alverton, Penzance, Cornwall TR18 4RE. 0736 61414
Locke & England, Walton House, 11 The Parade, Leamington Spa. 0926 27988
Lots Road Chelsea Auction Galleries, 71 Lots Road, Chelsea, London SW10 0RN. 01-351 7771
Michael G. Matthews, The Devon Fine Art Auction House, Dowel Street, Honiton, Devon. 0404 41872
McKenna's Auctioneers & Valuers, Bank Salerooms, Harris Court, Clitheroe, Lancashire. 0200 25446
Miller & Company, Lemon Quay Auction Rooms, Truro, Cornwall TR1 2LW. 0872 74211
Moore, Allen & Innocent, 33 Castle Street, Cirencester, Gloucestershire GL7 1QD. 0285 61831
Morphets, 4-6 Albert Street, Harrogate, North Yorkshire HG1 1JL. 0423 530030
D. M. Nesbit & Co., 7 Clarendon Road, Southsea, Hampshire PO5 2ED. 0705 864321
Michael Newman, The Central Auction Rooms, St Andrews Cross, Plymouth PL1 3DG.0752 669298
James Norwich Auctions Ltd., Head Office, 33 Timberhill, Norwich, Norfolk NR1 3LA. 0603 624817
Onslow's, Metrostore, Sands Wharf, Townmead Road, London SW6 2RZ. 01-793 0240
Osmond Tricks, Regent Street Auction Rooms, Clifton, Bristol, Avon BS8 4HG. 0272 737201
Outhwaite & Litherland, "Kingsway Galleries", Fontenoy Street, Liverpool, Merseyside L3 2BE. 051-236 6561
J. R. Parkinson Son & Hamer Auctions, The Auction Room, Rochdale Road, Bury, Lancashire. 061-761 1612
Phillips, 65 George Street, Edinburgh EH2 2JL. 031-225 2266
Phillips, 207 Bath Street, Glasgow G2 4DH. 041-221 8377
Phillips, Blenstock House, 7 Blenheim Street, New Bond Street, London W1Y 0AS. 01-629 6602
Phillips New York, 406 East 79th Street, New York, NY 10021, USA. (212) 570 4830
Phillips West Two, 10 Salem Road, London W2 4BU. 01-229 9090
Prudential Fine Art Auctioneers, Trinity House, 114 Northenden Road, Sale, Manchester. 061-962 9237
Prudential Fine Art Auctioneers, 71 Oakfield Road, Bristol. 0272 734052
Prudential Fine Art Auctioneers, 13 Lime Tree Walk, Sevenoaks, Kent. 0732 740310
Reeds Rains Prudential, Trinity House, 114 Northenden Road, Manchester M33 3HD. 061-962 9237
Rennie's, 1 Agincourt Street, Monmouth. 0600 2916
Riddetts of Bournemouth, Richmond Hill, Bournemouth. 0202 25686
Rosebery's Fine Art Ltd., 3 & 4 Hardwicke Street, London EC1R 4RB. 01-837 3418
Russell, Baldwin & Bright, The Fine Art Saleroom, Ryelands Road, Leominster HR6 8JG. 0497 820622
Sandoe Luce Panes, Wotton Auction Rooms, Wotton-under-Edge, Gloucestershire GL12 7EB. 0453 844733
Robt. W. Skinner Inc., Bolton Gallery, Route 117, Bolton, Massachusetts, USA. (617) 236 1700
Southgate Antique Auction Rooms, Rear of Town Hall, Green Lanes, Palmers Green, London N13. 01-886 7888
Henry Spencer & Sons, 20 The Square, Retford, Nottinghamshire DN22 6DJ. 0777 708633
Stephenson & Son, 20 Castlegate, York YO1 1RT. 0904 625533
Street Jewellery, 16 Eastcliffe Avenue, Newcastle-upon-Tyne NE3 4SN. 091-232 2255
G. E. Sworder & Sons, Northgate End Salerooms, 15 Northgate End, Bishops Stortford, Herts. 0279 651388
Taviner's of Bristol, Prewett Street, Redcliffe, Bristol BS1 6PB. 0272 265996
Tennants of Yorkshire, Old Chapel Saleroom, Market Place, Richmond, N. Yorkshire. 0969 23780
Thomson Roddick & Laurie, 60 Whitesands, Dumfries. 0387 55366
Tiffen King Nicholson, 12 Lowther Street, Carlisle, Cumbria CA3 8DA. 0228 25259
Duncan Vincent Fine Art & Chattel Auctioneers, 105 London Street, Reading RG1 4LF. 0734 589502
Wallis & Wallis, West Street Auction Galleries, West Street, Lewes, East Sussex BN7 2NJ. 0273 480208
Peter Wilson Fine Art Auctioneers, Victoria Gallery, Market Street, Nantwich, Cheshire. 0270 623878
H. C. Wolton & Son, 6 Whiting Street, Bury St Edmunds. 0284 61336
Woolley & Wallis, The Castle Auction Mart, Salisbury, Wiltshire SP1 3SU. 0722 411422

ANTIQUES
REVIEW 1990

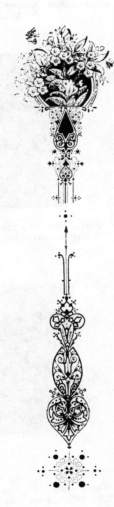

THE Lyle Official Antiques Review is compiled and published with completely fresh information annually, enabling you to begin each new year with an up-to-date knowledge of the current trends, together with the verified values of antiques of all descriptions.

We have endeavoured to obtain a balance between the more expensive collector's items and those which, although not in their true sense antiques, are handled daily by the antiques trade.

The illustrations and prices in the following sections have been arranged to make it easy for the reader to assess the period and value of all items with speed.

You will find illustrations for almost every category of antique and curio, together with a corresponding price collated during the last twelve months, from the auction rooms and retail outlets of the major trading countries.

When dealing with the more popular trade pieces, in some instances, a calculation of an average price has been estimated from the varying accounts researched.

As regards prices, when 'one of a pair' is given in the description the price quoted is for a pair and so that we can make maximum use of the available space it is generally considered that one illustration is sufficient.

It will be noted that in some descriptions taken directly from sales catalogues originating from many different countries, terms such as bureau, secretary and davenport are used in a broader sense than is customary, but in all cases the term used is self explanatory.

A rare advertising plaque by
Mayer, printed in the style
of Pratt, 'Rowland's Kalydor
for the complexion',
6 x 8½in. (David Lay)
$3,167

Faulkner's Sweet Rosemary
Empire Grown Tobacco, prin-
ted tin sign, 22 x 43cm.
(Onslow's) $51

Enamel sign for Motorine
Motor Oil, for longer, smoother,
easier running. (Onslow's)
$262

Wincarnis, 'The World's
Greatest Wine Tonic and Nerve
Restorative', 72 x 40in. (Street
Jewellery) $875

Aladdin Liquid Metal Polish,
'Shines Brightest and Longest',
36 x 24in. (Street Jewellery)
$262

Quaker Oats, 40 x 26in.
(Street Jewellery) $612

Chocolat Menier 'Eviter Les
Contrefacons', 24 x 10in.
(Street Jewellery)$437

Leica advertising poster,
27 x 34in., titled 'Leica',
showing cutaway views of a
Leica camera and a Hektor
f 1.9 7.3cm. lens, 1930's.
(Christie's) $231

Thorley's Food for Pigs,
28 x 18in. (Street Jewellery)
$175

Photographic advertisement for Continental Tyres featuring Boillot, winner of the Grand Prix, 1912. (Onslow's) $3,850

Nugget Boot Polish, tinplate counter display. (Onslow's) $129

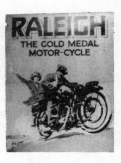

Enamel sign for Raleigh, The Gold Medal Motor-Cycle. (Onslow's) $1,312

Enamel advertising sign, Good Year tyres. (Millers) $157

Painted and decorated trade sign, signed 'T. M. Woodward', Worcester, Massachusetts, circa 1873, the rectangular bowed metal panel painted dark green and decorated in polychrome, 48in. high. (Robt. W. Skinner Inc.)$40,000

R. Geri, 'Exide The Long Life Battery', showcard, 30 x 22in. (Onslow's) $90

Zebra Grate Polish, 36 x 24in. (Street Jewellery) $350

Fry's 'Five Boys' Chocolate, 24 x 36in. (Street Jewellery) $612

Enamel sign for Texaco Motor Oil, Drain, Flush and Refill. (Onslow's) $437

After Gamy, 'Garros Gagne Le Grand Prix de L'Aero Club sur Monoplan Bleriot'. (Onslow's) $540

Flying scale model Puss Moth Monoplane, built by International Model Aircraft Ltd., in original box. (Onslow's) $270

C. H. Richardson, 'Spirit of St Louis', oil on board, signed, 43 x 62in. (Onslow's) $1,980

'S. E. Cody, F.R.M.S. of Texas, U.S.A. Inventor Of The Famous War Kite', color lithograph poster, by David Allen & Sons, Belfast, 30 x 20in. (Christie's) $344

An embroidered heavy silk banner of the Escadrille Lafayette Old Comrade Association, with tri-color and French Air Force roundel, framed, 37 x 39in.(Christie's) $1,720

T. L. Jouejelan, an Edwardian aviatrix in her Bleriot-type monoplane, color lithograph, indistinctly signed, 16½x11in. (Christie's) $404

A World War II German airman's watch in gray painted case, the matt gray dial with luminous hands and Arabic numerals. (Christie's) $1,416

Robert Taylor, Spitfire VB's just airborne for a sortie, Wing Cmdr. Robert Stanford Tuck leading 401 Squadron from Biggin Hill, circa 1941, signed and dated '81, unframed, 28 x 42in. (Christie's) $9,108

A 1-72 scale aluminium model of a Flying Fortress B17G, 9in. high. (Christie's) $1,113

J. Thompson, Three Spitfires from 602 Squadron, 'City of Glasgow' in the clouds, oil on canvas, signed and dated '86, 24 x 36in. (Christie's) **$1,012**

A chromium plated Avro Tutor biplane, circa 1930, 5½in. long. (Christie's) **$363**

Dion Pears, Lancaster limping home with Spitfire escort, oil on canvas, signed, 24 x 36in. (Christie's) **$526**

Desmond Nicholas, Boulton Paul P. 29 Sidestrand III in the clouds, watercolor, signed, 14¾ x 10½in. (Christie's) **$222**

'Defense Bonds Stamps', a colored World War II American publicity poster, 14 x 10in. (Christie's) **$90**

P. Melville, Packard-Le Pere Lusac above clouds, watercolor, signed and inscribed 'To Leonard Bridgman' and dated '23, 13½x8¼in. (Christie's) **$647**

Amy Polish, an unopened tin, produced by Amy Associates, Keswick Road, London SW15, 5in. high. (Onslow's) **$216**

Aeroplanes Bleriot, color lithograph poster depicting a Bleriot monoplane. inscribed G. Borel & Cie, 25 Rue Brunel Paris, 29¾ x 39in. (Christie's) **$404**

A chromium plated and enamelled Aero-Club Brooklands badge, stamped 164, 3¾in. high. (Onslow's) **$1,710**

An alabaster figure of a girl, carrying water pitchers, leaning against stone trough, signed Mozzanti, B, Florence, 62cm. high. (Phillips)
$1,496

A late 16th century Milanese pink alabaster and white marble figure of Christ lying on his shroud, attributed to Allesandro Masnago, 36cm. wide. (Phillips)
$2,275

A carved alabaster bust of a curly-haired young man in the neo-Classical style, eyes incised, on turned socle, 58cm. high. (Phillips) $1,662

An early 20th century Florentine colored alabaster bust, probably of Beatrice, from the workshop of Vichi, 11in. high. (Christie's)
$770

A late 19th century alabaster portrait bust of Joan of Arc, wearing a laced-up bodice, signed F. Guerrieri, 39in. high. (Christie's) $673

A sculpted alabaster bust of a young woman, a scarf around her head, 13½in. high, on a stepped base. (Christie's)
$437

An Italian alabaster lamp carved from a model by G. Gamboni as a mediaeval maiden in pleated robe, 32½in. high. (Christie's) $1,790

A pair of 19th century alabaster figures of classical maidens wearing flowing dresses, 21in. (Woolley & Wallis) $899

The Mermaid, a carved alabaster figure of a mermaid, by Sven Berlin, 24in. high. (Bearne's)
$2,904

AMERICAN INDIAN ART

Plateau American Indian beaded flatbag, white ground, red and blue abstract floral design, circa 1940-1950, 12 x 13in. (Du Mouchelles) $150

American South West Indian figural rug, white ground depicting Indian hunter with a deer, a monkey and a squirrel, 6ft.4in. x 4ft.8in. (Du Mouchelles) $700

Plateau American Indian beaded flatbag, blue ground, one side with crossing American flags, the verso with flower and bird, beaded strap, circa 1930, 7 x 9in. (Du Mouchelles) $400

American South West Indian runner, red ground having square and triangular medallions linked in barber pole fashion, 5ft. x 2ft. (Du Mouchelles) $300

Arapaho American Indian wood quirt with brass tacks, horsehair and beaded suspension, leather suspension at opposite end, circa 1910. (Du Mouchelles) $200

American Indian contemporary San Carlos design Apache vase by Manna, 17in. high. (Du Mouchelles) $300

American Indian Flathead tribe elk hide dress, circa 1930-40, red and black beadwork at top, with fringe, 49in. high. (Du Mouchelles) $400

Navajo striped Indian rug, circa 1900, vibrantly colored stripes of brick red, gray, bittersweet and black, 3ft.2in. x 4ft.6in. (Du Mouchelles) $550

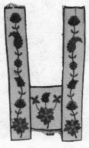

An American Indian beaded martingale from the Nez Perce tribe, with white ground, floral design and bells at bottom, circa 1910, 33in. high.(Christie's) $900

Nez Perce American Indian beaded stroud cradle hood cover, blue ground with colorful beaded sprays, red yarn fringe, demi-lune shape, 12 x 14in. (Du Mouchelles) $325

American South West Indian figural blanket, eagle attacking a serpent design in orange, black, brown, and yellow against white, 4ft. x 6ft.6in. (Du Mouchelles) $700

North Eastern American Indian water drum, wood with hide, black band decoration, circa 1900, 9in. high, 11in. diam. (Du Mouchelles) $95

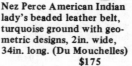

Plains Indian elk hide beaded lady's moccasins, circa 1900, 9½in. long. (Du Mouchelles) $85

Nez Perce American Indian lady's beaded leather belt, turquoise ground with geometric designs, 2in. wide, 34in. long. (Du Mouchelles) $175

A pair of American Indian Flathead tribe gauntlets, elk hide with yellow ochre, beaded floral design, 15in. long. (Du Mouchelles) $100

American South West Indian blanket, ivory ground having red, blue, green, wine, orange, yellow and black geometric clusters, 3ft.10in. x 6ft.4in. (Du Mouchelles) $200

American South West Indian rug, red ground with diamond design in center, 6ft. x 3ft2in. (Du Mouchelles) $700

Navajo blanket with a chocolate ground, lightning and zigzag designs in peach, ruby, tan and gray, 6ft.9in x 4ft. (Du Mouchelles) $1,000

AMUSEMENT MACHINES

Alwin de Luxe, British, 1935. (Brierley/Bates) $350

Bonanza Jackpot, Thompson, British, 1928.(Brierley/Bates) $875

Bryan's Fruit Bowl, British, 1960's. (Brierley/Bates) $280

Mills Extraordinary, USA, 1933. (Brierley/Bates) $525

Roulette Visible, Buzzoz, France, 1932. (Brierley/Bates) $875

'Beat the Goalie', British, 1933. (Brierley/Bates) $875

Circle Skill, British, 1928. (Brierley/Bates) $481

British version of Caille Pinwheel, Bollands, 1935. (Brierley/Bates)$656

British version of Mills Pinwheel, Clemence, 1935. (Brierley/Bates)$656

One of a set of six wrought iron balconettes. (Cantabrian Antiques) Six $1,200

A pair of Victorian terracotta garden urns, with leaf tip molded everted rims, raised upon waisted fluted cylindrical stems and panelled square socles, 70cm. diam. (Henry Spencer) $1,038

Corner basin on a decorative cast iron bracket, complete with taps. (Cantabrian Antiques) $400

Late Victorian cast iron fire place with swag motif and tiled splays. (Cantabrian Antiques) $960

Decorative cast iron wall fountain, dated 1873, 33in. wide, 66in. tall. (Cantabrian Antiques) $2,160

An ornately carved Victorian oak chimneypiece, decorated with ribbons, masks, flowers and fruit. (Cantabrian Antiques) $2,160

One of a set of four heavy cast iron garden chairs on cabriole legs. (Cantabrian Antiques)   Four $720

A fine pair of decorative cast iron brackets, with dragon supports, 15 x 18in. (Cantabrian Antiques) $320

One of a pair of very ornate etched plate glass door panels. (Cantabrian Antiques)   Two $400

ARCHITECTURAL FURNISHINGS

19th century washbasin with decorative splashback, shell-shaped soap trays and porcelain headed brass taps, 24in. across. (Cantabrian Antiques) $320

Pair of heavy Shanks' Deco style bath taps, with porcelain 'hot' and 'cold' tops. (Cantabrian Antiques) $120

Late 19th century roll-top cast iron bath with ball and claw feet. (Cantabrian Antiques) $360

Victorian finely carved oak chimneypiece, with grotesque masks on the capitals. (Cantabrian Antiques) $2,160

One of a pair of white painted cast iron conservatory plant stands, each with scroll edged vertical frame supporting five pierced circular plateaux, 104cm. high. (Henry Spencer) Two $484

Unusual 19th century polished steel register plate with shell motifs. (Cantabrian Antiques) $1,000

Typical late Victorian fireplace in white marble, with cast iron grate having splays of tiles depicting musical instruments. (Cantabrian Antiques) $1,400

A finely molded toilet decorated with roses and a border of blue on a white background. (Cantabrian Antiques) $400

One of a set of twenty oak mullioned windows of assorted sizes. (Cantabrian Antiques) Twenty $5,600

ARMOR

A Maximilian gauntlet, circa 1520, separate hinged thumb-piece, roped cuff. (Wallis & Wallis) $661

A pair of tassets from a late 16th century black & white armor , each of 7 lames. (Wallis & Wallis) $510

A German codpiece probably from a black and white armor , of bright steel, traces of tinning inside, mid 16th century, 6in. high. (Christie's) $2,032

A Cromwellian pikeman's armor , comprising: pot with two-piece skull of crude construction with turned rim, breastplate of peascod form with medial ridge. (Phillips) $972

An attractive Persian Qjar 19th century matching kulah khud, dhal and bazu band, the kulah khud skull of one piece, embos-sed with four human faces in relief within radial suns, chisel-led overall with flowers. (Wallis & Wallis) $1,575

An important suit of early 17th century Japanese black lacquered metal armor , circa 1620. (Prudential)
          $10,919

An etched Italian gothic pauldron for the right shoulder, of bright steel, covering the outside and back, the top-plate pierced with point holes, circa 1510. (Christie's) $2,400

A breast plate for a Knight of Malta in mid 16th century style, roped neck and articulated arm cusps, vertically ribbed ensuite with two lower plates and first skirt plate. (Wallis & Wallis)
          $1,440

An English Cromwellian period breast and backplate, struck with Commonwealth armorer's company mark of helmet over "A", maker's initials "F.O." (Wallis & Wallis) $1,050

ARMOR

A pair of spaulders from a late 16th century German Infantry Armor . (Wallis & Wallis) $302

A reinforcing bevor, made to fit over the side-bolts, the bands decorated with flowers, scrolls and leaves on a granular ground, mid 16th century, 11½in. (Christie's) $554

A well made Victorian copy of a Maximilian fluted and articulated right hand gauntlet, cuff with hinged plate. (Wallis & Wallis) $569

A good 17th/18th century Southern Indian chiselled steel armguard bazu-band, 14in. of polygonal form chiselled with bands of foliage in relief. (Wallis & Wallis) $216

A good French Guard Cuirassier officer's helmet and companion breast and back-plate, circa 1870, helmet with plated skull and large gilt comb with Medusa mask. (Wallis & Wallis) $4,325

A composite cuirassier's armor comprising: close helmet and large gorget plates, breast and backplate, mainly 17th century with Victorian and later elements. (Phillips) $3,380

A Cromwellian trooper's breast and backplate, breastplate with medial ridge, backplate struck with Commonwealth armorer's mark of helmet over "A" (Wallis & Wallis) $1,800

An English Cromwellian period trooper's gorget, intended to be worn over a buff coat, made in two parts. (Wallis & Wallis) $665

A well made Edwardian part suit of armor in the Milanese style comprising high peaked morion, breastplate, deep gorget, and articulated gauntlets. (Wallis & Wallis) $712

DAGGERS

A good Khanjar, 33cm. double fullered blade, jade hilt carved overall with foliage, contained in its leather scabbard. (Phillips)
$980

A Mondjembo (Ndjembo) chieftain's knife, 19½in., blade with ring shaped bifurcated tip 14¼in. with chiselled decoration. (Wallis & Wallis) $360

A Khanjar, 23.5cm. watered blade with twin fullers and reinforced point chiselled at the forte, the jade hilt lightly carved with leaves and decorated with native cut diamonds and cabochon rubies set in gold. (Phillips) $809

A rare Nazi Diplomat's dagger by Eickhorn, blade retaining some original polish, plated mounts. (Wallis & Wallis) $2,162

A late 19th century Indian combination Bowie knife, clipped back blade 8½in., damascened with 2 tigers and antelope, with stipple engraved foliage on reverse. (Wallis & Wallis) $540

A large Arab silver mounted Jambiya, 18in., blade 8¼in. with raised central rib, hilt and sheath of Eastern silver covered with silver wire. (Wallis & Wallis) $594

A gold damascened Indian thrusting dagger Katar, circa 1800, 19in., broad finely watered blade 10in., with swollen tip. (Wallis & Wallis) $178 £100

A silver mounted Bade bade, slim iron blade 7½in., foliate carved "tulip" horn hilt, in its wooden sheath with Eastern sheet silver foliate embossed mounts. (Wallis & Wallis) $126

DAGGERS

A well made Indo Persian dagger Kard, circa 1800, watered steel blade 8in., floral and foliate gold damascened bolsters and gripstrap. (Wallis & Wallis) $207

An attractive Nepalese silver mounted Kukri, blade 10¼in., polished with a little chiselled and brass inlaid decoration, one piece horn hilt. (Wallis & Wallis) $378

A Scottish silver mounted regimental dirk, the 30.5cm. blade by Brook & Son, George Street, Edinburgh, with faceted back edge, etched with scrolls and regimental badges, hallmarked Edinburgh, 1900. (Phillips) $1,521

An attractive gold mounted Kukri, blade 13in., horn hilt with gold ferule, in its black leather sheath with pierced gold mounts. (Wallis & Wallis) $648

A good late 19th century Russian silver mounted Kindjal, broad polished fullered blade 13in. with small signature. (Wallis & Wallis) $616

A Nazi army officer's dagger, by Luneschloss, plated mounts, white grip, bullion dress knot, in its plated sheath. (Wallis & Wallis) $188

An Indian 19th century Moghul jade hilted dagger Khanjar. curved watered blade 8½ in. (Wallis & Wallis) $1,246

A 1st Pattern F.S. fighting knife, blade 6½in. by Wilkinson Sword, also marked at forte "The FS Fighting Knife" plated hilt, reversed crosspiece diced grip. (Wallis & Wallis) $360

DAGGERS

A scarce 1st Pattern fighting knife, blade 6½in., etched at forte "The F.S. Fighting Knife", by Wilkinson Sword. (Wallis & Wallis) $396

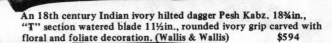

An 18th century Indian ivory hilted dagger Pesh Kabz, 18¾in., "T" section watered blade 11½in., rounded ivory grip carved with floral and foliate decoration. (Wallis & Wallis) $594

A good Victorian Bowie knife, clipped back blade 6¾in., by John Piggott Cheapside E.C., also marked at forte "Warranted Really Good". (Wallis & Wallis) $171

An Italian late 17th century gunner's stiletto, triangular section blade 11¼in. engraved with Cattaneo's scale from 1 to 120. (Wallis & Wallis) $534

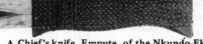

A Chief's knife, Empute, of the Nkundo-Ekonda tribe of the Central Basin of Zaire, broad blade 12¾ x 3¼in. at widest. (Wallis & Wallis) $252

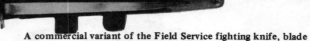

A commercial variant of the Field Service fighting knife, blade 6½in., with darkened finish, oval steel guard. (Wallis & Wallis) $144

An unusual silver mounted satanic dagger, 17cm. diamond section blade, the silver hilt modelled as the figure of Death clasping a victim in his arms and standing on the body of a naked woman which forms the crossguard. (Phillips) $670

A 19th century Indian Bowie style hunting knife, clipped back blade 9in., copper gilt hilt, crosspiece and sheath engraved overall with flowers and foliage. (Wallis & Wallis) $207

A 17th century Southern Indian Katar, double edged fullered blade 14½in. with chiselled forte and swollen tip, steel hilt with sail shaped guard chiselled with flowers and foliage. (Wallis & Wallis) $774

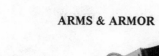

A good Nazi dagger, by "Remscheid Remue", blade retaining much original polish. (Wallis & Wallis) $222

A good Georgian officer's naval dirk, circa 1800, tapering flattened diamond section blade 8½in., retaining most blued and gilt etched decoration. (Wallis & Wallis) $640

A Scottish regimental dirk, 30.5cm blade by S.J.Pillin with faceted back edge, etched with scrolls and regimental badges and mottos of the Argyll and Sutherland Highlanders. (Phillips) $1,006

A good Nazi naval officer's dirk, by Horster, blade retaining all original polish, etched with fouled anchor, entwined dolphins and foliage. (Wallis & Wallis) $307

An all steel dagger stiletto, circa 1700, hollow ground triangular section blade 8¼in., nicely baluster turned steel crosspiece and grip. (Wallis & Wallis) $288

A Victorian bowie style hunting knife, clipped back blade 7in. stamped "Joseph Rodgers & Sons, 6 Norfolk Street, Sheffield England". (Wallis & Wallis) $198

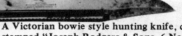

A Nazi Wehrmacht dress bayonet, plated blade 9½in., by Robert Klaas, etched with "Zur Erinnerung an Meine Dienstzeit". (Wallis & Wallis) $80

An attractive 19th century Ottoman Turkish silver mounted dagger bichaq, 14in., blade 9in., brass inlaid for full length with inscription. (Wallis & Wallis) $252

A second pattern Nazi Luftwaffe officer's dagger, gray metal mounts, wire bound yellow grip, original bullion dress knot. (Wallis & Wallis) $231

FLASKS

An unusually small bag shaped copper pistol flask 3in. steel ring on base, brass top with graduated charger. (Wallis & Wallis) $198

A good Persian tooled leather lacquered powder flask 11in., sides finely tooled with lions in relief. (Wallis & Wallis) . $83

A U.S. Revolutionary War period cow horn powder flask, 12in. overall, engraved "Liberty & Property" beneath tree. (Wallis & Wallis) $484

A very finely engraved polished staghorn powder flask, circa 1600, 5½in. engraved with a seated figure between a harpist with two maidens. (Wallis & Wallis) $472

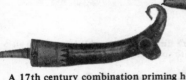

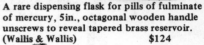

A 17th century combination priming horn, wheellock spanner and tinder lighter, 6in., body of chamois horn, fixed brass nozzle. (Wallis & Wallis) $222

A rare dispensing flask for pills of fulminate of mercury, 5in., octagonal wooden handle unscrews to reveal tapered brass reservoir. (Wallis & Wallis) $124

A 17th century staghorn powder flask, 8in., body engraved with a man and woman standing together in contemporary costume. (Wallis & Wallis) $540

A fine mid 19th century Afridi tribe powder horn from the North West Frontier, 9in. of polished horn. (Wallis & Wallis) $283

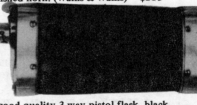

A good copper powder flask, 8¼in., embossed with 3 horses' heads, stamped "G. & J. W. Hawksley Sheffield". (Wallis & Wallis) $133

A good quality 3 way pistol flask, black leather covered body made by James Dixon and Sons, graduated charger. (Wallis & Wallis) $160

GUN LOCKS

A scarce detached Scandinavian flintlock lock, circa 1650, 7 in. engraved with perched bird and foliage. (Wallis & Wallis) $356

A scarce English detached matchlock lock from a musket, circa 1680, slightly rounded lockplate. (Wallis & Wallis) $453

A detached Scandinavian flintlock lock, circa 1650, 7¾in., mainspring acts on toe of hammer. (Wallis & Wallis) $356

A rare Continental military style detached self priming pill lock from a musket, 6¼in., pill reservoir with screw on stopper. (Wallis & Wallis) $391

An unusual detached flintlock lock, probably provincial Italian, circa 1700, 6¾in., tail chiselled with animal's head, plate with reclining figure. (Wallis & Wallis) $320

A scarce detached English dog lock from a flintlock musket, circa 1650, 8½in. horizontally acting scear, swivel dog safety catch, (Wallis & Wallis) $373

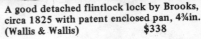

An unusual detached double flintlock lock, for use on a gun with 2 charges in the same barrel, probably early 18th century. (Wallis & Wallis) $338

A good detached flintlock lock by Brooks, circa 1825 with patent enclosed pan, 4¾in. (Wallis & Wallis) $338

A detached Italian snaphaunce gun lock, circa 1675, 6¼in., plate chiselled with figure, scrollwork and stylized face on tail in relief. (Wallis & Wallis) $284

A rare detached snap matchlock lock, circa 1600, plate 8 in., struck with maker's initials "H.M." within rectangle. (Wallis & Wallis) $410

HELMETS

A fine Prussian General Staff officer's Pickelhaube, silvered Guard helmet plate, with enamelled center to Guard star. (Wallis & Wallis) $2,076

A good Prussian Reservist Jager officer's shako, gilt shako plate with Landwehr cross. (Wallis & Wallis) $692

A good Wurttemberg Reservist Artillery officer's Pickelhaube, gilt helmet plate, gilt leather backed chinscales and mounts. (Wallis & Wallis) $735

A Wurttemberg infantryman's ersatz (pressed tin) Pickelhaube, gilt helmet plate, brass mounts with traces of gilt. (Wallis & Wallis) $409

An Edward VII officer's lancecap of the East Riding of Yorkshire Imperial Yeomanry, black patent leather skull and top. (Wallis & Wallis) $2,595

A fine Prussian Telegraph Company officer's Pickelhaube, fine gilt helmet plate of Line Eagle. (Wallis & Wallis) $605

A good Imperial German officer's Pickelhaube of the 94th Infantry Regt., arms of Saxe Weimar in white metal to gilt helmet plate. (Wallis & Wallis) $1,470

A fine Imperial German Wurttemberg General officer's Pickelhaube, with gilt and enamel star of the Order of the Wurttemberg crown. (Wallis & Wallis) $2,508

A fine Imperial German officer's Pickelhaube of a Reservist in the 1st or 2nd Battalion, Brunswick Infantry Regiment. (Wallis & Wallis) $2,076

HELMETS

A fine Imperial German officer's Pickelhaube of an Adjutant of the Lippe Detmold Infantry Regt. (Wallis & Wallis) $2,941

A good Imperial German officer's shako of the 14th Jager Battalion, silvered state arms upon gilt rayed star shako plate. (Wallis & Wallis) $865

A good Imperial German Artillery officer's Pickelhaube as worn by the 10th and 46th Field Artillery Regts. (Wallis & Wallis) $735

A good Prussian military official's Pickelhaube, fine gilt Line Eagle helmet plate, gilt leather backed chinscales and mounts. (Wallis & Wallis) $648

A rare Imperial German Garde du Corps Parade helmet, tombak skull with German silver mounts. (Wallis & Wallis) $10,034

A good Imperial German Mecklenburg Dragoon officer's Pickelhaube, gilt star helmet plate with white metal state arms. (Wallis & Wallis) $562

A fine and rare officer's Pickelhaube of the 1st Grand Ducal Hessian (Leibgarde) Infantry No. 115. (Wallis & Wallis) $4,325

A fine Bavarian Chevauleger Reservist officer's Pickelhaube, fine gilt helmet plate, leather backed chinscales and mounts. (Wallis & Wallis) $951

A fine Imperial German Reservist officer's Pickelhaube of the 2nd Battalion of the 96th Infantry Regt. (Wallis & Wallis) $2,941

35

An officer's blue cloth helmet of the Royal Army Medical Corps by J. B. Johnstone, Sackville Street London. (Christie's) $353

A good late 16th century Spanish morion, forged from one piece, of classic form with tall comb. (Wallis & Wallis) $1,557

A fine Imperial German officer's Pickelhaube of a Reservist officer in the 92nd Infantry Regt. (Brunswick) 3rd Battalion. (Wallis & Wallis) $1,903

A good Imperial German Hesse Reservist Infantry officer's Pickelhaube, gilt helmet plate with Landwehr cross. (Wallis & Wallis) $1,211

A rare Imperial German Colonial Garde Infantry officer's Pickelhaube, with gilt spike and gilt Garde eagle helmet plate. (Wallis & Wallis) $2,076

A fine Imperial German officer's Pickelhaube of the 109th Baden Leib Regiment. (Wallis & Wallis) $1,211

A scarce officer's 1878 pattern blue cloth spiked helmet of The 59th (2nd Nottinghamshire) Regiment. (Wallis & Wallis) $657

A Cabasset, circa 1600, formed in one piece with pear stalk finial, brass rosettes around base, the brim with traces of armorer's mark. (Wallis & Wallis) $320

A Victorian officer's blue cloth spiked helmet of the 5th Volunteer Battalion, The Royal Scots. (Wallis & Wallis) $1,081

HELMETS

A fine Imperial German officer's Pickelhaube (as worn by the 95th and 153rd Infantry Regts.). (Wallis & Wallis) $1,816

A Cromwellian period trooper's lobster tailed helmet "pot", one piece skull embossed with 6 radial flutes, small hanging ring finial. (Wallis & Wallis) $1,000

A scarce Saxony Reservist Dragoon Raupenhelm, circa 1865, black patent leather skull, with brass strip mounts and comb with wool crest. (Wallis & Wallis) $1,671

A fine Prussian General officer's Pickelhaube, gilt Guard Eagle helmet plate with silver and enamelled Garde Star. (Wallis & Wallis) $1,643

A good attractive 19th century Persian Qjar helmet Kulah Khud, steel bowl gold damascened overall with arabesques and 4 cartouches of inscription. (Wallis & Wallis) $1,157

A good Imperial German Dragoon officer's Pickelhaube of the 19th Dragoons (Oldenburg) silvered dragoon eagle with state arms. (Wallis & Wallis) $951

A good Imperial German officer's Pickelhaube of the State of Oldenburg, (91st Infantry Regt). (Wallis & Wallis) $778

A fine Saxony officer's Tschapka, fine gilt rayed star badge plate with silvered state badge to center . (Wallis & Wallis) $1,513

A Victorian officer's green cloth spiked helmet of the 1st Fifeshire Rifle Volunteer Corps. (Wallis & Wallis) $519

HELMETS

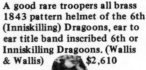

A German Naval OR's round cap, navy blue crown, small metal Prussian state roundel badge. (Wallis & Wallis) $273

A good rare troopers all brass 1843 pattern helmet of the 6th (Inniskilling) Dragoons, ear to ear title band inscribed 6th or Inniskilling Dragoons. (Wallis & Wallis) $2,610

A fine and rare painted ceremonial parade fire hat, American, inscribed Union Hose, the reverse dated 1856, 6¼in. high. (Christie's) $3,850

An Edward VII officer's lance-cap of The 5th (Royal Irish) Lancers, black patent leather skull, scarlet cloth top and sides. (Wallis & Wallis) $3,546

A fine and rare Imperial German officer's helmet of the Saxon Guard Reiter Regiment, tombak skull with fine helmet plate of silvered rayed star.(Wallis & Wallis) $17,300

A fine Prussian Uhlan officer's Tschapka with gilt Line eagle badge plate and black and white horsehair parade plume. (Wallis & Wallis) $1,167

A 19th century brass fireman's helmet, with crossed axes, firebrand and hoses badge, 33cm. (Osmond Tricks) $647

An officer's very rare Waterloo pattern shako bearing the gilt plate of the Kent Militia and with crimson and gold plaited cord with tassels. (Christie's) $7,276

An officer's 1847 (Albert) pattern gilt helmet of the Suffolk Yeomanry, gilt decoration, red leather backed chinchain with large ear rosettes. (Wallis & Wallis) $2,335

HELMETS

A fine Imperial German officer's busby of the Leib Garde Hussar Regt., silvered Guard star badge plate with enamelled center. (Wallis & Wallis) $1,211

A composite Imperial German Garde du Corps helmet, cuirassier tombak skull with edge mounts and studs, lobster tail neck guard. (Wallis & Wallis) $2,800

A fine Imperial German officer's busby of the 17th (Brunswick) Hussars, bearskin covered body, silver plated skull and crossbones badge plate. (Wallis & Wallis) $1,643

A fine Guard Uhlan officer's Tschapka (Lance Cap) fine silvered badge plate with enamelled center to Guard Star. (Wallis & Wallis) $1,600

An officer's shako, circa 1855, of the 10th (The Prince of Wales's Own Royal) Light Dragoons (Hussars), black velvet body, black patent leather front peak. (Wallis & Wallis) $2,941

A fine Prussian Grenadier's mitre cap of the 1st Guard Regiment of Foot, silvered helmet plate embossed with elaborate decoration of Prussian eagle. (Wallis & Wallis) $2,595

A very fine Victorian officer's blue cloth spiked helmet of the 1st Gloucester Volunteer Engineers, silver plated mounts. (Wallis & Wallis) $622

An officer's Victorian gilt helmet of the 7th (The Princess Royal's) Dragoon Guards with black and white hair plume. (Christie's) $1,351

An Edward VII troopers black leather helmet of the Kings Own Norfolk Imperial Yeomanry, brass peak bindings, ear to ear laurel wreath. (Wallis & Wallis) $702

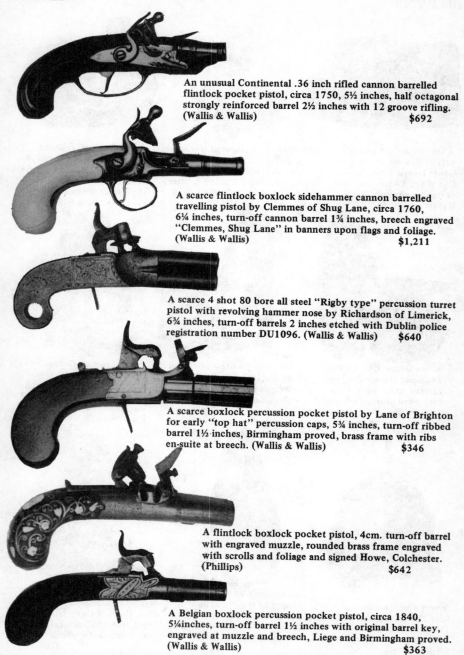

An unusual Continental .36 inch rifled cannon barrelled flintlock pocket pistol, circa 1750, 5½ inches, half octagonal strongly reinforced barrel 2½ inches with 12 groove rifling. (Wallis & Wallis)   **$692**

A scarce flintlock boxlock sidehammer cannon barrelled travelling pistol by Clemmes of Shug Lane, circa 1760, 6¼ inches, turn-off cannon barrel 1¾ inches, breech engraved "Clemmes, Shug Lane" in banners upon flags and foliage. (Wallis & Wallis)   **$1,211**

A scarce 4 shot 80 bore all steel "Rigby type" percussion turret pistol with revolving hammer nose by Richardson of Limerick, 6¾ inches, turn-off barrels 2 inches etched with Dublin police registration number DU1096. (Wallis & Wallis)   **$640**

A scarce boxlock percussion pocket pistol by Lane of Brighton for early "top hat" percussion caps, 5¾ inches, turn-off ribbed barrel 1½ inches, Birmingham proved, brass frame with ribs en-suite at breech. (Wallis & Wallis)   **$346**

A flintlock boxlock pocket pistol, 4cm. turn-off barrel with engraved muzzle, rounded brass frame engraved with scrolls and foliage and signed Howe, Colchester. (Phillips)   **$642**

A Belgian boxlock percussion pocket pistol, circa 1840, 5¼inches, turn-off barrel 1½ inches with original barrel key, engraved at muzzle and breech, Liege and Birmingham proved. (Wallis & Wallis)   **$363**

PISTOLS

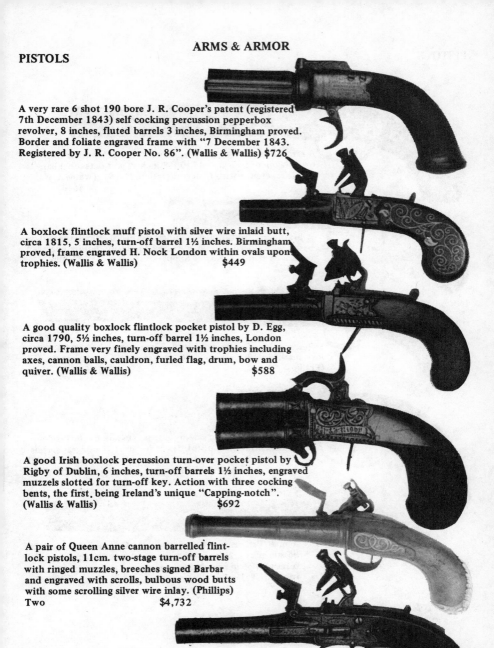

A very rare 6 shot 190 bore J. R. Cooper's patent (registered 7th December 1843) self cocking percussion pepperbox revolver, 8 inches, fluted barrels 3 inches, Birmingham proved. Border and foliate engraved frame with "7 December 1843. Registered by J. R. Cooper No. 86". (Wallis & Wallis) $726

A boxlock flintlock muff pistol with silver wire inlaid butt, circa 1815, 5 inches, turn-off barrel 1½ inches. Birmingham proved, frame engraved H. Nock London within ovals upon trophies. (Wallis & Wallis) $449

A good quality boxlock flintlock pocket pistol by D. Egg, circa 1790, 5½ inches, turn-off barrel 1½ inches, London proved. Frame very finely engraved with trophies including axes, cannon balls, cauldron, furled flag, drum, bow and quiver. (Wallis & Wallis) $588

A good Irish boxlock percussion turn-over pocket pistol by Rigby of Dublin, 6 inches, turn-off barrels 1½ inches, engraved muzzels slotted for turn-off key. Action with three cocking bents, the first, being Ireland's unique "Capping-notch". (Wallis & Wallis) $692

A pair of Queen Anne cannon barrelled flint-lock pistols, 11cm. two-stage turn-off barrels with ringed muzzles, breeches signed Barbar and engraved with scrolls, bulbous wood butts with some scrolling silver wire inlay. (Phillips) Two $4,732

A scarce and unusual flintlock boxlock double barrelled travelling pistol with selector slide by Bond of London, circa 1800, 8 inches, turn-off barrels 2½ inches, Tower proved. Frame engraved "Bond", "Corn Hill London" within borders upon trophies. (Wallis & Wallis) $882

41

PISTOLS

A rare 20 bore Belgian over and under flintlock holster pistol by C. Niquet of Liege — 1740, 18 inches, part octagonal barrels 11 inches etched with Irish registration ST-787. (Wallis & Wallis) $640

A brass barrelled flintlock blunderbuss pistol, 20cm. three-stage barrel with ringed muzzle, engraved Liverpool, border engraved brass lock signed J. Parr. (Phillips) $1,496

A flintlock long Sea Service pistol, 30cm. barrel, border engraved lock marked with a crown, G.R. cypher and Tower across the tail. (Phillips) $1,028

A good DB 80-bore side-by-side percussion boxlock side-hammer travelling pistol, 5½ inches overall, integral barrels 2 inches with B'ham proofs, the top rib engraved "E. Akrill, Beverley". (Wallis & Wallis) $778

A mid 18th century Scandinavian 12 bore military flintlock holster pistol, 20in. overall, barrel 13in. with large brass foresight, plain rounded banana shaped lock with unbridled frizzen. (Wallis & Wallis) $720

A flintlock boxlock cannon barrelled pistol, 5.5cm. 3 stage turn-off barrel with ringed muzzle, scroll engraved framed signed Barbar, London. (Phillips) $439

PISTOLS

A rare Belgian .30in. breech loading percussion pistol, 11in., twist barrels 6¾in., Liege proved, hinged breech block releases. (Wallis & Wallis) $338

A scarce 34 bore pellet lock pistol by Grierson, 8in. octagonal barrel 3in., fullstocked, foliate engraved lock with "Grierson London". (Wallis & Wallis) $712

A good 20 bore boxlock flintlock silver mounted cannon barrelled coaching pistol by Griffin & Tow, circa 1780, 12 inches, turn-off barrel 5½ inches London proved, with nicely turned reinforces. (Wallis & Wallis) $1,557

A Caucasian Migulet holster pistol, the 27.5cm. barrel chiselled and inlaid in gold with foliage. (Phillips) $732

A French 12 bore Model 1822 military percussion holster pistol, 13½in. overall, barrel 8in. stamped at breech "C. de 17,6 A", the breech marked "M 1822 bis", plain lock, walnut halfstock stamped "Chatelt. 162". (Wallis & Wallis) $432

A 6 shot 80 bore top hammer self cocking percussion pepperbox revolver, 8in., fluted cylinder 3in. Birmingham proved. (Wallis & Wallis) $306

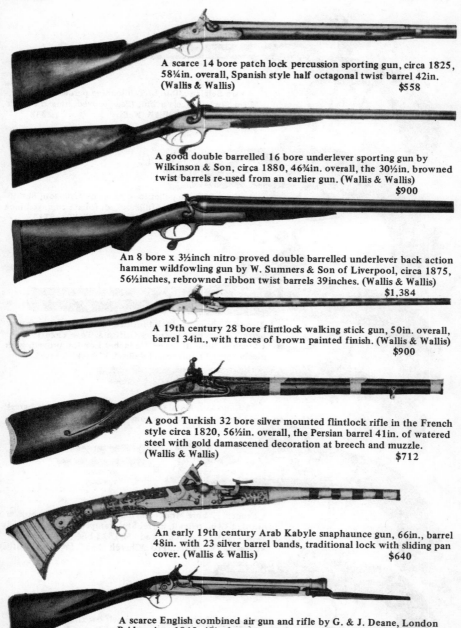

A scarce 14 bore patch lock percussion sporting gun, circa 1825, 58¼in. overall, Spanish style half octagonal twist barrel 42in. (Wallis & Wallis) $558

A good double barrelled 16 bore underlever sporting gun by Wilkinson & Son, circa 1880, 46¾in. overall, the 30½in. browned twist barrels re-used from an earlier gun. (Wallis & Wallis) $900

An 8 bore x 3½inch nitro proved double barrelled underlever back action hammer wildfowling gun by W. Sumners & Son of Liverpool, circa 1875, 56½inches, rebrowned ribbon twist barrels 39inches. (Wallis & Wallis) $1,384

A 19th century 28 bore flintlock walking stick gun, 50in. overall, barrel 34in., with traces of brown painted finish. (Wallis & Wallis) $900

A good Turkish 32 bore silver mounted flintlock rifle in the French style circa 1820, 56½in. overall, the Persian barrel 41in. of watered steel with gold damascened decoration at breech and muzzle. (Wallis & Wallis) $712

An early 19th century Arab Kabyle snaphaunce gun, 66in., barrel 48in. with 23 silver barrel bands, traditional lock with sliding pan cover. (Wallis & Wallis) $640

A scarce English combined air gun and rifle by G. & J. Deane, London Bridge circa 1845, 47inches, browned octagonal turn-off rifled twist barrel 29½inches. (Wallis & Wallis) $2,249

RIFLES

A brass-barrelled flintlock blunderbuss, 35cm. barrel with flared muzzle signed Wogdon, London, foliate scroll engraved lock signed Brander, full-stocked with brass mounts. (Phillips) $805

A silver mounted 14 bore flintlock sporting carbine by Newton of Grantham 1767, 41in. overall, half octagonal barrel 25in. (Wallis & Wallis) $890

A Maynard second model percussion breech-loading carbine, 51cm. rifled sighted tip-down two-stage barrel, frame stamped Edward Maynard Patentee, May 27 1851. (Phillips) $823

A fine .32 inch East German Wheellock Birding Rifle Tschinke, circa 1650, 43in., octagonal barrel 32¾in. with punched and engraved foliate decoration. (Wallis & Wallis) $7,785

A brass barrelled flintlock blunderbuss, 36.5cm. three-stage barrel with ringed muzzle signed John Richards, Strand London and fitted with spring bayonet beneath, brass signed, stepped and bolted lock engraved with foliage and stands of arms. (Phillips) $2,366

A 20 bore Arab Kabyle snaphaunce jezail, 67¾in. overall, barrel 52in. with inlaid plaques at breech, the lock also decorated with inlaid plaques. (Wallis & Wallis) $373

A 10 bore Volunteer flintlock musket by Staudenmayer, circa 1800, 55in. overall, barrel 39in. with break off breech, engraved "Staudenmayer, London", with its triangular socket bayonet by Harvey. (Wallis & Wallis) $1,335

ARMS & ARMOR

A Greene's breech-loading percussion carbine, 46cm. sighted three-stage rifled barrel released by secondary trigger and pivoting for loading back-action lock stamped Mass Arms Co., Chicopee Falls U.S.A. 1856. (Phillips) $1,189

A double-barrelled percussion sporting gun, 80.5cm. sighted barrels signed Joseph Manton, Hanover Square, London , stepped signed locks converted from flintlock engraved with scrolls and trophies. (Phillips) $785

A brass barrelled flintlock blunderbuss, 41cm. two-stage barrel with flared muzzle struck with the mark of John Bumford, plain lock, full stocked with brass mounts including flattened butt plate secured by square headed nails. (Phillips) $709

A Starr percussion breech-loading carbine, 53cm. rifled sighted barrel signed Starr Arms Co., Yonkers, N.Y., tip-down breech marked Starr's Patent Sept 14th 1858. (Phillips) $768

A brass barrelled Naval flintlock blunderbuss, 41.5cm. four-stage barrel with ringed muzzle, border engraved lock, full stock with flattened butt stamped with an ordnance mark beneath. (Phillips) $1,496

A mid 18th century 8 bore military style flint-lock musket, 56½in. overall, unusually heavy 3 stage barrel 39in., early banana shaped lock. (Wallis & Wallis) $605

RIFLES

An Enfield percussion prize rifle, 99cm. sighted barrel with ladder rear sight, lock engraved with a crown over V.R. cypher, 1863 and LA Co., full stocked with regulation brass and steel mounts. (Phillips) $1,183

A Spanish Migulet sporting gun, 91cm. sighted two-stage barrel decorated at the breech in gold with scrolling foliage, 'Ennaduras' and gold filled maker's mark of 'Y Rusta'. (Phillips) $1,215

A Naval flintlock blunderbuss, 55cm. barrel with flared muzzle, border engraved lock signed 'Sherwood', full stock with flattened butt fitted with iron swivel mount. (Phillips) $1,963

A wheel-lock Tschinke, 68.5cm. octagonal rifled barrel with some light engraved decoration, hooded rear sight, flat lock with external wheel and mainspring, engraved cock with spring covered by an engraved plate. (Phillips) $5,797

A .50 calibre rimfire Spencer repeating carbine, 51cm. sighted barrel with six-groove rifling marked M1865 and Spencer Repeating Rifle Co., Boston, Mass., Pat'd March 6, 1860. (Phillips) $768

A very rare Burnside breech-loading percussion military rifle, 86.5cm. sighted barrel with bayonet bar beneath, stamped Burnside's Patent March 25th 1856. (Phillips) $2,104

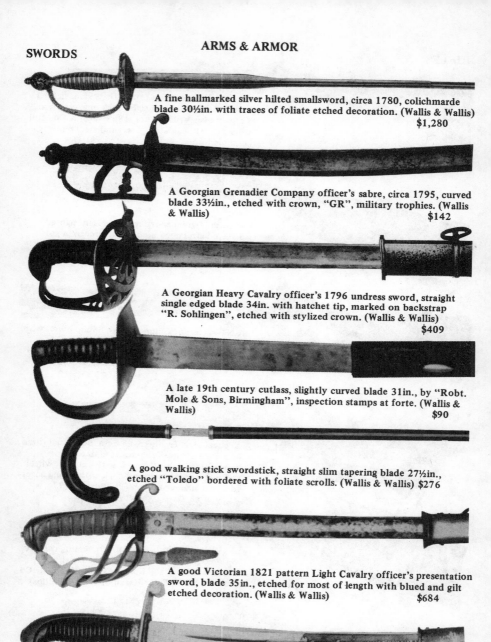

A fine hallmarked silver hilted smallsword, circa 1780, colichmarde blade 30½in. with traces of foliate etched decoration. (Wallis & Wallis) $1,280

A Georgian Grenadier Company officer's sabre, circa 1795, curved blade 33½in., etched with crown, "GR", military trophies. (Wallis & Wallis) $142

A Georgian Heavy Cavalry officer's 1796 undress sword, straight single edged blade 34in. with hatchet tip, marked on backstrap "R. Sohlingen", etched with stylized crown. (Wallis & Wallis) $409

A late 19th century cutlass, slightly curved blade 31in., by "Robt. Mole & Sons, Birmingham", inspection stamps at forte. (Wallis & Wallis) $90

A good walking stick swordstick, straight slim tapering blade 27½in., etched "Toledo" bordered with foliate scrolls. (Wallis & Wallis) $276

A good Victorian 1821 pattern Light Cavalry officer's presentation sword, blade 35in., etched for most of length with blued and gilt etched decoration. (Wallis & Wallis) $684

An Imperial Bavarian artillery officer's sword, curved, plated blade 33in. by A. Relfe, Augsburg, etched within panel "4. Bayr. Feld. Artill. Regt. Konig" bordered with cannon. (Wallis & Wallis) $119

SWORDS

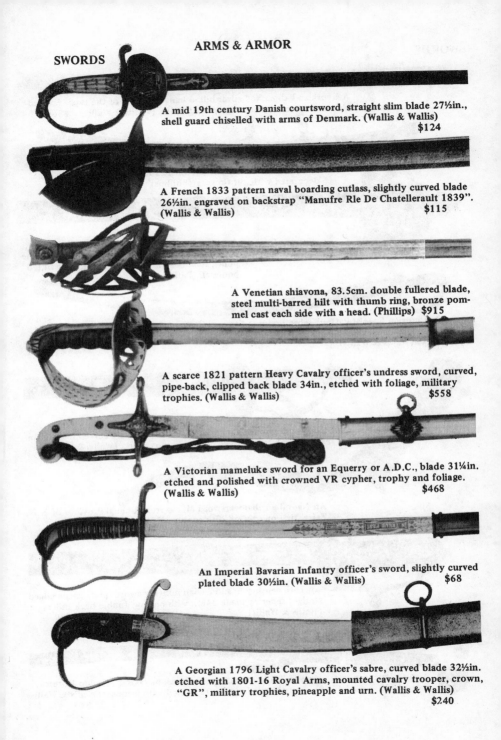

A mid 19th century Danish courtsword, straight slim blade 27½in., shell guard chiselled with arms of Denmark. (Wallis & Wallis)
$124

A French 1833 pattern naval boarding cutlass, slightly curved blade 26½in. engraved on backstrap "Manufre Rle De Chatellerault 1839". (Wallis & Wallis)
$115

A Venetian shiavona, 83.5cm. double fullered blade, steel multi-barred hilt with thumb ring, bronze pommel cast each side with a head. (Phillips) $915

A scarce 1821 pattern Heavy Cavalry officer's undress sword, curved, pipe-back, clipped back blade 34in., etched with foliage, military trophies. (Wallis & Wallis)
$558

A Victorian mameluke sword for an Equerry or A.D.C., blade 31¼in. etched and polished with crowned VR cypher, trophy and foliage. (Wallis & Wallis)
$468

An Imperial Bavarian Infantry officer's sword, slightly curved plated blade 30½in. (Wallis & Wallis)
$68

A Georgian 1796 Light Cavalry officer's sabre, curved blade 32½in. etched with 1801-16 Royal Arms, mounted cavalry trooper, crown, "GR", military trophies, pineapple and urn. (Wallis & Wallis)
$240

ARMS & ARMOR

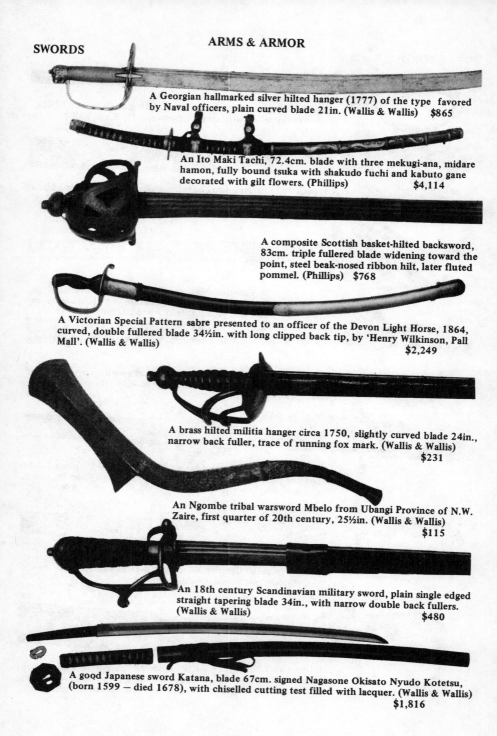

A Georgian hallmarked silver hilted hanger (1777) of the type favored by Naval officers, plain curved blade 21in. (Wallis & Wallis) $865

An Ito Maki Tachi, 72.4cm. blade with three mekugi-ana, midare hamon, fully bound tsuka with shakudo fuchi and kabuto gane decorated with gilt flowers. (Phillips) $4,114

A composite Scottish basket-hilted backsword, 83cm. triple fullered blade widening toward the point, steel beak-nosed ribbon hilt, later fluted pommel. (Phillips) $768

A Victorian Special Pattern sabre presented to an officer of the Devon Light Horse, 1864, curved, double fullered blade 34½in. with long clipped back tip, by 'Henry Wilkinson, Pall Mall'. (Wallis & Wallis)
$2,249

A brass hilted militia hanger circa 1750, slightly curved blade 24in., narrow back fuller, trace of running fox mark. (Wallis & Wallis)
$231

An Ngombe tribal warsword Mbelo from Ubangi Province of N.W. Zaire, first quarter of 20th century, 25½in. (Wallis & Wallis)
$115

An 18th century Scandinavian military sword, plain single edged straight tapering blade 34in., with narrow double back fullers. (Wallis & Wallis)
$480

A good Japanese sword Katana, blade 67cm. signed Nagasone Okisato Nyudo Kotetsu, (born 1599 — died 1678), with chiselled cutting test filled with lacquer. (Wallis & Wallis)
$1,816

SWORDS

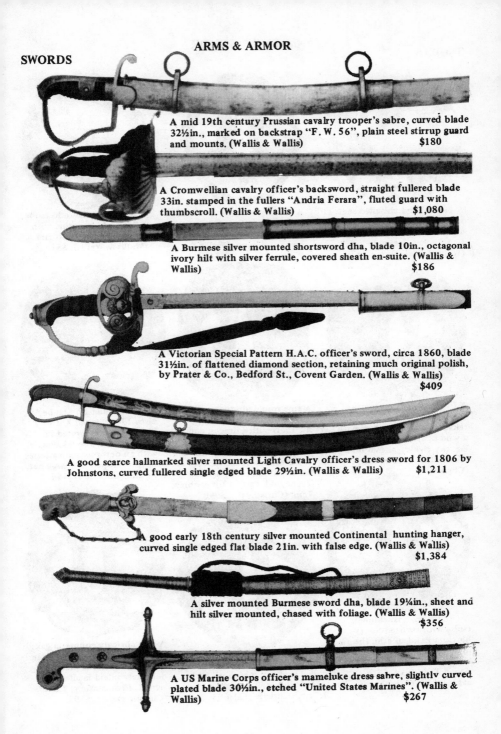

A mid 19th century Prussian cavalry trooper's sabre, curved blade 32½in., marked on backstrap "F.W. 56", plain steel stirrup guard and mounts. (Wallis & Wallis) $180

A Cromwellian cavalry officer's backsword, straight fullered blade 33in. stamped in the fullers "Andria Ferara", fluted guard with thumbscroll. (Wallis & Wallis) $1,080

A Burmese silver mounted shortsword dha, blade 10in., octagonal ivory hilt with silver ferrule, covered sheath en-suite. (Wallis & Wallis) $186

A Victorian Special Pattern H.A.C. officer's sword, circa 1860, blade 31½in. of flattened diamond section, retaining much original polish, by Prater & Co., Bedford St., Covent Garden. (Wallis & Wallis) $409

A good scarce hallmarked silver mounted Light Cavalry officer's dress sword for 1806 by Johnstons, curved fullered single edged blade 29½in. (Wallis & Wallis) $1,211

A good early 18th century silver mounted Continental hunting hanger, curved single edged flat blade 21in. with false edge. (Wallis & Wallis) $1,384

A silver mounted Burmese sword dha, blade 19¼in., sheet and hilt silver mounted, chased with foliage. (Wallis & Wallis) $356

A US Marine Corps officer's mameluke dress sabre, slightly curved plated blade 30½in., etched "United States Marines". (Wallis & Wallis) $267

TSUBAS

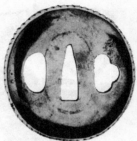

A pierced and chiselled sentoku tsuba, 7.2cm., mumei showing a hawk perched on prunus with two finches fleeing below. (Wallis & Wallis) $179

A Japanese sentoku sukashi tsuba, 6.6cm., signed Bushu Ju Masanao, carved with stylized dragon. (Wallis & Wallis) $153

A plain oval shakudo tsuba, 6.7cm., shiny patina with polished roped brass rim. (Wallis & Wallis) $81

A fine circular iron migakiji tsuba decorated in shakudo takazogan and nikubori with a wild boar breaking cover near a rocky rivulet, signed Ichiryusai Masamitsu, 19th century, 7.9cm. (Christie's) $633

A fine rounded square copper ishimeji tsuba decorated in nikubori with a dragon concealed in vapour ascending Mount Fuji, on the reverse a toy dragon suspended from a branch of bamboo, signed Tsuneyuki, early 19th century, 7cm. (Christie's) $990

A fine circular iron tsuba, circa 1748, signed Kato Shigemitsu, decorated in nikubori and iroe takazogan, with an octopus and varieties of fish trapped in a large net, 7.5cm. (Christie's) $594

A circular iron tsuchimeji tsuba with stylized cherry-blossom in kosukashi, the plate thinning towards the narrow shakudo pipe-rim, signed Tadatsugu, 18th century. (Christie's) $396

A shakudo tsuba formed as a coiled snake in marubori, with added gilt detail, unsigned, 7.7cm. (Christie's) $1,683

A fine aorigata copper migakiji tsuba with inome piercings and a shakudo rim, the plate delicately inlaid in silver, unsigned, 19th century, 7.8cm. (Christie's) $792

TSUBAS

A Mino Goto shakudo nanako mokko tsuba, 6.6cm., chiselled in relief with chrysanthemums and foliage, gilt details and rim. (Wallis & Wallis)$198

A copper tsuba of squared form, 6.1cm., signed Masachika, katakiri engraving of a boy playing a flute, some wear and a little distressing. (Wallis & Wallis) $180

An iron sukashi tsuba, 6.3cm., of regular cherry blossom form, lightly pitted. (Wallis & Wallis) $54

A fine circular iron migakiji tsuba decorated in nikubori with a group of Tartar hunters near a pine forest, signed Choshu Toyoura ju Torino Mobe Tomoshige saku, 19th century, 8cm. (Christie's) $743

A rounded square shakudo hari-ishimeji tsuba decorated in iroe takazogan with two Chinese scholars at a writing table watching a dragon materialise above them, 19th century, 6.4cm. (Christie's) $1,188

An oval iron migakiji tsuba decorated in takabori and takazogan with the Paragon of Filial Piety Taishun, on the reverse an elephant and two birds tilling and weeding the ground, signed Ukoku Oizumi Mitsuchika and dated 1849. (Christie's) $2,376

A rounded rectangular iron tsuba decorated in copper and gilt takazogan with Tenaga seated stretching beneath a pine tree, signed Ichiyoken Nagatsugu, late 19th century. (Christie's) $1,683

A good Soten shakudo tsuba, 7.5cms, signed Goshu Niudu Soten with Kakihan, pierced and chiselled with a sage at his writing table. (Wallis & Wallis) $189

An oval shakudo-nanakoji tsuba, 19th century, signed Sekisaido Hiroyuki, decorated in silver, gilt and shakudo takazogan with flowering plum branches, 6.6cm. (Christie's) $792

A clockwork musical auto-maton of a papier mache headed Japanese girl carrying tray and parasol, 33in. high, probably by Vichy. (Christie's) $8,514

A bisque headed clockwork clown standing on his hands dressed in original outfit, 16in. high. (Christie's) $570

A bisque headed musical automaton, modelled as a standing child holding a covered basket, 19in. high, by Lambert, the head stamped Tete Jumeau. (Christie's) $4,831

A clockwork automaton figure of a standing bear drummer, with moving lower jaw and front paws, 27in. high, probably Decamps, 1880. (Christie's) $1,903

A coin-in-the-slot automaton ship model, the three-masted vessel with all sail set, 42¾in. long. (Bearne's) $2,821

A marotte with three dancing children with bisque heads and wooden bodies in original clothing, 11in. high (music needs attention). (Christie's) $668

A printed paper on wood automaton toy of a house on fire, with two figures working a pump at the side, 10in. high, German. (Christie's) $570

A very fine Gustav Vichy musical automaton of a young woman playing the guitar, circa 1870. (Phillips) $12,168

Brass singing bird automaton, having a pair of feathered model birds on branches under domed cage, 7in. high. (Hobbs & Chambers) $445

A papier mache ginger jar musical automaton, French, late 19th century, the hinged cover opening to reveal a chinaman drinking tea, 12in. high.(Christie's) $3,080

A musical automaton doll in the form of a magician linking together a long chain of brass rings, wearing an exotic costume in the Turkish style, 15¼in. high. (Bearne's) $1,710

A Leopold Lambert musical automaton of a flower girl, the Jumeau bisque head with fair mohair wig over cork pate, 18½in. high. (Phillips) $5,746

A clockwork musical automaton of a papier mache headed North African girl, sitting on a stool inset with paste jewels and playing a lyre, 29in. high. (Christie's) $7,189

SFBJ bisque headed automaton doll seated playing a piano, the doll impressed SFBJ 60 Paris, with brown hair and fixed brown glass eyes, 13½in. wide. (Hobbs & Chambers) $700

An Armand Marseille bisque headed musical poupard, with blonde mohair wig, fixed blue glass eyes and open mouth, 38.5cm. long overall.(Henry Spencer) $676

The Reaper, a bisque headed clockwork musical automaton, modelled as a child in original red waistcoat, 17in. high, by Vichy, the head stamped in red Tete Jumeau. (Christie's) $5,636

Celluloid singing bird in a painted tinplate cage, with clockwork mechanism in base of cage, 4¼in. high, German, 1920's. (Christie's) $594

A bisque headed, hand operated automaton of a jester ringing handbells, dressed in original outfit, with musical movement, 15in. high. (Christie's) $798

Red and white cotton Bugatti driver's armband for the 1924 Grand Prix D'Europe. (Onslow's) $875

A chromium plated and enamelled B.R.D.C. badge, stamped 767 Boshier-Jones, 4¼in. high. (Onslow's) $504

'The Latest', 'Testing New Car for Width', by W. Heath Robinson, black ink, humorous cartoons, 2 x 5½in. (Onslow's) Two $612

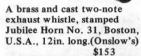

A petrol cigarette lighter modelled as the 1930 M.G. Midget, 6¼in. long.(Onslow's) $376

A brass and cast two-note exhaust whistle, stamped Jubilee Horn No. 31, Boston, U.S.A., 12in. long.(Onslow's) $153

Sir Malcolm Campbell's Bluebird, a clockwork tinplate toy by Kingsbury, repainted, 18in. long. (Onslow's)$396

Frederick Nevin, Giuseppe Campari in his Alfa Romeo Monza, charcoal, heightened with white, signed, 15½x20½in. (Christie's) $506

Poster by Andre Bermond, for the Grand Prix Automobile, Pau, 10 Avril 1950, 39 x 30cm. (Onslow's) $1,925

James Dugdale, 'Targa Florio 1964 Dan Gurney in the AC Cobra Campofelice', gouache, signed and dated 1980, 19½ x 22½in. (Onslow's) $720

Frazer Nash Car Club badge. (Onslow's) $280

A chromium plated Healey Car Club badge, 3¼in. high. (Onslow's) $216

An enamelled convex Bugatti radiator badge, slight chip, 1¾ x 3½in. (Onslow's) $216

Osterreichische Touren Trophae 1931, Steinfellner, a bronze plaque molded in relief with badge of the Austrian Automobile Club, 3¾in. wide. (Christie's)$104

Petrol pump globe for National Benzole Mixture. (Onslow's)
Two $315

Ferrari 275 GTB4, sales pamphlet, Italian, French and English text, 1964.(Christie's) $325

Sir Henry Segrave's Golden Arrow, a clockwork tinplate toy by Kingsbury, 20in. long. (Onslow's) $504

Bosch four cylinder magneto, brass and steel advertising table ornament, 3¼in. high. (Onslow's) $324

A chromium plated cigarette lighter modelled as an MG Midget, circa 1933, 6¼in. long. (Christie's) $364

A pair of Lucas 'King of the Road' headlamps, 8¾in. diam., and acetylene generator. (Christie's) $1,012

A sales brochure for Bentley 6½ Litre 6 Cylinder Standard Model, catalogue no. 27, October 1928. (Onslow's) $846

Petrol pump globe for Shell Benzol Mixture. (Onslow's) $367

James Dugdale, 'Auto Union C-Type cornering', gouache, signed and dated 1980, 14 x 20in. (Onslow's)$810

A chromium plated and enamelled Brooklands Automobile Racing Club badge, stamped 419, 3¾in. high. (Onslow's) $810

After Gamy, 'Coupe des Voitures Legeres 1911', Bablot le Gagnant sur Delage.(Onslow's) $612

Charles Pascarel, Le Mans, 1980, the Porsche leading a BMW, color lithograph poster, limited edition, signed, 25½ x 33½in. (Christie's) $283

'24 Heures du Mans', 1968, original poster, 24 x 15in. (Christie's) $306

'The Bluebird' at Daytona 24-26th February 1932, Speed 253.9 m.p.h., photograph, 7 x 9½in. (Onslow's) $540

Poster by F. Hugo d'Alesi, for Automobiles Bayard, 117 x 158cm. (Onslow's) $3,500

Shell petrol pump globe. (Onslow's) $455

Schenkel, 'Course Automobiles Internationale Anvers 14 Heures 22 Mai 1938', published by Patria, Anvers, on linen, 47 x 34in. (Onslow's)$720

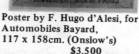

Roy Nockolds, 'Nuvolari at the Wheel of P3 Alfa Romeo', oil on board, signed, unframed, 10 x 12in. (Onslow's) $1,440

The Chequered Flag, a Tetley public house sign, with painted picture depicting a racing Bentley, 44½ x 30in. (Christie's) $556

One of twelve prints in color of various coachwork designs by Carrosserie Van Den Plas, circa 1925, 9¼ x 11in. (Christie's) Twelve $1,531

AUTOMOBILIA

Philippe Chapellier, 'Eclaireurs Bleriot', published by Philippe Chapellier, Paris, on linen, 38 x 48in. (Onslow's) $3,600

Ferrari Yearbook, 1953. (Onslow's) $702

Louis Klemantaski, 'Crowds and Cobbles Mille Miglia 1984 Ferrari Tour de France', color photograph, signed, 16 x 24in. (Onslow's) $180

Poster, Liege, Rome, Liege Rally, 1933, 73 x 53cm. (Onslow's) $822

Torbay and Totnes Motor Club English Riviera Trial 1935 Premier Award, a bronze figure of Victory, 10in. high. (Onslow's) $1,170

J. Jacquelin, Delage 1939, color poster showing an open two seater at speed, 32 x 23in. (Christie's) $910

An original oil painting by Guy Lipscombe, used as an advertisement for Rudge Whitworth featuring the Aurora Trophy, Elgin, Illinois, 1912, 45cm. square. (Onslow's) $12,250

One of a complete set of Monaco Grand Prix Posters, 1930-1957, post-war reproductions using the original lithographic method, approximately 37 x 25in. (Christie's) Set $1,518

'Study of a racing driver in cockpit', pastel, signed with initials and dated 1930, 16 x 12½in. (Onslow's) $1,350

BAROMETERS

Early Victorian
mahogany framed
barometer and ther-
mometer with carved
decoration.(British
Antique Exporters)
$525

A mahogany stick
barometer, signed
P. Grandi, fecit, the
herringbone veneered
case with open tube,
38¼in. (Lawrence
Fine Arts)
$1,465

Victorian carved oak
cased barometer and
thermometer in good
condition. (British
Antique Exporters)
$350

A Regency mahogany
stick barometer, by
Miller and Adie, Edin-
burgh, 85cm. (Phillips)
$1,122

A mahogany ship's
stick barometer,
the arched ivory
dial inscribed H.
Hughes, London,
38in. high. (Christie's)
$1,347

A mahogany wheel
barometer with
domed top, the 8½in.
silvered dial signed
Jos. Somalvico, Lea-
ther Lane, Holborn,
with domed base,
36in. high.(Chris-
tie's) $1,205

An early 19th cen-
tury mahogany cased
stick barometer, by
Adie and Son, 98cm.
(Phillips)
$2,618

A mahogany wheel
barometer with box-
wood stringing and
floral and shell in-
lays, the dial in-
scribed J.Polty,
fecit, 39in. high.
(Christie's)
$577

A mahogany stick barometer, the silvered register plate, signed Jno. Gatward, Hitchen, Herts., the case with open tube, 36in. (Lawrence Fine Arts) $1,424

An early George III mahogany angle barometer with thermometer framing a perpetual calendar, by F. Watkins, London, 41x25in. (Christie's) $37,840

An 18th century mahogany stick barometer, the concealed tube with silver register, signed J. Bennett, London, the case with fluted canted sides, (Lawrence Fine Arts) $6,105

A barometer and thermometer by C. Zambra, Holborn, in inlaid mahogany case, 38in. (Anderson & Garland) $363

A walnut wheel barometer with carved scroll top, the eight-inch dial signed D. Hayton, Hereford, with scroll base and applied carving, 36in. high. (Christie's) $457

A mahogany and boxwood strung stick barometer, signed Negretti & Co., fecit, London, with turned cistern cover, 38in. high. (Christie's) $731

A Victorian rosewood barometer, inlaid with mother-of-pearl, the eight-inch silvered dial signed John Hansford, Ilminster, 37in. high. (Christie's) $346

A rosewood stick barometer, with arched top above ivorine scales, signed T.Gath, Small Street, Bristol, 36½in. high. (Christie's) $770

An early 19th century mahogany stick barometer with broken classical pediment, signed Frans Pelegrino, 96cm. high.(Christie's) $1,443

A rare mahogany double tube angle barometer, circa 1850, signed Charles Howarth Fecit Halifax, 42in. high. - (Christie's) $6,600

A mahogany and boxwood-strung wheel barometer, the spirit level inscribed Warrented Correct, 37½in. high. (Christie's) $327

A rosewood marine stick barometer, signed MacGregor & Co., Glasgow & Liverpool, 37in. high. (Christie's) $1,636

A Victorian rosewood and mother-of-pearl inlaid wheel barometer, the spirit level signed A. Rivolta, 32 Brook Street, Holborn, 40in. high(Christie's) $962

An early 19th century mahogany checkered strung and kingwood cross-banded pillar barometer, signed Jas. Gatty, 32¾in. high. (Christie's) $2,805

A mahogany wheel barometer, the arched top above hygrometer, cased thermometer and engraved silvered dial, 40in. high. (Christie's) $693

A stained oak stick barometer, signed W. Armstrong & Co., Chichester, with cased thermometer and carved cistern cover, 41in. high. (Christie's) $770

BAROMETERS

A 19th century mahogany wheel barometer with broken arch pediment, 42in. high. (Christie's) $880

A mahogany Quare-type stick barometer, on engraved gilt folding feet, 42in. high. (Christie's) $3,850

An early 19th century mahogany and boxwood strung wheel barometer, signed Barnasconi and Co., Leeds, 45¼in. high. (Christie's) $770

A 19th century carved rosewood stick barometer, signed W. Cox, Devonport, 38½in. high.(Christie's) $880

An oak stick barometer in arched case with ivorine dial signed Henry Crouch, London, 37in. high. (Christie's) $673

A rosewood wheel barometer with swanneck pediment, signed Tagliabue & Casella, 25 Hatton Garden, London, 39in. high. (Christie's) $673

An early 19th century mahogany and checkered strung stick barometer, signed Js. Lyon, Lombard Street, 38in. high. (Christie's) $1,540

A fine rosewood and mother-of-pearl inlaid wheel barometer, the spirit level inscribed Gardner & Co., 21 Buchanan Street, Glasgow, 41in. high. (Christie's) $1,250

BASKETS

A woven splint storage basket, with sloped shoulders tapering to base, (some original paint) 8in. high. (Christie's) $88

Nantucket pocketbook basket, Jose Formoso Reyes, Nantucket Island, Massachusetts, circa 1949, deep sided oval form of woven splint on an oval base, 15.5 x 19cm. (Robt. W. Skinner Inc.) $1,400

A rye coil basket, with side handles released from overlay on circular base (some blue paint), 6½in. high. (Christie's) $88

Antique American Indian basket from Oregon, 9 x 7in., circa 1890. (Du Mouchelles) $100

One of a pair of mahogany paper baskets of octagonal form, the fret-pierced sides with gothic arches, on bracket feet, 17in. (Christie's) Two $4,857

Nantucket Basket, late 19th century, deep sides with turned base reinforced with four screws, 8½in. high. (Robt. W. Skinner Inc.) $650

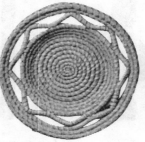

Oblong Nantucket basket, Nantucket Island, Massachusetts, late 19th century, bound oak rim above a woven rattan body, 11in. long. (Robt. W. Skinner Inc.) $1,500

A fine rye coil basket, late 19th/ early 20th century, the rye coils wrapped with oak ribbon, 10½in. diam. (Christie's) $55

Oblong Nantucket basket, Alfred D. Williams maker, Nantucket Island, Massachusetts, late 19th/early 20th century, 11in. long. (Robt. W. Skinner Inc.) $1,100

A blue-john cup and saucer with domed cover, 4½in. wide. (Christie's) $484

A blue-john cup with deep circular bowl on ring-turned stem and spreading base, 8in. high. (Christie's) $4,525

A mid Victorian blue-john inkwell with hinged lid and chamfered rectangular base with pen-groove, 3in. high. (Christie's) $473

A blue-john obelisk on square plinth edged with alabaster and black marble, 13in. high. (Christie's) $1,161

A George III ormolu and blue-john candelabrum by Matthew Boulton, the ovoid body mounted with herms issuing from acanthus foliage, 20¼in. high, 23in. wide. (Christie's) $79,464

A Regency blue-john urn, with black and white marble plinth base, 11in. high. (Christie's) $1,258

A pair of George III ormolu mounted blue-john cassolettes, by Matthew Boulton, 9¼in. high. (Christie's) $13,244

A good Derbyshire spa tazza, the shallow circular bowl raised upon a knopped cylindrical stem, 19cm. high. (Henry Spencer) $2,244

A pair of George III ormolu-mounted blue-john cassolettes, in the manner of Matthew Boulton, 10¼in. high. (Christie's) $14,190

The Middlesbrough and Guisbrough Railway Co. 1857, £25 share, vignette of an early train, industrial scene in background. (Phillips) $720

USA — American Express Company, 1858, 5 x $100 shares, Capital 7,500 shares, hand-signed by Wells as President, Fargo as Secretary and Holland as Treasurer. (Phillips) $1,557

Portugal — Comp Real dos Caminhos De Ferro Portuguezes, 1860, Wolfram Mining & Smelting Co., 1911-25. (Phillips) $54

Liverpool, Manchester and Newcastle-upon-Tyne Junction Railway Co. 1846, £20 share. (Phillips) $86

West Sunlight Reef Company, No Liability, Hillgrove, N.S.W. 1892, 10/- shares, Australian register. (Phillips) $88

Peru — Potosi, La Paz & Peruvian, Mining Association, 1827. One £15 bearer share with vignette of a city with large mountain in background. (Phillips) $371

Great Britain — Boston Tontine 1815, printed on vellum, large red seal slightly damaged. (Phillips) $540

Great Britain — Herne Bay Pier Company, 1832, one share on vellum. Large green seal on red wax. (Phillips) $271

Canada — The Province of Manitoba, 1885, £100 debenture with coupons, unsigned. (Phillips) $198

USA — The Cuba Company, 1903, 4 x $50,000 shares, issued to and endorsed by E. H. Harriman on reverse. (Phillips) $265

Imperial Australian Corpn. Ltd., 1895, £1 shares, three vignettes. (Phillips) $331

The Wharfdale Railway Co. 1840, £15 share. (Phillips) $126

Peru — The National Pisco To Yca Railway Co. 1869, £20 bond, Series "A" (3 examples) (Phillips) $140

USA — American Express Company, 1863, 1 x $500 share, hand-signed by Wells as President, Fargo as Secretary and Holland as Treasurer. (Phillips) $672

Shrewsbury and Hereford Railway Co. 1846, £20 share, panoramic vignette of a castle. (Phillips) $108

Canada — The Montreal and Bytown Railway Co. 1853, £100 bond. Several vignettes including one of Queen Victoria. (Phillips) $336

BOOKS

Edward Wells, 'A New Sett of Maps both of Antient and Present Geography', forty-one engraved double maps, Oxford 1700. (Henry Spencer) $2,244

Atlas; 31 maps colored in outline by Senex or Price. The Map of Asia by Kitchin. The Map Le Cours du Rhin by De Lisle; dated 1704-11, half calf and boards. (Prudential) $3,933

William Camden, 'Britannia; or a Chorographical Description of Great Britain and Ireland', volumes one and two, 1722. (Henry Spencer) $3,179

Louis Wain's Annual 1908, a paperback annual published by Bemrose & Sons. (Phillips) $185

Blaeu (Johannes): Novum Magnum Theatrum Urbium Belgicae Regiae, 2 vol.s, Amsterdam, 1647. (Phillips) $17,300

A Lalique bookbinding, Edmond Rostand: Chantecler, with an original drawing signed by Rostand on half title, Paris 1910, 24x17cm. (Christie's) $483

 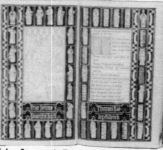 

Fun and Frolic by Louis Wain and Clifton Bingham, a children's poetry book published by Nister, circa 1902. (Phillips) $236

Friar Jerome's Beautiful Book, published by Houghton Mifflin and Company, Boston and New York, The Riverside Press, Cambridge, 1896, by Thomas Bailey Aldrich. (Robt. W. Skinner Inc.) $150

Curtis (William): The Botanical Magazine, First Series, vols. 1-53 incl. 1787-1826. (Phillips) $17,745

BOOKS

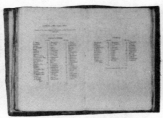

David Loggan, 'Oxonia Illustrata', engraved title page, thirty nine double page engravings, first edition, Oxford 1675. (Henry Spencer) $2,524

Bentley (H.): Cricket Matches 1786-1822, pub. 1823. (Phillips) $324

John Cary, 'New and Correct English Atlas', engraved general county map frontispiece, 1787. (Henry Spencer) $972

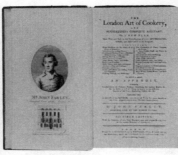

John Gerarde, 'The Herball or Generall Historie of Plantes', engravings, first Thomas Johnson edition, second edition, 1633. (Henry Spencer) $1,776

Speed (John): The Theatre of the Empire of Great Britaine, first edition, 4 parts in 1 vol., J.Sudbury & G.Humble, 1611. (Phillips) $17,473

Chivers (Cedric): Binder. Tennyson (Lord A.): Life and Works, 12 vol.s, limited edition of 1,050 copies, pale green end papers with stencilled decoration, 1898-99. (Phillips) $1,385

A Message to Garcia, by Elbert Hubbard, published by the Roycrofters, East Aurora, New York, 1899. (Robt. W. Skinner Inc.) $325

Farley (John), The London Art of Cookery, 6th edn, 12 engraved plates, 1789. (Phillips) $190

Gould (John): The Birds of Great Britain, 5 vols, 367 hand col. plates, approx. 18 with a few light spots on outer margins, 1873. A fine set in fitted oak case with glass front. (Phillips) $47,320

BOOKS

The Last Ride by Robert Browning, printed by the Roycrofters, East Aurora, New York, 1900, signed by Elbert Hubbard and illuminated by Lily Elss. (Robt. W. Skinner Inc.) $250

J. Marshall, publisher: A Garland of New Songs, 9 books bound together, each book comprising 9 woodcut vignette titles, Newcastle-upon-Tyne. (Phillips) $180

Richard F. Burton: Personal narrative of a pilgrimage to El-Medinah and Meccah, 3 vols, first edition, 1855-56. (Phillips) $1,215

Sir Sydney Cockerell: Autograph account book kept as trustee and executor to the estate of William Morris, begun immediately after Morris's death in October 1896 and carried on up until 1935. (Phillips) $10,846

William Cavendish, Duke of Newcastle, 'A General System of Horsemanship In All Its Branches', London 1743, Volumes one and two. (Henry Spencer) $6,171

Robert Hogg and Henry Gaves Bull: The Herefordshire Pomona, 2 vols, first edition, 77 color -printed lithographed plates, 1876-1885. (Phillips) $4,394

Giovanni Antonio Cavazzi: Istorica Descrittione De Tre Regni Congo, Matamba et Angola, 42 plates, Milan, 1690. (Phillips)$1,496

Infants Library: vols 2-16 (of 16) lacking vol 1, engravings and woodcut illustrations, circa 1801. (Phillips) $1,250

G. E. Shelley, 'A Monograph of the Nectariniidae, or Family of Sun-Birds', privately printed by the author, 1876-1880. (Henry Spencer) $7,106

BOOKS

Baron d'Eisenberg: Description du Manege Moderne dans sa Perfection, engr. title, 59 plates by B. Picart, 1727. (Phillips) $2,873

'A Closet for Ladies and Gentlewomen Or The Art of Preferuing, Conferving, and Candying', printed by John Haviland, 1632. (Woolley & Wallis) $1,000

David Roberts: Picturesque sketches in Spain, 25 tinted litho plates, 1837. (Phillips) $1,764

Peter Brown: New illustrations of Zoology, text in English and French, 50 hand-col. plates, 1776. (Phillips) $1,800

Lamb (Patrick), Royal Cookery; or, the Complete Court-Cook, first edn, half title, 1710. (Phillips) $1,350

J. J. Rousseau: La Botanique, 65 plates, 46 hand-col, Paris 1805. (Phillips) $990

Thomas Littleton Powys Lilford, 'Coloured Figures of the Birds of the British Islands', chromolitho plates by Archibald Thorburn, first edition, 1885-1897, seven volumes. (Henry Spencer) $2,244

F. Crisp, Mediaeval Gardens, 'Flowery Medes' and other arrangements of herbs, flowers and shrubs, with illustrations from original sources collected by the author, 2 vols, 1924. (Woolley & Wallis) $355

M. Seutter, and T. C. Lotter: A set of 37 hand-col. maps with cartouches, in green moroccan folders and contained in fitted green moroccan box, circa 1740.(Phillips)$3,024

BRONZE

'Golfer'. A cold-painted bronze and ivory figure, cast and carved from a model by Ferdinand Preiss, as a young woman with golden blouse and green skirt, 32cm. high. (Phillips) $7,106

A Western Asiatic bronze humped bull, the body of solid proportions, the thick neck with multiple incised folds, 12.5cm. high. (Phillips) $2,150

A bronze figure of a military gentleman, in ceremonial robes, the base inscribed F. W. Pomeroy, 1905, 29cm. high. (Phillips) $935

'Andalusian Dancer', a cold-painted bronze and ivory figure cast and carved from a model by P. Philippe, 35.3cm. high. (Phillips) $7,040

An impressive pair of Napoleon III French bronze lions, raised on shaped ormolu plinths, 36cm. x 42cm. (Phillips) $7,200

A Syro-Phoenician bronze figure of a woman standing with right hand cupped to breast and left hand placed upon the stomach, 11.5cm. high. (Phillips) $1,066

L. & J. G. Stickley dinner gong, circa 1907, the arched frame supporting circular bronze gong, signed with Handcraft label, 33¾in. high. (Robt. W. Skinner Inc.) $8,500

'Bubble Dance', a bronze and ivory figure by A. Goddard, of Georgia Graves at the Folies Bergere, 1930, the female figure in short silver-patinated dress, 52.5cm. high. (Christie's) $10,285

A French bronze table centerpiece, supported on the back of a young triton kneeling on a shaped base, 9¼in. high. (Lawrence Fine Arts) $632

A golden-patinated bronze figure cast from a model by Lorenzl, as a dancing girl wearing a long-sleeved dress, 49cm. high. (Phillips) $1,402

A large 19th century French bronze group of the dying Gaul, after the Antique, cast by Barbedienne, 75cm. long. (Christie's) $2,974

A Tibetan bronze and polychrome figure of a Buddhistic Yi-Dam, (God-protector), 18th century, the three-headed Sang-Dui seated in yab-yum, 6½in. high. (Robt. W. Skinner Inc.) $900

A cold painted bronze figure, attributed as a model by Colinet, of a naked girl with brown hair, poised above a stepped marble base, 49.5cm. high. (Phillips) $2,064

An Austrian cold-painted bronze elephant, 19th century, with mahout and bedecked in full riding gear, impressed mark, GESCHUTET, 9¼in. high. (Robt. W. Skinner Inc.) $2,100

'Fancy Dress', a cold-painted bronze and ivory group, cast and carved from a model by Demetre Chiparus, as a Pierrot wearing a green-silver costume dancing with his female companion, 48.5cm. high. (Phillips) $22,440

An inlaid bronze vase, with various colored bronzes, gold and silver, in high relief with a bear on a rocky outcrop, signed, 7in. high. (Lawrence Fine Arts) $4,065

A bronze fish group cast from a model by E.Smith, and fashioned as fish swimming in unison perched on the crest of a wave, 27.5cm. (Phillips) $748

An Art Nouveau bronze vase embellished at the top with two girls, faces in relief with flowers and foliage, 43.5cm. high. (Phillips) $561

BRONZE

A Regency bronze bust of the Prince Regent, after Chantrey, wearing military uniform with the Order of the Golden Fleece at his neck, 14.5cm. diam. (Christie's) $650

A 19th century French bronze equestrian group of a Berber drinking on horseback with a maiden, cast from a model by Dubucand, 67cm. high. (Christie's) $3,718

A 19th century English bronze statuette of the Eagle Slayer, cast by E.W.Wyon, from a model by John Bell, 62cm. high. (Christie's) $2,974

A rare late 19th century English New Sculpture bronze statuette of Perseus, cast from a model by F.W. Pomeroy, 51cm. high. (Christie's) $22,308

A pair of inlaid bronze vases of baluster shape, each applied in low relief, with sparrows in flight among leafless branches, signed, 6¼in. high. (Lawrence Fine Arts) $796

A 19th century French bronze statuette of Cupid, cast from a model by Bruchon, 45.5cm. high. (Christie's) $2,416

An Anglo-Australian early 20th century bronze figure of Diana wounded, cast from a model by Sir Bertram Mackennal, 42cm. high overall. (Christie's) $14,872

A late 19th or early 20th century French bronze group of a walking cow with a peasant girl knitting beside it, cast from a model by J. Garnier, 22.5 x 25cm. (Christie's) $930

'Skater', a silver-patinated bronze and ivory figure cast by Ferdinand Preiss, of a girl skating with one leg behind her, 33.4cm. high. (Christie's) $7,807

BRONZE

A Chinese gilt bronze figure of Guanyin depicted seated, 10½in. high, 17th century. (Bearne's) $440

A bronze censer and cover of rounded rectangular shape, the cover surmounted by a recumbent beast, 7½in. wide. (Lawrence Fine Arts) $716

'Pitcher', a bronze figure cast from a model by Pierre Le Faguays, of a young girl in a short dress, 25cm. high. (Christie's) $486

A bronze figure of a girl, cast from a model by P. Philippe, she stands above a shaped marble base with her arms upstretched, 53cm. high. (Phillips) $1,204

A magnificent pair of 19th century French bronze parcel gilt and enamelled busts with onyx drapery of 'La Juive d'Alger' and the 'Cheik Arabe de Caire', by Charles-Henri-Joseph Cordier, 86cm. high. (Christie's) $316,030

An early 19th century French bronze statuette of the King of Rome, in the style of Barre, the youth shown in military uniform, 33.5cm. high. (Christie's) $2,044

A large patinated bronze figure cast from a model by Lorenzl of a semi naked dancing girl, 16¼in. high. (Christie's) $1,028

A late 19th century Viennese bronze portrait bust of a young girl, cast from a model by Arthur Strasser, dated 1894, 42cm. high. (Christie's) $929

A bronze bust of William IV dated June 1, 1831, and indistinctly signed Sam Parker, 10in. high. (Christie's) $555

A bronze figure of a reclining deerhound, resting on a rounded base inscribed Gayrard London 1848, 12in. (Lawrence Fine Arts) $936

A 19th century bronze model of an elephant, its hide naturalistically cast and chased, signed, 9in. high. (Lawrence Fine Arts) $557

A 19th century French bronze group of a stag attacked by a panther, cast from a model by A.L. Barye, 36cm. high. (Christie's) $3,718

A 19th century English bronze group of the Tarpeian rock, cast from a model by George Halse, London 1860, 63cm. high. (Christie's) $2,044

A bronze figure of a monkey, seated, wearing a parcel-gilt trimmed jacket, his fur naturalistically chased, 2¼in. high. (Lawrence Fine Arts) $159

A late 19th century French bronze statuette of 'L' Industrie Moderne', cast from a model by Charley Perron, 63cm. high. (Christie's) $836

A bronze model of a farmer riding an ox, the detachable figure holding his tobacco pouch, signed Watanabe zo, 25cm. long. (Christie's) $1,175

An Art Nouveau bronze of a young woman wearing a long aubergine dress, signed L. Alliot, on a green marble base, 25in. high. (Hy. Duke & Son) $1,352

'Les Amis de Toujours', a bronze and ivory figure by Demetre Chiparus, of a standing lady, flanked by two borzois, on a rectangular amber- colored onyx base, 63cm. high. (Christie's) $22,440

BRONZE

A fine bronze koro on tripod feet inlaid in iroe hirazogan and takazogan with bowing branches of wisteria, signed Ichiyosai Atsumitsu koku, late 19th century, 13cm. diam. (Christie's) $4,895

An archaic bronze tripod libation vessel, jue, the body cast in four sections, Shang Dynasty 20.8cm. high. (Christie's) $9,955

A gilt bronze tray cast from a model by Maurice Bouval, formed as a leaf with the figure of a nymph holding flowers, signed M. Bouval, 17.5cm. high. (Christie's) $1,215

A 19th century bronze figure of a boy kneeling, 9in. high. (Lawrence Fine Arts) $706

A bronze model of an elephant being attacked by two tigers, one crawling up its back, signed Seiya zo, late 19th century, 19cm. long . (Christie's) $685

A gilt bronze and ivory figure of a young woman after Gregoire, 10in. high, signed, circa 1910. (Bearne's) $2,376

An early Ming gilt-bronze figure of Syamatara, finely cast seated on a triangular double lotus in lalitasana, Yongle period, 20.9cm. high. (Christie's) $23,892

'Rahda', a bronze and ivory figure by P. Philippe, of a dancer standing on tiptoe, arms outstretched, 43.4cm. high. (Christie's) $10,285

A mid 19th century English bronze inkwell, the lid cast with a group of cattle, stamped Messenger & Sons, 1850, Birmingham, 18cm. high. (Christie's) $743

77

BRONZE

'Panther', a dark patinated bronze figure, by M. Prost, of a stylized stalking panther, 37cm. long. (Christie's) $1,487

A cast bronze censer, of square tapering bucket form, cast to appear as if constructed from boldly grained wood, signed, 4¾in. wide. (Lawrence Fine Arts) $260

A 19th century French bronze model of a setter cast from a model by F. Delabrierre, on oval naturalistic base, 15.5cm. high. (Christie's) $1,115

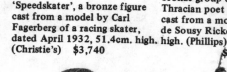

A large 19th century bronze group of a centaur with Cupid on his back, after the Antique, 76 x 49cm.(Christie's) $5,205

'Speedskater', a bronze figure cast from a model by Carl Fagerberg of a racing skater, dated April 1932, 51.4cm. high. (Christie's) $3,740

'Orpheus and Eurydice', a bronze group of the legendary Thracian poet and his wife, cast from a model by Charles de Sousy Ricketts, R.A., 34cm. high. (Phillips) $35,200

A 19th century French bronze group of a stag browsing at a branch, cast from a model by Pierre Jules Mene, 1843, 38cm. high. (Christie's) $2,416

A late 19th or early 20th century English bronze bust of a handsome youth, in the style of Brock, on turned red marble socle, 14.5cm. high. (Christie's) $167

A 19th century French bronze group of a mounted zouave with a dead gazelle, cast from a model by P.J. Mene, 51cm. high. (Christie's) $1,487

BRONZE

A 19th century French bronze group of a ewe suckling a lamb, after P.J. Mene, on oval naturalistic base, 15.5cm. high. (Christie's) $1,487

A bronze figure of an old man, seated on a mat holding a pipe, 14in. high. (Lawrence Fine Arts) $4,647

A bronze figure of a recumbent cow, a young boy perched on its back playing a flute, 7¾in. long. (Lawrence Fine Arts) $892

'Moth Girl', a bronze and ivory figure by Ferdinand Preiss, of a girl standing on tiptoe and examining a glass over her shoulder, 41.6cm. high. (Christie's) $8,415

A 19th century French bronze model of a long-horned bull, entitled Toro Romano, cast from a model by Jules Clesinger, 23 x 34cm. (Christie's) $1,137

A bronze figure by Cl. J. R. Colinet, modelled as a nude female standing on one foot, the other leg and both arms outstretched before her, supporting a ball on each, 26.7cm. high. (Christie's) $841

An early 20th century Belgian bronze bust of a stevedore, cast from a model by Constantin Meunier, inscribed Anvers, 58cm. high. (Christie's) $5,948

One of a pair of Regency bronze and ormolu figures with kneeling Egyptian figures holding lidded dishes, 4¾in. high. (Christie's) Two $1,954

'Source d'Or', a bronze sculpture by Ernest Wante of a gold patinated maiden standing in a rocky enclave, 25.4cm. high. (Christie's) $1,487

BRONZE

A bronze belt-hook unusually formed as two snakes twisted together, cast with scale markings, 4th/1st century B.C., 6.3cm. long. (Christie's) $2,190

A 19th century French bronze model of a seated boar, cast from a model by Christophe Fratin, 14cm. high. (Christie's) $2,481

A Bergman 'Egyptianesque' gilt bronze female figure, she stands naked with her arms folded across her chest, (Phillips) $1,020

An archaic bronze beaker, gu, with typical spreading foot and trumpet mouth, Shang Dynasty, 27.4cm. high, fitted box. (Christie's) $13,937

'Exotic Dancer', a gold-patinated bronze and ivory figure by Gerdago of a female dancer making a theatrical curtsey, 30.5cm. high. (Christie's) $22,440

A bronze oviform vase modelled in relief with carp in swirling waters, signed Jounkoku, late 19th century, 22.5cm. high. (Christie's) $940

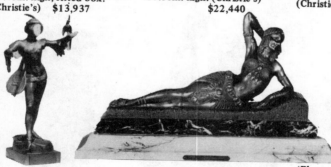

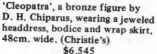

'The Strolling Minstrel', a bronze and ivory figure by Maurice Constant of a man dressed in mediaeval costume, 37cm. high. (Christie's) $743

'Cleopatra', a bronze figure by D. H. Chiparus, wearing a jeweled headdress, bodice and wrap skirt, 48cm. wide. (Christie's) $6,545

'Elegant', a gold patinated bronze and ivory group, cast and carved from a model by S. Bertrand, of a finely dressed woman standing with a grayhound at her side, 31.2cm. high. (Christie's) $3,740

BRONZE

A rare early 20th century English bronze statuette of the Spirit of Ecstasy, cast from a model by Charles Sykes, 60cm. high. (Christie's) $9,295

'Arab at Prayer', a Viennese bronze figure cast from a model by Chotka, on rectangular amber marble base, 31cm. long. (Christie's) $935

An early 20th century French bronze bust of Perseus, cast from a model by E. Hannaux, 56cm. high. (Christie's) $3,515

'Chinaman', a bronze bust cast from a model by Jean Mich, inscribed CHIH-FAN HAN YANG-CHINE, 43cm. high. (Christie's) $1,683

A pair of Persian bronze candle-sticks, chased with panels of figures, 8½in. high. (Lawrence Fine Arts) $185

A rare 19th century Irish bronze statuette of Mr Gladstone, cast from a model by Albert Bruce-Joy, 97cm. high. (Christie's) $5,205

'The Waiter', a bronze figure cast from a model by Engelhart of a waiter in tailcoat carrying dishes, dated 1904, 26.6cm. high. (Christie's) $374

A 20th century bronze model of a turtle, after Giovanni Antoniati, piped to emit water through mouth, 89 x 61cm. (Christie's) $3,102

'Gamin', a bronze and ivory figure by F. Preiss, of a girl dressed in a silver patinated short skirt suit, standing with her hands in her pockets, 34.3cm. high. (Christie's) $11,220

BRONZE

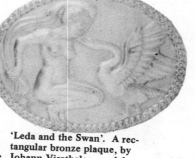

A late 19th or early 20th century Austrian bronze statuette of a huntsman, cast from a model by H. Muller, wearing traditional hunting clothing, 45cm. high. (Christie's) $520

A George IV bronze and brass tazza, in the manner of Vulliamy, the shallow dish supported by three addorsed dolphins, 6in. diam. (Christie's) $534

'Leaving the Opera', a bronze and ivory figure by D. Chiparus of a woman wrapped in a silver-patinated cloak, walking down a stepped brown onyx base, 23.4cm. high. (Christie's) $3,179

A 19th century French bronze statuette of Apollo Belvedere, after the Antique, on a circular base, 47cm. high. (Christie's) $1,757

'Leda and the Swan'. A rectangular bronze plaque, by Johann Vierthaler, modelled with a naked girl kneeling before a swan, 12.3cm. x 28.9cm., impressed 'J.V.'. (Phillips) $189

A late 19th century French bronze bust of a young cavalier, cast from a model by Ernest Rancoulet, 66cm. high. (Christie's) $1,447

'Valkyrie', a bronze and ivory figure, cast and carved from a model by Louis Chalon, as a warrior maiden wearing armor and a helmet, 52cm. high. (Phillips) $4,400

An unusual Austrian bronze and glass fish tank, cast from a model by Adolf Josef Pohl, surmounted by marabou storks looking expectantly into the water, 39cm. wide. (Phillips) $1,548

'Dancer', a bronze and ivory figure by H. Fournier of a girl standing on tiptoe, holding out her skirt, 35cm. high. (Christie's) $4,488

BRONZE

'Nubian Dancer', a bronze and ivory figure by D. H. Chiparus of a dancing girl in a silver-patinated bodice and headdress and black-patinated skirt in the Egyptian style, 42.3cm. high. (Christie's) $15,895

'Venetian Lady', a bronze and ivory figure by J. Lorimer of a maiden in a finely decorated and polychrome enamelled eighteenth century costume, 42cm. high. (Christie's) $9,350

Wal Law 'The Left Winger'. A cast bronze of a footballer, signed, inscribed and dated 1929, 24in. high. (Bearne's) $2,655

An early 20th century English bronze group of two naked youths playing leapfrog, by Arthur George Walker R.A., 31cm. high. (Christie's) $1,115

A pair of 19th century French rectangular bronze plaques with pendant trophies of game, cast from models by Pierre-Jules Mene, both signed, 30.5cm. (Christie's) $785

'Golfer', a bronze and ivory figure, by D. H. Chiparus, of a girl swinging a golf club and wearing a green-patinated skirt, 36.8cm. high. (Christie's) $16,830

A late 19th century French bronze group of a huntsman holding aloft a dead part-ridge, cast from a model by Paul Delabrierre, 53cm. high. (Christie's) $2,788

'Dancer', a bronze luminaire cast and carved from a model by Alex Kelety, of a naked fe-male running, her head thrown back and with one leg kicking backwards, 49.5cm. high. (Christie's) $11,220

A 19th century French bronze statuette of Cupid stringing his bow, after Lemire, 43cm. high. (Christie's) $1,240

BRONZE

A pair of ormolu candlesticks of rococo style, the foliate nozzles above shaped shafts, 10in. high. (Christie's) $4,477

A pair of Louis XV style ormolu chenets, mid 19th century, with a male and a female Oriental figure reclining, 18in. high. (Robt. W. Skinner Inc.) $6,000

A Tiffany Studios bronze candelabrum, with blown-out green Favrile glass in each holder, New York, 12in. high. (Robt. W. Skinner Inc.) $2,200

A pair of ormolu chenets, one with a seated figure of a boy in a turban, the other with a boy wearing a helmet, 18th century, 10¼in. high. (Christie's) $8,140

An Empire ormolu wall bracket, the turned nozzle flanked by lion mask lamps supported by a winged horse, 6½in. wide. (Christie's) $712

Pair of 19th century ormolu and green marble candelabra. (British Antique Exporters) $438

An American figure of a naked girl, cast from a model by Harriet W. Frishmush, inscribed with artist's name and Gorham Co., Founders, 29.8cm. high. (Phillips) $5,632

A pair of ormolu andirons of Louis XVI design, each with a large urn with flaming finial, 16¾in. wide. (Christie's) $3,053

'Pierrette', a cold-painted bronze and ivory figure, cast and carved from a model by P. Philippe, 37.8cm. high. (Phillips) $7,040

BUCKETS

A George III brass-bound mahogany plate-bucket with brass swing handle, 12in. diam. (Christie's) $1,851

A William IV green-painted coal-bucket with oval body and lid painted with flowers, 20½in. high. (Christie's)
$3,908

A Regency brass-bound mahogany peat bucket with swing handle and tapering cylindrical body, 18½in. high. (Christie's)
$2,710

A painted and decorated leather fire bucket, branded I. Fenno, Boston, Massachusetts, dated 1826, the painted ochre ground decorated with a shield-shaped reserve with standing figure of a Massasoit Indian, 13in. high. (Robt. W. Skinner Inc.)
$5,500

Two matching George III mahogany and brass bound peat buckets with brass swing handles. (Prudential)
$2,975

A painted and decorated leather fire bucket, Ipswich, Massachusetts, dated 1803, inscribed S. Newman, Ipswich Fire Society, 30.8cm. high. (Robt. W. Skinner Inc.) $1,300

A painted and decorated leather fire bucket, New England, 1806, decorated with oval reserve, with draped figure of Mercury, 12¾in. high. (Robt. W. Skinner Inc.) $27,000

A 'Lehnware' painted wooden bucket, Lancaster County, Pennsylvania, second half 19th century, 9½in. high. (Christie's)
$5,280

An oval brass-bound mahogany bucket with swing handle and brass liner, 19th century. 13in. high. (Christie's) $774

A George III mahogany tea caddy, the rectangular top with brass swan neck handle enclosing plain interior, 23cm. (Phillips) $168

A George III tortoiseshell tea caddy of octagonal shape with ivory and silver colored metal stringing, 6½in. (Lawrence Fine Arts) $1,039

A Regency tortoiseshell tea caddy, the casket top over double bowed front, on flange base, 20cm. (Phillips) $224

A William IV rosewood workbox with sarcophagus shaped cover lifting to reveal a fitted interior with mirror, 13in. wide. (Lawrence Fine Arts) $1,559

One of a pair of George III mahogany cutlery urns inlaid with checkered lines, 28½in. high. (Christie's)
    Two $2,468

A miniature painted blanket box, signed Edward Cornell and dated December 24, 1809, 13½in. high. (Robt. W. Skinner Inc.) $2,600

A mid Victorian ormolu mounted walnut games box, the slightly domed square top studded with 'cats' eyes', 7½in. wide. (Christie's) $537

An early Victorian painted and gilt papier-mache workbox, decorated with flowers and exotic birds, 11½in. wide. (Christie's) $744

An early Victorian rosewood casket tea caddy, with non-matching cut glass mixing bowl, length 30cm. (Osmond Tricks) $120

CADDIES & BOXES

A George III rolled paper tea caddy of elliptical shape, with wheatear and roundel design, 7¼in. (Lawrence Fine Arts) $1,205

A fine two-tiered suzuribako, decorated in gold and silver togidashi, detailed in nashiji, gyobu-nashiji and silver, Meiji period, 22.5 x 10.6 x 13.5cm. (Christie's) $5,874

A George III yew tea caddy, the canted rectangular top with box and harewood banding, 19cm. (Phillips) $262

A George III satinwood cutlery box, the crossbanded sloping flap inlaid with shells with later fitted interior, 8¾in. wide. (Christie's) $1,028

A French red tortoiseshell and boulle decanter box, the lock stamped Jean A Rennes, late 19th century, 14½in. wide. (Christie's) $1,861

A George III mahogany knife-box, the fall serpentine front revealing a fitted interior, 32cm. (Phillips) $449

An Edwardian tortoiseshell tea caddy in the form of a knife box, with silver banding and escutcheon, Birmingham Assay 1909, 10cm. (Phillips) $1,159

An Edwardian marquetry writing compendium with folding writing slope and fitted interior, 12in. wide. (Hy. Duke & Son) $676

A Victorian travelling dressing case by Parkins & Gotto, veneered in burr walnut and bound in brass, 13in. wide (hallmarked London 1866). (Bearne's) $2,389

CADDIES & BOXES

A 19th century Dutch Colonial amboyna and brass mounted box, the sides with brass carrying handles, on ball feet, 39cm. (Phillips) $598

An ormolu mounted scarlet leather work casket, on claw feet, early 19th century, 7¾in. wide. (Christie's) $308

An unusual tea caddy in the shape of a bowfront pedestal sideboard with bead style borders, 19th century, 18in. wide. (Lawrence Fine Arts)
$2,238

A Regency painted tin-plated coal scuttle, of sarcophagus shape, with chinoiserie decoration, 18½in. wide. (Christie's) $2,468

A birch pipe box, America, late 18th/early 19th century, shaped back and single thumb-molded drawer, 14¼in. high. (Robt. W. Skinner Inc.) $550

A Regency rosewood tea chest, the shaped hinged cover carved with anthemion motifs, 10¼in. (Lawrence Fine Arts)
$1,143

A George III yew tea caddy, the canted rectangular boxwood edged top over two-compartment interior, 18cm. (Phillips) $263

A George IV ormolu and ebonized pen tray with scrolled handles and two lidded inkwells, on winged claw feet, 13½in. wide. (Christie's) $1,851

A painted and decorated clock repairer's box, America, 19th century, painted dark red and decorated with polychrome eagle in flight grasping an American flag, 20in. wide. (Robt. W. Skinner Inc.) $4,200

A Regency mahogany marquetry workbox, the hinged rectangular lid inlaid with Prince-of-Wales' feathers, on scrolled feet, 8½in. wide. (Christie's) $781

A knife box, America, 19th century, rectangular form with outward flaring sides and shaped ends. (Robt. W. Skinner Inc.) $700

A painted and decorated document box, attributed to Heinrich Bucher, Reading, Bucks County, Pennsylvania, 1770-1780, the hinged domed lid lifting to an open compartment, 13in. wide. (Christie's) $6,600

An extensive Art Deco cased silver and enamelled toilet set, made by the Goldsmiths and Silversmiths Co. Ltd., all in blue crocodile leather case, 45cm. wide, London 1934. (Phillips) $3,440

A fine foliate shaped box decorated with the Nine-tailed Fox as a Chinese Princess, Dakki, seated, with an arm rest, in a Chinese room, 19th century, 12.5cm. wide. (Christie's) $5,482

A George III scrolled and gilt paperwork tea caddy, the hinged hexagonal top and sides inlaid with a geometric pattern, 7in. wide. (Christie's) $1,851

A Regency blond tortoiseshell tea caddy of rounded rectangular form, the lid revealing fitted interior, 18cm. (Phillips) $486

An inlaid and painted Masonic box, Lawrence, Massachusetts, dated 1858, the rectangular box decorated with Masonic symbols, 7¼in. wide. (Robt. W. Skinner Inc.) $800

A 19th century mother-of-pearl tea caddy, the domed rectangular top enclosing two lidded caddies. (Phillips) $711

A bird's-eye maple roll-top lap desk, America, circa 1820, tambour roll above fold-out writing leaf and single drawer, 9 x 14in. (Robt. W. Skinner Inc.) $1,000

A Victorian rosewood tortoiseshell and brass mounted stationery box by J.C.Vickery, Regent Street. (Greenslades) $761

An Anglo-Indian ivory and hardwood games board, the hinged rectangular lid with chess squares and enclosing a backgammon board, 19th century, 16in. wide. (Christie's) $1,628

A good late George III burr yew veneered and parquetry banded tea caddy of sarcophagus shape, 8in. wide. (David Lay) $651

A George III fruitwood tea caddy, third quarter 18th century, in the form of an apple, 4½in. high. (Robt. W. Skinner Inc.) $1,050

A George III maple and rosewood tea caddy of unusual shape, with curved tapering body and ring-and-basket handles, on claw feet, 11¾in. wide. (Christie's) $10,120

Early Victorian burr walnut stationery box with brass studded ivory decoration. (British Antique Exporters) $131

A rectangular Indian cigarette box, inset with a coloured oval miniature on ivory depicting a man and woman in fond embrace, 18cm. x 10cm. (Phillips) $321

An interesting Georgian Officer's campaign basin, the brass bound oval mahogany case with hinged lid and silver plated liner, the escutcheon with lifting handle engraved M. General Pack. (Phillips) $1,318

Early 19th century mahogany two-division tea caddy with mother-of-pearl inlay. (British Antique Exporters)
$175

19th century coromandel wood workbox with brass embellishments. (British Antique Exporters)
$219

A Regency bronze mounted rosewood ambassadorial inkstand, fitted with a pen trough flanked by canted wells, with an ivory bust of Voltaire, 20½in. wide. (Christie's)
$30,272

A Regency tortoiseshell tea caddy, with silver mounts, the hinged cover enclosing a two division lidded interior, on ball feet. (Geering & Colyer) $662

Victorian oak cased smoker's companion with earthenware tobacco jar and plated brass fittings. (British Antique Exporters) $175

A good William IV rosewood veneered and brass inlaid sarcophagus tea chest. (David Lay)
$261

A rare 18th century French straw-work tea caddy, the tinned body applied all over with colored straw-work, 6in. high. (David Lay)
$470

A Regency ebonized and boulle inkstand, fitted with two cut-glass inkwells, 16in wide. (Christie's) $781

A George III mahogany knife box with boxwood edging and fitted interior. (Greenslades)
$338

CAMERAS

Eastman Kodak Co., polished wood B Ordinary Kodak camera with string-set shutter and brass bound lens. (Christie's) $1,566

The Stereoscopic Company, rare 4½ x 6cm. 'Binocular Physiograph camera' no. 1776 with an E. Krauss, Paris Tessar-Zeiss f 4.5 52mm. lens. (Christie's) $1,174

An eighteenth century mahogany reflex camera obscura with sliding box focusing and hinged ground glass screen cover, lens diameter 1¼in. (Christie's) $9,398

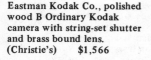

A 4½ x 6cm. Ermanox camera with an Ernemann Anastigmat Ernostar f 1.8 8.5cm. lens. (Christie's) $1,076

An Eastman Kodak Co., No. 3a Panoram-Kodak camera No. 1067. (Christie's) $395

Houghton-Butcher Mfg. Co. Ltd., London, an Ensign roll-film reflex camera Tropical model with an Aldis Uno Anastigmat. (Christie's) $430

A 4.14 x 6.35cm. 'Planovista' twin lens camera No. 991 with an upper viewing lens on to a ground glass screen and a lower Meyer Plasmat f 2.7 7.5cm. taking lens. (Christie's) $626

Marion and Co., 140 x 90mm. Tropical stereoscopic reflex camera with inset brass binding, red bellows and red leather viewing hood. (Christie's) $8,811

Child Guidance Products Inc., 126 cartridge 'Mick-A-Matic Deluxe' novelty camera in maker's original box. (Christie's) $97

A 3¼ x 4¼in. mahogany sliding box wet plate camera stamped 402 with a brass bound portrait lens.(Christie's) $1,409

Newman and Guardia, very rare 116 film 'Special stereoscope roll film Sibyl' camera No. A729 with a pair of Ross, London patent Xpres 75mm. f 4.5 lenses. (Christie's) $2,153

Horne & Thornthwaite, rare and unusual 6½ x 7½in. mahogany collapsible camera with brass fittings. (Christie's) $12,727

A quarter plate mahogany 'Loman's Patent Reflex Camera' with a brass bound Loman & Co., Amsterdam lens with rack and pinion focusing. (Christie's) $1,860

A Henry Park plate brass and mahogany tailboard camera with a brass bound Emil Busch rapid aplanat 10in. f 8 lens. (Christie's) $177

A twin lens Contaflex camera with a Zeiss Sucher-Objectiv f 2.8 8cm. viewing lens. (Christie's) $1,664

A rare quarter plate wooden bodied twin lens reflex camera with six integral mahogany double dark slides, maker's plaque 'H Park, Manufacturer'. (Christie's) $1,468

Mashpriborintorg, Narciss camera No. 6501138 with a Vega-M-1 f 2.8 35mm. lens. (Christie's) $783

W. Butcher and Sons, 3¼ x 4¼in. 'Royal Mail' camera with fifteen lenses mounted in five rows of three set into a simple shutter. (Christie's) $1,076

C. P. Goerz, 16mm. Minicord camera no. 7164 with a Goerz, Wien Helgar f 2 2.5cm. lens. (Christie's) $430

Newman and Guardia, quarter plate 'Nydia' camera no. 463 with a Ross, London symmetric Anastigmat 5½in., f 8 lens. (Christie's) $548

J. Richard, rare 35mm. 80 x 30mm. stereoscopic 'Homeos' camera no. 291 with a pair of Kraus/Zeiss Tessar f 4.5 28mm. lenses. (Christie's) $2,545

W. I. Chadwick, half plate brass and mahogany stereoscopic camera with a pair of brass bound lenses with wheel stops barrels. (Christie's) $979

H. Ernemann, Dresden, 9 x 12cm. tropical Heag II/II' camera with tan colored bellows, brass fittings and polished wood body. (Christie's) $1,272

Marion and Co., good and rare 1½ x 1½in. Academy camera in polished mahogany and brass fittings with plate holder and viewfinder. (Christie's) $6,265

Thornton-Pickard 4.5 x 6cm. Snappa camera with lens front panel marked 'Pat. No.26186 11'. (Christie's) $430

A Le Coultre Et Cie, Compass camera No. 2325 with a CCL 35mm. f 3.5 Anastigmat lens, all contained within a fitted pigskin case. (Christie's) $1,351

A Dollond half plate studio camera, the lens with irised diaphragm, f8 to f64, together with three mahogany double sided plate holders, (Lawrence Fine Arts) $244

CAMERAS

Horne and Thornthwaite, extremely rare and fine 3 x 3in. mahogany and brass 'Powell's Stereoscopic Camera' comprising a collapsible camera with detachable stereoscopic back that stores inside the camera mounting box. (Christie's) $5,874

An early 7 x 7in. wet plate mahogany sliding box camera with ground glass focusing screen and a brass bound Lerebours et Secretan a Paris lens. (Christie's) $939

A Seiki-Kogaku Canon S camera No. 10594 with a Nippon-Kogaku Nikkor f 2.8 5cm. lens. (Christie's) $2,494

Suzuki Optical Co., rare 5 x 8mm. 'Camera Lite' disguised camera with an f 8 lens, instant and bulb shutter. (Christie's) $685

A Stereo Kodak model 1 camera with a pair of Kodak Anastigmat f 7.7 130mm. lenses, set into an EKC Ball Bearing shutter. (Christie's) $395

An Eastman Kodak Co. red Vanity Kodak camera No. 96456 with 'Vest Pocket Kodak Series III' on catch. (Christie's) $270

Horne and Thornthwaite, rare and unusual 6½ x 4¾in. mahogany and brass combined single shot and stereoscopic wet plate camera. (Christie's) $3,132

An Eastman Kodak Co. original Brownie camera with cardboard body, push-on back and rotary shutter with detachable accessory clip. (Christie's) $498

A 45 x 107 'Photo-Stereo Binocular' camera with a pair of Goerz Doppel-Anastigmat III 75mm. lenses. (Christie's) $1,566

A chromium plated Rolls-Royce Spirit of Ecstasy, signed Charles Sykes, circa 1925, 5½in. high. (Christie's) $248

'Cinq Chevaux', a Lalique molded glass car mascot, commissioned by Citroen in 1925, modelled as the overlapping bodies of five spirited horses, 11.5cm. high. (Phillips) $6,336

A nickel plated baby's dummy, marked REG, circa 1926, 3½in. long. (Christie's) $535

A brass Felix the Cat, 1930's, 4in. high. (Christie's) $344

'Faucon', a Lalique car mascot, the amethyst tinted clear and satin finished glass with traces of black staining, molded as a falcon, 15.5cm. high. (Christie's) $1,683

A nickel plated Vauxhall griffin, the base stamped Joseph Fray Ltd., Birmingham, circa 1930, 3¼in. high. (Christie's) $325

'Grenouille', a Lalique molded glass car mascot, modelled as a small frog in crouched position, 5.8cm. high. (Phillips) $14,432

A brass dragonfly, the base stamped M. Bertin, circa 1920, 6½in. high. (Christie's) $421

A chromium plated Humber stylized horse on stepped base, circa 1935, 5¼in. high. (Christie's) $248

A chromium plated and mother-of-pearl inlaid Desmo dragonfly, circa 1935, 4¼in. long. (Christie's) $918

A nickel plated Amilcar Pegasus, the base stamped Darel, çirca 1920, 4in. high. (Christie's) $459

A chromium plated Schneider Trophy seaplane, circa 1930, 6in. long. (Christie's) $803

A chromium plated Vulcan, the figure standing by an anvil, 6in. high. (Christie's) $202

A nickel plated elephant hatching from an egg, the base stamped L'Oeuf d'Elephant depose, circa 1920, 5½in. high. (Christie's) $1,148

A riveted aluminium Voisin Cocotte, circa 1924, 9in. high. (Christie's) $535

A brass Alvis hare, 4½in. high. (Christie's) $191

A brass 'Telcote Pup', circa 1930, mounted on radiator cap, 4in. high. (Christie's) $421

A silver plated brass figure of a winged goddess, playing a harp, seated on a winged wheel, 6½in. high. (Onslow's) $1,980

A chromium plated Desmo winning greyhound, wearing red number 1 racing colors, circa 1950, 6in. long. (Christie's) $172

A chromium plated Packard swan, 7in. high. (Onslow's) $81

A chromium plated figure of a footballer, the base stamped Desmo copyright, 5¼in. high. (Onslow's) $171

A chromium plated figure of Dinky Doo with bow and arrow, mounted on radiator cap, 5¼in. high. (Christie's) $191

'Comete', a rare Lalique molded glass car mascot, moulded as a star with an angular vapor trail streaming behind it, 18.5cm. long. (Phillips) $8,800

A nickel plated caricature figure of a grinning cat, 3¾in. high. (Onslow's) $153

A nickel plated Rolls-Royce Spirit of Ecstasy, the base stamped Rolls-Royce Ltd Feb 6 1911, 5½in. high. (Christie's) $421

A chromium plated jumping salmon, the base stamped Desmo, 4½in. high. (Christie's) $95

A silver plated brass golfer, with head modelled as a golf ball, 6in. high. (Christie's) $3,238

A nickel plated Star with nymph in relief, circa 1922, 3¾ in. high. (Christie's) $861

'Faucon'. A Lalique frosted and polished glass car mascot, molded as a bird of prey with its wings tucked behind it and perched on a circular base, 15.5cm. high. (Phillips) $1,776

A chromium plated motorcycle mascot of Wilfred from Pip, Squeak and Wilfred, circa 1920, 3¼ in. high. (Christie's) $66

A nickel plated Gallia Oil Co., stylized cockerel, the base inscribed Chantecler, 5½ in. high. (Christie's) $161

A chromium plated girl riding a goose, mounted on radiator cap, 4¼ in. high. (Christie's) $803

A chromium plated bear eating honey, 31 in. high. (Christie's) $95

A silver plated young piping satyr, the base stamped DIT MAR, circa 1920, 3½ in. (Christie's) $172

A chromium plated Riley Ski Lady, circa 1930, 5½ in. high. (Christie's) $809

Touch Wud, a leather headed and brass good luck charm, 4½ in. high. (Christie's) $287

CHANDELIERS

A brass framed electrolier with six acanthus-cast branches, 23in. diam. (Bearne's) $910

A Roman key hanging chandelier, the whole overlaid with metal grid simulating leaded segments, 24in. diam. (Robt. W. Skinner Inc.) $1,100

An Art Deco two-tier chandelier in the style of Jacques Emile Ruhlmann, with gilt metal domed base and pendant bauble, 123cm. high. (Christie's) $3,718

A pair of cut-glass and ormolu six-light chandeliers each with a baluster stem and corona hung with swags of faceted drops, 19th century, 36in. high. (Christie's) $10,648

An Empire ormolu twelve light chandelier, the sconces supported by winged caryatid putti, the body hung with chains, 31½in. wide. (Christie's) $6,160

A Venetian glass chandelier, the shaped central stem with bulbous center, 19th century, 50in. high. (Lawrence Fine Arts) $4,158

19th century Victorian gilt bronze chandelier, with scrolled acanthus leaf decoration ringed by six scrolled arms, 60in. high. (Robt. W. Skinner Inc.) $4,700

A George IV ormolu fifteen-light chandelier with scrolling foliage and anthemion chased branches, 78in. high. (Christie's) $39,732

A cut-glass eight-light chandelier with baluster shaft and faceted scrolling branches, 35in. high. (Christie's) $10,696

100

CHANDELIERS

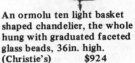

Early 19th century style six-branch glass lustre chandelier, 36in. drop. (Jacobs & Hunt) $2,450

A W.A.S. Benson brass and copper chandelier, the central copper circular fluted dish supported by a central brass rod with three brass arms, approx. 50cm. across. (Phillips)$2,494

An ormolu ten light basket shaped chandelier, the whole hung with graduated faceted glass beads, 36in. high. (Christie's) $924

An Italian giltwood twelve light chandelier with tasselled corona and ropetwist supports, 44in. high. (Christie's) $5,088

A Regency ormolu and cut-glass eight-light chandelier with spirally ribbed canopy, waterfall stem and corona, fitted for electricity, 36in. high. (Christie's) $10,973

An Empire ormolu and bronze six-light chandelier with pierced corona and three molded foliate supports. (Christie's) $2,442

An antique brass chandelier, with large brass ball base, 26in. diam. (Lawrence Fine Arts) $7,276

A gilt metal and glass three branch chandelier, the shades styled as green glass grape branches, 91cm. high. (Christie's) $1,301

A gilt metal and cut glass eight-light chandelier with open frame hung with faceted drops and stud-filled corona, early 19th century, 48in. high. (Christie's) $3,216

101

Teco pottery matt green vase, Illinois, circa 1908, with four open handles, 6½in. high. (Robt. W. Skinner Inc.) $850

Dedham pottery Night and Morning pitcher, early 20th century, 5in. high. (Robt. W. Skinner Inc.) $475

Cobalt decorated stoneware crock, J. & E. Norton, Bennington, Vermont, 10½in. high. (Robt. W. Skinner Inc.) $425

Grueby pottery monumental floor vase, Boston, Massachusetts, circa 1905, the body with repeating broad thumb molded and ribbed decoration, 21in. high. (Robt. W. Skinner Inc.) $4,000

Hampshire pottery vase, Keene, New Hampshire, circa 1900, with repeating molded tulip and running stem decoration, 9in. high. (Robt. W. Skinner Inc.) $350

Grueby pottery vase and Tiffany font, Boston, Massachusetts, circa 1905, with repeating leaves, artist initialled W. F., 10½in. (Robt. W. Skinner Inc.) $4,000

Decorated Marblehead pottery vase, circa 1905, decorated with overall brown latticework on green ground, 6in. high. (Robt. W. Skinner Inc.) $2,100

Two Cowan pottery figural candlesticks, Cleveland, Ohio, 1925, depicting beavers, 9¾in. high. (Robt. W. Skinner.Inc.) $425

Grueby pottery vase, Boston, Massachusetts, circa 1905, decorated with iris alternating with leaf blades, artist initialled by Ruth Ericson. (Robt. W. Skinner Inc.) $2,000

AMERICAN

One gallon stoneware jug, America, mid 19th century, straight sides, applied handle, 9¾in. high. (Robt. W. Skinner Inc.) $250

Saturday Evening Girls large decorated bowl, Boston, Massachusetts, 1914, with white geese outlined in black, dia 11½in. (Robt. W. Skinner Inc) $1,200

Dedham pottery polar bear plate, circa 1929-1943, stamped and the word 'Registered', 7in. diam. (Robt. W. Skinner Inc.) $475

A Tiffany Art pottery vase, New York, 1906, of cylindrical form with repeating molded lady slippers on stems, 12¼in. high. (Robt. W. Skinner Inc.) $3,750

Twelve handpainted porcelain plates, 1901, by Ella J. Libby, with shaped edge painted with seaweed and seashells, 9in. diam. (Robt. W. Skinner Inc.) $600

Large Toby pitcher, possibly Bennington, Vermont, 1849, seated gentleman with tricorn hat, 10¾in. high. (Robt. W. Skinner Inc.) $300

Important and unique stoneware crock with cobalt decoration of two deer flanking an eight-inch diameter pocket watch, 13in. high. (Eldred's) $39,600

Pair of Weller 'Ivory Ware' jardinieres on stands, Zanesville, Ohio, circa 1915, 35in. high, 18in. diam. (Robt. W. Skinner Inc.) $2,900

Four gallon Bennington jug with bird, Bennington, Vermont, 1859-1861, 18in. high. (Robt. W. Skinner Inc.) $700

AMERICAN

A Bennington flint-enamel pitcher, Lyman Fenton and Company, Bennington, Vermont, circa 1849-1853, 8¾in. high. (Robt. W. Skinner Inc.) $475

A painted chalkware lamb with ewe, Pennsylvania, mid 19th century, with red, yellow, black and green details, 7in. high. (Christie's) $385

A Bennington Toby pitcher, J. Norton, Bennington, Vermont, 1849-1858, in the form of a seated gentleman, 6½in. high. (Robt. W. Skinner Inc.) $475

An incised salt glazed stoneware presentation pitcher, attributed to Richard C. Remmy, Philadelphia, Pennsylvania, circa 1880, 10½in. high. (Christie's) $4,620

A Grueby pottery experimental drip glaze vase, Boston, Massachusetts, circa 1905, with wide rolled rim and short neck, 11¼in. high. (Robt. W. Skinner Inc.) $4,000

A cobalt decorated and incised jug, America, early 19th century, decorated with incised figure of standing bird, 15½in. high. (Robt. W. Skinner Inc.) $1,200

A Dedham Pottery covered Scottie dog jar, Dedham, Massachusetts, early 20th century, depicting three Scottie dogs (repaired), 6in. high. (Robt. W. Skinner Inc.) $1,200

A large cobalt decorated stoneware pitcher, Pennsylvania, late 19th century, salt glazed baluster form, 11in. high. (Robt. W. Skinner Inc.) $650

A three-colour Marblehead pottery vase, Massachusetts, circa 1905, the short flared rim on squat bulbous body, initialled by Hannah Tutt, 3½in. high. (Robt. W. Skinner Inc.) $800

ARITA

An Arita armorial bowl, the interior painted with birds, flowers and geometric designs, 29cm. diam. (Bearne's) $550

A handsome Arita model of a seated dog, decorated in iron-red, brown and black enamels and gilt, its mouth agape, late 17th century, 40cm. high. (Christie's) $62,656

A rare Arita blue and white octagonal teapot and cover, the lobed sides with two shaped panels containing scenes from O. Dapper, early 18th century, 26cm. wide. (Christie's) $4,308

A pair of Arita blue and white candlesticks, the bell shaped lower sections decorated with buildings in a forested landscape, late 18th/early 19th century, 25cm. high. (Christie's) $1,371

A fine Arita blue and white charger, the central roundel containing a vase of cascading peony sprays on a veranda, Genroku period, 55cm. diam. (Christie's) $7,832

A large Arita blue and white octagonal vase decorated with karashishi prowling beneath bamboo, pine and peony with ho-o birds hovering above, late 17th century, 60cm. high. (Christie's) $6,853

A large Arita blue and white charger, the central roundel decorated with peony and chrysanthemum sprays among fences, circa 1700, 63cm. diam. (Christie's) $3,133

A Japanese Arita life-size model of an eagle, the biscuit body painted in colors, circa 1700, 59cm. high. (Christie's) $33,462

A rare Arita blue and white shallow dish, the wide everted rim with stylized lotus and scrolling foliage, late 17th century, 24.7cm. diam. (Christie's) $9,398

BELLEEK

A late Belleek teapot in the form of a lobed pine cone. (Langlois) $449

An attractive Belleek porcelain two handled basket, with four strand woven base, impressed mark on applied ribbon, 30cm. wide. (Henry Spencer) $822

An early Belleek marine teapot and cover, the globular sides with molded panels and covered in an ivory lustre, the base with first period mark and registration mark for 1867 24cm. wide. (Christie's) $616

A Belleek vase, modelled as three thistles supporting a larger thistle, on circular base, 22.5cm. (Lawrence Fine Arts) $318

A Belleek center piece, modelled as a fluted circular shell supported by three dolphins, 26.5cm. (Lawrence Fine Arts) $318

A rare Belleek figure of a boy holding a basket on his shoulder, standing on circular base, 9in. high. (Langlois) $726

Belleek strapwork porcelain basket with impressed Belleek mark to base, approximately 9 x 6in. (G. A. Key)$210

One of a pair of Belleek tapering jugs with fluted bodies applied in high relief with bouquets of flowers, 9in. high. (Christie's)
Two $577

A Belleek tea kettle and cover, the overhandle bound with gilt tassels and with spreading leaf molded terminals, 8¼in. across. (Christie's) $230

BERLIN

A Berlin ornithological large lobed circular dish painted in colors with two parrots, circa 1770, 39cm. diam. (Christie's) $4,089

A Berlin blue and white cylindrical chocolate-pot and cover, circa 1775, 13cm. high. (Christie's) $650

A Berlin Zwiebelnmuster pierced two-handled blue and white basket, circa 1785, 21.5cm. diam. (Christie's) $557

A Berlin (Funcke Factory) blue and white faience octagonal baluster vase and cover painted with chinoiserie figures taking tea, circa 1760, 42cm. high. (Christie's) $3,532

A pair of Berlin Russian Ballet figures from models by Hubatsch, the figures in theatrical poses, each polychrome enamelled and with gilt decoration, 21.5cm high. (Christie's) $1,870

A Berlin porcelain rectangular paperweight, finely painted with flowers, printed and impressed marks, 16 x 8.5cm. (Bearne's) $309

A pair of Berlin porcelain figure groups of beggars, each raised upon a square base and highlighted in colors, 18cm. high. (Henry Spencer) $796

A Berlin porcelain plaque depicting a couple strolling through the countryside, 34 x 29cm., impressed K.P.M. and sceptre mark. (Bearne's) $6,960

Two Berlin faience polychrome flared octagonal vases, painted with birds perched and in flight among flowering shrubs, circa 1730, 29.5cm. high. (Christie's) $2,788

BOW

A Bow documentary blue and white octagonal plate, the center with the entwined monogram RC surrounded by trailing flowers, 21cm. diam. (Christie's) $3,872

A Bow fountain group, modelled as a sportsman and companion in flowered clothes, circa 1770, 21.5cm. (Christie's) $871

A pair of Bow figures of a shepherd and a shepherdess, on circular mound bases applied with colored flowers, circa 1758, 14.5cm. high. (Christie's) $2,821

A Bow figure of Pierrot with outstretched arms, wearing pale-yellow clothes edged in puce, circa 1762, 14.5cm. high. (Christie's) $1,258

A pair of Bow porcelain candlestick figures of a young boy and girl in elaborate garb. (A. J. Cobern) $1,443

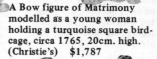

A Bow figure of Matrimony modelled as a young woman holding a turquoise square bird-cage, circa 1765, 20cm. high. (Christie's) $1,787

A pair of Bow white busts of Mongolians, she with her hair plaited, he with a moustache and pointed beard, circa 1750, 27.5cm. high. (Christie's) $85,140

A Bow figure of a seated tabby cat, a brown rat in its right paw, another disappearing into a rathole, circa 1758, 8cm. high. (Christie's) $3,574

A pair of Bow porcelain figures, representing Earth and Water, each with floral robes, 26.5cm., mid 19th century. (Bearne's) $1,575

BRISTOL

A Bristol delft polychrome small rectangular flower-brick, painted with yellow-centered iron-red flowers, circa 1750, 12cm. long. (Christie's) $1,501

A Bristol delft plate, painted in blue with a Chinese river scene, 22.5cm. (Lawrence Fine Arts) $185

A Bristol delft powdered manganese-ground bowl, the exterior with four blue fish swimming in a clockwise direction, circa 1740, 26cm. diam. (Christie's) $6,006

A Bristol delft Adam and Eve charger, boldly painted with the ill-fated couple holding iron-striped yellow leaves, circa 1740, 34cm. diam. (Christie's) $5,205

A Bristol delft blue and white dated miniature shoe, the date 1721 beneath the sole (crack to front, slight chips), 10cm. long. (Christie's) $2,069

A Bristol delft blue-dash Queen Anne portrait charger, boldly painted in bright blue, yellow and ochre, 1702, 35cm. diam. (Christie's) $6,006

A Bristol delft polychrome tea-bowl, painted in iron-red with a man and a stag, circa 1730, 7.5cm. diam. (Christie's) $1,601

A Bristol delft blue and white stand, painted in the manner of Bowen with a milkmaid and four cows, circa 1760, 23cm. diam. (Christie's) $1,501

A Bristol delft dated blue and white bleeding-bowl, the shaped flat handle pierced with two hearts and a circle, 1730, 19.5cm. wide. (Christie's) $1,901

CHINA

A documentary Bovey Tracey saltglaze scratch-blue inscribed and dated rectangular tea-caddy, 1768, 11.5cm. high. (Christie's) $3,403

A documentary creamware armorial quintal vase painted by William Absolon, with the Arms of Yarmouth in black beneath an iron-red ribbon, circa 1790, 20cm. high. (Christie's) $752

A Daisy Borne pottery group, modelled as a mother, sitting naked to the waist on a pedestal base, 29.3cm. high. (Phillips) $352

A 'Girl in a Swing' seal modelled as Harlequin in black mask and multi-colored checkered clothes, circa 1749-54, 3.2cm. high. (Christie's) $790

A blue glazed stoneware garniture comprising a pair of vases and a covered jar, mid 19th century, vases 39cm. and jar 35cm. (Bearne's) $963

A Copeland & Garrett porcelain fluted vase, painted with flowers on a light green ground, early 19th century, 15.5cm. (Bearne's) $249

An early 19th century English porcelain figure of a sheep shearer, wearing a wide brimmed hat, 16.5cm. high. (Henry Spencer) $561

A creamware cylindrical mug, painted in black and enriched in green and yellow with an Oriental standing beneath a shelter, Staffordshire or Yorkshire, circa 1780, 13.5cm. high. (Christie's) $1,137

A Machin coffee pot and cover, bat-printed and colored with buildings in landscape vignettes, circa 1815, 23.5cm. high. (Christie's) $527

BRITISH

A 19th century English drabware honey pot and cover in the form of a beehive, with attached dished circular stand, 9.5cm. high. (Henry Spencer) $149

A porcelain pastille burner in the form of a house, the gold tiled roof edged with moss, 16.5cm. (Bearne's) $653

A Cockpit Hill creamware globular teapot and cover, painted predominantly in iron-red and enriched in green and yellow, circa 1770, 14cm. high. (Christie's) $1,801

A 19th century English porcelain model of a sleeping shepherdess, wearing a bonnet, low cut bodice, long skirt and rouched apron, 14.5cm. high. (Henry Spencer) $187

A large blue glazed ironstone jardiniere with foliate handles, mid 19th century, 33cm. high. (Bearne's) $963

A Pilkington Lancastrian baluster vase, covered in a blue glaze, decorated in ruby and yellow lustre with stylized flowers, date code for 1908, 19.5cm. high. (Christie's) $520

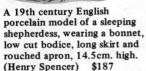

A rare Brameld type treacle glaze pottery figure of a cat, seated with free-standing forelegs, 28.5cm. high. (Henry Spencer) $449

A pair of Plymouth figures of musicians wearing pale clothes, he playing the recorder and his companion the mandolin, Wm. Cookworthy's factory, circa 1770, 14.5cm. high. (Christie's) $1,223

An early Carter and Co. Poole stoneware vase, flared cylindrical form with balcony collar and pinched neck, 19.9cm. high. (Christie's) $168

BRITISH

A Carlton ware orange ground bowl boldly decorated with flowers and multi-patterned quarter circle motifs, 9½in. diam. (Christie's) $192

An underglaze colored Toby jug of Winston Churchill, by 'Wilton Pottery of Cobridge', 17cm. high. (Phillips) $105

A highly unusual Carlton ware ceramic butter dish depicting a well proportioned couple in horizontal embrace, 26cm. across. (Phillips) $640

A Caughley shanked sugar bowl and cover painted with landscapes within gilt circular cartouches, circa 1792, 12cm. diam. (Christie's) $503

A Yorkshire pottery model of a horse, wearing a molded bridle, saddle cloth and surcingle, 15cm. high. (Henry Spencer) $3,287

A Herend porcelain model of a hen eating a berry with up-turned tail feathers, converted to a table lamp, 10in. long. (Christie's) $411

A Davenport fluted baluster jug, the exterior printed and painted with trailing bouquets of flowers, 14in. high.(Christie's) $494

A rare Burmantofts pottery plaque in shallow relief, depicting a heron in naturalistic setting, about to gorge himself on a family of frogs, 25in. approximately. (Geering & Colyer) $777

A Beswick pottery wall mask modelled as the face of a young woman, 9½in. high. (Christie's) $298

BRITISH

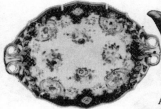

A Ridgway porcelain oval fruit dish with looped handles, and eight painted sprays of flowers, 11½in. wide, circa 1822/5. (Andrew Hartley) $391

A Shelley Intarsio teapot in the form of a caricature of Austin Chamberlain. (William H. Brown) $563

A Copeland and Garrett blue and white two-handled foot bath, the ribbed sides printed with the "Tower" pattern, 20½in. wide. (Christie's) $1,193

A Carlton Ware pottery advertising lampbase made for Guinness, 9½in. high. (Christie's) $303

An Obadiah Sherratt group of Polito's Menagerie, the stage with an organ grinder and companion and five other musicians wearing iron-red, blue and pink clothes, circa 1830, 35cm. wide. (Christie's) $25,168

A Caughley porcelain cabbage leaf molded jug, with rotund body and slant eyes to the mask spout, 22.5cm. high. (Henry Spencer) $486

A Brameld light buff stoneware jug, decorated with a stag at bay and equestrian figures, having an entwined serpent handle, 7in. high. (Woolley & Wallis) $281

A pottery figure of a mermaid, attributed to Daisy Borne, modelled as a naked female figure kneeling on a base of sea-shells and waves, 27cm. high. (Phillips) $281

19th century Sevres style chamber pot with gilt decoration. (British Antique Exporters) $53

An Enoch Wood model of a lion painted in shades of dark brown with his forepaw resting on a ball, 12in. wide. (Christie's) $1,161

Mid 19th century Mason's ironstone toilet set. (British Antique Exporters) $350

A George Jones 'Majolica' game tureen, cover and liner, with a frieze of fern and stiff leaves in shades of green on a dark brown ground, circa 1880, 28cm. wide. (Christie's) $527

Royal Lancastrian lustre pottery vase by W. S. Mycock, painted with galloping horses in jungle background, 5¾in. high. (Prudential) $642

A large pottery figure of a mermaid, attributed to Daisy Borne, she emerges from a wave-decorated base, embellished with fish, 29cm. high. (Phillips) $528

A Dillwyn & Co. oviform jug printed with a view of Pulteney Bridge, Bath, circa 1820, 7in. high. (Christie's) $500

A Susie Cooper wall mask modelled as the head of a woman with gray streaked black hair, 10¾in. long. (Christie's) $1,702

An early 19th century Yorkshire pottery figure of a horse, with green black sponged markings and with yellow saddle cloth, 15.5cm. high. (Henry Spencer) $2,610

A Copeland and Garrett blue and white water jug with the "Tower" pattern, 11½in. high. (Christie's) $350

CANTON

Rose Medallion Canton punch bowl, late 19th century, decorated with alternating scroll-edged reserves, 14½in. diam. (Robt. W. Skinner Inc.) $1,700

Antique Canton covered tureen with boar's head handles, length 12in., and matching platter. (Eldred's) $1,430

Canton square-cut corner bowl decorated with a boating scene, 5in. high, 10in. wide. (Eldred's) $1,760

Antique Canton rectangular deep platter decorated with a lake scene, length 12in. (Eldred's) $770

A good 19th century Cantonese enamelled vase, the waisted neck decorated with two panels of ladies, 24¼in. high. (David Lay) $905

Antique Canton drum-shaped teapot, 8in. high. (Eldred's) $1,100

Antique Canton two-handled sugar bowl, 4½in. high. (Eldred's) $77

A highly important pair of Canton vases, profusely figure decorated with sealion handles and gold serpents to the neck, 37½in. high. (Coles Knapp Fine Arts) $6,650

Antique Canton dish with scalloped edge, 9in. diam. (Eldred's) $303

A large stoneware rose bowl by Michael Cardew on circular foot, the interior covered in an iron speckled greenish-mushroom colored glaze, impressed MC and Wenford Bridge seals, 21.6cm. high. (Christie's) $752

A stoneware globular casserole by Michael Cardew with tall neck, two lug handles and a concave cover with knob finial, circa 1975, 20.7cm. high. (Christie's) $514

An earthenware coffee pot by Michael Cardew, covered in a pale brown glaze over which pale yellow, stopping short of the foot, 14.8cm. high. (Christie's) $316

A stoneware bowl by Michael Cardew, the interior with incised decoration and blue and brown brushwork of a bird amongst grasses, MC and Wenford Bridge seals, 24.5cm. diam. (Christie's) $1,287

A small earthenware cider flagon by Michael Cardew, covered in an amber and olive green glaze over which a mustard-green, stopping short of the foot, impressed MC and Winchcombe Pottery seals, 21cm. high. (Christie's) $198

An oval earthenware slip decorated dish by Michael Cardew, the interior covered in a dark toffee-brown glaze with trailed mustard-yellow slip, circa 1930, 21cm. wide. (Christie's) $277

An Abuja stoneware oil jar by Michael Cardew, with screw stopper, covered in a mottled olive-green glaze, impressed MC and Abuja seals, circa 1959, 33cm. high. (Christie's) $990

A large 'Gwari' stoneware casserole by Michael Cardew, covered in a translucent mottled olive brown and green glaze, 26.5cm. high. (Christie's) $1,683

An earthenware cider flagon by Michael Cardew, with olive-brown brushwork bands of stylized foliage, impressed MC and Winchcombe Pottery seals. 25.4cm. high $748

CHELSEA

A Chelsea tea bowl and trembleuse saucer, painted with bouquets and sprays of flowers, red anchor mark. (Lawrence Fine Arts) $780

A Chelsea coffee cup and saucer, painted with flowers on a molded artichoke ground, gold anchor mark. (Lawrence Fine Arts) $438

A Chelsea octagonal teabowl painted in iron-red and lightly gilt with two sinuous dragons, circa 1750, 9cm. wide. (Christie's) $2,129

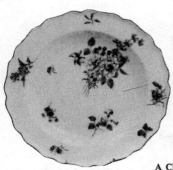

A Chelsea shallow soup plate painted with a bouquet and scattered flower-sprays, circa 1755, 23cm. diam. (Christie's) $677

A Chelsea figure of a Chinaman in black conical hat and long-sleeved robe (restored through waist), circa 1755, 11.5cm. high. (Christie's) $1,505

A fine Red Anchor period Chelsea porcelain 'Hans Sloane' plate, of shaped circular form, painted with panache in green, yellow, blue, puce, brown and burnt orange, 23.5cm. diam. (Henry Spencer) $11,832

A Chelsea figure of a musician playing the pipe and tambourine, leaning against a flower-encrusted tree, circa 1760, 27cm. high. (Christie's) $1,787

A Chelsea-Derby two-handled chocolate cup and saucer, painted with groups of flowers. (Lawrence Fine Arts) $398

A Chelsea figure of the Doctor after the Meissen original, on a circular base applied with flowers, circa 1756, 14.5cm. high. (Christie's) $715

CHINESE

An export "Blue Fitzhugh" basin, China, late 19th century, the interior decorated with central medallion, 15¾in. wide. (Robt. W. Skinner Inc.) $1,100

A painted gray pottery figure of a court lady with attenuated silhouette, (firing fissure, minor chips) Han Dynasty, 44cm. high. (Christie's) $21,901

A Cizhou polychrome pillow of kidney shape, the center carved and combed with a peony spray, the sides under a green glaze stopping above the base, Jin Dynasty, 30cm. wide. (Christie's) $7,565

A Chinese Chien Lung bulbous shaped vase, decorated in famille verte, iron-red and other colors with mythological beast reserves, 12in. high. (Geering & Colyer) $321

A large pair of Oriental vases, China, late 19th century, wide flared scalloped rims; on long tapered necks, 30in. high. (Robt. W. Skinner Inc.) $1,800

A large green-glazed 'Blue and Yellow Dragon' saucer-dish painted at the center with a striding dragon chasing a flaming pearl, Kangxi period, 32.2cm. diam, fitted box. (Christie's) $45,793

A Longquan celadon 'Twin-fish' dish, under an attractive lightly-crackled Kinuta-type glaze, Southern Song Dynasty, 22.6cm. diam. (Christie's) $5,574

A good 19th century Chinese celadon vase, the animal mask handles of carved "bronze", 10¼in. high. (David Lay) $336

A Doucai saucer-dish, the interior with a simple lotus flowerhead, Yongzheng period, 21.1cm. diam. (Christie's) $11,946

CHINESE

A rose Mandarin punch bowl, China, late 19th century, deep bowl decorated with colorful alternating panels, 15¾in. diam. (Robt. W. Skinner Inc.) $1,600

A fine Dehua blanc-de-chine group of the Bodhisattva Manjusri, seated on her recumbent Buddhistic lion, 18th century, 26.8cm. high. (Christie's) $18,914

An export Masonic punch bowl, China, circa 1800, deep bowl, the exterior decorated with Masonic symbols, (hairlines), 11½in. diam. (Robt. W. Skinner Inc.) $2,000

A Cizhou polychrome-enamelled baluster jar, guan, painted in iron-red, green and black, Yuan Dynasty, 30cm. high. (Christie's) $19,910

A fine transitional blue and white Gu-shaped beaker vase, delicately painted in brilliant blue tones with a lingzhi scroll, circa 1640, 41.7cm. high. (Christie's) $11,547

A 19th century Chinese hexagonal jardiniere painted with flowers in colored enamels, 13in. diameter. (Prudential) $6,840

A magnificent Yuan blue and white jar, guan, painted around the globular body with an arching peony scroll comprising six blooms, circa 1340-50, 39cm. high. (Christie's) $895,950

An Oriental export porcelain garden seat, China, late 19th century, barrel-shaped body molded with two rows of bosses, 18¼in. high. (Robt. W. Skinner Inc.) $2,000

A Henan black-glazed baluster vase, meiping, freely painted, Song Dynasty, 22cm. high. (Christie's) $5,574

CLARICE CLIFF

A Clarice Cliff Bizarre vase of cone shape with four triangular feet painted in pink, 6½in. high. (Christie's) $836

A Clarice Cliff Bizarre biscuit barrel and cover, painted with a band of stylized fruit and foliage, 6in. high. (Christie's) $438

A Clarice Cliff Bizarre Fantasque vase painted with a house amongst hills with flowers and leaves in the foreground, 10½in. high. (Christie's) $477

'Tulip' a Clarice Cliff Lotus vase, with ribbed relief signed Cafe-au-Lait, Hand-Painted Bizarre by Clarice Cliff, Newport Pottery, England, 30cm. high. (Christie's) $1,860

A Clarice Cliff plaque, the cavetto boldly painted with orange peonies and black leaves on a cream ground, 33cm. (Bearne's) $2,175

A Clarice Cliff Bizarre single-handled horizontally ribbed jug painted in the 'Delecia' pattern, 7in. high. (Christie's) $190

A Clarice Cliff conical 'Red Roofs' pattern sugar shaker, 14.1cm. high, printed factory marks and facsimile signature. (Phillips) $747

A rare Clarice Cliff vase shaped as a fish swimming amongst seaweed, 8¾in. high, 10½in. long. (David Lay) $531

A Clarice Cliff vase, painted in black, orange, blue, yellow and green with tumbling fruit, leaves and rods, 22.2cm. high. (Phillips) $1,496

CLARICE CLIFF

A Clarice Cliff 'Fantasque' vase of baluster form, brightly painted with a variation of the 'Chintz' design, 15cm.(Bearne's) $765

A Clarice Cliff Newport pottery bough pot, of flared stepped square form with similar fitted pierced center, printed Fantasque and Bizarre, 23cm. square. (Henry Spencer) $851

A Clarice Cliff 'Goldstone' lotus jug, painted in yellow, orange, pink, blue, turquoise and green, 28.5cm. high. (Phillips) $608

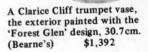

A Clarice Cliff vase, painted in yellow, brown, blue, green and orange with a cottage in a landscape, signed Hand-Painted, Bizarre by Clarice Cliff, Wilkinson Ltd., 46.5cm. high. (Christie's)$1,566

A set of three Clarice Cliff 'Age of Jazz' block ceramic figures, painted in bright colors of black, red, brown, lime-green and yellow. (Phillips) $5,425

A Clarice Cliff trumpet vase, the exterior painted with the 'Forest Glen' design, 30.7cm. (Bearne's) $1,392

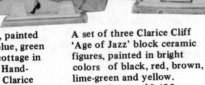

A Clarice Cliff jug of lotus form, boldly painted with the 'Alpine' design, 28.5cm. (Bearne's) $2,697

A Clarice Cliff Bizarre circular pottery plate designed by Dame Laura Knight, 10in. diam. (Christie's) $1,345

Clarice Cliff; a turquoise ground female nymph wall vase, 9½in. high. (David Lay) $467

CLARICE CLIFF

Clarice Cliff; a good sugar dredger, the ribbed body decorated with trees and flowers, 5in. high. (David Lay) $112

A Clarice Cliff 'Fantasque' bowl, painted on the rim with shaped oval stylized flowers and leaves, 30.5cm. diam. (Phillips) $574

Clarice Cliff; an 'Oriental' pattern turquoise ground baluster vase, 12in. high. (David Lay) $205

A rare miniature Clarice Cliff wall plaque molded as the head of a woman, 2¾in. high. (David Lay) $354

An unusual Clarice Cliff cat, naturalistically modelled with smiling expression and wearing a green bow-tie, 15.7cm. high. (Phillips) $1,575

A rare miniature Clarice Cliff wall plaque molded as the head of a woman with checkered scarf, 3¼in. high. (David Lay) $270

Clarice Cliff, an "Inspiration" plate decorated on a turquoise cloud ground with two groups of two trees, 10in. diam. (David Lay) $760

A good Clarice Cliff jug, the ribbed Isis body decorated with the 'Red Roofs' pattern, 11½in. high. (David Lay) $1,773

An "Inspiration" Clarice Cliff charger, decorated on a turquoise cloud ground with a knight on horseback, 18in. diam. (David Lay) $4,732

COALPORT

A Coalport Imari pattern rectangular teapot, cover and stand with gilt scroll spout and angular handle, circa 1815, 26cm. long. (Christie's) $1,129

A Coalport jewelled box and cover modelled as a pair of bellows, enamelled in colors in imitation of opalescent stone and gilt with a floral motif reserved on a gold ground, circa 1894, 23.5cm. long. (Christie's) $940

1897 Jubilee: A Coalport plate printed in blue with a statue and commonwealth members, cracked. (Phillips) $50

A Coalport two handled porcelain vase and cover, with a bud finial and raised upon a domed circular pedestal foot, 17.5cm. high. (Henry Spencer) $563

A pair of Coalport jewelled miniature ewers, enamelled with turquoise beading on gold grounds, the cream-ground shoulders with a band of gilt and red jewelled ornament, circa 1890, 7in. high. (Christie's) $940

A Coalport three handled porcelain pedestal vase of shaped tapering cylindrical form, with acanthus molded double scroll handles, 22.5cm. high. (Henry Spencer) $528

A Coalport (John Rose) breakfast cup and saucer from the Nelson Service, painted with the Admiral's Arms, circa 1800, (Christie's) $5,643

A Coalport tea kettle, cover and stand with green and gilt foliage-molded carrying handle and foliage-molded base to the spout and stand, Coalport mark in gold, circa 1830, 20.5cm. high overall. (Christie's) $3,198

A rare Coalport bust of a gentleman wearing a classical drape inscribed John Rose & Co., 10in. high, circa 1847. (Christie's) $398

COMMEMORATIVE

CHINA

1902 Coronation: A Wedgwood plate printed in blue with portrait and the Dominions. (Phillips) $126

A remarkable group modelled in wax, depicting Victoria and Albert on a gilt scroll-edged sofa, their costumes brightly colored and gilded, 34cm. high overall. (Phillips) $287

An octagonal nursery plate with embossed daisy border, printed in brown and colored with a scene entitled 'The Royal Christening', 16.5cm. (Phillips) $50

Edward VIII: A green jug with portrait and flags printed in colors, inscribed below '*Abdicated Dec. 11th, 1936*'. (Phillips) $270

A pearlware shallow bowl on a small foot, the interior printed in blue with a double portrait busts of George III and Charlotte inscribed '*A King Rever'd, A Queen Belovd, Long May They Live*', 19cm. (Phillips) $676

A 'Jackfield'-glazed pear shaped jug embossed with full length portraits of Victoria and Albert, 21cm. (Phillips) $84

A salt glazed stoneware spirit flask in the form of Prince Albert standing with one arm resting on a crown, 26cm. (Phillips) $338

A very rare pair of Staffordshire portrait busts of William IV and Adelaide finely modelled and colored with white and gold costumes. (Phillips) $1,352

A very rare creamware tea canister and cover of hexagonal section, embossed and colored with half-length portraits of George III and Queen Charlotte, 17.5cm. (Phillips) $1,267

COMMEMORATIVE

A tapering mug printed in black with a portrait of Victoria inscribed '*Liverpool Shipperies Exhibition, Opened...May 11th, 1886*'. (Phillips) $219

A rare pearlware water jug and bowl, probably London, decorated with embossed GR IV monograms within grooved bands, 22cm. and 29.5cm. (Phillips) $540

Edward VIII: A Crown Ducal pottery jug with Art Nouveau decoration, inscribed below '*Rhead*', 19cm. high. (Phillips) $76

Death of Edward VII: A plate printed in blue with portrait, with raised decorative border, chipped. (Phillips) $50

An attractive small jug of squat shape, with a double half-length portrait flanked by National Emblems and inscribed '*Long Live Queen Victoria and Prince Albert of Saxe Coburg*', 11cm. (Phillips) $388

A nursery plate, the border embossed with flowers, the center printed in blue with a half length double portrait of 'Queen Victoria and Prince Albert of Saxe Coburg', 17.5cm. (Phillips) $287

A rare baluster jug, with a profile double portrait of 'William IV and Queen Adelaide, ascended the British throne 26 June 1830', 15cm. (Phillips) $642

A plate printed in black with portraits inscribed to commemorate the Royal Visit to Canada in 1901. (Phillips) $84

Death of Edward VII: A jug printed in black, inscribed with dates on the reverse. (Phillips) $67

COPELAND

A Copeland tazza made for the Art Union of London in memory of Prince Albert, raised on a revolving foot, 41.5cm. (Phillips) $540

A Copeland parian figure of Narcissus modelled by John Gibson, the pensive nude youth looking downwards wearing Roman sandals and holding a horn, circa 1846, 31cm. high. (Christie's) $1,232

A Copeland ewer with pierced scroll handle and the shoulders to the globular body painted, 9in. high, circa 1855. (Christie's) $597

A large and important Copeland Alhambra vase with elaborate pierced handles to the oviform body, 18in. high, circa 1865. (Christie's) $1,500

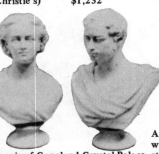

A pair of Copeland Crystal Palace Art Union parian ware busts, 'The Prince of Wales' and 'Princess Alexandra' by Marshall Wood and F. M. Miller. (Greenslades) $455

A Copeland figure of Apollo with a sheep-skin cape and standing before a tree stump, 17¼in. high, circa 1840. (Christie's) $956

A Copeland circular wall plaque, painted by R. R. Tomlinson, with a winged figure standing over a kneeling man, 47.5cm. diam., dated 1908. (Phillips) $299

A set of five Copeland 'Shakespeare' eight inch tiles, painted in colors with scenes and characters from Shakespeare's plays. (Phillips) $700

A bust of Daphne, the nude figure of a young girl with leaves in her hair and elaborate leaf-molded and glazed circular base, 23in. high, circa 1870. (Christie's) $1,710

COPER

A black glazed stoneware cup-form by Hans Coper, the spherical body on horizontal disc and conical foot, each section incised with spiral decoration, circa 1965, 16.2cm. high. (Christie's) $14,850

A rare early stoneware shallow dish by Hans Coper, covered in a matt manganese glaze, impressed HC seal, circa 1950, 37cm. diam. (Christie's) $37,202

A small stoneware black-glazed cup-form by Hans Coper, the sack-shaped cup with oval rim and four dimples to the base, impressed HC seal, circa 1972, 11cm. high. (Christie's) $5,940

A small black-glazed stoneware cup form by Hans Coper, incised with a spiral, covered in a matt-black textured and burnished ground, circa 1974, 11cm. high. (Christie's) $3,168

A stoneware composite vase form by Hans Coper, the compressed angular globular body with horizontal rib, impressed HC seal, circa 1965, 24.2cm. high. (Christie's) $23,496

A tall stoneware flattened tapering cylinder with spherical belly-form by Hans Coper on drum base, incised with spiral decoration, covered in a bluish-buff slip, circa 1968, 21.2cm. high. (Christie's) $13,860

A rare large black-glazed stoneware waisted cup form by Hans Coper, with incised spiral decoration, covered in a brownish-black burnish and textured glaze, impressed HC seal, circa 1965, 19.4cm. high. (Christie's) $14,850 £8,250

A small stoneware sack-form with spherical belly by Hans Coper, covered in a bluish-buff slip, burnished and textured to reveal areas of matt-manganese, impressed HC seal, circa 1969, 14.8cm. high. (Christie's) $8,316

A stoneware 'spade' form by Hans Coper, the gently swollen compressed body on cylindrical base, incised with spiral decoration, impressed HC seal, circa 1967, 27.4cm. high. (Christie's) $19,580

DELFT

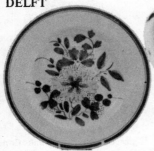

A delftware polychrome plate, painted in a bright Fazackerly palette, perhaps Delftfield factory, Glasgow, circa 1765, 23cm. diam. (Christie's)
$840

An English delft polychrome miniature mug, painted in iron-red, blue and green with stylised shrubs and rockwork, London or Bristol, circa 1730, 5cm. high. (Christie's) $3,003

A Dutch delft Dore plate painted in colors with a Chinese lady on horseback with three attendants, circa 1700, 23cm. diam. (Christie's)
$5,949

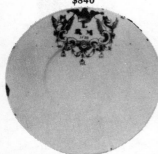

An English delft plate, monogrammed L.R.M. in blue, within heraldic surround, dated 1688, 10in. diam. (Hy. Duke & Son) $709

An English delft powdered manganese-ground plate, painted in underglaze blue with two Orientals, Bristol or Wincanton, circa 1745. (Christie's) $1,901

A Lambeth delft ballooning saucer-dish, painted in underglaze blue, gray/green and manganese, circa 1785, 22.5cm. diam. (Christie's) $1,601

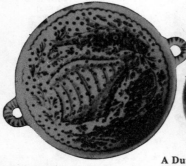

An English delft fish strainer, the shallow pierced bowl decorated with fish in cobalt blue, mid 18th century, 17in. (Hy. Duke & Son)
$828

A Dutch delft blue and white baluster table-fountain, painted in a bright blue, the lower part molded with a lion's mask to hold a tap, blue AK mark, circa 1690, 41.5cm. high. (Christie's) $1,673

A Dutch delft circular dish, painted in blue, in Chinese taste, 41cm., 18th century. (Lawrence Fine Arts)
$438

DELLA ROBBIA

'Water Avens Tile', a Della Robbia tile panel designed by Conrad Dressler and decorated by E. M. Wood, 51.5 x 34.2cm. (Christie's) $1,076

A Della Robbia vase of swollen cylindrical shape with flaring cylindrical neck, incised Della Robbia mark and decorators' monogram, 22.2cm. high. (Christie's) $178

A Della Robbia jardiniere, bulbous shape with incised and slip decoration of a scrolling foliate band between foliate rim and foot borders, 25.6cm. high. (Christie's) $1,068

A Della Robbia twin-handled vase, decorated by Charles Collis, with eight circular medallions, each with a sea-creature whose long tail curls round on itself, 35.8cm. high. (Christie's) $1,174

A Della Robbia vase decorated by Liz Wilkins, with incised and slip decoration of frogs, lily-pads, flowers and grasses, 38.8cm. high. (Christie's) $2,349

A Della Robbia vase decorated by Charles Collis, with an incised frieze of running hounds against a background suggesting grassy slopes with trees, 32.5cm. high. (Christie's) $822

A Della Robbia twin-handled vase, decorated by Liz Wilkins, with incised and slip decoration of daffodils framed by a leafy pattern, 41.3cm. high. (Christie's) $1,174

'The Third Day of Creation', a Della Robbia tile panel after a design by Edward Burne-Jones, 55.5 x 21.5cm. (Christie's) $5,090

A Della Robbia twin-handled vase decorated by Charles Collis, with a broad decorative frieze of stylized Tudor Roses, 31.6cm. high. (Christie's) $1,174

A William de Morgan bowl, painted in red lustre with a stylized design of fish against a scrolling foliage pattern, 25cm. diam. (Christie's) $1,487

A William de Morgan bowl, decorated by Charles Passenger, painted in red lustre with a stylized floral pattern, with artist's monogram C.P., 22.7cm. diam. (Christie's) $1,122

A William de Morgan lustre 'Italian style' bowl, decorated by Farini, supported on the backs of three stylized winged creatures, 25.5cm. diam. (Phillips) $516

A William de Morgan tile, painted in red lustre with two stylized carnations, with painted signature W. de Morgan & Co., Fulham, London, 20.5 x 20.5cm. (Christie's) $280

A William de Morgan vase decorated by Joe Juster, bulbous form with cylindrical neck, painted in red, pink and gold lustre with birds amid stylized foliage, 25.3cm. high. (Christie's) $2,431

A William de Morgan tile, square, painted in red lustre with a hippocampus on a white ground, impressed W. de Morgan on reverse (1872-1881), 20 x 20cm. (Christie's) $448

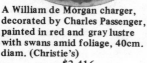

A William de Morgan charger, decorated by Charles Passenger, painted in red and gray lustre with swans amid foliage, 40cm. diam. (Christie's) $2,416

A William de Morgan lustre vase, painted in ruby tones against white with serpents, 16cm. high. (Phillips) $1,672

A William de Morgan lustre dish, painted in ruby lustre, pink and vivid mustard tones, 36cm. diam. (Phillips) $4,048

DERBY

A matched pair of Derby figures of a youth and girl, the man holding the remains of a letter in his hand, 21cm. and 21.5cm. (Lawrence Fine Arts) $966

An attractive Derby porcelain plaque by Thomas Steele, of rectangular form painted with fruits, contained in a glazed giltwood frame, together with an accompanying letter from the Royal Crown Derby Porcelain Company Limited. (Henry Spencer) $1,176

A pair of Derby vases of encrusted flowers, on white and gilt square-shaped bases, 16.5cm. (Lawrence Fine Arts) $637

An attractive early 19th century Derby porcelain cabinet plate, of dished circular form, the circular central panel painted with a view 'In Westmorland', 22.5cm. diam. (Henry Spencer) $422

A Derby baluster coffee pot and cover, painted with scattered cornflowers between gilt line rims, Wm. Duesbury & Co., circa 1785, 24.5cm. high. (Christie's) $940

An attractive early 19th century Derby porcelain cabinet plate, of dished circular form, the circular central panel painted with a view 'In North Wales', 22cm. diam. (Henry Spencer) $369

A Derby figure of a seated pugdog, wearing a gilt collar with red rosette, 6.5cm. (Lawrence Fine Arts) $517

A Derby oval plaque, painted with a group of flowers surrounding a classical vase, 18cm. wide. (Lawrence Fine Arts) $358

An attractive early 19th century Derby porcelain inkwell, raised upon the backs of three cats with free-standing forelegs, 9.5cm. high. (Henry Spencer) $912

DERBY

A Derby large jug, the spout modelled as a head of Lord Rodney, the ground with flowers in pink, 24cm. (Lawrence Fine Arts)　$676

A pair of Derby figures of a shepherd and shepherdess, on scroll- molded bases enriched in puce and green, Wm. Duesbury and Co., circa 1760, 26cm. and 27.5cm. high. (Christie's)　$2,445

A Crown Derby plate, painted with a view in Switzerland within an elaborate border, 22.5cm. (Lawrence Fine Arts)　$219

A Derby figure of Neptune standing beside a dolphin, on a high rocky base, 25cm. high. (Lawrence Fine Arts)　$632

A Derby rectangular plaque painted with a basket of flowers resting on a shaded purple slab, 14.5cm. by 19cm. (Lawrence Fine Arts)　$696

A Stevenson and Hancock Derby porcelain figure of a peacock, standing with gilt scaled plumage and blue and green enamelled tail feathers, 17.5cm. high. (Henry Spencer)　$692

A pair of Derby Stevenson & Hancock Imari pattern vases and covers, of bottle shape, circa 1870, 19in. (Hy. Duke & Son)　$1,521

A Derby porcelain side plate with gilt rim and reserves of painted flowers, 6¾in. wide. (Andrew Hartley)$338

A pair of Derby pedestal vases with swan handles, each painted with a bouquet of flowers, early 19th century, 24.8cm. (Bearne's)　$2,150

DOULTON

Doulton Lambeth two-tone saltglaze stoneware handled jug having raised hunting scene decoration, 7in. high. (Giles Haywood) $22

A large Royal Doulton character jug entitled 'Uncle Tom Cobleigh', withdrawn 1960. (Bearne's) $261

Doulton Lambeth saltglaze stoneware handled jug 'He That Buys', with four descriptive panels, 8in. high.(Giles Haywood) $74

Doulton Lambeth stoneware tobacco jar and cover with applied Art Nouveau decoration, 6in. high, circa 1925. (Peter Wilson) $129

A Doulton Lambeth faience circular wall plaque, painted with a head and shoulders of a red haired girl dressed in turquoise, 43.7cm. diam. (Phillips) $569

A Doulton Lambeth globular vase, by William Parker, carved with panels depicting classical warriors, 20.9cm. high. (Phillips) $338

'Baby', a Royal Doulton stoneware figural inkwell, designed by Leslie Harradine, 9.1cm. high. (Phillips) $498

A Royal Doulton group entitled 'St George', H.N.2051. (Bearne's) $226

'Votes for Women', a Royal Doulton stoneware figural inkwell, designed by Leslie Harradine, 9cm. high. (Phillips) $747

DOULTON

A Doulton Lambeth stoneware mug by Hannah B. Barlow incised with a central frieze of four running dogs, hallmarks for Sheffield 1873, 3¾in. high. (Christie's) $378

'Smuts', a large Royal Doulton character jug designed by H. Fenton, 7¼in. high, printed marks. (Christie's) $1,193

A Doulton Lambeth biscuit barrel, by Hannah Barlow, with plated cover incised with lions, 15.6cm. high, dated 1881. (Phillips) $925

A pair of Royal Doulton stoneware vases decorated by Hannah Barlow, each of shouldered cylindrical form with everted rim, with incised frieze of deer in a highland landscape, 34.5cm. high. (Christie's) $1,309

A glazed white Toby jug of Churchill with an accompanying photostat letter from Royal Doulton, stating that the jug is an unmarked prototype by Royal Doulton, circa 1940, 19cm. high. (Phillips) $4,048

A pair of Doulton Lambeth stoneware oviform vases by Hannah B. Barlow, each incised with a frieze of horses standing in a field, 16in. high. (Christie's) $851

A Doulton Lambeth cylindrical tobacco jar and cover modelled with a mouse, by George Tinworth, 17.8cm. high. (Phillips) $302

A large Royal Doulton character jug entitled 'Lord Nelson'. (Bearne's) $234

A Doulton Lambeth globular jug, by Eliza Simmance, incised with spear shaped motifs, 25.5cm. high, date shield for 1910. (Phillips) $356

DOULTON

A table lamp with the Royal Doulton figure Katrina on the base, H.N. 2327, total height 49.5cm. (Bearne's)
$292

Royal Doulton stoneware circular footed comport, with floral swags and mottled-blue. interior, 5in. high. (Giles Haywood) $149

1897 Jubilee: A Doulton Lambeth jug, the baluster body molded in green, blue and brown with portraits and inscriptions. (Phillips)
$236

A pair of Doulton Art Nouveau stoneware vases by Frank Butler, each damaged, 18½in. high. (David Lay) $540

A Royal Doulton pottery large character jug 'Regency Beau', numbered D6559. (Henry Spencer) $633

A pair of Doulton stoneware vases, each of baluster form, with applied and incised decoration of butterflies and beadwork within scrolling foliate and floral panels, 37.7cm. high. (Christie's)
$1,215

A Doulton Lambeth shouldered oviform vase, by Edith Lupton, decorated with a panel of pate-sur-pate white flowers and applied green leaves and berries, dated 1887. (Phillips)
$231

A Royal Doulton 'Sung' bowl, decorated with a central leaping deer amongst foliage with a spiral and diamond design, 13in. diam. (Christie's)
$822

A Doulton Lambeth stoneware figure attributed to George Tinworth modelled as a mouse playing a tuba, 3¼in. high. (Christie's)
$757

CHINA

DOULTON

A Royal Doulton porcelain figure 'Coppelia', HN2115, 18.5cm. high. (Henry Spencer) $490

A Doulton Lambeth stoneware silver-rimmed lemonade set comprising a jug and a pair of beakers. (GA Property Services) $595

A Royal Doulton porcelain figure of The Prince of Wales, later the Duke of Windsor, HN1217, 19cm. high. (Henry Spencer) $380

A Royal Doulton porcelain figure of 'Mr W. S. Penley as Charlie's Aunt', 17.5cm. high. (Henry Spencer) $484

A Royal Doulton Sung vase, decorated with broad irregular vertical bands of streaked purple glaze, framing panels of orange and yellow prunus, monogram for Harry Nixon, 27cm. high. (Lawrence Fine Arts) $1,161

'Spook', a Royal Doulton porcelain figure designed by H. Tittensor H.N.50 No.12, 7in. high. (Christie's) $1,173

A Royal Doulton globular vase, the body painted by J. H. Plant with a view of Windsor Castle, 10in. high. (Christie's) $411

A Doulton Lambeth stoneware cricketing jug, decorated in Art Nouveau taste with applied figures of cricketers, 15cm. high. (Phillips) $468

A good Hannah Barlow large Doulton Lambeth stoneware vase, decorated with a wide band incised with cattle, 18¼in. high. (David Lay) $676

DOULTON

'Clark Gable', a Royal Doulton character jug designed by S. Taylor D6709, 6¾in. high. (Christie's) $1,493

'The Bather', a Royal Doulton figure from a model by John Broad, of a nude maiden with flowers in her hair, 33.5cm. high. (Christie's) $2,230

'Guy Fawkes', a Royal Doulton limited edition jug decorated in shallow relief, 7½in. high. (Christie's) $637

'Bather', a Royal Doulton porcelain figure designed by L. Harradine H.N.1238, 7¾in. high. (Christie's) $341

A large Royal Doulton loving cup, commemorating the Coronation of King George VI and Queen Elizabeth, designed by Charles Noke and Harry Fenton. (Bearne's) $498

A Royal Doulton stoneware vase, decorated with an applied band of flowerheads and foliage, covered in a royal blue and shades of green and brown glazes, 30.6cm. high. (Christie's) $224

'Puppy Sitting', a Royal Doulton model of a puppy with one ear cocked, 10.4cm. high. (Phillips) $640

A table lamp with the Royal Doulton figure Genevieve on the base, H.N. 1962, total height 44.5cm. (Bearne's) $326

A Royal Doulton porcelain bust of H.M. Queen Elizabeth II designed by Peggy Davies, 4in. high. (Christie's) $497

DRESDEN

A pair of Dresden salts, each shaped oval, held by a reclining male and female figure respectively, 19th century, 6½in. (Lawrence Fine Arts) $1,006

A Dresden clockcase of arch form on three high scroll feet, surmounted by a putto emblematic of Autumn, circa 1880, 48cm. high. (Christie's) $1,551

A 'Dresden' large group of 'La Fete des Bonnes Gens' after the Sevres biscuit original, circa 1880, 43cm. wide. (Christie's) $3,115

An elaborate oval basket in Dresden style, with figures of a youth and girl on either side, 53cm. (Lawrence Fine Arts) $1,493

A pair of Dresden large groups of children playing round a wine press and a barrel, 30cm. and 34cm. (Lawrence Fine Arts) $8,551

A Dresden baluster vase and cover, painted with lovers at pastimes in landscape vignettes, late 19th century, 46cm. high. (Christie's) $868

A pair of vases and covers in Dresden style, surmounted by figures of a boy and girl. (Lawrence Fine Arts) $557

One of a pair of Dresden three-light candelabra each modelled with three young bacchantes seated on and around tree stumps, 10½in. high. (Christie's) Two $871

A pair of Dresden bottle vases and covers, the globular bodies painted with sportsmen at various pursuits, circa 1900, 33cm. high. (Christie's) $496

CHINA

A small Zsolnay lustre vase decorated with scrollwork and stylized foliage in golden-green lustre, 10cm. high. (Phillips) $227

A Ludwigsburg teabowl and saucer, painted with birds on branches, circa 1760. (Christie's) $836

A Zsolnay pottery lustre ewer decorated with sinuous silver-gray stems and ruby florets against a starred ground, 22.5cm. high. (Phillips) $1,435

A Westerwald stoneware Sternkanne, the oviform body impressed with a starburst enclosing a heart within a circular cartouche, circa 1700, 30cm. high. (Christie's) $1,487

A Ludwigsburg figure of a lady with a musical score, modelled by P. F. Lejeune, scantily clothed in a white blouse, circa 1770, 13.5cm. high. (Christie's) $1,208

A small Zsolnay figural lustre vase decorated on the shoulders with the partially clad Orpheus with his lyre beside him and an amorous mermaid, 13cm. high. (Phillips) $1,190

A Zsolnay lustre vase of tapering oviform with narrow neck supported on three sinuous stems rising from a ring base, 23.5cm. high. (Phillips) $840

A Goebel Art Deco ceramic figural group molded as three dancing girls leaning forwards, 11½in. high. (Christie's) $1,770

A Zsolnay oviform lustre vase painted in vivid reds, yellows and greens with exotic flowers and foliage, 26.5cm. high. (Phillips) $1,312

EUROPEAN

A stoneware 'Coleshill' bottle vase, by Katherine Pleydell Bouverie, covered in a rich streaked blue and green glaze, 17.1cm. high. (Phillips) $395

A Baltic faience lobed oval tureen and cover with foliate scroll handles and stalk finial, perhaps Stralsund, circa 1760, 42cm. wide. (Christie's) $3,160

An Art Pottery matt green umbrella stand, early 20th century, the domed top with triangular cut-outs, unsigned, 26½in. high. (Robt. W. Skinner Inc.) $325

A figure entitled the little Boat Builder, the young boy sucking his thumb having missed a nail with the hammer, modelled by E.B.Stephens, 1878 - 17½in. high. (Christie's) $557

A Massier art pottery jardiniere, sculpted to simulate ocean waves with a full-form nude woman perched amidst the breakers, 9½in. high. (Robt. W. Skinner Inc.) $2,900

A large Brannam pottery oviform vase, decorated in sgraffito on one side with stylized fish swimming amid aquatic foliage, 79cm. high. (Phillips) $688

A Reval rococo baluster vase with rib and feathered molding, encrusted with three branches, insects and flowers, circa 1780, 25.5cm. high. (Christie's) $7,436

A Continental tile picture painted in manganese and yellow with a two-handled urn on a pedestal, circa 1780, 37 x 25cm. (Christie's) $521

A Galle faience model of a cat, the smiling creature painted with blue and white circular and heart shaped motifs reserved against a yellow ground, 32.2cm. high. (Phillips) $642

EUROPEAN

An Art Pottery jardiniere, early 20th century, square body tapering toward base, with molded Art Nouveau design, 13in. high. (Robt. W. Skinner Inc.) $550

A Le Nove majolica shaped oval desk-set, painted with groups of fruit and flower-sprays, the tray also with an artichoke, circa 1770, the tray 18.5cm. wide. (Christie's) $1,766

A Samson porcelain and ormolu-mounted two-handled potpourri vase and cover, with high ormolu pineapple and foliage finial, blue cross mark, circa 1880, 53cm. high. (Christie's) $5,170

A large Dutch Art Nouveau jardiniere and stand, decorated in batik-style in colors with stylized flowers, 99cm. high, signed 'Corona Holland'. (Phillips) $894

A set of four Continental white and gilt figures of nymphs, symbolic of the Arts and Sciences, 43cm. to 45cm. (Lawrence Fine Arts) $503

A miniature Rozenburg 'Eggshell' vase, with bulbous base and flared neck of square section, possibly painted by R.Sterken, 8.9cm. high. (Phillips) $602

A Spanish lustre spirit barrel molded with two circular ribs, 18th/19th century, 23cm. high. (Christie's) $929

A Zsolnay ceramic jug, the handle formed as an Art Nouveau maiden with flowing hair and dress, 22.8cm. high. (Christie's) $371

A large Zsolnay lustre group, of two men possibly Cain and Abel, one lying prostrate on a domed rocky base with the other towering above him, 37.5cm. high. (Phillips) $946

FAMILLE ROSE

19th century famille-rose vase with gilt animal ring handles and reserve panels of figures, 10½in. high. (G. A. Key) $130

A bowl, modelled in relief with two bands of lotus petals in famille rose enamels, 26cm. Ch'ien Lung. (Lawrence Fine Arts) $1,791

A famille rose bottle vase with globular body, ribbed shoulder and long waisted neck, the rim with a band of ruyi-heads, 15in. high. (Christie's) $6,769

A 19th century Canton famille rose porcelain ovular vase painted in numerous reserves with groups of Royal and priestly figures, 23in. high. (Capes Dunn) $785

A pair of Chinese Canton famille rose baluster vases with reserved panels of processions and figures in an interior, 19th century, 24in. high. (Woolley & Wallis) $1,111

A rare famille rose gilt decorated blue-ground vase, with canted corners and a knotted sash painted in pink enamel, 12in. high. (Christie's) $25,384

A famille rose eggshell dish, delicately enamelled at the center with a seated lady painting a leaf at a table, 7¾in. diam. (Christie's) $5,358

A fine famille rose celadon-ground oviform vase, painted on the body and neck with richly fruiting gourd branches issuing fruit, Qianlong period, 53.7cm. high. (Christie's) $89,595

A famille rose yellow-ground teapot and cover, decorated at either side with an elaborate lotus scroll, the curling tendrils terminating in peony, 5½in. wide. (Christie's) $7,051

FOLEY

A set of six Foley bone china plates designed by Laura Knight, A.R.A., painted with two golden-haired young women picking fruit in colors and copper lustre, 21.5cm. diam., (Phillips) $1,575

A Foley Intarsio time-piece, designed by Frederick Rhead, in the form of a long-case clock, decorated with the profile head and shoulders of an Art Nouveau maiden, 33.5cm. high. (Phillips) $897

A Foley Intarsio ceramic clock, painted in blue, turquoise, green, brown and yellow enamels, with Art Nouveau maidens representing day and night, 29cm. high. (Christie's) $1,394

A Foley Urbato ware vase, of globular form, decorated in white slip trailing with pink flowers and green leaves, 22.3cm. high. (Phillips) $299

A Foley Intarsio oval teapot and cover printed and painted to represent a bald gentleman with beard, 8in. wide. (Christie's) $605

A Foley Intarsio pottery vase, with panels of foliage alternating with panels of seagulls, 22cm. high. (Phillips) $264

A Foley Intarsio circular wall plate, designed by Frederick Rhead, the center decorated in colors with two classical maidens, 36.8cm. diam. (Phillips) $860

A Foley jardiniere and stand, each decorated in alternate green and yellow ground spiralling panels patterned with flowers and foliage, 42in. high. (Christie's) $3,080

A Foley Intarsio circular wall plate, designed by Frederick Rhead, the centre with two classical maidens seated on a garden bench, 36.8cm.diam. (Phillips) $1,496

FRENCH

CHINA

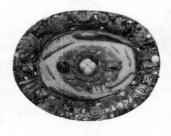

A Sarreguemines 'Egyptianesque' oviform vase, incised and decorated in colors with 'Egyptianesque' winged bird motifs, 39cm. high. (Phillips) $792

A Pallisy oval dish molded in relief with fishes swimming on a pale blue wavy ground, 16th century, 49.5cm. wide. (Christie's) $4,461

A Chantilly lobed beaker and saucer with foliate shaped rims, painted in the Kakiemon palette, circa 1735, (Christie's) $669

One of six plates from the Fontainebleau service made for Louis Phillipe, date code for 1846, one with dated code for 1874, 23cm. diam. (Christie's) Six $1,551

A large Clement Massier porcelain urn, the dark green glaze decorated with gold colored leaves and polychrome enamelled insects, 102cm. high. (Christie's) $4,833

A St Cloud white seau a demibouteille with mask handles, circa 1730, 11cm. high. (Christie's) $2,230

A Haviland art pottery vase by Chaplet, of red clay with whimsical sgraffito decoration of a young fisherman, 11¼in. high. (Robt. W. Skinner Inc.) $1,100

A Max Lauger pottery jug, decorated in slip with green wind blown tulip-like flowers against a deep-blue ground, 24cm. high. (Phillips) $516

A French oviform vase and cover, painted with roses on a blue ground, 38cm. (Lawrence Fine Arts) $501

GARDNER

A porcelain biscuit figure of a street vendor, by the Gardner Factory (impressed mark), circa 1885, 4¾in. high. (Christie's) $650

A porcelain figure of a blind beggar, by the Gardner Factory (red printed and impressed marks), circa 1885, 6¼in. high. (Christie's) $594

A porcelain group of a mother and child, by the Gardner Factory (impressed mark), circa 1885, 17.2cm. high. (Christie's) $743

A porcelain biscuit figure of an ice breaker, by the Gardner Factory (red printed and impressed mark), circa 1885, 11½in. high. (Christie's) $650

A porcelain biscuit group of Gogol's Dead Souls, portraying Chichikov haggling with two men, by the Gardner Factory, circa 1885, 5½in. high. (Christie's) $1,580

A porcelain biscuit figure of a Mezienskii Samoyed, by the Gardner Factory (red printed mark), circa 1885, 9¼in. high. (Christie's) $464

A porcelain biscuit group of a child seated on a trestle (hands repaired) and another playing a horn, by the Gardner Factory, circa 1885, 4¾in. high. (Christie's) $483

A porcelain figure of a peasant eating lunch, by the Gardner Factory (red impressed mark), circa 1885, 4½in. high. (Christie's) $892

A porcelain biscuit figure of a peasant, seated on a bench, by the Gardner Factory (impressed mark), circa 1885, 14cm. high. (Christie's) $1,022

GERMAN

CHINA

Two Volkstedt relief-modelled portrait plaques of the Duke of Saxe-Teschen and Maria Christina, circa 1785, 24cm. high. (Christie's) $26,955

A German porcelain pear-shaped scent-bottle and stopper, naturally modelled and colored and molded with two leaves in tones of green (slight chips to foliage), perhaps Furstenberg, circa 1770, gilt-metal mounts 7.5cm. high. (Christie's) $2,230

A large German Modernist ceramic group modelled as a warrior astride a large rearing horse emerging from the waves, 44cm. high. (Phillips) $540

A Crailsheim faience tankard (Walzenkrug) painted in colors with an exotic bird and pine trees, mid 18th century, 28.5cm. high. (Christie's) $1,487

A pair of German seated pug dogs, with blue ribbon-tied collars hung with yellow bells, possibly Braunschweig, circa 1750, 14.5cm. and 15.5cm. high. (Christie's) $5,577

A Kelsterbach gold-mounted etui modelled as a lady's leg wearing a buckled yellow shoe, circa 1775, 11.5cm. high. (Christie's) $1,394

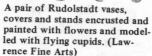

A Merkelbach stoneware flagon, designed by Paul Wynand, applied with black graduated beaded bosses and two floral roundels, 24.5cm. high. (Phillips) $722

A pair of Rudolstadt vases, covers and stands encrusted and painted with flowers and modelled with flying cupids. (Lawrence Fine Arts) $477

An Ehrfurt cylindrical tankard (Walzenkrug) painted in colors with St George killing the dragon, circa 1770, 26cm. high. (Christie's) $2,416

GERMAN

CHINA

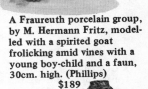

A Nymphenburg shaped oval dish, painted with fruit on a grassy mound, circa 1765, 28.5cm. wide. (Christie's) $2,044

A massive Kreussen armorial stoneware marriage Krug, molded all over and painted in enamels, possibly 17th century, with pewter mount, 49cm. high. (Christie's) $1,673

A Fraureuth porcelain group, by M. Hermann Fritz, modelled with a spirited goat frolicking amid vines with a young boy-child and a faun, 30cm. high. (Phillips) $189

An Art Deco Rosenthal figure of a young girl running with a leaping fawn to the base, 12in. (Hy. Duke & Son) $845

A pair of German porcelain figures of nodding Mandarins, modelled as a man and a woman seated cross-legged, late 19th century, about 30cm. high. (Christie's) $3,160

A Hannoversch-Munden reticulated baluster vase and pierced cover with rosehead finial and applied leaves painted in green and manganese, three crescents mark over painter's mark K in the manganese, circa 1770, 37cm. high. (Christie's) $5,577

A Sitzendorf pierced circular basket, the scroll base with three figures of cupids holding flowers, 31cm. high. (Lawrence Fine Arts) $676

A pair of Sitzendorf five-light candelabra, the flower encrusted branches set on a stem supported by figures, late 19th century, 41cm. (Bearne's) $860

A Wiener Keramik ceramic wall-mask, molded as a girl's head with a hat, painted in polychrome glazes, 24cm. high. (Christie's) $1,022

GOLDSCHEIDER

A Goldscheider Art Deco
female child figure wearing a
cape and a bonnet 'The New
Gloves', 8in. high. (Anderson
& Garland) $542

An unusual Goldscheider
pottery group, modelled as
a group of men, wearing
colorful medieval style
clothes, holding a large metal
and ceramic spear, 49cm.
long. (Phillips) $525

An Art Deco Goldscheider pottery figure designed by Dakon,
modelled as a girl holding a large
pink fan in front of her naked
body, 33cm. high. (Phillips)
$878

Goldscheider pottery mask
of an Art Deco lady, approx.
12in. (G. A. Key) $633

A Goldscheider pottery figure
of a young black boy, wearing
a shabby brown jacket,
grayish-brown trousers and
a red and white striped shirt,
56cm. high, impressed maker's
mark. (Phillips) $1,925

A small Goldscheider terracotta wall mask of the head,
neck and hand of a young
girl, 8in. high. (Christie's)
$350

A Goldscheider figure, the
design by J. Lorenzl, of a
striding girl, her head thrown
back, and holding her gray
dress behind her, 35.4cm. high.
(Christie's) $962

A Goldscheider pottery figure
designed by Lorenzl, the
standing young woman holding
butterfly wings, 11½in. high.
(Christie's) $1,828

A Goldscheider figure, of a
girl in a two-piece bathing suit,
with elaborate skirt draped
across her raised arm, 33cm.
high. (Christie's) $962

148

GOLDSCHEIDER

A Goldscheider terracotta wall mask modelled as the head of young girl holding a fan across her neck, 11in. high. (Christie's) $525

A Goldscheider figure, of a woman standing on tip-toe, holding the skirt of her dress, enamelled in pink, yellow and black, 28.8cm. high. (Christie's) $1,155

A Goldscheider pottery figure simply modelled as a Chinese child covered with a white crackled-glaze, 19.5cm. high. (Phillips) $350

A Goldscheider figure of a woman with one hand on her hip, one on her hat, with artist's monogram, 33.5cm.high. (Christie's) $1,487

A Goldscheider pottery figure of a dancer, in a floral lilac dress with bonnet, 12in. high, circa 1930. (Morphets) $523

'Suzanne', a Goldscheider figure, the design by J. Lorenzl, the nude figure loosely draped with a patterned gray enamelled robe, 33.6cm. high. (Christie's) $962

A Goldscheider ceramic wall mask fashioned as the face of a girl with black eyes and orange lips, 28.5cm. high. (Phillips) $676

A Goldscheider figure, of a dancing girl in bodice and split skirt which she holds out behind her, enamelled in pink and cerise, 27.1cm. high. (Christie's) $1,290

A Goldscheider ceramic wall mask modelled as the head of a girl with turquoise eyes and orange lips, 27cm. high, (Phillips) $473

GOSS

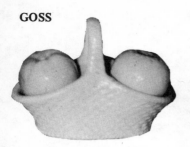

Fully colored Fruit in a Basket cruet set, 80mm. long. (Goss & Crested China Ltd.) $221

Large Dartmouth Sack Bottle with matching Arms of Dartmouth, 95mm. high. (Goss & Crested China Ltd.) $62

Goss Oven with brown or orange chimney, 75mm. (Goss & Crested China Ltd.) $460

Devil looking over Lincoln, brown, 150mm. high. (Goss & Crested China Ltd.) $177

Hythe Cromwellian Mortar, 40mm. (Goss & Crested China Ltd.) $18

Bust of Queen Victoria wearing mobcap, 130mm. (Goss & Crested China Ltd.) $221

Nut Tray with South Africa 1900 commemorative decoration, 145mm. diam. (Goss & Crested China Ltd.) $133

Durham Sanctuary Knocker in relief on two-handled mug, 120mm. high. (Goss & Crested China Ltd.) $168

Dr Samuel Johnson's House, Lichfield, 75mm. high. (Goss & Crested China Ltd.) $336

GOSS

First Period bust of Child of
Mirth, 210mm. high. (Goss &
Crested China Ltd.) $487

Caerleon lamp, 85mm. long.
(Goss & Crested China Ltd.)
$18

Preserve jar and lid with
grapefruit decoration, 110mm.
(Goss & Crested China Ltd.)
$133

Goss Flower Girl Joan,
135mm. high. (Goss & Crested
China Ltd.) $443

Model of Hastings Kettle,
55mm. with Barbadoes crest.
(Goss & Crested China Ltd.)
$16

Large Salisbury Jack, 135mm.
(Goss & Crested China Ltd.)
$35

Teignmouth Lighthouse, 115mm.
high. (Goss & Crested China Ltd.)
$80

The Great Pyramid, with
matching crest of Egypt,
60mm. high. (Goss & Crested
China Ltd.) $168

Shakespeare leaning on a
lectern, parian, 175mm. high.
(Goss & Crested China Ltd.)
$487

A stoneware bowl by Shoji
Hamada on shallow foot,
covered in a dark mushroom
colored glaze, with a gray
splash to rim, circa 1955,
11cm. high. (Christie's)
$5,940

A stoneware press-molded
rectangular bottle by Shoji
Hamada, brushed with panels
of tenmoku and brown glaze,
with printed label Made in
Japan, circa 1961, 19.8cm.
high. (Christie's)
$5,148

A stoneware bowl by Shoji
Hamada with circular base
and flared sides, covered in a
textured green and gray glaze,
23.1cm. diam. (Christie's)
$1,287

A stoneware waisted
cylindrical vase, by Shoji
Hamada, the exterior covered
in a mirrored black glaze with
combed bands through to a
khaki glaze, 21.5cm. high.
(Christie's) $3,960

A stoneware cut-sided vase by
Shoji Hamada, the square-
section body tapering to a
circular foot, circa 1960,
20.7cm. high. (Christie's)
$7,920

A stoneware cut-sided waisted
cylindrical vase by Shoji
Hamada, the exterior covered
in a lustrous iron-brown and
olive-green mottled glaze,
circa 1955, 17.4cm. high.
(Christie's) $5,940

A stoneware press-molded
rectangular bottle by Shoji
Hamada with tapering square
neck, covered in a speckled
olive green glaze, circa 1955,
20cm. high. (Christie's)
$5,544

A stoneware cylindrical jar by
Shoji Hamada, gently swollen
at the waist, with iron-brown
brushwork, 10cm. high.
(Christie's) $990

A stoneware press-molded
rectangular bottle by Shoji
Hamada with tapering square
neck, covered in a speckled
olive green glaze, circa 1960.
20.2cm. high. (Christie's)
$5,544

HISPANO-MORESQUE

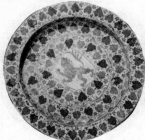

An Hispano-Moresque armorial large circular dish, painted in gold with a coat-of-arms of a rampant lion, third quarter of 15th century, 45.5cm. diam. (Christie's) $111,540

A 17th century Hispano-Moresque ruby lustre decorated circular dish with exotic peacock central motif, 1ft.3in. diam. (Geering & Colyer) $831

An Hispano-Moresque lustre dish with raised central boss, third quarter of 15th century, 34cm. diam. (Christie's) $929

HOCHST

Two Damm faience figures in the Hochst style, one modelled as an Oriental in conical hat, the other as a girl in black hat, circa 1840, 14.5cm. and 15.5cm. high. (Christie's) $929

A Hochst figure of a dancer, modelled by J. P. Melchior, as a youth with a garland of flowers, circa 1775, 16cm. high. (Christie's) $371

A pair of Damm faience figures of a baker and his wife in the Hochst style, circa 1840, 11.5cm. high. (Christie's) $1,859

A Hochst figure of Venus, modelled by J. P. Melchior, the nude goddess gracefully leaning against a tree-stump, circa 1771, 19.5cm. high. (Christie's) $5,577

A Hochst group of 'Der Bekranzte Schlafer', modelled by J. P. Melchior, circa 1770, 19cm. wide. (Christie's) $6,506

A Hochst figure of a drummer, modelled by J. P. Melchior, in black hat and pink clothes, circa 1775, 13cm. high. (Christie's) $1,487

IMARI

An Imari jardiniere, the ribbed body painted with panels of flowers and blossoming prunus trees, 12in. diam. (Hy. Duke & Son) $321

An 18th century Imari porcelain bowl and cover, decorated in underglaze blue, iron red and gilt with flowers and foliage, 25cm. high. (Henry Spencer) $1,593

An Imari barber's bowl decorated in iron-red enamel and gilt on underglaze blue with a vase containing flowers and foliage, Genroku period, 27cm. diam. (Christie's) $744

Imari baluster shaped vase painted, gilded and enamelled with kylins, exotic birds and trees, 19in. high. (Prudential) $429

A pair of 19th century Imari porcelain covered vases with Dog of Fo finials, 26in. high. (Geering & Colyer) $3,633

A rare Imari tureen and domed cover, the bowl with two applied foliate loop handles and decorated with branches of flowering peony and plum blossom, Genroku period, 23,5cm. high. (Christie's) $5,482

A fine and large Imari deep bowl decorated in the center with a bold design of a butterfly hovering above a karashishi prowling among branches of peony, Genroku period, 41.5cm. diam. (Christie's) $10,769

A 19th century Japanese porcelain Imari floor vase of baluster form decorated with panels of flowering shrubs and exotic birds, 24¾in. high. (W. H. Lane & Son) $2,100

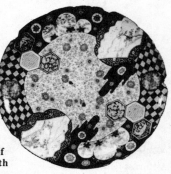

A late 19th century Japanese Imari porcelain large charger. (Henry Spencer) $700

IMARI

A 19th century Japanese Imari porcelain bowl of circular form, with a central circular panel enclosing a vase of flowers standing on a verandah, 30.5cm. diam. (Henry Spencer) $647

An Imari vase and cover, molded in low relief with two phoenix in flight with a net behind, late 17th/early 18th century, 9½in. high. (Lawrence Fine Arts) $522

An Imari molded teapot, the chrysanthemum-shaped body with chrysanthemum flower-heads and foliage in relief, circa 1700, 13.8cm. high. (Christie's) $2,741

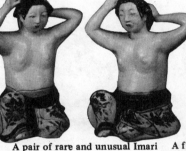

An Imari double-gourd bottle vase decorated with a profusion of chrysanthemum flower sprays and foliage, the flower-heads molded in relief, Genroku period, 26cm. high. (Christie's) $548

A pair of rare and unusual Imari bijin, the partially clad figures decorated in iron-red, green, aubergine and black enamels and gilt, Genroku period, 31.5cm. high. (Christie's) $24,475

A fine Imari tankard decorated in iron-red enamel and gilt on underglaze blue, the ovoid body with three shaped panels, the loop handle pierced for a mount, Genroku period, 22.5cm. high. (Christie's) $7,440

A molded Imari tureen and domed cover with loop handles, decorated on underglaze blue with chrysanthemums entwined among vertical lines, Genroku period, 17cm. high. (Christie's) $2,350

A pair of 19th century Japanese Imari porcelain chargers, each of dished circular form painted in underglaze blue, 55cm. diam. (Henry Spencer) $30,272

A rare Imari beaker decorated with two bijin standing beside floral sprays of cherry blossom, the interior with a single flower spray, Genroku period, 9.5cm. high. (Christie's) $1,179

ITALIAN

CHINA

A large blue and white Italian dish painted with David, crowned and playing a harp, mid 18th century, 49cm. diam. (Christie's) $1,394

A Montelupo wet-drug jar, with strap handle painted a foglie in blue, ochre and yellow, third quarter of the 16th century, 24.5cm.high. (Christie's) $1,487

A Pesaro fluted crespina painted with Christ on the road to Calvary, circa 1570, 23.5cm. diam. (Christie's) $6,134

A Montelupo blue ground wet drug jar with strap handle painted a foglie in ochre and green, the name of the contents *O. Volpino* in a cartouche beneath an ochre mask head, third quarter of the 16th century, 25cm. high. (Christie's) $2,788

An Italian late 19th or early 20th century alabaster relief of a girl playing her violin, 38cm. high. (Christie's) $723

A Bologna sgraffito trilobed jug, the bulbous body incised with scrolls of foliage, late 15th century, 20.5cm. high. (Christie's) $1,487

A Deruta tazza painted in colors   with Eros bearing the apple of love, circa 1620, about 26cm. diam. (Christie's) $3,160

A documentary Pesaro trilobed jug, inscribed in Greek, circa 1790, 22cm. high. (Christie's) $3,718

A Lodi plate painted in yellow, blue and brown with a whimsical scene of a ship and two tritons, circa 1760, 23cm. diam. (Christie's) $706

ITALIAN

CHINA

A Pesaro fluted crespina painted with the Sacrifice of Isaac, circa 1570, 24.5cm. diam. (Christie's) $9,295

An Italian ceramic figure designed by E. Mazzolani, of a young girl with bobbed hair, wearing a short dress and leaning against a post, 1929. (Christie's) $1,673

A Montelupo dish painted with a gentleman in a plumed hat brandishing two rapiers between trees, probably mid 17th century, 32cm. diam. (Christie's) $3,532

A Sicilian (Trapani) waisted armorial albarello painted in yellow, green and blue with an armorial device, circa 1620, 20.5cm. high. (Christie's) $1,487

A Venetian drug bottle painted with portraits of a Turk and a soldier, second half of 16th century, 23cm. high. (Christie's) $4,461

A Deruta documentary oviform drug jar with two serpentine handles, dated 1707, 32cm. wide. (Christie's) $1,301

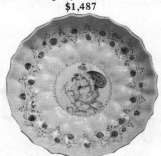

A Faenza documentary compendiaro crespina painted in the workshop of Maestro Virgiliotto Calamelli, with a falconer, circa 1565, 30cm. diam. (Christie's) $7,436

A Sicilian (Trapani) blue and white waisted albarello painted with stylized flowers, late 16th century, 21cm. high. (Christie's) $743

A Faenza shaped dish, Cn mark to base, Ferniani's factory, circa 1770, 32cm. diam. (Christie's) $650

A rare early enamelled Japanese bowl decorated in iron-red, green, blue and black enamels, circa 1660, 16cm. diam. (Christie's) $2,937

A Kinkozan type pottery koro and cover of globular lobed quatrefoil shape, signed, 7½in. high. (Lawrence Fine Arts) $2,886

A Kutani bowl, the interior and exterior each painted with a wrythen scroll of diapering, signed, 8½in. diam. (Lawrence Fine Arts) $251

A pair of 19th century Kutani-style shaped vases, with Oriental figure decoration to complete body in burnt orange and charcoal gray color, 14in. (Giles Haywood)$2,047

A fine pair of Kinkozan vases, painted with figures of women, children, warriors and room interiors, 18.2cms. (Bearne's) $13,572

A pair of large Japanese porcelain vases, each ovoid body painted with panels containing insects and garden flowers, mid 19th century, 44.5cm. (Bearne's) $1,548

An important Ko-Kutani dish decorated with chrysanthemum flowerheads and foliage scattered among stylized waves, late 17th century, 21cm. diam. (Christie's) $58,740

A Kinkozan oviform vase decorated with a panel of two ladies in a rocky fenced garden, a sleeping dog at their feet, signed on the base Kinkozan zo, 19th century, 11cm. high. (Christie's) $1,958

Japanese porcelain wall plaque, decorated with two birds on a pine tree, 18½in. diameter. (Hobbs and Chambers) $574

KAKIEMON

A fine Kakiemon dish decorated with cranes beneath stylized clouds, Ming six-character mark to the base (Chenghua), late 17th century, 20cm. wide. (Christie's) $9,790

A multi-faceted Kakiemon type vase decorated with sprays of peony, chrysanthemum and other flowers and foliage, late 17th century, 19.5cm. high. (Christie's) $12,727

A rare Kakiemon foliate rimmed dish decorated in vivid iron-red, green, blue and black enamels and gilt, late 17th century, 19cm. diam. (Christie's) $13,706

A Kakiemon ovoid jar decorated with a continuous wide band of butterflies hovering among peony, chrysanthemums and other flowers, circa 1660, 21.5cm. high. (Christie's) $78,320

A Kakiemon teapot and cover, the lobed sides with panels of various flowers and foliage, the cover with ho-o birds, circa 1680, 16.5cm. long. (Christie's) $6,853

A fine rare and unusual Kakiemon ewer decorated in iron-red, yellow, blue, green and black enamels, late 17th century, 16cm. high. (Christie's) $9,790

A rare Kakiemon deep bowl decorated in vivid colored enamels on underglaze blue, the central roundel with two large uchiwa, late 17th century, 26cm. diam. (Christie's) $3,133

A Kakiemon compressed globular kendi or gorgelet with short bulbous spout, decorated in iron-red, blue and green enamels, late 17th century, 20.2cm. high. (Christie's) $8,811

A Kakiemon type underglaze blue dish decorated with two herons in a central roundel, circa 1680, 18cm. diam. (Christie's) $2,154

LEACH, BERNARD

A rare stoneware bowl decorated by Bernard Leach, with lustrous tenmoku brushwork of Viking Longboats, the rim with pale blue glaze, circa 1955, 30.6cm. diam. (Christie's) $6,750

An early stoneware jug by Bernard Leach, the bulbous body on shallow foot with strap handle and pinched lip, circa 1930, 8.7cm. high. (Christie's) $237

A rare blue and white porcelain plate by Bernard Leach, the shallow well lightly incised with fishermen in boats before mountains, 19.5cm. diam. (Christie's) $3,366

A stoneware flattened rectangular slab bottle by Bernard Leach covered in a dark olive green tea-dust glaze, circa 1965, 18.5cm. high. (Christie's) $1,346

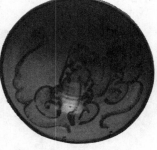

A rare slip trailed raku bowl by Bernard Leach on shallow foot covered in a pale sand colored, finely crackled, translucent glaze, circa 1923, 25.2cm. diam. (Christie's) $1,386

A St. Ives stoneware twin-handled vase, by Bernard Leach, with charcoal colored brush strokes reserved against a speckled olive glaze, 26cm. high. (Phillips) $722

A tenmoku stoneware pilgrim plate by Bernard Leach with a pilgrim before mountains, impressed BL and St. Ives seals, circa 1970, 32.4cm. diam. (Christie's) $10,890

A tall stoneware press-molded bottle vase by Bernard Leach with short neck and everted rim, circa 1966, 36.7cm. high. (Christie's) $4,356

A rare stoneware globular vase by Bernard Leach on circular foot and with short neck, covered in a pale celadon glaze with gray veining, circa 1930, 19.8cm. high. (Christie's) $5,148

LEACH

A porcelain bottle vase by David Leach, covered in a rich tenmoku glaze with two panels of khaki brushwork, 33.4cm. high. (Christie's) $396

A porcelain vase by David Leach on shallow foot, the cup-shaped body with vertical cut decoration on the exterior, 13.4cm. high. (Christie's) $99

A large stoneware vase, by Janet Leach, the dark brown body covered in a thin running milky gray slip over an iron-brown glaze, 49.7cm. high. (Phillips) $550

LEEDS

A Leeds creamware baluster coffee-pot and domed cover, the green striped body with entwined strap handle, circa 1775, 22.5cm. high. (Christie's) $5,205

A creamware punch-kettle and cover, painted in a famille rose palette with Orientals among furniture, vases and shrubs, probably Leeds, circa 1775, 21cm. high. (Christie's) $1,201

A Leeds creamware figure of a bird, with green splashes to its neck, tail and breast, standing astride a slender quatrefoil base, circa 1780, 21cm. high. (Christie's) $4,138

LENCI

A Lenci pottery figure, modelled as a girl wearing a long floral dress, painted in colors, 30.5cm. high. (Phillips) $387

A Lenci pottery figure of a nude girl with her knees raised, her arms folded behind her head resting on cushions, 44cm.long, signed. (Phillips) $4,900

A stylish Lenci pottery figure, modelled as a woman wearing a brown and beige striped dress, 23cm. high. (Phillips) $1,848

LINTHORPE

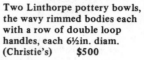

A Linthorpe pottery vase designed by Christopher Dresser, the red body covered with streaked green and milky-brown glazes, 10cm. high. (Phillips) $1,715

Two Linthorpe pottery bowls, the wavy rimmed bodies each with a row of double loop handles, each 6½in. diam. (Christie's) $500

A Linthorpe brown glazed pottery clock case, possibly designed by Christopher Dresser, 10in. high, impressed Linthorpe 1973. (Christie's) $250

A Linthorpe pottery ewer, designed by Christopher Dresser, the reddish body glazed on the shoulders with streaked milky-green and brown, 24cm. high. (Phillips) $344

A Linthorpe pottery pouring vessel, designed by Christopher Dresser, the domed vessel decorated with vertical beading, 16.5cm. high. (Phillips) $1,066

A Linthorpe pottery vase, designed by Christopher Dresser, decorated with stylized linear patterns, 21cm. high. (Phillips) $1,238

A Linthorpe pottery vase designed by Christopher Dresser, the red body streaked with milky-green and honey glazes, 24cm. high. (Phillips) $210

A Linthorpe pottery jardiniere designed by Dr Christopher Dresser, the swollen dimpled form with foliate rim, decorated with double loop handles and alternating rosettes, 13.8cm. high. (Christie's) $448

A Linthorpe earthenware jug designed by Dr Christopher Dresser, covered in a thick predominantly green and brown glaze, (slight restoration to lip rim) 16.7cm. high. (Christie's) $299

LIVERPOOL

A Liverpool creamware pitcher, England, early 19th century, ovoid body with black transfer printed scene of woman on shore waving to departing ships, 9½in. high. (Robt. W. Skinner Inc.) $1,300

A Liverpool delft blue and white dated bowl, the interior with a man holding an axe, with the date 1769, 18.5cm. diam. (Christie's) $3,003

A Liverpool creamware pitcher, attributed to Herculaneum Pottery, England, circa 1800, 12¾in. high. (Robt. W. Skinner Inc.) $17,000

A Liverpool mug, painted in underglaze blue, iron-red and gold with flowers and rocks and a bridge over a river, 9.5cm. (Lawrence Fine Arts) $1,742

A Liverpool delft transfer-printed tile by John Sadler, circa 1760, 13cm. square. (Christie's) $600

A Liverpool creamware ovi-form jug printed in black with figures on a quayside, 10½in. high, circa 1797. (Christie's) $1,193

A Liverpool delft polychrome coffee-cup, painted in blue and green with a building flanked by trees, circa 1760, 6cm. high. (Christie's) $1,301

One of a pair of Liverpool delft spirally molded wall pockets, the tops painted in blue, 7in. high, circa 1770. (Christie's) two $808

A Liverpool creamware pitcher, England, circa 1810, black trans-fer printed with 'Peace, Plenty and Independence', 9¾in. high. (Robt. W. Skinner Inc.) $2,000

A London delft dated blue and white armorial plate, painted in a dark blue with the arms of The Clothworkers Company, 1701, 23cm. diam. (Christie's) $19,019

A London delft white salt, the shallow circular bowl with flat rim and three scroll lugs, circa 1675, 12cm. diam. (Christie's) $12,012

A London delft dated blue and white oval royal portrait plaque of Queen Anne, the reverse with the date 1704, pierced for hanging (minute chips to beads), 23.5cm. high. (Christie's) $28,028

A London delft dated blue and white wet-drug jar, on a circular spreading foot (cracks to rim), 1666, 17.5cm. high. (Christie's) $5,605

A London delft blue and white two-handled beaker of flared form, painted with stylized flowers, circa 1720, 7cm. high. (Christie's) $560

A London delft blue and white drug-jar (rim chips and slight glaze flaking), circa 1680, 9.5cm. high. (Christie's) $1,101

A London delft blue-dash royal portrait charger painted with a full-length portrait of Charles II in his coronation robes, circa 1685, 32.5cm. diam. (Christie's) $29,040

A London delft blue and white octagonal pill-tile, boldly painted with the arms of The Worshipful Society of Apothecaries, late 17th century, 27.5cm. high. (Christie's) $6,006

A London delft blue and white dated barber's bowl, the center painted with a comb, scissors, shaving brush and other implements of the trade, 1716, 26cm. diam. (Christie's) $42,592

LOUIS WAIN

A Louis Wain porcelain cat vase, decorated in white, green, russet and black enamels, with impressed and painted marks, 15.5cm. high. (Christie's) $2,602

A Louis Wain porcelain Bulldog vase, decorated in cream, yellow, green, russet and black enamels, 14.5cm. long. (Christie's) $1,580

A Louis Wain porcelain vase, decorated in blue, green, yellow and russet enamels, with painted marks Louis Wain, Made in England, 14.5cm. high. (Christie's) $626

A Louis Wain porcelain lion vase, decorated in black, yellow, green and russet enamels, 11.8cm. high. (Christie's) $1,580

A Louis Wain porcelain animal vase, the stylized figure of a dog bearing a shield, with shaped aperture on its back, 14.2cm. high. (Christie's) $1,673

A Louis Wain porcelain pig vase, decorated in green, yellow, russet and black enamels, with impressed and painted marks, 12.4cm. high. (Christie's) $2,602

LOWESTOFT

A Lowestoft blue and white bell shaped tankard painted with Oriental buildings among trees, circa 1764, 4¾in. high. (Christie's) $1,250

A Lowestoft blue and white leaf-shaped pickle dish with molded | stalk handle and veins, circa 1765, 6in. wide. (Christie's) $840

Lowestoft jug, blue and white chinoiserie pattern of landscapes and figures, approx. 7in. (G. A. Key) $280

LUSTRE

A 19th century bronze lustre jug with floral decoration, 5in. diam. (Giles Haywood) $46

A pink lustre twin-handled chamber pot, printed with encouraging verses, a 'spy' inside exclaiming 'O! Me what do I See,' diam. 25cm. (Osmond Tricks) $629

A 19th century bronze lustre handled and footed jug with mask spout, 5in. diam. (Giles Haywood) $46

A large pink lustre jug, printed with a ship 'Northumberland 74', 'G' in a star, and a masonic verse, 20cm. (Osmond Tricks) $388

A Sunderland jug, printed with a view of Sunderland Bridge, the reverse with the Farmers Arms, by Dixon Austin & Co., 21.5cm. (Lawrence Fine Arts) $446

English, early 19th century antique pink and green lustre pitcher with floral decoration, 6in. high. (Eldred's) $154

Antique Sunderland pitcher with view of Iron Bridge on one side, masonic symbols on the other side, 7½in. high. (Eldred's) $303

'The Six Swans', a Maw and Co., two-handled lustre vase designed by Walter Crane, the base with enamelled monogram and dated 1890, 26.7cm. high. (Christie's) $6,853

A Sunderland pink lustre jug, printed with Wear Bridge, 'Friendship, Love & Truth' verse and painted 'Ann Gayley 1857' beneath spout, 18cm. (Osmond Tricks) $314

MARTINWARE

An early Martin Brothers vase, incised with birds and leafy branches in green, blue and brown, 23.3cm. high. (Phillips) $158

Two Martin Brothers stoneware jugs of rounded rectangular section, the body incised and painted in blue and green with flowering branches and stylized monogram CH&EA. (Christie's) $336

A rare and highly unusual Martin Brothers stoneware bird, modelled as a likeness of Benjamin Disraeli, 37cm. high. (Phillips) $14,960

A Martin Brothers 'Fish' vase, covered in a mottled gray-blue and green glaze and decorated with caricatures of fish, dated 1.1898, 16.1cm. high. (Christie's) $598

An unusual Martin Brothers stoneware toby jug, modelled as the full length seated figure of a bearded man, 25.5cm. high. (Phillips)$5,160

A Martin Brothers stoneware vase, swollen form with flared neck, decorated with caricatures of fish and eels swimming amid underwater plants, dated 6-1890, 18.9cm. high. (Christie's) $1,122

A large Martin Brothers stoneware bird, having broad brown beak and large slightly protruding eyes, 36.5cm. high. (Phillips). $8,944

A Martin Brothers jardiniere, incised and painted in blue with mythological figures in a flowering landscape, signed on the rim and base R. W. Martin & Brothers, London and Southall 1886, 31cm.high. (Christie's) $3,366

A Martin Brothers brown-glazed stoneware vase of swollen form with tapering cylindrical neck and flared base, with incised decoration of flowerheads, 15.7cm. high. (Christie's) $112

MEISSEN

A Meissen two-handled silver-shaped jardiniere, the fluted body painted with sprays of Manierblumen, circa 1755, 17cm. wide. (Christie's) $1,487

A Meissen group of four scantily clad children warming themselves by an open fire, 17.5cm. high. (Bearne's) $791

A Meissen figure of a recumbent pug dog on a baroque stool, modelled by J. J. Kandler, 11cm. high. (Christie's) $11,154

A Meissen figure of a gardener, modelled by P. Reinicke, standing using a watering can, circa 1760, 12.5cm. high. (Christie's) $836

A Meissen porcelain teacup, painted in puce enamel with a horseman blowing a horn, late 18th century. (Bearne's) $223

A Meissen group of two vintagers on a rocky outcrop, a young woman by their side filling a bottle from a barrel, 21 cm. (Bearne's) $1,307

A Meissen documentary teabowl with everted rim, molded with a band of stiff leaves, inscribed Dresden 1739. (Christie's) $408

A Meissen figure of a starling, naturistically modelled by J.J. Kandler, with black and green plumage, circa 1740, 15cm. high. (Christie's) $1,859

A Meissen Imari underglaze blue dish from the Bamburger Schloss service, circa 1735, 29.5cm. diam. (Christie's) $7,807

MEISSEN

A Meissen (Augustus Rex) baluster teapot and cover, painted in the manner of J. G. Horoldt with Orientals taking tea, circa 1728, 11.5cm. high. (Christie's) $39,039

A Meissen blue and white rectangular dish with indented corners, painted in the Transitional style, incised Dreher's mark 3R, circa 1732, 30cm. wide. (Christie's) $7,436

A Meissen brush-back painted in colors with a Watteaumalerei scene, circa 1745, 11.5cm. diam. (Christie's) $929

A Meissen hexagonal baluster teacaddy painted in the manner of P. E. Schindler with Orientals taking tea, circa 1725, 9cm. high. (Christie's) $3,346

An important Meissen white figure of an eagle, modelled after a Japanese Arita original, by J. J. Kandler, circa 1734-5, 56cm. high. (Christie's) $145,002

A Meissen coffee cup, painted in puce enamel with horsemen in an open landscape, late 18th century. (Bearne's) $172

A Meissen figure of a thrush, modelled by J. J. Kandler, circa 1745, 18cm. high. (Christie's) $5,205

A 19th century Meissen teapot and cover, painted with birds in landscapes, the cover with rose finial, 10cm. (Osmond Tricks) $416

A Meissen figure of a seated fisherboy, a fish in one hand and a basket of fish at his side, circa 1770, 12cm. high. (Christie's) $929

MEISSEN

A Meissen chinoiserie family group from the Delices de l'Enfance series, modelled by J. J. Kandler and P. Reinicke, circa 1755, 14cm. high. (Christie's) $2,788

A Meissen figure of a trinket-seller holding a box with her wares, circa 1745, 16.5cm. high. (Christie's) $2,602

A Meissen group of two scantily clad women and a child capturing Triton in a net, 30.5cm. (Bearne's) $825

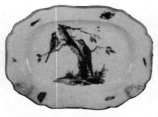

A Meissen circular bowl and cover painted with deutsche Blumen, the cover with seated youth finial, circa 1765, 18cm. diam. (Christie's)
$1,115

A Meissen ornithological ob-long octagonal dish, the center with woodpeckers on a tree, circa 1750, 38cm. wide. (Christie's) $1,859

A Meissen Augsburg Hausmale-rei pink lustre two-handled beaker painted by Auffenwerth, circa 1730. (Christie's)
$2,416

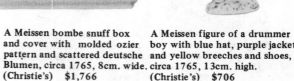

A Meissen figure of a seated harlequin playing the bagpipes, blue crossed swords mark to rear of base, circa 1750, 13.5cm. high. (Christie's)
$1,580

A Meissen bombe snuff box and cover with molded ozier pattern and scattered deutsche Blumen, circa 1765, 8cm. wide. (Christie's) $1,766

A Meissen figure of a drummer boy with blue hat, purple jacket, and yellow breeches and shoes, circa 1765, 13cm. high. (Christie's) $706

MEISSEN

A Meissen group of cherry pickers, modelled by J. J. Kandler, a young boy in the tree throwing the fruit down, circa 1770, 28.5cm. high. (Christie's) $4,461

A Meissen porcelain figure of a woman sitting in a chair, crossed swords mark, 16.5cm. (Bearne's) $619

A Meissen figure of a Dutch peasant, modelled by P. Reinicke, crossed swords mark at back, circa 1745, 13.5cm. high. (Christie's) $1,115

A Meissen shaped oval two-handled basket, boldly painted with specimen birds on branches and scattered insects, circa 1745, 36.5cm. wide. (Christie's) $4,275

A Meissen Hausmalerei two-handled beaker, painted by F.J. Ferner, with a gentleman playing the pipe and a lady playing the mandolin, circa 1730. (Christie's) $1,022

A Meissen Purpurmalerei ogival spoon tray painted with travellers in a gilt rococo scroll cartouche, circa 1745, 17.5cm. wide. (Christie's) $1,859

A Bottger Hausmalerei flared beaker and saucer painted by Ignaz Bottengruber with gilt and brown Laub-und-Bandelwerk, circa 1725. (Christie's) $42,757

A pair of Meissen detachable seven-light candelabra of triangular section, the lower parts with three scantily draped putti holding fruit and flowers, circa 1880, 65cm. high. (Christie's) $2,068

A Meissen pate-sur-pate covered vase, late 19th century, teal blue ground with reverse panel, 12½in. high. (Robt. W. Skinner Inc.) $1,400

MEISSEN

A Meissen bowl painted in the manner of J. G. Horoldt with Orientals brewing potions, circa 1725, 17cm. diam. (Christie's) $22,308

A pair of late Meissen figures of jays, perched upon tree stumps on rocky bases, their plumage naturalistically painted, 15¼in. high. (Christie's) $1,386

A Meissen oviform teapot and cover painted in colors in the manner of Hauer with continuous harbor scenes, circa 1745, 16.5cm. wide. (Christie's) $2,974

A Meissen porcelain crystalline oviform vase with incurved rim covered overall with a crystalline glaze, 16.5cm. high. (Phillips) $1,015

A small Meissen teapot and cover, with bird head spout, 18th century, 8cm. high. (Bearne's) $997

A Meissen figure of a girl carrying flowers in a basket and in her apron, circa 1755, 13cm. high. (Christie's) $517

A Meissen figure of a lady gardener standing on a shaped circular base applied with flowers, 4¼in. (Christie's) $539

A pair of late Meissen figures of a gallant and a lady, each standing on a shaped grassy base molded with gilt scrolls, 10½in. high. (Christie's) $3,080

A Meissen group of four figures standing playing musical instruments, 10¾in. high. (Christie's) $1,501

MING

An early Ming blue and white foliate-rim dish painted with a composite floral arabesque, 15in. diam. (Christie's) $49,358

A Ming blue and white square box and cover, the sides painted in bright blue tones with a lotus scroll, Longqing period, 11cm. square. (Christie's) $21,901

An important large early Ming blue and white dish, vividly painted, with two carp swimming amongst aquatic fern and weeds at the center Yongle, 53.6cm. diam. (Christie's) $378,290

A fine late Ming blue and white small jar painted in bright blue tones with three peacocks, 5¼in. high. (Christie's) $21,153

A Ming green enamelled engraved dragon dish, the center of the interior vigorously engraved with a scaly dragon, 21.6cm. diam. (Christie's) $11,987

A fine and rare Ming blue and white vase for the Japanese market, the lower section formed as a cube, 12¼in. high. (Christie's) $119,871

A very rare early Ming underglaze-blue yellow-ground saucer-dish, painted in strong cobalt tones with a spray of flowering pomegranate, Xuande period, 29.4cm. diam. (Christie's) $398,200

A very rare and important Ming blue and white large deep bowl, the shoulder with eight horizontal rectangular flanges, painted in vibrant blue tones, Yongle/Xuande, 36.8cm. wide. (Christie's) $378,290

A Ming 'Green Dragon' saucer-dish, the interior incised and painted in bright green enamel, Hongzhi period, 20cm. diam. (Christie's) $1,294

173

MINTON

A Minton majolica oval game dish and cover, factory mark for 1861. (Greenslades) $525

A pair of Minton candlesticks with cherubs supporting the candle holders. (Hobbs Parker) $700

A Minton majolica two-handled jardiniere, the handles modelled as entwined snakes, their heads resting on the shoulder, date code for 1869, 38cm. wide. (Christie's) $1,787

A pair of Minton pate-sur-pate two-handled vases of rectangular baluster section in the Oriental style, decorated by T. Mellor, with a bird hovering above flowering plants, circa 1880, 26cm. high. (Christie's) $940

A Minton blue and gilt vase modelled as a kneeling cherub supporting a leaf pattern vase on a circular base. (Greenslades) $367

Two Minton Secessionist vases each of inverted baluster form, one covered in violet and blue glazes, the other in red and brown, 23.8cm. high. (Christie's) Two $374

A Minton majolica garden seat of conical form, the sides pierced with shaped lappets edged with ochre and maroon strapwork, date code for 1883, 45cm. high. (Christie's) $564

A pair of Minton flower-encrusted vases, the flared bodies painted with exotic birds perched on branches in landscape vignettes, circa 1835, 35cm. high. (Christie's) $846

A Minton majolica garden seat, with pink and white flowerheads issuing from stylized foliage above a border of ochre S-scrolls, date code for 1867, 47cm. high. (Christie's) $1,881

MINTON

Victorian Minton pottery foot bath with carrying handles. (Hobbs & Chambers) $435

A Minton majolica sweet-meat dish supported by a seated Bacchanalian figure wearing a garland of vine leaves. (Greenslades) $427

A Minton game pie dish, with cover and liner, modelled with a hare and a pheasant in panels, 35cm. impressed mark. (Lawrence Fine Arts) $1,766

A pair of Minton vases with turquoise ground, modelled with pheasants standing on rocks, 35.5cm. (Lawrence Fine Arts) $597

A Minton porcelain elephant centerpiece with four candle holders. (Hobbs Parker) $1,300

A fine pair of Minton porcelain figures of Red Riding Hood and boy woodman, on green and gilt rococo bases, 6½in. high. (G.A.Property Services) $1,408

Minton octagonal garden seat having continuous wide band of Art Nouveau style floral decoration, 17½in. high. (Peter Wilson) $934

One of a pair of Minton porcelain plates each painted with scenes of country seat with several figures, 9in. wide. (Dacre, Son & Hartley) Two $2,250

A Minton Secessionist vase, covered in mustard-yellow and turquoise glazes, with green and brown piped slip decoration of stylized trees, 22.8cm. high. (Christie's) $317

MOORCROFT

A Moorcroft two-handled vase, designed for James MacIntyre & Co., circa 1904-1913, the white ground with trailing flowers in red, blue and green glaze, 23.3cm. high. (Christie's) $1,347

A Moorcroft 'Claremont' two-handled vase, circa 1930-1945, decorated in brilliant red and yellow with toadstools on a greenish glazed ground, 20.3cm. high. (Christie's) $3,080

A Moorcroft 'Claremont' elongated oviform vase, made for Liberty & Co., with short neck and everted rim, 20.5cm. high. (Christie's) $1,566

A Moorcroft white china baluster transfer vase with Coronation commemorative plaques to George V and Queen Mary 1911, 12in. high. (Langlois) $449

A 1960's period Moorcroft pottery 'Marine' pattern wall plate, glazed in naturalistic colors with seahorse, an exotic fish, shells and seaweed fronds, 26cm. diameter. (Henry Spencer) $236

A Moorcroft 'Florian' vase with white piped decoration of cornflowers and scrolling foliage, 26cm. high. (Christie's) $1,468

Moorcroft pottery vase painted with colored leaves and berries on blue ground, 6¼in. high. (Prudential) $253

An early 20th century tulip pattern Moorcroft 'Florian' ware jardiniere, of cylindrical form with slightly flared and crimped rim, 20cm. high. (Henry Spencer) $1,443

A Moorcroft 'Brown Cornflower' goblet/vase, supported on a spreading circular foot densely decorated with flowers and foliage, 21.5cm. high. (Phillips) $972

MOORCROFT

A Moorcroft 'Hazledene' inkwell, of square section with circular cover painted in the 'Eventide' palette with trees, 6.8cm. high. (Phillips) $561

A Moorcroft 'Flambe' candlestick, decorated in a flambe red with anemones against a blue ground, 8cm. high. (Phillips) $338

A 1960's period Moorcroft pottery 'Caribbean' pattern mug, slip trailed and glazed in greens, blues, and reds, with palm trees on sand dunes and yachts at sea, 10cm. high. (Henry Spencer) $152

A Moorcroft large baluster vase, the white ground piped with mountainous landscape, 37cm. high. (Christie's) $3,524

A Moorcroft 'Claremont' jardiniere, decorated in tube-lining with large mushrooms, painted in clear colors of maroon, yellow, green and blue, 24.8cm. high. (Phillips) $3,179

A 1920's period Moorcroft pottery 'Landscape' pattern large vase, in sombre blue and brown saltglazes. (Henry Spencer) $3,042

A Moorcroft 'Claremont' vase made for Liberty & Co., with white piped decoration of mushrooms, covered in green, blue and crimson glaze, 21cm. high. (Christie's) $1,468

A Moorcroft 'Flambe' pottery plate, painted with a colorful fish and a jellyfish, circa 1935, 25.8cm. (Bearne's) $894

MacIntyre Moorcroft vase, painted with red and purple cornflowers with green foliage, 9¾in. high. (Prudential) $1,149

NANTGARW

A Nantgarw London-decorated gold-ground circular two-handled sauce tureen and stand, the body and stand painted with garden flowers on a gilt band, circa 1820, the stand 18.5cm. diam. (Christie's) $4,891

A Nantgarw oblong dish, painted by Thomas Pardoe, with a basket of flowers on a ledge, circa 1820, 28cm. wide. (Christie's) $1,693

A Nantgarw coffee cup and saucer with pierced heart-shaped handle, painted by Thomas Pardoe, circa 1820. (Christie's) $564

A Nantgarw plate, the center painted by James Plant with a yokel and companion with cattle, circa 1820, 23.5cm. diam. (Christie's) $3,198

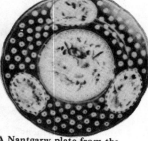

A Nantgarw plate from the Duke of Cambridge service, the center painted with a bouquet of flowers, circa 1820, 24cm. diam. (Christie's) $2,069

A Nantgarw London-decorated plate, the center painted with a bouquet within a border of flower-sprays, circa 1820, 25cm. diam. (Christie's) $3,010

A Nantgarw plate, painted by James Plant with sailing ships by a lighthouse on a calm sea, circa 1820, 24cm. diam. (Christie's) $2,821

A Nantgarw armorial cabinet-cup and saucer, the central arms within a garter with the motto *Deus et Patria*, circa 1820. (Christie's) $3,574

A Nantgarw green-ground plate painted by J. Martin Randall, the center with hounds attacking a wolf in a wooded landscape, circa 1820, 24cm. diam. (Christie's) $2,633

PARIAN

Good quality 19th century parian ware group 'Haymaking', 19in. high. (Prudential) $732

A Rockingham biscuit bust of William IV on a waisted cylindrical socle, 18cm. high. (Henry Spencer) $392

A Minton parian figure of Miranda sitting barefoot on a rocky outcrop, after a model by John Bell, 36.5cm., circa 1860. (Bearne's) $469

Late 19th century parian figure composition depicting Bacchus and Ariadne embracing, 20in. high. (Peter Wilson) $346

A white bisque bust of Venus modelled with head turned to her left, 17½in. high. (Christie's) $432

A parian ware bust after Paul Duboy of a young girl with floral garland in her hair, 21in. high. (GA Property Services) $1,870

PARIS

A Paris inkstand, surmounted by a seated figure of a greyhound wearing a collar and padlock, 21.5cm. wide. (Lawrence Fine Arts) $580

A pair of Paris ovoid vases each reserved on oval panels with figures in a river landscape, late 19th century, 13in. high. (Woolley & Wallis) $540

A Paris porcelain veilleuse, the globular teapot and cylindrical holder painted with peasant lovers in landscape vignettes, circa 1830, 24cm. high overall. (Christie's) $464

PEARLWARE

A Yorkshire pearlware figure of a sportsman in green-brown hat, blue jacket, spotted waistcoat and yellow breeches, circa 1800, 26.5cm. high. (Christie's) $7,524

A pearlware oval plaque molded in high relief and colored with two recumbent lions, circa 1790, 28.5cm. wide. (Christie's) $1,223

An interesting pearlware coffee pot, of baluster form, painted with scattered sprays of flowers and foliage in underglaze blue, beige, green and cream, 31cm. high. (Henry Spencer) $1,196

A Staffordshire pearlware group of a dandy and companion wearing their finest clothes, circa 1820, 21cm. high. (Christie's) $962

A pearlware flattened oviform jug with loop handle, molded and colored with the Miser, perhaps Yorkshire, circa 1800, 13cm. high. (Christie's) $451

A Staffordshire pearlware group of Departure modelled as a sailor in blue jacket and brown hat, circa 1820, 23.5cm. high. (Christie's) $619

A pearlware circular plate transfer printed with a half length portrait of J. C. J. Van Speyk and a Dutch inscription, 22cm. diam. (Henry Spencer) $92

'Heroes Bearded and Beardless', a Wedgwood pearlware shaving pot, designed by Richard Redgrave, of tapering form, mark for 1847, impressed mark Wedgwood, 20.5cm. high. (Christie's) $1,058

A pearlware figure of a horse sponged in brown and ochre, on a sponged green rectangular base, Yorkshire or Staffordshire, circa 1800, 19cm. long. (Christie's) $4,514

PILKINGTON

A Pilkington Royal Lancastrian two-handled lustre vase decorated by W. S. Mycock, with a frieze of running hounds against a foliate background, dated 1917, 18cm. high. (Christie's) $1,664

A Pilkington Royal Lancastrian lustre bowl, the exterior decorated with six rectangular cartouches of stylized foliate design, code for 1910, 19.3cm. diam. (Christie's) $685

A small Pilkington Royal Lancastrian lustre vase, with a formal pattern of dots, wavy lines, spiral motifs and stylized leaves, 1905, 9cm. high. (Christie's) $195

A Pilkington Royal Lancastrian lustre vase decorated by Richard Joyce, with stylized floral and foliate bands, 22.5cm. high. (Christie's) $980

A fine Burmantofts faience charger with domed center, decorated in the Isnik manner in blue, turquoise, green and amethyst with dragons, 45.6cm. diam. (Christie's) $5,090

A Pilkington Royal Lancastrian lustre vase decorated by Richard Joyce, with a Tudor Rose motif in four rectangular cartouches, 22.1cm. high. (Christie's) $391

A Pilkington Lancastrian lustre vase and cover decorated by Richard Joyce with a frieze of antelopes and stylized trees, 15.5cm. high. (Christie's) $979

A Pilkington Royal Lancastrian lustre vase decorated by Gordon Forsyth, with a pattern of silvery-yellow stylized cornflowers with their stems against a green ground with red spots, 1910, 23cm. high. (Christie's) $1,960

A Pilkington Royal Lancastrian lustre vase, decorated by Richard Joyce, of shouldered, flaring, cylindrical form with everted neck, 24.4cm. high. (Christie's) $875

PRATTWARE

A Prattware creamer in the form of a dappled cow with hind legs tied, a milk maid sitting on a stool, 10.3cm. high, tail and cover missing. (Bearne's) $626

An unusual 18th century Prattware tobacco pipe, the bowl molded with four grimacing masks, 10in. long. (Prudential) $676

A Prattware pepperette in the form of the bust of a gentleman with black hair, wearing a bowler hat and a sash with a leopard's head shoulder clasp, 10.5cm. high. (Henry Spencer) $452

A Prattware vase bearing 'Tria Juncta in Uno and Alma', with Feast stamp. (Phillips) $1,131

18th century Pratt figure of a cat with blue, green and ochre splashed decoration, 3in. high. (Prudential) $475

A vase of flattened form bearing 'Cattle and Ruins' and 'The Queen! God Bless Her'. (Phillips) $382

A Prattware fish paste jar, 'Reception of H.R.H. The Prince of Wales and Princess Alexandra at London Bridge 7th March 1863'. (Phillips) $260

A Prattware plaque, "Felix Edwards Pratt", olive green background. (Phillips) $870

A Prattware jar, "Great Exhibition 1851". (Phillips) $870

REDWARE

A glazed and decorated redware water cooler by Peter Bell, Hagerstown, Maryland, first quarter 19th century, 10¾in. high. (Christie's)
$990

A glazed redware lion by Henry Gast, Lancaster County, Pennsylvania, mid/late 19th century, 10½in. long. (Christie's)
$385

A rare glazed Wagner redware bank, probably Pennsylvania, 19th century, modelled as a seated dog, 6½in. high. (Christie's) $1,430

A G. E. Ohr molded pitcher, Biloxi, Mississippi, late 19th century, with Grover Cleveland on one side and his wife on the reverse (some chips), 8in. high. (Robt. W. Skinner Inc.)
$700

A slip decorated pierced and incised redware tobacco jar, Pennsylvania, first half 19th century, with flaring scalloped rim, 6in. high, with lid. (Christie's) $4,950

A redware glazed and decorated wallpocket, American, 1875, with pierced holes for mounting, 10in. high. (Christie's) $286

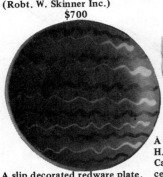

A slip decorated redware plate, Pennsylvania, mid 19th century, with crimped edge, 10in. diam. (Christie's) $1,045

A glazed redware grotesque jug, H. F. Rhinhardt, Vale, North Carolina, late 19th/early 20th century, squat form with applied facial features, 7¼in. high. (Robt. W. Skinner Inc.)
$1,400

A glazed redware cake mold, Pennsylvania, 19th century, with scalloped edge and fluted channels, 9in. diam. (Christie's)
$110

RIE, LUCIE

A stoneware salad bowl with pulled lip by Lucie Rie, covered in a finely pitted bluish-white glaze with iron-brown flecks, circa 1954, 14.3cm. high. (Christie's) $1,584

An inlaid porcelain bowl by Lucie Rie, the interior and exterior inlaid with double pale amethyst bands, covered in a pinkish-white matt glaze, circa 1979, 24cm. diam. (Christie's) $3,960

A stoneware bowl by Lucie Rie, covered in a pinkish-white pitted and mottled glaze, impressed LR seal, circa 1955, 22.9cm. diam. (Christie's) $2,970

A stoneware vase by Lucie Rie, covered in a gray-lavender pitted glaze with iron-brown flecks, circa 1970, 17cm. high. (Christie's) $1,089

A large stoneware bowl by Lucie Rie on shallow foot, covered in a rich pitted yellow-uranium glaze, impressed LR seal, 35.6cm. diam. (Christie's) $7,524

An important large stoneware vase by Lucie Rie, with areas of bluish buff thinning and pooling in places, to reveal body beneath, impressed LR seal, circa 1960, 47cm. high. (Christie's) $5,148

A stoneware bowl by Lucie Rie with compressed flared sides, the exterior carved with fluted decoration, impressed LR seal 14cm. high. (Christie's) $3,564

A stoneware coffee pot and cover by Lucie Rie, the bulbous body with pulled handle and tall cylindrical neck with pulled lip, impressed LR seal, circa 1966, 22.9cm. high. (Christie's) $792

A porcelain bottle vase by Lucie Rie, covered in an off-white glaze, with gray veining and a mottled pinkish-green spiral, circa 1965, 27.5cm. high. (Christie's) $4,752

ROCKINGHAM

A Rockingham miniature lavender-ground teapot and cover, applied with trailing white flowers, Puce Griffin mark and Cl. 2 in red, circa 1835, 6.5cm. high. (Christie's) $677

A Rockingham blue-ground rectangular tray, the center painted with a bouquet within a periwinkle-blue border, circa 1835, 36.5cm. wide. (Christie's) $1,505

A Rockingham blue-ground ring holder, painted with a band of pink roses within a gilt line rim, Red Griffin mark, circa 1826-30, 9cm. diam. (Christie's) $658

A Rockingham spill holder modelled as the corner of a thatched cottage, a cat gazing from a bush by a pile of logs below, circa 1835, 16.5cm. high. (Christie's) $1,317

A Rockingham miniature plate encrusted with three flower-sprays, Puce Griffin mark, circa 1835, 9.5cm. diam. (Christie's) $339

A Rockingham green-ground hexagonal baluster vase and cover, painted with bouquets and scattered flowers and insects, circa 1826-30, 46cm. high. (Christie's) $1,599

A Rockingham puce-ground flared cylindrical spill vase painted with a loose bouquet within a gilt rectangular cartouche, circa 1835, 8.5cm. high. (Christie's) $470

A Rockingham hexagonal basket, the center painted with Salisbury Cathedral named below within a trailing gilt foliage surround, circa 1835, 31cm. wide. (Christie's) $1,505

A Rockingham campana-shaped pot-pourri vase and pierced cover with gilt scroll handles, painted with bouquets, circa 1835, 34.5cm. high. (Christie's) $3,198

ROOKWOOD

A Rookwood pottery basket, by artist Artus Van Briggle, decorated in slip underglaze with blossoms, berries and leaves, 6½in. high. (Robt. W. Skinner Inc.) $700

Rookwood pottery jewelled porcelain vase, Cincinnati, Ohio, 1922, 8½in. high. (Robt. W. Skinner Inc.) $1,000

Rookwood iris glaze pansy vase, Cincinnati, Ohio, 1901, decorated with white pansies on lavender and blue ground, 6¾in. high. (Robt. W. Skinner Inc.) $400

A Rookwood earthenware vase, possibly decorated by Edward Diers, with a riverscape in shades of blue and green in a 'Vellum' glaze, 8½in. high. (Christie's) $577

Three Rookwood pottery standard glaze mouse plates, Cincinnati, Ohio, circa 1893, each depicting a mischievous mouse, 7in. diam. (Robt. W. Skinner Inc.) $650

Rookwood pottery standard glaze vase, Cincinnati, Ohio, circa 1902, decorated with daffodils and blades on shaded brown ground, 11¼in. high. (Robt. W. Skinner Inc.) $600

A Rookwood stoneware vase, the compressed globular body painted in browns, amber and green with three wild roses, 21cm. high. (Christie's) $486

Rookwood pottery standard glaze pitcher, Cincinnati, Ohio, 1890, decorated with clover and grasses, 12¼in. high. (Robt. W. Skinner Inc.) $900

Rookwood standard glaze vase, Cincinnati, Ohio, 1900, pansy decoration on shaded brown and orange ground, 10¼in. high. (Robt. W. Skinner Inc.) $250

ROYAL COPENHAGEN

A Royal Copenhagen group by Gerhard Henning, depicting an 18th century courting couple, 24cm. high. (Christie's) $1,260

A Royal Copenhagen vase of faceted globular outline, having a pierced 'spider web' protrusion to the rim, 14cm. high. (Phillips) $805

A Royal Copenhagen group by Gerhard Henning, depicting a courting couple in finely detailed 18th century costume, 22cm. high. (Phillips) $1,050

A Royal Copenhagen figure by Gerhard Henning, of a naked girl with nodding head seated cross-legged upon a large detachable cushion, 32.5cm. high. (Phillips) $2,362

A Royal Copenhagen Fairy Tale group, the embracing figures in brightly colored costume, 8¼in. high. (Christie's) $363

A Royal Copenhagen figure by Gerhard Henning, of a naked woman in a bathing cap standing with towel clenched to her chest, 33cm. high. (Phillips) $525

'The Chinese Bride'. A Royal Copenhagen group by Gerhard Henning, depicting a mandarin-type figure in ritualistic embrace with his bride, painted marks to base. (Phillips) $1,925

A Royal Copenhagen porcelain vase decorated with blue-bells against a white glazed background, 16cm. high. (Phillips) $175

'Faun and Nymph', a Royal Copenhagen group by Gerhard Henning, the crouched figures embracing on a grassy knoll, 28cm. high. (Phillips) $1,487

ROYAL DUX

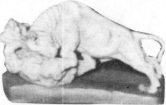

Royal Dux figure of Pierrot and Pierrette, on circular base, 6½in. high. (Prudential) $429

Royal Dux porcelain ornament of a wild bull fighting a grizzly bear, predominantly cream and brown, 12in. (G. A. Key) $704

One of a pair of Royal Dux figures modelled in the form of a peasant boy and girl, 16in. high. (Peter Wilson) Two $588

A colorful Royal Dux group in the form of a young woman alighting from a sedan chair, two grooms in smart uniforms and tricorn hats at her side, 38cm. high. (Bearne's) $490

A Royal Dux Art Deco porcelain figure, modelled as a girl with red hair, naked except for a blue cap tied with a ribbon at the side, 27.25cm. high. (Phillips) $437

A Royal Dux porcelain figure group of a Roman charioteer, the chariot drawn by two rearing horses, 46cm. overall. (Henry Spencer) $1,458

A large Royal Dux figure group, modelled as two embracing lovers, applied pink triangle marks, 69cm. high. (Lawrence Fine Arts) $968

An impressive pair of Royal Dux porcelain large figures, the young goatherd standing wearing a brown tunic; and a young shepherdess, wearing a brown blouse and fleece skirt, 67cm. and 64cm. high. (Henry Spencer) $1,218

A Royal Dux figure of a girl, seated, nude, upon a foliage encrusted rocky base tinted in pink, beige, green, and gilt, 48cm. high. (Henry Spencer) $743

RUSKIN

A Ruskin high-fired porcelain ginger jar and cover, glazed in sang-de-boeuf shading through mauve to white, 25cm. high, 1925. (Phillips) $3,150

A Ruskin lustre vase covered with a variegated green/gray glaze exhibiting a silver sheen, 17.1cm. high. (Phillips) $227

A Ruskin high-fired porcelain vase covered with a rich sang-de-boeuf glaze thinning to white at the neck, 18.5cm. high, impressed 'Ruskin Pottery 1910'. (Phillips) $1,225

A Ruskin high fired pottery vase, with everted rim in mottled deep red and white glazes, 8½in. high. (Christie's) $616

A Ruskin high-fired porcelain ewer, covered overall with a sang-de-boeuf glaze shading to plum with random green speckling, 21cm. high. (Phillips) $598

A Ruskin high-fired vase of flaring cylindrical form with everted rim, 10in. high. (Christie's) $393

A Ruskin high-fired porcelain vase, glazed in sang-de-boeuf and having random spots of green, 21.8cm. high. (Phillips) $792

A Ruskin high-fired porcelain bowl glazed in sang-de-boeuf thinning to white, 20cm. diam., and a Ruskin porcelain stand. (Phillips) $1,190

A Ruskin high-fired porcelain vase, with a rich sang-de-boeuf glaze shading through mottled areas of plum mauve and gray-green, 23.5cm. high. (Phillips) $774

RUSSIAN

CHINA

A commemorative porcelain covered cup and saucer, with Russian inscription *'In memory of 200 years of the Founding of St. Petersburg'*, by the Gardner Factory, circa 1903. (Christie's) $557

A porcelain figure of a dancing peasant, with unrecorded Cyrillic impressed initials GE, circa 1850. (Christie's) $929

A porcelain tazza from the service of Grand Duke Konstantin Nikolaevich, by the Imperial Porcelain Factory (period of Nicholas I), 8in. high. (Christie's) $4,275

A pair of Gardner Factory bisque porcelain figures of Russian peasants, raised upon square bases, 25 and 20.5 cm. high. (Henry Spencer) $1,309

A Russian porcelain figure of a pierrot from the Commedia dell'Arte standing on a spill-vase base, 19th century, 8½in. high. (Christie's) $575

A pair of porcelain figures of a couple dancing, by the Kornilow Factory, 1843-1860, 7¾in. high. (Christie's) $1,673

A large Suprematist dish, after a design by K. Malevich, circa 1926, with underglaze mark of the Imperial Porcelain Factory, 11¼in. diam. (Christie's) $18,590

A large tapering cylindrical porcelain vase, by the Imperial Porcelain Factory (period of Nicholas II), dated 1904, 18½in. high. (Christie's) $3,903

A Soviet porcelain propaganda plate 'The Red Star', with gold borders enclosing a hammer and a plough, by the State Porcelain Factory, circa 1922, 9½in. diam. (Christie's) $20,449

SATSUMA

A Japanese Satsuma earthenware bowl, the interior decorated with numerous figures in colored enamels and gilt, 19cm. wide. (Henry Spencer) $1,487

A Satsuma earthenware bowl, painted in colors with an X florette motif, Satsuma mark, 6½in. diam. (Lawrence Fine Arts) $909

A Japanese Satsuma earthenware circular bowl, decorated on the interior and exterior with numerous chrysanthemum and other blossoms, 15cm. diam. (Henry Spencer) $708

A Japanese Satsuma earthenware vase, finely painted in colors with a continuous mountainous river landscape, 23.5cm. high. (Henry Spencer) $1,385

A Satsuma style pottery bowl, the interior painted with two birds inspecting a spider's web, signed, 7in. diam. (Lawrence Fine Arts) $238

A Japanese Satsuma ware barrel shape vase and cover, decorated with two shaped panels of figures in landscapes, Meiji, 6.7in. (Woolley & Wallis) $657

A late 19th century Japanese Satsuma earthenware large vase, the body molded in high relief with grim faced immortals seated on the banks of a river, 45cm. high. (Henry Spencer) $5,075

A Satsuma style earthenware bowl, the interior painted with pavilions beside waterfalls in a mountainous landscape, signed, 8½in. diam. (Lawrence Fine Arts) $348

A Kyo-satsuma oviform vase decorated with Hotei surrounded by numerous boys in Chinese costume, signed Ryokuzan, late 19th century, 12.3cm. high. (Christie's) $979

SEVRES

A Sevres shaped circular plate from the Charlotte-Louise service, painted in colors ·with the floral monogram CL, blue date letter Z for 1777, 24cm. diam. (Christie's) $2,602

One of a pair of Sevres Chateau de Tuileries, two handled porcelain cachepots, painted with continuous bands of spring and summer flowers in colors, 21cm. wide.(Henry Spencer) Two $692

A Sevres fond ecaille plate, the center painted with a female head, date mark for 1805, 23.5cm. diam. (Christie's) $1,673

A Sevres pot a tabac and cover with rose finial painted in imitation of contemporary cloth with pink stripes on alternating bands of white and seeded pink, 14.5cm. high. (Christie's) $13,244

A pair of Sevres pattern cachepots, the bleu-celeste grounds reserved with panels of figures in gardens, 5¼in. high. (Christie's) $866

One of a pair of Sevres-pattern blue and white vases and covers, of slender fluted form with everted rims, late 19th century, 38cm. high. (Christie's) Two $2,068

A Sevres biscuit figure of The Butter Churner, circa 1754, 21cm. high. (Christie's) $1,860

A pair of large Sevres-style vases, each painted on one side with a couple in a country landscape, late 19th century, signed Maglin. (Bearne's) $3,784

A Sevres porcelain urn and cover, painted in pale and dark amber and white with animals amidst vines and grapes, gilt borders, 47.5cm. high. (Christie's) $935

SEVRES

An ormolu-mounted jewelled Sevres pattern baluster vase decorated with two ovals, one of 18th century figures, the other of a bouquet of flowers, late 19th century, 17½in. high. (Christie's) $892

A Sevres bleu nouveau two handled ecuelle, cover and quatrefoil stand painted with garlands of ribbon-tied flowers, the stand 26cm. wide. (Christie's) $4,275

A Sevres tasse a chocolat, cover and saucer, painted with pairs of exotic birds, date letter h for 1760 and painter's mark of Jean Pierre Ledoux. (Christie's) $2,974

A Sevres (Louis XVIII) royal blue ground cup and saucer painted with a named view of the factory, circa 1819, 20cm. high. (Christie's) $9,306

A Sevres-pattern gilt-metal-mounted two-handled casket, the gilt metal finial modelled as two children holding a mirror, last quarter of the 19th century, 34cm. wide. (Christie's) $1,199

A Sevres gold ground cup and trembleuse saucer painted by Le Guay with the portrait of Marie la Grande Duchesse de Bade, Stephanie Napoleon, date MC juin 1816. (Christie's) $27,885

A Sevres vase and cover, painted with a portrait of a lady, 40cm. (Lawrence Fine Arts) $594

A large pair of Sevres-pattern turquoise-ground baluster vases, painted with ladies and gentleman in 18th century dress at various pursuits, late 19th century, 98.5cm. high. (Christie's) $5,577

A Sevres-pattern ormolu-mounted two-handled vase and cover, the turquoise ground reserved and painted with Europa, circa 1875, 57cm. high. (Christie's) $1,394

SPODE

A Spode blue and white narrow rectangular cheese coaster printed with the Italian ruins pattern, 11½in. wide, circa 1815. (Christie's) $1,000

A Spode stone china table centrepiece, with hand painted floral sprays and pierced border, circa 1805-1815, 20in. diam. (Hy. Duke & Son) $3,211

A good Spode octagonal vase and cover by Abbeydale China commemorating Churchill's 90th birthday and Honorary Citizenship of the USA, 28cm. high. (Phillips) $193

A Spode ironstone two-handled slender oviform vase with spreading neck and foot, 5½in. high. (Christie's) $346

Spode trio set finely painted in the Imari taste. (Prudential) $201

A Spode coffee pot and cover of tapering cylindrical form, gilt all over with trailing foliage, circa 1805, 25.5cm. high. (Christie's) $226

A Spode tapering cylindrical coffee pot and cover, painted with bouquets beneath a border of molded foliage and scrolls, circa 1815, 27cm. high. (Christie's) $376

A Spode porcelain pastille burner in the form of a large house with two windows in the gable end. (Bearne's) $2,236

A Victorian Spode pottery pot-pourri vase, baluster shape with pierced domed cover having bud finial, 12in. high. (Hobbs & Chambers) $330

STAFFORDSHIRE

A Staffordshire pearlware clock group and cover, of Walton type, molded with a clock-dial flanked by the Royal supporters and surmounted by a crown, circa 1820, 20cm. high. (Christie's) $1,505

A Staffordshire creamware figure of a shepherdess of Ralph Wood type, holding a flower to her bosom, a sheep at her feet, circa 1780, 22.5cm. high. (Christie's)
$1,129

A Staffordshire small green-glazed plate, with molded diaper-pattern border, circa 1770, 19.5cm. diam. (Christie's)
$700

A Staffordshire jug, decorated with a band of silver lustre with a pattern of scrolling flower branches, 12cm. (Lawrence Fine Arts)
$271

A Staffordshire solid-agate tapering hexagonal chocolate-pot and domed cover, (cover restored) circa 1750, 22.5cm. high. (Christie's)
$11,011

Late 19th century Staffordshire jug and basin set with floral decoration. (British Antique Exporters) $123

A Staffordshire creamware leaf-shaped dish of Whieldon type, crisply molded with two racemes of pea flower resting on three veined leaves, circa 1760, 18cm. wide. (Christie's)
$1,317

A Staffordshire phrenology bust by L. N. Fowler, the cranium printed with divisions named with character interpretations, 19th century, 30cm. high. (Christie's) $1,045

A Staffordshire saltglaze bear-jug and cover of conventional type, covered in chippings and clasping a dog, circa 1750, 26.5cm. high. (Christie's)
$6,969

CHINA

A Staffordshire creamware bowl of Whieldon type, applied with trailing vine beneath a streaked brown glaze, circa 1755, 14cm. diam. (Christie's) $715

A Staffordshire creamware globular teapot and cover of Whieldon type, with crabstock-molded spout, circa 1755, 9.5cm. high. (Christie's) $2,069

A Staffordshire model of a greengage, of Ralph Wood type, naturally modelled and resting on an oval basket, circa 1780, 8cm. wide. (Christie's) $715

A Staffordshire pearlware group of a gallant and companion, she in a spectacular plumed yellow bonnet (her neck repaired), circa 1820, 22cm. high. (Christie's) $1,035

A pair of Staffordshire pottery figures of reclining cherubs, circa 1800, 6½in. high. (Robt. W. Skinner Inc.) $300

A Staffordshire creamware baluster cream jug and cover of Whieldon type, applied with trailing fruiting branches, circa 1760, 12cm. high. (Christie's) $2,069

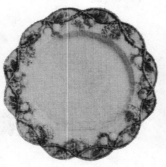

A Staffordshire creamware pineapple-molded milk jug of Wedgwood-Whieldon type, the naturistically molded body with serrated green leaves, circa 1760, 13cm. high. (Christie's) $846

A Staffordshire creamware plate of Whieldon type with a molded diaper-pattern ground, circa 1760, 23.5cm. diam. (Christie's) $1,035

A Staffordshire creamware tea caddy of Whieldon type, the molded panelled sides framed by ropetwist pattern, circa 1760, 9.5cm. high. (Christie's) $846

STAFFORDSHIRE

A Staffordshire slipware dated shallow drinking-vessel, with small loop handle, 1700, 13.5cm. wide. (Christie's) $8,008

A Staffordshire creamware cow-creamer milking group, of Whieldon type, spotted in brown and the milkmaid in a brown coat, circa 1765, 18cm. long. (Christie's) $1,411

A Staffordshire pottery trans-fer printed commemorative chamber pot with a printed vignette of Victoria & Albert inscribed *Married, February 10th 1840,* 7in. (Hy. Duke & Son) $371

A Staffordshire pearlware group of a country woman with a boy, standing before puce foliage on a green oval base, 23.5cm. high. (Christie's) $1,035

A pair of colorful Staffordshire pottery zebra vases, each animal with head held high, 27.5cm. high. (Bearne's) $860

A Staffordshire pottery figure of Andromache in a cream robe, leaning on an urn, circa 1790, 22.5cm. (Ormond Tricks) $157

A Staffordshire pearlware group of a town lady with a boy, standing before green foliage on a marbled rectangular base, circa 1800, 21.5cm. high. (Christie's) $978

A Staffordshire creamware melon-shaped teapot and cover of Wedgwood-Whieldon type with leaf-molded spout, circa 1760, 12.5cm. high. (Christie's) $7,148

A Staffordshire toby jug in the form of a man seated holding a jug of foaming ale, the base marked Walton, 10¼in. (Lawrence Fine Arts) $696

A Staffordshire saltglaze white miniature teapot and cover with crabstock- molded spout and handle, circa 1750, 9.5cm. high. (Christie's) $1,601

A Staffordshire saltglaze white teapot-stand, on a circular spreading base pierced with hearts, circa 1760, 13.5cm. diam. (Christie's) $1,601

A Staffordshire saltglaze polychrome globular punch pot, with green crabstock handle and foliage molded spout, circa 1760, 19cm. high overall. (Christie's) $8,408

A Staffordshire saltglaze white miniature pear-shaped coffee pot and cover with angular loop handle, circa 1760, 11.5cm. high. (Christie's) $846

A Staffordshire saltglaze polychrome baluster pepper pot, painted in a famille rose palette with Orientals, circa 1755, 12cm. high. (Christie's) $9,609

A Staffordshire saltglaze white heart-shaped pickle dish, molded with anthemion and scrolls (restored), circa 1760, 10.5cm. wide. (Christie's) $600

A Staffordshire saltglaze white bucket-shaped piggin, with ropetwist carrying handle, circa 1755, 7cm. high. (Christie's) $1,091

A Staffordshire saltglaze white figure of Chung-li Ch'uan, the bearded Immortal, holding a fan and a peach, circa 1750, 18.5cm. high. (Christie's) $12,012

A Staffordshire saltglaze white heart-shaped teapot and cover, with bird's head spout, circa 1755, 12.5cm. high. (Christie's) $5,205

STAFFORDSHIRE SALTGLAZE

A Staffordshire saltglaze poly-chrome creamboat with green scroll handle, molded and colored with cattle and black fleeced sheep, circa 1760, 11.5cm. long. (Christie's) **$1,901**

Three Staffordshire saltglaze white fish-molds naturally modelled with incised scales, fins and tails, circa 1760, 12.5cm. and 9cm. long. (Christie's) **$919**

A Staffordshire saltglaze poly-chrome oval sauceboat, the exterior crisply molded and painted in natural colors with trailing vine, circa 1755, 18cm. long. (Christie's) **$6,406**

A Staffordshire saltglaze white snuffer figure, modelled as a lady wearing a peaked bonnet, (two cracks to skirt) circa 1745, 9.5cm. high. (Christie's) **$3,603**

A Staffordshire saltglaze balu-ster coffee pot and cover, pain-ted with loose bouquets and flower-sprays within puce and iron-red loop and foliage rims, circa 1755. (Christie's) **$9,029**

A Staffordshire saltglaze small leaf dish with green stalk handle, circa 1755, 15cm. wide. (Christie's) **$489**

A Staffordshire saltglaze white miniature conical chocolate-pot and domed cover, circa 1760, 14.5cm. high. (Christie's) **$6,006**

A Staffordshire saltglaze white molded footed bowl, the ex-terior with crisply molded panels depicting 'The Seven Champions of Christendom', circa 1745, 28cm. diam. (Christie's) **$11,011**

A Staffordshire saltglaze white teapot and cover in the form of a camel, with molded bird's head and foliage spout, circa 1755, 15cm. high. (Christie's) **$14,014**

A Swansea Pottery kidney shape dessert dish and cover, painted with a man and woman fishing, (Lawrence Fine Arts) $260

A Swansea oviform vase, painted with a wooded landscape vignette and a lakeland scene, circa 1815, 26cm. high. (Christie's) $6,772

A Swansea chamber candlestick with bird's head handle and campana-shaped nozzle, the saucer-shaped base painted by William Pollard, circa 1815, 12.5cm. diam. (Christie's) $2,633

A Swansea pot-pourri vase and pierced cover of campana shape, painted by David Evans, with a frieze of garden flowers, circa 1820, 13.5cm. high. (Christie's) $3,574

A Swansea porcelain plate from the Lysaght service, painted by Henry Morris, 24.3cm., early 19th century. (Bearne's) $696

A Swansea London-decorated flared cylindrical cabinet cup, painted with a continuous band of garden flowers, circa 1815, 9cm. high. (Christie's) $846

A Swansea miniature cabinet cup and saucer painted by William Pollard with bands of wild flowers, circa 1815. (Christie's) $1,129

A Swansea oviform vase with flared neck and gilt eagle handles, painted by David Evans, red stencil mark, circa 1815, 15cm. high. (Christie's) $3,010

A Swansea Pottery circular center dish, the bowl painted with a sportsman in a landscape, 26cm. (Lawrence Fine Arts) $353

TANG

A Sancai glazed buff pottery model of a boar standing four-square on a pierced rectangular base, Tang Dynasty, 20cm. long. (Christie's)$4,977

A fine Sancai glazed buff pottery shallow bowl, the exterior applied with quatrefoil florettes on a ground of slip-trailed diagonals, Tang Dynasty, 9.8cm. diam. (Christie's) $10,950

An ochre glazed buff pottery model of a ram standing four-square on a pierced rectangular base, (legs restored) Tang Dynasty, 20cm. long. (Christie's) $2,787

An important massive glazed buff pottery figure of a Bactrian camel, extremely well modelled standing four-square on a rectangular plinth, (restored, primarily to the legs) Tang Dynasty, 82cm. high. (Christie's) $278,740

Two painted red pottery figures of standing matrons, both with hands held before their chests, Tang Dynasty, both about 37cm. high. (Christie's) $23,892

A fine Sancai glazed buff pottery figure of a hound, standing four-square on an oval pedestal, Tang Dynasty, 17.2cm. high. (Christie's) $21,901

A massive Sancai glazed buff pottery figure of a caparisoned horse standing almost four-square on a trapezoidal base, Tang Dynasty, 76cm. high. (Christie's) $179,190

A fine blue glazed footed bowl, with thinly potted rounded sides, Tang Dynasty, 11cm. diam. (Christie's) $4,778

A Sancai glazed buff pottery figure of a camel standing four-square on a rectangular base, Tang Dynasty, 57.1cm. high. (Christie's) $17,919

TERRACOTTA

French terracotta figure of a classical maiden, 19th century, after Clodion, signed Fernand Cian, Paris, 12½in. high. (Robt. W. Skinner Inc.)
$650

A late 19th century French terracotta group of two allegorical putti, by Albert Ernest Carrier-Belleuse, possibly representing Earth and Water, 36 x 65cm. (Christie's) $2,974

A 19th century French terracotta bust of Mademoiselle Marguerite Bellanger, by Albert Carrier-Belleuse, 69cm. high, on a glazed terracotta socle. (Christie's)
$14,872

A terracotta jug with silver mounts designed by Dr Christopher Dresser, with the cover inscribed East Sussex Entry 1873, 23cm. high. (Christie's)
$935

A Davenport terracotta two-handled jardiniere, decorated in relief with a portrait of Admiral Lord Nelson, the handles in the form of dolphins' heads, 9¾in. high. (Geering & Colyer)$1,145

A Belgium terracotta face mask by L. Nosbusch modelled as Rudolf Valentino, 14in. high. (Christie's) $77

A late 19th century French terracotta statuette of the Art of Painting, by Alfred Drury, 39.5cm. high. (Christie's) $836

A mid 19th century French terracotta maquette for a monumental group of three classical females, 21cm. high. (Christie's) $1,168

A 19th century French terracotta bust of Louise Brogniart, after Houdon, 50cm. high. (Christie's) $1,034

URBINO

An Urbino Istoriato saucer dish painted in the Patanazzi workshop with the Menapians surrendering to Caesar, circa 1580, 27cm. diam. (Christie's) $33,462

An Urbino Istoriato dish painted in the Fontana workshop with Proserpine and her companions, circa 1570, 27.5cm. diam. (Christie's) $27,885

An Urbino Istoriato charger painted in the Fontana workshop with the legend of Deucalion and Pyrrha, circa 1560, 40.5cm. diam. (Christie's) $31,603

VENICE

A Venice Istoriato saucer dish painted with Apollo slaying the children of Niobe, circa 1560, 29.5cm. diam. (Christie's) $29,744

A Venice (Vezzi) chinoiserie teapot and cover painted in colors, one side with a Chinese archer aiming his arrow at a pair of swans, circa 1725, 17.5cm. wide. (Christie's) $20,812

A Venice plate painted in colors with the Children of Venus, 23.5cm. diam. (Christie's) $2,788

VIENNA

A 19th century Vienna porcelain tea caddy and cover of vertical rectangular form, painted in colors with 'Romeo and Juliet' and 'Ulysses, Achilles and Thetis', 17cm. high. (Henry Spencer) $270

A 'Vienna' circular dish, the center painted with the Three Graces, imitation blue beehive mark, circa 1900, 35.5cm. diam. (Christie's) $1,115

A Vienna figure of a milliner from the Cris de Vienne series modelled by J. J. Niedermeyer, 19.5cm. high. (Christie's) $1,135

WEDGWOOD

A Wedgwood fairyland lustre bowl, the interior with pixies and goblins beneath trees with gilt goblin's webs between, circa 1925, 16cm. diam. (Christie's) $564

A pair of Wedgwood & Bentley black basalt griffin candlesticks, seated on their haunches, their wings raised towards the fluted nozzles, circa 1775, 33cm. high. (Christie's) $7,524

A Wedgwood stoneware vase designed by Keith Murray, covered in a turquoise-green glaze, inscribed with facsimile signature, 16.6cm. high. (Christie's) $897

A Wedgwood creamware fish slice of pierced spade form, painted with pendant pink flowers and green foliage, circa 1810, 30cm. long. (Christie's) $1,317

A garniture of four Wedgwood white stoneware vases, each applied with lilac pilasters terminating in lions heads, 18cm. and 13.3cm. (Bearne's) $1,496

A Wedgwood black basalt vase designed by Keith Murray, of flaring cylindrical form with everted rim, 8in. high. (Christie's) $3,405

Very rare Wedgwood 'Woodland Elves' fairyland lustre bowl signed by Daisy Makeig-Jones, 8¾in. diam., circa 1923. (Du Mouchelles) $7,500

A Wedgwood and Bentley black basalt oval portrait medallion of Minerva in high relief, circa 1775, 20cm. high. (Christie's) $1,129

A Wedgwood ceramic ewer and basin designed by George Logan, covered in a lilac glaze and decorated with stylized yellow floral designs, 29.6cm. height of ewer. (Christie's) $1,370

WEDGWOOD

'Bison', a Wedgwood earthenware cream glazed sculpture from a model by John Skeaping, 9in. high. (Christie's) $605

A Wedgwood fairyland lustre malfrey pot and cover designed by Daisy Makeig-Jones and decorated with pixies and elves, 1920's, 22cm. diam. (Christie's) $9,680

John Skeaping Wedgwood figure of a kangaroo seated on a rectangular base, 8½in. high, circa 1930. (Peter Wilson) $519

Pair of Wedgwood three-colour jasper covered urns, 19th century, with floral motifs, trophies and mythological medallions, 14in. high. (Robt. W. Skinner Inc.) $1,300

A rare Wedgwood bust of Lord Zetland wearing medals of Freemasonry, 1868, 20in. high. (Christie's) $896

A pair of Wedgwood flame fairyland lustre tapering oviform vases, designed by Daisy Makeig-Jones, decorated with pixies, elves and bats crossing bridges, 1920s, 29.5cm. high. (Christie's) $6,772

Wedgwood fairyland lustre 'Candlemas' vase, decorated with panels of heads and candles, 9½in. high.(Prudential) $845

A pair of Wedgwood black basalt Triton candlesticks, the bearded gods holding shells terminating in foliate nozzles, circa 1860, 28cm. high.(Christie's)$1,496

Wedgwood bust in moonstone glaze, of Princess Elizabeth, the present Queen, modelled as a young girl in 1937, 15in. high. (Henry Spencer) $782

WEDGWOOD

A Wedgwood & Bentley black basalt oval portrait medallion of Solon in high relief, circa 1775, 16cm. high. (Christie's) $564

A Wedgwood lustre Mei Ping vase and domed cover gilded with an oriental dragon, 11½in. high. (Christie's) $454

'Travel', a Wedgwood dinner plate designed by Eric Ravilious, transfer-printed in black with a sailing boat within a landscape, 25.3cm. wide. (Christie's) $352

An interesting Wedgwood creamware veilleuse, the upper section containing an inverted cone, with two spouts, 43cm. high. (Henry Spencer) $570

A Wedgwood/Whieldon cauliflower teapot and cover in shaded green colors. (A. J. Cobern) $1,388

A Wedgwood flame fairyland lustre tapering oviform vase with flared neck designed by Daisy Makeig-Jones, 1920's, 30cm. high. (Christie's) $1,742

A Wedgwood bone china powder-blue ground massive yanyan vase, outlined in gilt and painted in natural colors with a polar bear and cub, circa 1920, 56.5cm. high. (Christie's) $2,069

Wedgwood pottery mug commemorating the Coronation of Queen Elizabeth II, designed by Eric Ravilious. (G.A.Key) $200

A Wedgwood black basalt bust of Voltaire on a pedestal, his shoulders draped, circa 1810, 23cm. high overall. (Christie's) $704

WEMYSS

A Wemyss pig, of small size and in seated pose, its flanks painted with flowering thistles, 15.5cm. from snout to tail. (Lawrence Fine Arts) $1,064

A Wemyss ware pottery fruit basket, the body painted with cockerels and hens in brown, black, pink and green enamels, 30cm. wide. (Henry Spencer) $1,385

A Wemyss preserve pot and lid painted with oranges and foliage, green painted mark, 4in. high. (G. A. Key)$122

A Wemyss vase of panelled baluster form, the shoulders with eight pierced circular panels, 38cm. (Lawrence Fine Arts) $1,375

A rare signed Karel Nekola Wemyss comb tray, painted with mallards and ducks by reed pond, 29.5cm. long. (Phillips) $4,550

A large Wemyss pig, the seated animal painted with pink leafy roses, 43.5cm. from snout to tail. (Lawrence Fine Arts) $5,420

WHIELDON

A creamware globular teapot and cover of Whieldon type, with entwined strap handle and foliage-molded spout, circa 1765, 10cm. high. (Christie's) $715

A Staffordshire creamware figure of a Turk, of Whieldon type, wearing a turban and in flowing cloak, circa 1760, 14cm. high. (Christie's) $12,012

A Staffordshire creamware figure of a leveret, of Whieldon type, with brown slip eyes, circa 1760, 8.5cm. long. (Christie's) $11,011

A First Period Worcester globular teapot and cover, with polychrome enamel floral decoration, 16cm. (Osmond Tricks) $144

A Worcester porcelain coffee cup and saucer painted by 'The Spotted Fruit Painter', saucer 5¼in. wide. (Dacre, Son & Hartley) $792

A Worcester oblong-shaped basket with pierced cover, painted with flowers, 14.5cm. (Lawrence Fine Arts) $1,991

A Chamberlains Worcester porcelain cup and saucer with a painted scene of a castle framed in gilt and inscribed 'Sherbourn', saucer 5½in. wide, circa 1815. (Dacre, Son & Hartley) $2,700

A Chamberlains Worcester spill vase, with an elongated panel depicting Cardinal Wolsey, 8cm. (Lawrence Fine Arts) $1,487

A First Period Worcester sweetmeat stand with three scallop shaped dishes, painted with flowers in underglaze blue, 9in. (Lawrence Fine Arts) $1,936

A First Period Worcester globular teapot and cover, polychrome enamel decorated with sprays of flowers, 13.5cm. (Osmond Tricks) $579

A Royal Worcester pierced oviform two-handled vase, painted by H. Chair, with swags of roses suspended from a band of pierced ornament, date code for 1909, 16cm. high. (Christie's) $1,505

A Chamberlains Worcester circular basket and pierced cover with floral finial, 16cm. diam. (Lawrence Fine Arts) $517

WORCESTER

A Worcester (Grainger & Co.) Imari pattern oval teapot and cover boldly painted with iron-red flowers with blue and gilt foliage, circa 1810, 28cm. long. (Christie's) $658

A Worcester taper stick, painted with flower sprays on a royal blue ground, 10cm. (Lawrence Fine Arts) $398

A Worcester group of shells and coral forming a mound, on circular base modelled and gilt with scrolls, 12cm. diam. (Lawrence Fine Arts) $871

A Worcester leaf dish with a butterfly hovering above flowering branches, circa 1758, 18.5cm. wide. (Christie's) $940

A pair of Worcester shagreen-ground Imari pattern tapering hexagonal vases and domed covers, painted with fabulous winged beasts sinuously entwined about flowering shrubs, circa 1770, 30.5cm. high. (Christie's) $45,144

A Worcester porcelain scalloped shallow dish, the center painted with sprays of flowers, 8¼in. wide. (From the Marchioness of Huntly service) circa 1770. (Dacre, Son & Hartley) $792

A Worcester bust of the Veiled Bride on a circular socle, 11½in. high, impressed mark, circa 1855. (Christie's) $1,792

A First Period Worcester coffee cup and saucer, painted in an orange Japan pattern. (Lawrence Fine Arts) $367

A Worcester blue and white faceted baluster cream jug, painted with The Root Pattern, circa 1758, 9cm. high. (Christie's) $1,411

WORCESTER

A Royal Worcester porcelain jardiniere by John Stinton, with painted highland cattle watering in a mountainous lakeland landscape, 25 cm. diam. (Henry Spencer) $4,114

A pair of Royal Worcester parian figures of scantily clad maidens. (Hobbs Parker) $1,575

One of a pair of Flight, Barr & Barr porcelain shallow circular dishes with gros bleu borders, in the manner of J. Barker; 7¾ in. wide. (Dacre, Son & Hartley)
Two $1,116

One of a pair of fine Worcester polychrome plates, each painted with the 'Old Mosaic Japan' pattern, 21.5 cm., late 18th century. (Bearne's)
Two $1,392

Three Royal Worcester 'Ivory' figures from The Countries of the World series after James Hadley, modelled as a Yankee, John Bull and an Irishman, date codes for 1881, 1889 and 1897, about 17.5 cm. high. (Christie's) $1,223

A Worcester polychrome teapot and cover, painted with sprigs and sprays of garden flowers, 14.5 cm., late 18th century. (Bearne's) $1,252

An attractive pair of Royal Worcester porcelain vases painted by John Stinton, with scenes of a pair of highland cattle watering and a pair of cattle grazing, 31 cm. high. (Henry Spencer) $4,350

A Worcester jardiniere by Flight & Barr, painted with a mountain finch perched on a rock. (Lawrence Fine Arts)
$4,977

A pair of Royal Worcester lobed vases potted in the Persian manner, with pierced rims and foliage handles, 49.5 cm., 1885. (Bearne's)
$1,218

WORCESTER

A rare early Worcester leaf-shaped pickle dish, decorated in underglaze blue with flowers and a moth in Oriental style, circa 1752, 4 x 3in. (Woolley & Wallis) $704

A pair of Royal Worcester figures in the form of Eastern water carriers, each on one knee pouring the contents from a large jar, 25.5cm., printed mark, circa 1891. (Bearne's) $1,496

A Royal Worcester figure of a negro man dressed in trousers and shirt and wearing a hat, 1882. (Greenslades) $594

A Worcester large bulbous mug printed with three flowers and four butterflies, 6in. high. (G.A.Property Services) $525

A set of three Worcester vases by Grainger, painted with flowers in panels, 24cm. and 20cm. (Lawrence Fine Arts) $637

A fine Royal Worcester porcelain two handled vase by Harry Davis, the handles molded with grotesque mythical beasts heads, 1899, 32cm. high. (Henry Spencer) $3,710

A pair of Royal Worcester polychrome figures of semi-naked women, representing 'Joy' and 'Sorrow', 25.5cm., circa 1885. (Bearne's) $435

A Royal Worcester 'Aesthetic' teapot and cover, one side modelled as a youth wearing mauve cap, the reverse as a girl in mauve bonnet, 1882, 15cm. high. (Christie's) $2,112

A pair of Royal Worcester figures of a Japanese lady and gentleman after the models by James Hadley, each standing beside vases supported on tables, impressed and puce printed marks and date code for 1874, 42cm. high. (Christie's) $6,019

CIGARETTE PACKETS

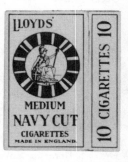

Musk Rose, packet of 5 unscented cigarettes, Wm. Clarke, circa 1905. $20

Mitchell's Golden Dawn, packet of 12 cigarettes, circa 1910. $14

Navy Cut, packet of 10 medium cigarettes, made in England, Richard Lloyd, circa 1930. $3.50

Black Cat, packet of 10 medium cigarettes, Carreras Ltd., London, circa 1930. $3.50

Guards' Parade, packet of 20 selected Virginia cork tipped cigarettes, Playfair Tobacco Co., circa 1912. $18

Navy Cut, packet of 5 medium cigarettes, John Player & Sons, circa 1930. $1

Argosy, packet of 10 for 2d, W. & F. Faulkner, circa 1900. $20

Wartime Raleigh, 20 plain end cigarettes, manufactured U.S.A. circa 1940. $1

Sport cigarettes, manufactured by The United Tobacco Co. (South) Ltd., packet of 10, circa 1930. $5

(R. Brocklesby)

CIGARETTE PACKETS

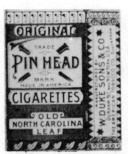

Mild Richmond Gem cigarettes, 10 pieces, signed Allen & Ginter, 'None genuine without this signature', circa 1915. $5

Original Pin Head cigarettes, Old North Carolina leaf, W. Duke Sons & Co., circa 1900. $20

Pirate, packet of 10 cigarettes, W. D. & H. O. Wills, Bristol & London, circa 1915. $7

Scented Lily, packet of 10 high-class cork-tipped Virginia cigarettes, Miranda Ltd., circa 1915. $7

Clown, 20 balanced blend cigarettes, manufactured by The Axton-Fisher Tobacco Co., Louisville, Kentucky, circa 1935. $1

Taddy's Myrtle Grove medium cigarettes, packet of 10, circa 1910. $20

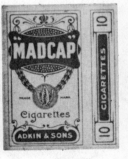

Gulland's Latch-Key, J. Gulland & Son, cigarette specialist, Bolton, circa 1900. $26

Miss Blanche Virginia cigarettes No. 1, packet of 20, W. Hill (Holland), circa 1925. $3.50

Madcap cigarettes, packet of 10, Adkin & Sons, circa 1905. $9

(R. Brocklesby)

213

BRACKET CLOCKS

A rare mid 18th century ebony and silver mounted miniature bracket clock, signed on an oval cartouche, Charls Clay, London, the movement with engraved backplate, 7½in. high. (Phillips) $17,765

An early 18th century ebonised bracket clock, the five ringed pillared movement reconverted to verge escapement, signed Saml Pitts, London, 1ft. 4in. high. (Phillips) $3,910

A Regency rosewood bracket clock, the case with gadrooned top, the shaped silvered dial signed G.Searle, London, the twin fusee movement with anchor escapement, 1ft. 4in. high. (Phillips) $2,210

A 19th century mahogany and brass inlaid bracket clock, anchor escapement signed Thos Glase, Bridgnorth, 1ft 7in. high, together with a wall bracket. (Phillips) $1,436

An ebonised musical bracket clock, the three train fusee movement with anchor escapement, chiming two tunes on eight bells, 21in. (Lawrence Fine Arts) $3,256

A George III mahogany and ormolu musical bracket clock, the silvered dial signed John Taylor London, triple fusee movement chiming on eight bells, 28in. high. (Christie's) $11,352

A substantial Edwardian bracket clock with arched brass dial, fronting a three-train movement with Westminster chime. (Osmond Tricks) $1,737

A Charles II ebony striking bracket clock, the plinth case with carrying handle and gilt metal foliate mounts to the cushion-molded top, the tulip engraved backplate signed John Knibb London Fecit, 11¼in. high. (Christie's) $34,056

An ebonised bracket clock, the two train fusee movement now with anchor escapement, signed on a silvered arc Wm. Threlkeld, London, 36½in. (Lawrence Fine Arts) $1,831

BRACKET CLOCKS

An early 18th century ebony bracket timepiece, with silvered chapter ring signed C. Gretton London, now converted to anchor escapement, 1ft. 3½in. high. (Phillips) $3,549

A late 19th century three-train musical bracket clock, in the 18th century manner, inscribed Henry Ruttiman Lucerne, 50cm. (Phillips) $2,057

A good 19th century mahogany and gilt brass mounted bracket clock of small size, the circular enamel dial signed Vulliamy, London, with anchor escapement, 9in. high. (Phillips) $9,802

A late Victorian burr walnut chiming bracket clock, the arched engraved silvered dial signed Thwaites & Reed London, 22½in. (Christie's) $1,419

A late Stuart ebonized timepiece repeat bracket clock by Francis Robinson in Ye Temple, the case with handle and cast foliate mounts of Knibb pattern, restoration, 12in. high. (Christie's) $10,406

A George III ebonised striking bracket clock, the break-arch case with bracket feet, backplate signed Lynford Paddington, 14in. high. (Christie's) $1,797

A Regency ebonised striking miniature bracket clock, the border engraved backplate signed Kenth. Maclennan London, behind the bell, 10½in. high. (Christie's) $2,270

A George II bracket clock, by Thomas Satcher, London, with 7in. arched brass dial, 15¾in. high (with pendulum and keys). (Bearne's) $2,035

A late 19th century bracket clock in ebonized case with gilt metal mounts, full chimes of Westminster and Eight Bells, 34in. high overall, by Canova, Halesworth and Southwold. (Prudential) $3,933

BRACKET CLOCKS

A boulle bracket clock of Louis XIV design, inscribed J. Le Lacheur, Guernsey, with an eight-day bell-striking movement, 15in. high. (Hy. Duke & Son) $929

A walnut bracket clock with verge escapement and pull quarter repeating on two bells, the florally engraved backplate signed in a cartouche Johannes Fromanteel Londini Fecit, 12½in. high. (Phillips) $5,440

A good Victorian blonde oak and ebony bracket clock by Charles Frodsham of London, the arched silvered dial with black Roman numerals to the chapter ring. (Henry Spencer) $2,835

A 19th century rosewood and inlaid quarter chiming bracket clock, the arched case inlaid with an urn, the three train movement with anchor escapement, 1ft.8in. high. (Phillips) $1,215

A Regency mahogany brass and ebony inlaid quarter chiming bracket clock, with circular enamel dial signed Grimalde & Johnson, Strand London, 12in. high.(Phillips) $3,060

A Georgian mahogany bracket clock, the arched painted dial with pierced gilt hands, signed D.Evans London, now converted to anchor escapement, 1ft 8½in. high. (Phillips) $1,859

A late Stuart ebonized striking bracket clock with gilt metal repousse basket top, carrying handle and pressed door mounts, engraved backplate signed Isaac Papavoine Londini Fecit, 14½in. (Christie's) $7,189

An 18th century French boulle-work bracket clock, the circular gilt metal dial cast with acanthus leaves and scallop shells, blue Roman numerals to the white enamelled chapters and with engraved Arabic minutes. (Henry Spencer) $2,492

An Edwardian mahogany bracket clock, the 19cm arched gilt brass dial with black Roman numerals and Arabic seconds, stylized paw feet, 73cm high. (Henry Spencer) $1,890

BRACKET CLOCKS

A Georgian style mahogany bracket clock, the arched case, surmounted by a carrying handle, decorated with two raised panels, 1ft.1in. high. (Phillips) $3,400

A Louis XV premiere and contre partie boulle bracket clock with shaped circular face, signed Calon a Paris, 48in. high. (Christie's) $3,460

A Georgian ebonized bracket clock with engraved spandrels and date aperture signed Peter Nichols, Newport, the twin fusee movement converted to anchor escapement, 1ft.8in. high. (Phillips) $1,275

A Georgian ebonized and brass mounted bracket clock, the square silvered dial with mock pendulum and date apertures, signed Edward Clarke, London, 1ft. 5½in. high. (Phillips) $2,992

A mahogany bracket clock in cushion-topped case surmounted by pineapple finials, signed Dwerrihouse, Berkley Square, 19in. high. (Christie's) $2,806

A Georgian mahogany bracket clock, signed Joseph Pomroy, London and with strike/silent subsidiary in the arch, the five pillared movement with verge escapement and engraved backplate, 1ft.8½in. high. (Phillips) $3,927

A brass inlaid mahogany bracket timepiece, the single train fusee movement with anchor escapement, 12¾in. (Lawrence Fine Arts) $915

A Louis XV ormolu mounted boulle bracket clock, the movement signed G. I. Champion A Paris, the shaped case surmounted by a figure of Father Time, 43in. high. (Christie's) $6,105

A Victorian mahogany eight-day chiming and striking bracket clock with 7¼in. arched brass dial, 23¼in. high. (Bearne's) $1,456

BRACKET CLOCKS

A Regency gothic mahogany bracket clock, the lancet case with brass and ebony line inlay, signed Bentley & Beck Royal Exchange London, 23in. high. (Christie's) $1,608

A Georgian mahogany bracket clock, signed Daniel Prentice, London, the twin fusee movement with engraved backplate, 1ft 5in. high. (Phillips) $2,112

An ebonised quarter chiming bracket clock, the arched brass dial with silvered chapter ring inscribed Delander, London, 1ft. 6in. high. (Phillips) $3,740

A Georgian ebonized bracket timepiece, signed on a cartouche in the arch Robt Gymer, Norwich, the five pillared movement with verge escapement and pull quarter repeating on two bells, 1ft.7¼in. high. (Phillips) $1,683

A late George III mahogany miniature bracket timepiece alarm, the engraved silvered dial signed Perigal, Coventry Street, London, chain fusee movement with verge escapement, 9½in. high. (Christie's) $5,297

A George III ebonized and brass mounted bracket clock, the arched brass dial with silvered chapter ring and date aperture, signed James Tregent, London, 1ft 8in. high, together with a wall bracket. (Phillips) $4,394

A George III ebonized bracket clock, signed on a plate Thos Hughes, London, the twin fusee movement with engraved backplate, 1ft.7in. high. (Phillips) $2,431

An 18th century mahogany bracket clock, signed on a recessed cartouche Wm Fothergill, Knaresbro, with verge escapement and engraved backplate, 1ft. 4in. high. (Phillips) $6,120

A Regency mahogany bracket clock, the arched silvered dial with alarm set disc, signed John Walker, London, 1ft. 5¼in. high. (Phillips) $3,740

CARRIAGE CLOCKS

A 19th century French grande sonnerie carriage clock, the movement now with lever platform escapement, signed Paul Garnier, 7in. high. (Phillips) $2,992

A Swiss miniature silver and enamel carriage timepiece, the lever movement with circular enamel dial, 5cm. high, signed for Asprey. (Phillips) $578

A French 19th century gilt brass carriage clock, the movement with replaced lever platform, the case with curved side panels, 7½in. high. (Phillips) $878

A gilt brass grande sonnerie carriage clock, enamel dial, signed Collin Paris and subsidiary alarm ring below VI within a gilt metal mask, Corinthian case, 7in. high. (Christie's) $2,270

A gilt brass striking carriage clock, the enamel dial signed Goldsmiths Company 112 Regent St. London and Paris, Corinthian case, stamp of Margaine, 6½in. high. (Christie's) $1,513

A 19th century French gilt brass carriage clock, the movement with Soldano lever platform, in an engraved gorge case, 7in. high. (Phillips) $1,272

A gilt-brass carriage clock, inscribed J. C. Vickery, *to their majesties*, with subsidiary alarm dial striking on a bell, 11cm. (Phillips) $374

A 19th century English gilt brass travelling clock, the twin fusee movement with maintaining power and lever platform, signed Viner, London, 6½in. high. (Phillips) $2,890

A 19th century French miniature gilt brass and porcelain mounted carriage timepiece, the lever movement stamped on the backplate, A.Dumas, 3¾in. high. (Phillips) $3,549

CARRIAGE CLOCKS

An unusual miniature carriage timepiece, late 19th century, the movement with platform lever escapement, signed Bigelow, Kennard & Co., Boston. (Christie's)$1,650

An early 19th century brass timepiece carriage clock, by James McCabe, Royal Exchange, London, in plain case, 16cm. (Phillips) $2,992

A repeating carriage clock in anglaise case, the eight-day movement with silvered lever platform escapement striking on a gong, 5½in. high. (Christie's)
$616

A gilt brass and enamel striking carriage clock with cut bimetallic balance to lever platform, signed Edward & Sons Glasgow, Paris made, 6¼in. high. (Christie's) $4,351

An unusual 19th century French gilt bronze and porcelain mounted carriage clock, bearing the Drocourt trademark on the backplate, in an ornate rococo case, 9in. high. (Phillips)$7,098

A gilt metal bamboo striking carriage clock with cloisonne enamel dial, case with naturalistic bamboo angles and Chinese fret handle, 7in. high. (Christie's)
$2,459

A brass miniature carriage timepiece, with gilt chapter ring signed Wm. Drummond & Sons Melbourne, bamboo case, 3½in. high. (Christie's) $2,838

A 19th century French gilt brass grande sonnerie carriage clock, with enamel dial in a cannalee case, 7in. high. (Phillips) $1,774

A fine 19th century gilt brass repeating carriage clock, inscribed Ch. Oudin, the movement striking the hours and half hours, 15cm. (Phillips)
$4,488

CARRIAGE CLOCKS

A 19th century French gilt brass and silvered carriage clock, the lever movement striking on a gong, with alarm and push repeat, 8¼in. high. (Phillips) $1,496

A French brass carriage clock, the movement with lever escapement, bearing the trade stamps of Hy. Marc and Japy Freres, 6¾in. (Lawrence Fine Arts) $1,526

A silver gilt carriage timepiece, the case with colored stone corner decorations, the lever movement with circular enamel dial, 4in. high. (Phillips) $850

A 19th century Continental silver miniature carriage timepiece, the lever movement with enamel dial, 4in. high, marked London 1895. (Phillips) $676

A gilt brass striking carriage clock with later lever platform, strike/repeat on gong, the porcelain dial signed Walsh Brothers Melbourne, 7½in. high. (Christie's) $3,216

An unusual gilt brass carriage timepiece, the fusee movement signed Viner on the backplate, rectangular case with turned corner columns, 5¼in. high. (Christie's) $1,135

A 19th century French gilt brass and enamel carriage clock, bearing the Drocourt trademark, in an engraved gorge case, 6¾in. high. (Phillips) $2,366

A gilt brass miniature carriage timepiece with uncut bimetallic balance to silvered lever platform, the caryatid case with harpies to the angles, 2¾in. high. (Christie's) $1,797

A 19th century French gilt brass grande sonnerie carriage clock, the movement with replaced lever platform, 7in. high. (Phillips) $1,645

CARRIAGE CLOCKS

A 19th century French brass and enamel mounted carriage clock, bearing the Drocourt trademark, in a bamboo case, 7½in. high. (Phillips) $2,197

An oval Drocourt grande sonnerie calendar and alarm carriage clock, the engine turned and silvered mask with white enamel dials, 5½in. high. (Christie's)　$3,080

A 19th century Austrian grande sonnerie gilt brass carriage clock, the lever movement striking on two gongs, signed J.Jessner in Wien, 6¼in. high. (Phillips) $1,700

A French champleve enamelled repeating carriage clock with 2in. enamelled dial, 6¼in. high. (Bearne's)　$2,024

A 19th century French gilt brass carriage clock, the movement with two plane escapement, signed on the backplate, Paul Garnier, Paris, 6¾in. high. (Phillips)　$4,675

A French gilt brass carriage clock, the repeating movement with lever escapement, gong striking and signed John P. Cross, Paris, 6½in. (Lawrence Fine Arts)　$2,543

A French brass carriage timepiece, the movement with replacement lever platform escapement, contained in a pillared rectangular case, 6in. (Lawrence Fine Arts) $651

A 19th century French brass grande sonnerie carriage clock, the lever movement chiming on two gongs, 7in. high. (Phillips) $2,197

A French brass carriage clock, the movement with lever escapement and gong striking, signed James Murray, Glasgow, contained in a corniche case 6¾in. (Lawrence Fine Arts) $1,058

CARRIAGE CLOCKS

A 19th century French gilt brass miniature timepiece, the enamel dial signed for Payne & Son, London, with Roman and Arabic numerals, 3¾in. high. (Phillips) $507

A gilt brass oval striking carriage clock with strike/repeat on gong, enamel dial with Breguet style hands, 4½in. high. (Christie's) $1,135

A repeat/alarm carriage clock in gorge case, the eight-day movement with silvered pointed lever platform escapement striking on a bell, 5in. high. (Christie's) $1,143

A 19th century French gilt brass carriage clock, signed on the backplate for Ch. Frodsham, Paris, in an engraved one-piece case, 5in. high. (Phillips)$2,125

A silver and enamel carriage timepiece, decorated in blue enamel with circular enamel dial, signed for H.Gibbs, London, 4½in. high. (Phillips) $612

A striking carriage clock in Corinthian case, the eight-day movement with lever platform escapement, bearing the trademark LF, Paris, 6¼in. high.(Christie's) $415

A miniature French brass carriage timepiece, with enamel dial within a gilt mask with pierced decoration, in an anglaise case, 3in. high. (Phillips) $972

A good English gilt brass carriage clock, the twin fusee movement with lever platform escapement, signed Chas Frodsham, London, 8in. high. (Phillips) $8,500

A silver-cased minute-repeating carriage clock, inscribed E. White, London, with lever platform escapement striking the quarters on two gongs, 3½in. high. (Christie's) $5,821

Mid 19th century black marble garniture de cheminee with ormolu mounts and Continental movement. (British Antique Exporters) $438

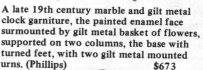

A late 19th century marble and gilt metal clock garniture, the painted enamel face surmounted by gilt metal basket of flowers, supported on two columns, the base with turned feet, with two gilt metal mounted urns. (Phillips) $673

A French white marble and gilt metal mounted composite clock garniture, the mantel clock on column supports with drum shaped case surmounted by an urn finial and a pair of twin-branch candelabra, 11in. high. (Christie's) $730

A clock garniture in the Louis XVI style, signed in the center 'Goldsmiths' Alliance Ltd./Cornhill, London', 12½in. high. (Bearne's) $728

A French veined rouge marble and ormolu mounted clock garniture, the mantel clock in four-glass case flanked by cylindrical columns, 18½in. high; and a pair of matching ornamental vases, 14½in. high. (Christie's) $1,443

A 19th century French ormolu and porcelain mounted clock garniture, the case decorated with flowers and a bird, raised on a shaped base decorated with naked putti, 10½in. high, together with the associated pair of three branch candelabra. (Phillips) $1,589

CLOCK SETS

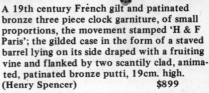

1930's black and brown marble clock set in the Art Deco style. (British Antique Exporters. **$175**

A 19th century French gilt and patinated bronze three piece clock garniture, of small proportions, the movement stamped 'H & F Paris'; the gilded case in the form of a staved barrel lying on its side draped with a fruiting vine and flanked by two scantily clad, animated, patinated bronze putti, 19cm. high. (Henry Spencer) **$899**

A French 19th century clock garniture, the mantel clock in architectural gothic case, stamped Villamesens, Paris, with gilt cast pendulum, 20¼in. high, and a pair of similarly decorated cassolettes, on cylindrical plinths and square bases, 11½in. high. (Christie's) **$1,540**

An ormolu, bronze and white marble garniture de cheminee comprising: a clock with circular glazed enamel dial signed James Aitchison, and a pair of three-light candelabra. (Christie's) **$3,346**

An ormolu and bronze garniture de cheminee of Louis XV style, with a group of three putti playing musical instruments, second half 19th century. (Christie's)
$2,974

A Charles X Siena marble and bronze mounted composite clock garniture, the rectangular shaped case surmounted by a bronze group depicting 'The Oath of Horatii', 19¼in. high, and a pair of tazze on square plinths, 11¼in. high. (Christie's)
$3,307

FOUR GLASS CLOCKS

A French four glass regulateur de table, the twin going barrel movement striking on bell with 3-rod grid iron pendulum, 22in. high. (Christie's) $4,540

A gilt and enamel French four glass clock, surmounted by a multi-colored enamelled dome, the pendulum with a portrait of a lady, 16½in. high. (Christie's) $1,251

A mid 19th century brass four glass mantel clock, with mercury compensated pendulum, the glazed sides on shaped base, 30cm. (Phillips) $673

A 19th century French brass, enamel and green onyx mantel clock, of four glass form, on a green onyx base, 9¾in. high. (Phillips) $935

A rosewood four glass mantel timepiece, silvered chapter ring signed Vulliamy London, chain fusee movement, 7¼in. high. (Christie's) $9,081

A good 19th century French mantel regulator, the gilt brass case of four glass form, signed Chs Oudin, with an annular dial below, 1ft 7in. high. (Phillips) $8,112

A mid 19th century brass four glass mantel clock, inscribed Seth Thomas, the movement striking the hours and half hours on a coiled gong, 28cm. (Phillips) $748

A 19th century French ormolu and enamel four glass mantel clock, decorated Corinthian columns, 12in. high. (Phillips) $1,521

A 19th century French gilt brass mantel clock, of four glass form, the circular enamel dial signed Callier, Horloger de la Marine Imperiale, 22 Bould Montmatre 22, 14in. high. (Phillips) $1,272

LANTERN CLOCKS

A brass lantern clock, the posted movement surmounted by a bell, the dial signed Thos Mortlock, Stradishall, the twin-train movement with anchor escapement, 14½in. high.   (Phillips) $2,720

A late 17th century brass "winged" lantern clock with pierced dolphin fret above the Roman chapter ring, 14½in. high. (Christie's) $1,870

An early 18th century brass wing lantern clock, the dial with brass chapter ring and single steel hand, the movement with verge bob pendulum escapement, 1ft.3½in. high.(Phillips) $2,890

A brass miniature lantern clock, signed D. Robinson Northampton on the chapter ring, 9in. high.   (Christie's) $4,730

A Louis XV quarter chiming lantern clock, with circular chased gilt dial signed below Le Bel a Orbec, the three train movement with verge escapement, 1ft.8½in. high. (Phillips) $2,244

An interesting late 17th century English brass lantern clock with pierced and engraved decoration of entwined dolphins and foliage, 34cm. high. (Henry Spencer) $1,691

A fine Charles II gilt brass lantern clock of small size with rare indirect wind line-and-barrel drive within standard frame, signed Thomas Ford de Bucks Fecit, 12½in. high. (Christie's) $9,625

A brass lantern clock, the substantial movement with verge and double foliot escapement, European-hour countwheel strike on pork-pie bell above, 18th century, overall 120cm. high. (Christie's) $9,398

A Japanese brass lantern clock, the posted frame movement with verge and single foliot escapement and European hour countwheel strike on bell above, 7¾in. high. (Christie's) $2,648

LONGCASE CLOCKS

A George III oak and mahogany longcase clock, by Willm. Latham Macclesfield, circa 1775, rack striking on the hour, 80in. high. (Robt. W. Skinner Inc.)
$1,600

A month going longcase clock, now with a late 18th century 12in. arched silvered dial, inscribed Tompion London, in a mahogany case, 7ft 2½in. high. (Phillips)
$15,210

A mahogany and marquetry longcase clock with domed hood, the 12in. square brass dial signed Brounker Watts, London, with pendulum and two weights, 83in. high. (Christie's)
$3,742

A George III Lancashire mahogany longcase clock on bracket feet, the painted dial signed William Wilson Kendal round the moonphase in the arch, 8ft. high. (Christie's)
$4,919

An unusual lacquered 30-hour longcase clock with stylized pagoda top surmounted by a gilt cockerel finial, the rectangular door painted with religious scenes, 85in. high. (Christie's)
$2,182

A Louis XV kingwood and ormolu mounted longcase clock, the 10in. circular convex enamel dial signed J.S. Chauvet a Paris, 6ft. 7in. high. (Phillips)
$13,600

A Georgian mahogany longcase clock, the pagoda topped hood with pierced brass fret, signed on a cartouche David Rivers, London, 7ft. 11in. high. (Phillips)
$3,740

A Georgian mahogany longcase clock, the 13in. square brass dial signed Chars Morgan, Dublin, the twin train movement with anchor escapement, 7ft. 8½in. high. (Phillips)
$3,927

LONGCASE CLOCKS

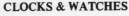

A George III mahogany longcase clock, the dial signed John Berry London, five-pillar rack striking movement with anchor escapement, 7ft.11in. high. (Christie's) $9,460

A celebrated Queen Anne astronomical longcase clock of long duration signed Edward Cockey, Warminster, in an ebonised, parcel-gilt and silvered case, 10ft.2in. high. (Christie's) $113,520

A mid 18th century inlaid walnut longcase clock, inscribed Stenard, Henley, the trunk with arched door, parquetry inlaid with herringbone, 6ft.8in. high. (Hobbs & Chambers) $9,050

A grain painted tall timepiece, Pennsylvania, circa 1820, the hood with molded swan's neck cresting with rosette carved terminals, 105in. high. (Robt. W. Skinner Inc.) $1,100

A Dutch walnut longcase clock by Joseph Norris Amsterdam, the movement with five ringed pillars, inside countwheel Dutch strike on single bell and anchor escapement. (Christie's) $17,028

A Regency mahogany striking half-regulator in a Graeco-Egyptian revival case, 12in. circular engraved silvered dial signed Widenham No.13, Lombard Street London, 6ft.10in. high. (Christie's) $6,243

A George III mahogany longcase clock by Barker, Wigan, the eight day bell-striking movement with brass dial and silvered chapter ring, 96in. high. (Hy. Duke & Son) $4,394

A Regency mahogany longcase clock, inscribed Christopher Lawson, Edinburgh, with subsidiary seconds dial, the drum hood over molded plinth, 214cm. (Phillips) $1,776

A Regency mahogany longcase clock, the white painted dial with subsidiary seconds and calendar dials, 216cm. (Phillips) $1,776

An early Victorian mahogany longcase clock, inscribed J. D. Reid, Airdrie, with subsidiary seconds and calendar dials, 230cm. (Phillips) $1,402

An early Victorian mahogany longcase clock, inscribed Thos. McGregor, Ayton, the eight-day movement striking on a single bell. (Phillips) $1,683

An early 18th century month going lacquered longcase clock, signed in an oval cartouche John Miller, London, 7ft.2½in. high. (Phillips)$4,394

A walnut and marquetry longcase clock, the 10in. sq. dial signed Joseph Stripling in a lambrequin in the florally engraved center, the movement with anchor escapement, 7ft. high. (Christie's) $7,946

A Regency mahogany longcase clock, the arched hood surmounted by a spire and turned wood finial, the 12in. convex painted dial signed Barraud, Cornhill, London, 87½in. high. (Phillips) $4,760

A Charles II burr walnut month going longcase clock, the 9½in. sq. dial with winged cherub spandrels and signed Joseph Knibb Londini fecit in florid script at the base, circa 1673-5, 6ft.8in. high. (Christie's) $104,060

A late 19th century mahogany longcase clock, in the 18th century style, surmounted by carved and pierced swan neck pediment, inscribed William Alexander & Son, Glasgow, 230cm. (Phillips) $4,488

LONGCASE CLOCKS

A George II oak longcase clock, by Arthur Hurt, Ashford, mid 18th century (reduced in height), 77½in. high. (Robt. W. Skinner Inc.)
$800

A Federal inlaid mahogany longcase clock, dial signed by Simon Willard, Roxbury, Massachusetts, circa 1810, 97in. high. (Christie's)
$34,100

A Georgian mahogany and inlaid longcase clock, the 13in. arched painted dial signed Bancroft, Scarbro', 7ft.11½in. high. (Phillips)
$3,366

A Federal cherry tall case clock, Luther Smith, Keene, New Hampshire, circa 1810, the hood with pierced finials, 92½in. high. (Robt. W. Skinner Inc.) $16,000

A 19th century mahogany longcase clock, the pagoda topped hood decorated with three ball and spire finials, signed on a circular cartouche in the arch, Pridgin, Hull, 8ft. 1in. high. (Phillips)
$3,910

Tho. Tompion London No. 542, a Queen Anne burr walnut longcase clock, the finely veneered case with plain foot and concave moldings, the flat top hood with brass capped quarter columns, 6ft.8in. high. (Christie's)
$75,680

A 19th century mahogany regulator, the 12in. circular brass dial, signed Joseph Sewill, Liverpool, the substantial six pillared movement with maintaining power, 6ft.7½in. high. (Phillips)
$4,590

A good early 18th century longcase clock by Joseph Millis of London, the arched brass dial with subsidiary seconds dial, and two-train bell-striking eight-day movement. (Osmond Tricks)
$7,240

LONGCASE CLOCKS

A Regency mahogany longcase clock, the white painted dial decorated with figures depicting the Four Seasons and Peace and Plenty, 227cm. (Phillips) $1,309

A Georgian Irish mahogany longcase clock, the 13½in. square brass dial with silvered chapter ring, signed Geoe Walker, Dublin, 7ft 7in. high. (Phillips) $3,740

An 18th century walnut longcase clock, the hood with stepped dome top, the 12in. arched brass dial signed Martin Jackson, London, 8ft. high. (Phillips) $7,106

A late Regency mahogany longcase clock, the drum head with relief husk border over tapered trunk, inscribed Whitelaw, Edinburgh, 200cm. (Phillips) $3,179

A Charles II walnut longcase clock with bun feet to crossbanded convex molded case, the silvered chapter ring signed Cha. Gretton London, case extensively restored, 6ft.3½in. high. (Christie's) $20,812

A 30 hour longcase clock, the 10in. square brass dial signed at the base Thomas Tompion Londini, with winged cherub's head spandrels and silvered chapter ring, 7ft 8in. high. (Phillips) $13,520

An early 18th century walnut and panel marquetry longcase clock, the 11in. square brass dial with silvered chapter ring signed Nat Hodges, Londini Fecit, 6ft.8½in. high. (with some restorations) (Phillips) $14,960

A Victorian mahogany half-regulator with barometer and thermometer by Bryson Edinburgh, the movement partly with deadbeat escapement and wood rod pendulum, 6ft.3in. high. (Christie's) $2,838

LONGCASE CLOCKS

A George III mahogany longcase clock, the 12in. arched brass dial with brass chapter ring, signed Ellicott, London, 7ft 6in. high.
(Phillips)
$5,070

An early 19th century mahogany longcase clock, inscribed J. Durward, Edinburgh, the eight-day movement striking on a single bell, 201cm.
(Phillips)
$1,402

An early Victorian mahogany longcase clock, inscribed George Lumsden, Pittenweems, and decorated with shipping scenes, 225cm.
(Phillips)
$2,992

A late 17th/early 18th century walnut and panel marquetry longcase clock, the 10in. square brass dial signed Robert Fenn, London, 6ft.10in. high.
(Phillips)
$10,285

A George I burr walnut longcase clock, the crossbanded case with double-footed plinth, dial signed Willm. Manlove London on a silvered arc in the matted center with subsidiary seconds, 8ft.5in. high. (Christie's)
$7,568

A Charles II burr walnut and marquetry month-going longcase clock, the 10in.sq. dial signed John Ebsworth Londini fecit on a lambrequin in the tulip engraved center, restoration, 6ft.6in. high. (Christie's)
$28,380

A Georgian mahogany longcase clock, the 12in. arched silvered dial signed H.J.Tymms, Vauxhall, Surry, the five pillared movement with anchor escapement, 7ft 10in. high. (Phillips)
$5,915

A Queen Anne burr walnut and marquetry longcase clock, the dial signed Dan le Count London on the silvered chapter ring, now rack strike and anchor escapement, 7ft.1in. high. (Christie's)
$9,081

LONGCASE CLOCKS

An Irish George IV longcase clock, signed Donegan, Dublin, the mahogany case with carved hood. (David Lay) $905

A good early 18th century Dutch walnut longcase clock by Willem Redi of Amsterdam, with black Roman numerals and Arabic minutes, 245cm high. (Henry Spencer) $14,175

A Scottish longcase clock, signed A. McMillan, Glasgow, the mahogany hood on tapering column trunk. (David Lay) $1,719

A George III mahogany longcase clock, the 29cm arched brass dial inscribed Robert Bunyan, Lincoln, with a silvered strike/silent dial to the arch, 226cm high. (Henry Spencer) $5,481

John Wise, London, eight-day marquetry longcase clock with 11in. square brass dial, 87in. high, with brass cased weights. (Bearne's) $4,186

Walter Harris, London, George II eight-day lacquered longcase clock with 12in. arched brass dial, 84in. high. (Bearne's) $2,548

A Queen Anne ebonised longcase clock, the 12in. square brass and silvered dial inscribed 'Jno Hughes, London', 88½ins. high. (Dreweatt Neate) $2,376

An early 19th century longcase clock, the 8-day movement by R.Roberts, Bangor, 7ft.9in.high. (Greenslades) $2,467

LONGCASE CLOCKS

An 18th century green japanned longcase clock, the 29cm broken arched brass dial with the inscription John Long, of London to the chapter ring, 232cm high. (Henry Spencer) $1,512

An early 19th century mahogany longcase clock, the 32cm arched cream painted dial inscribed 'Thomas Pearce Bourne', the spandrels painted with sprays of roses, 218cm high. (Henry Spencer) $1,417

A carved and painted longcase clock in the form of a woman standing with arms akimbo, with glazed convex painted dial signed Joh Ylie Konnig Tlmola, late 19th century, 7ft. high. (Christie's) $7,623

An early 18th century walnut and mulberry longcase clock, signed 'Joseph Knibb, Londini Fecit', the eight day movement with outside count wheel striking on a bell, 192cm high. (Henry Spencer) $6,426

An early 20th century musical longcase clock, bearing the date 1925, the three-train movement with deadbeat escapement. (Phillips) $2,992

A George III longcase clock, the arch painted with scene of a girl and her dog, 7ft. 3in. high. (Greenslades) $1,078

A mahogany longcase clock, the 29cm broken arched brass dial with fielded panelled base and stepped plinth, 254cm high. (Henry Spencer) $3,024

Thomas Bartholomew, London, eight-day chiming clock with 14½in. arched brass dial, 110in. high. (Bearne's) $4,004

MANTEL CLOCKS

A 19th century ormolu and porcelain mounted mantel clock, the rectangular case surmounted by a figure of a boy riding a dolphin, 12in. high. (Phillips) $1,221

A Napoleon III brass and champleve lighthouse clock, late 19th century, with spring wound mechanism, on a green onyx base, 20in. high. (Robt. W. Skinner Inc.) $4,500

A boulle mantel clock in the Louis XV taste, in waisted tortoiseshell and brass inlaid case, 42cm. (Phillips) $935

A 19th century French ormolu and porcelain mantel clock, the case surmounted by an urn and flanked by naked putti, 1ft 2in. high. (Phillips) $1,352

A Gustav Stickley oak mantel clock, early 20th century, the door with faceted cut-out framing brass dial, Seth Thomas movement, 13¾in. high. (Robt. W. Skinner Inc.) $3,000

A French ormolu and bronze mantel clock flanked by seated cherubs, mid 19th century, 30¾in. high, 26½in. wide. (Christie's) $4,136

A French ormolu mantel clock in the style of Louis XV, inscribed Julien Leroy a Paris, the eight-day movement with outside count-wheel strike on a bell, 21in. high. (Christie's) $924

A Jaeger-Le Coultre eight day mantel clock, with Roman chapters, the transparent glass discuss-shaped body with chrome rim and foot, 23.3cm. diam. (Christie's) $897

A late 19th century gilt metal French mantel clock in the Louis XV manner, inset with pink porcelain panels, 46cm. (Phillips) $524

MANTEL CLOCKS

A boulle mantel clock in the Louis XV taste, the gilt metal face in waisted tortoiseshell and brass inlaid case, 30cm. (Phillips) $411

A Continental 'Zappler' timepiece, the movement mounted behind a chased gilt frame decorated with two griffins, 2in. high. (Phillips) $598

A 19th century French porcelain mantel clock, the circular enamel dial signed Hry Marc a Paris, on a shaped base bearing the mark of Jacob Petit, 12in. high. (Phillips) $673

A Liberty and Co. hammered pewter clock, the body decorated with stylized tree and foliate panels, the copper clock face with black enamel Roman chapters and turquoise enamel center, 18.2cm. high. (Christie's) $1,122

An Empire bronze mantel clock, early 19th century, the circular enamelled dial surmounted by a bust of Socrates, 25in. high. (Robt. W. Skinner Inc.) $2,000

A good French ormolu mantel regulator, signed Lepaute, the movement with pin wheel escapement mounted on the backplate, 1ft.3in. high. (Phillips) $15,895

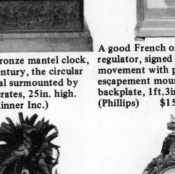

A gilt metal boudoir timepiece and thermometer of cheval form attributed to Thos. Cole London, the case of typical cast layered construction, 7in. high. (Christie's) $4,540

A Black Forest 'cuckoo' mantel clock, the two train fusee movement with anchor escapement and skeletonized back plate. (Lawrence Fine Arts) $520

A red tortoiseshell boulle mantel clock in waisted case, the eight-day movement striking on a bell, with sunburst pendulum, 14½in. high. (Christie's) $1,247

MANTEL CLOCKS

A 19th century French brass and enamel mantel clock, the arched case surmounted by a pierced spire finial and with turned corner columns decorated with three winged cherubs, 1ft.9in. high. (Phillips) $972

A 19th century French gilt brass mantel clock with blue porcelain panels, signed Miller & Sons, London. (Greenslades) $1,176

An electroplated pewter presentation clockcase, surmounted by an Art Nouveau maiden standing contraposto, her arms raised against an elaborate pierced trellis superstructure, 50cm. high. (Christie's) $1,301

A French white marble and ormolu mounted lyre shaped clock in the style of Louis XV, with sunburst finial, 16½in. high. (Christie's) $2,502

An ormolu mantel clock with enamel circlet dial, signed Bausse Rue de Richilieu, in globe shaped case supported by the winged figure of Aurora, 20½in. high. (Christie's) $3,256

A French torchere ormolu mounted mantel clock in the style of Louis XIV, the eight day movement striking on a gong, 11¼in. high. (Christie's) $962

An Empire ormolu mantel clock in the form of a plinth shaped bookcase with dial in the upper half, 13in. high. (Christie's) $2,849

A good French mantel clock, the movement by Vincenti & Cie, enamelled to three sides, 12¾in. high. (David Lay) $1,049

An ormolu and bronze mantel clock the glazed enamel dial signed Duot a Paris, the pedestal case surmounted by Cupid, 15½in. high. (Christie's) $2,646

MANTEL CLOCKS

An ormolu, white marble and soft-paste porcelain mantel clock with circular glazed enamel dial in a waisted basket of flowers and foliage, late 19th century, 11¼in. high. (Christie's) $1,394

Liberty & Co., an "English Pewter" plain arch mantel timepiece with enamelled dial. (David Lay) $280

A Louis XV ormolu mounted kingwood mantel clock, the glazed enamel dial signed Baret a Brevanne, 17½in. high. (Christie's) $916

A Charles X ormolu and mahogany mantel clock, the silvered dial with scrolling floral bezel, 19½in. high. (Christie's) $814

A 19th century French porcelain mantel clock, the shaped case applied with flowers, the circular enamel dial signed Hry Marc, a Paris, 1ft 1½in. high. (Phillips) $1,088

A Charles X mantel clock with 3½in., diameter silvered dial, Roman numerals and eight-day movement, 20½in. high. (Bearne's) $819

A Second Empire ormolu and bronze mantel clock, the chased dial signed Michelez Eleve de Breguet, with a frieze of emblematic putti, 19in. high. (Christie's) $2,646

A substantial 19th century French ormolu mantel clock, the case lavishly decorated with foliage and sun rays and with three naked winged putti, 2ft.9½in. high. (Phillips) $5,423

An unusual French 19th century bronze and gilt brass mantel timepiece, the case in the form of a lighthouse, with circular enamel dial, 10in. high. (Phillips) $1,700

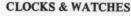

A Victorian mahogany mantel clock with stepped chamfered top, inscribed Yonge and Son, Strand, London, the twin fusee movement with shaped plates and engraved border, 18½in. high. (Christie's) $2,079

A George III ormolu, Derby biscuit porcelain and white marble mantel clock by Vulliamy, with later enamelled dial, London, 1785, the porcelain damaged and restored, 19½in. high. (Christie's) $60,544

A Regency rosewood mantel timepiece, the case of Gothic style, the fusee movement with anchor escapement, 12½in. high. (Phillips) $766

A French porcelain panelled mantel clock, the movement with Brocot suspension, the dial decorated in the Japanese manner with herons, butterflies and other birds, 13in. (Lawrence Fine Arts) $1,261

A rare mixed metal mantel clock by Tiffany & Company, New York, 1880-1885, the front with mokume panels of silver mixed with niello, brass and red metal, 9in. high. (Christie's) $18,700

A 19th century rosewood mantel timepiece, the silvered dial signed Frodsham & Son, Gracechurch Street, London, the fusee movement with anchor escapement, 30cm. high. (Phillips) $2,618

An Odd Fellows carved box with clock, America, early 20th century, shaped upper section crested with carved eagle, 13½in. high. (Robt. W. Skinner Inc.) $400

An English Regency black and white marble mantel timepiece, flanked by bronze recumbent lions, on a rectangular black marble base, signed Vulliamy, 11½in. wide. (Christie's) $4,235

A 19th century gilt brass and malachite mantel timepiece by Thomas Cole, the case in the form of a miniature chiffonier, the lever movement now converted to eight day duration, 5½in. high. (Phillips) $10,985

MANTEL CLOCKS

A 19th century gilt metal strut clock, after Thomas Cole, in scrolling oval case, 13cm. (Phillips) $449

A Continental silver gilt miniature timepiece, the shaped case decorated with repousse scrolls and flowers, 4in. high, in a fitted tooled leather travelling case. (Phillips) $1,326

A 19th century mahogany mantel timepiece, of balloon form, the circular painted dial signed Daldorph, Croydon, the fusee movement with anchor escapement. (Phillips) $411

A 19th century rosewood and brass inlaid mantel timepiece, signed Thwaites & Reed, Clerkenwell, London, the fusee movement with anchor escapement, 8in. high. (Phillips) $2,720

An impressive 19th century French ormolu and white marble mantel clock, the circular enamel dial with pierced gilt hands, 2ft 3½in. high. (Phillips) $1,774

A 19th century mantel clock, the front incorporating a rectangular porcelain panel painted with an Arab street scene, 11¾in. high overall. (Bearne's) $1,203

A 19th century French gilt brass and white marble mantel timepiece, the rectangular case surmounted by a rooster, 7½in. high. (Phillips) $841

A late 19th century brass cased mantel clock in the French taste, striking the hours and half hours on a coiled gong, 28cm. (Phillips) $430

An impressive French 19th century ormolu mantel clock, the case in the form of an urn flanked by grotesque masks, 1ft 9½in. high. (Phillips) $1,216

A 19th century ebonised mantel timepiece, the enamel dial signed Archd Haswell, London, the fusee movement with anchor escapement, 26cm. high. (Phillips) $1,384

A Lalique clock, the satin-finished glass molded with two pairs of love-birds in blossoming branches, with brown stained decoration, 21.8cm. wide. (Christie's) $1,496

A 19th century French ormolu mantel clock, the circular enamel dial signed Henry Voisin A Paris, the movement with silk suspension, 1ft. 1in. high. (Phillips) $816

A late 19th century gilt metal French mantel clock in the Louis XIV manner, with celeste bleu porcelain panels, 37cm. (Phillips) $299

A 19th century rosewood mantel timepiece, the square silvered dial signed Frodsham Gracechurch Street, London, the fusee movement with anchor escapement, 9in. high. (Phillips) $1,436

A French ormolu and bronze mantel clock, the circular glazed enamelled dial signed Brenzes...? the case signed Aug. Moreau, 9in. high. (Christie's) $1,394

A 19th century French bronze, porcelain and gilt mantel timepiece, the movement mounted in a circular case on the back of an elephant, 8½in. high. (Phillips) $972

A green lacquer mantel timepiece, the later single fusee movement with anchor escapement, 24¾in. high. (Lawrence Fine Arts) $773

A late 19th century mantel clock, with back plate signed 'J.W.Benson, London', surmounted by a bronze group of a young man and woman holding a tambourine, 22¼in. high. (Bearne's) $1,062

MANTEL CLOCKS

A French Siena marble and ormolu mounted mantel clock, the drum-shaped case with lyre finial, 15½in. high. (Christie's) $481

A 19th century mahogany and brass inlaid clock, with anchor escapement chiming the quarters on two bells, 1ft.10in. high. (Phillips) $1,352

A 19th century French ebonised pillar clock, on gilt metal applied block base, with glass dome, 41cm. (Phillips) $411

A Regency mahogany, ebonised brass-inlaid timepiece, the circular white painted dial with Roman numerals, eight day single fusee movement, 15½in. high. (Christie's) $1,155

A leather covered travelling timepiece, the later lever movement signed Le Coultre Co., the ivory dial signed Cartier, France, 'Eight Days', 4in. high. (Phillips) $486

A late George III satinwood mantel timepiece by Grant Fleet Street London No. 476, the architectural breakfront case with side volutes, brass angle quarter columns and ball finials, 13½in. high. (Christie's) $9,460

A 19th century Austrian gilt metal repeating mantel clock, in shaped rococo case, 20cm. high. (Phillips) $411

A mid Victorian burr elm Gothic mantel clock, inscribed Webster, Cornhill, London, the base with trefoil panels supporting obelisk pilasters, height 62cm. (Phillips) $1,122

A Charles X mahogany and ormolu mounted mantel clock, with stepped top surmounted by a two handled urn, 16in. high. (Christie's) $731

MANTEL CLOCKS

A gilt timepiece and barometer desk set in oval case surmounted by a carrying handle, with timepiece movement and platform escapement, 6¾in. high. (Christie's) $616

Victorian pollard oak cased mantel clock with eight day Continental movement. (British Antique Exporters) $219

Late 19th century ebonised mantel clock in the Arts and Crafts style with porcelain face and eight day movement. (British Antique Exporters) $263

A Viennese silver gilt and enamel monstrance watch with verge movement signed Gudin A Paris with champleve guilloche enamel dial, 6½in. high. (Christie's) $2,270

A German brass hexagonal stackfreed table clock, stamped M.L. on the backplate of the brass movement, with walnut parquetry veneered hexagonal case with glazed dial aperture, 14.8cm. diam. (Christie's) $7,189

A Viennese enamel desk clock, mid 19th century, the whole supported by Hercules, decorated with polychrome classical scenes over a pink ground, 8in. high. (Robt. W. Skinner Inc.) $1,500

Late 19th century red and black marble mantel clock with strike. (British Antique Exporters) $105

A fine hardstone and enamelled silver desk clock, signed Cartier, on agate base, 63mm. high. (Christie's) $6,050

A 19th century Japanese table clock in glazed shitan wood case, with chain fusee going and spring barrel striking train with outside countwheel, 7½in. (Christie's) $6,652

MANTEL CLOCKS

A Meissen porcelain clockcase, the circular gilt metal dial with blue Roman numerals, blue crossed swords and incised numeral marks, circa 1880, 60cm. high. (Christie's) $5,577

A miniature silver and enamel timepiece, the rectangular case decorated with blue guilloche enamel, the dial signed for Harrods Ltd, 1½in. high. (Phillips) $711

An ormolu mounted malachite mantel clock and urn, supported by foliate capped paw feet, inset with a circular clock, 19th century, 19¼in. high. (Christie's) $4,089

An unusual Jaeger LeCoultre table clock in Art Deco style, the straight line eight day movement jewelled to the center with monometallic balance, 7½in. diam. (Christie's) $457

An ormolu mantel clock, supported by a satyr seated on a tree stump, mid 19th century, the clock signed Paul Buhre, St. Petersbourg, 29¼in. (Christie's) $3,718

A Germanic late Renaissance quarter-striking hexagonal table clock signed Michael Fabian Thorn, the movement with baluster pillars, steel great wheels, chain fusee for the going, 6in. diam. (Christie's) $7,946

An early electric Eureka table clock in glazed mahogany case, the signed white enamel dial with Roman numerals and subsidiary seconds, dated 1906, 13¼in. high. (Christie's) $1,351

Victorian rouge marble mantel clock with eight-day French movement and brass dial. (British Antique Exporters) $306

A guilloche enamel desk clock, the split seed-pearl bezel enclosing a white enamel dial with black Arabic chapters, white metal, marked Faberge, 1899-1908, 5in. high. (Christie's) $24,167

MYSTERY CLOCKS

A belle epoque mystery timepiece, 25in. high. (Christie's) $5,082

SHELF CLOCKS

A Federal stained maple shelf-clock, O. Brackett, Vassalboro, Maine, 1815-1825, with molded cornice above a square glazed door with floral painted corners, 29¼in. high. (Christie's) $26,400

An early 19th century American mahogany shelf timepiece, signed Aaron Willard, Boston, the whole surmounted by scroll crestings. (Lawrence Fine Arts) $7,326

A chromium plated Smiths electric mystery clock, inscribed Smith Electric, with dagger hands, 8in. high. (Christie's) $500

A hammered copper shelf clock, by Tiffany & Co., New York, early 20th century, on rectangular brass platform base, 11in. high. (Robt. W. Skinner Inc.) $1,100

A Federal mahogany shelf clock, labelled Seth Thomas, Plymouth, Connecticut, first quarter 19th century, the swan neck pediment above a rectangular case with double glazed door, 29in. high. (Christie's) $1,540

A South German giltwood calendar mystery clock, signed Joseph Holtzel, 18th century, 32in. high. (Christie's) $10,527

A Federal walnut shelf timepiece, possibly rural Massachusetts, circa 1820, the hood with molded cornice above a glazed kidney door, 32in. high. (Robt. W. Skinner Inc.) $4,250

A Federal mahogany inlaid shelf timepiece, Joseph Chadwick, Boscawen, New Hampshire, circa 1810, on ogee bracket feet, 40in. high. (Robt. W. Skinner Inc.) $5,500

SKELETON CLOCKS

A 19th century French brass skeleton timepiece with alarm, the A-frame movement with enamel chapter ring, 9½in. high. (Phillips) $884

A 19th century French skeleton timepiece, the plates of inverted Y form, the three pillars terminating in floral cast nuts, 37cm. high. (Phillips) $6,290

A 19th century brass skeleton timepiece, the fusee movement with six spoked wheels and anchor escapement, 1ft. 2¾in. high. (Phillips)

$765

A brass skeleton timepiece, the chain fusee movement with anchor escapement, probably by Haycock of Ashbourne, 17in. (Lawrence Fine Arts) $773

A brass skeleton timepiece, the chain fusee movement with anchor escapement, the pierced silvered chapter with Roman numerals, 13in. high. (Lawrence Fine Arts)$520

A 19th century brass skeleton timepiece, the pierced scroll plates with silvered chapter ring, the fusee movement with six spoked wheels, 1ft 3in. high. (Phillips)

$1,014

A brass skeleton clock, the pierced scroll frame surmounted by a bell, the twin fusee movement with anchor escapement, 1ft. 6½in. high. (Phillips) $1,156

An unusual 19th century brass skeleton timepiece, the fusee movement with maintaining power and lever platform escapement, 1ft.1¾in. high. (Phillips) $782

An unusual brass skeleton timepiece, the pierced plates with shaped silvered chapter, signed on an oval plate Brown & Co., London, 6¼in. high. (Phillips) $935

WALL CLOCKS

An Edwardian mahogany wall clock, inscribed Evans & Sons, Birmingham, over panelled pendulum cover, 162cm. (Phillips) $1,028

An 18th century German wooden wall clock, the shaped painted dial with giltwood hands and center alarm set, 1ft.2¾in. high. (Phillips)
$5,984

A George III mahogany wall clock, 11in. round brass dial inscribed John Newman, Piccadilly, 47in. high overall. (Dreweatt Neate)
$3,256

A 19th century walnut and ebonised Vienna style wall timepiece, 5ft.7¾in. high. (Phillips) $2,975

An early 18th century longcase clock movement, the 10in. square brass dial with silvered chapter ring, subsidiary seconds, date aperture and engraved centre, (Phillips)
$1,870

A 19th century grande sonnerie Vienna wall clock, 4ft. 1in. high. (Phillips)
$5,070

A Georgian brass pantry clock, 30-hour movement, the dial signed Wm. Brice, Sandwich on a silvered disc, 4½in. high. (Christie's) $4,162

A mahogany wall timepiece, the repainted white enamel convex dial with Roman numerals, moon hands and signed Middleton, London. (Lawrence Fine Arts)$600

An unusual chiming oak hooded wall clock with verge movement, signed on a silvered plaque in the arch George Prior, London, 26in. high. (Christie's)
$1,540

WALL CLOCKS

A mahogany wall timepiece, the chain fusee movement with anchor escapement, mottled plates signed Dent, London. (Lawrence Fine Arts) $504

An interesting late 18th century French cartel clock by Etienne Baillon of Paris, the white enamel dial plate with Roman numerals, 27cm. high. (Henry Spencer) $2,136

A Georgian black lacquered tavern wall timepiece, the shield-shaped dial with gilt chapter, the weight driven movement with anchor escapement, 5ft.2½in. high. (Phillips) $6,358

A Georgian tavern clock signed Will[m]Murrell Horsham, 4ft.8½in. high.(Phillips) $4,080

A small engraved gilt brass weight driven chamber clock, German, dated 1625, with maker's punch 'LP', the iron posted frame movement with pillars of square section, 97mm. high. (Christie's) $4,180

A 19th century Dutch oak Staartklok, the painted dial with automaton figures, 4ft.1in. high.(Phillips) $1,436

A walnut veneered striking Vienna regulator, the movement with dead beat escapement, 52¾in. high. (Lawrence Fine Arts) $1,600

An early 18th century longcase clock movement, the 11in. square brass dial with silvered chapter ring signed Chr Gould, Londini Fecit. (Phillips) $3,740

A good mahogany striking drop-dial wall clock, with hexagonal bezel, the white painted dial indistinctly signed, 29½in. high. (Christie's) $1,039

WATCHES

An 18th century Swiss silver pair cased verge watch, signed Philippe Terrot, with signed silver champleve dial, the outer case decorated with a repousse design, 50mm. diam. (Phillips) $680

An 18ct. gold keyless lever chronograph, the movement with compensated balance, signed J. W. Benson, London, the case marked London 1882, 53mm. diam. (Phillips) $1,122

An Austrian silver and horn pair-cased coach clockwatch with alarm, signed Joseph Derchinger Wienn, with chain fusee, basically circa 1700, 106mm. diam. (Christie's) $5,297

A silver pair-cased verge watch, signed W. Graham London, with pierced carved mask cock and foot, outer case plain, 51mm. diam. (Christie's) $2,649

A silver and tortoiseshell triple case Turkish market verge watch, the enamel dial signed Isaac Rogers, London, 71mm. diam. (Phillips) $850

A silver gilt and enamel Chinese duplex watch, the polished steel movement with shaped Lepine calibre cocks, plain steel batwing balance, 62mm. diam. (Christie's) $1,324

A Continental silver verge watch, the enamel dial mounted with the seated figure of an automated cobbler hammering, 51mm. diam. (Phillips) $442

A gold repousse pair-cased quarter repeating verge watch, signed Jon. Magson, embossed with a Trojan War scene within asymmetrical scroll border, 48mm. diam. (Christie's) $2,459

A Swiss gold and enamel cylinder watch, the gilt bar movement signed Grohe Geneve, 36mm. diam. (Phillips) $338

WATCHES

A Swiss verge watch, with eccentric chapter ring above a painted landscape scene, 55mm. diam. (Christie's) $1,135

A gold quarter repeating cylinder watch, the enamel dial signed Courvoisier & Compe, 54mm. diam. (Phillips) $1,122

A French gold cylinder watch, the movement with silver dial, offset chapter and machined decoration, 42mm. diam. (Phillips) $449

An 18th century French gilt metal verge watch, inscribed Gribelin A Paris, the gilt dial with enamel numerals and chapter, 60mm. diam. (Phillips) $2,380

A 'Dutch import' silver and tortoiseshell triple case verge watch, signed Samson, London, decorated at the center with a river scene, 57mm. diam. (Phillips) $1,054

A French gold quarter repeating erotic Jaquemart watch, with a panel below opening to reveal two lovers, 55mm. diam. (Phillips) $5,610

An 18ct. gold keyless lever Karrusel watch, the movement signed Charles Fox, Bournemouth, the case marked Chester 1895, 55mm. diam. (Phillips) $3,718

An 18th century silver pair cased quarter repeating verge watch, signed Martineau, London, the signed silver champleve dial with arcaded chapters, 50mm. diam. (Phillips) $2,244

A silver pair cased quarter repeating verge watch, the movement with pierced cock signed Eardley Norton, London, 62mm. diam. (Phillips) $935

WATCHES

A Swiss gold hunter cased keyless lever watch, the steel bar movement signed Henry Hoffman, Locle, 54mm. diam. (Phillips) $1,069

An 18ct. gold minute repeating perpetual calendar chronograph hunter pocket watch with moonphase, by S. Smith & Sons Ltd, in plain case, 50mm. diameter. (Christie's) $10,010

A Swiss gold hunter cased quarter repeating keyless lever watch, the blue enamel dial with figures of Father Time and two winged cherubs, 55mm. diam. (Phillips) $2,915

A heavy 18ct. gold open-face Duplex pocket watch in plain case with small cartouche to the rear and foliate scroll decoration to the band, signed James Lytle, Sligo, 52mm. diameter. (Christie's) $1,058

A Swiss silver Masonic watch, the circular movement with triangular mother-o'-pearl dial inscribed *Love Your Fellow Man Lend Him A Helping Hand*, 58mm. high. (Phillips) $1,267

An 18th century gold pair-cased verge watch, signed Wm Plumley, Ludgate Hill, the outer case of repousse work depicting a classical scene, 50mm. diam. (Phillips) $1,605

A Swiss nickel keyless lever watch of very large size, the enamel dial with subsidiary seconds signed for J.C. Vickery, 13.5cm. diam. (Phillips) $591

An Austrian silver verge watch, the movement with pierced bridge cock, the enamel dial with offset chapter and subsidiary date, 58mm. diam. (Phillips) $612

An unusual cigarette lighter mounted with a watch, signed 'The Golden Wheel Lighter', fitted with adjusted 6-jewel lever movement, signed Cyma, 52mm. high. (Christie's) $418

WATCHES

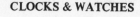

A gold half-hunter minute repeating keyless lever watch, the
half-plate movement signed
Donne & Son, London, repeating
on two gongs, 58mm. diam.
(Christie's) $5,676

A gold hunter-cased physician's
chronograph, the keyless nickel
finished lever movement with
chronograph train, 51mm. diam.
(Christie's) $1,320

A 19th century Austrian silver, enamel and rock crystal
verge watch, the circular
movement signed F.S.
Lompejo in Wien, 60mm.
diam. (Phillips)$1,496

A gilt-metal and enamel watch,
signed Bouvier A Geneve, the
reverse enamelled with an Arca-
dian couple by an altar of love,
54mm. diam. (Christie's)
$1,135

An 18ct. gold combined watch
and lighter by Dunhill, engine-
turned silvered Deco dial with
Arabic numerals set in a hinged
reeded octagonal frame, 1930,
49mm. high. (Christie's)
$4,162

A gilt-metal musical alarm watch,
pin barrel playing on 27mm.
steel comb (lacking two teeth),
case reverse florally engraved,
64mm. diam. (Christie's)
$1,324

A silver sector watch, signed
Sector Watch, Tramelan, with
shaped lever movement jewelled to the third wheel, 60mm.
diam. (Christie's)$1,650

A Swiss silver Masonic watch,
the circular movement signed
Solvil, the enamel dial decorated with Masonic symbols,
68mm. high. (Phillips)
$2,524

An early 19th century French
gold and enamel form watch,
the circular verge movement
with pierced bridge cock and
enamel dial. (Phillips)
$1,014

WRISTWATCHES

A circular Swiss silver Service wristwatch, the enamelled dial with subsidiary seconds, the front cover pierced to reveal the numerals, 35mm. diam. (Phillips) $340

A rectangular Swiss gold lady's wristwatch, by Patek Philippe, the signed gilt dial marked Gubelin, 23mm. long. (Phillips) $1,776

A gent's steel and gilt metal circular wristwatch, by Baume & Mercier, the quartz movement with signed dial and date aperture, 33mm. diam. (Phillips) $642

A World War II German pilot's wristwatch in base metal circular case, the frosted gilt movement signed Laco, jewelled to the center with 22 jewels, 55mm. diam. (Christie's) $790

An unusual gold wristwatch, signed Hamilton Electric, the battery-powered nickel movement with electro-magnetic balance. (Christie's) $1,100

A rectangular Swiss gold gent's electronic wristwatch, by Omega, the gilt dial marked Constellation Chronometer, with center seconds, 36mm. long. (Phillips) $1,122

A Swiss gold square gent's wristwatch, by Rolex, the movement stamped Rolex Prima, 25mm. square. (Phillips) $371

A circular Swiss gold gent's wristwatch, by Patek Philippe, the signed movement jewelled to the center, 32mm. diam. (Phillips) $1,870

A Swiss gold gent's wristwatch, by Patek Philippe, the signed circular steel bar movement jewelled to the center, 25mm. square. (Phillips)$2,244

WRISTWATCHES

A Swiss gold circular lady's wristwatch, by Rolex, the stamped movement with painted dial with Arabic numerals, 27mm. diam. (Phillips) $473

A very rare gold and diamond-set skeletonized automatic wristwatch by Patek Philippe, Geneve, the bezel with 12 diamonds, the case with sapphire crystal to the front and back, 34mm. diameter. (Christie's) $34,650

A Swiss gold oval lady's wrist-watch, by Chopard, signed black dial with baton numerals, 26mm. wide, on a fancy link bracelet. (Phillips) $608

A circular Swiss gold gent's wristwatch, by Patek Philippe, Geneve, the signed dial with subsidiary seconds and raised gilt numerals, 34mm. diam. (Phillips) $3,226

A rectangular Swiss two-color gold Rolex Prince wristwatch, the silvered dial with Arabic numerals and subsidiary seconds below, 42mm. long. (Phillips) $5,610

A stainless steel Omega Flight-master wristwatch, the outer scale in five-minute divisions from 5 to 60, with screw back case, 53 x 42mm. (Christie's) $395

A cushion-shaped Swiss gold wristwatch, by Rolex, the move-ment signed Rolex Extra Prima, with subsidiary seconds, 32mm. long. (Phillips) $1,496

A Swiss gold 'Mystery' wrist-watch by Jaeger-le-Coultre, with backwind movement, the bezel with enamelled baton numerals, 30mm. diam. (Phillips) $5,049

A Swiss gold oyster perpetual day-date wristwatch, by Rolex, the signed gilt dial with center seconds and with diamond numerals, (Phillips) $5,408

WRISTWATCHES

A gent's Swiss gold Oyster perpetual wristwatch, by Rolex, the signed gilt dial with baton numerals, 29mm. diam. (Phillips) $929

A circular steel gent's wristwatch, by Pierce, the silvered dial with center seconds, date, and Arabic numerals, 32mm. diam. (Phillips) $270

A gent's circular steel automatic wristwatch, by Blancpain, with perpetual calendar, the white dial with subsidiaries for day, date and month, 34mm. diam. (Phillips) $4,114

A stainless steel Breitling Navitimer in circular case with milled bezel and adjustable calculator scale, with expanding steel bracelet, 40mm. diam. (Christie's) $582

A gold Audemars Piguet perpetual calendar automatic wristwatch, the signed movement with 36 jewels adjusted to heat, cold, isochronism and five positions, diam. 35mm. (Christie's) $14,437

A 19ct. gold chronograph wristwatch in circular case, the matt silvered dial signed Universal, Geneve, 33mm. diam. (Christie's) $1,058

An 18ct. gold circular gent's wristwatch, by J.W.Benson, the enamel dial with Roman numerals, the case marked London 1916, 34mm. diam. (Phillips) $709

A Swiss gold cushion shaped gent's wristwatch, by Rolex, with Arabic numerals and subsidiary seconds, 36mm. long. (Phillips) $422

A fine gold calendar wrist chronograph with perpetual calendar, signed Patek Philippe, Geneve, No. 869392, the nickel 23-jewel movement with monometallic balance. (Christie's) $41,800

WRISTWATCHES

A gent's Swiss gold Oyster perpetual day-date wristwatch, by Rolex, the signed chocolate colored dial with center seconds, (Phillips) $4,394

A Swiss gold circular gent's wristwatch, by Patek Philippe & Co, Geneve, the signed gilt dial marked Gobbi Milano, 32mm. diam. (Phillips) $2,873

A steel Oyster perpetual bubble back gent's wristwatch, by Rolex, Arabic numerals, 39mm. long. (Phillips) $574

An 18ct. gold automatic wristwatch in oval case, the white enamel dial signed Baume & Mercier, Geneve, with very slim automatic movement. (Christie's) $1,455

A square white gold diamond and baguette sapphire set wristwatch signed on the silvered dial Cartier, Paris, 23mm. square. (Christie's) $8,855

An 18ct gold wristwatch in circular case, the black dial signed Van Cleef & Arpels, the movement signed Piaget, 33mm. (Christie's) $962

A Swiss gold circular gent's wristwatch, by Movado, the signed silvered dial with subsidiary seconds, 36mm. diam. (Phillips) $473

An 18ct. gold Rolex chronograph wristwatch with black bezel, calibrated in units per hour, the silvered dial with applied gold luminous baton numerals, 37mm. diameter. (Christie's) $7,315

A stainless steel calendar and moon phase wristwatch, inscribed 'Universal, Geneve', the signed movement jewelled to the third, diam. 34mm. (Christie's) $481

257

A Japanese cloisonne vase of slender baluster form decorated with a dragonfly resting on an iris, 12in. high. (Hamptons) $525

A cloisonne enamel bowl decorated with an arching lotus scroll around a central lotus flower-head below ruyi-heads at the rim, Jingtai nianzhao mark, 17th century, 19.4cm. diam. (Christie's) $1,155

A Japanese cloisonne enamelled wine pot and cover, the shoulders decorated with a dragon and a Ho-o bird, 5½in. high. (Bearne's) $345

A pair of cloisonne enamel deer in mirror image, each seated recumbent on a brocade mat with key-fret borders, Qianlong, 24.6cm. high. (Christie's) $14,437

A Hattori moriage slender trumpet vase with widely flared foliate rim with metal edging, impressed Hattori seal to the base, late 19th century, 19cm. high. (Christie's) $1,958

A pair of Japanese cloisonne enamelled vases decorated with cranes among waterlilies, 12in. high. (Bearne's) $1,092

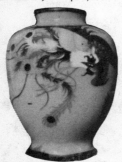

Good quality Japanese cloisonne vase, yellow ground with finely worked figure of a bird of paradise and foliage, 5in. high.(G. A. Key) $315

Pair of Japanese cloisonne enamel on copper vases, late 19th century, decorated with spring blossoms under a flowering tree, 12in. high. (Robt. W. Skinner Inc.) $800

One of a pair of Chinese cloisonne vases in late Ming style of ovoid form, with waisted necks and splayed cylindrical feet, late 19th century, 15½in. high.(Woolley & Wallis) Two $2,450

CLOISONNE

A cloisonne enamel pear-shaped vase, yuhuchunping, entirely decorated with a lotus scroll, 17th century, 30cm. high. (Christie's) $7,964

A shaped rectangular cloisonne box and cover decorated in various colored enamels and thicknesses of silver wire, brocade lining, Meiji period, 9.3cm. wide. (Christie's) $2,350

A Chinese cloisonne incense burner, the body of tapering rectangular form, standing on four fish like legs, early 20th century, 12in. high. (Woolley & Wallis) $420

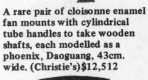

A pair of Japanese cloisonne vases of semi ovoid form decorated with sprays of chrysanthemum, peony, wisteria and lilies, 16in. high. (Hamptons) $2,362

A gilt bronze mounted Ming cloisonne enamel pear-shaped bottle decorated with scrolling lotus on a turquoise ground, 15th/16th century, 29cm. high. (Christie's) $5,775

A rare pair of cloisonne enamel fan mounts with cylindrical tube handles to take wooden shafts, each modelled as a phoenix, Daoguang, 43cm. wide. (Christie's) $12,512

A Chinese 24in. circular cloisonne enamel plaque with chrysanthemum and crane decoration. (Anderson & Garland) $579

Massive Chinese cloisonne enamel Ding-form temple vase, bearing Qianlong reign mark, probably 19th century, 29in. wide. (Robt. W. Skinner Inc.) $3,800

A Japanese cloisonne enamel vase, late 19th century, enamelled with a continuous scene of finely detailed brown sparrows and water-fowl, 18in. high. (Robt. W. Skinner Inc.) $3,000

A heavy brass footman, on front cabriole shaped supports, 20½in. wide. (Lawrence Fine Arts) $415

An Arts and Crafts white metal and copper jewelry casket designed by E. Creswick, with curved hinged cover, set with two cabochon chrysoprases, 1902, 28.8cm. long. (Christie's) $2,244

A Hagenauer brass bowl, supported on a broad cylindrical stem pierced with golfing figures, 11cm. high. (Phillips) $633

19th century brass jelly pan with cast iron fixed handle. (British Antique Exporters) $79

A hammered copper and repousse serving tray, attributed to Gustav Stickley, circa 1905, with simple leaf decoration, unsigned, 20in. diam. (Robt. W. Skinner Inc.) $650

Early 20th century brass firescreen with stylized flame decoration. (British Antique Exporters) $79

Late 18th century copper kettle with gadrooned lid and wooden handle. (British Antique Exporters) $219

A pair of brass fire dogs, the design attributed to C. F. Voysey, on splayed trestle feet. 39.4cm. high. (Christie's) $1,028

A Morris & Co. whistling copper and brass kettle, the asymmetrical conical vessel with cylindrical spout and cover, 24cm. high. (Phillips) $292

A 19th century brass needlework box, applied with engraved cross motif set with agates, and signed Howell James & Co., Regent Street, 8in. (Greenslades) $371

A good large Newlyn copper rosebowl decorated with fish, 9in. diam. (David Lay) $187

A 19th century brass fender fireguard with brass twist pattern frame, 3ft.6in. wide. (Greenslades) $507

19th century copper kettle with nicely shaped handle. (British Antique Exporters) $219

A French Art Deco circular copper wall plaque by Claudius Linossier, with hammered and silvered surface inlaid with geometric motifs, 50cm. diam., signed. (Phillips) $860

A Hagenauer brass twin branch candelabrum of interlaced form, the cylindrical sconces with gadrooned oval drip pans, decorated with a stylized dog, 35.5cm. high. (Christie's) $523

A Dutch copper and brass pail, the removable cover with urn shape finial, 17½in. high. (Lawrence Fine Arts) $374

A pair of French brass candlesticks with faceted nozzles and baluster drip pans, 18th century, 9½in. high. (Christie's) $1,221

Gustav Stickley hammered copper chamberstick circa 1907, with removable flared bobeche and strapwork handle, 9in. high. (Robt. W. Skinner Inc.) $400

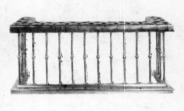

A set of brass measures from West Riding County Council, dated 1880, contained in a fitted mahogany case. (Hamptons) $1,330

A Regency copper hot water urn of small size, the ovoid body supported on tapering fluted monopodiae, 13½in. high. (Christie's)$385

A 19th century brass club fender of typical form, with ring turned uprights, 55in. wide. (Christie's)$1,664

A brass and steel firegrate, the shaped pierced basket mounted with laurel.wreaths and acanthus leaves, 21in. wide. (Christie's) $2,129

A brass bedwarmer, the circular lid with folded rim and punched decoration of a peafowl enclosed by scrolls, above a conforming pan, with a turned and painted handle, 43in. long. (Christie's) $495

A George III copper and brass coal helmet with swing handle. (A. J. Cobern) $123

A harlequin pair of brass and Wedgwood candlesticks with overhanging drip-pans, 9½in. high. (Christie's) $774

Early 19th century brass candlestick with pusher, on square base. (British Antique Exporters) $26

A pair of ornamental French brass ewers, decorated with cavorting bacchanalian figures and chased with fruiting vines, 22½in. high. (Christie's) $673

COPPER & BRASS

A rare 17th century brass English tavern bell candlestick with ribbed stem and flared bell base with iron clapper, 6in. high. (Boardman) $2,704

An early 19th century brass tavern tobacco box, with central fixed loop carrying handle flanked by two compartments, engraved 'William Hickton, Greyhound Inn, Mansfield', 25.5cm. wide. (Henry Spencer) $845

A Hagenauer brass figure of a tennis player, the stylized male figure in serving position, stamped marks Hagenauer, Wien, wHw, Made in Austria, 27.5cm. high. (Christie's) $1,309

A late 18th century brass tapering beaker, inset with George III halfpennies, 7½in. high. (Christie's) $173

A Regency steel register-grate, the beaded surround engraved with ribbon-tied bellflower swags and scrolling foliage, 38in. wide. (Christie's) $3,097

An early 19th century brass parrot cage, of square form, with eagle finial and ring suspension loop, 42in. high. (Christie's) $924

A 16th century style Nuremburg brass alms bowl, the center repousse with black letter inscription, 17½in.diam (Christie's) $1,155

A pair of brass figures of cavaliers, one holding a mallet, the other a scroll, with inscribed plaques, 19in. high overall. (Christie's) $308

An Edwardian satin brass coal receiver on claw feet. (A. J. Cobern) $97

A 19th century brass standish, fitted with two covered pots with acorn finials, a pen holder and circular dish, 11¾in. wide. (Christie's) $308

A pair of brass andirons in the 17th century style, with a ball and spire mounted on a baluster form column, with a broad bladed knop on twin supports, centering a lion's mask with paw and ball feet, 18½in. high. (Bearne's) $735

A Regency brass fender with D-shaped rails on turned supports above a wire grille on paw feet, 39in. wide. (Christie's) $2,710

A good pair of George II brass candlesticks, each with scalloped sconce, knopped stem and shaped base, 8in. high. (Tennants) $787

A 19th century brass and cast iron serpentine grate, the architectural backplate incised and raised with ribbon swags, 33in. high. (Christie's) $2,021

Pair of 19th century brass candlesticks on square bases with canted corners. (British Antique Exporters) $105

A George III style brass coal receiver with lion mask handles and claw feet. (A. J. Cobern) $194

A Dutch brass warming pan, the lid embossed with Adam and Eve, late 17th/early 18th century, 43in. (Bearne's) $739

An iron and brass firegrate, the serpentine-fronted basket with urn finials, 36in. wide. (Christie's) $3,484

A Continental corkscrew of 18th century style, the baluster stem chased with masks and scallops and capped by a parrot handle. (Phillips) $558

A fine four-pillar King Screw corkscrew, the vertical rach driven by a metal-handled ratchet. (Christie's) $374

An 18th century Dutch corkscrew with fluted kidney-shaped handle and fluted baluster stem, probably by Cornelis Hilberts, Amsterdam, 1749. (Phillips) $710

A pair of German folding legs corkscrew, with green and white stockings. (Phillips) $211

An unusual George IV silver mounted corkscrew, the ivory handle with tapering reeded ends and a brush, 1821 by Charles Fox II. (Lawrence Fine Arts) $962

A German novelty erotic folding corkscrew, the bone handles carved in the form of a scantily-clad woman. (Christie's) $1,028

A fine quality four-pillar nickel-plated King Screw corkscrew with bone handle, marked 'Mechi Leadenhall'. (Christie's) $462

An unusual late 19th century plated steel German figural corkscrew of a soldier in uniform and lady in under-garments embracing, 7cm. long. (Phillips) $528

A 19th century brass corkscrew, the twin turned handles held by a cloven footed devil, 19cm. high. (Osmond Tricks) $801

A navy silk dress printed with red, yellow and white circles, labelled Paquin, Paris and London, 1940's. (Christie's) $243

A mid 18th century Spitalfields silk open robe, brocaded with bold flower blooms, circa 1750's.(Phillips) $3,460

A dress of black georgette, the skirt with looped floating panel, labelled Doeuillet, circa 1922. (Christie's) $770

A late 19th century pink and blue brocade silk dress designed with swags and plumes, circa 1890's.(Phillips) $356

A strapless evening dress of black pleated chiffon, molded to the body hips, by Balmain, early 1956. (Christie's)$523

An evening dress of black chiffon and georgette, the skirt worked with floating panels, labelled Chanel, circa 1928. (Christie's) $2,695

A brushed blue wool dress, with matching short tailored jacket, labelled Jacques Heim, 1956-7. (Christie's) $168

A blue crepe bias cut evening dress, the bodice worked as a jacket, labelled Schiaparelli, 1937. (Christie's) $1,732

A stunning dress of peach colored velvet, densely worked with silver, white and peach colored beads 1920's. (Christie's) $243

A turn of the century black satin pleated tea gown, the pagoda sleeves and neck with tambour lace trim. (Phillips) $249

A dress of ivory silk velvet, the straps embroidered with diamante beadwork, 1920's. (Christie's) $198

An Empire dress with a chemise bodice of fine silk gauze, circa 1800-1805. (Christie's) $2,244

A banyan of yellow cotton woven with narrow pink-brown stripes, late 18th century. (Christie's) $1,732

An evening dress of raspberry pink gazar marked Aout 67, Mona Lucia, 158 by Balenciaga, 1967. (Christie's) $1,374

A dress of yellow, white, blue and black striped silk, circa 1810 (slightly altered) (Christie's) $385

A suit of blue and white striped 'silk', labelled Schiaparelli 21 Place Vendome Paris, circa 1953. (Christie's) $2,310

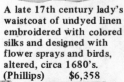

A boned corset of brown canvas lined with white linen, with tabbed waist, circa 1770. (Christie's) $4,620

An early 19th century waist-coat of undyed linen, printed in brown and fawn with a striped and foliate design, circa 1810. (Phillips)$696

A bolero jacket of black ribbed silk, with a large cape collar, labelled Balenciaga, 10 avenue George V, Paris, 1950's. (Christie's)$1,402

One of three pairs of gaiters comprising one of natural linen and one of white fustian and a pair of fine linen with black buttons, circa 1800. (Christie's) Three $462

A Chinese court vest of midnight blue silk, embroidered in colored silks and couched gilt thread, with a civil rank badge on the back and front embroidered with the fourth-rank goose, fringed. (Christie's)
$654

A late 17th century lady's waistcoat of undyed linen embroidered with colored silks and designed with flower sprays and birds, altered, circa 1680's. (Phillips) $6,358

A pair of white linen cut hose with drawstring ties, circa 1800. (Christie's) $539

A mid 19th century Chinese coat of silk and gold thread K'o-ssu, the midnight blue ground designed with archaic characters. (Phillips)
$4,394

A mid 19th century French shawl woven in mainly red, blue and green, 3.28x1.64m. circa 1860's. (Phillips)
$208

COSTUME

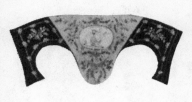

A black and blue silk wedding belt embroidered with flowers and cartouches with silver and gold metal thread, circa 1790, Swiss or French. (Christie's) $173

A pair of moschettos of unbleached linen, the gaiter type lower leg closing with silver metal buttons, circa 1800. (Christie's) $3,176

A late 19th century Rajasthani embroidered skirt-piece of magenta silk satin, 85 x 410cm., circa 1900's. (Phillips) $190

A waistcoat of black satin, lined with white glazed cotton, with notched lapels embroidered with a garland of flowers, circa 1840. (Christie's) $317

A Chinese robe of sage green silk damask embroidered in colored silks with sprays of flowers. (Phillips) $740

A nightshirt of fine linen reputed to have belonged to H.M. King Charles I, the deep square collar and the cuffs trimmed with lace, English, second quarter of the 17th century. (Christie's) $1,870

A late 19th century black Chantilly lace tie, designed with flowers, and meandering foliate sprigs, 290cm.(Phillips) $151

A 19th century Chinese robe of red cut and uncut velvet, designed with peaches and bats, bordered in black silk. (Phillips) $1,606

A tunic top of cream wool with very short sleeves, a high collar and run-through belt, labelled Martial & Armand. (Christie's) $269

A suit of pink and fawn wool, with metallic thread wefts, unlabelled, Chanel, 1950's. (Christie's) $243

A dress of fawn ribbed silk, with bell sleeves and skirt trimmed down the front with bows, circa 1870. (Christie's) $317

A black velvet evening dress with narrow velvet straps, labelled Chanel, circa 1934. (Christie's) $1,155

A fine marriage coat of white goatskin, stamped with leaves and flowers, 1887. (Christie's) $1,090

A dress of apple green muslin, embroidered overall with clear bugle beads, 1920's. (Christie's) $168

An early 19th century girl's dress of pale pink silk, with capped sleeves and flounced hem, circa 1820's. (Phillips) $623

A coat of cisele velvet woven with brown carnation type flowers and berries, circa 1740. (Christie's) $1,683

A summer suit of white cotton, with a high collar decorated with broderie anglaise, circa 1905. (Christie's) $130

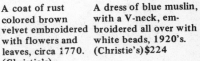

An open robe and petticoat of green silk damask woven with a design of flowers, berries and leaves, circa 1775. (Christie's) $5,049

An evening dress of florescent pink silk labelled Gres, Rue de la Paix, Paris, early 1960's. (Christie's) $693

A coat of rust colored brown velvet embroidered with flowers and leaves, circa 1770. (Christie's) $1,028

A dress of blue muslin, with a V-neck, embroidered all over with white beads, 1920's. (Christie's) $224

A wedding dress of ivory spotted silk, the blouse pouched above the waist, 1909. (Christie's) $205

A dress of brown shot silk taffeta, the bodice woven with brown, black and white silks, circa 1865. (Christie's) $731

A sleeveless wrapover shift of peach velvet, labelled Becker Fils, 1930's. (Christie's) $299

A dress of royal blue silk, with ribbons of ivory silk printed with black chine leaves, circa 1875. (Christie's) $2,021

DOLLS

A bisque headed doll with open mouth, sleeping eyes and brown hair, stamped with a monogram 'GW', Germany, 16in. (Anderson & Garland)
$337

A waxed shoulder composition doll, c. 1840, with closed mouth, in original glazed case, 16in. (Lawrence Fine Arts)
$298

Schoenau and Hoffmeister 'Princess Elizabeth' bisque headed doll impressed Porzellanfabrik Burggrub Princess Elizabeth 6½ Made in Germany, 23in. high. (Hobbs & Chambers) $897

A poured wax child doll with fixed blue eyes, the long blonde hair inset in groups into head, 21½in. high, with Lucy Peck oval stamp on body. (Christie's)
$831

A large Festival doll of a seated samurai in armor, with cloth covered kabuto, and an attendant figure with jingasa similarly dressed, the figures 19th century with 18th century brocade, 96cm. and 54cm. high respectively. (Christie's)
Two $13,706

A bisque swivel headed bebe with closed mouth, brown paperweight eyes, molded feathered brows, pierced ears, 18½in. high, marked BRU Jne 6 (one finger damaged). (Christie's) $18,711

A cloth doll with black button eyes, painted facial features and stuffed body, in Highland dress, 10in. (Lawrence Fine Arts) $59

A cloth and leather figural grouping, Lucy Hiller Lambert Cleveland, Salem, Massachusetts, 1840, 15in. high. (Robt. W. Skinner Inc.) $3,000

A Chad Valley doll of Winston Churchill, the molded rubber head with painted facial features, 14in. (Lawrence Fine Arts) $99

DOLLS

A papier-mache headed doll with molded ringlets, the stuffed body with wooden limbs, 11in. high, circa 1840. (Christie's) $540

A 19th century pedlar doll standing beside a table cluttered with her wares. (Greenslades) $2,450

A 20th century bisque headed doll with brown hair and jointed limbs, 22in. (Anderson & Garland) $173

Danel et Cie bisque headed doll impressed E5D Depose with fixed blue glass eyes, painted mouth, fair hair wig, 16in. high. (Hobbs & Chambers) $841

A long-faced bisque headed bebe with closed mouth, pierced and applied ears, blue paperweight eyes, 19½in. high, head impressed 9, body marked with blue Jumeau Medaille d'Or stamp. (Christie's) $15,592

Simon and Halbig bisque headed doll, having brown sleeping eyes, open mouth with two molded upper teeth, 23½in. high. (Hobbs & Chambers) $561

A bisque headed doll with open mouth, blonde hair and sleeping eyes, stamped '21, Germany, R6/OP', 14in. (Anderson & Garland) $121

Kammer and Reinhardt/Simon and Halbig bisque headed character doll, with brown glass sleeping eyes, molded closed mouth, 21¼in. high. (Hobbs & Chambers) $5,236

A Grodnertal wooden doll, the domed painted head with black hair, finely painted features and rings for earrings, 29cm. (Phillips) $785

DOLLS

A Lenci fabric girl doll with fair mohair wig and painted brown eyes looking left, 12in. high. (Phillips) $642

An Armand Marseille bisque doll, with sleeping blue eyes, brown wig and cream apron and hat, 10in. high. (Lawrence Fine Arts) $104

A composition mask faced googlie eyed doll, with smiling watermelon mouth, 13in. high, Hug Me Kiddies, circa 1914. (Christie's) $456

A late 18th century wooden doll with natural brown plaited wig, the straight legs peg jointed at the hip, 12in. high. (Phillips) $777

A set of Madame Alexander Dionne Quins, the composition dolls with painted facial features, 7in. high. (Lawrence Fine Arts) $639

A bisque headed doll with blue sleeping eyes, blonde wig and jointed body, 17in. high, marked '390 A ½ M', in original box stamped 'Toyland, Hull'. (Christie's) $557

A painted felt doll, the felt body jointed at shoulders and hips, dressed in purple silk gown trimmed with organdie and felt, 15in. high, marked Lenci. (Christie's) $391

A flesh tinted china shoulder head with dark brown mohair wig, 19in. high. (Christie's) $3,160

An early 19th century painted wooden Grodnertal doll with yellow comb, dressed in contemporary rose silk dress, 5½in. high. (Christie's) $799

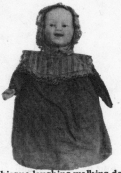

A bisque laughing walking doll with the walking talking mechanism concealed under original outfit of blue and cream lace, 9in. high, marked with Gebruder Heubach Square. (Christie's) $470

A Lenci fabric boy doll with fair mohair wig and painted brown eyes looking right, 18in. high. (Phillips) $1,014

A bisque headed bebe with closed mouth, pierced ears and fixed blue yeux fibres, 10in. high. (Christie's) $2,230

An early Alt, Beck & Gottshalck bisque shoulder and head doll, with painted facial features, 12in. high. (Lawrence Fine Arts)$131

A set of Madame Alexander Dionne Quins, in original romper suits, bonnets, shoes and socks, 7in. high, marked Alexander. (Christie's) $905

A Bru Jeune bisque headed doll with original sheepskin wig, blue paperweight eyes and pierced ears, 19in. high. (Phillips) $25,350

A bisque headed child doll, with brown lashed sleeping eyes, pierced ears and jointed body, 12½in. high, marked S&H. (Christie's) $1,006

J. D. Kestner bisque headed 'Hilda' doll, with combed hair, open mouth and upper molded teeth, 20½in. long. (Hobbs & Chambers) $2,275

'Dancing Sailor', a printed and painted tinplate sailor, in blue cloth uniform, 7½in. high, by Lehmann, circa 1912. (Christie's) $190

DOLLS

A Lenci fabric boy doll with short fair mohair wig, painted brown eyes and features, 14in. high. (Phillips)$743

A bisque headed child doll with blue lashed sleeping eyes, pierced ears and blonde mohair wig, 20in. high, marked S & H K*R 50. (Christie's) $1,115

A bisque headed child doll with blue sleeping eyes, pierced ears and fair mohair wig, 17in. high, marked Simon & Halbig. (Christie's) $743

A bisque headed character child doll with closed pouting mouth, painted blue eyes and blonde mohair wig, marked K*R. (Christie's)$1,208

A bisque figure of a seated boy, wearing a cream and orange bathing cap, 11½in. high, impressed with the Gebruder Heubach Sunburst and 4859. (Christie's) $1,141

A ventriloquist's dummy modelled as a school girl with moving eyes and lower jaw, in original gym slip and skirt, 34in. high. (Christie's) $190

A poured wax doll, the stuffed body with wax limbs in spotted muslin dress trimmed with lace and pink ribbon, 13½in. high. (Christie's) $783

A Simon & Halbig mulatto bisque doll, with open mouth and upper teeth, 10in. high. (Lawrence Fine Arts) $282

A Lenci pressed felt girl doll, circa 1930, with molded and painted facial features and blonde wig, 49cm. high. (Osmond Tricks) $391

DOLLS

A turned and carved painted wooden doll, the wooden body with kid arms, dressed in original organza skirt, 13in. high, circa 1840. (Christie's) $1,673

A bisque headed googlie eyed doll, with water melon mouth, brown mohair wig, and painted shoes and socks, 7in. high. (Christie's) $913

A Kammer and Reinhardt bisque headed character doll, the jointed composition body dressed in red cotton dress, 12½in. high. (Phillips) $1,690

A painted felt doll dressed in the costume of Sicily, 15in. high, marked on foot, by Lenci, circa 1941. (Christie's) $321

A bisque swivel headed Parisienne with closed mouth, fixed blue eyes and Geslard body with bisque limbs, 14in. high. (Christie's) $3,044

A bisque swivel headed doll, with fixed blue eyes, pierced ears, blonde wig and cloth body, 15½in. high. (Christie's) $783

A shoulder composition doll, with closed mouth, fixed blue glass eyes, fair wig, dressed as a parlor maid. (Lawrence Fine Arts) $188

A bisque swivel headed Parisienne with blue fixed eyes, pierced ears, fair mohair wig with cork pate, 16½in. high, with Cremer, 210 Regent Street stamp on body.(Christie's) $1,859

A Kathe Kruse fabric boy doll with short wig, dressed in red cotton shorts, white shirt and raincoat, 20in. high. (Phillips) $980

A bisque swivel headed Parisienne modelled as a child with blue eyes, pierced ears and blonde mohair wig, 9½in. high. (Christie's) $2,013

A bisque swivel headed Parisienne with blue fixed eyes, feathered brows and sheepskin wig, 16in. high, probably by Jumeau. (Christie's) $2,230

A bisque headed child doll with blue sleeping eyes, blonde wig and jointed body, 23in. high, probably Alt Beck & Gosschalk. (Christie's) $1,022

A bisque headed bebe with fixed brown eyes, closed mouth, pierced ears and blonde wig, 19in. high, stamped in red Depose Tete Jumeau. (Christie's) $4,833

A good Lenci cloth doll, Italian circa 1930, the stiffened felt head with painted features, eyes looking to the right and blonde short curly mohair wig, 56cm. high. (Henry Spencer) $878

A painted felt portrait doll modelled as HRH The Princess Elizabeth, with original pink frilled rayon dress, 17½in. high, by Chad Valley. (Christie's) $342

A papier mache headed doll, the molded black hair arranged in a loose bun at the nape, 9in. high, circa 1840. (Christie's) $190

A good Edwardian pedlar doll on ebonised stand under glass dome, the wax covered boy sailor standing on his one leg. (David Lay) $470

A wooden character doll with carved and painted features, in pink velvet and organza dress and original underwear, 14½in. high, by Schoenhut. (Christie's) $764

A white enamel box, painted with reserves of flowers, the cover portraying lovers, 3in. wide. (Christie's) $616

A jewelled guilloche enamel cigarette case, lilac enamel bands alternating with white plain enamel bands, marked Faberge, 1908-1917, 8.5cm. long. (Christie's) $5,577

A Birmingham rectangular enamel snuff-box, the cover printed and painted with two lovers, circa 1755-60, 3¼in. long. (Christie's) $1,513

A Birmingham circular enamel snuff-box, painted with fruits and flowers on a white ground, circa 1755, 2¼in. diam. (Christie's) $340

A pair of early Surrey enamel and bronze candlesticks each with slender baluster column, flared sconce and circular base, 5¾in. high. (Hamptons) $3,500

A Birmingham or South Staffordshire circular enamel snuff-box, painted with the Stag over the Gate, after Wotton, circa 1755-60, 2½in. diam. (Christie's) $983

A Birmingham rectangular small enamel snuff-box, the cover painted with a macaw and fruits, circa 1755, 2½in. long. (Christie's) $946

A South Staffordshire enamel etui painted with flowers and figures in landscapes, circa 1765-70 (chips to enamel) 4in. long. (Christie's) $1,419

A very attractive late 19th century Russian enamel plaque depicting a wedding feast, the lining printed with the retailer's name Bolin, Moscow, 6 x 4.5cm. (Phillips) $726

A late 18th century fan, designed with a cartouche of lovers flanked by maidens and inset with diamante, circa 1770's, 26,5cm. long. (Phillips) $1,225

A mid 18th century French fan, the vellum leaf painted with Minerva greeted by the Muses on Mount Helicon with Apollo hovering above, circa 1760's, 29.5cm. long. (Phillips) $770

A fan, the leaf painted with a classical scene, with ivory sticks, 11in., Italian, circa 1940. (Christie's) $1,022

A mid 19th century Chinese tortoiseshell brise fan, carved and pierced both sides with figures, 19cm. long. circa 1840's. (Phillips) $420

A fan, the leaf painted with a goddess appearing to a shepherd, mother-of-pearl sticks, 11½in., Flemish with German sticks, circa 1750. (Christie's) $743

A fan, the shaped leaf painted with a woman wearing a violet trimmed bonnet, signed Jebagnes, 9½in., circa 1905. (Christie's) $2,788

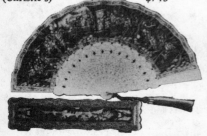

A mid 19th century Chinese fan with ivory sticks, carved and pierced with figure scenes, in original black and gilt lacquer box, circa 1850's, 27.5cn. long. (Phillips) $735

An early 18th century fan with Italian carved ivory sticks designed with a pair of lovers flanked by vases and scrolling leaves, probably German, in brocade box, circa 1700's 29.5cm. long. (Phillips) $875

FANS

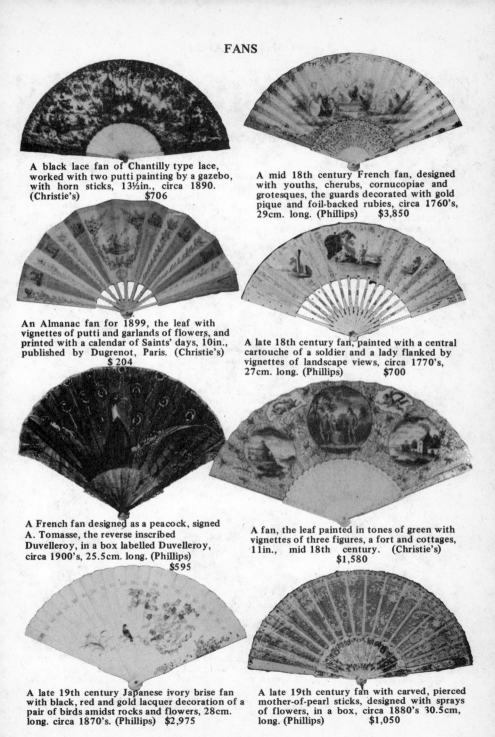

A black lace fan of Chantilly type lace, worked with two putti painting by a gazebo, with horn sticks, 13½in., circa 1890. (Christie's) $706

A mid 18th century French fan, designed with youths, cherubs, cornucopiae and grotesques, the guards decorated with gold pique and foil-backed rubies, circa 1760's, 29cm. long. (Phillips) $3,850

An Almanac fan for 1899, the leaf with vignettes of putti and garlands of flowers, and printed with a calendar of Saints' days, 10in., published by Dugrenot, Paris. (Christie's) $204

A late 18th century fan, painted with a central cartouche of a soldier and a lady flanked by vignettes of landscape views, circa 1770's, 27cm. long. (Phillips) $700

A French fan designed as a peacock, signed A. Tomasse, the reverse inscribed Duvelleroy, in a box labelled Duvelleroy, circa 1900's, 25.5cm. long. (Phillips) $595

A fan, the leaf painted in tones of green with vignettes of three figures, a fort and cottages, 11in., mid 18th century. (Christie's) $1,580

A late 19th century Japanese ivory brise fan with black, red and gold lacquer decoration of a pair of birds amidst rocks and flowers, 28cm. long. circa 1870's. (Phillips) $2,975

A late 19th century fan with carved, pierced mother-of-pearl sticks, designed with sprays of flowers, in a box, circa 1880's 30.5cm, long. (Phillips) $1,050

Metro-Goldwyn-Mayer Studios — Tom and Jerry, 'Robin Hoodwinked', gouache on full celluloid applied to a water-color background, 7¼ x 10in. (Christie's) $1,115

A bowler hat, the inside leather band with manuscript inscription in black ink 'Thanks Harry! Stan Laurel', allegedly worn by Stan Laurel during his 1947 stage tour of Britain. (Christie's) $15,801

Metro-Goldwyn-Mayer Studios — Tom and Jerry, 'Muscle Beach Tom', gouache on full celluloid applied to a water-color background, 8½ x 11½in. (Christie's) $1,208

A 'Marilyn Monroe Drawing Aid', the perspex draftsman's 'aid' shaped as the seated figure of Marilyn Monroe with instructions in red lettering, 8½ x 4¼in. (Christie's) $1,022

A decollete full-length evening dress of gold lame in 'Grecian style', owned by Marilyn Monroe and worn by her on the occasion of the Royal Film Premier for 'The Battle of the River Plate', October 29th, 1956, when she was presented to H.M. Queen Elizabeth II. (Christie's) $5,205

A model of the head of the fantasy half man, half fish, from the 1954 film 'The Creature from the Black Lagoon', of molded rubber, 11 x 9½in., possibly a prototype for the head of 'The Creature'. (Christie's) $1,487

A good half-length portrait photograph by Coburn with manuscript inscription 'To Pat Dixon Sincerely Gary Cooper', 13½ x 10½in. (Christie's) $520

Alec Guinness — a good half-length portrait photograph by Cecil Beaton, mounted on card with photographer's signature, 10 x 9½in. (Christie's) $316

An original Paco Rabanne leather jacket, the collar, cuffs and hem of black leather, made for Brigitte Bardot in the 1960's. (Christie's) $1,766

Walt Disney Studios — Der Fuehrer's Face, 'Donald Duck speaking into a telephone', gouache on celluloid, stamped 'Original WDP', 7½ x 9in. (Christie's) $9,024

A bowler hat allegedly owned by Oliver Hardy and given by him to Max Miller. (Christie's) $2,230

Walt Disney Studios — Peter Pan, 1953, 'Peter Pan and Wendy flying', gouache on full celluloid, framed and glazed, 12½ x 15in.(Christie's) $1,115

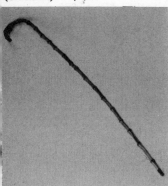

A bamboo cane with metal tip, allegedly given by Charlie Chaplin to a relative of the vendor, 33¾in. long. (Christie's) $1,078

A promotional thermometer for the United Artists film 'Some Like It Hot', decorated with a picture of Marilyn Monroe, her white dress blowing in the breeze, circa 1959, 39 x 8in. (Christie's) $6,507

Ken Konno, two portrait studies of Lauren Bacall and Humphrey Bogart, signed by artist, airbrush, pen and acrylic, both 29½ x 22in. (Christie's) $297

A head and shoulders portrait photograph with manuscript inscription 'Marilyn Monroe', 5 x 4in. (Christie's)$1,115

A theatre programme for 'The Teahouse Of The August Moon' at the Martin Beck Theatre, signed on the cover by Marilyn Monroe and Joe Di Maggio. (Christie's) $1,115

Marilyn Monroe — a poly-chrome film poster for 'Bus Stop', 20th Century Fox, printed in England by Stafford & Co., Nottingham and London, 30 x 20in. (Christie's) $1,208

An Art Deco style Mickey Mouse figure of cast iron finished in gilt, 5¾in. high. (Christie's)　$651

George Bernard Shaw/Danny Kaye — a rare 16mm. black and white film, 10 minutes long, sold with copyright. (Christie's) $35,321

Walt Disney Studios — Sleeping Beauty, 1959, 'Malificent with Crow', gouache on celluloid, 8 x 10in., window mounted and Walt Disney production label on reverse. (Christie's)　$2,974

A half-length still of Mae West signed and inscribed in white ink 'Miss Seena Owen Come up and see me sometime, Mae West', 10 x 8in. (Christie's) $297

Eight hand-painted Wadeware figures of Snow White and the Seven Dwarfs, largest 7in. high. (Christie's)　$650

Emile T. Mazy, 'Portrait of Charlie Chaplin', signed, dated 1917, oil on canvas, framed, 27¼ x 21¼in. (Christie's) $1,022

One of a complete set of eight 1970 reproduction front of house stills for 'Giant', with four original 1956 front-of-house stills, for the same film. (Christie's)Twelve $167

James Dean — one of a complete set of eight front-of-house stills for 'Rebel Without A Cause', 1955. (Christie's)
　　　　Eight　　$260

Ronald Reagan — a poly-chrome film poster, for 'Hell's Kitchen', printed in America by Continental Litho Corp., Cleveland, 41 x 27in.(Christie's) $483

Walt Disney Studios — Peter Pan, 1953, two similar multi-cel set ups, both gouache on full celluloid, one framed and glazed, 12½ x 15¾in. (Christie's) $836

A stetson of fawn-colored hatter's plush with indistinct signature 'Tom Mix' on brim, the inside leather band stamped 'Made by John B. Stetson Company especially for Tom Mix'. (Christie's) $1,022

Walt Disney Studios — Peter Pan, 1953, 'Wendy', a half-length close-up, gouache on celluloid, 12½ x 16in., framed and glazed; with three other celluloids of Wendy.(Christie's) $520

A piece of paper signed 'Marilyn Monroe Miller' attached to the reverse of a previously unpublished photograph of Marilyn Monroe with her husband Arthur Miller arriving at London airport 1956. (Christie's) $1,394

An autograph letter signed from Eli Wallach to a fan, dated Oct. 3rd, 1960, telling him 'I'm currently filming "The Misfits" with Clark Gable, Marilyn Monroe, and Montgomery Clift — since you're collecting autographs, I took the liberty of asking them to sign as well — Sincerely, Eli Wallach'. (Christie's) $8,923

A half-length publicity photograph, signed and inscribed 'To Honey Frances thanks for the pointers Antony Curtis', 10 x 8in. (Christie's) $74

Walt Disney Studios — Snow White and the Seven Dwarfs, 1937, 'Dopey and Animals', gouache on celluloid with air-brush background, 5¾ x 5½in. (Christie's) $4,089

James Dean — one of a complete set of eight front-of-house stills for 'Rebel Without A Cause', 1955.(Christie's) Eight $260

A good head and shoulders portrait photograph with manuscript inscription 'Montgomery Clift', 10x8in. (Christie's) $223

Lead, clasped hands, small cuffs, with open crown above, policy no. 75165 on panel below. (Phillips) $518

Church of England Life and Fire Assurance, copper, circular, arms of the Church raised on convexed center. (Phillips) $481

Lead, open portcullis with Prince of Wales' feathers above, policy no. 31212. (Phillips) $555

Hibernian Fire Insurance, lead, Irish harp raised on oval with raised border, with open crown above. (Phillips) $740

London Assurance, copper, seated figure of Britannia with shield, spear and harp, original paint, lacks spear tip. (Phillips) $444

Kent Insurance, copper, raised horse forcene on octagonal panel 'Invicta' raised on small panel above. (Phillips) $629

Lead, open portcullis with Prince of Wales' feathers above, policy no. 23829 on panel below, lacks rings. (Phillips) $407

London Assurance, lead, seated figure of Britannia with shield, spear and harp, policy no. 36327 on panel below. (Phillips) $703

Union Fire Office, lead, four clasped hands, with 'Union' raised on panel above, policy no. 27617. (Phillips) $999

United Firemen's Insurance Company, Philadelphia, Pennsylvania, USA, cast iron, oval, raised steam fire engine in high relief, circa 1877. (Phillips) $2,220

Lead, open portcullis with Prince of Wales' feathers above, policy no. 36044 on panel below. (Phillips) $592

Edinburgh Friendly Insurance, lead, the shaped panel raised with clasped hands, policy no. 8769. (Phillips) $370

Lead, impressed portcullis with Prince of Wales' feathers above, policy no. 53252 on panel below. (Phillips) $407

The General Insurance Company of Ireland, lead, square, raised phoenix, torse and borders. (Phillips) $518

Lead, open portcullis with Prince of Wales' feathers above, policy no. 28341 on panel below. (Phillips) $407

Copper, raised with a standing figure of King Alfred, 'West of England' raised around, 'Exeter' raised on panel below. (Phillips) $185

Lead, clasped hands, small cuffs, with open crown above, policy no. 76444 on panel below. (Phillips) $518

Licensed Victuallers and General Fire and Life Insurance, copper, bunch of grapes raised in convexed oval. (Phillips) $185

BEDS

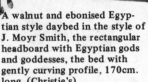

An oak cradle with arched hood and panelled sides surmounted by turned finials, on rockers, 41 in. wide. (Christie's) $1,082

A walnut and ebonised Egyptian style daybed in the style of J. Moyr Smith, the rectangular headboard with Egyptian gods and goddesses, the bed with gently curving profile, 170cm. long. (Christie's) $8,041

A mahogany four-poster bed with pleated ivory silk canopy on two spirally and ring turned columns, 78in. wide, 74in. high. (Christie's) $6,582

An Elizabethan oak, walnut and painted tester bedstead, the panelled canopy with lunette and foliate molded cornice, late 16th century, restorations, 66in. wide. (Christie's)$59,070

A French white painted wickerwork cradle, decorated with spandrels and scrolls, with a swing bed beneath a coronet cresting, 42in. (Christie's) $1,347

A Victorian mahogany half tester double bed, the shaped footboard decorated with applied fielding and scallop motif, 4ft.6in. wide. (Anderson & Garland) $1,176

A mahogany and cane cradle with arched top and square frame, the two ends joined by stretchers, first half 19th century. (Lawrence Fine Arts) $876

A Regency rosewood bed, the head and foot-end panelled with ormolu ripple moldings between freestanding paired fluted columns, 71in. wide. (Christie's) $94,600

An oak tester bedstead of panelled construction carved throughout with stylised scrolls and foliage, the canopy with a dentilled cornice, 62in. wide. (Christie's)$9,845

BEDS

A George II oak cradle, with fielded side panels and arched canopy with ball mounted rocker finials, 38in.(Christie's) $1,058

L. & J. G. Stickley day bed, circa 1910, the straight rail over four vertical side slats, signed with Handcraft decal, 80in. long. (Robt. W. Skinner Inc.) $1,800

A George III mahogany cradle of rectangular form, the scrolling side panels applied with roundels, 39in. wide.(Christie's) $866

An English Art Deco Egyptian style bed, the tall headboard with beaten copper panel of Egyptian style foliage, 108cm. wide. (Christie's) $935

A Victorian walnut half-tester bed, with tasselled molded canopy hung with printed cotton drapes, 67 x 68in. (Christie's) $1,636

A fine Federal mahogany carved and inlaid canopy bed, probably New Hampshire, circa 1810, the arched canopy on two turned swelled and reeded posts with acanthus leaf carving. (Robt. W. Skinner Inc.) $8,500

A Wylie and Lockhead mahogany bed, the design attributed to George Logan, the toprail inlaid with mother-of-pearl and wood peacock-eye motifs, 122cm. high. (Phillips) $1,084

A mahogany four-poster bed in the manner of Chippendale, the molded canopy, 62 x 84in. (Christie's) $5,775

A small inlaid oak Heal's double bed, the design attributed to Ambrose Heal, with panelled footboard, 148cm. across. (Phillips) $1,496

BOOKCASES

Mid 19th century mahogany bookcase with glazed doors to the upper section and panelled cupboard doors below. (British Antique Exporters) $2,100

A Morris & Co. oak bookstand, the sloping rectangular rest surmounted with carved and turned ball and foliate finials, above panelled sides and open recess, 185.5cm. wide. (Christie's) $7,480

An unusual mahogany center bookcase, each side with two glazed doors, 21¼in. square. (Lawrence Fine Arts) $5,762

A 19th century carved walnut library bookcase, decorated with masks, lyre, foliate scrolls and motifs, 6ft.10in. wide, 10ft. high. (Geering & Colyer) $4,056

A George III mahogany breakfront bookcase with molded cornice above two pairs of gothic-glazed doors, on a plinth base, 100in. wide. (Christie's) $32,912

L. & J. G. Stickley single door bookcase, circa 1907, the single door with sixteen panes, signed with Handcraft decal, 30in. wide. (Robt. W. Skinner Inc.) $3,250

A George III mahogany bookcase with molded gothic arcaded cornice and open shelves, 92in. wide. (Christie's) $6,582

A rare and important Gustav Stickley inlaid two door bookcase, designed by Harvey Ellis, circa 1903-1904, signed with red decal in a box, 55¾in. wide. (Robt. W. Skinner Inc.) $48,000

An ormolu mounted plum pudding mahogany dwarf open bookcase of Louis XVI style, on toupie feet, stamped Krieger, third quarter, 19th century, 22in. wide. (Christie's) $2,230

BOOKCASES

A Victorian walnut and marquetry bookcase inlaid throughout with boxwood lines and foliate arabesques, on a plinth base, 48½in. wide. (Bearne's) $3,717

An early George III mahogany breakfront bookcase, attributed to Thomas Chippendale, of double breakfront outline, 149½in. wide. (Christie's) $104,060

A George III mahogany double-sided dwarf open bookcase, on plinth base, 30in. wide. (Christie's) $5,142

Early 19th century mahogany bookcase with astragal glazed upper section and panel cupboard doors. (British Antique Exporters) $1,925

A George III mahogany breakfront bookcase with dentilled cornice surmounted by an arched central pediment, 172in. wide. (Christie's) $34,969

A William IV rosewood bookcase with molded cornice above a pair of panelled cupboards, doors filled with leather bookspines, 34½in. wide. (Christie's) $4,114

A late 19th century mahogany breakfront bookcase, the fitted adjustable shelves enclosed by four panel doors, 8ft.6in. high. (Anderson & Garland) $2,508

An Edwardian satinwood revolving bookcase, on stand with cabriole legs and platform stretcher, 46cm. (Phillips) $2,992

A fine George III period mahogany breakfront library bookcase having a central drawer fitted with a lined adjustable writing surface and stationery compartments, 7ft.3in. wide. (Geering & Colyer) $34,222

BOOKCASES

A George III mahogany book-case with molded dentilled gothic arcaded cornice above a pair of geometrically glazed cupboard doors, 65in. wide, 92in. high. (Christie's) $5,420

A late 19th century 12ft. wide breakfront bookcase, enclosed by six glazed panel doors with pilaster supports. (Anderson & Garland) $7,958

A George III mahogany standing bookcase, the apexed molded cresting above graduating open rectangular shelves. (Christie's) $1,925

A figured mahogany bookcase, the top section with a molded cornice above two glazed panelled doors, on bracket feet, 48in., 19th century. (Christie's) $3,080

A late Victorian carved oak library bookcase with brass drop handles, fielded panel-led doors and plinth base, 130in. wide. (Dacre, Son & Hartley) $2,405

A small Federal carved cherry glazed bookcase on chest, probably Connecticut, circa 1800, the upper case with mold-ed and dentilled broken pedi-ment, 32½in. wide. (Robt. W. Skinner Inc.) $45,000

A late George III mahogany breakfront library bookcase of small size with an architec-tural pediment, 58½in. wide. (Lawrence Fine Arts) $20,449

A handsome George II carved mahogany breakfront book-case, with foliate carved broken architectural pediment above rectilinear glazed doors, 99in. wide. (Bonhams) $32,940

A mahogany breakfront book-case with molded cornice above four glazed panel doors each with a hinged fall panel below, 92in. wide, early 19th century. (Christie's) $7,946

BOOKCASES

A William IV golden mahogany small bookcase, the recessed upper part enclosed by a pair of glazed doors, 2ft.10½in. wide. (Tennants)$5,250

A Regency mahogany breakfront bookcase with stepped gothic arcaded cornice above two pairs of geometrically glazed doors, 91½in. wide. (Christie's) $13,464

One of a pair of Regency mahogany bookshelves, each with four stepped shelves, 26in. wide. (Christie's)
Two $10,648

A Victorian mahogany breakfront library bookcase, the dentilled cavetto molded cornice above four glazed lattice astragal doors, three central drawers and four inset panelled cupboard doors, on plinth base, 90in. (Christie's) $6,160

One of two early Victorian mahogany bookcases by Holland and Sons, each with triangular pediment, 92½in. high. (Bearne's)
Two $18,375

One of a pair of rosewood dwarf bookcases with rectangular tops, the friezes applied with gilt metal berried, foliate and flowerhead clasps, early 19th century, 36¼in. wide. (Christie's) Two $3,564

A burr walnut and gilt metal mounted dwarf bookcase, banded in tulipwood and inlaid with boxwood lines, 29in. (Christie's)$1,925

A Regency mahogany library bookcase, the top section with molded cornice above four, glazed doors. 95in. wide. (Christie's) $12,584

A mahogany bookcase cupboard with writing drawer, the molded cornice above two geometric reeded astragal doors, 19th century, 58in. wide. (Lawrence Fine Arts) $2,602

BUREAU BOOKCASES

A fine and rare carved rose-wood and satinwood Gothic Revival desk and bookcase, by J. and J. W. Meeks, New York, 1836-1850, 48½in. wide. (Christie's) $28,600

A Venetian early 18th century style painted lacca bureau cabinet, decorated with flower-sprays and foliate scrolls, on scroll feet, 30in. (Christie's) $4,235

A George III mahogany bureau bookcase with a pair of geometrically glazed cupboard doors, the sloping flap enclosing a fitted interior, on bracket feet, 48in. wide. (Christie's) $6,171

A Georgian mahogany bureau bookcase with a molded and dentil cornice above two bevelled mirror doors, 42in. wide. (Lawrence Fine Arts) $5,948

An early George III mahogany bureau cupboard in three sections, inlaid with stringing and above four long graduated drawers, 42in. wide. (Lawrence Fine Arts) $8,547

An Edwardian mahogany inlaid bureau bookcase with two glazed doors, on bracket feet, 39in. wide. (Lawrence Fine Arts) $3,118

A George III mahogany bureau bookcase, with broken pediment and dentil molded cornice above a blind fret carved frieze, on ogee bracket feet, 47in. (Christie's) $5,775

A German stained birch bureau cabinet, with hinged slope above a concave kneehole, on bracket feet, mid 18th century, 44in. wide. (Christie's) $16,280

A George II mahogany bookcase with associated bureau, the swan neck pediment terminating in carved rosettes, 242 x 109cm. (Phillips) $7,480

BUREAU BOOKCASES

A George III mahogany bureau bookcase with quarter veneered and inlaid fall front, fully fitted marquetry inlaid interior, 48in. wide. (Andrew Hartley) $5,340

A George II scarlet and gold lacquer bureau cabinet, possibly supplied by Giles Grendey, 40in. wide; 93in. high. (Christie's) $416,240

A George III mahogany bureau and associated bookcase with two thirteen-pane astragal glazed doors, on bracket feet, 40¼in. wide. (Bearne's) $1,783

A Victorian mahogany bureau bookcase, the cylinder enclosing sliding writing surface and fitted interior, 230cm. (Osmond Tricks) $1,900

A fine George II mahogany and brass inlaid bureau bookcase in the manner of John Channon the upper part with a broken pediment and a dentil cornice, on ogee bracket feet, 4ft.9in. wide. (Phillips) $21,600

An early George II walnut bureau bookcase, the upper section with cavetto cornice above a pair of mirrored doors and candle slides, 40in. wide. (Bonhams) $10,248

An early 19th century inlaid mahogany bureau bookcase with molded dentil carved top, astragal glazed doors and ogee bracket feet, 48in. wide. (Dacre, Son & Hartley) $3,060

A George II mahogany bureau cabinet with cavetto cornice, two doors with fielded panels, on bracket feet, 38¼in. wide. (Bearne's) $3,062

A George I walnut bureau bookcase, with molded double domed cornice, on bun feet, the feet possibly replaced, 40½in. wide. (Christie's) $14,190

FURNITURE

BUREAUX

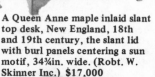

An ormolu mounted king-wood, tulipwood and marquetry bureau de dame of bombe outlines, on tapering cabriole legs, late 19th century 31½in. wide. (Christie's) $10,410

A Queen Anne maple inlaid slant top desk, New England, 18th and 19th century, the slant lid with burl panels centering a sun motif, 34¾in. wide. (Robt. W. Skinner Inc.) $17,000

A Louis XVI walnut cross-banded marquetry and parquetry bureau de dame, the sloping fall of shaped outline inlaid with flowers, 2ft.11½in. wide. (Phillips) $3,960

A George II walnut bureau inlaid overall with chevron bands, on a later undulating bracket base, 37½in. wide. (Christie's) $4,114

A Biedermeier figured maho-gany cylinder bureau, the stepped superstructure fitted with a cupboard and a pair of drawers, on bracket feet, 43in. wide. (Bonhams) $2,960

A George III mahogany bureau, with a fitted interior and four long drawers, on later ogee bracket feet, restored, 41½in. (Lawrence Fine Arts) $2,035

A Country Chippendale cherry slant front desk, probably Charlestown, New Hampshire, 1760-1780, 36in. wide. (Robt. W. Skinner Inc.) $22,000

A French mahogany and Vernis Martin bureau a cylindre with rectangular red and white mottled marble top, above a cy-linder and slide painted with romantic figures, 35½in. wide. (Christie's) $2,230

A Chippendale mahogany slant front desk, Massachusetts, circa 1780, with shaped bracket feet and remnants of central drop, 40in. wide. (Robt. W. Skinner Inc.) $12,000

BUREAUX

A painted Country birch slant top desk, probably Western Massachusetts, circa 1780, the fall front reveals a stepped interior of valanced compartments, 38in. wide. (Robt. W. Skinner Inc.) $14,000

An Art Deco plastic veneered lady's bureau, the drop front enclosing compartments with single drawer below, 64cm. across. (Phillips)
$1,408

A Chippendale tiger maple slant lid desk, Rhode Island, circa 1780, the slant lid opens to reveal an interior of valanced compartments and small end-blocked drawers, 38in. wide. (Robt. W. Skinner Inc.) $17,000

An unusual George III mahogany and sycamore bureau, the leather lined shaped spreading fall-flap enclosing a fitted interior, 30in. wide. (Christie's)
$3,291

A fine Queen Anne tiger maple slant lid desk, Massachusetts, circa 1750, on scrolled cabriole legs ending in pad feet, 37½in. wide. (Robt. W. Skinner Inc.)
$53,000

A George II figured walnut bureau inlaid overall with chevron bands, on later bracket feet, 36in wide. (Christie's)
$7,199

A Chippendale tiger maple desk, New England, circa 1780, the thumb-molded fall front opens to an interior of small drawers and valanced compartments, 38¾in. wide. (Robt. W. Skinner Inc.) $7,000

A Scandinavian burr walnut, kingwood and marquetry bureau, third quarter 18th century, 32in. wide. (Christie's)
$10,406

A walnut veneered bureau crossbanded and inlaid with feather stringing throughout, on bracket feet, 40in. wide. (Bearne's) $3,520

BUREAUX

A George II oak bureau, the crossbanded sloping flap enclosing a fitted interior, on bracket feet, 28½in. wide. (Christie's) $2,879

A fine Chippendale carved mahogany block-front desk, Boston, 1760-1780, the case with four graduated and blocked long drawers, 43in. wide. (Christie's) $71,500

A 19th century chinoiserie laquered bureau, in the 18th century manner, the top and fall-front decorated with a Chinese riverscape, 92cm. (Phillips) $2,337

A George II oak bureau of elegant small proportions having three long and two short graduated drawers, 36in. wide. (Morphets) $1,538

An 18th century Piedmontese walnut and ivory marquetry serpentine front bureau, decorated with rinceaux foliate scrolls, 3ft.6in. wide. (Phillips) $17,100

A George III mahogany bureau, crossbanded and inlaid with stringing and with a satinwood faced interior of unusual design, 40in. (Lawrence Fine Arts) $5,494

A George III mahogany bureau, the fall front revealing a fitted interior, on bracket feet, 36in. wide. (Morphets) $3,801

An 18th century Dutch walnut and marquetry bombe front bureau profusely inlaid in a design of flowers, scrolls, urns and cockatoos, 40in. wide. (Morphets) $7,783

A Georgian oak bureau with fitted interior enclosed by flap and above four long graduated drawers, 36in. (Lawrence Fine Arts) $2,645

BUREAUX

A George I walnut veneered bureau outlined with feather stringing and crossbanding, on bracket feet, 34½in. wide. (Bearne's) $2,992

A Louis XV Provincial bureau en pente, mid 18th century, with two short drawers over a long drawer, on cabriole legs, 39in. high. (Robt. W. Skinner Inc.) $4,000

A George II figured walnut bureau with sloping flap inlaid with boxwood and ebonised lines, 34¼in. wide. (Christie's) $9,256

A George III mahogany bureau with sloping flap enclosing a cupboard, drawers and pigeon holes, on bracket feet, 37in. wide. (Bearne's) $2,832

A George I walnut bureau with hinged top enclosing an interior fitted with drawers and pigeon-holes, on shaped bracket feet, 37in. wide. (Christie's) $16,082

An early 18th century oak bureau in two sections, applied throughout with double-ovolo carcase moldings, 35½in. wide. (Bearne s) $3,363

A 19th century Dutch mahogany and marquetry bombe bureau in two parts, on ogee bracket feet, 37¾in. wide. (Dreweatt Neate) $10,208

A George III mahogany bureau with rectangular sloping flap enclosing a fitted interior, shaped bracket feet, 26in. wide. (Christie's) $3,085

A George I walnut, cross-banded and featherstrung bureau of small size, on bracket feet, 2ft.10in. wide. (Phillips) $8,640

CABINETS

A late George III dwarf mahogany side cabinet of breakfront D shape with one fielded panel door, 40½in. wide. (Lawrence Fine Arts) $4,833

A mid 19th century Italian ebony side cabinet, with well executed bone inlays of arabesques and vases of flowers, 96cm. (Phillips) $1,122

A 19th century 3ft. walnut cabinet with foliated scroll inlay and ormolu shell and foliated mounts, 3ft.3in. high. (Anderson & Garland) $1,072

A Gordon Russell walnut side cabinet, with open top shelf above a panelled door enclosing shelves, 76cm. high. (Phillips) $633

A William IV rosewood breakfront side cabinet with mottled white marble slab, on plinth base, 84½in. wide. (Christie's) $2,879

A fine Aesthetic Movement ebony and lacquer cabinet, set with lacquered rosewood panels of Japanese landscapes with parquetry borders, stamped Gregory & Co. 212 & 214, Regent St., London 944, 202cm. high. (Christie's) $3,179

A William and Mary walnut, crossbanded and oyster veneered cabinet on stand, crossbanded in acacia, terminating in bun feet, 5ft. 2in. wide. (Phillips) $19,800

A late 17th century Anglo-Dutch walnut, rosewood banded and inlaid cabinet on stand, with two drawers enclosed by a pair of panel doors with oval panels with vases of flowers, on spirally turned supports, 5ft.9in. wide. (Phillips) $12,600

A Gustav Stickley work cabinet, circa 1905-7, with two cabinet doors over two drawers with square wooden pulls, 36in. high. (Robt. W. Skinner Inc.) $14,000

CABINETS

An Austrian Secessionist black lacquer and pewter inlaid cabinet, the shaped rectangular top above bowed and glazed cupboard door enclosing red stained interior, 161.6cm. wide. (Christie's) $9,350

A Flemish tortoiseshell and ebony cabinet veneered in geometric design, 18th century, on a mahogany stand with one drawer, the cabinet 17in. wide. (Lawrence Fine Arts)
$1,208

A Regency parcel gilt and simulated rosewood breakfront side cabinet, on bun feet, 49in. wide. (Christie's) $6,582

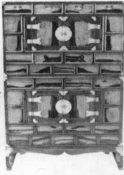

An Austrian neo-Classical mahogany and satinwood cabinet, circa 1830, on a molded base with bracket feet, 50½in. wide. (Robt. W. Skinner Inc.)
$2,900

A late 17th century Continental ebony, ivory and tortoiseshell table cabinet, on base with single long drawer, height 45cm. (Phillips)
$4,862

A Korean paulownia wood tansu, 19th century, on bracket feet, brass mounts, (piece missing) 50½in. high. (Robt. W. Skinner Inc.) $700

One of a pair of Regency ormolu mounted mahogany sidecabinets, each with D-shaped top mounted with ormolu pierced roundel gallery, 41in. wide. (Christie's)
Two $22,704

A J. P. White oak inlaid dwarf cabinet designed by M. H. Baillie-Scott, the rectangular top above open recess with pierced sides and a cupboard door, 50.8cm. wide. (Christie's)
$4,114

A Victorian ebonised and porcelain mounted side cabinet, applied throughout with gilt brass moldings,   59½in. wide. (Bearne's) $1,492

CABINETS

An Italian baroque walnut
credenza, mid 18th century,
the serpentine crossbanded
top over a pair of similar
drawers, on bun feet, 52in.
long. (Robt. W. Skinner Inc.)
$8,200

An Art Nouveau stained wood
cabinet carved with tulips and
ducks, 4ft.8in. high. (Anderson
& Garland) $813

A George III carved maho-
gany collector's cabinet,
fitted with twenty-six drawers, 3ft. x 1ft.8in. (Phillips)
$990

A Victorian amboyna D-shape
side cabinet with rounded glass
door sides flanking a central
panel door, 57in. wide.
(Lawrence Fine Arts)
$3,866

A fine 18th century Vigiza-
patan padouk and ivory
inlaid collector's cabinet
with engraved foliate borders, 57cm. wide. (Phillips)
$21,600

A Japanese hardwood cabinet,
19th century, on block legs,
mounted with engraved brass
plaques and paktong lock,
40in. high. (Robt. W. Skinner
Inc.) $2,250

A Regency mahogany side
cabinet with a frieze drawer and
pair of panelled doors filled with
gilt trellis, 25in. wide.
(Christie's) $4,114

A Regency rosewood serpentine side cabinet with brass
acanthus leaf borders to the
top and base, 51in. wide.
(Lawrence Fine Arts)
$4,070

One of a pair of 19th century
red tortoiseshell boulle side
cabinets, the whole with gilt
metal mounts, 87cm.
(Phillips)
Two $2,618

CABINETS

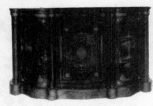

A fine Victorian serpentine fronted figured walnut credenza with burr walnut and string work border, 3ft.7in. high. (Anderson & Garland) $5,709

A rosewood side cabinet, the rectangular verde antico marble top with inverted front, on plinth base, 71¾in. wide. (Christie's) $6,582

A South German baroque walnut table cabinet, with shaped scrolled crest over central crossbanded drawer, on turned feet, 39¼in. wide. (Robt. W. Skinner Inc.) $850

A Charles II black and gilt lacquer cabinet on silvered stand, with chased lacquered brass lockplate and hinges, 42in. wide. (Christie's) $30,272

A large oak buffet designed by M. H. Baillie-Scott, the shaped rectangular top above shaped superstructure with beaten repousse copper panel, with three adjustable candle holders and small shelf flanked by two shaped cupboards, 327.9cm. wide. (Christie's) $5,984

A Queen Anne walnut veneered cabinet on chest outlined throughout with feather banding, 66½in. high by 46½in. wide. (Bearne's) $9,735

A Rowley walnut and marquetry cabinet and stand, the design attributed to Frank Brangwyn, with two marquetry panels inlaid in various fruitwoods with toiling farm labourers, 85.1cm. wide. (Christie's) $1,309

An Italian Renaissance style walnut cabinet on stand, on a scroll cut trestle base, 49½in. high. (Robt. W. Skinner Inc.) $600

A William and Mary walnut and marquetry cabinet, the two front doors inlaid with oval panels, 42in. wide. (Lawrence Fine Arts) $3,014

CANTERBURYS

A Regency mahogany canterbury, the rectangular top with slatted divides, 17¾in. wide. (Christie's) $4,114

A William IV rosewood canterbury with four bowed compartments and ring turned supports above a shallow drawer, 20in. wide. (Bonhams) $1,830

A Victorian walnut music canterbury with foliate scroll pierced divisions joined by turned grips, 22in. wide. (Lawrence Fine Arts) $1,557

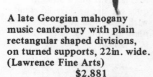

A George III period mahogany three division canterbury, having inverted baluster legs with brass caps and castors, 20¾in. wide. (Geering & Colyer) $2,173

A Regency mahogany canterbury with four compartments with dividers of column profile above a drawer, on ring turned feet, 21in. wide. (Christie's) $3,097

A late Georgian mahogany music canterbury with plain rectangular shaped divisions, on turned supports, 22in. wide. (Lawrence Fine Arts) $2,881

A Regency mahogany canterbury, with four divisions above one frieze drawer on ring turned tapering legs, 19in. wide. (Christie's) $5,142

A William IV mahogany canterbury with X-shaped dividers each side carved with a wreath of flowers, 20in. wide. (Christie's) $2,710

A mid Victorian carved rosewood four section canterbury with pierced leaf carved divisions, 20½in. wide. (Dacre, Son & Hartley) $1,248

FURNITURE

DINING CHAIRS

One of a pair of early 19th century mahogany framed bar back chairs with Trafalgar seats. (British Antique Exporters) Two $175

A pair of George II mahogany Ribband Back side chairs, after a design by Thomas Chippendale, on foliate cabriole legs. (Christie's) $141,900

Early 19th century mahogany framed bar back side chair with tapestry upholstered drop-in seat. (British Antique Exporters) $61

A William and Mary maple side chair, Boston, Massachusetts, circa 1710, the carved, molded crest rail over molded square stiles, 45½in. high. (Robt. W. Skinner Inc.) $11,000

One of a set of five Dutch elm dining chairs and an armchair of similar design, late 19th century and later. (Christie's) Six $3,080

One of a set of four late Victorian mahogany framed dining chairs with shaped front supports. (British Antique Exporters) Four $525

One of a set of six good mahogany William IV dining chairs, with turned and fluted legs. (David Lay) Six $1,810

Two of a set of six mahogany and parcel gilt side chairs in the manner of Robert Manwaring, on cabriole legs carved with cabochons. (Christie's) Six $302,720

One of a set of four mahogany-framed turned leg dining chairs with tapestry upholstery. (British Antique Exporters) $438

DINING CHAIRS

One of a set of six Victorian mahogany drawing room chairs, with elegant foliate carved cameo backs and on cabriole knopped legs. (Morphets)

Six $3,439

Two of a set of eight Victorian mahogany dining chairs, including two with arms, with solid curved cresting rails. (Lawrence Fine Arts)

Eight $3,459

A Federal mahogany carved side chair, New York, circa 1800, the square, beaded stepped crest rail above a plume and drape carved splat. (Robt. W. Skinner Inc.) $750

One of a set of six late Victorian painted satinwood side chairs, with bowed padded seats and turned tapering legs. (Christie's)

Six $4,319

Two of a set of eight brass inlaid mahogany dining chairs, including two with arms, each with a solid cresting rail above rope twist bar, lift-off seat and sabre supports inlaid with brass lines, seven Regency period and one later. (Lawrence Fine Arts) Eight $7,484

One of a set of four mahogany dining chairs in the Queen Anne style with cabriole front supports and pad feet. (Lawrence Fine Arts)

Four $790

One of a set of ten mahogany ladder back dining chairs, with cabriole front supports with pad feet. (Lawrence Fine Arts)

Ten $3,256

Two of a set of eight mahogany dining chairs of George III design, stamped HOLLAND & SONS, circa 1870's. (Christie's)

Eight $6,171

One of a set of six early Victorian mahogany chairs, the broad toprails above plain horizontal splats, circa 1840. (Bonhams)

Six $1,157

DINING CHAIRS

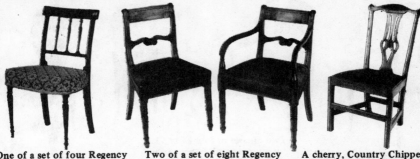

One of a set of four Regency mahogany dining chairs, on reeded turned tapering legs. (Christie's)
Four $1,234

Two of a set of eight Regency mahogany dining chairs, with ring turned tapering legs. (Christie's)
Eight $9,256

A cherry, Country Chippendale, upholstered side chair, Upper Connecticut River Valley, circa 1790, 38in. high. (Robt. W. Skinner Inc.) $475

One of a set of five Windsor yew-wood single wheelback chairs, early 19th century. (Lawrence Fine Arts)
Five $2,910

Two of a set of eight George III mahogany dining chairs, on square section tapering legs with intersecting stretchers. (Phillips)
Eight $6,358

One of a set of five mid Georgian mahogany dining chairs, on chamfered legs. (Christie's)
Five $1,645

A George II walnut side chair, the toprail carved with a shell and scrolling acanthus above a solid splat, on claw and ball feet, restored. (Bearne's)
     $743

Two of a good set of eleven Regency mahogany dining chairs, on turned legs and intersecting stretchers. (Phillips)
Eleven $9,911

One of a set of six Victorian rosewood dining chairs, with shaped waisted backs, raised on turned supports. (Osmond Tricks)
Six $1,520

DINING CHAIRS

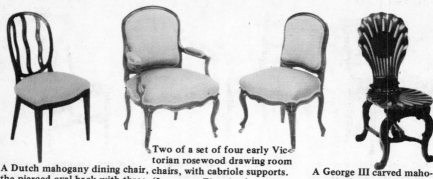

A Dutch mahogany dining chair, the pierced oval back with three waved splats, late 18th century. (Christie's) $284

Two of a set of four early Victorian rosewood drawing room chairs, with cabriole supports. (Lawrence Fine Arts)
Four $4,647

A George III carved mahogany hall chair of grotto design with pierced shell shaped back and solid seat. (Phillips) $9,900

One of a set of six J. Walden oak painted side chairs, the design attributed to William Burgess, on tapering legs joined by plain stretchers, with black and red painted bands. (Christie's)
Six $935

Two of a set of ten early Victorian oak dining chairs and a pair of early Victorian oak bergeres en suite, with leather upholstered drop-in seats on panelled legs. (Christie's) Twelve
$10,285

One of a pair of George I scarlet japanned chairs, each with a shaped splat decorated with a Chinese figure. (Christie's)
Two $34,056

A Louis XV beechwood chair with cartouche shaped padded back and serpentine seat, formerly caned. (Christie's)
$611

A pair of Regency giltmetal mounted ebonized chairs, each with a deep U-shaped top rail. (Christie's) $3,702

One of a set of five George III dining chairs, each with a pierced arched ladderback. (Christie's)
Five $3,188

DINING CHAIRS

One of a set of six Victorian rosewood dining chairs with drop-in seats and on lotus carved baluster legs. (Bearne's)
Six $1,783

A Federal mahogany carved upholstered side and armchair, probably New York, 1800-1810, square backed with a rectangular carved tablet. (Robt. W. Skinner Inc.) $800

One of a set of six Victorian walnut dining chairs with balloon backs, on molded cabriole legs. (Bearne's)
Six $1,820

One of a set of six mahogany 19th century Queen Anne style dining chairs with fiddle pattern back splats. (County Group)
Six $374

One of a set of five Dutch mahogany and floral marquetry dining chairs, on sabre legs, early 19th century, and a similar open armchair, (Christie's)
Six $5,291

An early Scandinavian painted single chair with wide bar back painted with name and date. (Greenslades)
$483

An Adirondack hickory chair, probably New York, early 20th century, stick construction with six spindles in back and twelve in seat. (Robt. W. Skinner Inc.)
$400

Two of a set of eight mahogany dining chairs on foliate cabriole legs and scrolling feet. (Christie's)
Eight $22,704

A fine carved walnut hall chair, the back scroll and guilloche carved with central satyr mask. (Hobbs and Chambers)
$202

DINING CHAIRS

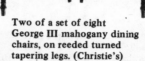

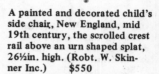

One of a set of six Queen Anne gilt gesso dining chairs, the tall arched backs and shaped baluster splats carved in low relief with flowersprays. (Christie's) Six $18,920

Two of a set of eight George III mahogany dining chairs, on reeded turned tapering legs. (Christie's) Eight $15,427

A painted and decorated child's side chair, New England, mid 19th century, the scrolled crest rail above an urn shaped splat, 26½in. high. (Robt. W. Skinner Inc.) $550

An oak side chair by A. W. N. Pugin, the carved and pierced backrests with gothic tracery, the square solid seat on rounded X-shaped trestle ends with stylized paw feet. (Christie's) $11,220

A set of six oak side chairs and two armchairs, the design attributed to Alfred Waterhouse, the rectangular backs with carved frieze of stylized flowers, on brass castors. (Christie's) Eight $2,992

One of a set of four Regency brass inlaid rosewood dining chairs, on sabre legs. (Christie's) Four $3,496

One of a set of six Regency mahogany dining chairs, the anthemion splats on arched scrolling supports. (Bearne's) Six $7,040

Two of a set of eight mahogany dining chairs, in the Chippendale style, with ball and claw feet. (Lawrence Fine Arts) Eight $4,158

A George III mahogany dining chair, the pierced splat with a roundel, on chamfered square legs. (Christie's) $1,131

DINING CHAIRS

One of a set of six Regency brass inlaid mahogany dining chairs, on ring turned tapering legs. (Christie's)
Six $5,348

One of a set of six George III mahogany dining chairs, each with rectangular railed back and padded seat and one of a pair of George III mahogany open armchairs (same lot), on square tapering legs, one with later arms and blocks. (Christie's) Eight $6,171

One of a set of six early Victorian mahogany dining chairs on turned and lobed front supports. (Lawrence Fine Arts)
Six $2,442

One of a pair of Wylie and Lockhead beech chairs, possibly designed by E.A. Taylor, tapering supports united by stretchers. (Phillips)
Two $299

Two of a good set of ten Regency mahogany and ebony inlaid dining chairs in the manner of Thomas Hope, on sabre legs. (Phillips)
Ten $49,680

A Chippendale walnut side chair, America, probably Southern 1760-1790, the serpentine crest rail with molded raked terminals. (Robt. W. Skinner Inc.)
$900

One of a set of six Victorian mahogany dining chairs, the rectangular backs with turned toprails. (Bearne's)
Six $1,443

Two of a fine set of eight Chippendale period carved mahogany dining chairs in the Director taste, on cabriole legs. (Phillips)
Eight $97,200

One of a set of four Georgian mahogany dining chairs in the Chippendale style, with C scroll brackets, restored. (Lawrence Fine Arts)
Four $1,767

EASY CHAIRS

One of a pair of Anglo-Indian satinwood bergeres, on short cabriole legs, mid 19th century. (Christie's)
Two $6,582

A Regency simulated rosewood bergere armchair with padded U-shaped seat on turned and reeded legs. (Hy. Duke & Son) $1,521

One of a pair of giltwood bergeres of Empire style, each with a rectangular padded back, sides and squab, on square tapering panelled legs. (Christie's)
Two $5,948

A George II wing armchair with high shaped back, on front cabriole legs carved with shells and leafage, 44in. high. (Lawrence Fine Arts) $8,954

A Herman Miller laminated rosewood lounge chair designed by Charles Eames, upholstered in black hide, on swivel, five-pronged, aluminium base. (Christie's) $1,402

An early Victorian mahogany armchair, the spoon-shaped padded back, sides and squab covered in green leather, (Christie's) $2,788

A George III mahogany bergere, the arched padded back, arms and serpentine seat covered in close-nailed brown suede. (Christie's) $2,057

A George IV rosewood library armchair with scrolled buttoned olive green leather back and seat, on arched legs. (Christie's) $3,908

A mahogany bergere with rectangular caned back and seat in a channelled frame, late 19th century. (Christie's) $925

EASY CHAIRS

One of a set of four William IV mahogany tub chairs, on turned tapering legs. (Christie's)
Four $12,342

A George III mahogany open armchair with rectangular padded back and seat. (Christie's) $7,816

A George IV mahogany desk chair with horseshoe shaped padded back. (Christie's)
$3,291

An adjustable gothic oak armchair, designed by Charles Bevan, with upholstered back and seat with crossed sides. (Phillips) $1,091

A Regency cream and green painted bergere, on turned tapering front, and sabre back legs. (Christie's)
$13,370

A George I walnut framed wing armchair upholstered in lozenge pattern needlework, on lappet-headed cabriole legs. (Bearne's)
$29,920

One of a pair of mahogany open armchairs, upholstered in patterned repp, with spade feet, later blocks. (Christie's)
Two $3,702

A Morris & Co. oak armchair to a design by Philip Webb, with horizontal spindles and arms supported by turned beaded spindles. (Phillips)
$2,408

A small Art Deco gilt and upholstered salon chair attributed to Jules Leleu, the curved back and arm rests upholstered in beige fabric. (Christie's)
$2,618

EASY CHAIRS

One of a set of six oak side chairs and two armchairs, attributed to Alfred Waterhouse, the rectangular backs with carved frieze of stylized flowers. (Christie's)
Eight $2,991

George I walnut frame wing easy chair with floral pattern upholstery and loose cushion. (Hobbs & Chambers)
$3,740

One of a pair of Chippendale mahogany upholstered armchairs, Charlestown, New Hampshire, circa 1795, attributed to Bliss and Horswill. (Robt. W. Skinner Inc.)
Two $28,000

A William and Mary walnut wing armchair with high arched padded back, on later baluster legs. (Christie's)
$1,028

A Victorian walnut framed open armchair upholstered in maroon velour, and a matching nursing chair. (Bearne's) $1,419

An unusual giltwood fauteuil with winged lion monopodia, early 19th century, possibly Scandinavian. (Christie's)
$4,477

A mid 18th century giltwood framed armchair, (without upholstery), with hairy lions paw feet. (Phillips)
$1,776

A Louis XV walnut fauteuil, the cartouche shaped padded back and bowed seat upholstered in floral tapestry. (Christie's) $3,256

A George III mahogany open armchair, on molded square legs joined by stretchers. (Christie's) $2,468

EASY CHAIRS

A rare William IV reclining mahogany chair with upholstered buttoned back, with maker's stamp "R. Daws Patent". (David Lay) $1,183

A Victorian mahogany framed armchair on cabriole leg supports. (Greenslades) $726

A cream painted and parcel gilt bergere, with cartouche shaped padded back, on channelled cabriole legs. (Christie's) $6,105

Early Victorian nursing chair in carved mahogany show wood, on scroll and claw feet. (County Group) $523

A Victorian walnut framed armchair, the oval buttoned back surmounted by foliage, and a matching nursing chair. (Bearne's) $4,071

A George III style mahogany framed open armchair with reeded underframe and on leaf carved tapering reeded legs. (Bearne's) $1,274

An unusual Maltese rosewood and olivewood open armchair, the frame edged with checkered lines, on square tapering legs. (Christie's) $8,140

A scarce good quality Victorian folding mahogany campaign chair, upholstered in original black leatherette. (Wallis & Wallis) $2,162

Victorian carved walnut framed library chair, upholstered in old gold velour. (British Antique Exporters) $350

FURNITURE

EASY CHAIRS

An early George III mahogany elbow chair, the mahogany frame carved with blind fret. (Lawrence Fine Arts) $10,582

A Queen Anne walnut and maple easy chair, probably Massachusetts, circa 1760, on cabriole legs ending in pad feet. (Robt. W. Skinner Inc.) $42,000

A George III giltwood open armchair with padded drop-in back and seat. (Christie's) $863

L. & J. G. Stickley fixed back armchair, circa 1912, with up-holstered spring cushion seat with back cushion, unsigned, 32in. high. (Robt. W. Skinner Inc.) $4,750

A Gustav Stickley willow armchair, circa 1910, the tall back with square cut-outs centered by flat arms, unsigned, 42¾in. high. (Robt. W. Skinner Inc.) $3,500

A Regency mahogany bergere with padded rectangular back, sides and cushion, on turned tapering baluster legs. (Christie's) $1,851

A George III mahogany library armchair, with plain square chamfered legs joined by stretchers. (Christie's) $4,525

One of two George III mahogany open armchairs, each with an arched cartouche shaped padded back, on cabriole legs. (Christie's)
Two $141,900

A directoire style green painted and partial gilt bergere, 19th century, raised on fluted tapering legs, 32in. high. (Robt. W. Skinner Inc.) $1,200

EASY CHAIRS

A Regency carved mahogany library bergere, having a stuff-over seat, on ring turned tapered legs. (Phillips)
$5,040

A walnut and oak wing arm-chair, lacking all upholstery, on cabriole legs, early 18th century and later. (Christie's)
$2,262

One of a pair of George III tub chairs upholstered in brown hide and on tapering square mahogany legs. (Bearne's)
Two $2,024

American 19th century style spoon back armchair, on squat cabriole legs and scrol-led feet, upholstered in red and ivory fabric. (County Group) $561

One of a pair of Howard easy armchairs, each with an over-stuffed back, on square tapered legs, stamped and labelled Howard. (Christie's)
Two $3,657

Victorian carved mahogany hoopback drawing room chair, on scroll supports, scroll feet and castors. (Hobbs and Chambers)
$642

A Regency mahogany bergere, the reeded arm supports and seat-rail on turned tapering legs. (Christie's)
$1,234

One of a pair of Italian perspex and chromium plated tubular steel chairs, designed by Harvey Guzzini, with original label. (Christie's)
Two $561

One of a pair of George III gilt-wood open armchairs, on panel-led tapering legs carved with guilloches and fluted feet, 27in. wide. (Christie's)
Two $56,760

ELBOW CHAIRS

A Classical mahogany armchair, New York, circa 1822-1825, down-scrolled arms above a trapezoidal seat, 37in. high. (Christie's) $6,050

One of a composite set of five Windsor yew-wood elbow chairs, with crinoline stretchers, 19th century. (Lawrence Fine Arts)
Five $8,316

A Victorian child's elbow chair with seat and backrest upholstered in original petit point floral pattern tapestry. (Greenslades)
$735

A Charles I oak armchair, the plain rectangular panelled back with an arched cresting, on baluster supports, mid 17th century, 45in. high. (Lawrence Fine Arts) $1,208

One of a set of six Macassar ebony Art Deco armchairs, attributed to Paul Kiss, upholstered in brown hide. (Christie's)
Six $10,224

A George III carved mahogany elbow chair, the back with undulating toprail and pierced interlaced splat, on square legs united by stretchers. (Phillips) $3,600

A Lancashire mahogany spindle back armchair with slightly bowed arms, on square legs, circa 1790. (Bonhams) $647

A Regency mahogany metamorphic library chair, opening to form library steps with four treads. (Christie's)
$20,812

A Dutch marquetry elbow chair, with shaped arms, serpentine front lift-off seat and cabriole legs. (Lawrence Fine Arts) $650

ELBOW CHAIRS

A French Empire miniature mahogany elbow chair, the concave back with pierced interlaced splat, 42cm. high. (Phillips) $720

A George III mahogany open armchair with pierced foliate shield shaped back, on square tapering legs. (Christie's) $5,348

A walnut open armchair with flat spirally twisted arms supported on female busts, third quarter of the 17th century. (Christie's) $5,698

A George III mahogany elbow chair, the back formed of Chinese lattice-work with undulating top-rail. (Phillips) $2,700

One of a pair of laminated birch-wood open armchairs designed by Gerald Summers, with central splat and curvilinear arm-rests. (Christie's) Two $24,167

An Egyptian hardwood X - framed armchair inlaid throughout in ivory with geometric motifs. (Bearne's) $655

A George III carved mahogany elbow chair, the cartouche shaped back with paterae decorated pierced vase splats. (Phillips) $4,140

Chippendale birch high chair, probably Massachusetts, circa 1780, the shaped crest rail above vase splat, 36½in. high. (Robt. W. Skinner Inc.) $2,900

A good Regency mahogany library chair, the bulbous upholstered seat, on turned front supports with brass castors. (Phillips) $8,415

One of a pair of George IV mahogany elbow chairs with lift-out seats and plain front sabre supports. (Lawrence Fine Arts)
Two $2,645

One of a pair of Victorian rosewood elbow chairs, on X-shaped underframes and stretchers. (Lawrence Fine Arts)   Two $1,017

A William IV mahogany library chair, the curved paper scroll back with upholstered panel and drop-in seat. (Phillips) $1,402

A William and Mary painted banister back armchair, probably Massachusetts, circa 1750, the cut out splat above five split banister spindles, 46in. high. (Robt. W. Skinner Inc.)
$1,500

One of a pair of George II black and gold lacquer open armchairs by William and John Linnell, with black and gold Chinese paling, 40¾in. high. (Christie's)
Two $189,200

A George I walnut open armchair with vase shaped splat and shaped scroll ended arms. (Christie's) $17,028

A Windsor yew-wood elbow chair, the hooped back with three splats, reduced in height. (Lawrence Fine Arts)
$1,351

An Anglo-Indian mahogany elbow chair of X shape, with curved cane panel back and seat, 19th century. (Lawrence Fine Arts) $976

A George I figured walnut open armchair, on X-shaped cabriole front legs and pad feet. (Christie's)
$24,596

ELBOW CHAIRS

A Regency mahogany open armchair, with pierced trellis pattern back with reeded uprights, on reeded tapering legs, 22½in. wide, 35in. high. (Christie's)
$9,460

A brass-mounted mahogany hall chair of Regency style, the solid seat on sabre legs, with registry mark for 1883, 22in. wide. (Christie's) $2,468

A Gimson design yew-wood adjustable ladder back open arm chair, with shaped cross-rails. (Hobbs & Chambers)
$941

A yew-wood and elm, low comb back armchair, with shaped seat, on turned legs tied by bowed stretcher, late 18th century. (Bonhams)
$1,295

An important oak lath armchair designed by Marcel Breuer for the Bauhaus, Weimar, 1924, constructed from vertical and horizontal strips of stained oak, 94.8cm. high. (Christie's)
$48,620

One of a pair of Regency rosewood open armchairs, on ring turned and ribbed tapering legs. (Christie's)
Two $6,171

A George I walnut writing elbow chair with solid cartouche shaped back with paper scroll cresting, on cabriole legs. (Phillips)
$20,700

A Country Queen Anne transitional tiger maple armchair, New England, mid 18th century, the yoked crest above vasiform splat, 41¼in. high. (Robt. W. Skinner Inc.)
$4,500

A George III mahogany framed open armchair with oval padded back, on leaf headed tapering fluted legs. (Bearne's)
$1,380

ELBOW CHAIRS

A stained wood and embossed leather Art Nouveau chair, circular panelled seat with brass studs, on square legs joined by stretchers. (Christie's) $962

A pair of George III mahogany open armchairs, each with a shield shaped curved back with five reeded splats. (Christie's) $71,896

An early George III mahogany open armchair with a pierced interlaced splat. (Bearne's) $1,237

A Thonet bentwood rocking chair, the rounded rectangular back and seat with canework panels, on elaborate supports, stamped Thonet. (Christie's) $411

An Italian parcel gilt and painted rocking chair, the arms and rectangular seat on supports in the form of lions, late 19th century, labelled Countess of North Brook. (Christie's) $3,465

An oak wainscot lambing armchair, the serpentine cresting and panelled back above a box seat, basically 17th century. (Christie's) $2,695

A painted bow back Windsor rocking chair, probably New England, circa 1830, the bowed crest rail above seven tapering incised spindles. (Robt. W. Skinner Inc.) $700

A pair of open armchairs, designed by Ernest Gimson, with shaped arms above turned legs and turned double stretchers. (Christie's) $1,487

A fine and rare black painted high chair, Delaware River Valley, 1730-1760, with four graduated and arched slats, on turned front feet, 38in. high. (Christie's) $6,050

ELBOW CHAIRS

A George III mahogany ladder back open armchair on square legs joined by stretchers. (Bearne's) $946

Two of a set of eight Regency mahogany dining chairs, including a pair of open armchairs, on turned tapering legs. (Christie's)
Eight $10,285

A Gimson design yew open arm rocking chair with straight top and crossrail, on platform supports. (Hobbs & Chambers) $1,049

An Empire mahogany fauteuil de bureau, the yoke shaped curved toprail with scrolling arm terminals. (Christie's) $2,849

A bentwood rocking chair, with rounded back and seat, on scrolling bentwood frame (slightly cracked). (Christie's) $748

Satinwood and painted open armchair in late 18th century style, on turned legs. (Prudential) $1,750

One of a pair of American hickory open armchairs, on simple turned legs, stamped 'Old Hickory, Artinsvill, Indiana'. (Bearne's)
Two $709

A pair of Russian, Alexander I open armchairs, with drop-in padded seats on scrolling tapering legs. (Christie's) $4,681

One of a set of eight Chippendale design ball and claw dining chairs having finely carved backs. (Michael G. Matthews)
Eight $2,745

CHESTS OF DRAWERS

A George III satinwood and mahogany bow-fronted chest, on later square tapering feet, 37½in. wide. (Christie's) $12,342

A Federal inlaid walnut tall chest of drawers, Pennsylvania, 1790-1810, on flared French feet, 43¾in. wide. (Christie's) $5,280

A Regency mahogany bow-fronted chest in the manner of Gillows, with molded eared top, 42in. wide. (Christie's) $3,702

Early 19th century bow front mahogany chest of drawers on slightly splayed feet. (British Antique Exporters) $481

A Victorian walnut Wellington chest fitted with seven graduated drawers flanked by acanthus carved corbels, 20½in. wide, circa 1870. (Bonhams) $1,157

1930's oak chest of four drawers with blind fret decoration and turned wooden knobs. (British Antique Exporters) $88

A 19th century mahogany bow-fronted chest of two short and two long drawers, on splay feet, 2ft.11in. wide. (Greenslades) $687

A George III mahogany gent's enclosed dressing and writing cabinet, on plinth base, 31in. wide. (Lawrence Fine Arts) $11,154

A George II mahogany chest of drawers, on ogee bracket feet, brass drop handles, 89cm. (Phillips) $3,085

CHESTS OF DRAWERS

A Federal cherry inlaid bureau, possibly Massachusetts, circa 1800, the rectangular top above cockbeaded case of four graduated drawers, 40in. wide. (Robt. W. Skinner Inc.) $2,800

A Classical Revival maple and birch carved bureau, circa 1820, the scrolled carved backboard above six cockbeaded small drawers, 42¾in. wide. (Robt. W. Skinner Inc.) $950

A 17th century oak Jacobean chest with panelled ends and three drawers with molded edges and brass furniture, on bun feet, 35in. wide. (Duncan Vincent) $1.275

A George III mahogany serpentine chest, fitted with a brushing slide, on bracket ·feet, 3ft.3½in. wide. (Phillips) $5,400

19th century mahogany chest of five drawers with pressed brass handles and bracket feet. (British Antique Exporters) $438

A Federal cherry inlaid bureau, New England, circa 1810, the rectangular top with bow front and on inlaid cut-out base, 40in. wide. (Robt. W. Skinner Inc.) $2,500

A George III mahogany bow-fronted chest of two short and three long drawers raised on splay bracket supports, 3ft. 7½in. (Greenslades) $1,050

A Georgian rectangular mahogany chest of four long graduated drawers with pierced brass escutcheons and loop handles, 3ft.1in.wide. (Greenslades) $2,044

A George III black lacquer chest decorated throughout in gilt and red with figures in landscapes, 45½in. wide. (Bearne's) $3,276

CHESTS OF DRAWERS

A burr elm bachelor's chest with
hinged rectangular top above
four graduated long drawers,
30in. wide. (Christie's)
$7,816

An Army and Navy oak military chest with inset brass
bindings and handles, on
turned feet, 45in. wide,
circa 1900. (Bonhams)
$1,459

A Betty Joel Art Deco burr walnut chest of drawers, with six
short drawers, on four short
fluted legs of rectangular-section,
71cm. wide. (Christie's)
$748

A Federal inlaid mahogany bow
front chest of drawers, New
England, 1790-1810, on flared
French feet, 42in. wide.
(Christie's) $2,640

A George II walnut chest of
two short and three long
drawers, on bracket feet, 38in.
wide. (Lawrence Fine Arts)
$4,477

A Federal inlaid cherrywood
bow-front chest of drawers,
Pennsylvania, 1800-1810,
on French feet, 40in. wide.
(Christie's) $8,800

A Regency mahogany chest
of drawers with a crossbanded
rectangular top, on short sabre
legs, 39in. wide. (Hy. Duke &
Son) $3,887

A Dutch marquetry chest of six
long drawers with canted angles,
19th century, 36½in. wide.
(Lawrence Fine Arts)
$2,494

A George III mahogany serpentine chest with molded top
above a slide, on splayed bracket
feet, 40in. wide. (Christie's)
$18,920

CHESTS OF DRAWERS

A Chippendale birch reverse serpentine chest of drawers, Massachusetts, circa 1780, on claw and ball feet, 41in. wide. (Robt. W. Skinner Inc.) $9,500

A George II oak bookpress on chest, the arched framework supporting a fruitwood screw-wind mechanism, 65in. high. (Bearne's) $2,212

A George II walnut chest with four graduated long drawers flanked by fluted angles, 32in. wide. (Christie's) $6,582

A mid-Charles II oak chest, the molded rectangular plank top above four graduated molded panelled long drawers, 37½in. wide. (Bonhams) $1,068

An Edwardian satinwood serpentine fronted collector's chest of ten graduated drawers, 17in. wide. (Greenslades) $875

Chippendale wavy birch bowfront chest of drawers, Massachusetts, circa 1780, the rectangular top with bow front and beaded edge, 35in. high. (Robt. W. Skinner Inc.) $11,000

A mid-Georgian burr elm and oak chest, the rectangular molded top above two short and three long drawers, 36¾in. wide. (Christie's) $1,748

A Federal tiger maple tall chest, Pennsylvania, circa 1810, the rectangular top with flaring cornice, 40in. wide. (Robt. W. Skinner Inc.) $3,750

Early 18th century oak chest of two short and three long drawers, on bracket feet, 3ft. 3¼in. wide. (Hobbs and Chambers) $642

CHESTS ON CHESTS

A Georgian oak chest on chest with a cavetto cornice, two plain quarter round pilasters, and ogee bracket feet, 39in. wide. (Lawrence Fine Arts) $2,974

A George III mahogany tallboy, with a key-pattern cavetto cornice, on bracket feet, 44in. wide. (Bearne's) $2,552

A George I walnut veneered tallboy crossbanded and outlined throughout with feather stringing, on bracket feet, 44in. wide. (Bearne's) $9,152

A George III mahogany chest on chest with three short drawers and three long drawers, 42in. wide. (Lawrence Fine Arts) $2,645

A good early George III mahogany chest on chest, the lower part with a slide above three long drawers, 42in. wide. (Lawrence Fine Arts) $5,577

An early George III secretaire tallboy, the base with a well-fitted secretaire drawer, on ogee bracket feet, 48in. wide. (Christie's) $39,732

A Georgian inlaid mahogany double chest of six long and two short drawers, 6ft.8in. high. (Anderson & Garland) $1,124

A George I walnut, feather banded and crossbanded tallboy chest, on bracket feet, 3ft.8in. wide. (Phillips) $19,800

A George I walnut veneered tallboy with a cavetto cornice, fluted canted corners, and on bracket feet, 45in. wide. (Bearne's) $5,632

CHESTS ON STANDS

A Queen Anne tiger maple high chest of drawers, Salem, Massachusetts, 1730-1760, the center fan carved above a scalloped skirt, 38¼in. wide. (Christie's) $27,500

An early 18th century walnut chest on stand, with baluster turned legs joined by curved stretchers, 104cm. wide. (Phillips) $5,236

A Japanese parquetry chest on 17th century style walnut stand, the two doors enclosing eight small drawers, 54¼in. high. (Bearne's) $1,593

A Flemish and ebonized cabinet on stand, the molded cornice above eight drawers each with pietra paesina marble panel, late 17th century, 46in. wide. (Christie's) $7,123

A mahogany chest on stand in the Chippendale manner with dentil cornice, on a later stand, 3ft,7in. wide. (Greenslades)

$706

A figured walnut foliate marquetry and penwork chest on stand, decorated throughout with flower swag panels, 40in. wide, late 17th century. (Christie's) $4,235

A Queen Anne oak chest on stand, with shaped apron and cabriole supports with scrolls at the knees, 36½in. wide. (Lawrence Fine Arts)
$5,087

A Queen Anne walnut and burr elm chest on stand, with molded cornice and convex frieze drawers, on later cabriole legs, 40in. wide. (Christie's)
$3,908

A Goanese ivory, ebony and hardwood cabinet on stand inlaid with interlaced geometric roundels, on stylized mermaid caryatids upon block and bun feet, 40in. wide. (Christie's)
$50,875

CHIFFONIERS

A William IV rosewood chiffonier, the front of unusual concave shape with a drawer above two cupboard doors, 44in. wide. (Lawrence Fine Arts) $1,424

A 19th century French coromandel wood chiffonier, the mirror upstand with gilt and pierced foliate frame, 196cm. wide. (Osmond Tricks) $1,267

A fine quality rosewood and inlaid chiffonier, the main bevelled mirror plate flanked by subsidiary arched mirrors and inlaid panels, circa 1890, 56in. wide. (Bonhams) $2,035

A George IV mahogany chiffonier, the raised back with shelf and C-scroll supports, 36in. wide. (Lawrence Fine Arts) $2,136

A cherrywood pie safe, possibly Tennessee, circa 1820, the rectangular top above a cabinet of single cockbeaded drawer and tin panels of decoratively pierced designs of urns, 50½in. wide. (Robt. W. Skinner Inc.) $3,500

A Regency rosewood chiffonier, with single shelf and pierced gilt metal gallery, above two open shelves, 43in. wide. (Christie's) $3,702

A Regency rosewood small chiffonier, the raised shelf with a pierced brass gallery, 33½in. wide. (Dreweatt Neate) $6,336

A Regency rosewood chiffonier inlaid with brass lines, with eared rectangular white marble top, on gadrooned feet, 45¾in. wide. (Christie's) $3,908

A Regency brass inlaid rosewood chiffonier, the frieze inlaid with foliate arabesques above a pair of gothic panelled doors, 27in. wide. (Christie's) $8,639

COMMODES & POT CUPBOARDS

A set of late Regency mahogany library commode steps, with two hinged treads and a lower tread, on turned tapered legs, 20in. (Christie's) $3,080

A George II mahogany corner commode chair with leather covered padded horseshoe toprail, on squat cabriole legs. (Bearne's) $1,026

One of a pair of mahogany cylindrical bedside step commodes each on a fluted support fitted with a single drawer, 16in., 19th century. (Christie's) Two $808

Late 19th century mahogany pot cupboard with carved and panelled door. (British Antique Exporters) $105

A George III gentleman's mahogany toilet commode with box top, fitted interior with mirror, 28in. wide. (Dacre, Son & Hartley) $1,942

An unusual George III pollard oak bedside cabinet with rectangular tray top, 21in. wide. (Christie's) $4,525

A Regency mahogany bedside cupboard with tray-top, the concave front with a tambour shutter, on square legs, 18in. wide. (Christie's) $1,839

A Victorian mahogany box seat armchair commode, enclosed by a hinged panelled lid, on turned bun feet, 24in. (Christie's) $539

A George III mahogany bedside cupboard with rectangular tray top, on shaped bracket feet, 24½in. wide. (Christie's) $2,262

A North Italian rococo walnut commode, mid 18th century, raised on cabriole legs with scroll feet (repairs), 50in. long. (Robt. W. Skinner Inc.) $5,100

A Louis XV/XVI style Vernis Martin commode, circa 1900, on cabriole legs with bronze sabots, 36½in. wide. (Robt. W. Skinner Inc.) $1,900

A George II mahogany commode of bombe outline, the cabriole angles and legs carved with rockwork and foliate scrolls, 50in. wide. (Christie's) $700,040

A George III mahogany commode in the manner of Thomas Chippendale with eared molded serpentine top, on bracket feet, 46in. wide. (Christie's) $56,760

A Dutch ormolu mounted kingwood and tulipwood bombe commode with serpentine mottled gray marble slab and two drawers inlaid sans traverse, 39in. wide. (Christie's) $26,455

A Dutch walnut and marquetry bombe commode inlaid throughout with urns of flowers, scrolling foliage, figures, birds and ribbon-entwined poles, 40in. wide. (Bearne's) $7,434

A small Continental marquetry commode with mottled marble top, on short turned tapering supports, possibly Swedish, 19th century, 29¼in. wide. (Lawrence Fine Arts) $1,152

One of a pair of George III satinwood commodes, each with semi-circular top crossbanded with mahogany, on tapering feet, 47in. wide. (Christie's) Two $98,384

A Dutch marquetry bombe commode inlaid with flowers and birds, the serpentine top with a checkered line, 28in. wide. (Christie's) $4,884

COMMODE CHESTS

A George III tulipwood and kingwood marquetry commode, attributed to Pierre Langlois, of bombe outline, 57in. wide. (Christie's) $141,900

A George III mahogany commode with serpentine molded top above three drawers, on cabriole legs and scroll toes, 45½in. wide. (Christie's) $41,624

An ormolu mounted king-wood and marquetry com-mode a encoignures after the model by J.H. Riesener, on massive foliate sabots headed by foliate panels, circa 1900, 80in. wide. (Christie's) $15,801

An Empire mahogany and brass mounted rectangular commode with galleried marble inset top and pro-jecting rounded corners, 3ft.10in. wide. (Phillips) $8,100

A kingwood commode of Louis XV style with bowed molded mottled oxblood marble top, late 19th century, 32in. wide. (Christie's) $3,532

A Regence rosewood and brass mounted commode of bowed outline, the over-hanging quarter-veneered top inlaid with feather stringing, 4ft.1in. wide. (Phillips) $9,000

 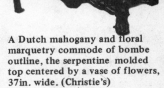

A George III mahogany com-mode, the bowed concave sided top crossbanded with rosewood and framed by ebony and box-wood lines, 44in. wide. (Christie's) $37,840

A black and gold japanned bombe commode of Louis XV style, decorated with a red oval panel of pavilions and Chinese figures, 44¼in. wide. (Christie's) $4,647

A Dutch mahogany and floral marquetry commode of bombe outline, the serpentine molded top centered by a vase of flowers, 37in. wide. (Christie's) $6,919

COMMODE CHESTS

A George III mahogany commode with molded eared serpentine top above three drawers, on splayed bracket feet, 47in. wide. (Christie's) $12,144

A Louis XVI mahogany commode chest of two long and two short drawers with brass handles, 4ft.¾in. wide (marble surmount missing) (Geering & Colyer) $3,591

An Empire figured mahogany and gilt metal mounted commode, the rectangular gray marble top above a single frieze drawer, 49½in. wide. (Christie's) $2,310

A French Provincial walnut commode, with serpentine front, the top crossbanded and inlaid with geometric motifs, supported upon short bracket feet, 105cm. wide. (Henry Spencer)$2,237

A Louis XV style kingwood commode, inlaid with marquetry and rosewood bands in boxwood line borders, on splayed legs with sabots, 42in. wide. (Christie's)$2,695

A George II mahogany commode, the waved molded top with carved border above three drawers, 38in. wide. (Christie's) $52,624

A Dutch walnut and marquetry bombe commode, decorated with ribband tied baskets of flowers, 28½in. wide. (Christie's) $4,235

A cream painted commode of Louis XVI style, with eared rectangular top and three fluted long drawers, 50in. wide. (Greenslades) $5,088

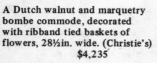

A tulipwood and amaranth banded petite commode, inlaid with boxwood lines and applied with gilt metal mounts, 32in., late 18th century. (Christie's) $3,465

COMMODE CHESTS

A North Italian burr walnut bombe commode with cross-banded top and three long drawers, 18th century and later, 51in. wide. (Christie's) $8,563

A George III harewood and satinwood banded commode of serpentine outline, fitted with three mahogany lined drawers between slightly bombe keeled angles, 37½in. wide. (Christie's) $16,192

A French Provincial walnut commode crossbanded with yew-wood, the eared serpentine top above four graduated drawers between quadrant angles, early 18th century, 56½in. wide. (Christie's) $6,891

A Dutch mahogany commode with chamfered rectangular mottled gray marble top, on tapering feet, 41in. wide. (Christie's) $1,628

A Regence kingwood commode with bow-fronted mottled gray marble top, on bracket feet, 45½in. wide. (Christie's) $8,140

A brass mounted mahogany commode of rectangular shape with canted corners, the stepped top above a secret frieze drawer, stamped twice A.(I). on the back, circa 1870, 33½in. wide. (Christie's) $24,167

A French small commode in Louis XV style, with veined rouge marble top, supported upon slender tapering legs with gilt metal capped feet, 72cm. wide. (Henry Spencer) $1,110

A Transitional tulipwood commode banded in amaranth, inlaid with checkered lines, stamped F.Sche(y)(?) 53¾in. wide. (Christie's) $13,701

A 19th century French kingwood and ivory parquetry inlaid toilet commode with leaf and mask ormolu mounted decoration, 23in. wide. (Dacre, Son & Hartley) $2,775

CORNER CUPBOARDS

Tiger maple glazed corner cupboard, probably Pennsylvania, mid 19th century, the frieze above two glazed doors with canted corners, 82¾in. high. (Robt. W. Skinner Inc.) $3,800

A mahogany standing corner display cabinet, the top section with a dentil molded cornice, 34in. wide, basically early 19th century. (Christie's) $3,080

A Chippendale walnut corner cupboard, in two parts, the upper section with coved cornice, on bracket feet, 88½in. high. (Christie's) $1,870

Country Federal poplar corner cupboard, possibly Pennsylvania, circa 1825, in two sections, the projecting molded cornice above cockbeaded glazed door, 45in. wide. (Robt. W. Skinner Inc.)$2,300

A Georgian mahogany hanging corner cabinet with wide canted angles flanking a glazed door, 42½in. high. (Lawrence Fine Arts) $1,791

A George III mahogany corner cabinet the top section with a dentil molded cornice and two geometrically glazed doors, 42in. wide. (Christie's) $6,582

An Edwardian mahogany and satinwood inlaid standing corner cupboard, with broken arch pediment, 70cm. wide. (Phillips) $2,618

An early 19th century Dutch marquetry and rosewood dwarf corner cabinet, with shaped front, enclosed by a panel door with interior lozenge marquetry panel, 2ft.9in. wide. (Geering & Colyer) $1,647

An Edwardian satinwood and kingwood banded corner cabinet painted with trailing foliage in naturalistic colors, on square tapered legs, 36in. wide. (Christie's)$9,081

CORNER CUPBOARDS

A Russian mahogany and brass corner cabinet, the molded cornice above a glazed door with brass astragals and a panelled door, on bracket feet, circa 1830. (Bonhams) $7,320

Antique oak corner wall cupboard with single panelled door enclosing four shaped fitted shelves, 2ft. 7in. wide. (County Group) $374

A Federal grain-painted corner cupboard, Pennsylvania, early 19th century, with scalloped cornice above a glazed cupboard door, 84in. high. (Christie's) $6,600

A George III mahogany and box-wood strung hanging corner cupboard, the molded cornice above a geometrically glazed door, 30in. wide. (Bonhams) $1,017

19th century pine corner cupboard with shaped shelves and panelled cupboard door with brass knob. (British Antique Exporters) $525

Late 18th century pine two-door corner cupboard with shaped shelves and panelled doors. (British Antique Exporters) $1,400

An Edward Barnsley walnut corner cabinet with ebony stringing and panelled fall flap, on stepped plinth, circa 1930, 126.3cm. wide. (Christie's) $8,976

A green painted bow-fronted standing corner cabinet, painted with an oval medallion of a flower girl, lover and spaniel, 28¼in. wide. (Christie's) $2,057

A grain painted corner cupboard, mid-Atlantic States, mid-19th century, with coved cornice above an egg-and-dart molding, 87in. high. (Christie's) $2,860

CUPBOARDS

A Renaissance style oak press, carved with cherubs and lion masks in gadrooned and strapwork borders, on block feet, 73in. (Christie's)$1,347

A Genoese blue and cream painted cupboard of bombe shape, the serpentine top with three-quarter gallery, on cabriole legs, 18¼in. wide. (Christie's) $2,340

A Jacobean style oak press, with chip and carved strapwork borders, the dentilled cornice above three cupboard doors, 58½in. (Christie's) $1,251

Late 18th century pine bacon cupboard with ornate pediment and bracket feet. (British Antique Exporters) $875

A Georgian mahogany cupboard on chest with two panel doors, two short and three long drawers, 40in. wide. (Lawrence Fine Arts) $1,767

A George III mahogany, satinwood and inlaid dwarf side cupboard of broken and D-shaped outline, on square tapered legs, 4ft.3in. wide. (Phillips) $11,700

An ormolu mounted kingwood parquetry and red lacquer meuble d'appui by Henry Dasson, with foliate clasps reaching to scrolled sabots, 62¼in. wide. (Christie's) $11,525

One of a pair of satinwood bedside cupboards crossbanded with rosewood, on turned tapering legs, 17¼in. wide. (Christie's) Two $3,085

An oak court cupboard, the upper section with fluted frieze above panelled cupboards, 61in. wide. (Bonhams) $1,281

CUPBOARDS

A Dutch mahogany and marquetry cupboard, of rectangular form, the frieze drawer above a pair of recessed doors, circa 1820, 49in. wide. (Bonhams) $3,111

A late George III mahogany bedside cupboard, the rectangular tray-top with carrying handles, on square tapering legs. (Christie's) $1,258

An oak press, carved with strapwork panels and bands, the finialled crenellated canopy top above five cupboard doors, 65in., 1687. (Christie's) $5,005

One of a pair of late Chinese red lacquered cabinets in two sections, decorated with applied hunting scenes in ivory, soapstone, lacquer and mother of pearl, 4ft. 1in. high. (Lambert & Foster)
Two $1,443

A Charles II oak court cupboard with a low waved cornice on baluster supports, Yorkshire, 59in. high. (Lawrence Fine Arts)$2,602

An oak and mahogany press, the top section with a molded cornice above two panelled doors each with a bone diamond escutcheon, 49in., early 19th century.(Christie's) $1,540

A 17th century oak dole cupboard with double arched open frieze molded frame 32½in. wide. (Dacre, Son & Hartley) $6,480

Painted and stencil decorated poplar cupboard, 'Manufactured by Jeremiah H. Stahl', Soap Hollow, Somerset County, Pennsylvania, circa 1850, 54in. wide. (Robt. W. Skinner Inc.) $44,000

A 17th century oak court cupboard, the lower section with two panelled cupboard doors with diamond lozenge decoration, 148cm. (reconstructed) (Phillips) $1,215

DAVENPORTS

A Victorian walnut davenport with brass gallery above a shaped fall-front with fitted interior, 25in. wide. (Lawrence Fine Arts) $4,070

Victorian walnut davenport whatnot with turned supports and leather lined lid. (British Antique Exporters) $656

A Victorian walnut veneered harlequin davenport, on tapering spiral turned columns, one side fitted with four drawers. (David Lay) $1,605

A rare George IV rosewood davenport of exceptionally small size, on four short supports with brass castors, 14in. (Lawrence Fine Arts) $10,582

A late Victorian rosewood davenport, inlaid with marquetry and geometric box-wood lines, on square splayed tapering legs, 23in. wide. (Christie's) $1,193

An early Victorian oak davenport, the sliding rectangular box top enclosed by a hinged panelled lid below a three-quarter baluster gallery, 20in. (Christie's) $1,540

An Anglo-Chinese hualiwood davenport carved with cabochons, acanthus scrolls and applied with S-scroll moldings, 21½in. wide. (Christie's) $1,732

Early Victorian burr walnut davenport with shaped front supports, brass gallery and tooled leather insert. (British Antique Exporters) $963

A good William IV rosewood davenport with brass gallery and bead edge to the sliding desk, on bun feet, 20in. (Lawrence Fine Arts) $7,326

DAVENPORTS

A late Regency rosewood davenport with a leather lined writing slope enclosing a fitted interior, on four turned feet, 26in. wide. (Hy. Duke & Son) $1,690

A late Regency rosewood davenport, on tapering turned supports and arched feet, terminating in roundels and castors, 20in. (Hy. Duke & Son) $845

A Burmese padouk davenport pierced and carved throughout with foliage, fruit, flowers and birds, 36½in. wide. (Bearne's) $844

An Edwardian oak davenport, having interior drawers and pigeon holes and four drawers to one side, 25in. wide. (Morphets) $597

An early Victorian finely figured walnut davenport, having fluted and barley twist supports, stamped C. Hindley & Sons, London, 1ft.9in. wide. (Geering & Colyer) $3,132

A William IV rosewood veneered davenport with sloping flap and shaped three-quarter gallery. (David Lay) $995

Fine Victorian walnut veneered davenport having fitted interior and four drawers to side. (Michael G. Matthews) $1,134

A good Regency rosewood davenport of tapering pedestal form with canted corners and boxwood bandings, 1ft.8in. wide. (Tennants) $6,300

A Victorian figured walnut davenport, with lidded pen compartment above a lined serpentine slope, 21in. wide. (Christie's) $1,828

DISPLAY CABINETS

An Art Deco mahogany, maple and chromium plated display cabinet, on solid mahogany side supports united by an undertier. (Phillips) $1,760

An Art Deco walnut veneered circular display cabinet, with glazed doors enclosing glass shelves, 120.5cm. high. (Phillips) $516

A Dutch oak cabinet with molded arched cornice above a pair of glazed doors, mid 18th century, 89½in. high. (Christie's) $12,210

One of a pair of mid-Victorian burr walnut display cabinets, the molded crossbanded tops above glazed doors, 31in. wide. (Christie's) Two $5,205

An Art Nouveau mahogany display cabinet, with recessed top shelf held by front supports heavily carved with fruit and leaves, 106.8cm. across. (Phillips) $1,267

A Victorian mahogany display stand, the four graduated open shelves with scroll supports, 3ft.6in. (Greenslades) $1,226

A French rosewood and ormolu serpentine vitrine, painted with romantic panels and on six cabriole shaped legs, 54in. wide x 75in. high. (Morphets) $4,706

A Louis XV/XVI style mahogany and ormolu mounted vitrine, with trapezoidal mottled red marble top, 63in. high. (Robt. W. Skinner Inc.) $1,500

A good walnut display cabinet in the French Provincial manner, by Whytock & Reid, on characteristic short cabriole legs. (Phillips) $3,927

342

DISPLAY CABINETS

A Louis XV style mahogany vitrine with Vernis Martin panels and on cabriole legs, 84in. high by 42in. wide. (Bearne's) $2,552

A 19th century crossbanded figured walnut and inlaid breakfront credenza, enclosed by three glazed doors, flanked by molded brackets, 5ft.6in. wide. (Geering & Colyer) $3,024

An Edwardian rosewood display cabinet, the mirrored back with foliate and fret carved pediment, 93½in. high. (Bearne's) $1,548

A George III style satinwood display cabinet, the two conforming doors and sides with gothic style astragals, on splayed bracket feet, 44¾in. wide. (Bearne's) $7,280

An ormolu mounted kingwood display cabinet with serpentine purple and white molded marble top, 66¾in. wide. (Christie's) $14,476

An Edwardian mahogany display cabinet outlined with satinwood banding, boxwood and ebony stringing, 35¾in. wide. (Bearne's) $1,365

A Dutch walnut and marquetry vitrine, inlaid throughout with flowers and foliage, on lion paw feet, 60½in. wide. (Bearne's) $17,346

A finely decorated gilt and black lacquered display cabinet, with serpentine ends, decorated in the chinoiserie manner with figures and bird in a water garden, 4ft.8½in. wide. (Geering & Colyer) $1,352

An Edwardian mahogany display cabinet inlaid with cornucopias, scrolling foliage, urns and patera, on tapering square supports joined by an undertier, 83in. high. (Bearne's) $4,071

DISPLAY CABINETS

A French kingwood Vernis Martin vitrine of small size with shaped sides and front, late 19th century, 29in. wide. (Lawrence Fine Arts) $4,680

An Edwardian mahogany display cabinet inlaid with ribbon-tied bellflowers and foliage, on cabriole legs, 79in. high. (Bearne's) $1,050

A late 19th century rosewood vitrine, in the French taste, surmounted by three quarter gilt metal gallery with Siena marble top, 69cm. wide. (Phillips) $1,776

A Louis XV transitional style kingwood standing vitrine, applied with gilt metal mounts, the coffered swan neck cresting with an acanthus scroll centre, 35¼in. (Christie's) $1,732

A Chinese hardwood display cabinet, pierced and carved throughout with animals, birds, flowers, fruit and foliage, 74in. high by 40in. wide. (Bearne's) $1,681

Louis XVI style kingwood and ormolu mounted vitrine, the rectangular yellow and grey mottled marble top with chamfered corners over glazed bevelled door, 26in. wide. (Robt. W. Skinner Inc.) $2,400

A walnut display cabinet, of Queen Anne design, the domed upper section enclosed by a glazed door and side panels, 27in. wide. (Christie's) $1,925

A Russian Karelian birch cabinet with molded cornice, two panelled and glazed cupboard doors edged with giltwood foliage, early 19th century, 46in. wide. (Christie's) $5,577

An ormolu mounted tulipwood and marquetry serpentine corner vitrine with molded cornice, 29in. wide. (Christie's) $2,481

DRESSERS

A Georgian style oak small dresser, with boarded plate rack, raised on turned supports with potboard base, 195cm. (Osmond Tricks)
$1,628

An early 19th century oak dresser base with a later raised back, 72in. wide. (Bearne's) $4,576

An early 18th century oak dresser and later plate rack with a molded cornice, 74½in. wide. (Bearne's)
$3,872

An oak dresser with a molded cornice, two open shelves flanked by fret carved uprights, 69in. wide, the base mid-18th century. (Bearne's) $2,093

A handsome oak and mahogany banded dresser, the cavetto molded cornice above three narrow open shelves, late 18th century, 82in. wide. (Bonhams)
$3,145

An inlaid oak Welsh dresser outlined throughout with crossbanding on cabriole legs, 73in. wide. (Bearne's)
$4,224

A 17th century oak dresser having molded edge and panelled sides fitted with three frieze drawers and cupboards under, 57in. wide. (Duncan Vincent) $7,480

Small oak Welsh dresser, carved and decorated in period style with shaped canopy and side panels, 30in. x 64in. (County Group)
$93

Antique oak breakfront dresser having three drawers and two cupboards with turned knob handles. (Michael G. Matthews) $2,745

DUMB WAITERS

A late George III mahogany dumb waiter with two circular drop leaf tiers on turned column supports, 33½in. high. (Christie's) $6,424

A Victorian mahogany two tier serving buffet, each rounded rectangular molded tier on solid end standards, 51½in. wide. (Christie's) $1,443

A George III mahogany dumb waiter, the three graduated circular tiers on vase turned supports, 49¾in. high. (Bearne's) $1,327

A George III mahogany dumb waiter with three stepped molded circular tiers on spirally fluted baluster shaft, 43in. high. (Bonhams) $5,676

A late Regency mahogany dumb waiter, the two rectangular tiers each with a pierced brass gallery, 46in. wide. (Christie's) $7,920

A mahogany three tier dumb waiter, each circular dished graduated tier on ring turned spiral twist carved supports, 25½in. high. (Christie's) $962

Mid-19th century mahogany circular three tier dumb waiter with three molded swept feet. (Peter Wilson) $1,625

A William IV mahogany dumb waiter with three rectangular tiers on lotus carved side supports, 39½in. high. (Bearne's) $2,975

A George III mahogany dumb waiter with three stepped tiers on baluster turned stem and cabriole tripod, 46in. high. (Christie's) $2,226

KNEEHOLE DESKS

A good mahogany twin pedestal desk in 18th century style, the lift-off top with recessed center above three frieze drawers, 4ft.6in. wide. (Tennants) $3,150

A late Victorian mahogany cylindrical bureau, with rectangular molded top above a front opening to a bird's-eye maple fitted interior, 54in. wide.(Christie's)$1,636

An Edwardian mahogany kneehole pedestal desk, inlaid with satinwood and fluted bands, with boxwood line borders, 48in. (Christie's) $1,540

A George III mahogany kneehole desk with crossbanded molded rectangular top, the frieze with a drawer above a shaped kneehole drawer and recessed cupboard flanked by six drawers on shaped bracket feet. (Christie's)$2,710

A George III mahogany kneehole desk of unusually long narrow form, on six short square tapering legs with brass castors, 66in. wide. (Lawrence Fine Arts) $5,577

A mid Georgian mahogany kneehole desk with crossbanded molded rectangular top above a frieze drawer. (Christie's) $5,033

A walnut kneehole desk with molded rectangular top, the frieze with a fitted secretaire drawer on bracket feet, 31in. wide. (Christie's)$1,673

A satinwood partner's desk, with nine drawers around the knee-hole one side, the other side with three drawers and a pair of panelled cupboards, 59in. wide. (Christie's) $8,639

A walnut kneehole pedestal desk of kidney shaped outline, with a pierced spindled three-quarter gallery, 54in. wide. (Christie's) $1,892

KNEEHOLE DESKS

A mahogany partner's desk, fitted with the usual arrangement of nine drawers either side, 54½ x 43in. (Lawrence Fine Arts) $2,747

An oak kneehole writing table with inset brown leather to top and fitted drawers to center with brass drop handles, 60in. wide. (Lambert & Foster) $616

A mahogany partner's desk, the rectangular molded top lined with gilt tooled brown leather, 61 x 61in. (Christie's) $2,695

A George III mahogany desk, with a leather lined and crossbanded rectangular top opening on hinges and supported on a ratchet, 44½in. wide. (Hy. Duke & Son) $5,408

An ormolu mounted kingwood and parquetry kidney shaped kneehole desk with painted leather lined top, 48in. wide. (Christie's) $7,064

A rare Queen Anne japanned kneehole bureau, probably Boston area, 1730-1750, with a central recessed bank of five graduated drawers, 34¼in. wide. (Christie's) $264,000

An early Georgian walnut kneehole desk crossbanded in yew with molded and quarter-veneered rectangular top, 32in. wide. (Christie's) $11,352

A Georgian mahogany kneehole desk, containing seven drawers about the recess, on bracket feet, 2ft.10in. wide. (Phillips) $2,340

A Victorian mahogany kneehole desk with raised gallery, having three drawers to each side and a cupboard to the kneehole, 45in. wide. (Morphets) $1,049

KNEEHOLE DESKS

A mahogany kneehole desk with rectangular leather lined top and nine drawers, 47½in. wide. (Christie's) $3,085

A George I style walnut kneehole desk with tooled leather inset and molded edge to the top, 48in. wide. (Bearne's) $1,575

A Victorian mahogany pedestal cylinder bureau, the interior with pull-out writing slide, 60in. wide. (Bearne's) $2,625

A walnut veneered kneehole desk, with an arrangement of seven crossbanded drawers around a cupboard in the recess, 33in. wide, early 18th century. (Bearne's) $3,894

An ormolu mounted mahogany pedestal desk of Empire style, the eared rectangular top inset with green leather, on turned feet, circa 1880, 56in. wide. (Christie's) $7,064

A mid Georgian gentleman's mahogany desk and toilet stand, the hinged rectangular lid enclosing a baize lined writing panel, on bracket feet, 36in. (Christie's) $2,310

19th century pedestal writing desk with nine drawers, having a leather lined top and plinth base. (British Antique Exporters) $1,400

An unusual early George III mahogany kneehole desk, the back with a pair of hinged cupboard doors, on bracket feet, 50in. wide. (Christie's) $3,702

19th century mahogany cylinder top pedestal desk with fitted interior and plinth base. (British Antique Exporters) $1,488

LINEN PRESSES

A George III mahogany linen press with two panel doors crossbanded and inlaid with oval bands, 48in. wide. (Lawrence Fine Arts) $3,866

A Victorian mahogany linen press with ogee cornice, the top section having five sliding shelves enclosed by a pair of arched framed panel doors, 4ft. wide. (Hobbs & Chambers) $868

An early 19th century mahogany linen press with a molded cornice, on splayed bracket feet, 50½in. wide. (Bearne's) $1,760

A late George II mahogany linen press with a dentil cornice and bracket feet, 47¼in. x 73in. high. (Lawrence Fine Arts) $3,326

A William IV mahogany linen press, with deep panelled secretaire drawer enclosing fitted interior, on turned feet. (Phillips) $2,057

A George III mahogany linen press, with two short and two long drawers, on ogee bracket feet, 123cm. wide. (Phillips) $1,496

A mahogany and satinwood banded linen press, the projecting cornice over two panelled doors, each inlaid with urns. (Phillips) $1,870

An early George III mahogany linen press with architectural pediment above two panelled doors, 48in. wide. (Lawrence Fine Arts) $3,160

A well coloured early George III mahogany linen press, the upper section with dentil cornice, 49½in. wide. (Bonhams) $2,670

LOWBOYS

A walnut lowboy inlaid with feather banding, the rounded rectangular top above three drawers, on club legs and pad feet, mid-18th century. (Christie's) $2,559

An 18th century oak lowboy, the rectangular top with molded edge and re-entrant corners, on cabriole supports with pad feet, 2ft. 6½in. wide. (Greenslades) $4,461

A George II padouk lowboy with molded rectangular top above a drawer and shaped apron on cabriole legs, 28½in. wide. (Christie's)$3,544

A mahogany lowboy, on cabriole legs with claw and ball feet, 32in. wide, basically 18th century. (Christie's) $2,791

A walnut lowboy, the quarter-veneered crossbanded rectangular top above a frieze drawer, on square-section cabriole legs, 29½in. wide. (Christie's) $4,331

A George I style burr walnut lowboy, with featherbanded inlay, on cabriole legs with pad feet, 31in. (Christie's) $962

A walnut lowboy with molded rectangular top above three drawers and shaped apron on cabriole legs, 29in. wide. (Christie's) $1,969

An early 18th century style walnut lowboy, on bold cabriole legs with braganza feet, 81cm. (Phillips) $2,992

A Dutch walnut lowboy, in-laid with marquetry arabesques, the coffered rectangular top above an undulating frieze fitted with a drawer, 33in., basically 19th century. (Christie's) $1,131

SCREENS

A Dutch leather six leaf screen painted with chinoiserie scenes on a gilt and black ground, 18th century, each leaf 83½ x 22¾in. (Christie's) $11,313

An early Victorian black lacquered and painted pole screen, the rectangular panel painted with fishermen and figures, 4ft.high. (Greenslades)
$427

A George III painted four panel screen, late 18th century, one side featuring panels representing various landscapes, the other various genre scenes, 66½in. high. (Robt. W. Skinner Inc.) $2,200

A Chinese amboyna wood screen, each panel mounted with porcelain plaques depicting figures, animals, foliage, flowers and insects, 74¼in. high. (Bearne's) $2,912

An Empire mahogany cheval firescreen and secretaire, the leather lined pleated silk flap enclosing a hinged fitted interior, 24in. wide. (Christie's)
$916

An early 18th century japanned five fold screen decorated with chinoiserie figures, each panel 9ft. x 1ft.10in. (Phillips) $7,200

A Russian ormolu mounted burr birch three leaf screen, the central rectangular leaf with two upholstered panels, early 19th century, the central leaf 70 x 22½in. (Christie's)
$9,158

A Chinese export black and gold lacquer four leaf screen, each leaf with a shaped arched cresting, early 19th century, each leaf 75¼ x 17¾in. (Christie's) $4,114

A four fold screen representing the Four Seasons, carved and pierced with birds among flowering plants, 63in. high. (Lawrence Fine Arts)
$706

FURNITURE

SCREENS

An Arts and Crafts oak framed
fire screen, the plain oak frame
having a toprail pierced with
oval shapes, 77.4cm. high.
(Phillips) $167

A Chinese coromandel lacquer
eight leaf screen decorated with
courtly figures and pavilions in
landscapes, early 19th century,
each leaf 84 x 16in. (Christie's)
$5,759

A Regency bronze mounted
mahogany cheval firescreen,
with central rectangular red silk
panel, 34in. wide. (Christie's)
$4,540

A late 19th century French
gilt metal framed fireguard,
the oval glass panel painted
with trailing roses. (Greenslades) $241

A Napoleon III gilt three
fold screen, the crests carved with cornucopiae and
a basket of flowers, 145cm.
wide. (Bonhams)
$925

A Chinese hardwood table screen
set with a circular famille verte
panel enamelled with sages and
other figures, 33in. high.
(Hy. Duke & Son)
$354

A walnut firescreen of Regence
style, with a panel of silver
thread embroidered silk in a
molded frame. (Christie's)
$2,137

Pair of Chinese spinach green
nephrite jade table screens, decorated
with landscapes in gilt and lacquer,
18th century, 11¼ x 8½in. (Lambert
& Foster) $457

An 18th century style mahogany framed firescreen, the
arched rectangular panel set
with a gros point chair seat
cover, 40½in. high.
(Bearne's) $424

SCREENS

A late Victorian walnut four leaf screen, each leaf incorporating two arched scrapwork panels depicting contemporary literary figures and aristocracy, each leaf 32 x 79in., dated 1885 and initialled J.F. (Christie's) $8,085

20th century wrought iron firescreen in the gothic style. (British Antique Exporters) $61

A six leaf screen painted in oils on canvas with figures and classical ruins in an extensive Italianate landscape. 88in.high (Christie's) $2,904

Edwardian mahogany framed firescreen with embroidered floral panel. (British Antique Exporters) $61

A Chinese coromandel lacquer eight leaf screen decorated in gilt and colors on a black ground, on brass bound feet, each leaf 96 x 17½in. (Christie's) $5,775

A Victorian cartouche shaped papier-mache firescreen, the scrollwork surround heightened in gilt, painted with a scene of the Giudecca in Venice, signed Jennens and Bettridge, 41in. high. (Christie's) $2,310

19th century Chinese hardwood two leaf screen with ivory and mother of pearl decoration. (British Antique Exporters) $788

A pair of oak polescreens designed by Anthony Salvin, each adjustable square panel with a fret carved edge, 61in. high. (Bearne's)$2,712

A Victorian walnut framed firescreen with an arched cresting carved with flowers and foliage, 54in. high.(Bearne's) $525

SECRETAIRE BOOKCASES

A good George III mahogany secretaire bookcase, the base with single frieze drawer folding to reveal writing surface, on French splay feet, 238 x 120cm. (Phillips) $7,480

An early 19th century mahogany secretaire bookcase, the lower section with secretaire drawer enclosing drawers, cupboards and pigeonholes, 294cm. high. (Phillips) $1,496

A George III mahogany secretaire bookcase with later fretwork architectural pediment above astragal glazed doors, 33½in. wide. (Bonhams) $5,340

A Regency mahogany secretaire bookcase, the base with a fitted secretaire drawer, on bracket feet, 46in. wide. (Christie's) $8,639

A Georgian mahogany breakfront secretaire bookcase. with a molded and cavetto cornice, 97in. wide. (Lawrence Fine Arts) $20,790

An early Victorian mahogany secretaire bookcase, the two glazed doors with lotus carved astragals, 47in. wide. (Bearne's) $3,009

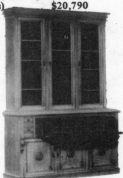

An Edwardian mahogany and satinwood inlaid secretaire bookcase, the two panel doors with oval patera of musical muses, 91cm. wide.(Phillips) $5,984

A Victorian oak secretaire bookcase, the secretaire drawer below flanked by four small drawers, 66 x 101in. high. (Anderson & Garland) $2,179

An attractive Regency mahogany secretaire bookcase, on splayed feet (restorations to the upper section), 36½in. wide. (Bonhams) $1,757

SECRETAIRES

A Regency mahogany secretaire cabinet, the rectangular top with solid three-quarter gallery, 33in. wide. (Christie's) $10,285

A Continental mahogany secretaire a abattant, with fitted interior above three further long drawers, 19th century, 46in. wide. (Lawrence Fine Arts) $1,975

A Heals red lacquered bureau cabinet, the fall flap enclosing fitted interior of eight pigeonholes and two small drawers, on four turned feet, circa 1918, 76.5cm. wide. (Christie's) $748

An early 19th century German mahogany secretaire a abattant, the stepped cornice with drawer over single frieze drawer, 108cm. (Phillips) $2,244

Attractive Edwardian mahogany escritoire, with cockbeading to drawer fronts and circular brass drop handles, original keys, 37in. wide. (County Group) $1,496

An early 19th century mahogany Continental secretaire a abattant, with single frieze drawer over fall-front writing surface, 98cm. wide. (Phillips) $3,927

A North Italian ivory inlaid walnut and marquetry secretaire a abattant, the fall-flap inlaid with Neptune and consort, 37in. wide. (Christie's) $8,547

A Queen Anne scarlet lacquer cabinet, the upper part from a bureau cabinet, 45½in. wide. (Christie's) $49,192

A walnut secretaire cabinet, the fall-flap enclosing a fitted interior with drawers and pigeonholes, late 17th century, possibly Dutch, 44in. wide. (Christie's) $4,936

SECRETAIRES

A Federal glazed veneered and inlaid lady's writing desk and bookcase, probably North Shore, Massachusetts, circa 1815, 107.4cm. wide. (Robt. W. Skinner Inc.) $4,250

An early 19th century inlaid mahogany secretaire chest, three drawers under with brass handles, on turned feet, 3ft.9in. high. (Anderson & Garland) $1,816

A George III satinwood, mahogany, marquetry and painted secretaire cabinet, on turned tapering legs, 28½in. wide. (Christie's) $20,812

A fine Augsburg walnut, marquetry and ebonized secretaire writing cabinet in three sections, 3ft.6in. wide. (Phillips) $15,300

A good Edwardian mahogany secretaire chest of small proportions, on splayed bracket feet, 33½in. wide. (David Lay) $3,982

A George III mahogany and walnut cabinet, the base with fitted secretaire drawer above two drawers and on ogee bracket feet, 245cm. (Osmond Tricks) $3,529

A late 18th century Dutch marquetry and satinwood secretaire a abattant, the fall-front enclosing plain interior, 106 x 157cm. (Phillips) $3,927

A Queen Anne walnut, crossbanded and featherstrung secretaire cabinet of comparatively small size, the upper part with a molded cornice, 3ft.3½in. wide. (Phillips) $16,200

A George III mahogany secretaire writing cabinet with shelved Chinese lattice fret superstructure, on bracket feet, 2ft.8½in. wide. (Phillips) $15,300

SETTEES & COUCHES

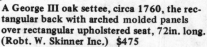

A Classical carved mahogany and maple veneered sofa, New York, 1815-1825, on carved paw feet, 85½in. wide. (Christie's) $2,420

A George III oak settee, circa 1760, the rectangular back with arched molded panels over rectangular upholstered seat, 72in. long. (Robt. W. Skinner Inc.) $475

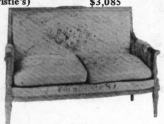

A Regency mahogany and ebony sofa with scrolled buttoned leather back and padded seat, on turned tapering legs, 90in. wide. (Christie's) $3,085

One of a pair of 19th century gilt frame canapes, in the Louis XV manner, the molded top-rail centered by scrolling leaves, 219cm. wide. (Phillips) Two $5,236

A Louis XVI style carved giltwood canape, the rectangular back centered by a ribbon tied floral crest, late 19th century, 52in. wide. (Bonhams) $740

A George III mahogany sofa with rectangular back, on square tapering legs headed by paterae, 72½in. wide. (Christie's) $3,908

Rare L. & J. G. Stickley spindle 'Prairie' settle, circa 1912, no. 234 the broad even sided flat crest rail over spindles, two section seat, unsigned, 86in. wide. (Robt. W. Skinner Inc.) $85,000

A three seater Gimson design yew settee, having drop-in rush seat, on bobbin supports. (Hobbs & Chambers) $2,443

SETTEES & COUCHES

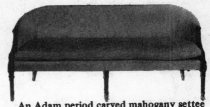

A painted Windsor rod back settee, New England, circa 1800, the circular crest rail above twenty-five tapering spindles, 83in. wide. (Robt. W. Skinner Inc.) $9,000

An Adam period carved mahogany settee with arched stuffover back and seat, on ringed fluted tapered legs, 5ft.9in. wide. (Phillips) $8,694

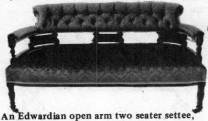

An Edwardian open arm two seater settee, having inlaid and buttoned upholstered back and stuffover seat. (Hobbs & Chambers) $760

A late Regency mahogany framed couch, the shaped and gadrooned top rail over upholstered back and seat with scroll-over arms, 137cm. (Phillips) $1,028

A Morris & Co ebonized and rush settle, the rectangular turned back and arms above rectangular rush seat, on eight turned legs, 122cm. wide. (Christie's) $598

A Regency mahogany settee, with scroll hand grips and slightly tapering square supports with brass castors, 63in. wide. (Lawrence Fine Arts) $1,394

A George IV rosewood sofa with arched back, the frame with gadrooned cresting and roundel arm terminals, 83½in. wide. (Christie's) $1,234

A William IV mahogany framed settee, the toprail carved with acanthus and lotus, 90in. wide. (Bearne's) $1,724

FURNITURE

SETTEES & COUCHES

A Victorian oak framed settee, the serpentine
toprail centered by a cartouche and carved
with scrolling acanthus, 75in. wide.(Bearne's)
$1,837

A fine quality bergere settee, in the Hepple-
white style, the highly decorative back with
three ovals centered by paterae and surrounded
with continuous harebell and ribbon outline,
76in. wide. (Boardman) $4,901

A Chippendale style mahogany open arm
settee, profusely carved with acanthus
scrolls and cabochons, on cabriole legs with
scroll pad feet, 46in. wide. (Christie's)
$2,695

A giltwood daybed of Louis XV style, upholstered in faded olive green velvet with
channelled frame on cabriole legs, 75in. wide.
(Christie's) $2,849

A tubular chromium plated chaise longue
designed by Le Corbusier and Charlotte
Perriand, the adjustable seat upholstered
in brown and white pony skin.
(Christie's) $4,114

A Biedermeier brass inlaid mahogany sofa,
with drop-in seat and pierced arm supports
upon sphinx legs, 53½in. wide. (Christie's)
$4,477

An early Victorian mahogany couch with a
shaped three-quarter back to a right hand
outward scroll, 79in. wide. (Lawrence Fine
Arts) $1,394

A Classical Revival carved mahogany sofa,
Boston, circa 1825, on legs with curving reeds
terminating in hairy paw feet, 94in. wide.
(Robt. W. Skinner Inc.) $1,900

SETTEES & COUCHES

A mahogany and parcel gilt daybed of George II style, on shell-headed cabriole legs with hairy paw feet, 99in. wide. (Christie's) $39,732

A Regency ebonized and gilt chaise longue with over-scrolled ends, conforming back rail and on sabre legs with brass caps and castors,79in. wide.(Bearne's)$5,250

A Flemish baroque style walnut settee, the arched rectangular back and seat upholstered with a 17th century Flemish tapestry, 62½in. long. (Robt. W. Skinner Inc.) $1,500

Fine Victorian walnut framed chaise longue having carved decoration and standing on cabriole legs. (Michael G. Matthews) $1,098

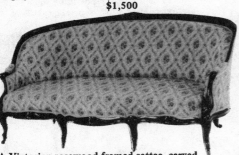

A Victorian rosewood framed settee, carved with foliage and ivy tendrils, on molded cabriole legs with castors, 76in. wide. (Bearne's) $1,601

A beechwood triple chairback settee, the shield shaped chair backs flanked by arched arms, on square tapering legs, 64¾in. wide. (Christie's) $2,674

'Boxing Glove', a chaise longue, by De Sede, the frame upholstered and covered in brown and beige leather, 173cm. long. (Phillips) $4,725

A Classical mahogany veneered carved sofa, probably Boston, circa 1835, the rolled raking veneered crest over carved eagle's heads on acanthus leaves, 81in. wide. (Robt. W. Skinner Inc.) $1,300

SIDEBOARDS

A large Regency mahogany pedestal sideboard with curved back and two center drawers, on six brass hairy paw supports. (Greenslades) $5,577

A George III mahogany breakfront sideboard with satinwood banding and line inlay, 102in. wide, 37in. deep. (Prudential) $8,550

A George IV mahogany bow-front sideboard with a brass curtain rail, on tapering square legs with spade feet, 36½in. high by 66in. wide. (Bearne's) $4,956

A George III mahogany and satinwood banded demilune sideboard, on square section tapered and stopped legs, 167cm. (Phillips) $3,366

A George III mahogany, boxwood strung and tulipwood crossbanded bowfront sideboard, on square tapered legs, 6ft. wide. (Phillips) $11,160

A fine George III mahogany and marquetry serpentine sideboard, containing a central and two deep drawers, on square tapered legs, 5ft.5½in. wide. (Phillips) $26,100

A 17th century oak sideboard on turned supports with block and turned feet, fitted three drawers and brass drop handles, 78in. wide. (Duncan Vincent) $3,400

A George III style mahogany serving table and pair of urns on pedestals, 67in. overall height. (Bearne's) $6,864

SIDEBOARDS

A mahogany sideboard with rectangular bow-fronted top, on square tapering legs, 59½in. wide. (Christie's) $2,674

A Regency mahogany sideboard with cross-banded rectangular breakfront top, on spirally-reeded turned tapering front legs, 60½in. wide. (Christie's) $4,525

A Regency mahogany ebonized and inlaid serving table in the manner of Thomas Hope, with molded arched ledge back, 6ft.11in. wide. (Phillips) $15,300

A Federal inlaid mahogany sideboard, Pennsylvania, 1790-1810, on square tapering legs, 72in. wide. (Christie's) $16,500

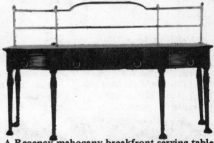

A George III mahogany and satinwood banded sideboard, the bow-front top over concave central frieze drawer, 154cm. wide. (Phillips) $2,805

A Regency mahogany breakfront serving table in the style of George Smith, with brass railed back, 95in. wide. (Christie's) $4,114

An Edwardian mahogany serpentine-fronted sideboard, in the Sheraton manner, on square section tapered legs. (Phillips) $4,488

A Federal mahogany inlaid sideboard, probably Charlestown, New Hampshire, circa 1805, the top with bow front, concave corners, 70in. wide. (Robt. W. Skinner Inc.) $19,000

SIDEBOARDS

A late Georgian mahogany break-front sideboard, the top edge inlaid with a brass band, on six turned reeded supports, 73in. (Lawrence Fine Arts) $3,866

A Regency mahogany bow-fronted sideboard, on canted square tapering legs and spade feet, 54in. wide. (Christie's) $10,696

A George III mahogany sideboard, inlaid with boxwood lines and crossbanded with rosewood, on square tapering legs with spade feet, 71in. wide. (Christie's) $12,342

A French gilt metal mounted mahogany meuble d'appui with a panelled Vernis Martin cupboard door, 32½in. wide. (Christie's) $3,722

A mahogany bow-fronted sideboard, inlaid with satinwood and foliate spandrels, on canted square tapering legs and spade feet, 54in. wide. (Christie's) $4,114

A large sideboard cabinet, the cupboard over with scroll fret carved doors and brass lion mask and drop ring handles, 7ft.10in. high. (Greenslades) $1,747

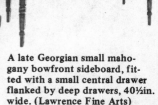

A mahogany half round sideboard, the center drawer flanked by cupboards, on four squared tapering supports and spade feet, 3ft. 5in. (Greenslades) $1,191

An early Victorian D-shaped side cabinet, covered overall with paper scrap design, on plinth base. (Lawrence Fine Arts) $3,663

A late Georgian small mahogany bowfront sideboard, fitted with a small central drawer flanked by deep drawers, 40½in. wide. (Lawrence Fine Arts) $2,416

SIDEBOARDS

A George III mahogany bow-front sideboard with kingwood crossbandings and edged with stringing, partly distressed, 72in. wide. (Lawrence Fine Arts) $5,087

A Victorian burr walnut and marquetry credenza with ormolu mounts and a central rectangular door inlaid with a classical urn, 60in. (Hy. Duke & Son) $2,704

A good ebonized and painted sideboard, the painted panels attributed to Henry Stacy Marks, on turned supports and painted with gilt stylized borders, 198cm. long. (Phillips) $5,504

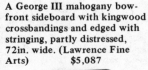

An unusual 6ft. serpentine fronted oak sideboard, richly inlaid with satinwood and rosewood checker work, 7ft.3in. high. (Anderson & Garland) $1,816

A Regency mahogany sideboard of unusually small size, on ring turned tapering feet, 37½in. wide. (Christie's) $8,228

A George IV mahogany breakfront pedestal sideboard outlined with boxwood stringing, to the tapering pedestals, 39¾in. wide. (Bearne's) $1,911

A fine Victorian figured walnut serpentine fronted side cabinet, the whole inlaid with urns of flowers and floral sprays, 80in. wide. (G.A.Property Services) $8,050

A late Georgian mahogany sideboard with bow-front, inlaid with ebony stringing and fitted with two central drawers, on six turned supports, 60½in. wide. (Lawrence Fine Arts) $4,884

A Gordon Russell oak and chestnut sideboard, with chestnut tapering handles, shaped apron below, on octagonal supports, 1927, cabinet maker P. J. Wade, 4ft.5½in. wide. (Hobbs & Chambers) $3,077

STANDS

A Regency mahogany bookstand, with tooled leather bookspine divisions, on hipped splayed tripod base, 62in. high. (Christie's) $39,732

A George IV mahogany pot-stand with circular dished top on four lappeted cabriole legs, 22in. wide, 17¾in. high. (Christie's) $1,851

A late 19th century fruitwood sewing accessory stand with table clamp stay. (Phillips) $245

A Regency mahogany, ebonised and parcel gilt torchere with in-set circular white bordered Portor marble top, 36½in. high. (Christie's) $14,190

A pair of George III mahogany pedestals, the molded tops above fluted friezes, some repairs, each 25¼in. wide. (Lawrence Fine Arts) $6,134

A Country Chippendale cherry carved candlestand, Connecticut, circa 1780, the square tray top with applied molded edge, 26in. high. (Robt. W. Skinner Inc.) $3,100

A County Federal tiger maple light stand, New England, circa 1810, the square overhanging top above four square tapering legs, 27¾in. high. (Robt. W. Skinner Inc.) $850

A pair of ormolu mounted satinwood and marquetry pedestals of Louis XV style with serpentine mottled pink marble tops, 42½in. high. (Christie's) $6,692

An early Victorian mahogany folio stand, on splayed feet with scroll toes, 31in. wide. (Christie's) $3,908

STANDS

A George IV mahogany duet stand, the easel flaps filled with lyres, tripartite platform and scrolled feet, 20in. wide. (Christie's) $5,759

A pair of Venetian painted and gilded blackamoor stands, each in the form of a negro boy doing a handstand, 31in. high. (Christie's) $26,455

A Country Federal mahogany and cherry inlaid candlestand, Upper Connecticut River Valley, 1800, 28½in. high. (Robt. W. Skinner Inc.) $1,300

A Bentwood hall stand, possibly made by Thoret and possibly designed by Josef Hoffman, 194.5cm. high. (Phillips) $1,028

A Biedermeier tapestry frame with adjustable open rectangular top on adjustable trestle ends, on splayed feet, 41in. wide. (Christie's) $2,646

A Gramophone & Typewriter Ltd. oak gramophone pedestal with Angel trademark plaque, accessories drawer and cupboard below, 40in. high, circa 1905. (Christie's) $2,190

A giltwood torchere, the hexagonal top inset with a slab of mottled purple marble, 44in. high. (Christie's) $951

A pair of 19th century French ebony and pietra dura pedestals, inset with black marble panel tops, 4ft. high. (Phillips) $5,400

A William IV rosewood duet stand, the two lyre pierced stands supported by a tapered column, 113cm. high. (Osmond Tricks) $1,810

FURNITURE

A Dutch fruitwood and parquetry jardiniere of serpentine bombe shape with detachable tin liner and cabriole legs, 20in. high. (Christie's) $1,730

A Regency parcel gilt, maple and brass music stand, the adjustable stand with lyre shaped back, 43½in. high. (Christie's) $3,085

A late Federal figured maple two drawer stand, Pennsylvania, 1810-1820, on tapering baluster and ring turned legs, 17½in. wide. (Christie's) $2,640

An early Victorian carved rosewood polescreen with leaf and scroll decorated frame, 60½in. high. (Dacre, Son & Hartley) $540

A gilt metal mounted kingwood and tulipwood jardiniere, of large size, with detachable tin liner, on shaped feet, 49in. wide. (Christie's) $6,105

Edwardian ebonized corner display stand with delicate fretwork decoration. (British Antique Exporters) $875

A late Federal carved mahogany tilt-top candlestand, New York, 1815-1835, on sabre legs, 30½in. high. (Christie's) $1,210

1930's oak framed corner umbrella stand. (British Antique Exporters) $35

A Federal mahogany tilt-top candlestand, Western New Hampshire, circa 1810, oval top on an incised vase and ring turned stem, 22in. wide. (Robt. W. Skinner Inc.) $4,000

STANDS

A Country Federal tiger maple inlaid tilt top candlestand, New England, circa 1810, the rectangular top with ovolo corners, 28¼in. high. (Robt. W. Skinner Inc.) $1,100

A late Victorian ormolu mounted rosewood and mahogany pedestal with a square brown and gray marble top, 45¾in. high. (Christie's) $2,068

A Gordon Russell walnut linen bag and frame, with a linen bag suspended within, 82.5cm. high. (Phillips) $563

A Crimean campaign shaving stand, on turned supports with turned candle nozzles. (David Lay) $261

Art Nouveau style oak umbrella stand on gutta feet. (British Antique Exporters) $131

A rare fine Federal birch inlaid candlestand, probably New Hampshire, circa 1800, the oval top outlined and edged with stringing, 18in. wide. (Robt. W. Skinner Inc.) $53,000

A Regency brass inlaid rosewood reading stand with shaped shaft on splayed quadripartite base, 18in. wide. (Christie's) $1,028

A plain mahogany early 19th century rectangular butler's tray, on baluster turned folding stand. (David Lay) $845

A Russian mahogany hatstand with pierced circular top, the fluted shaft carved with ribbons and acanthus, 75in. high. (Christie's) $305

A walnut and parcel gilt fender stool, on cabriole legs carved with shells and claw and ball feet, 31½in. wide. (Christie's) $2,468

A late Federal mahogany window bench, New York, 1820-1830, the rounded opposing crest rails above rectangular flame veneer solid splats, 40¼in. long. (Christie's) $4,400

An English Art Deco walnut and painted Egyptian style stool, the rectangular concave seat upholstered in brown leather. (Christie's) $448

An early George III mahogany clover leaf stool, the upholstered top over bellflower and acanthus leaf carved cabriole legs, 48cm. (Phillips) $1,776

A small Liberty & Co. oak 'Thebes' stool, the shaped seat supported on three splayed legs, with Liberty & Co. label. (Phillips) $371

A Herman Miller laminated rosewood ottoman designed by Charles Eames, upholstered in black hide. (Christie's) $654

A George I walnut stool, on cabriole legs headed by scrolled brackets, with pad feet, 19½in. wide. (Christie's) $7,946

One of a pair of William IV oak stools in the style of Daniel Marot, on S-scroll legs, joined by an X-shaped S-scroll stretcher, 20½in. wide. (Christie's) Two $4,936

An inlaid mahogany Moorish stool, the apron inlaid in ivory with banding, on turned legs. (Phillips) $792

STOOLS

A William IV mahogany X-framed stool with rectangular padded drop-in seat, on scrolling legs, 32½in. wide. (Christie's) $2,057

A Regency ebonized window seat with dished rectangular padded seat, the reeded X-frame on splayed legs, 45in. wide. (Christie's) $3,908

A George III mahogany window seat, with scrolled ends, on tapering legs headed by stiff leaves, 41½in. wide. (Christie's)
$35,948

An Art Deco stained black and limed oak Ashanti style stool, possibly French, on five turned supports, 51.5cm. high. (Phillips)
$412

A Gordon Russell walnut and ebony stool with shaped eared handles, on octagonal section legs with ebony chamfered bulbous feet. (Christie's)
$6,171

One of a pair of Liberty oak folding stools, each consisting of ten slats forming X-shaped frames. (Christie's)
Two $408

A mahogany stool with solid panelled dished rectangular seat with molded edge, the frieze carved with pendant rockwork, 22¾in. wide. (Christie's)
$20,812

A Regency simulated rosewood and parcel gilt stool after a design by Thomas Hope, the X-frame with lion mask and ring finials, 34in. wide. (Christie's)
$24,596

A Liberty and Co. oak stool with square curved seat, on straight square section legs joined by plain stretchers and diagonal struts. (Christie's)
$1,028

STOOLS

A George II mahogany stool, the padded rectangular seat upholstered in yellow velvet, on cabriole legs, 24in. wide. (Christie's) $3,872

A mahogany window seat of Louis XV style with scrolling ends and bowed seat, 53in. wide. (Christie's) $1,954

A George I walnut stool, the ring turned cabriole legs and pad feet headed by unusual pierced and scrolling angle brackets 22¼in. wide. (Christie's)
$41,624

A Victorian walnut piano stool with adjustable circular seat on well carved tripod base. (David Lay)
$380

A pair of George III mahogany stools with rectangular red leather upholstered seats on square panelled legs, 22in. wide. (Christie's) $12,298

A Liberty & Co. 'Thebes' stool, the square shallow seat with pierced panels on four turned and waisted legs. (Christie's)
$353

A Neo-Classical white painted and parcel gilt stool, the X-shaped frame with lion mask terminals and monopodia with cleft feet, early 19th century, possibly Austrian, 28in. wide. (Christie's) $6,919

A Regency mahogany piano stool, the circular revolving seat upholstered in horsehair, on splayed feet, 13½in. (Christie's) $731

A Barcelona chromium plated stool designed by Mies van der Rohe, with curved cross legs, (Phillips)
$223

STOOLS

A Regency ormolu mounted rosewood footstool, supplied by George Bullock for Napoleon's use and New Longwood, the padded seat upholstered in green velvet, 13¾in. wide. (Christie's)
$21,252

One of a pair of Victorian oak window seats, each with raised sides on C-scroll supports, 60in. wide.(Bearne's)
Two $4,375

A Gustav Stickley mahogany footstool, circa 1904-1906, with upholstered seat, arched seat rail and exposed tenons, 20¼in. wide. (Robt. W. Skinner Inc.) $500

A Louis XV Provincial walnut tabouret, mid 18th century, on carved cabriole legs, 19¼in. long. (Robt. W. Skinner Inc.)
$475

A padded stool of Second Empire style, upholstered with silk covered cushion and bracket feet, 20in. wide. (Christie's)
$1,323

A Regency rosewood and mahogany framed dressing stool, the rectangular seat with bone and brass inlaid frieze, 19in. wide. (Greenslades) $743

A George IV gilt window seat of X shape, the scroll ends carved with acanthus leaves, 32in. wide. (Lawrence Fine Arts)
$8,923

A Stickley Bros. spindle sided footstool, circa 1907, with stretchers centering seven spindles each side, unsigned, 20½in. wide. (Robt. W. Skinner Inc.)
$2,600

A Charles II silvered wood stool, the padded circular seat with an applique crest surmounted by a coronet, 17in. diam. (Christie's)$2,277

A three piece gilt frame drawing room suite, in the Louis XV manner, with floral Aubusson tapestry, on molded cabriole legs. (Phillips) $2,992

An Art Nouveau pearwood salon suite, comprising a three seater settee, 175cm. long, two elbow chairs and four upright chairs. (Phillips)   Seven $4,576

A Roman style giltwood suite comprising: a sofa and two side chairs, with padded backs and seats upholstered in distressed silk, mid 19th century, sofa 76in. wide. (Christie's)
$3,867

SUITES

A suite of gilt frame seat furniture in the Louis XV style, comprising a small settee, two arm chairs and six side chairs, all with molded frames enriched with flowerheads and leafage, the settee 49½in. (Lawrence Fine Arts)   Nine $3,561

A 19th century three piece beech frame drawing room suite, in the Louis XVI manner, on turned and fluted tapering legs, 185cm. (Phillips) $2,992

A Victorian walnut framed drawing room suite comprising a settee with oval padded back on a pierced scrolling foliate framework, a similarly carved open armchair and a nursing chair. (Bearne's) $5,278

CARD & TEA TABLES

A mahogany and satinwood card table, the baize lined crossbanded demi-lune top with a bat's wing motif, 37in. wide. (Christie's) $2,982

An Edwardian rosewood envelope-top card table, each flap inlaid with bowls of fruit, cornucopiae and scrolling foliage, 23¾in. square. (Bearne's) $2,640

A George II walnut veneered card table, with projecting corners and feather stringing, on carved cabriole legs with claw and ball feet, 34in. wide, restored. (Bearne's) $2,655

A George III mahogany tea table in the manner of Thomas Chippendale, with well figured folding serpentine top, 36in. wide. (Christie's) $12,298

A Regency rosewood card table inlaid in cut brass with stylized foliage within strapwork, on four S-scroll feet, 35¾in. wide. (Bearne's) $3,717

A George III satinwood card table of D shape on four square tapering supports, 36in. wide. (Lawrence Fine Arts) $2,849

A Classical carved mahogany card table, New York, 1815-1825, on carved hairy paw feet, 36½in. wide (leaves open). (Christie's) $1,980

A George III mahogany card table of D-shape, with satinwood crossbanded top inlaid with stringing, 36in. (Lawrence Fine Arts) $1,628

A William IV mahogany card table on a concave sided platform with acanthus scroll feet, 36in. wide. (Bearne's) $1,760

CARD & TEA TABLES

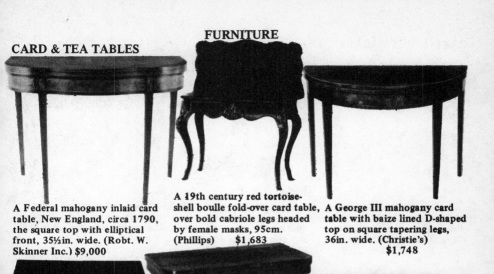

A Federal mahogany inlaid card table, New England, circa 1790, the square top with elliptical front, 35½in. wide. (Robt. W. Skinner Inc.) $9,000

A 19th century red tortoise-shell boulle fold-over card table, over bold cabriole legs headed by female masks, 95cm. (Phillips) $1,683

A George III mahogany card table with baize lined D-shaped top on square tapering legs, 36in. wide. (Christie's) $1,748

An 18th century South German walnut and marquetry card table with projecting round corners, on cabriole legs, 2ft. 10in. wide. (Phillips) $3,060

A William IV rosewood card table, on an unusual base with three scroll supports carved with leafage, 36in. wide. (Lawrence Fine Arts) $1,951

A Federal mahogany inlaid veneered card table, New Hampshire, circa 1798, the hinged rectangular top with elliptical front and sides and ovolo corners, 35½in. wide. (Robt. W. Skinner Inc.) $2,500

A George IV satinwood card table with a hexagonal stem and on a triangular platform with reeded bun feet, 35in. wide. (Bearne's) $1,408

A Victorian inlaid walnut card table, the shaped swivel fold-over top raised on four turned supports and four carved feet, 3ft.1in. wide. (Greenslades) $2,275

A Regency mahogany fold-over tea table, with molded sabre legs and well cast brass shoes, 90cm. (Phillips) $1,683

CARD & TEA TABLES

A satinwood and rosewood card table, with D-shaped baize lined top, on square tapering legs, 38in. wide. (Christie's) $9,462

A George IV rosewood card table, on spreading hexangular shaft with concave gadrooned platform base and claw feet, 36in. wide. (Christie's) $1,439

A George III mahogany card table with serpentine folding top, on cabriole legs, 37in. wide. (Christie's) $1,645

A Georgian mahogany tea table with projecting eared corners, on cabriole legs with scrolls, 34in. wide. (Lawrence Fine Arts) $2,602

A Victorian walnut card table, with four shaped legs with scroll toes, 37in. wide. (Hy. Duke & Son) $2,028

A fine quality George III style satinwood demi-lune card table, on square tapered legs, 35½in. wide, circa 1890. (Bonhams) $2,492

A George III small mahogany card table, inlaid with narrow bands and stringing and on four square tapering supports, 28¾in. (Lawrence Fine Arts) $2,602

A fine and rare Classical painted card table, Baltimore, circa 1815, on an X-frame base with foliate gilt mounts, 36in. long. (Christie's) $17,600

A George III mahogany card table with serpentine baize lined folding top on chamfered legs, 35¼in. wide. (Christie's) $1,028

CARD & TEA TABLES

A Regency simulated bamboo mahogany card table, on ring turned legs and spreading feet, 32in. wide. (Christie's) $9,256

A late Regency mahogany tea table on a turned pillar with four reeded and fluted sabre legs, 36in. wide. (Lawrence Fine Arts) $3,256

A George I mahogany card table, the rectangular top with projecting corners above lappet-headed tapering turned legs with pad feet, 35½in. wide. (Bearne's) $3,520

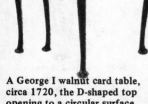

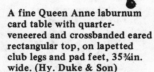

A George I walnut card table, circa 1720, the D-shaped top opening to a circular surface over three short drawers, 31in. wide. (Robt. W. Skinner Inc.) $850

A fine Queen Anne laburnum card table with quarter-veneered and crossbanded eared rectangular top, on lapetted club legs and pad feet, 35¾in. wide. (Hy. Duke & Son) $16,562

A George III mahogany semi-circular card table with baize lining and spade feet, restored, 36in. (Lawrence Fine Arts) $1,871

A George II walnut card table, opening in a concertina action with four cabriole supports, 33in. wide. (Lawrence Fine Arts) $8,551

A late Regency rosewood and brass inlaid card table with D-shaped fold-over top, 35½in. wide. (Lawrence Fine Arts) $1,221

A George III mahogany card table with serpentine folding top and plain frieze, 35½in. wide. (Christie's) $1,851

CENTER TABLES

A Regency center table, the rounded rectangular top fitted with two drawers either end, 42 x 29¾in. (Lawrence Fine Arts) $31,542

A Regency rosewood center table, the circular tip-up top inlaid with brass lines, 52½in. diam. (Christie's) $16,082

A Regency rosewood center table, the rectangular white marble top inlaid with a central roundel of lapis lazuli, bar supports with paw feet, 42in. wide. (Christie's) $18,920

A Chinese hardwood center table, 19th century, the round top with mottled rose marble insert, 33in. diam. (Robt. W. Skinner Inc.) $1,500

An ormolu mounted red tortoiseshell and boulle center table, on cabriole legs with female clasps and scroll sabots, mid-19th century, 62in. wide. (Christie's) $1,859

A Napoleon III Sevres pattern porcelain and ormolu center table, the circular top with a dished centre painted with a bust of Louis XIV, 28¾in. diam. (Christie's) $16,731

A giltwood and rosewood center table with molded circular white marble top, mid 19th century, 40in. diam. (Christie's) $4,136

An English Art Deco walnut center table, the octagonal top on a pedestal base consisting of four shaped rectangular compartments with open recesses, 70.5cm. high. (Christie's) $1,122

A Victorian walnut and marquetry center table with octagonal tip-up top veneered in a segmented design, 38½in. (Lawrence Fine Arts) $2,598

FURNITURE

CENTER TABLES

A Regency rosewood center table, on lyre-shaped trestle end supports headed by anthemion and lozenge plaques, 32½in. wide, 30¼in. high, 19in. deep. (Christie's) $17,028

A George IV style mahogany center table with pink marble inset to the circular top, 60in. diameter. (Bearne's) $1,770

An ebony and marquetry center table, the octagonal tilt-top profusely inlaid with ribbon-tied stylized Medici foliate panels, third quarter 19th century, 49½in. wide. (Christie's)$13,942

An early Victorian gilt and composition center table, the circular specimen marble top in an entrelac and flowerhead molded border. (Christie's) $2,602

A mid Victorian rosewood center table, in the Louis XV taste, on molded cabriole legs, 152cm. (Phillips) $2,431

An Italian micro mosaic center table, Rome, second quarter 19th century, inlaid with a scene depicting 'The Doves of Pliny', 31½in. high. (Robt. W. Skinner Inc.) $26,000

A Louis XV style kingwood veneered center table, the shaped circular marble top with molded brass edge, 37in. diameter. (Bearne's) $1,628

A George IV mahogany center table with finely figured circular segmented tilt-top, 47¼in. diam. (Christie's) $5,759

A Regency rosewood center table, on ormolu framed trestle end supports, the arched bar feet inlaid with brass lines, 29¾in. wide. (Christie's) $60,544

CENTER TABLES

An early Victorian black lime-stone center table from Adam's Original Royal Museum, Mat-lock, 29in. high. (Christie's) $6,811

A tiger maple hutch table, North America, 18th century, on mold-ed stepped, shoe feet, 45½in. wide. (Robt. W. Skinner Inc.) $5,100

An ormolu mounted maho-gany center table by Wright and Mansfield in the style of Adam Weisweiler, 36in. diam. (Christie's) $10,224

A Russian Nicholas I mahogany center table, the oval top with gadrooned border, on shaped platform base with claw feet, 56in. wide. (Christie's) $2,442

A Scandinavian mahogany center table with circular top centered by an inlaid fan medallion, second quarter 19th century, 36in. diam. (Christie's) $2,239

A Regency rosewood center table with circular tip-up top and plain frieze, 52¼in. diam. (Christie's) $2,057

An Empire mahogany center table with molded circular black fossil marble top, 32½in. diam. (Christie's) $5,291

A pollard oak veneered center table in the style of Thomas Hope, the concave sided tri-angular pedestal inlaid in ebony, 66in. diam. (Bearne's) $23,660

A Gillows small oak center table, the octagonal molded top on four chamfered and molded legs joined by X-shaped mold-ed platform, 66.4cm. high. (Christie's) $1,776

CENTER TABLES

A Biedermeier birchwood, ebonised and mahogany center table, inlaid with a seated Etruscan lady and two attendants, 44in. diam. (Christie's) $22,385

A Victorian rosewood center table, with oblong top, on trestle base with scroll feet, on castors, 74cm. (Osmond Tricks) $684

A Louis Philippe mahogany center table, on a hexagonal baluster shaft and scroll carved triform base with paw feet, 39in. diam. (Christie's) $2,035

A German parcel gilt mahogany and ebonized center table, the frieze painted with various Masonic symbols, early 19th century, 36¼in. diam. (Christie's) $16,280

A William IV rosewood center table, the rounded rectangular top with bead edging, on a platform base with massive paw feet, 48in. wide. (Lawrence Fine Arts) $4,573

An early Victorian papier-mache center table, the molded circular tip up top painted with a romantic lakeside scene, 48in. diam. (Christie's) $7,807

A Regency rosewood center table, the circular top inlaid with a specimen marble chessboard, 29in. high. (Christie's) $4,114

A Limbert octagonal table, circa 1905, the overhanging top on flat splayed legs with spade cut-outs, 29¼in. high. (Robt. W. Skinner Inc.) $1,400

A Victorian walnut center table with a well figured segmentally veneered circular tip-up top, 47in. diameter. (Bearne's) $2,184

FURNITURE

A satinwood, marquetry and parcel gilt pier table, the rectangular segmented breakfront top crossbanded with rosewood, 53¾in. wide. (Christie's) $28,380

A Regency rosewood and parcel gilt pier table with mirror-backed superstructure, 56in. wide. (Christie's) $2,879

A 19th century Italian rococo style giltwood console table, with mottled rose marble top over pierced scroll carved frieze, 54in. wide. (Robt. W. Skinner Inc.) $2,900

One of a pair of Louis XV style carved giltwood serpentine console tables, the detachable simulated marble tops above a pierced foliate carved frieze, 20in. wide. (Christie's) Two $1,155

A baroque giltwood console table, upon carved figure supports with foliate X-shaped stretchers, late 17th century, probably Austrian, 55in. wide. (Christie's) $6,105

A Louis XVI carved giltwood console table with semi-elliptical mottled gray marble top, on a scrolling leg, 34½in. wide. (Christie's) $1,425

A George III small mahogany console table of D shape, on two square tapering supports, 33½in. wide. (Lawrence Fine Arts) $3,625

A George III carved giltwood and gesso console table, having beaded and fluted frieze with central ribband, 3ft.10in. (Phillips) $10,800

One of a pair of Louis XV style giltwood and composition console tables, each with a serpentine shaped onyx top, 21½in. wide. (Christie's) Two $2,459

CONSOLE TABLES

One of a pair of oak console tables designed by Anthony Salvin, each with a molded edge to the rectangular top, 41½in. wide.(Bearne's)
Two $10,850

A cream painted console table, carved with foliage and flower-heads upon scrolling foliate legs, 72in. wide. (Christie's)
$1,628

A Regency parcel gilt and blue painted console table with mott-led salmon pink and ochre D-shaped marble top, 48in. wide. (Christie's) $5,965

An 18th century Italian baroque blackamoor console table, supported by a crouching figure with strained expression holding a cloth on his lap. (Robt. W. Skinner Inc.)
$9,750

A Charles X mahogany console table, upon lion monopodia support and concave sided base, the back with pilasters, 30in. wide. (Christie's) $3,256

A marble top and gilt plaster console table, supported by three bacchanal cherub figures, 19th century, 54in. wide. (Lawrence Fine Arts)
$1,673

An Italian painted console table, the shaped pietra dura marble top inlaid in various stones with a cartouche and flowers, second quarter 19th century, 25in. wide. (Christie's)
$4,477

A pair of George III carved giltwood corner console tables, with shaped marble tops. (Greenslades)$1,310

A Louis XV style giltwood console table, of serpentined outline, the eared later rectangular marble top above a profusely carved frieze, 33in. early 19th century. (Christie's)
$2,887

DINING TABLES

A William IV rosewood and parcel gilt breakfast table, on a square spreading pillar with concave sided base and four sabre shaped supports, restored, 51in. diam. (Lawrence Fine Arts) $5,698

A Regency mahogany breakfast table, the figured rectangular top with a bead type under edging, 47 x 42in. (Lawrence Fine Arts) $3,742

A William IV parcel gilt and mahogany breakfast table, on a canted triangular pillar with large gilt paw feet, 58in. diam. (Lawrence Fine Arts) $7,068

A mahogany breakfast table with circular tip-up top on a baluster pillar with tripod base, 18th century, 50in. diam. (Lawrence Fine Arts) $1,119

An unusual Regency mahogany and crossbanded library table, on turned urn shaped column and quadruped reeded splayed legs, 4ft.6in. x 3ft.2in. (Phillips) $6,840

A late Regency rosewood breakfast table with a tilting circular top, on a circular base with three hairy paw feet, 52in. diam. (Hy. Duke & Son) $2,366

A Victorian mahogany dining table, the coffered circular molded top on fluted turned tapering legs, extending to 108in. (Christie's) $4,235

A Victorian walnut and marquetry breakfast table, with a circular floral and butterfly center panel, 54in. diam. (Lawrence Fine Arts) $5,577

A figured mahogany dining table, the circular tilt-top with a bead molded frieze on a triform pedestal with concave sided platform base, on scroll feet, 53in., 19th century. (Christie's) $1,732

DINING TABLES

A late Regency circular breakfast table, the circular plumpudding mahogany top on a turned pillar, 48in. diam. (Lawrence Fine Arts)
$2,079

A Regency mahogany breakfast table, the tilting rectangular top with rounded corners and crossbanded in rosewood, 58 x 38in. (Hy. Duke & Son) $3,042

A William IV rosewood breakfast table, with circular tilttop, on lions paw feet, 52in. (Christie's) $2,695

A well figured Regency snaptop breakfast table, quadripartite fluted sabre legs, brass shoes and castors, 153 x 113cm. (Phillips) $2,618

A late George III mahogany large breakfast table, the rectangular top with rounded corners, 65¼in. x 47¼in. (David Lay) $3,077

A Regency brass inlaid rosewood breakfast table, on concave sided tripartite base with brass claw feet, 48in. diam. (Christie's) $4,936

A fine late 18th century circular rosewood tip-up table on center pedestal and platform with three feet. 49in. diameter. (Lambert & Foster) $2,816

A Regency rosewood snap-top breakfast table, on octagonal column and platform base with sabre legs, 101cm. (Phillips) $2,431

A rosewood and brass inlaid breakfast table, the circular banded tilt-top on a turned quadripartite support, 42in. (Christie's) $6,737

An Edwardian rosewood and inlaid dressing chest with swing mirror flanked by superstructure with drawers and shelves, on turned feet, 138cm. (Phillips) $1,870

A Louis XV Provincial fruitwood dressing table, mid 18th century, the kneehole flanked by a pair of panelled cabinet doors, 51in. long. (Robt. W. Skinner Inc.) $1,200

A George IV satinwood and parcel gilt dressing table, attributed to Morel and Seddon, inlaid with mahogany lines and beading, 42in. wide. (Christie's) $30,272

A Queen Anne cherry dressing table, Upper Connecticut River Valley, circa 1785, 34½in. wide. (Robt. W. Skinner Inc.) $11,000

A Dutch mahogany serpentine kneehole dressing table, profusely inlaid with urns, birds and foliate marquetry, on cabriole legs with sabots, 30½in. 19th century. (Christie's) $2,599

An Art Deco walnut dressing table, the removable shaped top having a glass cover and three drawers, 88cm. long. (Phillips) $152

An Edwardian mahogany inlaid kidney dressing table with insert leather top and fitted with nine drawers, 48in. wide. (Lawrence Fine Arts) $4,647

An Empire mahogany bonheur du jour, the panelled fall-flap enclosing a fitted interior, on square tapering legs, 34in. wide. (Christie's) $2,340

A Queen Anne walnut veneered dressing table, Massachusetts, circa 1740, the overhanging, molded top on a walnut veneered base, 32in. high. (Robt. W. Skinner Inc.) $6,500

DRESSING TABLES

Queen Anne cherry dressing table, probably Connecticut, circa 1770, the rectangular overhanging top with shaped corners and molded edge, 35¾in. wide. (Robt. W. Skinner Inc.) $15,000

An Empire mahogany dressing table on a U-shaped support carved with swan's heads, 32½in. wide. (Bearne's) $1,128

A Victorian mahogany knee-hole dressing table by Holland & Sons, London, on a plinth base, 48in. wide. (Bearne's) $1,408

A late Federal figured maple dressing table, New England, 1820-1830, with a rectangular bolection molded mirror, 65in. high. (Christie's) $1,320

A Queen Anne inlaid walnut dressing table, New England, 1730-1750, the rectangular top with molded edge above one long drawer over three short drawers, 32½in. wide. (Christie's) $3,080

A late George III mahogany dressing table with divided top enclosing bowl apertures and a rising ratcheted toilet mirror, possibly by Gillows, 20in. wide. (Christie's) $1,174

An Art Deco mahogany dressing table, having three pivot domed mirrors, 130cm. wide. (Phillips) $1,066

A late Federal mahogany dressing table, New York, 1815-1825, on a reeded curule base joined by a baluster and ring turned stretcher, 36½in. wide. (Christie's) $8,250

A 19th century lady's walnut bonheur du jour in the French manner, on turned and fluted legs, 43in. wide. (G.A.Property Services) $2,625

DROP LEAF TABLES

A Queen Anne maple drop leaf table, Massachusetts, 1730-1750, with shaped skirts and cabriole legs, 42½in. wide, extended. (Robt. W. Skinner Inc.) $61,000

A Queen Anne style tiger maple drop leaf table, the rectangular top with two oval drop leaves above a shaped skirt, 53in. wide. (Christie's) $1,760

A George II mahogany drop leaf table, circa 1740, on circular tapered legs with pad feet, 39in. diam. (Robt. W. Skinner Inc.) $850

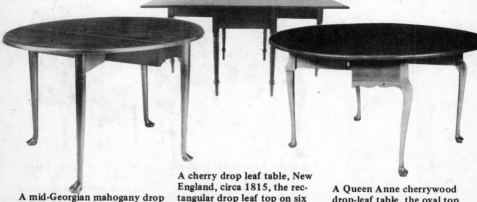

A mid-Georgian mahogany drop leaf table, on club legs and pad feet, 47½in. wide, extended. (Christie's) $1,234

A cherry drop leaf table, New England, circa 1815, the rectangular drop leaf top on six ring turned tapering legs, 59in. long, extended. (Robt. W. Skinner Inc. $800

A Queen Anne cherrywood drop-leaf table, the oval top with two drop leaves, 53½in., extended. (Christie's) $1,320

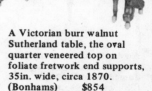

A small Gordon Russell oak drop leaf gateleg occasional table with plank sides and pull-out supports, 51 x 82cm., extended. (Phillips) $1,144

A mid-Georgian mahogany two flap table, with one drawer and on four cabriole supports with pointed pad feet, 50in. extended. (Lawrence Fine Arts) $2,044

A Victorian burr walnut Sutherland table, the oval quarter veneered top on foliate fretwork end supports, 35in. wide, circa 1870. (Bonhams) $854

DROP LEAF TABLES

A George II mahogany drop leaf dining table, with deep elliptical leaves, on plain turned tapered legs with pad feet, 54in. x 56in. (Bonhams) $2,136

A late George II mahogany two-flap table, on four cabriole supports with pointed pad feet, 48 x 57in. extended. (Lawrence Fine Arts) $4,989

Queen Anne maple and birch dining table, Rhode Island, circa 1760, tapering legs ending in high pad feet, 59in. wide. (Robt. W. Skinner Inc.) $4,900

A George II red walnut drop leaf table, the oval top over plain frieze and turned tapering legs terminating in pad feet. (Phillips) $935

An early 19th century Dutch marquetry drop leaf table, the oval top profusely inlaid with foliage, 115cm. wide. (Phillips) $2,992

A Dutch rosewood, mahogany and floral marquetry drop leaf table, on cabriole legs and pointed pad feet, 47in. wide open. (Christie's) $3,460

Late 19th century mahogany Sutherland table with square flaps. (British Antique Exporters) $306

A Queen Anne maple drop leaf dining table, New England, 1740-1760, on cabriole legs with pad feet, 44in. wide. (Christie's) $2,420

Early 19th century mahogany breakfast table on a central column with splay legs with brass claw feet. (British Antique Exporters) $656

DRUM TABLES

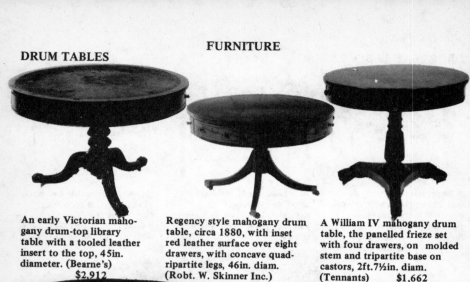

An early Victorian mahogany drum-top library table with a tooled leather insert to the top, 45in. diameter. (Bearne's)
$2,912

Regency style mahogany drum table, circa 1880, with inset red leather surface over eight drawers, with concave quadripartite legs, 46in. diam. (Robt. W. Skinner Inc.)
$2,900

A William IV mahogany drum table, the panelled frieze set with four drawers, on molded stem and tripartite base on castors, 2ft.7½in. diam. (Tennants) $1,662

A Regency mahogany drum table on an urn shaped pedestal and reeded quadripartite splayed base, 45in. diam. (Christie's)
$9,256

A mahogany drum table with circular leather lined top, basically early 19th century, 23½in. diam. (Christie's)
$5,553

A Regency mahogany library table with eight frieze drawers and splayed quadripartite base with brass dolphin caps, 46¼in. wide. (Christie's)
$5,759

A George III mahogany drum table, on later turned spreading column and splayed quadripartite base, 32in. diam. (Christie's) $5,759

A Regency mahogany drum table with circular top and eight drawers in the frieze, 44½in. diam. (Christie's)
$6,171

A mahogany drum table, the circular revolving top with a frieze fitted with four short drawers and four dummy drawers, 35in. diam. (Christie's)
$1,443

GATELEG TABLES

A Commonwealth oak double gateleg table, the oval top on columnar legs, 59½in. long. (Bearne's) $7,040

An oak gateleg table, the oval twin flap top of planked construction, on baluster turned legs, 57in., 17th century. (Christie's) $1,540

An early Georgian solid yew-wood gateleg dining table, on ring turned legs joined by square and turned stretchers, 69½ x 58½in. (Christie's) $20,812

20th century oak gateleg table with half-round leaves. (British Antique Exporters) $131

A mid-18th century solid walnut gateleg table in American New England style, 28in. high. (David Lay) $724

20th century oak gateleg table with barley twist supports and half-round flaps. (British Antique Exporters) $131

A Queen Anne oak gateleg table with oval drop leaf top fitted with one drawer and raised on turned supports, 54½ x 63½in. (Lawrence Fine Arts) $6,715

A mid-Georgian mahogany gateleg table, the folding triangular top with a small frieze drawer, on club legs, 39in. (Christie's)$1,347

An oak gateleg table, with oval twin flap top, on ring turned baluster supports and splayed feet, 35in., 17th century. (Christie's)$924

LARGE TABLES

A Regency mahogany three pedestal dining table, on turned shafts and molded splayed legs. 147½ x 60in., including two extra leaves. (Christie's) $109,736

A mahogany three pedestal dining table with molded D-shaped end sections, on ring turned shafts and splayed bases, 45 x 150in. (Christie's) $7,816

A pine painted table, probably New England, early 19th century, the overhanging scrubbed two board top with breadboard ends, 50in. wide. (Robt. W. Skinner Inc.) $1,900

A Regency mahogany breakfast table with rectangular tip-up top on baluster shape turned pillar, 40½ x 52in. (Lawrence Fine Arts) $2,950

A red painted tilt-top hutch table, American 19th century, on trestle feet, the top 46in. long. (Christie's) $3,300

A mahogany two pillar dining table on two turned pillars, each with four sabre legs and brass feet, 106in. extended. (Lawrence Fine Arts) $7,436

A mahogany twin pedestal dining table, on turned pedestals and quadripartite bases, basically early 19th century, 75½in. long. (Christie's) $4,114

A 19th century rosewood scroll table, the rectangular top above a pierced frieze and brackets. (Bonhams) $1,513

LARGE TABLES

A late Regency mahogany extending dining table, with a concertina action center portion and five leaves, 174½in., extended. (Lawrence Fine Arts) $33,264

A Betty Joel walnut refectory table, with canted corners, raised on two supports with chamfered edges, 208cm. long x 74cm. across. (Phillips) $2,200

A Spanish walnut two drawer table with two frieze drawers carved with stylized flower-heads, 61½in. wide. (Christie's) $4,274

A Regency mahogany breakfast table, on a cylindrical turned pillar and four sabre shape supports, 54 x 39½in. (Lawrence Fine Arts) $4,070

A Regency mahogany breakfast table, the rounded rectangular tip-up top crossbanded with rosewood, 50½in. wide. (Christie's) $6,582

A 19th century red tortoiseshell boulle bureau plat, in the Louis XV manner, gilt metal female mask headed cabriole legs, 149cm. (Phillips) $2,805

A Victorian mahogany extending dining table, 154in. long, the five extra leaves within a standing case, on castors, 70in. high. (Bearne's) $5,808

A Regency mahogany breakfast table with rounded rectangular tip-up top with later crossbanding, 51in. wide. (Christie's) $4,731

LARGE TABLES

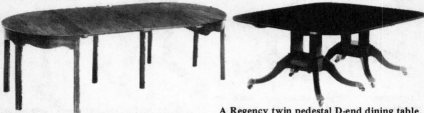

A Georgian mahogany D-end dining table, on square canted supports, with repairs and alterations, 47½in. (Lawrence Fine Arts) $4,275

A Regency twin pedestal D-end dining table, each pedestal with two rectangular supports and quadripartite splayed base, 118½in. long. (Christie's) $75,680

A late 19th century mahogany D-end dining table, in the 18th century manner, with tripod sabre legs terminating in brass shoes and castors, 208cm. (Phillips) $4,114

A mahogany extending dining table, on four rectangular supports, each with two reeded splayed legs with giltmetal paw feet, 214½ x 50¼in. (Christie's) $11,313

A pine and ash sawbuck table, probably New England, early 19th century, the overhanging two-board top with breadboard ends, 43½in. wide. (Robt. W. Skinner Inc.) $450

An Art Deco walnut dining table, the rounded rectangular top with mirrored walnut veneer, on curved V-shaped trestle ends, 179.5cm. long. (Christie's) $1,122

A Regency mahogany twin pedestal dining table, each with ring turned baluster shaft and quadripartite base, 60in. long. (Christie's) $10,285

A late Regency mahogany extending dining table on tapering reeded legs with brass castors, 90in. long (including two extra leaves). (Bearne's) $2,552

LARGE TABLES

A William IV mahogany twin pedestal dining table, the triangular pedestals with scrolled feet, 52in. x 114½in., including three extra leaves. (Christie's) $16,456

A George III period mahogany D-end dining table, with drop leaf center section, on square tapering legs, 3ft.8½in. by 9ft.2¼in. extended. (Geering & Colyer) $5,670

A Classical cherry dining table, probably Connecticut, circa 1820, two identical drop leaf tables joined by metal cleats, both extended 81in. (Robt. W. Skinner Inc.) $750

An antique oak drawleaf dining table, the oblong top on massive spherical supports, having shaped molded stretcher, opening to 9ft.3in. (Hobbs & Chambers)
$2,534

A fine Regency mahogany extending dining table with telescopic action in the manner of Gillows, including six extra leaves, 14ft. 1in. x 5ft. extended. (Phillips)
$14,400

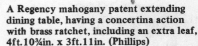

A Regency mahogany patent extending dining table, having a concertina action with brass ratchet, including an extra leaf, 4ft.10¾in. x 3ft.11in. (Phillips)
$3,240

A Gordon Russell quartered oak dining table, with octagonal panelled supports and pierced cross stretcher, made by G. Cooke, 1923, 5ft.6in. x 2ft.9in. (Hobbs & Chambers)
$4,344

A Victorian mahogany extending dining table with molded edge, on tapering octagonal legs with china castors, 167in. long. (Bearne's) $5,310

OCCASIONAL TABLES

A mid 19th century ebonized and porcelain mounted petit table, the square top centered by two figures, signed Lervas, 44cm. (Phillips) $898

A Regency satinwood tripod table, on concave sided platform and bronzed feet, 24in. wide. (Christie's) $7,816

A George III mahogany reading table with crossbanded rectangular easel top and square tapering legs, 25in. wide. (Christie's) $5,142

A French kingwood, marquetry and porcelain mounted table a ouvrage with shaped top lifting to reveal an interior mirror, 19th century, 20in. (Lawrence Fine Arts) $1,831

A quartetto nest of mahogany coffee tables, on slender turned supports with splayed legs, the largest 22in. (Lawrence Fine Arts) $6.715

A George III mahogany tea table, the rectangular folding top above a fluted frieze, 20¾in. wide. (Christie's) $24,596

A George III mahogany lamp table with oval crossbanded top, on square tapering legs, 28¼in. wide. (Christie's) $2,674

A Victorian brass and cast iron pedestal table, the circular thuyawood top with lotus cast brass edge, 29½in. high. (Bearne's) $637

A gilt metal mounted kingwood and parquetry two tier table on fluted supports and cabriole legs, 24in. wide. (Christie's) $1 861

OCCASIONAL TABLES

A George III mahogany artist's table, with hinged baize lined ratcheted adjustable top, on square legs, 2ft.1½in. wide. (Phillips) $2,520

A George II mahogany snap-top wine table, on turned and gadrooned column and tripod base, 72cm. (Phillips) $1,870

A George III figured mahogany urn table, on molded cabriole legs with shell headings and pendant flowerheads, 27½in. high. (Christie's) $37,840

A walnut occasional table, on spirally turned shaft and S-scroll tripartite base, 19¼in. wide. (Christie's) $9,256

A George II walnut corner table, on lappet-headed tapering turned legs with pointed pad feet, 36in. wide. (Bearne's) $873

A Louis XV style mahogany bombe display table with a sloping and curved glazed top, on cabriole legs, 31in. high. (Bearne's) $1,232

A William IV tripod occasional table with rectangular burrwood top with a bead edge, 22in. wide. (Lawrence Fine Arts) $3,296

A mid-Georgian mahogany tripod table with birdcage action on ring turned spreading shaft and carved Manx base, 38in. wide, 28¼in. high. (Christie's) $7,199

An ebonised occasional table by E.W.Godwin, on turned tapering legs united by an undertier, 66cm. high. (Phillips) $411

FURNITURE

An early Victorian mahogany games table with a mid-Georgian circular tilt-top lined in red baize, 48in. diam. (Christie's) $2,262

A Regency mahogany serving table, in the manner of Gillows, on ribbed tapering legs joined by a platform, 48in. wide. (Christie's) $5,142

A George II mahogany tripod table, the waved tip-up top on swivelling birdcage support, 31in. diam. (Christie's) $35,948

A William IV mahogany two tier table, the overlapping top with a bead type border. (Lawrence Fine Arts) $1,559

A Finmar laminated birch two tier table, designed by Alvar Aalto, painted black, the rectangular tiers with curved sides supported by rounded square shaped trestle ends, printed manufacturer's label, 58.6cm. high; 60cm. wide; 50.1cm. deep. (Christie's) $481

A satinwood and amaranth tricoteuse inlaid overall with trellis and dot pattern, on splayed legs, 29¼in. high. (Christie's) $9,873

A George III mahogany architect's table, the rectangular top with detachable book rest on a double ratchet, 4ft.4in. extended. (Phillips) $4,680

A Classical marble top gilt stencilled mahogany pier table, New York, 1820-1830, on foliate carved black painted paw feet, 39½in. wide. (Christie's) $6,600

A Regency rosewood jardiniere table, with ring turned stretcher and arched feet, 20in. wide. (Christie's) $1,851

OCCASIONAL TABLES

A George III mahogany reading table crossbanded in kingwood with a rising rectangular screen filled with an embroidered panel, 23½in. wide. (Christie's) $6,054

A Chinese hardwood altar table with overscrolled ends, 33in. high by 47in. wide. (Bearne's) $1,196

A Gustav Stickley table with twelve Grueby tiles, circa 1902-4, with four flat rails framing twelve four-inch green tiles, signed, 24in. wide. (Robt. W. Skinner Inc.) $29,000

A Georgian mahogany silver table, on chamfered legs with pierced fret spandrels, 2ft. 10in. x 1ft.10in. (Phillips) $3,312

An ormolu mounted kingwood and marquetry two tier Sutherland table, the two-eared sepentine rectangular twin flap tiers inlaid with sprigs of foliage, late 19th century, 31in. wide, open; 28¼in. high; 25¾in. deep. (Christie's) $6,320

An early George III mahogany architect's table, the mitred adjustable top above a frieze drawer, 42in. (Lawrence Fine Arts) $4,368

An ormolu mounted kingwood etagere crossbanded with tulipwood, on tapering cabriole legs with foliate clasps reaching to pieds de biche sabots, 37in. wide. (Christie's) $4,833

A George III satinwood reading table crossbanded with fiddle back mahogany and rosewood, on square tapering legs, 22½in. wide. (Christie's) $4,936

An ormolu mounted kingwood, mahogany, parquetry and marquetry table a ecrire, on cabriole legs with foliate clasps, 33½in. wide. (Christie's) $3,718

PEMBROKE TABLES

A George III mahogany and inlaid Pembroke table, the oval satinwood crossbanded hinged top fitted with a bowed frieze drawer, 1.09m. x 82cm. (Phillips) $4,320

A Regency mahogany Pembroke breakfast table, on a vase turned column and outswept legs, 39in. wide, circa 1810. (Bonhams) $979

A George III sycamore, satinwood and marquetry oval Pembroke table, containing a drawer in the bowed frieze with shell, palm and anthemion headed angles, 3ft. 2in. x 2ft. 4½in. (Phillips) $16,200

A George III plum-pudding mahogany Pembroke table with butterfly top, on square tapered legs, 3ft. x 2ft. 6in. (Phillips) $3,600

A George III mahogany Pembroke table with rounded rectangular twin flap top, on chamfered square legs, 42in. wide. (Christie's) $3,702

19th century mahogany Pembroke table on turned leg supports with brass cap casters. (British Antique Exporters) $263

A Federal inlaid mahogany Pembroke table, New York, 1790-1810, the rectangular top with bowed ends and line inlaid edge, 41in. wide (leaves open). (Christie's) $5,500

A George III mahogany Pembroke table, crossbanded with satinwood, on square tapering legs, 44¾in. wide, open. (Christie's) $1,645

A mid Georgian mahogany Pembroke table, one end with a drawer with a writing slope and pen and ink drawer, 21in. wide. (Lawrence Fine Arts) $3,903

SIDE TABLES

A Victorian oak side table, the canted rectangular marbleized top above a frieze carved with stylised foliage, 100in. (Christie's) $2,117

A George III mahogany side table, with rectangular molded top above three frieze drawers, on square moulded legs, 71in. (Christie's) $2,117

A Spanish chestnut side table, the rectangular molded top above a pair of walnut banded frieze drawers, 63¼in., 18th century. (Christie's) $731

A George I burr walnut side table with quartered and cross-banded rectangular top, on cabriole legs and pad feet, 30in. wide. (Christie's) $9,256

An important Chippendale period carved mahogany sideboard table in the gothic taste based on a design in the Director, feet with quatrefoil blind fret ornament, 6ft.6in. wide. (Phillips) $72,000

A 19th century Chinese hardwood half round table, the four legs with carved knees and floral carved feet, 36in. wide. (David Lay) $845

A William IV rosewood side table, on baluster legs with lappeted foliage joined by a concave-fronted undertier, 50½in. wide. (Christie's) $3,085

A Regency mahogany side table, on square channelled end standards with scrolling volutes, 38in. wide. (Christie's) $4,114

A Regency mahogany, ebony molded and strung side table of breakfront D-shaped outline in the manner of Gillows, 3ft.6in. wide. (Phillips) $6,480

SIDE TABLES

One of a pair of George II
grained side tables, the Italian
molded rectangular quartered
and mottled purple and yellow
marble tops with channelled
brass borders, 70in. wide.
(Christie's)
Two $340,560

A George IV ebonized and parcel gilt side table, the rectangular top inset with two Italian
micro-mosaic panels, 20in. wide.
(Christie's) $5,553

An oak refectory or side table
with cleated three plank top,
on simple turned legs joined
by stretchers, 76in. long.
(Bearne's) $1,557

Antique oak side table, the
top with thumb mold edge ,
the scroll shaped frieze fitted
single drawer with brass loop
handles, 1ft.8¾in. wide.
(Hobbs & Chambers)
$1,306

One of a pair of Irish Georgian
mahogany side tables with oval
tops, 24in. wide. (Christie's)
Two $3,085

An 18th century Portuguese
rococo carved rosewood
side table, containing two
drawers in the shaped apron,
3ft.11in. wide. (Phillips)
$15,300

A George I gilt gesso side
table in the manner of James
Moore, on cabriole legs
terminating in scroll feet,
3ft. wide. (Phillips)
$10,800

A Galle walnut and marquetry
side table, the eared rectangular
top inlaid in various fruitwoods
with a spray of flowers, with inlaid signature Galle, 73.1cm. high.
(Christie's) $935

A George IV rosewood and
brass inlaid side table of unusual design, with the top of
exaggerated serpentine outline,
52in. wide. (Lawrence Fine
Arts) $4,461

SIDE TABLES

A George II giltwood side table with rectangular mottled gray scagliola top, 51in. wide. (Christie's) $32,164

A brass inlaid rosewood side table with rectangular gray marble slab, on square tapering legs, 25¼in. wide. (Christie's) $1,119

A massive giltwood side table, on a foliate molded frieze hung with swags centered by a bearded mask of Hercules on imbricated S-scroll legs carved with female masks, joined by shaped stretchers supporting an eagle, on turned feet, 72in. wide. (Christie's) $18,513

A French Empire mahogany side table with a rectangular tray top, on S-shaped legs, 19in. wide. (Bearne's) $1,091

A 19th century English Colonial rosewood side table in George IV style, the low back intricately carved with birds, 57in. wide. (David Lay) $507

An early Victorian burr walnut small side table, on a square pillar and concave sided base, 25in. (Lawrence Fine Arts) $1,424

An early 18th century oak side table on simple turned legs joined by squared stretchers, 30in. wide. (Bearne's) $3,256

An early Georgian crossbanded oak side table, on angled cabriole legs with shaped apron, 2ft.9½in. wide. (Geering & Colyer) $2,280

A George III mahogany side table with serpentine crossbanded top centered by an oval fan medallion, 31½in. wide. (Christie's) $8,228

A Regency mahogany sofa table with rounded rectangular twin flap crossbanded top, on molded splayed legs, adapted, 50¼in. wide. (Christie's)
$2,879

A fine and rare painted and gilt rosewood sofa table, New York, circa 1815, lion's paw feet with acanthus knees, 57¼in. long (leaves up). (Christie's) $209,000

A Regency pollard oak, ebony and ebonized sofa table in the manner of George Bullock, 60in. wide, open. (Christie's)
$6,622

A Regency rosewood sofa table, the two flap top with canted corners, on four sabre supports with brass claw feet, 61in. extended. (Lawrence Fine Arts) $15,801

A Regency solid yew-wood sofa table, on solid end standards and reeded splayed legs, 57in. wide, open. (Christie's)
$5,142

A Regency mahogany sofa table fitted two drawers opposite two dummy drawers, with splayed legs with brass claw feet, 61in. extended. (Lawrence Fine Arts) $17,102

A Classical carved mahogany and mahogany veneer sofa table, probably New York, circa 1820, 35½in. wide. (Robt. W. Skinner Inc.) $7,500

A Regency satinwood sofa table, the rounded rectangular twin flap top crossbanded with coromandel, 64in. wide, open. (Christie's) $34,056

A Regency rosewood sofa table, on trestle base with beaded border and carved scrolling feet, 86cm. (Phillips)
$4,488

SOFA TABLES

A Regency brass inlaid rosewood sofa table, on stepped square shaft and splayed quadripartite base, 59in. wide. (Christie's) $9,050

A Regency mahogany sofa table, on reeded curved X-framed supports joined by a turned stretcher ending in paw feet, 65in. wide. (Christie's) $75,680

A George III mahogany sofa table, on solid end standards, the square tapering splayed legs with paw feet and castors, 56½in. wide, open. (Christie's) $7,405

A Regency mahogany sofa table, on solid trestle shape end supports joined by square stretcher and with reeded sabre legs, 57½in. extended. (Lawrence Fine Arts) $5,391

A Regency rosewood sofa table, on rectangular trestle ends with channelled splayed feet, 58in. wide open. (Christie's) $9,873

A fine Regency calamander veneered and brass inlaid sofa table, the frieze containing two drawers and dummy drawers to the reverse, 4ft.10in. x 2ft.6in. (Phillips) $28,800

A Regency rosewood sofa table, on ring turned trestle base joined by shaped pole stretcher, 93cm. wide. (Phillips) $6,732

A Regency rosewood sofa table, on a U-shaped pedestal and quadripartite splayed base, 59in. wide, open. (Christie's) $14,399

A Regency mahogany sofa table, on reeded sabre legs joined by flying stretcher, brass shoes, 92cm. (Phillips) $3,740

WORKBOXES & GAMES TABLES

A Chinese export black and gold lacquer work table, on ring turned trestle ends joined by a conforming stretcher with claw feet, 25in. wide. (Christie's) $1,851

A late Federal mahogany work-stand, Philadelphia, 1800-1820, on baluster turned and reeded legs on peg feet, 16¾in. wide. (Christie's) $2,090

A late Regency mahogany games and work table, on a U-shaped support, 23in. wide. (Lawrence Fine Arts) $1,767

Federal mahogany and mahogany veneer work table, Massachusetts, circa 1800, the rectangular top with ovolo corners, 21½in. wide. (Robt. W. Skinner Inc.) $2,900

A Victorian walnut work table, the octagonal top with partitioned interior and octagonal tapered stem, 17½in. wide, circa 1860. (Bonhams) $712

A late Federal mahogany drop leaf work table, New England, 1810-1830, on spirally reeded and ring turned legs, 44½in. wide, leaves open. (Christie's) $1,210

A Classical mahogany and mahogany veneer work table, probably Boston, circa 1820, the rectangular top with rounded oval leaves. (Robt. W. Skinner Inc.) $800

A Dutch walnut and marquetry games table, the fold-over top with rounded corners, 18th century with later legs and feet, 33½in. wide. (Lawrence Fine Arts) $3,160

A Classical mahogany work table, Philadelphia, 1810-1830, on a shaped base with leaf and paw feet, 19½in. wide. (Christie's) $935

A Federal mahogany work table, Boston, Massachusetts 1810-1820, on molded sabre legs with castors, 51.1cm. wide, closed. (Christie's) $3,300

An Academy painted tiger maple work table, New England circa 1815, the rectangular over hanging top edged in tiny flowers, 43,5cm. wide. (Robt. W. Skinner Inc.) $7,250

A Regency mahogany and brass inlaid drop flap work table, quadruped splayed scroll supports, 2ft.10in. x 1ft. 5in. (Phillips) $6,120

A William IV period mahogany concave front work table, on quadruple scrolls and leaf carved column support, with triangular base, 20in. wide. (Geering & Colyer) $1,140

A Victorian walnut games table, with fold-over swivel top with checker inlay, backgammon inlay, and cribbage inlay, 28in. wide. (Duncan Vincent) $2,040

A satinwood games table inlaid with checkered lines, on square tapering legs, 19in. wide. (Christie's) $1,234

A Biedermeier maple and ebony work table, the hinged square top enclosing a fitted interior including a silk lined folding pin-cushion, 20in. wide. (Christie's) $6,105

A watered ash games table, the reversible rectangular top inlaid with chess squares, Scandinavian or Russian, basically late 18th century. (Christie's) $4,070

A rare Federal mahogany veneered inlaid work table, probably Seymour workshop, Boston, Massachusetts, 1795-1810, 18in. wide. (Robt. W. Skinner Inc.) $44,000

WORKBOXES & GAMES TABLES

A George III satinwood games and writing table, crossbanded in rosewood, the rounded rectangular twin flap top with a reversible center, 34in. wide. (Christie's) $4,259

An Anglo-Indian Regency padoukwood games table, on end standards and splayed legs with stiff leaf brass caps, 51in. wide. (Christie's)
                    $22,704

A fine George III mahogany and inlaid envelope games table, on square tapered legs terminating in cross stretchers, stamped C.Toussaint several times, 1ft.6in. (Phillips)
                    $12,600

A Victorian 16in. rosewood work box with nulled borders and a shaped base on bun feet. (Anderson & Garland)
          $1,038

Victorian games/work table, the top with inlaid games board, on platform base with hairy lion paw feet. (Prudential) $700

A satin and marquetry work-table, the frieze with a pierced fringe and fitted with a drawer, on a lyre support, 19½in. wide. (Christie's) $2,239

A Regency mahogany work table with rounded rectangular twin flap top above two drawers on ring turned legs. 28½in. wide. (Christie's) $1,936

A mid Victorian walnut games/work table, the shaped rectangular fold-over top enclosing chess and backgammon boards, 69cm. (Phillips) $1,870

A Regency pollard oak work-table with hinged canted rectangular top enclosing lidded compartments, with down-swept legs and brass paw feet. 26in. (66 cm.) wide. (Christie's)
          $3,872

WRITING TABLES & DESKS

A Chippendale style mahogany kidney shaped writing desk carved with swag hung acanthus scrolls, paterae and gadrooning, on squat cabriole legs and hairy paw feet, 48in. wide. (Christie's) $4,730

A Victorian burr walnut kidney shaped writing table, profusely carved with blind fret foliate trails, 50in. (Christie's) $4,042

A figured mahogany and satinwood banded Carlton House style desk, the rectangular top fitted with a superstructure on square tapered legs, 52in. wide. (Christie's)$1,797

A late Victorian rosewood writing table, inlaid with marquetry arabesques, boxwood lines and bellflower festoons, on square tapering legs, 42in. (Christie's) $3,657

A George III mahogany cheveret with carrying handle and three-quarter solid gallery, 18¾in. wide. (Christie's) $2,674

An early Victorian oak writing table in the manner of A. W. Pugin, on spirally turned column supports joined by H-stretchers, 41½in. wide. (Christie's) $1,636

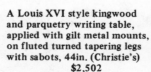

A mahogany partner's writing table, inlaid with ebonized lines, the rectangular molded top lined in gilt tooled green leather, 48½in., early 19th century. (Christie's) $3,657

A Louis XVI style kingwood and parquetry writing table, applied with gilt metal mounts, on fluted turned tapering legs with sabots, 44in. (Christie's) $2,502

A Louis XV style walnut veneered bonheur du jour applied throughout with gilt brass foliate mounts, 48in. wide. (Bearne's)$5,075

WRITING TABLES & DESKS

A late George III mahogany secretaire writing table, with a molded top fitted with two shallow drawers, 1ft.10½in. (Phillips) $1,620

A Regency mahogany writing-table, on solid end-standards and reeded splayed legs, 36in. wide. (Christie's) $11,313

A late 19th century rose-wood and kingwood banded bonheur de jour, the whole decorated with floral marquetry and gilt metal mounts, 78cm. (Phillips) $1,402

A mahogany Carlton House desk, with leather lined writing surface, on square tapering legs, 54½in. wide. (Christie's) $14,399

An Edwardian rosewood and inlaid writing and work table, designed by John Bagshaw & Son, inlaid with flowers and leafage, 26½in. (Lawrence Fine Arts) $3,052

A late George III satinwood Carlton House desk, fitted with six drawers around a green leather lined writing surface, 37in. wide. (Christie's) $49,192

An attractive walnut clerk's desk, the sloping fall front enclosing a simple interior, on square tapered legs, 34in. wide. (Bonhams) $1,110

A George III rosewood, satin-wood crossbanded and inlaid serpentine bonheur du jour with ebony and boxwood stringing, 3ft. wide. (Phillips) $3,240

An early Victorian gilt metal and porcelain mounted oak architect's table with rectangular leather lined easel-supported top, 31½in. wide. (Christie's) $5,205

WRITING TABLES & DESKS

A mid-Victorian rosewood and marquetry writing table with rectangular leather lined top, on cabriole legs, 36½in. wide. (Christie's) $2,468

A mid-Victorian walnut bonheur du jour, the rear superstructure with pierced three quarter gallery over arrangement of shelves and drawers, 81cm. (Phillips) $2,244

A Louis XV style kingwood veneered bureau plat labelled Druce & Co., on cabriole legs, 55in. wide. (Bearne's) $2,552

A George III satinwood work and writing table with rising screen, adjustable hinged top, pull-out leather covered slide, 23in. wide. (Lawrence Fine Arts) $2,788

A fine Regency mahogany library table, on four reeded tapering supports, headed by brass overlapping bands, 63 x 42in. (Lawrence Fine Arts) $48,334

A Regency mahogany bonheur du jour with two open shelves above a folding writing flap, 2ft.6in. wide. (Greenslades) $4,025

A George III mahogany writing table, with a double easel, a fitted frieze drawer and two candleslides, 22in. wide. (Christie's) $3,702

A walnut writing table by Peter Waals, with barber's pole inlay, on molded tapering legs, 94cm. wide. (Christie's) $3,160

A good Edwardian satinwood bonheur du jour, surmounted by gilt metal gallery over tambour front, 74cm. (Phillips) $4,488

WRITING TABLES & DESKS

A mahogany library table with rectangular leather lined top, on partly chamfered square tapering legs, 55in. wide. (Christie's) $8,639

A George IV oak writing table, fitted each side with two gothic panelled drawers, on gothic panelled tapering legs, 63in. wide. (Christie's) $15,136

A mahogany library table, on molded trestle ends, arched legs and claw feet, 49½in. wide. (Christie's) $5,759

An early Gustav Stickley chalet desk, circa 1901-2, the arched gallery top with pierced corner cut-outs and keyed tenon sides, 45¾in. high. (Robt. W. Skinner Inc.) $1,600

A Gordon Russell mahogany desk, with five short drawers and solid trestle end joined by molded stretcher, with chair en suite, 106cm. wide. (Christie's) $1,122

An Arts and Crafts oak writing cabinet, the shaped rectangular top with curved three-quarter gallery above open recess, fall flap and short drawers, 94cm. wide. (Christie's) $654

A Regency ormolu mounted rosewood bonheur du jour attributed to John McLean, on turned supports, 32½in. wide. (Christie's) $15,136

A Louis XV style walnut and ormolu mounted desk, with three-quarter gallery, on cabriole legs with chutes and sabots, 43in. high. (Robt. W. Skinner Inc.) $1,600

A late Biedermeier mahogany and parcel ebonised writing table with canted rectangular top, on incurved legs and paw feet, 35in. wide. (Christie's) $5,499

414

WRITING TABLES & DESKS

An early Victorian maple
writing table, on shaped
trestle ends and bun feet, 36in.
wide. (Christie's)
$1,954

A William IV pollard oak
veneered library table on
splayed end supports with
lotus carved feet, 60in. wide.
(Bearne's) $3,168

A William IV oak writing table,
on twin ring turned trestle ends
joined by a conforming stretcher, 48½in. wide. (Christie's)
$2,674

A George III harewood, kingwood and marquetry writing
table in the manner of John
Cobb in the Transitional style,
18in. wide. (Christie's)
$12,298

A Victorian small writing table
veneered with bird's eye maple,
on tapering spiral turned legs,
38½in. wide. (David Lay)
$980

An Arts and Crafts writing table,
the shaped superstructure with
castellated back panel above a
three-quarter gallery with overhanging top, 111.2cm. wide.
(Christie's) $841

A George III mahogany cylinder bureau with rectangular top
and tambour shutter, on square
tapering legs with later angle
brackets 39¾in. wide.
(Christie's) $6,171

An Edwardian inlaid mahogany
bonheur du jour, the raised
back with brass galleried shelf,
all with satinwood herringbone
inlay and shell patera, 3ft. wide.
(Hobbs & Chambers)
$724

A Regency ormolu mounted
mahogany writing table, on
ring turned tapering legs, joined
by a galleried platform, 39in.
wide. (Christie's)
$18,920

TEAPOYS

A Regency mahogany pedestal teapoy of sarcophagus form, the hinged top enclosing a later divided interior, 22½in. wide. (Christie's) $1,468

A Regency satinwood teapoy of sarcophagus form, the rectangular lid enclosing two canisters, 16½in. wide. (Christie's) $871

A William IV rosewood teapoy, the rectangular molded lid enclosing four hinged compartments, 17½in. wide. (Bonhams) $665

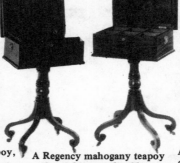

A Regency exotic wood teapoy, veneered with pieces of contrasting woods in a geometric pattern within banded borders, 15¾in. wide. (Hy. Duke & Son) $2,535

A Regency mahogany teapoy and matching work table, each on a turned stem with four S-scroll supports and brass castors, 31½in. high. (Bearne's) $2,920

A Regency mahogany teapoy crossbanded in rosewood and with ebony and boxwood stringing, on square tapering splayed legs, 32in. high. (Christie's) $1,617

A Regency mahogany teapoy, circa 1830, opening to fitted compartment over tapering sides, tripartite legs, 32½in. high. (Robt. W. Skinner Inc.) $1,900

An unusual William IV maple teapoy, the circular hinged top enclosing a fitted interior with two cylindrical canisters, 19½in. diam. (Bonhams) $1,050

A William IV Colonial carved rosewood teapoy with hinged cavetto top with radiating reeded fan panels, 48cm. wide. (Phillips) $1,400

TRUNKS & COFFERS

A 17th century panelled oak coffer with geometrically carved frieze, on channel molded stiles, 26in. high by 53in. wide. (Bearne's) $682

A 17th century panelled oak mule chest, with brass handles, 5ft. wide. (Greenslades) $525

An oak mule chest, the rectangular hinged lid above a foliate carved frieze, with lunette carved apron and shaped feet, 57in. (Christie's) $770

A Country Chippendale pine blanket chest, New England, circa 1780, the molded lift top above a case of two false thumb-molded drawers and three working drawers, 36¾in. wide. (Robt. W. Skinner Inc.) $1,500

A mid-Georgian lacquered coffer on stand, of boarded construction with hinged cover, 39½in. (Lawrence Fine Arts) $2,442

A large Louis Vuitton wardrobe trunk, fitted with wooden hangers, rails and a pull-out box, 44 x 22 x 22in. (Christie's) $2,618

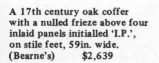

A 17th century oak coffer with a nulled frieze above four inlaid panels initialled 'I.P.', on stile feet, 59in. wide. (Bearne's) $2,639

A Roycroft oak bridal chest, East Aurora, New York, circa 1912, with extended serpentine sides, 36½in. wide. (Robt. W. Skinner Inc.) $6,750

A mid-18th century North Country oak mule chest with a rectangular hinged top enclosing a compartment, 62in. wide. (Bearne's) $1,443

An oak coffer with domed rectangular hinged lid, the interior with a small lidded compartment to either side, 16th century, 55½in. wide. (Christie's) $7,482

A Victorian ottoman, the hinged rectangular lid upholstered in floral gros point needlework, 62in. wide. (Christie's) $6,054

A Spanish walnut coffer, with hinged rectangular lid above decorated, fielded and carved tracery panels, 18th century. (Christie's) $1,732

A French brass bound kingwood cofret forte with gilt metal clasps, probably late 17th century, 14 x 9¼in. (Lawrence Fine Arts) $2,974

A mahogany chest on stand, with a projecting apron carved with acanthus and centered by a shell; 48in. wide, 19th century. (Christie's) $962

A 17th century panelled oak coffer, 4ft.6in. wide with plank top. (Greenslades) $520

An Italian walnut cassone, the hinged rectangular lid above fielded front panels and two base drawers, 60 in., late 16th century. (Christie's) $2,021

Dower chest, Pennsylvania, early 19th century, the rectangular molded top over a dovetailed case with painted decorations, on molded base, 51in. wide. (Robt. W. Skinner Inc.) $1,500

A red painted blanket chest, possibly Pennsylvania, 19th century, the rectangular top with batten edges, 43in. wide. (Christie's) $1,980

418

TRUNKS & COFFERS

A North Italian walnut and pine coffer, the later hinged rectangular molded top above an arcaded front, on flattened bun feet, 69in., early 18th century. (Christie's) $1,347

A Chinese black and gold lacquer coffer decorated with chinoiserie and pavilions, the domed lid enclosing a red lacquer interior, 18th century, 41½in. wide.(Christie's) $8,096

A Jacobean oak planked coffer, having four panels to the top with molded surround, 57in. wide. (Locke & England) $840

A Spanish walnut coffer with hinged rectangular top, the front carved with two geometric roundels, 17th century, 66½in. wide. (Christie's) $1,526

A Spanish walnut coffer with hinged rectangular lid, three locks and carrying handles, on plinth base, 40½in. wide. (Christie's) $916

A Chippendale blue painted and decorated blanket chest, signed Johannes Rank, Dauphin County, 1794, the blue painted rectangular top with two orange bordered square reserves, 51½in. wide. (Christie's) $4,620

Painted pine blanket box, probably Connecticut River Valley, circa 1840, the rectangular hinged top opens to an interior with lidded till, 25¾in. high. (Robt. W. Skinner Inc.) $1,400

An Indian padouk and brass bound coffer on stand, with carrying handles to the sides, the stand on ogee bracket feet, 50in., 19th century. (Christie's) $1,732

A George II oak mule chest, the hinged rectangular lid above fielded front panels, on bracketed plinth base, 52in. (Christie's) $1,443

WARDROBES & ARMOIRES

A Federal inlaid and carved mahogany wardrobe, New York, 1800-1820, on short reeded baluster turned legs, 56½in. wide. (Christie's) $6,050

A George III mahogany wardrobe, with two short and six long drawers flanked by a pair of cupboard doors, 95in. wide. (Christie's) $3,702

A French Provincial walnut armoire with arched molded cornice, panelled sides and scrolled feet, 61in. wide. (Christie's) $6,105

A Victorian mahogany compactum, the upper central section enclosed by a pair of framed arched panel doors, 6ft.7½in. wide. (Hobbs & Chambers) $930

A Dutch figured walnut armoire, the canted corners with flat pilasters, 8ft.10in. high, early 19th century. (Anderson & Garland) $6,228

20th century oak wardrobe with central oval mirror and Spanish feet. (British Antique Exporters) $88

An Arts and Crafts oak wardrobe with broad everted top above a central mirrored door flanked by panelled sides, 198.5cm. high. (Phillips) $561

A fine Art Nouveau walnut wardrobe, designed by Georges de Feure, with shaped and carved pediment above twin central panelled doors, 200cm. wide. (Phillips) $8,800

A Chippendale red gum linen press, New York State, 1750-1800, on a molded base with bracket feet, 51½in. wide. (Christie's) $4,180

WARDROBES & ARMOIRES

19th century flame mahogany corner wardrobe with shaped apron. (British Antique Exporters) $700

An early 19th century mahogany breakfront wardrobe with a molded cornice, on a plinth base, 100in. wide. (Bearne's) $2,640

A Dutch walnut floral marquetry armoire, the bombe base fitted with two short and two long drawers, 78in. wide. (Christie's) $32,560

Early 20th century mahogany gentleman's wardrobe with pressed brass handles and a plinth base. (British Antique Exporters) $525

A Louis Philippe ormolu mounted kingwood armoire, with double panelled doors now filled with brocade, 58in. wide. (Christie's) $4,461

An impressively large Dutch figured walnut veneered wardrobe, on bracket feet. (Woolley & Wallis) $3,335

An Arts and Crafts mahogany wardrobe, attributed to Kenton & Co., possibly to a design by Arthur Blomfield, the doors enclosing drawers and shelves, 149cm. wide. (Phillips) $880

A mid-18th century mahogany wardrobe with two doors each with three fielded panels, 54¾in. wide. (Bearne's) $2,212

A Huntingdon Aviation & Co. aluminium wardrobe designed by P.W. Cow, with twin doors and amber plastic pulls, 122cm. across. (Phillips) $258

WASHSTANDS

A late Federal mahogany washstand, New York, 1815-1825, the shaped splashboard above a medial shelf over a pierced and fitted D-shaped top. (Christie's) $1,320

An early 19th century mahogany cylinder front washstand, later inlaid with intertwined husk chains and foliage, 25½in. wide. (Bearne's) $1,593

A George III mahogany washstand geometrically inlaid with boxwood strings and edgings on partly replaced square tapering legs, 17½in. wide. (Christie's) $1,903

A Louis XV style tulipwood poudreuse, inlaid with amaranth bands and boxwood lines, on cabriole legs with knob feet, 31in. wide. (Christie's) $2,310

A Georgian mahogany opening toilet commode with integral slide up mirror, on square tapering legs, 19in. wide. (Dee & Atkinson) $437

A French ormolu mounted kingwood vitrine table, the hinged kidney shaped glazed top enclosing green velvet interior, late 19th century, 31¾in. wide. (Christie's) $2,788

A George III mahogany washstand with folding rectangular top enclosing basin apertures, on square legs joined by an undertier, 16in. wide. (Christie's) $648

A William IV mahogany nursery washstand, having a high gallery back and center provision for washbasin, 33in. (Locke & England) $280

A Regency mahogany gentleman's toilet stand, the folding rectangular top enclosing bowl apertures and a telescopic mirror frame, 22in. wide. (Christie's) $1,058

WHATNOTS

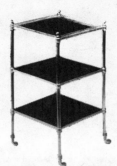

A William IV parcel gilt and dark stained bird's-eye maple whatnot, on paw feet, 34¼in. high. (Christie's) $1,645

A brass and rosewood etagere with three tiers, the top with pierced gallery, 15in. wide. (Christie's) $2,468

A good 19th century rosewood three tier whatnot, with broken bow front shelves, 40½in. high. (David Lay) $897

Attractive Victorian inlaid burr walnut corner whatnot of five tiers, on china castors, 32in. wide overall, 5ft. high. (Lambert & Foster) $1,012

A pair of marquetry etageres, each of three oval shaped tiers with straight turned supports, 19th century, 31in. high. (Lawrence Fine Arts) $1,831

Early Victorian burr walnut four tier corner whatnot with carved supports and pressed brass gallery. (British Antique Exporters) $788

A rosewood whatnot of three tiers joined by slender turned supports, first half 19th century, 39in. high. (Lawrence Fine Arts) $2,747

Early Victorian rosewood what not with barley twist supports and carved galleries. (British Antique Exporters) $1,400

One of a pair of William IV mahogany whatnots, joined by baluster uprights with finials. on turned tapering legs, 16in. wide. (Christie's) Two $9,256

A Regency mahogany wine cellaret, the hinged cover in a fluted fan design, 30in. wide. (Lawrence Fine Arts) $10,968

A George III brass bound mahogany wine cooler, the octagonal hinged top enclosing a lead lined interior, 20½in. wide. (Christie's) $5,142

A Regency mahogany wine cellaret of sarcophagus shape with bead borders and raised on four square curved supports, 27in. (Lawrence Fine Arts) $2,035

A George III mahogany and brass bound octagonal cellarette on square tapered splayed legs. (Phillips) $2,520

A mid 19th century mahogany wine cooler, of sarcophagus form, the stepped panelled lid over tapered base, 97cm. (Phillips) $2,431

A George III mahogany wine cooler, with hinged cover and two brass bands (third band missing), 24in. wide. (Lawrence Fine Arts) $5,019

A Sheraton period mahogany rectangular wine cooler, with satinwood oval and line inlay, on square tapering legs, 21¾in. wide. (Geering & Colyer) $1,323

A good Regency mahogany oval cellaret, the hinged cover with raised central boss, 27in. wide. (Prudential) $13,338

A Regency mahogany cellaret inlaid with boxwood lines and with square channelled legs, 18¼in. wide. (Christie's) $1,542

WINE COOLERS

A Regency mahogany sarcophagus shaped wine cooler, the chamfered domed lid inlaid with rosewood, on ormolu paw feet, 27in. wide. (Christie's) $2,648

A William IV mahogany wine cooler of sarcophagus shape, the hinged top enclosing a lead lined interior, 30½in. wide. (Bearne's) $2,112

A George III, 27½in. wide, mahogany brass bound oval wine cooler with brass handles. (Anderson & Garland) $1,211

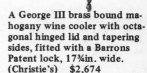

A Regency mahogany cellaret, on square tapering legs edged with boxwood, 12½in. wide. (Christie's) $2,159

A Victorian large wine cistern, on leafage S-scroll corbels, 38in. wide. (Lawrence Fine Arts) $4,089

A George III brass bound mahogany wine cooler with octagonal hinged lid and tapering sides, fitted with a Barrons Patent lock, 17¾in. wide. (Christie's) $2,674

A George III mahogany cellaret on stand of rectangular form, with brass side handles, 17in. wide. (Bearne's) $873

A Georgian crossbanded mahogany and line inlaid octagonal wine cooler, having tap to base on a stand with chased brass claw and ball feet, 18in. diameter. (Geering & Colyer) $2,685

A George III mahogany wine cooler, the later stand with square splayed legs and pierced angle brackets, 23½in. wide. (Christie's) $2,468

WINE COOLERS

A George III Sheraton mahogany wine cooler, the irregular eight sided top with boxwood inlay over a tapering body, 25in. wide. (Boardman) $2,028

A massive William IV ash wine cooler of sarcophagus form with hinged rectangular lid, tapering sides and plinth base, 44in. wide. (Christie's) $1,234

A Victorian mahogany rectangular cellaret, on turned and carved feet, 2ft.1in. wide. (Anderson & Garland) $1,072

A George III brass bound mahogany wine cooler, the octagonal tapering body with carrying handles, 19in. wide. (Christie's) $5,348

A mahogany wine cooler or jardiniere of oval shallow form with two brass bands, on four fluted and chamfered supports, 29in. wide. (Lawrence Fine Arts) $5,841

A George III brass bound mahogany wine cooler of oval form with hinged lid, 25in. wide. (Christie's) $4,936

A George IV mahogany wine cooler of sarcophagus form, the front line inlaid and the flat topped lid with ebonized edges, 1ft.11½in. wide. (Tennants) $1,225

A George III mahogany and brass bound octagonal cellaret with a hinged top and brass carrying handles. (Phillips) $3,600

A William IV mahogany sarcophagus wine cooler, the hinged cavetto molded rectangular top enclosing compartments, 28in. wide. (Bonhams) $2,745

ALE GLASSES

A dwarf ale glass, the slender funnel bowl with wrythen molded lower part edged with flammiform ornament, circa 1730, 13.5cm. high. (Christie's) $398

An engraved and cut cylindrical ale vessel, inscribed Iron Bridge Near Coalbrook Dale, mid 19th century, 15cm. high. (Christie's) $995

An early ale glass, the slender funnel bowl with crisply ribbed lower part, on a folded conical foot, circa 1700, 13.5cm. high. (Christie's) $995

BEAKERS

A Bohemian beaker in clear glass with amber flashed panels on the hexagonal faceted bowl, on a massive hexagonal lobed foot, 13.8cm. (Phillips) $560

A Bohemian beaker, of cut blue and clear glass with panels of gilt foliage, 12.5cm. (Lawrence Fine Arts) $446

A German beaker of tapering cylindrical form, the body engraved with four medallions with figures, late 18th century, 7¼in. (Lawrence Fine Arts) $658

A North Bohemian transparent enamelled topographical beaker, the flared body painted in colors with a view of Bieberich, circa 1840, 12cm. high. (Christie's)$2,616

A Bohemian engraved beaker and cover, the cylindrical body engraved with two equestrian figures in combat beneath a sun, late 17th century, 19cm. high. (Christie's)$1,107

An important transparent-enamelled and signed topographical beaker by Samuel Mohn, 10cm. high. (Phillips) $26,250

BOTTLES

Mount Washington peachblow bottle, flared and raised rim on vertically ribbed body of rose pink to blue, total height 5in. (Robt. W. Skinner Inc.) $625

'E. G. Booz's/Old Cabin/Whiskey' cabin bottle, honey amber, sloping collared lip, smooth base, quart, Whitney Glassworks, New Jersey, 1860-1870. (Robt. W. Skinner Inc. $1,000

'Red Star/Stomach Bitters' bottle, fluted shoulder and base, amber, sloping collar, smooth base, 11½in. high, America, circa 1900. (Robt. W. Skinner Inc.) $225

Rare 'Bennington/Battle' figural book bottle, brown, cream and green flint enamel, 11in. high, 1840-1880. (Robt. W. Skinner Inc.) $600

Twelve early gin bottles with original wooden case, most bottles green with a few olive green and olive amber, 9¼in. high, 1780-1810. (Robt. W. Skinner Inc.) $550

A green tinted bottle gilt by James Giles, the facet-cut tapering body with flower-head, dot and sunray ornament, circa 1765, 14.5cm. (Christie's) $536

Double Eagle historical flask, vertically ribbed body, emerald green, double collared lip, pontil scar, Louisville Glass works, Kentucky, 1855-1865. (Robt. W. Skinner Inc.) $1,500

An 18th century green glass sealed wine bottle, initialled I.G. and dated 1732, the base with a deep kick, 21cm. high. (Henry Spencer) $487

'Turner Brothers, New York' whiskey bottle, barrel shaped, brownish amber, flattened collared lip, smooth base, 10in. high, America, 1860-1880. (Robt. W. Skinner Inc.) $100

BOTTLES

Three miniature green bottles and stoppers for soy, catsup and kyan, named in gilt within oblong octagonal cartouches, early 19th century. (Christie's) $1,408

Early cologne bottle of unusual form, with three bands of diamonds running up the side, 7¼in. high, America, possibly Sandwich Glass Co., 1850-1870. (Robt. W. Skinner Inc.) $50

Rare 'W. Ludlow' seal spirits bottle, dark olive green, sheared mouth with wide string rim, pontil scar, 12½in. high, possibly America, circa 1760. (Robt. W. Skinner Inc.) $450

'A.B.L. Myers AM/Rock Rose/ New Haven' medicine bottle, emerald green, crude blob lip, iron pontil, 9½in. high, America, 1860-1870. (Robt. W. Skinner Inc.) $450

Square oak cased, 19th century, four bottle decanter box, having cast brass corner mounts and carrying handle. (Michael G. Matthews) $350

Cathedral type pickle bottle, minor stain along 1in. of bottom, 33cm., America, 1870-1875. (Robt. W. Skinner Inc.) $125

Rare 'Bennett & Carroll/ No. 120 Wood St./Pitts Pa' flattened whiskey bottle, golden amber, 8¼in. high, America, 1845-1860. (Robt. W. Skinner Inc.) $225

Rare 'E. Smith/Elmira/N.Y.' soda bottle, cylindrical, cobalt blue, heavy collared mouth, iron pontil mark, half pint, America, 1845-1860. (Robt. W. Skinner Inc.) $300

An early sealed globe and shaft wine bottle, with a seal of St. George and The Dragon, late 17th century, 22.5cm. high, found in the Thames at Wapping. (Christie's) $3,168

BOTTLES

'Poland/Water' Moses figural spring water bottle, aqua, smooth base, 11¼in., quart, America, 1870-1890. (Robt. W. Skinner Inc.) $60

An early sealed and dated 'onion' wine bottle of dark-green tint, applied with a seal inscribed *'John Lovering Bidiford 1695'*, 12.5cm. high. (Christie's) $4,576

'J. Lake/Schenectady N.Y.' ten pin soda bottle, cobalt blue, heavy collared mouth, iron pontil mark, 8in. high, America, 1845-1860.(Robt. W. Skinner Inc.) $300

A South Staffordshire opaque small bottle, the globular body enamelled in bright colors with two exotic birds perched on a flower-spray, circa 1765, 12cm. high. (Christie's) $792

A sealed and dated wine bottle of olive-green tint, the cylindrical sides applied with a seal inscribed *'Kirktoun 1734'*, 21.5cm. high. (Christie's) $792

'Tr. Cannab. I' label under glass apothecary bottle, cylindrical, base embossed 'W. N. Walton Patd Sep 23 1862', cobalt blue, 8½in. high, America, 1860-1890. (Robt. W. Skinner Inc.) $300

Rare 'Fortune Sequattir' sealed spirits bottle, deep olive green, sheared mouth with applied string rim, pontil scar, 9in. high, Europe, 1760-1780. (Robt. W. Skinner Inc.) $225

A sealed and dated wine bottle of onion shape and olive-green tint, the seal inscribed Auchen Leck, 1717, 16.5cm. high, (Christie's) $2,616

'Browns Celebrated Indian Herb Bitters' bottle, Indian figural, honey amber, smooth base, 12¼in., America, 1865-1880. (Robt. W. Skinner Inc.) $210

BOTTLES

Mount Washington amberina bottle, flared flat rim, dark fuchsia to amber color, faceted amber stopper, total height 5½in. (Robt. W. Skinner Inc.) $175

A sealed and dated wine bottle of onion shape and green tint, the seal inscribed 'Joseph King 1733', 20cm. high. (Christie's) $792

A moulded cruciform bottle, the body of deeply indented rectangular section, circa 1725, 25cm. high. (Christie's) $457

Huckleberry bottle, tall cylinder with upper body, neck ribbed, deep golden amber, 11in. high, New England, 1850-1870. (Robt. W. Skinner Inc.) $350

Large demijohn, oval, olive green, crude lip, smooth indented base, 13½in. high, America, circa 1850. (Robt. W. Skinner Inc.)$100

'Dr H. B. Skinner/Boston' medicine bottle, rectangular with bevelled corners, olive amber, flared mouth, 6in. high, New England, 1840-1860. (Robt. W. Skinner Inc.) $100

'Old Sachem/Bitters/Wigwam Tonic' bottle, barrel shaped, light golden yellow, 9½in. high. America, 1860-1880. (Robt. W. Skinner Inc.) $500

A sealed and dated wine bottle of olive-green tint, the cylindrical body applied with a seal inscribed 'Col. John Folliott 1743', 22.5cm. high. (Christie's) $844

Fancy peppersauce bottle, square with five stars vertically placed in three panels, 21.92cm. high, probably Midwest America, 1845-1860. (Robt. W. Skinner Inc.) $150

GLASS

An Austrian art glass bowl, of bright pink cased to opal with iridescent mauve interior, 5¼in. high. (Robt. W. Skinner Inc.) $325

A Loetz type art glass mounted center bowl, of brilliant green with roundel texture and iridescent surface, 11in. high. (Robt. W. Skinner Inc.) $100

A green stained Lalique bowl, the clear and satin finished glass molded with a pattern of birds and foliage, 23.4cm. diam. (Christie's) $486

A Daum cameo glass jardiniere, the mottled amber tinted body overlaid with two tones of ruby glass acid etched with exotic lilies and grasses, 25cm. (Phillips) $1,533

A Kosta glass bowl designed by Evald Dahlskog, with cut and engraved decoration of women on horseback, 16.5cm. high. (Christie's) $935

A large and colorful cased glass bowl by the American studio glass maker, Samuel J. Herman, 51.5cm. wide, inscribed and dated 1971. (Bearne's) $1,426

A Loetz bowl, the bulbous body with a drawn trefoil rim, the clear glass internally decorated with a pattern of blue and glittery-green spots, 14.6cm. high. (Christie's) $486

A Daum acid etched and enamelled verrerie parlante ashtray, the clear and amber tinted glass with ribbon motto amid mistletoe on an acid textured ground, 14cm. diam. (Christie's) $785

An Orrefors footed bowl designed by Simon Gate and engraved by Wilhelm Eisert, 1932, the body with engraved decoration of two women in a constructivist city, 15cm. high. (Christie's) $1,683

BOWLS

A Loetz iridescent glass bowl with an everted rim and having six loop handles, exhibiting a green, gold and mauve iridescent skin, 21.3cm. diam. (Phillips) $1,548

A Decorchemont pate-de-verre bowl, short cylindrical foot and straight sided flaring body, 6.5cm. high. (Christie's) $2,416

A Galle enamelled glass bowl, the slightly smoky body acid etched with foliage, 15cm. wide. (Phillips) $704

A Haida bowl and cover, the clear glass decorated with green, blue and red flowers, 12.5cm. high. (Christie's) $334

An Austrian art glass metal mounted bowl, of brilliant yellow-green, mounted in four pronged bronzed metal holder, 10½in. high. (Robt. W. Skinner Inc.) $125

An Orvit cameo glass, mounted punch bowl, cameo carved with four stylized designs of alternating grapes on vines and grape leaf clusters, 12in. high. (Robt. W. Skinner Inc.) $1,500

An Austrian art glass bowl, of yellow-green iridescent glass decorated with red-purple threading, diam. 9½in. (Robt. W. Skinner Inc.) $75

An Argy-Rousseau pate-de-verre bowl, with molded decoration of three reserves with a ballerina in white taking her bow, surrounded by stylized rose border, on a mottled yellow ground, 6.3cm. high. (Christie's) $5,984

A Tiffany Favrile intaglio cut bowl, with gold iridescence and pink and blue highlights, 9½in. diam. (Robt. W. Skinner Inc.) $900

CANDLESTICKS

GLASS

Two dolphin candlesticks, both colorless, probably Boston & Sandwich Glassworks, Sandwich, Massachusetts, 1845-1870, 10in. high. (Robt. W. Skinner Inc.) $125

A Waterford candlestick, the sconce and baluster column cut with faceting, 24cm. (Lawrence Fine Arts) $318

Pair of vaseline candleholders, 7in. high, probably Boston & Sandwich Glassworks, Sandwich, Massachusetts, 1836-1860. (Robt. W. Skinner Inc.) $70

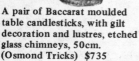

A pair of Baccarat moulded table candlesticks, with gilt decoration and lustres, etched glass chimneys, 50cm. (Osmond Tricks) $735

A pair of Steuben threaded candlesticks, squat holders of bright Bristol yellow accented with dramatic black threading, 4½in. high. (Robt. W. Skinner Inc.) $225

A pair of Steuben candlesticks, swirled sticks of clear green with hollow teardrop shaft, 10in. high. (Robt. W. Skinner Inc.) $275

A pair of Tiffany Favrile pastel candle holders, lavender opalescent optic pattern with squared bobeche rim, 3½in. high. (Robt. W. Skinner Inc.) $325

Early candlestick, rare color, translucent purple-blue, probably Boston & Sandwich Glassworks, Sandwich, Massachusetts, 1850-1865. (Robt. W. Skinner Inc.)$250

Pair of early white pressed glass candlesticks, 7in. high, probably New England Glassworks, Boston, Massachusetts, 1840-1850. (Robt. W. Skinner Inc.) $300

CHAMPAGNE GLASSES

A moulded pedestal stemmed champagne glass, the ovoid bowl with everted rim molded with 'nipt diamond waies', circa 1745, 15cm. high. (Christie's) $756

An engraved baluster champagne glass, the bell bowl with a border of single birds perched among arabesques, circa 1720, 21.5cm. high. (Christie's) $756

A molded champagne glass, supported on a ribbed hollow swelling stem above a ribbed domed foot, circa 1765, 15.5cm. high. (Christie's) $1,095

A molded pedestal stemmed champagne glass, the double-ogee bowl with vertically ribbed sides, circa 1740, 18cm. high. (Christie's) $995

A champagne glass, the large cup shaped bowl molded with vertical ribbing and a domed and folded foot, 17.8cm. (Christie's) $700

A molded pedestal stemmed champagne glass, the ogee bowl with everted rim, circa 1740, 19cm. high. (Christie's) $895

CHARGERS

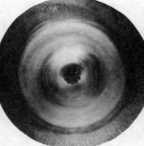

'Trepied Sirene', a satin finished and opalescent charger, decorated with a sea sprite, 36.5cm. diam. (Christie's) $3,718

Tiffany decorative rondel, the round flat disc of dark cobalt blue favrile glass with strong blue iridescence,16¼in. diam. (Robt. W. Skinner Inc.) $1,900

A large Lalique charger, circular, heavily molded with three nymphs among vine branches, signed Lalique, France, 40cm. diam. (Christie's) $1,487

DECANTERS

An oak and brass locking tantalus, fitted with three cut glass decanters and stoppers, 16in. wide. (Christie's) $385

A shipping decanter and stopper for 'White Wine', of mallet shape named within a quatrefoil cartouche, circa 1781, 28cm. high. (Christie's) $1,610

A mahogany liqueur casket, fitted with three ruby red decanters with silvered metal stoppers, on bun feet. (Christie's) $808

A Venini 'Vetro Pesante Inciso' decanter and stopper, designed by Paolo Venini, with short cylindrical neck and mushroom shaped stopper, orange glass cased in clear glass, 18cm. high. (Christie's) $557

A set of four Victorian silver mounted brown glass decanters, each with molded scroll handle, by H. H. Dobson & Sons, 32 Piccadilly, London. (Christie's) $5,108

An amethyst gilt decorated decanter and stopper for 'Wine', of club shape, named within a lozenge shaped diaper pattern cartouche, perhaps Irish, circa 1800, 29cm. high. (Christie's) $1,711

A George III double ring neck mallet decanter, engraved with the motto 'The Land we Live In', with bull's-eye stopper, 28cm. high. (Henry Spencer)$730

A late Victorian silver mounted walnut veneered combination tantalus and humidor, fitted with a games drawer, Charles Boyton, London 1899, 15¾in. wide. (Christie's) $1,347

A Webb rock crystal decanter and stopper engraved by William Fritsche, the double gourd shaped body engraved in an intaglio technique, circa 1890, 27cm. high. (Christie's) $4,928

DECANTERS

A Webb tricolor cameo glass decanter, of frosted glass overlaid with white over bright pink layers, 9½in. high. (Robt. W. Skinner Inc.)
$2,600

An oak and brass mounted locking tantalus, carved with anthemion leaves, fitted with three cut glass decanters, 13in. wide. (Christie's)
$539

A Cork Glass Co. decanter, engraved with oval panels and stars, 22.5cm, and a stopper. (Lawrence Fine Arts)
$159

One of a pair of silver mounted cut-glass decanters, each cut-glass body with stellar motifs, by Lorie, maker's mark Cyrillic E. Ch, Moscow, 1899-1908, 12¾in. high, 4490gr. gross. (Christie's) Two $9,295

An Edwardian electro plated tantalus, with three square section decanters and stoppers and the original keys, by Daniel and Arter of Birmingham, 42.7cm. across. (Lawrence Fine Arts) $946

A Bohemian armorial spirit-decanter of rectangular section with canted angles, circa 1730, 23cm. high. (Christie's)
$836

A polychrome enamelled decanter and stopper for beer from the Beilby Workshop, of mallet shape, circa 1775, 28.5cm. high. (Christie's) $11,946

A pair of Richardson's vitrified flask decanters and stoppers for 'Port' and 'Sherry', designed by Richard Redgrave, circa 1848, 35cm. high. (Christie's) $4,579

A Powells 'Whitefriars' glass decanter of green tone, having hammered silver top with ball finial, 26.5cm. high, mark for Hutton & Sons, London 1901. (Phillips) $584

DISHES

A sulphide and cut glass circular dish, the center set with a sulphide plaque showing Ganymede and the Eagle, perhaps Apsley Pellatt, circa 1825, 18cm. diam. (Christie's) $796

Steuben blue Aurene bonbon, crimped extended rim on round bowl of cobalt blue, signed 'Aurene', 6¼in. diam. (Robt. W. Skinner Inc.) $1,300

'Ondines', a Lalique opalescent plate, the wide rim molded with a frieze of water-nymphs, 27.5cm. diam. (Christie's) $1,234

Mount Washington Crown Milano bride's basket, tricon crimped rim on round opal body, silver plated pedestal base dated 'Feb. 6, 1896', 12½in. high. (Robt. W. Skinner Inc.) $2,100

A Lalique opalescent dish, moulded with a radiating pattern of eight carnations and leaves, 35.8cm. diam. (Christie's) $935

A Viennese gilt metal and engraved glass tazza, encrusted with turquoise jewelled beads, possibly Lobmyer, circa 1880, 10½in. high. (Christie's) $2,068

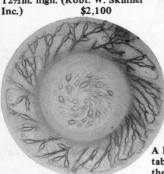

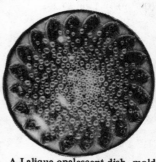

'Anvers', a large Lalique opalescent glass dish, molded on the underside with carp amid seaweed, 39.5cm. diam. (Phillips) $4,224

A Bohemian cranberry glass table centerpiece painted with the bust portraits of three children alternating with foliage roundels on a ground of gilt leafy tendrils, 20.5cm. high. (Henry Spencer) $487

A Lalique opalescent dish, molded with a radiating pattern of twenty fish and bubbles, with a slightly undulating rim, 35.2cm. diam. (Christie's) $1,215

DRINKING SETS

A Bohemian part lemonade set, decorated with arabesque frosted panels, comprising a globular jug, one goblet and a trafoil tray, 9½in. high. (Christie's) $1,386

A seventeen piece Lalique drinking set, each piece with molded motif incorporating two male nudes, with acid-stamped and engraved signatures. (Christie's) $3,405

Gold decorated glass decanter and eight wine goblets having round reserves with courting scenes. (Du Mouchelles) $350

A Richardson's 'Waterlily' water set, each piece painted with a continuous frieze of flowering waterlilies, marked Richardson's Vitrified, and with registry mark of 1848, the jug 24cm. high.(Christie's) $2,816

A Loetz drinking set, designed by Richard Teschner, comprising a jug and five tumblers, the smokey white glass with polychrome applied decoration, 17.7cm. high. (Christie's) $529

A 19th century Bohemian glass ewer of classical shape, together with a pair of matching goblets, height 8½in. (David Lay) $1,135

One of a set of eight cups and saucers of blue tinted glass, decorated with white dot border. (Christie's)
Set $327

Bohemian cobalt blue and gilt decorated glass punch set, late 19th century, 15in. high. (Robt. W. Skinner Inc.) $1,000

An armorial decanter of mallet shape, engraved with a coat-of-arms and an armorial cylindrical mug with scroll handle en suite, circa 1775. (Christie's) $1,056

A mammoth baluster goblet, the large round funnel bowl supported on an inverted baluster stem, circa 1700, 29cm. high. (Christie's) $5,973

A baluster goblet, the round funnel bowl with a solid lower part, on a folded conical foot, circa 1710, 21cm. high. (Christie's) $756

A Jacobite composite stemmed goblet, the bell bowl engraved with a rose, bud and half opened bud, the reverse with a butterfly, on a conical foot, circa 1750, 18cm. high. (Christie's) $1,294

A baluster coin goblet, the funnel bowl supported on a hollow ball knop containing a Charles II three-pence piece dated 1673, early 18th century, 18.5cm. high. (Christie's) $2,986

A John Hutton glass goblet, the tulip shaped cup on a cylindrical stem, with engraved design showing two naked female figures, 31cm. high. (Christie's) $486

A Dutch-engraved armorial light baluster goblet, supported on a multi-knopped stem above a domed foot, circa 1755, 19.5cm. high. (Christie's) $1,393

A mammoth baluster goblet, the round funnel bowl with a solid base, on a folded conical foot, circa 1710, 28cm. high. (Christie's) $3,384

A Sunderland Bridge rummer, the flared bucket bowl engraved with a sailing ship passing beneath Sunderland Bridge, 19th century, 17.5cm. high. (Christie's) $696

A Dutch-engraved armorial light baluster goblet, the bell bowl engraved with the arms of Dordrecht, circa 1740, 20cm. high. (Christie's) $895

An engraved baluster goblet, the round funnel bowl with a border of fruiting vine, circa 1730, 17cm. high. (Christie's) $796

A moulded pedestal stemmed goblet, the generous double-ogee bowl with allover honeycomb molding, circa 1735, 18cm. high. (Christie's) $1,294

A Dutch-engraved light baluster armorial goblet, the funnel bowl with the crowned arms of Amsterdam, circa 1750, 18cm. high. (Christie's) $1,393

A pedestal stemmed goblet, supported on an hexagonally molded tapering stem enclosing an elongated tear, circa 1715, 17cm. high. (Christie's) $398

A Wiener Werkstatte enamelled goblet designed by M. von Brunner, the clear glass enamelled in black, blue and red with male and female figures by fruit trees, 15.4cm. high. (Christie's) $935

An engraved 'Excise' goblet, the round funnel bowl engraved and polished with a trailing branch of fruiting vine, mid 18th century, 18cm. high. (Christie's) $1,692

A Dutch-engraved armorial baluster goblet, the stem with a wide angular knop enclosing a tear above a basal knop, circa 1710, 18cm. high. (Christie's) $1,393

A baluster goblet, the stem with shoulder and waist ball knops, on a folded conical foot, circa 1715, 18cm. high. (Christie's) $696

A baluster goblet, the tulip shaped bowl with a solid lower part supported on a drop knop, circa 1710, 19.5cm. high. (Christie's) $1,294

441

GOBLETS

A Bohemian amber flashed goblet, the deep cylindrical bowl engraved with a panoramic scene of a stag and does in a wooded, hilly landscape, 22.2cm. (Phillips) $840

A Netherlands façon-de-Venise engraved color-twist goblet, the funnel bowl decorated with a frieze of Cupid riding on a lion, circa 1660, 16cm. high. (Christie's) $13,937

A painted glass goblet by Richard Redgrave, the bell shaped cup painted in yellow, white and green with a daisy, registration mark for 25 October 1847, 20cm. high. (Christie's) $1,271

A Saxon armorial goblet for the Russian market, engraved with the Royal Arms of Russia, on a knopped and similarly faceted baluster stem, 25.2cm. (Phillips) $1,218

A Dutch-engraved goblet, the flared bucket bowl finely engraved with a ship in full sail, on a plain folded foot. 21cm. (Phillips) $904

A large Saxon engraved goblet, on a faceted, knopped and inverted baluster stem and folded conical foot, circa 1740, 30.5cm. high. (Christie's) $1,194

A Dutch-engraved light baluster royal armorial goblet, on a conical foot, circa 1750, 19cm. high. (Christie's) $3,583

A pair of goblets of ruby and clear glass, engraved with views of the Crystal Palace, in panels on a ground of fruiting vine, 23cm. (Lawrence Fine Arts) $1,006

A Netherlands diamond engraved dated royal portrait goblet, in the manner of Mooleyser, engraved with a crowned bust portrait of Queen Mary (1662-1695), 1695, 21.5cm. high overall. (Christie's) $3,185

GOBLETS

A Bohemian engraved ruby flash goblet and cover, the bell shaped bowl with a continuous stag-hunting scene on a ruby flash ground, circa 1865, 35cm. high. (Christie's) $1,393

A Netherlandish 'Roemer' of pale-green tint, the generous cup shaped bowl merging into a hollow cylindrical stem, 17th century, 13cm. high. (Christie's) $8,362

A four sided pedestal stemmed goblet, the round funnel bowl with a tear to the solid lower part, circa 1715, 15.5cm. high. (Christie's) $796

A Bohemian mammoth fluted 'spa' goblet, the flared bowl engraved with ten named views, circa 1850, 35.5cm. high. (Christie's) $1,592

A Bohemian stained ruby engraved goblet and cover, the bowl engraved with a galloping stallion, circa 1865, 42cm. high. (Christie's) $3,185

A goblet with bucket shape bowl, teared stem and folded foot, 7¾in. (Lawrence Fine Arts) $193

A 'Newcastle' engraved light baluster goblet, the slightly waisted funnel bowl with a border of floral swags, circa 1740, 18.5cm. high. (Christie's) $1,294

A Dutch-engraved light baluster royal armorial goblet, the slightly waisted funnel bowl engraved and polished with the crowned arms of Willem V of Orange and Nassau within the Garter, circa 1760, 18.5cm. high. (Christie's) $3,384

A Dutch-engraved light baluster goblet attributed to Jacob Sang, on a conical foot, circa 1755, 18cm. high. (Christie's) $1,991

JELLY GLASSES

An hexagonal jelly glass with applied scroll handle, mid-18th century, 11.5cm. high. (Christie's) $557

A two handled posset pot, the slender bowl with an everted rim and applied with two scroll handles, circa 1740, 10cm. high. (Christie's) $704

A molded jelly glass with applied scroll handle, with all-over honeycomb ornament, circa 1735, 12cm. high. (Christie's) $796

JUGS

A Gunderson Burmese pitcher, of delicate Burmese pink to pastel yellow coloring, 13in. high. (Robt. W. Skinner Inc.) $100

A Dutch silver and cut glass flagon, circa 1900, with rococo reserves, scrolls and busts on a stippled ground, 14in high. (Robt. W. Skinner Inc.) $1,700

A Moser oviform jug, with amber tinted handle and tri-corn rim, the body graduating from red to amber and decorated in raised enamels. (Christie's) $2,117

MEAD GLASSES

A baluster mead glass, supported on a shoulder-knopped stem with basal knop, circa 1720, 14cm. high. (Christie's) $796

A baluster mead glass, the cup shaped bowl with gadrooned lower part, early 18th Century, 11cm. high. (Christie's) $1,194

A baluster mead glass, the stem with a triple annulated waist knop and a basal knop, circa 1715, 14.5cm. high. (Christie's) $597

MISCELLANEOUS

A Mount Washington/Pairpoint cracker jar, decorated in the Crown Milano manner with blossoms and leaves, 6½in. high. (Robt. W. Skinner Inc.)
$450

'Houppes'. A Lalique opalescent glass circular box and cover, molded on the inside with powder-puffs, 14cm. diam. (Phillips)
$972

A rare early cameo glass teapot, very delicate small pedestalled tankard form pot, of Persian, Roman and Oriental influence, 6¾in. high. (Robt. W. Skinner Inc.)
$4,500

A Pairpoint art glass pickle jar and holder, cranberry colored jar decorated with enamelled aster blossoms, 13in. high. (Robt. W. Skinner Inc.)
$225

A pair of French glass drops in green and opaque white, with glass lustres, 32.5cm. (Lawrence Fine Arts) $716

'Source de la Fontaine', a Lalique statue, the clear and satin-finished glass molded as a standing maiden holding a fish in front of her, 54cm. high without base. (Christie's)
$8,365

A silver mounted cut glass tazza, the dish with rosette motif, by Orest Kurliukov, Moscow, circa 1880, 7¾in. high, 531gr. without glass dish. (Christie's) $929

'Quatre Papillons'. A Lalique frosted glass powder box and cover, the slightly domed top molded with four moths, 8cm. diam. (Phillips)
$822

A Webb cameo glass silver mounted flask, of yellow amber glass heavily layered with opal white, 10in. high. (Robt. W. Skinner Inc.) $1,200

MISCELLANEOUS

A Loetz type art glass covered jar, of clear simulated crackle glass decorated with four applied prunts of emerald green, 7¼in. high. (Robt. W. Skinner Inc.) $75

A Lalique frosted swan figure, with head erect in swimming position, signed "Lalique/France" on base, 9¾in. high. (Robt. W. Skinner Inc.) $1,500

A pale blue-green glass jar of bulbous form with broad mouth and collar rim, 3rd-4th century A.D., 9.4cm. high. (Phillips) $223

A.J.F. Christy (Lambeth) 'Well Spring' water carafe, the decoration designed by Richard Redgrave for the 'Summerly's Art Manufactures', circa 1847, 16.5cm. high. (Christie's) $1,493

A Venini glass picture frame with brass stand, the clear glass of corrugated rectangular form, 18.5cm. high. (Christie's) $1,215

"La Donna Somersa" art glass sculpture, by Da Rossi of Murano, Italy, with gold leaf wrapped figure, 16½in. high. (Robt. W. Skinner Inc.) $1,400

A large Galle carved and acid etched double overlay hanging light, globular form overlaid with green and dark amber pendant clematis, 35.2cm. high. (Christie's) $13,090

A pair of glass confitures and covers, probably Waterford, each cut with bands of diamonds, slight damage, 30cm. (Bearne's) $464

A hookah base, the wrythen molded neck with an applied collar and folded everted rim, first half of the 18th century, 19.5cm. high. (Christie's) $1,294

MISCELLANEOUS

An amberina syrup pitcher with silverplated undertray, New England Glass Company, 5½in. high. (Robt. W. Skinner Inc.) $475

An amberina bride's basket and holder, set into a silver plated basket with applied leaves and cherries, 9in. high. (Robt. W. Skinner Inc.) $650

A rare Webb cameo glass framed clock, the shield-shaped frame of yellow overlaid opal white, Birmingham, England, 7in. high. (Robt. W.. Skinner Inc.) $3,500

An engraved bell with folded rim, decorated with a view of the High Level Bridge at Newcastle on Tyne, circa 1849, 19.5cm. high. (Christie's) $895

Victorian cut glass and plated biscuit box, on four bun feet. (Hobbs and Chambers) $92

'Suzanne', a Lalique opalescent glass statuette of a naked maiden, her arms outstretched and holding her robes, 22.6cm. high. (Christie's) $14,872

An engraved water glass, the triple ogee bowl with a border of stylized flowers, mid-18th century, 12.5cm. high. (Christie's) $497

'Profile', a glass sculpture in the manner of Stanislav Libensky, the pierced rectilinear form in violet molded glass, 16.7cm. high (Christie's) $317

A Bohemian millefiori and latticinio wafer stand, the upper part with a flared tray, mid-19th century, 14cm. high. (Christie's) $756

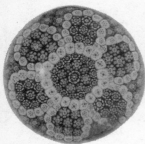

A Baccarat panelled blue carpet-ground weight, on a ground of dark blue and white canes, star cut base, mid-19th century, 8cm. diam. (Christie's) $6,968

A Clichy paperweight, patterned multicolored millefiori canes with central Clichy rose, 2½in. diam. (Robt. W. Skinner Inc.) $375

A Clichy lime-green checker weight, the two concentric circles of canes including a pink rose, mid-19th century, 6.3cm. diam. (Christie's) $597

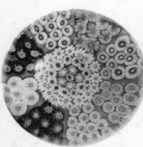

A Clichy green ground patterned millefiori weight, the eight clusters of canes in shades of red, white, pale blue, dark blue and pink, mid-19th century, 8.2cm. diam. (Christie's) $1,393

A Max Erlacher 1971 American Indian paperweight, from limited edition of 100, 3½in. diam. (Robt. W. Skinner Inc.) $225

A St Louis wild strawberry weight, the flower with five white ribbed petals, mid-19th century, 6.7cm. diam. (Christie's) $1,149

A Baccarat gilt decorated double overlay faceted concentric millefiori mushroom weight, mid-19th century, 8cm. diam. (Christie's) $3,384

A Clichy pink ground patterned millefiori weight, the trefoil garland in shades of pale green, blue and white, mid-19th century, 8cm. diam. (Christie's) $716

A Clichy swirl weight with alternate bright blue and white staves, mid-19th century, 6.5cm. diam. (Christie's) $1,393

GLASS

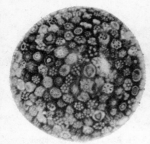

A Baccarat dated close mille-fiori weight, the brightly color-ed tightly packed canes revea-ling latticinio thread in places, 1847, 8cm. diam. (Christie's) $1,891

A Baccarat miniature white double clematis and bud weight, mid-19th century, 5cm. diam. (Christie's) $836

A Clichy blue ground garlanded millefiori weight, the hexafoil garland in shades of pink and white, mid-19th century, 7.8cm. diam. (Christie's) $637

A Baccarat miniature yellow pom-pom weight, the flower with many recessed yellow petals, mid-19th century, 4.2cm. diam. (Christie's) $895

A Max Erlacher 1972 Charging Elephant paperweight, from limited edition of 100, 3½in. diam. (Robt. W. Skinner Inc.) $200

A St Louis jasper ground pink clematis weight, the flower with ten striped petals, mid-19th century, 7.7cm. diam. (Christie's) $836

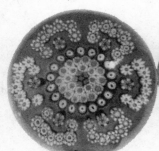

A Clichy colored ground pat-terned concentric millefiori weight, in shades of pink, tur-quoise and pale yellow, mid-19th century, 8.5cm. diam. (Christie's) $1,095

An overlaid paperweight, con-centric rings of multicolored millefiori canes centered and suspended within faceted rounds, 3½in. diam. (Robt. W. Skinner Inc.) $100

A St Louis fuchsia weight, the blue and red flower and two red buds pendant from an ochre stalk, mid-19th century, 7cm. diam. (Christie's) $2,787

A Baccarat garland weight with a central green cane within a circle of blue canes, 7cm. (Phillips) $490

A Baccarat close millefiori mushroom paperweight, the tuft encircled by a blue and white torsade, 7.7cm. (Phillips) $805

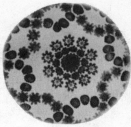

A St. Louis garland paperweight with a central pink cogwheel cane within two rows of pink and green canes, 7.5cm. (Phillips) $560

A Baccarat mushroom weight, the tuft of closely packed colored canes set within a torsade of white gauze, mid 19th century, 8.2cm. diam. (Christie's) $1,107

A St Louis fuschia weight, the three fully opened flowers, two red buds and four green leaves flanking a slender green stalk, mid 19th century, 6.5cm. diam. (Christie's) $2,013

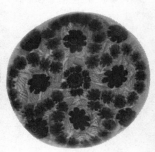

A Clichy paperweight with latticinio 'upset muslin' ground with a cruciform design of pink and red canes, 7.8cm. (Phillips) $770

A St Louis blueberry weight, the two dark blue berries pendant from an ochre branch with three serrated green leaves, mid 19th century, 7.8cm.diam. (Christie's) $3,824

A St Louis faceted upright bouquet weight, the bouquet with a large white and two smaller pink gentian-type flowers, mid 19th century, 8cm. diam. (Christie's) $1,449

A Clichy blue flower weight, the flower with seven pale blue ribbed petals about eight turquoise stamens, mid-19th century, 7.2cm. diam. (Christie's) $6,441

PAPERWEIGHTS

A Paul Ysart garlanded butter-fly weight, the insect with an aventurine body, lime-green and pink wings, inscribed 'PY', 20th century, 7cm. diam. (Christie's) $563

A Clichy close millefiori paper-weight, the multi-colored canes closely set, 7.8cm. (Phillips) $735

A St Louis pom-pom and pansy weight, the pink pom-pom with many recessed petals about a yellow stamen center, mid 19th century, 7.2cm. diam. (Christie's) $6,039

A Clichy close millefiori paper-weight with the multi-colored canes set in a basket of dark blue and white staves, 6.5cm. (Phillips) $1,050

A St Louis aventurine ground dahlia weight, the white flower with fifteen ribbed petals about a green, yellow and red center, mid 19th century, 7.1cm. diam. (Christie's) $7,045

A Clichy green ground con-centric millefiori weight, the three circles of canes in pre-dominant shades of pink and white, mid-19th century, 7.5cm. diam. (Christie's) $805

A Paul Stankard faceted bouquet weight, the arrange-ment of three apple-blossoms set among loosestrife and heather, signed with a black 'S' on a yellow dot, 1982, 8cm. diam. (Christie's) $2,415

A Baccarat green flash faceted patterned millefiori weight, the central red, white, blue and green arrow's head within a circle of green-centered white star canes, mid 19th century, 8.2cm. diam. (Christie's) $4,831

A Baccarat garlanded red and white flower weight, the double clematis type flower with six small dark iron-red petals, mid-19th century, 6.8cm. diam. (Christie's) $2,415

GLASS

A rare Webb gem cameo perfume bottle, designed and executed by George Woodall, of opaque opal white overlaid with coral, 4½in. high. (Robt. W. Skinner Inc.)
$5,500

A Galle carved and acid-etched cameo scent bottle, the clear and pale green glass overlaid with red fruit blossom, 11.5cm. high. (Christie's) $1,122

'A Cotes Bouchon Papillon', a Lalique amber stained scent bottle and stopper, 6.5cm. high. (Christie's) $743

A Galle enamelled glass perfume bottle and stopper, enamelled in colors with a butterfly hovering above delicate flowers, 16cm. high. (Phillips)
$2,464

Amusing mid Victorian Samuel Mordan double scent flask in the form of a pair of opera glasses, 3in. high, London 1868. (Prudential) $878

An 18th century English clear glass scent bottle of flattened pear shape with gold cagework mount in the manner of James Cox, circa 1775. (Phillips)
$1,346

'Quatre Soleils', a Lalique frosted glass scent bottle and stopper, of almost conical shape molded with linear decoration, 7.2cm. high. (Phillips)
$12,320

'Panier de Roses'. A Lalique frosted glass scent bottle, molded with basket-work enclosing rosebuds spilling over the top, 10cm. high. (Phillips) $3,179

An unusual Lalique frosted glass atomiser modelled in high relief with two birds nesting together, 9.5cm. wide. (Phillips)
$791

452

SCENT BOTTLES

A Webb gem cameo perfume bottle, of bright blue layered in white, cameo cut and carved overall with a wide band of five-petalled blossoms, 4½in. high. (Robt. W. Skinner Inc.) $1,800

A Lalique scent bottle and stopper, each face molded with a flowerhead heightened with brown staining, 5.7cm. high. (Phillips) $1,870

A Webb gem cameo perfume/ cologne bottle, of luminous red overlaid opal white, fitted with original glass stopper, 5in. high. (Robt. W. Skinner Inc.) $1,200

A rare Lalique glass perfume bottle, the stopper molded as the full figure of a maiden wearing a long dress studded with flowers, 10cm. high. (Phillips) $1,892

A very attractive Victorian Scottish scent bottle of horse-shoe shape, set with panels of different colored agates, unmarked, circa 1880. (Phillips) $561

A Galle enamelled glass perfume bottle and stopper, enamelled with an insect amid foliate branches, 15cm. high. (Phillips) $1,320

'Flacon Deux Fleurs', a Lalique frosted glass scent bottle, formed as two overlapping flowerheads with beaded centers, 9cm high. (Phillips) $475

A Lalique black glass scent bottle and stopper made for Ambrl D'Orsay, molded in each corner with a woman in long dress holding a garland, 5in. high. (Christie's) $2,674

A Galle scent bottle, with enamel painted decoration of a landscape, seaweed and seashell decoration, 11cm. high. (Christie's) $1,580

'Acanthus', a Lalique frosted glass hanging shade heavily molded with stepped feather-like pattern, 17¾in. diam. (Christie's) $1,645

Two Quezal gas light shades, both of opal glass in squat bulbed form, 5in. diam. (Robt. W. Skinner Inc.) $300

A Galle carved and acid etched double overlay plafonnier, of shaped circular form, overlaid with a green ground and dark amber marguerites, 34.2cm. diam. (Christie's) $7,807

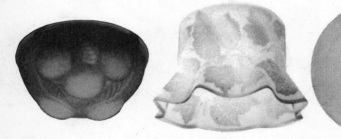

'Dahlia', a Lalique opalescent and frosted hanging shade molded with large flower heads, 12in. diam. (Christie's) $1,439

Unusual English cameo glass lamp shade, fluted shaped rim on frosted clear glass, 6in. high. (Robt. W. Skinner Inc.) $525

A 1930's plafonnier, the half-round blue tinted bowl moulded with coquilles, signed R. Lalique, France, 17½in. full diam. (David Lay) $371

A Daum hanging shade, the milky and frosted acid treated ground overlaid with acid cut decoration of coral colored berries and leaves. (Christie's) $3,718

A Burmese art glass lamp shade, with black "etched" scene of birds, insects, dragonflies, crickets and bees, 5¾in. high. (Robt. W. Skinner Inc.) $350

A Sabino glass hanging shade, the clear glass molded with an interlocking circular motif and a frieze of stylized roses in high relief, 46.2cm. diam. (Christie's) $635

STAINED GLASS

A stained glass window, the design attributed to E. A. Taylor, of a blue bird amidst stylized curvilinear pink blooms, above a field of bluebells, 81 x109.5cm. (Christie's) $929

Leaded glass window with central portrait of a young woman with colorful flowers and a bird at each side, 50in. long. (Robt. W. Skinner Inc.) $1,200

A circular stained glass panel, by W. Aikman, depicting a rural landscape with a plough-man and horses in the foreground, 1924, 45cm. diam. (Phillips) $352

One of a pair of stained glass windows, the design attributed to E. A. Taylor, each with a blue bird amidst stylized curvilinear pink blooms, 82 x 56.4cm. (Christie's) $1,208

A lead and stained glass window designed by M. H. Baillie-Scott consisting of four large and four small rectangular panels, in green, blue and puce-colored glass, (1897-1898). (Christie's) $24,310

A stained glass and leaded roundel by Jessie Jacobs, painted with two birds above a kidney shaped pane inscribed 'I would Rather be than seem to be', 24.3cm. diam. (Phillips) $344

John LaFarge leaded glass panel, of 'stained', painted and layered segments of textured mottled and multi-colored glass, 16½ x 13¼in. (Robt. W. Skinner Inc.) $13,000

A stained glass window, depicting a shepherd with crook and pipe sitting beneath a tree, 56cm. x 85cm. (Phillips) $774

Tiffany leaded glass window, full figure portrait of an angel with a field of spring flowers and intricately designed landscape beyond, 34 x 29in. (Robt. W. Skinner Inc.) $14,000

SWEETMEAT GLASSES

An opaque twist sweetmeat glass, the shallow double ogee bowl with everted molded dentil rim, circa 1770, 15cm. high. (Christie's) $1,493

A baluster sweetmeat glass, on a short angular knopped stem above a domed foot, circa 1720, 14cm. diam. (Christie's) $637

An opaque twist sweetmeat glass, the double ogee bowl with molded dentil rim, circa 1765, 17.5cm. high. (Christie's) $1,891

TUMBLERS

A Baccarat molded sulphide cylindrical tumbler, set with a profile portrait of Napoleon I in the guise of a Roman Emperor, circa 1845, 10cm. high. (Christie's) $696

A Baccarat molded Legion d'Honneur cylindrical tumbler, the medal enamelled in colors circa 1845, 9cm. high. (Christie's) $756

A French molded octagonal sulphide tumbler, inset with a sulphide portrait of St Anne, circa 1845, 10cm. high. (Christie's) $278

An opaque flared tumbler finely painted in a brilliant palette with a bouquet of flowers including a pink rose, perhaps London, 1760-65, 10cm. high. (Christie's) $53,757

A pair of Bohemian engraved 'Annagelb' tumblers, the waisted hexagonal sides engraved with horses in various stances, mid-19th century, 12cm. high. (Christie's) $1,294

A Bohemian topographical stained ruby tumbler, the octagonal waisted sides engraved with a view of Dresden, circa 1850, 14.5cm. high. (Christie's) $557

VASES

An enamel decorated Burmese vase, decorated in the Crown Milano manner with handpainted autumn colored flowers and leaves, 8in. high. (Robt. W. Skinner Inc.) $450

A tall Daum cameo vase, overlaid in mottled amber, brown and green with flowers, broad leaves and corn, 17¼in. high. (Anderson & Garland) $2,422

A Webb gem cameo exhibition vase, of clear cased raspberry red layered white, deeply carved and cut with cat's tails, exotic blossoms and leaves, 1889, 10¼in. high. (Robt. W. Skinner Inc.) $11,000

A Webb gem cameo vase, overlaid in stunning Chinese red, cameo cut and carved, 6¾in. high. (Robt. W. Skinner Inc.) $4,300

A Galle cameo glass vase with tall slender neck and a similar vase with paler coloring and cameo signature 6¾in. high. (Dacre, Son & Hartley) $1,406

A Daum carved and acid etched cameo vase, the milky-white and yellow acid textured glass overlaid in green with trees beside a lake, 16.8cm. high. (Christie's) $1,122

A Lalique green glass globular vase, catalogued 'Formose', 17cm., inscribed R. Lalique, France. (Bearne's) $6,612

A Daum 'Solifleur' glass vase, gilded with thorny branches of leaves and painted en grisaille with a lone figure walking through a bleak rural landscape, 37cm. high. (Phillips) $6,880

A rare Webb tricolor hand-carved gem cameo vase, on bulbous body of brilliant teal blue overlaid with white, 12in. high. (Robt. W. Skinner Inc.) $16,000

VASES

A Quezal art glass vase, with gold iridescence, the surface decorated with "King Tut" swirls of green and gold, 11in. high. (Robt. W. Skinner Inc.) $750

A Fritz Heckert enamelled glass vase, the green tinted iridescent vessel painted in naturalistic colors with daisies, 9.7cm. high, signed. (Phillips) $223

A Galle cameo glass vase, the grayish body having a pinkish tint, overlaid with apple green and blood-red glass, 31cm. high. (Phillips) $1,320

A tall Daum double overlay and wheel carved martele vase, the yellow tinted glass overlaid with orange and green lilies and clover leaves, 40cm. high. (Christie's) $7,854

A Webb tricolor cameo glass vase, of bright yellow overlaid with opal white over brilliant red, 12in. high. (Robt. W. Skinner Inc.) $10,000

A Lalique vase, modelled in high relief with pairs of opalescent budgerigars perched on oval panels, 24cm. (Lawrence Fine Arts) $1,991

An Austrian art glass vase, of brilliant green decorated by stretched iridescent surface separations, 13¼in. high. (Robt. W. Skinner Inc.) $125

An unusual iridescent glass 'Elephant' vase, attributed to Loetz, the globular base forming the creature's head, 29cm. long. (Phillips) $915

A Loetz iridescent glass oviform vase decorated with random splashes of golden iridescence, painted in colored enamels, 22.5cm. high. (Phillips) $602

VASES

A simulated ivory carved vase, of ivory colored glass enhanced with brown, Thomas Webb & Sons Limited, 8½in. high. (Robt. W. Skinner Inc.)
$1,900

A Webb simulated ivory cameo glass vase, designed by George Woodall in the Oriental manner, with handpainted polychrome and gilt enhancements, 7½in. high. (Robt. W. Skinner Inc.)
$5,000

An Austrian enamelled glass vase, probably Fachschule Haida, painted in black, green, yellow and red with stylized florets and foliage, 21.3cm. high. (Phillips)
$275

A Webb cameo glass vase, of lustrous red layered in opal white, carved on base "Gladiolus", 16¼in. high. (Robt. W. Skinner Inc.)
$4,500

A Loetz shell shaped iridescent vase, modelled as a conch shell resting on a spiky base, 21cm. (some chips) (Phillips)
$748

A Daum carved and double overlay martele solifleur vase, overlaid with ruby and dark amber lily of the valley, 29cm. high. (Christie's)
$5,577

A Daum carved, acid textured and enamelled vase, the mottled yellow ground decorated with polychrome flowering convolvulus; 29.5cm. high. (Christie's)
$5,762

A Mount Washington lustreless vase, opal glass handpainted with clusters of pink and white forget-me-nots, 11in. High. (Robt. W. Skinner Inc.)
$150

A Daum carved and acid textured vase, overlaid in purple with a flowering iris, 19.3cm. high. (Christie's)
$3,903

VASES

A Muller Freres carved and acid textured cameo vase, the mottled orange, yellow and brown cased glass overlaid with a green fruiting vine, 12.5cm. high. (Christie's)　$966

A small Galle carved and acid etched triple overlay vase, the light pink glass cased in clear glass and overlaid with white, blue and green umbel flowers, 8.5cm. high. (Christie's) $673

A Venini handkerchief vase, designed by Fulvio Bianconi, the folded rim pulled up into three points, white glass cased in red glass, 20.5cm. high. (Christie's) $836

A Daum vase, with acid cut decoration of coral colored berries and leaves, 17.5cm. high. (Christie's)　$2,788

A Galle vase, the opaque jade green glass overlaid with sang de boeuf, with carved and acid etched decoration of a tiger lily, 22cm. high. (Christie's) $9,295

A Loetz vase, with two lug handles, internally decorated with tiny air bubbles and cased in blue glass, 23.3cm.high. (Christie's) $561

A Daum vase, the sombre pink ground overlaid with amethyst, with carved and acid etched decoration of bats, 26cm. high. (Christie's)　$4,089

'Formose', a Lalique blue stained vase, molded with a shoal of goldfish, with molded signature R. Lalique, 17.5cm. high. (Christie's)　$1,394

A Lalique brown stained vase, of flared form, molded with relief decoration of birds amid foliage, 22.7cm. high. (Christie's) $1,766

'Marisa', a Lalique vase, the milky-white glass molded with four graduated bands of fish, (minute rim chip), 22.7cm. high. (Christie's) $4,488

'Avallon', a Lalique opalescent glass vase, heavily molded with birds perched amongst fruit-bearing cherry branches (rim chip), 15.8cm. high. (Christie's) $748

A Loetz vase of swollen dimpled form with everted rim, the yellow glass with a blue-green iridescent trailed design, 10.7cm. high. (Christie's) $1,496

A Leerdam enamelled vase, designed by Andreas Dirk Copier, the pale red glass with black enamel decoration, 27.8cm. high. (Christie's) $966

A Barovier and Toso patchwork vase designed by Ercole Barovier, the clear glass internally decorated with graduated rectangles inside each other, circa 1955, 14.5cm. high. (Christie's) $935

A Lamartine acid textured and enamelled vase, the clear glass internally decorated with blue-white flecks and polychrome enamelled with an extensive wooded landscape, 13.4cm. high. (Christie's) $561

A Val St Lambert vase, the 'soapstone' ground overlaid with streaked crimson and green glass , 18cm. high. (Christie's) $836

A Loetz footed vase, the swollen body with applied arch decoration, with iridescent purple and golden-green decoration, 24.3cm. high. (Christie's) $935

A Daum Art Deco vase, the auburn tinted clear glass decorated with a pattern of ribs, 26.3cm. high. (Christie's) $557

GLASS

A Loetz cased glass vase, the green glass decorated with a webbed silvery-blue design, 28.3cm. high. (Christie's)
$929

A Galle vase, the frosted ground overlaid with white and mauve glass with acid etched and carved decoration of bellflowers, 15.5cm. high. (Christie's)
$1,301

One of a pair of fine Beijing blue glass bottle vases, the color of deep violet-blue, circa 1850, 23cm. high. (Christie's)
Two $7,964

A Loetz vase, the golden-green iridescent body on a green base with silvery-blue iridescent decoration, 22cm. high. (Christie's) $92

A Daum Art Deco acid etched vase, the topaz glass decorated with lines of graduated squares on an etched ground, 29.4cm. high. (Christie's)
$748

A Galle carved and acid etched cameo vase, the light blue and milky-white glass overlaid in orange with pendant flowering branches, 24.2cm. high. (Christie's) $785

A large Loetz vase, the clear glass decorated in an iridescent golden-green and blue oil splashed pattern, 22cm. high. (Christie's) $743

'Cala Lily', a Galle molded-blown, carved and acid etched double overlay vase, with large flowering cala lilies, 37cm. high. (Christie's) $37,180

'Ceylan', a Lalique opalescent glass vase molded with eight budgerigars perched amid foliage, 24 cm. high. (Christie's)
$4,488

An Italian glass vase, the rose-pink glass cased in clear and pulled over at the top with palest pink glass edged in black, 1985, 24.8cm. high. (Christie's) $336

A Delatte vase, the milky glass overlaid with pink and dark green glass with acid etched and carved decoration of budding branches, 17cm. high. (Christie's) $1,115

A Webb cameo glass vase, carved in relief in white with flowering branches, 21cm. high. (Lawrence Fine Arts) $1,152

'Coqs et Plumes', a Lalique vase, with blue stained and satin finished glass molded with twelve cockerels, 15.6cm. high. (Christie's) $929

A Lobmeyr vase designed by Josef Hoffmann, the clear glass bowl on twelve-side fluted base, with wheel engraved oval view of Vienna, 1858, 13.1cm. high. (Christie's) $561

A Le Verre Francais acid etched cameo vase, the pink and white mottled glass overlaid in red with stylized flowers, 16.5cm. high. (Christie's) $204

A Daum enamelled and acid etched vase, the milky-white and purple acid textured glass enamelled in purple and green with violets, 12cm. high. (Christie's) $2,057

'Milan', a Lalique blue stained vase, molded with stylized leafy branches, 28.2cm. high. (Christie's) $2,602

A Daum vase, with acid etched and enamel painted decoration of a rampant lion and a fleur-de-lys, 12cm. high. (Christie's) $1,951

A gilt decorated opaque twist wine glass, the ogee bowl gilt with a flower-spray, circa 1775, 15cm. high. (Christie's) $895

A green tinted wine glass, the cup shaped bowl supported on a hollow cylindrical stem above a domed foot, circa 1765, 13.5cm. high. (Christie's) $439

A quadruple knopped airtwist wine glass the stem with four knops and filled with airtwist spirals, circa 1750, 16cm. high. (Christie's) $995

An airtwist Jacobite wine glass, the round funnel bowl engraved with a rose and two buds, circa 1750, 14.5cm. high. (Christie's) $1,991

An opaque twist pale green tinted wine glass, with three raspberry prunts, 18th century, 15.5cm. high. (Christie's) $1,095

An engraved wine glass of drawn trumpet shape, the plain stem with a tear, circa 1740, 16.5cm. high. (Christie's) $2,190

A color-twist wine glass with a round funnel bowl, on a conical foot, circa 1765, 15cm. high. (Christie's) $2,588

An airtwist Jacobite wine glass of drawn trumpet shape, on a folded conical foot, circa 1750, 16cm. high. (Christie's) $895

A Dutch-engraved light baluster wine glass, the funnel bowl engraved and polished with a scantily draped winged figure, circa 1748, 17cm. high. (Christie's) $2,190

464

WINE GLASSES

A balustroid wine glass, the slender drawn trumpet bowl set on a beaded inverted baluster stem, circa 1730, 17.5cm. high. (Christie's) $597

A gilt decorated emerald-green wine glass, in the manner of James Giles, circa 1765. 11.5cm. high. (Christie's) $1,393

A Beilby enamelled opaque twist wine glass, the stem with a double-series core above a conical foot, circa 1770, 15.5cm. high. (Christie's) $1,194

A 'Lynn' opaque twist wine glass with horizontally ribbed round funnel bowl, circa 1770, 14.5cm. high. (Christie's) $995

An Anglo-Venetian wine glass, the flared funnel bowl with lightly ribbed lower part with pincered fringe, late 17th century, 12cm. high. (Christie's) $696

An airtwist Jacobite wine glass of drawn trumpet shape, the stem filled with spirals above a conical foot, circa 1750, 16.5cm. high. (Christie's) $796

An opaque twist presentation wine glass, on a double series stem and conical foot, circa 1770, 15.5cm. high. (Christie's) $696

A baluster wine glass with a bell bowl, the stem with a triple annulated knop, circa 1715, 16cm. high. (Christie's) $438

A gilt decorated facet stemmed wine glass, in the manner of James Giles, circa 1770, 14.5cm. high. (Christie's) $398

A 'Newcastle' engraved light baluster wine glass, with a basal knop above a conical foot, mid-18th century, 18.5cm. high. (Christie's) $796

A white enamelled small opaque twist wine glass, the round funnel bowl with floral swags, Beilby Workshop, circa 1770, 11cm. high. (Christie's) $1,791

A light baluster wine glass with a generous bell bowl, the stem with a spreading knop, circa 1735, 16.5cm. high. (Christie's) $637

An opaque twist wine glass, the stem with four knops enclosing a gauze core, circa 1775, 16.5cm. high. (Christie's) $756

A commemorative wine glass, the pedestal stem inscribed in relief *God Save King George* and the shoulder with a crown at each angle, 1715-20, 16cm. high. (Christie's) $8,959

A Beilby enamelled plain stemmed wine glass, the ogee bowl decorated in white with a border of fruiting vine, circa 1770, 14.5cm. high. (Christie's) $1,493

An airtwist wine glass, the stem with four knops and filled with airtwist spirals, circa 1750, 16cm. high. (Christie's) $597

A baluster wine glass, the bell bowl with a tear to the lower part, circa 1715, 16.5cm. high. (Christie's) $1,294

A Jacobite light baluster wine glass, the flared funnel bowl engraved with a rose and a bud, circa 1750, 17.5cm. high. (Christie's) $2,968

WINE GLASSES

A Dublin Volunteers wine glass, the round funnel bowl inscribed *Dublin Volunteers/pro Patria*, circa 1785, 16cm. high. (Christie's) $2,389

An engraved airtwist wine glass, the funnel bowl engraved and polished with a growing vine, circa 1750, 15.5cm. high. (Christie's) $517

A Jacobite airtwist wine glass, the bell bowl engraved with a rose, bud and half opened bud, the reverse with the motto *Fiat*, circa 1750, 16.5cm. high. (Christie's) $1,592

A baluster wine glass with a flared thistle shaped bowl, on a domed and folded foot, circa 1715, 17cm. high. (Christie's) $955

A green tinted wine glass, the cup shaped bowl supported on a hollow knopped stem, circa 1765, 15cm. high. (Christie's) $298

An engraved opaque twist wine glass, decorated with a rustic house and a figure suspended from gallows, circa 1775, 14.5cm. high. (Christie's) $915

A baluster wine glass with a bell bowl, the stem with a plain section above an inverted baluster knop, circa 1720, 16cm. high. (Christie's) $597

A Beilby opaque twist wine glass of drawn trumpet shape, the border enamelled in white, circa 1765, 17cm. high. (Christie's) $3,982

A colour twist wine glass with a bell bowl, the stem with a gauze core, circa 1760, 15.5cm. high. (Christie's) $1,393

A Swiss enamelled gold octagonal snuff box, the cover painted with a figure of Hope, Geneva, circa 1815, 3¾in. long. (Christie's) $7,946

An English oval gold mounted citrine vinaigrette, the facet cut cover and base in reeded gold borders, circa 1830, 1½in. long (Christie's) $2,763

A Swiss enamelled gold octagonal snuff box, the cover painted with Venus and Cupid, Geneva, circa 1795, with prestige marks (restored), 8cm. long. (Christie's) $5,297

A Swiss shaped oval enamelled gold snuff box, the cover and base painted with fruit and flowers, circa 1820, 3in. wide. (Christie's) $8,703

An Austrian imperial presentation gold mounted hardstone octagonal snuff box, Vienna, 1806, probably by Johann Karl Retzer, 3¾in. long. (Christie's) $16,082

A jewelled gold mounted amethyst vinaigrette, set with turquoise, circa 1830, 1¾in. long, in original fitted case. (Christie's) $6,622

A George III enamelled gold aide memoire, closed by a reeded pencil, circa 1770, 8cm. high. (Christie's) $8,514

An Asprey three colored 9kt. gold cigarette box, with maker's mark and London hallmarks for 1924, in original fitted case, 14cm. long, 651 grams gross. (Christie's) $7,106

An 18th century French gold souvenir, the cover set with a miniature of a gentleman in light-blue coat, Paris, 1768. (Christie's) $2,992 £1,600

A Louis XVI narrow rectangular gold snuff box, by Jean-Bernard Cherrier, Paris, 1774-75, 6.5cm. long, in case. (Christie's) $9,460

A George IV vari-colored gold, silver gilt and hardstone paper knife, the handle formed of chevrons of various hardstones mounted in gold, by Joseph Angell, 1824, 9in. long. (Christie's) $2,763

A William IV rectangular gold snuff box, with concave sides, by Alexander James Strachan, 1835, 3¼in. long. (Christie's) $5,676

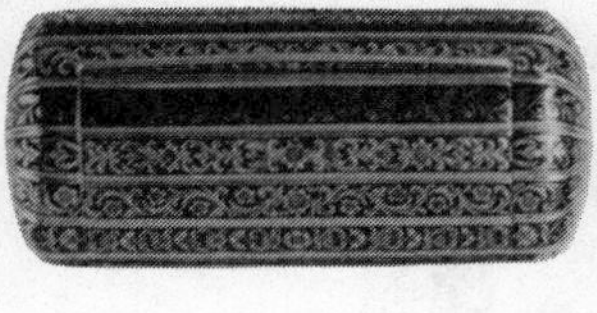

A Swiss oblong gold snuff box of bolster form, by Bautte et Moynier, Geneva, circa 1820, 3½in. long. (Christie's) $3,027

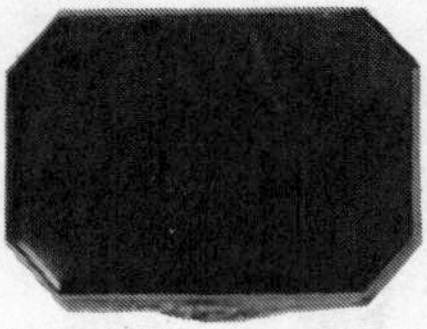

A George II gold mounted octagonal snuff box, the cover and base formed of panels of honey colored agate, circa 1740, 2½in. long. (Christie's) $1,554

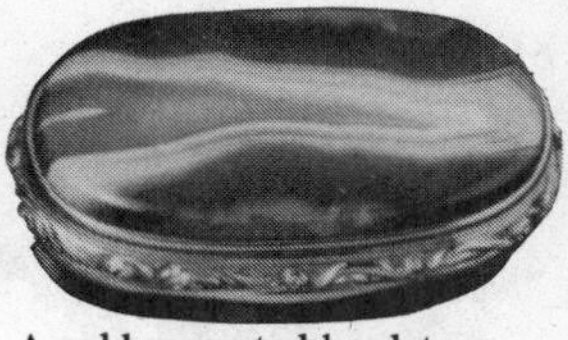

A gold mounted hardstone vinaigrette, the base and cover of striated gray agate, circa 1830, 2in. long, in fitted case. (Christie's) $2,175

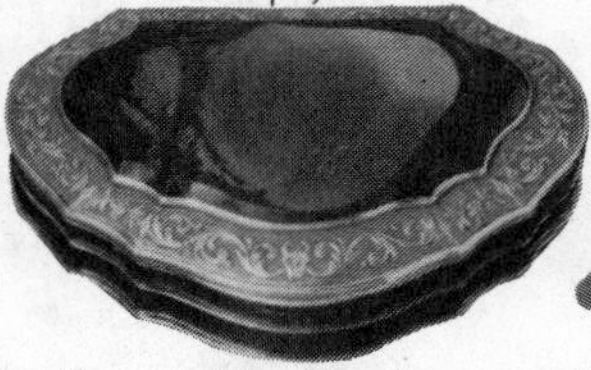

A George III gold and hardstone cartouche shaped snuff box, by A. J. Strachan, date letter indistinct, probably 1804, 3¼in. long. (Christie's) $5,297

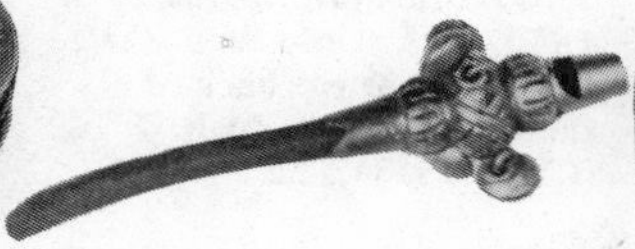

A late 18th or early 19th century gold miniature rattle and whistle, unmarked, circa 1800, 5.4cm. long. (Phillips) $785

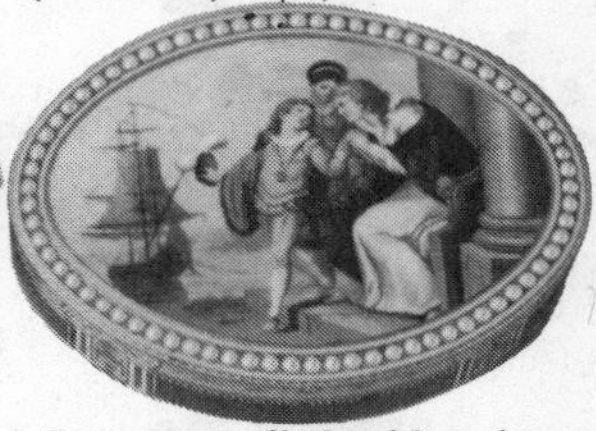

A Swiss enamelled gold oval snuff box, the cover painted with a young man taking leave of his mother, by George Remond et Cie., Geneva, circa 1815, 3½in. long. (Christie's) $11,730

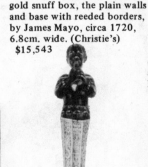

A Swiss enamelled gold etui a tablettes, with four engine turned panels bordered by enamelled foliage and flowers, circa 1790, 8.5cm. (Christie's) $2,935 £1,870

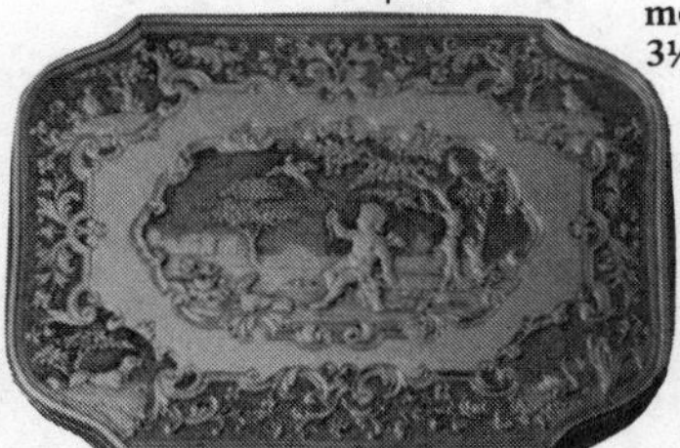

A rare George I shaped oblong gold snuff box, the plain walls and base with reeded borders, by James Mayo, circa 1720, 6.8cm. wide. (Christie's) $15,543

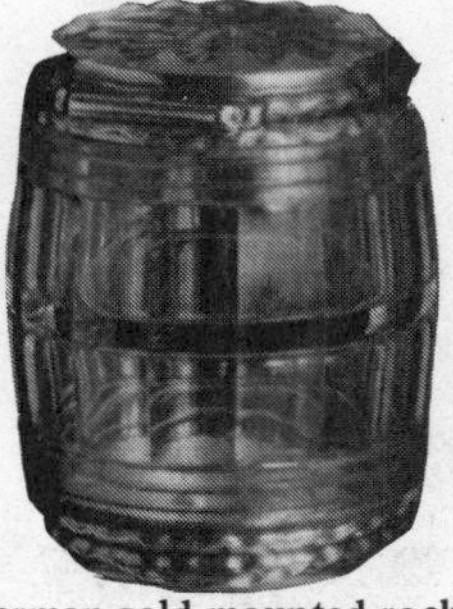

A German gold mounted rock crystal double snuff box, formed as a barrel, circa 1740, 2¼in. high. (Christie's) $13,244

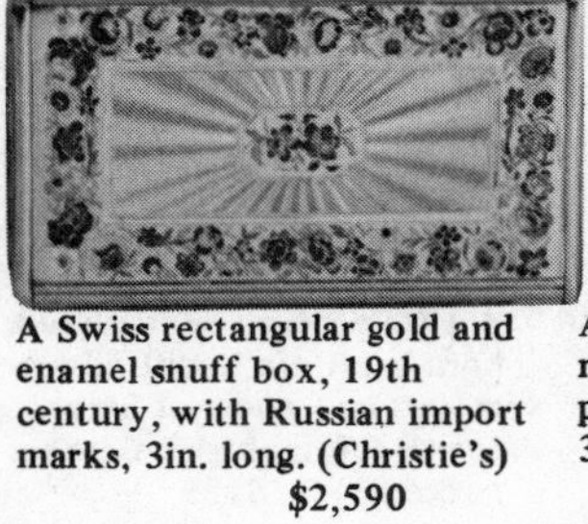

A Swiss rectangular gold and enamel snuff box, 19th century, with Russian import marks, 3in. long. (Christie's) $2,590

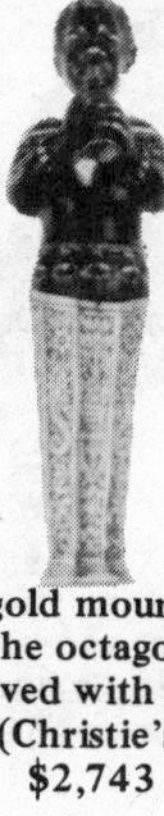

A jewelled gold mounted blackamoor etui, the octagonal flaring plinth engraved with flowers, 3¼in. high. (Christie's) $2,743

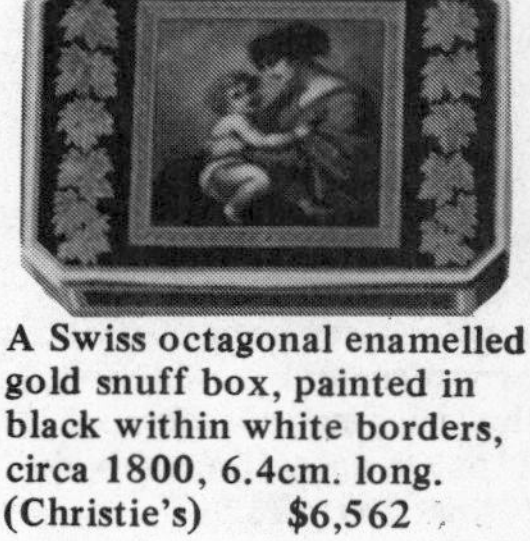

A Swiss octagonal enamelled gold snuff box, painted in black within white borders, circa 1800, 6.4cm. long. (Christie's) $6,562

A rhinoceros horn libation cup of tapered rectangular form, carved to each face with archaistic bats, 17th century, 13.8cm. high. (Christie's)
$10,353

Two erotic horn figures, circa 1800, both semi-naked, their hair coiled at the back of their heads, 4¼in. high. (Christie's) $4,512

A late Victorian oak desk stand, incorporating a timepiece supported on silvered metal mounted horns, 17¾in. wide. (Christie's) $673

A George III horn beaker, with fitted Old Sheffield plate liner and silver rim, Sheffield 1812, by John Roberts and Company, 4½in. high. (Bonhams) $262

A rhinoceros horn libation cup of tapered square shape, carved on the body with two pairs of confronted kui dragons, 17th century, 14.6cm. wide, carved fitted wood base. (Christie's) $5,973

A carved pierced rhinocerous horn, on teak carved stand, 14½in. high. (Du Mouchelles) $900

A rhinoceros horn libation cup carved around the sides with flowering magnolia branches, 17th century, 16.6cm. wide. (Christie's) $3,583

A German horn armchair with red velvet padded back and seat with gilt studs and five pairs of horns. (Christie's) $1,522

A 19th century Scottish ram's horn snuff mull, with silvered mount and agate set hinged cover, 6.7cm. high. (Geering & Colyer) $135

A two case brown lacquer inro decorated in gold and red taka-zogan, a sea-bream inlaid in mother-of-pearl, signed Kyu-koku, 19th century, 7.9cm. wide. (Christie's) $1,566

An unusual circular natural wood three case inro decorated with a kirin in finely carved takazogan, unsigned, 19th century, with an attached ivory ojime, 7.3cm. diam. (Christie's) $5,184

A single case inro decorated with revellers in a pleasure boat, the reverse with another boat full of people, unsigned, 19th century, 7.8cm. wide. (Christie's) $2,056

A four case Kinji inro richly decorated in various techniques with boys and fighting cockerels, signed Kajikawa, 19th century, 8.5cm. (Christie's) $4,752

A single case Roironuri inro with fitted double compartment decorated in takamakie, sabiji and ivory and shell inlay with arrows in an archer's quiver, 18th/19th century, 5cm. (Christie's) $1,485

A fine Roironuri five case inro decorated with an eagle flying above water plants, the reverse with an egret flying in terror, signed Kanshosai, late 18th/early 19th century, 10.2cm. high. (Christie's) $3,524

A four case Nashiji inro decorated in hiramakie with cranes in flight, signed Inagawa saku, 19th century, 6.7cm. (Christie's) $2,178

A Roironuri four case inro decorated with a crow on a flowering plum branch, signed Inagawa and tsubo seal, 19th century, 8cm. high. (Christie's) $4,308

A fine four case Roironuri inro decorated with a group of attendants seated beside a torii and surrounded by brushwork fences, signed Shiomi Masanari, 18th century, 7.2cm. high. (Christie's) $3,329

A 19th century two inch four draw brass refracting telescope, signed on the first draw Dollond, London, 12½in. (Lawrence Fine Arts) $854

A 19th century barograph, inscribed Lennie, Edinburgh, with drawer to base, 37cm. (Phillips) $524

A brass surveyor's vernier compass, signed Benj'n Pike Jr., 294 Broadway, N.Y. N.Y., mid-19th century, the shaped strap with two detachable slit sights, 14¾in. (Christie's) $880

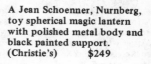

A brass compound microscope for the American market, signed I. P. Cutts, Sheffield, retailed by McAllister & Bro., Philadelphia, circa 1825, on folding tripod base, 31cm. length of box. (Christie's) $2,090

A rare George III mahogany waywiser with 7in. silvered dial, by William Watkins, St. James's Street, London, wheel diameter 32in. (Prudential) $3,249

A Jean Schoenner, Nurnberg, toy spherical magic lantern with polished metal body and black painted support. (Christie's) $249

An ivory tablet dial with the trademark of Hans Tucher, Nuremberg, dated 1611, the underside of the base with scale for age and aspect of the moon, 91mm. long. (Christie's) $1,760

A Lane's pocket terrestrial globe, the sphere applied with printed gores depicting Cook's, Anson's and King's voyages, 3in. diameter, late 18th century. (Bearne's) $2,376

A brass Culpepper type microscope, signed Troughton, London, late 18th century, on molded mahogany base with drawer. (Christie's) $715

INSTRUMENTS

A Thatcher's calculating instrument by Keuffel & Esser Co., Serial No. 4012, on oblong mahogany base, with engine turned brass supports. (Christie's) $880

A one day marine chronometer signed on the dial Harris late Hatton & Harris, London, the gilt full plate fusee movement with Earnshaw spring detent escapement, 75mm. diam. of dial. (Christie's)
$1,980

An interesting small Gregorian reflecting telescope, mid-18th century, signed 'Made by George Adams at Tycho Brahe's Head in Fleet Street, London', the eyepiece signed 'Repaired by F.. Nairne 1770 London', 15in. length of body tube. (Christie's) $1,870

A 19th century brass monocular microscope, inscribed Charles Perry, Northolme Rd., London, 35cm. (Phillips)
$243

A mahogany microscope slide cabinet of twenty-one drawers, containing a collection of mainly entomological, botanical, diatomaceous and micro-photographic interest, 11¾in. (Lawrence Fine Arts)
$325

A 19th century brass and ebony octant, with ivory inset calibrated scale, 36cm. (Phillips)
$411

An early 19th century T.M. Bardin 12in. celestial globe, on four turned baluster legs joined by stretchers. (Lawrence Fine Arts) $1,994

A ship's magnetic detector by Marconi's Wireless Telegraph Co., No. 71335, in polished teak case. (Christie's)
$8,362

A brass universal ring dial, signed T. Wright fecit, 18th century, with folding brass Roman chapter ring, 5in. diam. (Christie's) $2,640

A 19th century amputation part set, the three Liston knives stamped Z. HUNTER with bone saw, pincers, finger saw and other items, 16½in. wide. (Christie's) $718

A fine and rare early 18th century walnut Hauksbee-Papin pattern air pump, with 18th century glass bell jar, 135cm. high overall. (Phillips) $7,160

A French lacquered brass barograph, in hinged mahogany case, the annular ring dial with enamelled numbers. (Phillips) $537

An upright cylinder lantern with red and gilt decoration on barrel with chimney by Ernst Planck, Nuremberg. (Christie's) $1,076

An unusual 19th century teak mineralogical prospector's chest, 30cm. wide, with stamp of Max Hildebrand fruher August Lingke & Co, Freiberg in Sachsen, containing chamois lined fitted tray and two cases, 30cm. wide, circa 1880's. (Phillips) $1,700

A Persian brass astrolobe, with rete for twelve stars, the mater with decorated and inscribed kursi, 28cm. diam. (Phillips) $805

A terrestrial globe by G. & J. Cary, the globe set in a brass mount calibrated through four sectors inscribed 'Cary's New Terrestrial Globe'. (Bearne's) $2,625

A good late 18th century brass 4in. Gregorian reflecting telescope, signed Mackenzie, 15 Cheapside, London, sighting telescope and dust cap, body tube 61cm. long. (Phillips) $1,253

A rare Baby-rem typewriter, in case, circa 1920. (Phillips) $114

INSTRUMENTS

A rare mid-19th century plated brass Harrington's Patent clockwork dental drill, No. 146, with controls switch and thumb operated clutch, 6cm. long, in fitted walnut veneered case. (Phillips) $3,043

A W. W. Rouche and Co., rare and good wet-plate photographers portable dark tent with mahogany case with inset red glass window. (Christie's) $2,079

A mid-19th century electro-medical shock machine, the brass wheel molded with dolphins, on marble base, 10in. wide. (Christie's) $321

A gun metal pocket roulette wheel, the circular white enamel dial signed Roulette Ideale, with red and black numerals, 68mm. diam. (Christie's) $1,650

An early 19th century lacquered brass 'Jones's Most Improved Compound Monocular Microscope', signed on folding tripod base 'W. & S. Jones, 30 Holborn, London, 30.5cm. wide. (Phillips) $1,969

A 19th century lacquered brass Sorby-Browning micro-spectroscope, signed Smith, Beck & Beck, 31 Cornhill, London, 9. (Phillips) $429

An 18th century brass 2¼in. Gregorian reflecting telescope, with rod for focusing secondary mirror, on decorative baluster stand with augur. (Phillips) $859

A 19th century black enamelled brass transit theodolite signed on the silvered compass dial R.W. Street, Commer Rd Lambeth, London, in mahogany case, 12½in. wide. (Christie's) $851

F. E. Ives/The Photochromo-scope Syndicate Ltd., London, Kromskop viewer with viewing hood and diffusing screen. (Christie's) $1,468

INSTRUMENTS

A 19th century lacquered brass Stellar goniometer, the eyepiece mounted with geared disc, signed Rothwell, Manchester, 19cm. wide, in wooden box. (Phillips) $286

A late 18th century brass universal equinoctial dial, the silvered compass box with eight cardinal points, signed Adams, London, 16cm. wide. (Phillips) $1,074

A fine 19th century anodised and lacquered brass 8in. double frame sextant, signed Allan, London, with five telescopes, 32cm. wide. (Phillips) $1,611

An 18in. Malby's terrestrial globe, the colored sphere inscribed, the whole supported in a brass meridian engraved with degrees, 42in. high. (Lawrence Fine Arts) $6,230

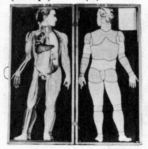

Anatomical teaching device, 'Smiths's New Outline Map of the Human System, Anatomical Regions, No. 2', manufactured by American Manikan Co., Peoria, Illinois, 1888, 44in. high. (Robt. W. Skinner Inc.) $900

A rare 'The Pocket Typewriter, Swan Arcade, Bradford', with name and characters on circular white enamel dial, 10cm. long, circa 1887. (Phillips) $1,936

English brass and rosewood marine chronometer, Parkinson & Frodsham, Change Alley, London, 1801-1842, in a brass bound rosewood case. (Robt. W. Skinner Inc.) $1,700

A rare Munson typewriter, the three row keyboard with octagonal keys, horizontal type-sleeve and wide ribbon, (Phillips) $1,496

Negretti and Zambra, a mahogany stereoscope with focusing section, hinged top lid and hinged rear reflector. (Christie's) $1,664

A French mid-19th century lacquered and plated brass cannon, 9cm. diam., signed Louis Guerin, Opticien a Alger. (Phillips) $1,790

A rare Lambert typewriter, with type-ring and gilt decorated body, in original leather case. (Phillips) $809

A Brewster pattern stereoscope in mahogany with inset metalwork, ivory and semi-precious stone decoration. (Christie's) $587

A lacquered brass French theodolite, the telescope with rack and pinion focusing on a three screw tripod attachment, in mahogany case, 15in. high. (Christie's) $1,040

A modern lacquered brass 'Perpetual Motion' machine, mounted on four turned pillars, 45cm. wide. (Phillips) $286

A 19th century lacquered brass Wenham compound binocular microscope, the base signed J. Swift, 43 University St., London W.C., in mahogany case. (Phillips) $1,163

A burr walnut pedestal stereoscope with focusing eye-pieces and internal mechanism. (Christie's) $626

A 200 x 140mm. Polyrama Panoptique viewer with focusing lens section, opening lid and label 'Polyrama Panoptique, Brevet d'Invention SGtie du Govt'. (Christie's) $1,566

A 19th century French pewter enema douche with accessories in fitted oval japanned case, 8in. wide. (Christie's) $454

A pair of George III polished steel andirons with pierced obelisk supports surmounted by vase finials, 29in. high. (Christie's) $1,645

A wrought iron foot scraper, probably Pennsylvania, mid-19th century, modelled in the form of a ram, 34.6cm. long. (Christie's) $4,620

A steel bridle or scold, of conventional strap form, the front strap with tongue depressor, surmounted by a ring, 9½in. overall height. (Lawrence Fine Arts) $358

A cast iron architectural ornament, American, early 20th century, modelled in the form of a Classical head, 22in. high. (Christie's) $770

A reticulated brass and iron kettle stand, probably English, late 18th century, on cabriole front legs with penny feet, 13in. high. (Christie's) $330

A cast iron panel by Hector Guimard for the entrance to the Paris Metro, 74cm. high. (Christie's) $1,859

A cast iron funeral gate by James Monahan, Savannah, Georgia, late 19th century, centering a reticulated weeping willow tree, 33 x 27¾in. (Christie's) $1,210

A Gordon Russell polished steel set of fire irons, the stand with square section column, arched legs and trefoil feet. (Christie's) $1,496

A pair of cast iron figural andirons, America, late 19th/early 20th century, caricature figures of a black man and woman, 16½in. high. (Robt. W. Skinner Inc.) $1,200

One of a pair of cast iron garden urns of campana shape, with loop handles, 19th century, 30½in. high. (Lawrence Fine Arts) Two **$1,039**

A pair of Arts and Crafts polished steel firedogs, designed by Ernest Gimson and made by Alfred Bucknell, 58.5cm. high. (Phillips) $3.010

A wrought iron snake sculpture by Edgar Brandt, of a king cobra coiled in a circle with its head raised to strike, dark patina, stamped E. Brandt, 11.5cm. high. (Christie's) **$1,122**

A Regency blackened iron fire surround and grate, the pierced basket with vase finials, 43in. wide. (Christie's) $4,731

A wrought iron Conestoga wagon box hasp, Pennsylvania, early/mid-19th century, the triangular crest above a double row of two pierced circles, 14½in. long. (Christie's) $462

A cast iron stove plate, probably by Mary Ann Furnace, York County, Pennsylvania, circa 1761, depicting two tulip and heart decorations, 24½in. high. (Christie's) $990

A brass mounted steel basket grate with arched rectangular cast iron back, late 19th century, 34½in. wide. (Christie's) $3,702

A cast iron tea kettle, the sides cast in low relief with numerous chrysanthemum blooms, 5¼in. diam. (Lawrence Fine Arts) $167

A cast iron painted mill weight, American, late 19th/early 20th century, modelled as a bob-tailed standing horse, 16½in. high. (Christie's) $440

A Regency polished steel, brass and cast iron fire grate in the manner of George Bullock, the arched backplate with scrolling foliage and flowerheads, the guard 37in. wide. (Christie's) $16,192

A 20th century, white painted wrought iron gazebo, worked with tubular members in the form of a painted arch, 120in. wide. (Robt. W. Skinner Inc.) $4,300

A good fire grate, the wrought iron basket with integral brass andirons. (David Lay) $935

A set of three brass and steel fire irons, comprising a poker, tongs and a shovel, 27¾in. long. (Christie's) $987

A set of three steel fire irons comprising: a long handled poker, tongs and shovel with brass capitals in the form of flowerheads, 29in. long. (Bearne's) $297

An attractive 17th century German crossbow, 25¼in., span 18in., foliate finialled steel rearsight with hinged adjustable view. (Wallis & Wallis) $3,806

One of a pair of French enamelled cast iron urns, decorated with geometric foliage and flowerheads on a cream ground, late 19th century, 15in. high. (Christie's)
Two $5,698

A pair of Victorian white painted cast iron campana shaped garden urns, the fluted bodies with raised foliage, 22in. high. (Christie's) $1,155

An 18th century design steel and brass serpentine fronted fire grate, the frieze pierced with foliage, 21¼in. wide. (Christie's) $1,076

A set of three early 19th
century steel and bronze
mounted fire irons, the
octagonal shafts fitted with
foliage chased handles.
(Christie's) $385

A Victorian cast iron garden
seat, and a cast iron garden
chair, the legs and back cast
in the form of foliage and
flower heads, 33½in. high.
(Bearne's) $1,225

A set of three George III
polished steel fire irons each
with turned finials and shaft,
the shovel pierced with a
rising sun. 29in. long. (Christie's)
$968

A Regency polished steel fender, the D-shaped
body with pierced geometric strapwork and
bun feet, 46½in. wide. (Christie's)
$1,028

A Regency ormolu, bronze and polished steel
fender, with sleeping lions on plinths, 40¼in.
wide. (Christie's) $3,291

A rare Hodges patent sporting bow constructed of six stiff steel wires with white metal
mounts and nocks, tubular steel handle, 64cm. overall. (Phillips) $422

Cast iron State Seal of New
York, America, late 19th
century, the figure of an eagle
with outstretched wings
perched upon a scrolled cartouche, 34in. wide. (Robt. W.
Skinner Inc.) $2,200

A pair of good cast iron urns
and pedestals, each of classical
fluted shape, full height 54in.
(David Lay) $3,085

A George III steel and brass
firegrate, the shaped arched
backplate with a molded
circular panel, the basket with
serpentine front surmounted
by finials, 38in. wide.(Christie's)
$21,252

IVORY

A 19th century French ivory group of a cavalier putting his arm round a lady, by J. J. Soute, 1851, 17cm. high. (Christie's) $1,861

A late 19th century French ivory figurine of Cupid ensnared, possibly after a model by L. Samain, 10cm. high. (Christie's) $427

A rare elephant tusk humidor by Tiffany & Company, New York, the body formed by an oval shaped section of an elephant's tusk, repousse and chased in stylized floral motifs in the Indian taste, 10½in. high. (Christie's) $10,450

An ivory figure carved from a model by Ferdinand Preiss, the seated naked young woman with legs dangling over a shaped onyx rectangular base, 3¾in. high. (Christie's) $1,234

A 19th century German or Austrian ivory group of an aristocratic couple accosted on their travels by two fortune tellers, 29cm. high. (Christie's) $20,449

An Art Deco ivory bust of a nude maiden, her head turned sideways, on a flaring shaped ebony plinth, 24.3cm. high. (Christie's) $1,859

A wood and ivory carving of Ebisu kneeling beside a large floundering sea bream, signed on a rectangular reserve Ryumei Meiji period, 17cm. high. (Christie's) $3,720

A 19th century Dieppe ivory tankard carved with the birth of Venus, after Raphael, with a figure of Venus on the lid after Botticelli, 48cm. high. (Christie's) $11,897

A well carved ivory okimono of an elegantly dressed lady holding a scarf, signed Kazusane, late 19th century, 15cm. high. (Christie's) $1,958

IVORY

A fine ivory group of a man holding one of his sons in his arms, another kneeling beside a basket of peaches, signed Seiga, late 19th century, 15cm. high. (Christie's) $2,937

An ivory group of a farmer and his family, gathered together on a raft of bundles of reeds, 10in. high. (Lawrence Fine Arts) $1,394

An ivory and carved wood figure of a wood carrier, the old man crossing a log bridge, 13in. high. (Lawrence Fine Arts) $2,416

An early 20th century English ivory bust of Mrs. Emmeline Pankhurst, by A.G.Walker, signed on the back, on a gray marble pedestal, 16.5cm. high. (Christie's) $4,647

A well carved ivory group of a cockerel, hen and three chicks on wood stand, late 19th century, overall 18cm. wide. (Christie's) $1,958

A small 19th century French silver mounted ivory tankard, with scenes of classical maidens dancing before elders, 10.5cm. high. (Christie's) $2,230

A turned ivory mortar, the egg cup shaped body with ring turned decoration, 16.8cm. high, 17th century. (Bearne's) $2,288

A fine ivory and lacquer figure of a seated Tea Master, his kimono decorated in gold and silver hiramakie on a Kinji ground, signed Komin. late 19th century, 15.7cm. high. (Christie's) $8,811

A finely carved ivory figure of an old man feeding grain to a hen and two chicks at his feet, signed Seirin, late 19th century, 15cm. high. (Christie's) $2,545

IVORY

An ivory mounted casket with domed hinged cover, the protruding base on bun feet, late 19th century, 13in. wide. (Lawrence Fine Arts) $1,301

A 19th century Dieppe ivory figurine of a musketeer on a turned ebonized wood base, 12cm. high. (Christie's) $408

A 19th century ball, stained and carved in relief with rats among tassles and objects, 2½in. diam. (Lawrence Fine Arts) $418

A 19th century Anglo-Indian ivory watch stand, decorated with stained inlay work, 11in. high. (Phillips) $219

An ivory and silver vase, the lobed ivory body decorated with cockerels and hens and their chicks among a bamboo grove, the silver mounts decorated in various colored cloisonne enamels, signed Hidetomo, late 19th century, 20cm. high. (Christie's) $3,139

A fine 18th century German ivory tankard with silver gilt mounts, by Johann Benno Canzler, Munich, 1742. 9½in. high. (Prudential) $25,650

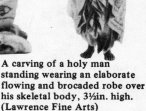

A 19th century Dieppe ivory statuette, possibly of Mary Queen of Scots, in period costume with a rosary on turned ebony base with moldings, 18cm. high. (Christie's) $1,078

An okimono of the Takara-bune, the Seven Gods of Good Fortune, crammed into the open boat, signed, 3½in. wide. (Lawrence Fine Arts) $597

A carving of a holy man standing wearing an elaborate flowing and brocaded robe over his skeletal body, 3½in. high. (Lawrence Fine Arts) $517

IVORY

An okimono of a court figure, seated wearing engraved robes, signed, 2½in. high. (Lawrence Fine Arts) $278

A mid-19th century French ivory figurine of a boy violinist, in Van Dyck costume, on a turned circular base (bow separate), 19cm. high. (Christie's) $1,078

An okimono carved as an elaborately coiffeured man with an unrolled scroll, squatting on the back of a demon holding an axe, signed, 3¼in. high. (Lawrence Fine Arts) $338

'Ecstasy', an ivory figure by Ferdinand Preiss, of a nude maiden standing on tiptoe with her arms outstretched above her, 36cm. high. (Christie's) $14,872

One of a pair of ivory bezique markers, each carved and stained in low relief with monkeys and insects. (Lawrence Fine Arts) Two $398

A Japanese carved ivory tusk depicting many figures on a river bank, 12¾in. high, Meiji period. (Bearne's) $1,584

A carving of a nobleman, standing wearing stained robes, 3½in. high. (Lawrence Fine Arts) $258

A 19th century Cantonese ivory watch stand, decorated to the front and sides in high relief. (Phillips) $544

A fine ivory tusk vase and cover carved in high relief with a multitude of quail among millet, late 19th century, 25.2cm. high. (Christie's) $7,636

An ivory tusk paperweight, carved with the bust of an Art Nouveau maiden amid poppies, 32.1cm. long. (Christie's) $594

An octagonal handscreen applied with a group of four ladies with ivory faces and padded silk clothes, 15½in., Canton, circa 1830, in silk covered box. (Christie's) $1,022

A Japanese carved ivory figure of a man attempting to fend off a dragon, signed, 7in. high. (Bearne's) $297

A Continental carved ivory group of a lightly draped female figure carrying a cherub on her shoulder, 9½in. high. (Bearne's) $1,015

A pair of Continental carved ivory allegorical female figures, each lightly draped, 7¼in. high. (Bearne's) $1,575

A fine lacquered leather and ivory kiseruzutsu, decorated in takamakie with a Dutchman walking his dog, signed, Hisamine. (Christie's) $7,049

A Japanese ivory figure of a man shown standing wearing a dragon robe and voluminous trousers, 9½in. high, signed. (Bearne's) $665

Early 20th century Japanese ivory boat, hull with veneered carved and stained rectangular panels, 15¼in. high, on shaped wooden base. (Robt. W. Skinner Inc.) $900

Chinese ivory carving of Guan Yin standing and holding a mirror, 19th century, 21½in. high. (Lambert & Foster) $1,056

Very ornate Chinese ivory tusk carving of figures in high relief, on carved wood stand, 17½in. high. (Lambert & Foster) $220

A Japanese carved ivory group of a goose and a gosling on a rocky base, signed, 4¾in. long. (Bearne's) $770

Late 19th century carved ivory okimono of a child with a rolled scroll watching a man holding a cloth banner aloft, 9in. high. (Robt. W. Skinner Inc.) $200

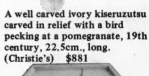

An ivory and fruitwood bust carved from a model by I. Sosson, of an Art Nouveau maiden, on striated marble pedestal, 27.4cm. high. (Christie's) $841

A fine Japanese Shibayama style ivory standing caparisoned elephant with trunk raised, surmounted on the top with two flowerheads, signed Toshikazu, Meiji period, 8½in. long. (Christie's) $11,900

A well carved ivory kiseruzutsu carved in relief with a bird pecking at a pomegranate, 19th century, 22.5cm., long. (Christie's) $881

A 19th century French ivory quadrilobed fluted vase, the body carved with grapes and vine leaves, 4¼in. high. (Christie's) $539

An ivory figure carved from a model by P. Phillipe, modelled as a nude maiden standing with her arms crossed, 22.7cm. high. (Christie's) $4,114

An ivory plaque of Nicholas I, in the uniform of the Gardes a Cheval regiment, signed in Cyrillic and dated, Ia. Seriakov, 3¾ x 2¾in. (Christie's) $2,044

A pale celadon jade square tapering censer, with handles formed as vigorous chilong clambering over the rim, 17th/18th century, 12.3cm. square, fitted wood stand. (Christie's) $17,919

A very pale celadon jade model of a boat crossing a shallow sea of turbulent breaking waves, 18th century. (Christie's) $15,928

A lavender and pale apple-green jadeite figure of a horse, carved in the Ming style, 3¾in. long. (Christie's) $3,525

A very rare calcified jade figure of a seated man, the knees folded with both hands resting on them, Han Dynasty, 5.5cm. high, box. (Christie's) $79,640

A white jade group of three cranes on rockwork by a lotus pond, with minor pale brown inclusions, Qianlong, 15cm. high. (Christie's) $35,838

A dark celadon and russet jade small boulder mountain, well carved, with three monkeys in a grotto, 17th century, 15cm. high, fitted wood stand. (Christie's) $11,946

A Mughal pale spinach jade dish carved at the center with a stylized chrysanthemum flower-head, the Qing Dynasty, 21.6cm. diam. (Christie's) $4,977

A very pale celadon jade circular censer and domed cover, and a spinach jade lotus base elaborately carved and pierced with flowering bush peony, 18th century, 18cm. wide, box. (Christie's) $18,914

A very fine Imperial spinach jade cylindrical brush pot, Qianlong, on five short feet, 7½in. diam. (Christie's) $105,769

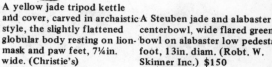

An Imperial white jade teapot and cover, with compressed globular body, mid Qing Dynasty, 18cm. wide. (Christie's) $59,730

A yellow jade tripod kettle and cover, carved in archaistic style, the slightly flattened globular body resting on lion-mask and paw feet, 7¼ in. wide. (Christie's) $5,358

A Steuben jade and alabaster centerbowl, wide flared green bowl on alabaster low pedestal foot, 13in. diam. (Robt. W. Skinner Inc.) $150

An apple-green streaked pale lavender jadeite flattened baluster vase and domed cover, late Qing dynasty, 6¾in. high. (Christie's) $6,346

A pair of pale green and apple jadeite carvings of parrots, each pierced and cut in the round, 7½in. high, on elaborately carved fixed wood bases. (Christie's) $59,230

A very fine pale celadon jade double cylinder vase and cover, 18th century, 20.1cm. high. (Christie's) $43,802

A fine celadon jade bowl, carved in crisp relief, with a roundel of leafy flowering lotus rising in a cluster, 18th century, 16.2cm. diam. (Christie's) $8,959

A white and mottled green jade carving of two pheasants with heads turned slightly to the side, 8½in. high.(Christie's) $1,974

A very fine Imperial green jadeite circular two handled tripod censer and low domed cover, incised Qianlong seal mark within a square, width across handles 6¾in. (Christie's) $592,307

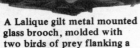

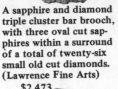

A Lalique gilt metal mounted glass brooch, molded with two birds of prey flanking a cabochon, 9.5cm. long. (Phillips) $1,760

A sapphire and diamond triple cluster bar brooch, with three oval cut sapphires within a surround of a total of twenty-six small old cut diamonds. (Lawrence Fine Arts) $2,473

A stylish Georg Jensen silver bracelet designed by Henning Koppel, formed by six heavily wrought amoebic like links, 21cm. long, 1957. (Phillips) $825

A pate de verre pendant, the mottled yellow and amber glass decorated in high relief with a red and green beetle. 4.6cm. diam. (Christie's) $1,028

An antique gold canetille work brooch, set with pear shaped foiled pink beryls, circa 1840. (Bonhams) $637

A Victorian pietra-dura and gold brooch, with a mosaic flower spray in colors. (Lawrence Fine Arts) $863

A diamond monogram pendant, the center with diamond chip EFS monogram. (Lawrence Fine Arts) $370

A diamond stylized flower spray brooch, sef through-out with various brilliant and baguette cut stones. (Lawrence Fine Arts) $6,660

A lapis, coral and gold brooch by Cartier in the form of a stylized scarab beetle, the head a cabochon coral. (Lawrence Fine Arts) $2,854

A very attractive diamond set, yellow colored gold bracelet, signed Cartier, circa 1950. (Bonhams) $7,257

A diamond, ruby and sapphire butterfly brooch, the diamond chip wings capped with rubies and sapphires. (Lawrence Fine Arts) $1,398

An Edwardian diamond and enamel panel brooch, of oblong shape with canted corners, one stone deficient. (Bonhams) $3,717

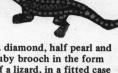

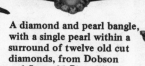

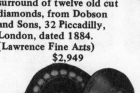

A diamond, half pearl and ruby brooch in the form of a lizard, in a fitted case from Elkington and Co. Ltd., 73 Cheapside, E.C. (Lawrence Fine Arts) $2,188

A diamond and pearl bangle, with a single pearl within a surround of twelve old cut diamonds, from Dobson and Sons, 32 Piccadilly, London, dated 1884. (Lawrence Fine Arts) $2,949

An antique diamond flower spray brooch in the form of leafage, ferns and a flowerhead, London. (Lawrence Fine Arts) $2,674

A pearl and diamond roundel brooch, the central pearl within a surround of nine small old cut diamonds. (Lawrence Fine Arts) $1,998

A Victorian turquoise and gold buckle brooch, in the form of a scroll with central buckle. (Lawrence Fine Arts) $1,069

An amethyst and diamond brooch, centered by a circular cut amethyst within a band of diamond chip. (Lawrence Fine Arts) $1,028

A Lalique brooch, the clear and satin finished glass molded with marguerites, on rose pink foil ground. (Christie's) $2,788

A late Victorian diamond star brooch, with a central cluster of a brilliant collet within a surround of eight similar smaller diamonds. (Lawrence Fine Arts) $3,291

A rare enamelled Lalique glass ring, of blue color with domed cabochon top, 2.5cm. wide. (Phillips) $2,992

An antique two color gold bracelet, composed of seven shaped square panels and a similar larger locket clasp. (Lawrence Fine Arts) $1,645

A white metal and plique a jour scarab brooch, the green gem scarab with wings enamelled in shades of green and pink, set with a ruby. (Christie's) $929

A Victorian cabochon garnet bangle, with three oval cabochon garnet collets within a corded wire surround. (Lawrence Fine Arts) $1,069

A fine lacquer kodansu decorated in silver, red, black and green togidashi and nashiji depicting various scenes from the story of the 'Tongue Cut Sparrow', 19th century, 11 x 10 x 8cm. (Christie's) $5,874

A Regency lacquered, black, gold and maroon table casket with shaped hinged top, 10in. wide. (Christie's) $1,851

A gold lacquer kogo of square shape with a domed lid, the gilt dusted ground with scattered circular mon, 3¼in. wide. (Lawrence Fine Arts) $597

A fine lacquer tray decorated in the center with a lobed panel with a group of figures including a monkey trainer, signed Somei (Muneaki), late 19th century, 30.5cm. wide. (Christie's) $6,853

A lacquerware tea tray, Japan, early 19th century, the oval tray inlaid with mother-of-pearl and oval reserve with gilt American spreadwing eagle, 31in. wide. (Robt. W. Skinner Inc.) $24,000

An Oriental lacquered tea caddy, China, 19th century, scalloped melon shaped body with a stem finial handle, 7¼in. high. (Robt. W. Skinner Inc.) $950

A large red papier-mache lacquer Easter egg, composed of two halves, one depicting the Resurrection, the other the full length figure of Saint Peter, Russian, 19th century, 16cm. high. (Christie's) $4,275

A lacquered tray, China, late 19th century, the rectangular form decorated with figures within a walled garden, 19½ x 27in. (Robt. W. Skinner Inc.) $2,500

A rare Ming red lacquer mallet shaped vase deeply carved with lush flowering peony, probably early 15th century, 15.8cm. high. (Christie's) $14,932

A Handel brass table lamp, with silvered reflective interior on brass finished three socket standard, 26in. high. (Robt. W. Skinner Inc.) $600

A Steuben Cintra sculptured lamp, of clear frosted glass with pink, blue, white and occasional yellow granules, 21in. high. (Robt. W. Skinner Inc.) $800

A Pairpoint boudoir lamp, with panels of floral sprays mounted on silvered metal standard, 15in. high. (Robt. W. Skinner Inc.) $550

An ormolu and cut glass lantern with foliate corona and shaped faceted body, 15½in. high. (Christie's) $2,057

A Durand art glass lamp, with domed shade and baluster base, fitted with two socket lighting, 15in. high. (Robt. W. Skinner Inc.) $1,100

A French pewter hour lamp, with glass reservoir and passage of time scale indicator, 18th century, 13½in. high.(Christie's) $182

A Quezal candle lamp, bronzed metal Art Nouveau standard with bell form gold iridescent glass shade signed on rim, 19¼in. high. (Robt. W. Skinner Inc.) $350

A rare George I walnut and gilt embellished lantern with mirrored back and glazed hinged door, 2ft.4in. x 1ft. (Phillips) $13,500

A Quezal desk lamp, with curved shaft adorned by a full bodied dragonfly, signed on rim, 17½in. high. (Robt. W. Skinner Inc.) $1,500

LAMPS

A William IV colza oil lamp, supported by the Three Graces, on a scrolling foliate base. 31½in. high. (Christie's) $3,496

A Galle cameo and bronze mounted 'Veilleuse', the globular frosted glass shade with bronze dragonfly finial, resting within a mount of three further dragonflies, 18cm. high. (Phillips) $6,192

A Regency ebonized plaster oil lamp modelled as a scantily draped neo-Classical female, 42½in. high. (Christie's) $2,057

'Rudolph', a robot light fitting designed by Frank Clewett, the head formed by spherical glass shade, the adjustable arms with light bulbs forming the hands, 149cm. high. (Christie's) $1,580

A Daum Art Deco glass table lamp with geometric panels enclosing stylized foliage and berries, supported on three chromed arms, 53.5cm. high. (Phillips) $10,664

A de Vez cameo and acid etched landscape night light, the yellow and pink glass overlaid in purple with tropical palms and islands at sunset, 17.2cm. high. (Christie's) $748

A glass and metal floor lamp by Gae Aulenti, the cylindrical wirework cage with blown glass forming column and bulbous shade, 60cm. high. (Christie's) $650

A pair of Regency ormolu colza oil lamps, each with a vase shaped fluted reservoir, fitted for electricity, 27¾in. high. (Christie's) $7,405

One of a set of four Sabino wall lights, with molded decoration, 38cm. high. (Christie's) Four $2,230

LAMPS

A 1930's Modernist chromium plated table lamp, the domed metal stepped shade with white painted reflector, 42cm. high. (Christie's) $1,580

'Batwomen', a large bronze and ivory table lamp by Roland Paris, the body modelled with three female figures gold patinated in bat-winged costume and ruffs, 94cm. high. (Christie's) $14,960

A green glazed red pottery Phoenix lamp, with cup shaped mouth, Han Dynasty, 33cm. high. (Christie's) $6,371

A Daum acid etched, carved and enamelled landscape table lamp, of acid textured and cased polychrome glass, enamelled with a Dutch village in a snowy wooded landscape, 39cm. high. (Christie's) $24,310

One of a pair of bronze colza oil lamps, each with a covered cornucopia with a boar's head spout, 19th century, 10½in. high. (Lawrence Fine Arts)
Two $4,365

A bronze lamp base with a Loetz shade cast from a model by M. Csadek, the base modelled as two lions seated by a tree trunk, the hemispherical shade with iridescent mother-of-pearl finish, 46cm.high. (Christie's) $2,431

A bronzed spelter lamp in the form of a warrior youth wearing a skin loincloth, 68in. high overall. (Bearne's)$1,760

An important and rare Tiffany Studios leaded glass table lamp, the shallow domed shade edged with the bodies of bats, 48cm. high. (Phillips)
$105,600

A brass table lamp with a Loetz glass shade, the lightly iridescent green glass shade applied with trailed amethyst bands, 38cm. high. (Christie's) $743

495

A Murano panelled glass oil lamp, with caramel and green slag glass panels, 1905, 19in. high. (Robt. W. Skinner Inc.) $800

A Steuben table lamp, classic form of lustrous blue Aurene mounted in Art Deco fittings, vase 11in. high. (Robt. W. Skinner Inc.) $700

A mica and hammered copper table lamp, possibly Benedict Studios, New York, early 20th century, 19in. diam. (Robt. W. Skinner Inc.) $2,500

A Moe Bridges parrot lamp, with reverse handpainted scene of two exotic birds centered in a summer landscape, 23in. high. (Robt. W. Skinner Inc.) $4,600

A Tiffany bronze table lamp with lotus shade, of Oriental umbrella form with brilliant blue rectangular glass segments, 26in. high. (Robt. W. Skinner Inc.) $32,000

A Pairpoint scenic table lamp, handpainted with four nautical scenes of tall ships separated by seashell panels, 23in. high. (Robt. W. Skinner Inc.) $2,600

A Tiffany bronze lamp with spider and web shade, of mottled muted gray-green colored rectangular panels divided into six segments, 19in. high. (Robt. W. Skinner Inc.) $18,000

A leaded slag glass and oak table lamp, early 20th century, the square hipped shade with colored glass panels, 22in. high. (Robt. W. Skinner Inc.) $1,300

An art glass table lamp, open Tam o' Shanter shade of green iridescent pulled and swirled damascene design cased to opal-white glass, 19½in. high. (Robt. W. Skinner Inc.) $1,700

A mica and hammered copper table lamp, possibly Benedict Studios, New York, early 20th century, unsigned, 16in. high. (Robt. W. Skinner Inc.) $1,200

A Handel scenic table lamp, handpainted on the interior with a scenic landscape of summer birches and poplar trees, 23in. high. (Robt. W. Skinner Inc.) $2,600

A Handel leaded glass lamp shade with Hampshire Pottery base, early 20th century, signed, 1851, 21in. high. (Robt. W. Skinner Inc.) $3,750

A Tiffany Studios table lamp, on four-pronged spider ring attached to matching insert, 17in. high. (Robt. W. Skinner Inc.) $2,000

An art glass table lamp, with gilt metal fittings supporting two glass shades of opal and gold, 28in. high. (Robt. W. Skinner Inc.) $500

A Handel parrot lamp, handpainted with three brilliantly colored parrots, against a flower strewn background, 24in. high. (Robt. W. Skinner Inc.) $22,000

A Tiffany leaded glass lamp shade on Grueby pottery base, early 20th century, with dome shaped shade in acorn pattern, artist initialled A. L. for Annie Lingley, 17¾in. high. (Robt. W. Skinner Inc.) $20,000

A desk lamp with Steuben Aurene shade, bronzed metal standard, mirror lustre at top, 13½in. high. (Robt. W. Skinner Inc.) $550

A Fulper pottery and leaded glass table lamp, New Jersey, signed Vasekraft, stamped "Patents pending in United States and Canada, England, France and Germany", 20½in. high. (Robt. W. Skinner Inc.) $11,000

MARBLE

An early 20th century Welsh marble portrait bust of John Cory, by Sir William Goscombe John, R.A. (1860-1952), dated 1906, 72cm. high. (Christie's)
$929

A fine 19th century English marble figure of Eve sitting on an oval rocky base, by John Warrington Wood, signed, 107cm. high. (Christie's)
$37,224

An early 20th century English marble bas relief of a girl, by Richard Garbe, holding a knot of drapery on her left shoulder, 60cm. high. (Christie's)
$929

An Indian carved marble Buddha seated in virasana, a smaller figure before him, 19½in. high. (Bearne's)
$528

A George II Carrara marble fireplace, the tablet centered frieze with sheep, ram and lambs, 64½in. wide. (Christie's)
$26,488

One of a pair of ormolu mounted and pink mottled marble urns, with winged caryatids holding cornucopiae, 12¼in. high. (Christie's)
Two $15,510

A 19th century English or Italian marble statue of a nymph dipping her toe into a stream, 104cm. high. (Christie's)
$8,272

A pair of ormolu mounted red and white marble cassolettes with reversible domed tops, 9½in. high. (Christie's)
$723

A 19th century English marble bust of a Grecian lady, by R.Physick, her hair with diadem falling over her left shoulder, 1866, 63.5cm. high. (Christie's)
$1,673

Early 19th century marble bust of the First Earl of Stradbroke by Joseph Nollekens, signed and dated 'Nollekens 1811', 27½in. high. (Prudential) $27,360

One of a pair of ormolu mounted green marble urns of baluster form, the sides with goats' masks, 13½in. high. (Christie's) Two $2,044

A 19th century Italian marble bust of a young veiled woman, looking down to dexter, by E. Ferrarini, 56cm. high. (Christie's) $650

A French 19th century marble group of cupids disputing over a heart, after an 18th century original, 64cm. high. (Christie's) $2,788

A pair of George III ormolu and white marble tripod cassolettes, the supports headed by Mercury masks, 9¾in. high. (Christie's) $7,568

A rare early 19th century English marble bust of Lady Antonina Le Despenser, by John Bacon, shown in Classical guise, with her hair in a band and chignon behind, 71cm. high. (Christie's) $25,096

A 19th century Irish marble bust of Lady O'Hagan, by Joseph Watkins, signed on the rim, Dublin 1869, 52cm. high. (Christie's) $413

A fine 19th century British marble statue by John Gibson R.A., showing a Classical shepherd boy leaning asleep on a tree stump, 112 x 104 x 55cm. (Christie's) $89,232

A 19th century French marble bust of Louise Brogniart, after Houdon, 46cm. high. (Christie's) $1,819

A Roman marble head of a young satyr with uptilted narrowed eyes, full lips and a deeply incised mass of locks, 17cm. high. (Phillips) $5,504

A marble stonecutter's sample, America, 19th century, oblong stone carved with male profile, a hand, reclining lamb, roses, bird, engine and tender, 21in. long. (Robt. W. Skinner Inc.) $5,700

A George III ormolu mounted white marble urn by Matthew Boulton, mounted with Classical figures in relief, 16in. high. (Christie's) $35,948

A Roman marble torso of a woman wearing a chiton and himation draped around her, 1st-2nd century A.D., 74cm. high. (Phillips) $13,760

A massive pair of 19th century marble urns of campana form, on circular socles and stepped square bases, 69in. high. (Bearne's) $24,640

A marble bust of an English nobleman, portrayed in Classical style in the manner of Matthew Noble, 28¾in. high. (Bearne's) $1,183

One of a pair of ormolu and verde antico marble urns, with twin swan handles and square plinths, one restored, 12½in. high. (Christie's) Two $6,512

A white marble bust of Prince Alexander Borisovich Kurakin, possibly by F. I. Chubin, 29in. high. (Christie's) $13,942

A white marble sculpture of a little girl, by J. A. Cipriani, Italian, 19th century, 21in. high. (Du Mouchelles) $1,000

A painted miniature pine blanket chest, attributed to Joseph Long Lehn, Pennsylvania, circa 1890, decorated with floral decals and landscapes, 8½in. wide. (Christie's) $935

Bird's-eye maple cannon ball doll's bed, America, circa 1830, the turned base on ball posts, 8¾in. high. (Robt. W. Skinner Inc.) $400

A William and Mary miniature walnut veneered and marquetry chest, 16in. wide. (Henry Spencer) $1,750

A brocade covered display case in the form of a miniature sedan chair, 16in. high. (Christie's) $423

A fine early 19th century miniature dressing chest, 14in. wide, and a similar chest of drawers. (Henry Spencer) $1,365

A miniature Dutch gilt metal mounted mahogany armoire, the top with a pierced gallery, late 18th century, 18½in. wide. (Christie's) $5,291

A Dutch marquetry miniature bureau with hinged slope enclosing drawers and pigeon holes, 16in. wide. (Christie's) $4,884

A 19th century Continental miniature bone piano, fitted with shelves above the keyboard, carved with the name Badenweler, 6½in. high. (Christie's) $519

A Danish parcel gilt and stained elm miniature commode with molded waved top, 14in. wide. (Christie's) $4,681

A Regency mahogany toilet mirror with rectangular plate and partridgewood cresting inlaid with a fan oval, 20½in. wide. (Christie's) $3,027

A George III mahogany toilet mirror, the shield-shaped plate surmounted by an ivory vase finial, 19in. wide. (Christie's) $1,542

A fine Federal inlaid maple and mahogany dressing mirror, Philadelphia, 1800-1810, on ogee bracket feet, 22½in. wide. (Christie's) $1,320

A George III mahogany fret carved mirror with contemporary rectangular plate, and scroll surround, 2ft.7½in. x 1ft.1½in. (Phillips) $1,620

A small giltwood mirror with shaped bevelled plate, 19th century, 12 x 14¼in. (Christie's) $413

A George II carved giltwood and gesso mirror in the William Kent taste, with later projecting feather and foliate cartouche cresting, 5ft.2in. x 3ft. (Phillips) $9,900

A Victorian overmantel mirror with scrolling pediment centered by a scallop motif, 55 x 64in. high. (Anderson & Garland) $726

A giltwood mirror with bevelled rectangular plate, the frame crisply carved with ribbon-tied berried foliage, late 19th century, 59 x 49½in. (Christie's) $1,240

A George III giltwood mirror with rectangular plate, in a cavetto frame with beading, 66¾ x 43¼in. (Christie's) $7,199

MIRRORS

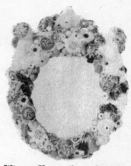

A Regency giltwood convex mirror with fluted ebonized slip, the molded frame with ring turned strapwork clasps, 30in. diam. (Christie's) $822

An unusual Colonial ivory and silvered metal hardwood toilet mirror, on claw feet, early 19th century, 29in. wide. (Christie's) $4,114

A Wiener Keramik oval mirror, designed by Michael Powolny, formed as a multi-colored floral garland surmounted at the top with a yellow sparrow, 29.5cm. long. (Phillips) $481

A Regency brass inlaid rosewood looking glass in the manner of George Bullock, 42½in. high by 29½in. wide, originally part of a cabinet. (Bearne's) $1,681

An Arts and Crafts pewter and mother-of-pearl wall mirror, decorated with rectangular panels inlaid in mother-of-pearl, 60.3 x 87cm. (Phillips) $1,496

A Biedermeier mahogany dressing mirror, the rectangular glass plate on column supports, 18in. wide. (Bearne's) $616

A Regency mahogany cheval mirror with oval plate, the spandrels carved with foliage, 68in. high. (Christie's) $2,468

A pair of William and Mary parcel gilt mirrors, each with a canted rectangular divided bevelled plate, 34¾in. x 26in. (Christie's) $26,488

A Classical giltwood mirror, probably Boston, 1815-1830, with broken cornice hung with acorn pendants, 68in. high. (Christie's) $3,300

A Regency giltwood convex mirror, surmounted by griffin perched on rockwork. (Phillips) $2,150

An Art Nouveau electroplated mirror and stand, the cartouche form decorated with two maidens with trumpets amid scrolling foliage, 42.8cm. long. (Christie's) $523

A George I giltwood mirror, the shaped cresting centered by a mask, 45 x 24in. (Christie's) $8,228

A Venetian gilt brass framed looking glass, within an engraved mirror glass border, 52in. high. (Bearne's) $3,872

A 17th century carved walnut wall mirror surmounted by armorial cartouche cresting with a bishop's mitre, 3ft.11in. x 3ft.1½in. (Phillips) $3,600

A Chippendale mirror, late 18th century, the shaped and pierced crest centering gilded foliate device over molded frame, 19½in. wide. (Robt. W. Skinner Inc.) $1,800

A carved gilt frame wall mirror, with rococo style foliate scrolls, 19th century, 53in. high. (Lawrence Fine Arts) $3,014

A Carlo Bugatti ebonized and vellum covered mirror, the rectangular plate with circular top, 177.5cm. high; 90cm. wide. (Christie's) $2,057

A giltwood and composition mirror with oval plate, the apron with three scrolling branches 57½in. x 40in. (Christie's) $1,022

MIRRORS

A William IV gilt frame convex mirror, the eagle surmount perched on rocky base over molded frame, 145 x 100cm. (Phillips) $3,927

An Italian rococo giltwood mirror, 18th century, the rectangular mirror plate with pierced leaf carved crest, 20in. wide. (Robt. W. Skinner Inc.) $1,900

A Regency giltwood convex mirror with circular plate in an ebonized slip and cavetto frame, 32½ x 27in. (Christie's) $1,851

A giltwood mirror of George III style with shaped rectangular plate, 59 x 36¼in. (Christie's) $2,468

A mid 19th century gilt frame overmantel mirror, with boldly scrolling surmount flanked by turned columns, 180 x 150cm. (Phillips) $1,122

One of a pair of George III giltwood mirrors, each with an oval plate in a carved frame, 42 x 27in. (Christie's)   Two $30,272

A George III oval giltwood mirror with later plate, the pierced frame carved with rockwork and flowerheads, 30½ x 21½in. (Christie's) $3,291

A Bennington flint enamel frame with mirror, Bennington, Vermont, 1849-1858, of rectangular form with shaped edge, 11½in. high. (Robt. W. Skinner Inc.) $850

A Louis XVI cream and pink painted mirror, the panelled surround with basket-of-flower cresting and ribbon-tied oval cartouche, 51½ x 36in. (Christie's) $3,052

An Egyptian New Kingdom black granite part male figure, the head with bag wig, 9 in. high. (David Lay) $9,350

An unusual 'Egyptianesque' ashtray, fashioned in Swiss lapis embellished with plique a jour and hardstone scarabs, 10.5cm. wide. (Phillips) $1,056

A Victorian silk floral bouquet under a glass dome. (Greenslades) $385

A fine Victorian shell floral bouquet under a glass dome. (Greenslades) $735

An early Victorian papier-mache tray, painted with a bird of paradise perching on the rim of a goblet, 31¾in. long. (Bearne's) $800

A pale soapstone carving of a Luohan seated with one hand resting on the right knee, signed *Xu Xuan*, 18th century, 8.7cm. high. (Christie's) $14,932

A late 18th or early 19th century Spanish-Mexican wax equestrian model of King Carlos IV of Spain, by Manuel Tolsa, 15.3cm. high. (Christie's) $836

Fuessli (R.H.), Les Costumes Suisses les plus origineaux et les plus interessants, hand colored costume plates, circa 1830. (Phillips) $4,671

A 19th century pietra dura fold-out photograph frame, the pierced scrolling surmount over floral inlaid doors, 51cm. high. (Phillips) $1,421

MISCELLANEOUS

An Egyptian 23rd Dynasty Canopic jar lid in buff pottery, molded as a male head. (David Lay) $1,683

A French scarlet and parcel gilt leather portefeuilles, lacking inkwells, with silver plate hinges and lock, 18th century, 17in. wide. (Christie's) $651

A silkwork floral arrangement, in painted vase, on circular base, with glass dome, 52cm. (Phillips) $355

A stone model of a phallus, in an Australian cedar wood box, engraved with the inscription 'Resting in Piece, John Thomas who died stiff in the exececution of his duty, Dais Natalis 31247 (sic)', 7¼in. long overall. (Christie's) $616

An Egyptian carved stele engraved with hieroglyphic inscription, of the Ramses II period, XVIII Dynasty, 60cm. x 66cm. (Phillips) $4,816

A Victorian taxidermic specimen, of exotic colored birds and insects, on tree, all on oval stained wood base, with glass dome, 22½in. high. (Hobbs & Chambers) $244

A moss agate tazza with everted lip and deep bowl on domed base, 7¼in. high. (Christie's) $1,439

A 19th century Barbadian shell souvenir, the mahogany case hingeing open to show a sailing boat, 14¼in. closed. (David Lay) $1,028

An unusual Perry & Son ewer designed by Dr. Christopher Dresser of conical shape with exaggerated tapering spout, 32cm. high. (Phillips) $1,892

A hat of white elaborately knotted macrame, trimmed with a ball fringe, labelled Balenciaga, early 1950's. (Christie's) $243

Sir Ernest Henry Shackleton: The Heart of the Antarctic, 3 vols including The British Antarctic Expeditions Winter Quarters 1907-1909, signed by all members of the Shore Party, 1909. (Phillips) $2,740

A carved root cane, possibly the Balley Carver, Mount Pleasant, Berks County, Pennsylvania, carved as a dog's head, 35¼in. long. (Christie's) $352

A shaded enamel parcel gilt icon of Saints Basil The Great and Anisia, Moscow, 1908-1917, maker's initials Cyrillic, 12½ x 10½in. (Christie's) $5,019

John Field (1772-1848) - James Lander, in profile to the right, in coat, waistcoat and tied cravat, bronzed silhouette painted on card, oval, 73mm. high. (Christie's) $299

Charles Dickens: Early autograph letter signed, about autograph collecting, to Miss Catherine Hutton of Bennett's Hill, near Birmingham, 29 July 1839. (Phillips) $1,028

An interesting engraved seashell, bearing a representation of the S.S. Great Eastern. (Wallis & Wallis) $273

A painted toleware coffee pot, attributed to Louis Zeitz, Pennsylvania, early 19th century, the stepped dome lid with brass finial, 12in. high. (Christie's) $2,090

A horsehair wig with a queue and side curls, with a black grosgrain silk wig bag trimmed with a black silk rosette, circa 1770. (Christie's)$1,116

A carved maple cane, possibly by John Simmons, Virginville, Berks Co., Pennsylvania, 19th century, carved as a steer's head, 36in. long. (Christie's) $264

A silver mounted brick match holder, by Faberge, workmaster Julius Rappaport, St. Petersburg, circa 1880, 12.5cm. long. (Christie's) $11,154

A carved and painted cane, possibly the Balley Carver, Mount Pleasant, Berks County, Pennsylvania, carved as two faces, 38in. long. (Christie's) $660

Aleister Crowley: Autograph letter signed to the actor Ernest Thesiger, written on the back of a printed prospectus for Foyle's twenty-third literary luncheon, 15 September 1932. (Phillips) $158

Two gentlemen's mannequins, 50in. and 54in. high, and a lady's bust mannequin on a stand, 30in. high, circa 1905. (Christie's) $935

An ormolu and malachite candlestick, modelled as a female caryatid, on crenellated circular base, late 19th century, 10¼in. high. (Christie's) $446

A very rare 19th century brass and ebony fire engine foreman's tipstaff of The Protector Fire Insurance Company, 1825-1835, 18cm. long, circa 1830. (Phillips) $4,070

A Suprematist porcelain inkwell, of Planit design, by the Lomonosov Porcelain Factory, circa 1926, 5½ x 5½in. (Christie's) $17,660

An umbrella of blue silk, with white border, curving between the wooden spokes tipped with brass, marked Hobday, Francis and Co., circa 1820. (Christie's) $102

A fully planked and rigged model of the 'Wasa' of circa 1628, built by J. M. R. Brown, Darwen, 31 x 40in. (Christie's) $2,069

A finely detailed and well presented 3/32in.:1ft. scale fully rigged model of the clipper ship 'Timaru', of circa 1874, built to drawings of H. A. Underhill by E. V. Fry, Cowes, 16 x 27½in. (Christie's) $6,019

A well detailed and presented waterline display model of the Thames Sprit's'l sailing barge 'Emma' of London, No. 221, built by W. H. Crook, York, 13½ x 16in. (Christie's) $837

A finely detailed and well presented fully planked and framed, fully rigged ¼in.:1ft. scale model of the frigate H.M.S. 'Endymion', of circa 1792, built by M. Salville-Smithin, Bristol, 43 x 67in. (Christie's) $4,138

A fully planked and rigged model of the clipper 'Cutty Sark', of circa 1869, built by J. M. R. Brown, Darwen, complete with masts, spars, standing and running rigging and full suit of stitched linen sails, 25½ x 44in. (Christie's) $2,069

A well detailed fibreglass, wood and metal ¼in.:1ft. scale model of the armed trawler H.M.S. 'Sir Agravaine' Pennant No. T230, built by N. Howard-Pritchard, Blackpool, 18½ x 35in. (Christie's) $1,692

A wood and metal unrigged model of the
Royal Naval 90-gun ship of the line H.M.S.
'Albion', built by A. Brown, St Austell,
18 x 44in. (Christie's) $1,128

A fine and detailed planked and framed, fully
rigged model of the screw/sail man of war
H.M.S. 'Rattler', complete with masts, yards,
standing and running rigging with scale
blocks and deck details, 35 x 60in. (Christie's)
$4,890

A well detailed and presented 3/8th in.:1ft.
scale model of a Royal Naval gaff-rigged
schooner of circa 1760, built by I. H. Wilkie,
Beardisely, 29 x 36in. (Christie's)$752

A well detailed 3.32 scale wooden model of
the three masted barquentine 'William
Ashburner', built in Barrow, 1876, and modelled by J. Kearon, Southport, 10 x 15in.
(Christie's) $1,128

A well detailed and presented fully planked
and rigged model of the bomb ketch H.M.S.
'Firedrake', of circa 1741, built by P. N.
Smith, London, 20½ x 34in. (Christie's)
$3,385

A well detailed free rigged and planked
model of H.M.S. 'Victory', built by J. M. R.
Brown, Darwen, complete with masts, yards
with stun's'l booms, standing and running
rigging and deck details, 27 x 40in.
(Christie's) $2,445

Early Hornby gauge 0 rolling stock, including a 'Carr's Biscuits' van and an LNER Gunpowder van, circa 1924. (Christie's) $494

A well detailed and finished model of an unusual L.M.S. (ex L.N.E.R.) twin bogie 3rd driving/trailer coach of circa 1901, 3½ x 15in. (Christie's) $407

A live steam spirit fired model of the L.N.E.R. Class A4 4-6-2 locomotive and tender No. 4468 'Mallard', by Aster for Fulgurex, 5 x 28in. (Christie's) $6,105

A Bing clockwork model of the L.S.W.R. 0-4-4 'M7' tank locomotive No. 109, circa 1909. (Christie's) $1,831

An early and rare Marklin M.R. 1st class bogie coach, with opening roof and side doors, circa 1904. (Christie's) $1,119

A Bassett-Lowke gauge 0 clockwork BR Goods Set, including a 4-4-0 'Compound' locomotive and tender No. 62453 'Prince Charles', in original display box, with instructions, circa 1960. (Christie's) $535

A gauge '0' three rail electric model of the B.R. Class 7P 4-6-2 locomotive and tender No. 70004 'William Shakespeare', by Bassett-Lowke, 3¾ x 19½in. (Christie's) $4,070

An early Marklin station 'Harrogate', the painted tinplate building with opening doors and painted adverts, circa 1902, 40in. wide. (Christie's) $3,052

The L.M.S. Class 5XP 4-6-0 locomotive and tender No. 5500 'Patriot' built by P. Hammond and painted by L. Richards, 3¾ x 17½in. (Christie's) $2,238

A rare Marklin electric model of the G.W.R. 4-6-2 'Pacific' locomotive and bogie tender, circa 1909. (Christie's) $7,122

A Hornby (3-rail) electric model of the LMS 4-6-2 locomotive and tender No. 6201 "Princess Elizabeth", in original paintwork, circa 1937. (Christie's) $1,851

5in. gauge live steam 0-6-0 tank locomotive in British Rail black livery No. 1505. (Hobbs & Chambers) $1,487

A Hornby clockwork L.M.S. 'No. 1 Tank Good Set', comprising an 0-4-0 tank locomotive, a 'Shell Motor Spirit', an open wagon, a brake van and a circle of track, in original box, circa 1926. (Christie's) $386

Wells clockwork 'Mickey Mouse Circus Train', comprising an 0-4 0 A4 locomotive No. 2509 'Silver Link', a tender with Mickey Mouse and a lithographed 'Circus Dining Car', circa 1948, (Christie's) $1,628

A well detailed two-rail electric model of the G.W.R. 48XX Class 0 4-2 side tank locomotive No. 4837 and auto coach No. 187 built by B. Miller, 3¼ x 25¾in. (Christie's) $10,175

A rare Marklin Jubilee Set No. AR12930/35/3, comprising a 'Planet' locomotive and tender, a stage type coach and an open carriage, all in original paintwork, circa 1935. (Christie's) $7,122

A rare Marklin electric model of the Paris-Orleans Railway E.1. electric locomotive, with glass windows, circa 1919. (Christie's) $1,221

A (3-rail) electric 'Coronation Scot' train set, comprising the L.M.S. 4-6-2 class HP streamlined 'Pacific' locomotive and tender, by Trix Twin Railways, circa 1937. (Christie's) $2,238

A rare gauge 0 (3-rail) electric model of the SBB CFF 'Re 4/4' No. 427 diesel electric locomotive, by H. and A. Gahler, Switzerland, circa 1947. (Christie's) $1,131

A Leeds Model Company clockwork model of the S.R. 0-6-0 goods locomotive and tender, in original box, circa 1933. (Christie's) $651

One of two Bing lithographed bogie coaches No. 62/190/0 G.W.R. passenger coach No. 3295, with tables and chairs, circa 1924, in original box. (Christie's) Two $407

The L.M.S. 'Jinty' 0-6-0 side tank locomotive No. 7469 built by Duchess Models and painted in L.M.S. black livery by L. Richards, 3½ x 8½in. (Christie's) $1,119

The L.M.S. Streamlined Pacific 4-6-2 locomotive and tender No. 6220 'Coronation' built by Duchess Models, 3¾ x 20¾in. (Christie's) $2,035

An Exhibition Standard two-rail electric
model of the L.N.W.R. Webb 0-6-2 coal
tank locomotive No. 588 built by J. S.
Beeson, Ringwood, 3½ x 9in. (Christie's)
$4,477

A rake of three Hornby S.R. No. 2 passenger coaches, in original boxes, circa 1936
(boxes lids torn, one lid missing).(Christie's)
$1,729

A rare early Hornby gauge 0 clockwork
model of the LNWR 0-4-0 No. 00 locomotive and tender No. 2663 'George the Fifth',
circa 1924. (Christie's) $185

'Central-Bahnhof', an early Marklin railway
station, with central arch and platform
canopy, ticket office and waiting room,
circa 1901. (Christie's) $5,291

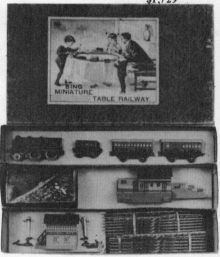

A Bing 'Miniature Table Railway', a lithographed tinplate railway set, comprising a
L.M.S. 2-4-0 locomotive and tender, circa
1925. (Christie's) $712

'Hamburg Flyer' a Marklin (3-rail) electric
model of the two-car diesel unit Ref. No.
T.W.12970, with operating front and rear
lights, circa 1937. (Christie's) $1,119

A Bassett-Lowke remodelled gauge 0 (3-rail)
electric model of the LNER 4-6-2 'Pacific'
class locomotive and tender No. 4472
'Flying Scotsman', circa 1937. (Christie's)
$494

MODELS

A well engineered display model of a twin overhead camshaft, fuel injected V-8 car engine, finished in red, black and polished brightwork, 4¼ x 5½in. (Christie's) $577

3in. scale model of Aveling & Porter steam road roller, by Bishop-Ellis, Birmingham, with boiler test certificate, 4ft.6in. long. (Peter Wilson) $7,350

Water mill, one of three Marklin working models, in original paintwork, German, circa 1936. (Christie's) Three $288

3in. scale model of a Wallis & Stevens 'Simplicity' road roller, 35½in. long. (Peter Wilson) $2,187

A rare late nineteenth live steam, spirit fired, stationary steam set, with brass pot boiler and fretwork firebox, 8½in. high, possibly American. (Christie's) $288

A Schoenner live steam spirit fired tinplate overtype engine, with brass boiler and original fittings, 17½ x 15¾in., circa 1910. (Christie's) $1,732

A German spirit fired model of a horizontal steam engine, bearing the trademark M.G. & Cie, Wurtemberg, size of base 18½in x 20½in. (Lawrence Fine Arts) $1,991

A Bing live steam spirit fired portable engine, with japanned pot boiler, chain drive to rear wheel and turning lock, circa 1928, 10 x 8½in.(Christie's) $866

A Marklin live steam, spirit fired horizontal stationary steam engine, with brass boiler and chimney, 13¼ x 11 x 16½in., German, circa 1920. (Christie's) $2,310

Cast iron money bank, 'The lion and two monkeys', 23cm. high. (Phillips) $219

A 20th century English cast iron 'Dinah' mechanical bank, by John Harper & Co. Ltd., 6½in. high. (Phillips) $220

"I Always Did 'Spise a Mule", a cast iron mechanical bank of a negro jockey riding a mule, probably by J. Harper and Co., circa 1910, 10½in. long. (Christie's) $576

Owl cast iron mechanical bank, by J. & E. Stevens Co., pat. 1880, 7.5/8in. high. (Robt. W. Skinner Inc.) $265

A William Tell cast iron money bank, 1896, the figure firing coins placed on his crossbow into a slot above a boy's head, 10½in. (Lawrence Fine Arts) $398

A painted cast iron mechanical money box in the form of a seated man, 'Pat d. Dec 23 1873 and Tammany Bank', 14.5cm. (Osmond Tricks) $271

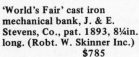

'World's Fair' cast iron mechanical bank, J. & E. Stevens, Co., pat. 1893, 8¼in. long. (Robt. W. Skinner Inc.) $785

Late 19th century American 'Uncle Sam' mechanical bank, by Shepard Hardware Co., 11½in. high. (Robt. W. Skinner Inc.) $435

American cast iron money bank, 'Hall's Lilliput Bank'. (Phillips) $473

An enamelled gold singing bird box, probably Les Freres Rochat, Geneva, early 19th century, the base, sides and top with blue enamel panels, 9.2cm. long. (Christie's) $38,500

A Gramophone & Typewriter Limited Senior Monarch gramophone, in oak case with carved moldings, 12-inch rocking turntable, 23in. diam., circa 1907. (Christie's)
$796

A Swiss gilt metal singing bird box, of oval form, the stepped lid with oval enamel aperture depicting an alpine scene, 11.5cm. wide. (Phillips)
$3,740

An upright coin-in-slot 19½-inch Polyphon disc musical box in typical walnut case with glazed door, 38in. high. (Christie's) $6,371

A New Style No. 3 gramophone by the Gramophone & Typewriter Ltd., with plated zinc horn, 14in. long, with three Nicole 7 inch records. (Christie's) $1,592

A 24½-inch Lochmanns 'Original' coin-operated disc musical box with twelve bar glockenspiel, and disc-bin stand with hinged door and sixteen discs, 90in. high. (Christie's) $15,928

A Bergman cold painted bronze musical box, inscribed 'Nam Greb', modelled as an amorous young beau kneeling beside his willing consort, 13½in. (Lawrence Fine Arts)
$3,782

An Edison class M electric phonograph, in oak case with accessories drawer and North American Phonograph Co. patent plate. (Christie's)
$1,891

A late 19th century walnut and kingwood banded cased lever wound musical box, a 13in. barrel playing twelve airs, 60cm. (Phillips) $1,402

A Columbia Regal (Sterling, Type B1) disc graphophone in panelled oak case with engaged corner columns, circa 1908. (Christie's) $1,891

A Tyrela oval cabinet gramophone in mahogany case with replacement tone arm, Thorens soundbox and internal horn, 22in. wide. (Christie's) $338

An EMG Mark X gramophone with spring motor, EMG four spring soundbox on gooseneck (early type), 33½in. diam. (Christie's) $2,588

A Deccalian bijou cabinet gramophone in mahogany case of eighteenth century design, with accessories drawer, fretwork side rails and open shelf below, 34in. high, circa 1922. (Christie's) $995

An Edison Concert (Opera) phonograph, No. 4298, with Diamond A reproducer and traversing mandrel in oak case. (Christie's) $796

A gramophone in the form of a miniature grand piano with Thorens soundbox, in mahogany case on paired tapered legs, 54in. long. (Christie's) $1,095

A late 19th century rosewood case musical box, 33cm. barrel and tune change lever, length 54cm. (Phillips) $841

An HMV mahogany Intermediate Monarch horn gramophone, with single spring motor, 18in. diam., circa 1911. (Christie's) $1,294

A musical box playing ten airs accompanied by eighteen key organ, with double spring motor, tune indicator, and inlaid front and lid, 26in. wide. (Christie's) $2,588

MUSICAL BOXES

An eight-air forte-piano key-wind musical box by Nicole Freres, with two-per-turn cylinder, endflap and inlaid lid, 17in. wide. (Christie's) $2,389

A New Melba gramophone by the Gramophone & Typewriter Limited, with triple spring worm drive motor, 1907-8. (Christie's) $2,190

A Gramophone & Typewriter Limited double spring Monarch gramophone in oak case, 10in. turntable, G & T Exhibition soundbox. (Christie's) $836

A 13½-inch Symphonion disc box with twin combs, monochrome print in lid and rectangular walnut case. (Christie's) $1,891

An upright coin-in-slot 19½in. Polyphon disc musical box in typical glazed walnut case with replacement pediment, coin drawer and disc-bin, 82in. high, with six discs. (Christie's) $5,574

A Swiss bells-in-sight organette musical box playing eight airs with 16in. cylinder, six bells and three-piece comb, 32in. long. (Bearne's) $4,375

A musical box playing eight airs accompanied by fourteen-key organ, with double spring motor, 25in. wide. (Christie's) $1,791

A Gramophone & Typewriter New Style No. 3 gramophone with oak case, 7in. turntable and brass horn. (Christie's) $1,592

A mahogany single spring Monarch gramophone (Doric) by the Gramophone Company Limited, the Morning Glory horn with original maroon paintwork, 1909. (Christie's) $756

A lever wind musical box by Nicole Freres, playing twelve operatic airs, with tune sheet and inlaid lid, 21in. wide. (Christie's) $2,588

A Columbia Regal/Sterling disc graphophone in panelled oak case with engaged corner columns, aluminium tone-arm and nickel plated flower horn, circa 1907. (Christie's) $1,393

A bells-in-sight musical box with 14in. cylinder and six bells playing ten airs and with original air sheet, two-part comb lacks one tooth. (Bearne's) $2,800

A disc Pathephone with single spring motor in oak case, accelerating starter, 10in. turntable, ebonite reproducer, brass flower horn. (Christie's) $995

A Polyphon vertical disc musical box, playing 19 7/8in. discs, contained in a white painted case with glazed door to front, 77cm., together with four discs. (Osmond Tricks) $3,500

A musical box playing ten popular tunes of the 1890's accompanied by six engine turned bells, 21in. wide. (Christie's) $1,891

A Star Model 50 external horn talking machine with bevel drive double spring motor in mahogany case, 10in. turntable. (Christie's) $955

An organette by J.M.Draper, Blackburn, with eleven paper rolls in an inlaid case. (Greenslades) $297

An Edison Bell Electron Model 248 cabinet gramophone with Edison Bell Electron soundbox on S-shaped tone-arm, 35½in. high. (Christie's) $1,095

An Italian violin by Annibale Fagnola in Turin, circa 1910, unlabelled, in case with cover by W. E. Hill & Sons, London. (Phillips) $20,700

A violin by Gilkes probably Samuel, first quarter 19th century, bearing the manuscript label 'Gilkes Maker, Westminster', length of back 359mm. (Phillips) $4,400

A violin by Vincentius Postiglione bearing the label Me fecit Neap 1887 and inscribed on the label in manuscript, the table is antique wood from a church. (Phillips) $11,440

A rare violin by Enrico Catenri bearing the label Henricus Catenar fecit Taurini anno 1684, length of back 354mm. (Phillips) $35,200

A violoncello by William Forster, circa 1770, bearing the signed label, length of back 29in. with cover. (Phillips) $14,760

A viola by Walter H. Mayson, bearing the maker's label in Manchester, dated 1890 and named Molique. (Phillips) $2,880

A fine violin by Charles Jacquot in Paris, circa 1840, length of back 357mm. (Phillips) $10,208

A fine violin by Benigno Saccani, bearing the maker's signed label in Milan Anno 1913, Liuteria Italiana. (Phillips) $8,460

A violin by Alfredo Gianotti in Milan bearing the maker's label with signature fecit A.D. 1975. (Phillips) $3,520

A good violin by George Craske bearing the label Made by George Craske (born 1795, died 1888) and sold by William E. Hill & Sons, length of back 360mm. (Phillips) $5,632

A fine violin by Joannes Baptista Guadagnini in Piacenza, bearing the label Joannes Baptista filius Laurentii Guadagnini fecit Placentiae 1743, length of back 355mm. (Phillips) $140,800

A good viola by Mark William Dearlove in Leeds, 1847, bearing a pencil inscription Dearlove Maker Leeds below the button, length of back 385mm. (Phillips) $1,672

A fine viola by Charles Jacqot in Paris, circa 1860, bearing the maker's label at 48 Rue de L'Echiquier, length of back 415mm. (Phillips) $11,440

A violin by Paolo Castello in Genoa, circa 1790, length of back 360mm., in a black oblong double case. (Phillips) $20,240

A violin by Tomaso Eberle bearing the label Thomas Eberle fecit Neap, 1793, length of back 354mm. (Phillips) $22,880

A fine violin by George Pyne bearing the maker's label in London, anno 1914 and branded G. Pyne, length of back 356mm. (Phillips) $2,816

A late Victorian rosewood lute-harp with gilt decoration to the front, on oval foot. (Christie's) $808

A brass cornopean by Gisborne stamped on the bell 'at 27 Suffolk Street, Birmingham', circa 1850. (Phillips) $1,476

The Anaconda, the only known example of a contra-bass C serpent, by Joseph Richard Wood in Upper Heaton, Yorks, circa 1840, overall length 475cm. (Phillips) $8,700

An engraved silver mounted flute, bearing a cartouche on the head joint of Card, '29 St James St., London', circa 1840-61. (Phillips) $990

An ivory mounted boxwood clarinet by Goulding & Co., with six brass keys, square flaps. (Phillips) $126

A rare ivory single key flute by Frederico Haupt in Lisbon, circa 1720, branded on all joints 'F. Haupt' between two stars. (Phillips) $6,760

A rare double flageolet by Thomas Scott (Inventor) 17 Holborn Bars, London, circa 1806, of boxwood with double action and silver cutout in one barrel, overall length 480mm. (Phillips) $338

A violin by a maker of the Kloz family, circa 1780, labelled Sebastian Kloz in Mittenwald. (Phillips) $4,680

A viola by the William Piper Workshop, Birmingham, bearing their label, Copy Gand Freres, Paris. (Phillips) $1,440

An ivory mounted boxwood clarinet by Key in Charing Cross, London, circa 1820. 17¾in. long. (Phillips) $252

A Spanish model guitar by C. Frederick Martin in Nazireth, New York, circa 1870, length of back 465mm. (Phillips) $1,080

A Tyrolean Concert zither, circa 1880, in fitted velvet lined case the body of rosewood. (Phillips) $828

A set of Regency period musical glasses, in the original mahogany veneered rectangular case with divided interior, 3ft.9in. (Woolley & Wallis) $3,500

A rope-tension side drum of the 4th (Carms.) Bn., The Welch Regiment emblazoned with regimental devices. (Christie's) $498

A fine stand of Irish Union bagpipes by R. L. O'Mealy in Belfast, circa 1920, the mounts of heavy nickel plate, all collars and surmounts of finely turned ivory. (Phillips) $1,253

An ivory mounted figured boxwood flute by Goulding, D'Almaine, Potter & Co., Soho Square, London, circa 1811-15. (Phillips) $288 £160

A rare early bass recorder, attributed to Dupuis in Paris, circa 1690, of ebony with heavy ivory collars and mounts, inset with stained green and black colored ivory spot decoration. (Phillips) $9,048

A rare ivory flute by Thomas Cahusac the Elder, circa 1750, branded on all joints 'Cahusac, London'. (Phillips)$5,746

A violin bearing the label Joseph Gagliano filius Nicolai fecit Neap 1761, length of back 352mm.(Phillips) $52,800

A good violin by Hart & Son bearing their label at 28 Wardour Street, London, dated 1928. (Phillips) $3,420

A viola by Guiseppe Calace bearing the maker's manuscript label in Napoli 1935. (Phillips) $3,600

A fine violin by Arthur Richardson bearing the maker's label in Crediton Devon, dated 1940. (Phillips) $4,500

Hozan (late 19th century), Mask of Okina, netsuke, box-wood, 4.2cm. high, signed Hokkyo Hozan. (Christie's) $1,650

Hirado Kilns (late 19th century), Mouse, netsuke, white glazed porcelain with black enamel details, 5.5cm. long, unsigned. (Christie's) $1,210

A well carved wood netsuke of a sleeping shojo, signed in a rectangular reserve Masakazu, 19th century, 3cm. high. (Christie's) $3,133

Anonymous (20th century), A humanoid kirin, netsuke, wood, 6.5cm. high, unsigned. (Christie's) $880

Anonymous (19th century), Cranes in flight, netsuke, natural gourd with lacquer decoration, silver fittings, 6cm. high, unsigned. (Christie's) $2,090

Ouchi Sosui (1907/11-72), Lady Tokiwa Gozen with her children fleeing through the snow, netsuke, ivory, 5cm. high, signed Sosui to, in inscribed wood box signed Sosui koku. (Christie's) $7,700

Anonymous (19th century), Oni tugging his fundoshi from a clam shell, netsuke, coral with stained details, 6cm. high, unsigned. (Christie's) $1,320

Morita Soko (1879-1942), A crate of tangerines, netsuke, boxwood with dark wood inlay, 4cm. high, signed Soko. (Christie's) $22,000

A finely carved ivory netsuke of an ama and a kappa embracing, signed Akihide (born 1934), 6.2cm. high. (Christie's) $2,350

Suzuki Tokoku (1846-1931), Daruma yawning, netsuke, wood with amber and soft metal inlaid details, 2.8cm. high, signed Tokoku. (Christie's) $5,280

Nakamura Takakazu, known as Kuya (1881-1961), Neck wrestlers, netsuke, ivory stained details, 3.5cm. diam., signed Kuya. (Christie's) $2,530

A well carved ivory netsuke of a monkey holding an octopus under a pan, signed Kangyoku (born 1944), 3.7cm. high. (Christie's) $1,664

Anonymous (late 18th century), Hotei with a karako on his shoulders, netsuke, stained ivory, 7cm. high, unsigned, age cracks and minor wear. (Christie's) $1,760

An ivory netsuke of a horse, grazing on a slight hummock, its tail and mane stained brown. (Lawrence Fine Arts) $669

Anonymous (18th century), Grazing horse, netsuke, stained ivory with horn inlay, 6.8cm. high, unsigned, age cracks. (Chrsitie's) $4,180

Ozaki Kokusai (1861-1911), Samurai ningyo, netsuke, stag antler, 4.5cm. high, signed Koku. (Christie's) $3,080

Anonymous (19th century), Eel in split bamboo basket, netsuke, stained stag antler and iron, 3.8cm. high, unsigned. (Christie's) $2,640

A well carved lightly stained ivory netsuke of a standing baku looking up, signed Kangyoku (born 1944), 4.8cm. (Christie's) $1,468

NETSUKE

Anonymous (18th century), Minogame and young, netsuke, stained ivory, 5cm. long, unsigned — age cracks and slight wear. (Christie's) $2,420

Sukenaga (19th century), Daruma yawning, netsuke, wood (chosen matsu), 4.3cm. wide, signed Sukenaga. (Christie's) $2,420

Anonymous (18th century), Dog with blanket and belt, netsuke, stained ivory, 4.1cm. high, unsigned. (Christie's) $2,420

Kagetoshi (early/mid 19th century), Wild boar and young on coin (Tenpo tsuho), netsuke, ivory, 4.7cm. long, signed Kagetoshi on a rect-angular reserve. (Christie's) $3,520

Nakamura Tokisada, known as Masatoshi (b. 1915), Net ripper (amikiri) with hoshu, netsuke, ivory with black coral inlay and gold, 6cm. long, signed Masatoshi to.(Christie's) $3,300

Fukai Soju (b. 1918), Stone-mason relaxing with pipe in hand, netsuke, wood with inlaid ivory detail, 3.8cm. high, signed Soju. (Christie's) $4,950

Risuke Garaku (second half of 18th century), Seated baku, netsuke, stained ivory with dark horn inlaid details, 4.2cm. long, signed Garaku.(Christie's) $24,200

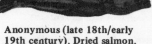

Anonymous (late 18th/early 19th century), Dried salmon, netsuke, ivory, 12cm. long, unsigned, age cracks. (Christie's) $1,320

Inada Ichiro (b. 1891), Oxherd seated on an ox, netsuke, boxwood, 3cm. high, signed Ichiro. (Christie's) $3,960

Meikeisai Hojitsu (d.1872), Manzai dancers, Manju netsuke, ivory with stained details, 4cm. diam., signed Hojitsu. (Christie's) $2,090

Shunkosai Anraku of Osaka (mid 19th century), Taira no Tadamori capturing the oil thief, netsuke, ivory, with stained details, 5.1cm. high, signed Anraku on the reverse. (Christie's) $1,320

An ivory netsuke of a cat peering into a flattened paper lantern, a rat emerging through the paper of the lantern, sig-ned Meigyokusai, 19th century, 4.5cm. long. (Christie's) $1,762

NETSUKE

An ivory netsuke of Moso seated holding a mattock on a large bamboo shoot, signed, 19th century, 3.5cm. high. (Christie's) $1,175

Ouchi Gyokuso (1879-1944), Female hand with diamond ring making an obscene gesture, netsuke, boxwood and ebony with soft metal and diamond detail, 4.5cm., signed Gyokuso koku.(Christie's) $4;180

Kaigyokusai Masatsugu (1813-92), Flying plover, kogo, ivory with coral and horn inlay, 6.5cm. diam., signed Kaigyoku.(Christie's) $3,080

An ivory netsuke of a recumbent frog, its foot resting on a shell enclosing a spider, two further spiders on the shell of a snail crawling on the back of the frog, signed Goho (Mitani Goho), early 19th century, 4cm. high. (Christie's) $5,874

Masanao of Kyoto (second half of 18th century), Dog on cushion, netsuke, stained ivory, with dark horn inlay, 4.5cm. wide, signed Masanao. (Christie's) $20,900

An ivory netsuke of Tekkai, breathing out his spiritual essence in the form of a miniature figure, signed Mitsuyuki, 19th century, 4cm. high. (Christie's) $1,566

An ivory netsuke of a shi-shi seated, scratching its left ear with a rear paw. (Lawrence Fine Arts) $483

Seikanshi (19th century), Namahage dancer playing a drum, Manju netsuke, ivory, 4.6cm. diam., signed Seikanshi. (Christie's) $1,320

A wood netsuke, carved as a skeleton kneeling beating a large mokugyo, ivory hole rims, signed. (Lawrence Fine Arts) $387

Anonymous (late 19th century), Seated dog, netsuke, (Chinese) glazed porcelain, 5cm. long, unsigned, minor chips. (Christie's)$605

Fukumoto Homin (mid 19th century), An anamorphic figure of Fukurokuju masquerading as a turtle, netsuke, wood with ivory inlay, 5cm. high, signed Homin. (Christie's) $1,265

A well carved wood netsuke modelled as a cicada, signed Seiyodo, 19th century, 6.5cm. long. (Christie's) $3,524

Bahamas — 18--, Bank of Nassau unissued £1 in blue with central vignette of Queen Victoria. (Phillips) $243

Trinidad — Royal Bank of Canada, 1920 $100, rust traces from paper clip showing mainly on back upper left edge. (Phillips) $990

Bank of England, E. M. Harvey, £50 note, 29 August 1918, issued at Leeds. (Phillips) $849

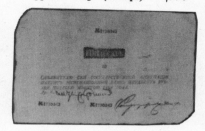

Russia — 1808 50 roubles State Assignat. (Phillips) $354

Turkey — 1908 Banque Imperiale Ottomane 50 livres, hole at center, edge damage and missing piece from bottom margin. (Phillips) $162

Great Britain — Anti-Hanging note by George Cruikshank. (Phillips) $371

Australia — 1877 Union Bank of Australia £1 proof on card in black on yellow and orange, with portrait of Queen Victoria at left. (Phillips) $495

Bank of England, E.M. Harvey, £100 note, 19 November 1918, numerous spots of foxing and some small holes. (Phillips) $407

Bahamas — 1905 Bank of Nassau 4/- unissued. (Phillips) $180

Bank of England, £1 error 1948, missing prefix and serial numbers. (Phillips) $180

General Bank Plymouth — £5. (Phillips) $212

Trinidad — $20. (Phillips) $351

South Africa — 1900 Siege of Mafeking £1, no center crease and therefore an unusually good example of this note. (Phillips) $990

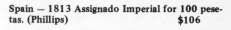

Spain — 1813 Assignado Imperial for 100 pesetas. (Phillips) $106

Rhodesia — 1917 African Banking Corporation 10/- Specimen, date inked in along top margin. (Phillips) $566

South Africa — 1890 Natal Bank £5 Specimen by Skipper & East in black on white. (Phillips) $123

Mexico — Banco de Guanajuato 50 pesos.
(Phillips) $176

Uruguay — 1889 El Banco Italo-Oriental 100
pesos specimen. (Phillips) $234

North Wilts. Banking Company — £5 proof on
card for Westbury. (Phillips) $141

Bradford (Wiltshire) Bank — £1 180-, unissued.
(Phillips) $168

South Africa — 1917 Natal issue 10/- Specimen
of the African Banking Corporation. (Phillips)
$230

Uruguay — 1887 Banco Nacional 500 pesos unissued. (Phillips) $225

Trinidad — 1938, $20. (Phillips) $396

Mozambique — 1909 1 mil reis. (Phillips)$88

Bermuda — 1947 £5. (Phillips) $297

United States of America — 1977 $100 error
with inverted serial numbers. (Phillips)
$180

Torpoint, Plymouth Dock — £5, 180-, unissued. (Phillips) $566

Southern Rhodesia — 1944 £5. (Phillips)
$396

Scotland — Union Bank, £5, 1920. (Phillips)
$146

South Africa — 1892 De Nationale Bank £1,
has been split and rejoined. (Phillips)
$168

Portugal — 1918, 100 escudos, missing lower
left corner tip, other small tears around edges.
(Phillips) $165

Bank of New South Wales £1 Specimen by C.
Skipper & East for Auckland, stain on part of
counterfoil. (Phillips) $189

A Liberty & Co. 'Tudric' pewter timepiece, showing the influences of C.F.A. Voysey, in the form of a dwelling, 34cm. high. (Phillips) $3,182

A WMF pewter centerpiece, decorated with flowerheads and butterflies, with cobalt-blue shaped glass liner, 42.3cm. long. (Christie's)$1,215

A pewter porringer, New England, late 18th/early 19th century, with a crown handle, unmarked, 13cm. diam. (Christie's) $286

A pewter basin by William Will, Philadelphia, 1764-1798, with molded everted rim, marked in the center with Laughlin touch 542, 16.2cm. (Christie's) $3,190

A WMF electroplated pewter vase mount, modelled with a seated male figure holding up a rose to a scantily clad maiden, on four openwork feet, (liner missing) 40.4cm. high. (Christie's) $935

A pewter plate, by William Kirby, New York, 1760-1793, with single reed brim and a hammered booge, 9in. diam. (Christie's) $935

An Art Nouveau electroplated pewter candlestick, formed as a freestanding scantily clad maiden holding a curvilinear branch, on pierced floral base, 32cm. high. (Christie's) $523

A W. M. F. electroplated pewter teaset, of domical form with chased bands of decoration and pierced circular finials. (Christie's) $483

A W. M. F. electroplated pewter lamp stand, modelled as an Art Nouveau maiden holding aloft a bulbous stand, 32.3cm. high. (Christie's) $743

PEWTER

A pewter charger with wide everted rim, the pennant inscribed *'Dieu et Mon Droit'*, 20¼in. diameter. (Bearne's) $492

One of a pair of W. M. F. electroplated pewter candelabra, each modelled as a scantily clad Art Nouveau maiden, with usual W. M. F. marks, 26.5cm. high. (Christie's) $1,859

A W. M. F. electroplated pewter tray, with pierced and raised decoration of an Art Nouveau maiden with flowing hair and an iris, 33.1cm. diam. (Christie's) $353

A Palme Konig und Habel vase mounted in a pewter stand, with pierced mount formed by three Art Nouveau maidens on pierced tripartite stand, 24.3cm. high. (Christie's) $897

A WMF pewter coupe, the pierced oval body formed by two Art Nouveau butterfly-maidens, with shaped green glass liner, , 17.8cm. high. (Christie's) $523

A W. M. F. pewter mirror and stand, cast with a partially draped maiden admiring herself in the glass and with molded decoration of marguerites, 37.3cm. long. (Christie's) $1,022

A fine and rare pewter teapot by Peter Young, New York, 1775-1785, or Albany, 1785-1795, the domed cover with a beaded edge, 7¼in. high. (Christie's) $30,800

A rare pewter funnel, by Frederick Bassett, New York or Hartford, 1761-1800, marked with Laughlin touch 465 (bruises), 6½in. long. (Christie's) $1,980

A WMF electroplated pewter sweetmeat dish, the trefoil scalloped form with handle formed by a freestanding Art Nouveau maiden, stamped with usual WMF marks, 31.3cm. long. (Christie's) $523

PEWTER

A WMF electroplated pewter desk tray, the bi-partite form with scalloped edges, with central loop handle molded as a butterfly-maiden, stamped 80, 31cm. wide. (Christie's) $523

A Liberty & Co. 'Tudric' pewter and enamel time-piece, embellished with a stylized tree with leaves, the roots tied in celtic knot. (Phillips) $2,524

A WMF electroplated pewter letter tray, with pierced and scrolling floral decoration and modelled with a maiden reading a letter, 34.3cm. long. (Christie's) $594

A fine pewter quart tankard, by John Will, New York, 1752-1774, with a double-domed cover, 18.1cm. high, overall. (Christie's) $16,500

One of a pair of Art Nouveau pewter three light candelabra, each with flowerhead sconces with foliate drip-pans, 25.5cm. high. (Phillips)
Two $1,021

A rare pewter pint infusion pot, probably by Robert Pale-thorp, Jr., Philadelphia, 1817-1821, the scroll handle with three piercings, 13cm. high. (Christie's) $176

An 18th century German pew-ter flagon, the reeded body engraved with a coat of arms, 13¼in. high. (Christie's) $962

A Liberty and Co. pewter four piece tea service designed by Archibald Knox, the teapot with compressed globular body, stamped Made in England, Eng-lish Pewter. (Christie's) $841

Large pewter flagon, by Samuel Danforth, Hartford, Connecticut, circa 1800, the domed molded cover over cylindrical body, 12in. high. (Robt. W. Skinner Inc.) $500

536

A pair of 19th century pewter fire dogs, on scroll supports, 26in. (Greenslades) $613

A WMF pewter dish, of shaped oval section, in the form of a river, a frog playing the flute sitting on the bank, 23cm. long. (Christie's) $241

Two of a set of six WMF pewter tea-glass holders, each with scrolling handle and pierced entrelac and ivy decoration, on four feet, stamped with usual WMF marks, 7.5cm. high. (Christie's) Six $561

A pewter pint mug, by William Will, Philadelphia, 1764-1798, the scroll handle with a bud terminal, 4½in. high. (Christie's) $8,250

A pewter plate, "Love" Touch, Philadelphia, 1750-1800, with single reed brim, 21.3cm. diam. (Christie's) $286

A rare early 19th century pewter Dr John Mudge-pattern inhaler, with a pewter pint tankard with spout, proof marked for William IV, lacks mouthpiece. (Phillips) $447

A Liberty & Co pewter timepiece, designed by Archibald Knox, with copper colored numerals, 8in. high. (Christie's) $3,908

A pewter coffee pot, by John H. Palethorp, Philadelphia, 1826-1845, with a black painted scrolled handle, 10¼in. high. (Christie's) $220

A late 18th century Swiss pewter flagon or wine kanne, with heart shaped cover, 13in. high. (Christie's) $808

Sacha Stone — Lady painting numbers — Gelatin silver print. 6¾ x 8½in., early 1920's. (Christie's) $685

Francis Bruguiere — New York Theatre Studies — Eight gelatin silver prints, approx. 8¾ x 10in. to 10¼ x 12½in. 1920/30's. (Christie's) $979

F. M. Sutcliffe — His Son's Son — one of four albumen prints, each approx. 7½ x 5½in. late 19th century. (Christie's) $979

J. Frish — London river scenes — Five gelatin prints, image size approx. 8 x 12in., 1940's. (Christie's) $215

Baron Adolf de Meyer — Still life with parasols, hat stands and flowers — Gelatin silver print, 7 x 9 in., after 1914. (Christie's) $391

Bill Brandt — Nude — Mammoth gelatin silver print, 23 x 27½in., July 1960, printed early 1970's. (Christie's) $1,410

William Klein — New York 1954 — Gelatin silver print, image size 13¾ x 9½in. photographer's signature and print date '1977'. (Christie's) $881

Govt. Printer, N.S.W. — New South Wales 1911 — One of sixty-eight gelatin silver prints, each approx. 11 x 14in. (Christie's) $1,566

Bisson Freres — Facade detail — Albumen print, 17½ x 13in. with red facsimile signature on card mount, 1850's. (Christie's) $313

PHOTOGRAPHS

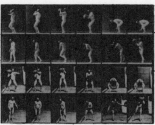

C. R. Jones — 59 Colosseum — One of three calotypes, each hand-coloured, the former titled in pencil on reverse, later card mounts, 1846. (Christie's) $3,524

Eadweard Muybridge — Animal Locomotion: men — Eleven photogravure prints, approx. image sizes 9½ x 12¼, 1887.(Christie's) $783

Heinz Loew — Corsets — Three gelatin silver prints, 3 x 7in, 3 x 4½, 2 x 4½in., mounted together on card, late 1920's. (Christie's) $940

Dominique Roman — Roman architecture, Arles — Albumen print from waxed paper negative, 11 x 8in., mounted on card, late 1850's. (Christie's) $489

Count Zichy — Celebrity and society portraits commercial and personal photographs — eight albums containing approx. 300 gelatin silver prints, 1940's and 1950's. (Christie's) $431

Albert Renger-Patszch — Untitled, metal castings — Gelatin silver print, 9 x 6¾in. numbered within copyright stamp on reverse, 1930's. (Christie's) $822

Margaret Bourke-White — In a Korean village, a wife, mother and grandmother lament the death of their boy — Gelatin silver print, 10¾ x 14¼in., early 1940's. (Christie's) $822

Dorothy Hickling, George Bernard Shaw — Portraits of George Bernard Shaw and correspondence with photographer, ninety gelatin silver prints, each overprinted as postcard. (Christie's) $1,664

Mr Mendenhall — Photos of San Franciso Earthquake taken for Government Record by Mr Mendenhall of the Geodetic Survey 1906 — Forty-one gelatin silver prints. 1906. (Christie's) $1,469

PHOTOGRAPHS

USA: Richmond, Virginia, view of main street during flood, with crowds of onlookers, signed and dated in negative 'Rees & Co., Oct 1 1870', 27 x 34cm. (Phillips) $3,026

T. R. Williams, Still life of vegetables and game, stereoscopic daguerreotype, 1850's. (Christie's) $1,076

USA: Cleveland, Ohio-Cleveland baseball team, with crowd of onlookers and carriages beyond, 29 x 42cm. $979

Gustave Le Gray — The Harbour, Sete — Albumen print, 12¼ x 16¼in., archival matt, 1856/59. (Christie's) $6,853

A rare hinged wooden sample case containing sixteen ninth-plate daguerreotype portraits, 1845. (Christie's) $822

USA: Cincinnati, Ohio, one of a fine four section panorama, looking north across the Ohio River, dated 1865, each 31 x 39cm., 152cm. long overall.(Phillips) Four $4,984

Xie Kitchin, 'Chinese Merchant', sitting on pile of chests, in Chinese costume, by Lewis Carroll, 10.5 x 15cm. (Phillips) $1,068

Xie Kitchin sitting on chaise longue, in white dress with ribbon in hair, whole plate negative by Lewis Carroll, 8½ x 6½in. (Phillips) $2,136

H. Negretti & Zambra, Crystal Palace, one of four stereoscopic daguerreotypes with photographer's printed paper pictorial advertising label, 1850's. (Christie's) $822

T. R. Williams — Still-life including Brewster stereoscope and studio reflection, mid 1850's. (Christie's) $1,174

Anon, The basket maker, stereoscopic daguerreotype, black glass surround, 1850's. (Christie's) $548

A signed portrait photograph by D.Wilding of King George VI, Queen Elizabeth, Princess Elizabeth and Princess Margaret in Coronation robes, dated 1937, 20cm. x 28cm. (Phillips) $878

Xie Kitchin, leaning on back of chair, negative, 5 x 6in., also numbered '291', by Lewis Carroll. (Phillips) $1,424

1887: A photograph of Queen Victoria, seated, signed bottom right 'Victoria...1887', framed and glazed. (Phillips) $1,183

Negative for Xie Kitchin, lying barefoot on sofa, in white dress, by Lewis Carroll, 6 x 5in. (Phillips) $1,424

Captain Scott and the Polar Expedition, album containing thirty-nine gelatin silver prints, various sizes, 1901. (Christie's) $735

Family group portrait, a halfplate daguerreotype with gilt highlights, in folding morocco case, 1850's. (Christie's) $372

PIANOS

A harpsichord by William de Blaise, London, the walnut case on tapering turned legs, 6ft.7½in. long. (Bearne's) $1,091

An early 19th century rectangular mahogany table piano, inscribed Thomas Tomkinson, Dean Street, Soho, on turned tapering legs, 67 x 34in. high. (Anderson & Garland) $795

An overstrung grand pianoforte by C. Bechstein, in a rosewood case on octagonal tapering legs and castors. (Christie's) $2,625

A Bluthner boudoir grand piano, the ebonized case on tapering square legs with brass castors, 6ft. 4in. (Bearne's) $4,071

A Steinway & Sons boudoir grand piano, No. 138781, the rosewood case on tapering square legs. (Bearne's) $7,392

Late Georgian mahogany grand piano having inlaid decoration, dated 1803, by John Broadwood, London. (Michael G. Matthews) $11,550

Ritzmar mahogany baby grand piano, no. 1801, excellent condition, on square tapered legs. (Giles Haywood) $1,925

A John Broadwood & Sons upright piano, the mahogany case with a panelled front, 58½in. wide. (Bearne's) $1,443

A Bechstein boudoir grand piano Model A, No.108650, the mahogany case with three pairs of tapering square legs, on brass castors, 6ft.(Bearne's) $3,872

An early 19th century Italian plaster bust of a gentlewoman, in the style of Canova, on integral socle, 66cm. high overall. (Christie's) $4,478

Pair of patinated plaster busts, after Jean-Antoine Houdon, depicting a young boy and girl, 16in. high. (Robt. W. Skinner Inc.) $500

A 19th century French tinted plaster bust of Antoine-Louis Caumartin, after Houdon, 79cm.high. (Christie's) $5,376

A late 19th century painted plaster of Paris male medical torso, the insides detachable, 30in. high. (Christie's) $192

One of a pair of oval cream-painted plaster and wood plaques, the molded frames with foliate cresting, 34 x 27in. (Christie's) Two $2,849

An early 20th century French figure of a lady, by Alphonse Saladin, the lady bent over by the wind and clutching at her hat, 21cm. high. (Christie's) $545

A 19th century Swiss plaster cast of a Greek dancer, after James Pradier, nude and looking down to her right with a garment behind her, 30.5cm. high. (Christie's) $1,050

A pair of 19th century French terracotta colored plaster busts of Bacchantes, with indistinct signature on one (marbled wood socles), 16cm. high. (Christie's) $962

A plaster figure, patinated terracotta, in the Directoire style, 69cm. high. (Christie's) $4,645

Thomas Richmond (1771-1837) - A gentleman, facing right, in blue coat with gold colored buttons, white waistcoat and frilled cravat, gilt metal frame, oval 2¾in. high. (Christie's)$748

Attributed to Samuel Shelley (1750/58-1808) - A lady, nearly full face, in decollete blue dress with white fichu, oval, 42mm. high. (Christie's) $523

French School, circa 1806 - A French officer of Hussars, in scarlet uniform, wearing the Knights Cross of the Legion d'Honneur, gilt metal frame, oval, 2¼in. high. (Christie's) $935

Francois Dumont (1751-1831) - A lady, full face, in white dress with blue ribbon tied in bow at corsage, oval, 61mm. high. (Christie's) $2,142

Jeremiah Meyer (1735-1789) - A gentleman, in maroon-colored coat with silver buttons, white chemise and lace cravat, with the monogram CHL, oval, 48mm. high. (Christie's) $935

Edward Miles (1753-1828) - Viscount Newark, in blue coat, yellow waistcoat and tied white cravat, oval, 2½in. high. (Christie's)$748

George Engleheart (1750/3-1829) - A gentleman with the initials JWH, facing right, in blue coat with white waistcoat and tied cravat, powdered hair, signed with cursive E, oval, 3in. high. (Christie's) $1,496

Charles Shirreff (b. 1750) - A lady, in white dress with blue ribbon sash, fine black lace shawl and white turban headgear, with gold monogram RJB, oval 2¾in. high. (Christie's) $1,309

John Hoskins (d. 1664/5) - Mrs. Street, nearly full face, in fur stole, decollete black dress with white underslip, oval, 61mm. high. (Christie's) $5,984

Francois Meuret (1800-1887) - A young gentleman, facing left, in black coat with fur collar, signed on obverse, oval, 4¼in. high. (Christie's) $1,084

James Scouler (1740-1812) - A fine miniature of an Infantry officer, in scarlet uniform with buff colored facings, gold bracelet clasp frame, oval, 42mm. high. (Christie's) $2,618

William Marshall Craig (fl. 1787-1827) - An officer, in white-bordered scarlet uniform of the 53rd Regiment, with gold lace and epaulettes, oval, 3in. high. (Christie's) $1,309

Peter Edvard Stroely (1768-1826) - Charles, 8th Earl of Haddington (1753-1828), full face, in military uniform, gilt metal frame, oval, 3in. high. (Christie's) $2,057

John Comerford (1770-1832) - A gentleman, in dark blue coat, white waistcoat and cravat, gilt-metal frame, oval, 3¼in. high. (Christie's) $1,028

Andrew Robertson (1777-1845) - A gentleman, with black hair and sideburns, facing left in black coat and tied white cravat, signed with monogram and dated (18)05, oval, 79mm. high. (Christie's) $841

Andrew Plimer (1763-1837) - A fine portrait of a gentleman, facing left, in black coat, white waistcoat and frilled cravat, gold frame, oval, 3in. high. (Christie's) $2,057

John Wright (c. 1745-1820) A gentleman, full face, in black coat, white waistcoat and stock, signed on the reverse, oval, 60mm. high. (Christie's) $841

Charles Robertson (1760-1821) - A charming portrait of a young boy, in blue coat, beige colored waistcoat and white chemise with large frilled collar, oval, 2¾in. high. (Christie's) $1,028

William Marshall Craig (fl. 1787-1827) - A lady, facing right, in white dress trimmed with lace and fichu, trade label on the reverse, gilt metal frame with basket weave border, oval, 87mm. high. (Christie's) $748

Gervase Spencer (d. 1763) Dorothy Taylor (nee Rumbold), facing right, in yellow surcoat and white dress, signed with initials and dated 1756, oval, 1¾in. high. (Christie's) $467

Horace Hone (1745/6-1825) - Lady Elizabeth Araminta Monck, facing right, in white dress with frilled border, signed with monogram and dated 1794, oval, 2¾in. high. (Christie's) $897

Attributed to Claude Jean Besselievre, circa 1810 (b. Paris 1779) - A fine portrait of a lady, facing right, in black Empire-line dress, rectangular, 4¼in. high. (Christie's) $1,870

The Painter 'V' (fl. c. 1778) - A fine portrait of a lady, seated half length, holding the paw of a spaniel, in decollete mauve dress, gold frame with rose cut diamond border, oval, 2½in. high. (Christie's) $10,285

Andrew Robertson (1777-1845) - John Trumbull, in black coat, vermilion colored waistcoat and white cravat, inscribed on the reverse in the artist's hand, rectangular, 3¼in. high. (Christie's) $2,992

Edward Robertson (b. 1809) - Captain Charles Robertson (1808-89), facing right, in dark blue coat, beige waistcoat with small gold colored buttons, oval, 3in. high. (Christie's) $4,675

Reginal Easton (1807-1893) - A fine portrait of a lady, seated half length, in white dress with wide falling lace frill, gilt metal frame, oval, 92mm. high. (Christie's) $2,244

Archibald Robertson (1765-1835) - An unknown officer, of the United States Infantry, facing right, in blue uniform with red facings, signed with monogram, oval, 3¼in. high. (Christie's) $3,366

Mrs. Diana Hill (later Mrs Harriot) (d. 1844) - A fine portrait of a gentleman, in brown coat, white waistcoat and lace cravat, signed and dated 1788, oval, 2½in. high. (Christie's) $2,805

Miss Sophia Smith (fl. 1760-1769) - A young lady, full face, in decollete white dress with blue bodice, signed and dated 1769, oval, 42mm. high. (Christie's) $841

John Bogle (1746-1803) - An elderly lady, in white dress with frilled border, and jewelled stick pin, signed with initials and dated 1786, oval, 1¾in. high. (Christie's) $1,309

A miniature portrait of a young lady, circa 1835, attributed to Justus Dalee (American, active 1826-1847), inscribed on back Susan Miller, 3 x 2½in. (Robt. W. Skinner Inc.) $1,700

Andrew Robertson (1777-1845) - An extremely fine portrait of Jenny Robertson, in red tunic dress with blue ribbon at corsage, signed with monogram, rectangular, 7in. high. (Christie's) $8,415

Moritz Michael Daffinger (1790-1849) - A lady, seated half length before a drapery background, in decollete blue dress, rectangular, 4in. high. (Christie's) $2,992

Andrew Robertson (1777-1845) - Thomas A. Shaw, facing right, in navy coat, white waistcoat and frilled cravat, signed and dated 10 May, 1816, oval, 80mm. high. (Christie's) $1,589

George Engleheart (1750/3-1829) after Sir J. Reynolds - 'The Little Thief', original gilt mounted rectangular black papier-mache frame, oval. 73mm. high. (Christie's) $3,553

Horace Hone (1745/6-1825) Edward Gibbon, in gold bordered white coat, gold bordered red waistcoat and cravat, signed with monogram and dated 1785, oval, 3in. high. (Christie's) $11,220

George Engleheart (1750/3-1829) - A gentleman, in black coat, white waistcoat and frilled cravat, signed with cursive E on obverse, dated 1803, oval, 3¼in. high. (Christie's) $3,366

Peter Cross(e) (c. 1645-1724) - Henry Lord Capell, facing right, in red robes and lace jabot, on prepared card, oval, 86mm. high. (Christie's) $2,618

Charles Shirreff (born 1750) - A gentleman, in brown coat, white waistcoat and tied cravat, powdered hair en queue, signed and dated 1797, oval, 3in. high. (Christie's) $710

William John Thomson (1771/3-1845) - An officer, facing right, in scarlet uniform with blue facings and gold lace, gilt metal frame, oval, 3in. high. (Christie's) $841

John Smart (1742-1811) - An extremely fine and important miniature of Major Richard Gomonde, in the staff officer's uniform of the Madras Presidency, signed and dated 1790, oval, 2½in. high. (Christie's) $26,180

Attributed to Thomas Hull (fl. 1775-1827) - A young boy, facing right, in blue coat with gold colored buttons, gilt metal frame, oval, 60mm. high. (Christie's) $561

Richard Crosse (1742-1810) - A fine portrait of Lieutenant Farnham Hill, facing right, in the blue uniform of the 19th Light Dragoons, signed and dated 1793, oval, 2¾in. high. (Christie's) $2,057

Thomas Richmond (1771-1837) - A fine miniature of a lady, facing right, in white dress with frilled border, gold frame with gilt metal mount, oval, 74mm. high. (Christie's) $1,870

George Engleheart (1750/3-1829) - An extremely fine portrait of a young boy, facing right, in dark blue coat with gold colored buttons, signed with cursive E, oval, 3¼in. high. (Christie's) $10,659

Richard Cosway R.A. (1742-1821) - A fine portrait of Sarah Anne, Countess of Westmorland, facing left, in white dress with green sash, with plaited hair reverse, oval, 2¾in. high. (Christie's) $11,220

John Bogle (1746-1803) - A young boy, facing left, in blue coat with gold colored buttons, signed with monogram and dated 1797, oval, 2in. high. (Christie's) $1,122

Jeremiah Meyer, R.A. (1735-1789) - A fine portrait of a lady, in decollete white dress with frilled border and green ribbon sash, gilt metal frame, oval, 3in. high. (Christie's) $2,244

William Sherlock (1738-d. after 1806) - A self-portrait, in dark blue coat with gold colored buttons, yellow and white striped waistcoat, oval, 73mm. high. (Christie's) $1,028

Johann Christian Schoeller (1782-1851) - A fine portrait of Emperor Napoleon I, facing left, in the uniform of the Chasseur a Cheval de la Guarde, 3in. diam. (Christie's) $7,854

Andrew Robertson (1777-1845) - A lady, believed to be Mistress Macallister, in red cloak and white dress with ruffled border, verre eglomise border, oval, 74mm. high. (Christie's) $1,309

Charles Robertson (1760-1821) - A gentleman, in blue coat with black collar, and white cravat, gold frame with plaited hair reverse, oval, 2½in. high. (Christie's) $841

English School, 17th century - A gentleman, wearing a pink cloak and white jabot, full-bottomed wig, oil on card, oval, 73mm. high. (Christie's) $561

John Cox Dilman Engleheart (1782-1826) - A fine portrait of a lady, in blue dress, the sleeves slashed to reveal white, signed and dated 1821, oval, 73mm. high. (Christie's) $1,496

Claude Flight, Speed, linocut printed in colors, circa 1925, on thin Japan, signed in pencil, 220 x 205mm. (Christie's) $4,259

Henri de Toulouse-Lautrec, 'Le Photographe Sescau', lithograph printed in colors, 1894, on wove paper, Adreani's second state, 607 x 782mm. (Christie's) $23,650

Henri Matisse, 'Le Repos du Modele', lithograph, 1922, on Chine volant, signed in pencil, 220 x 304mm. (Christie's) $7,568

Rembrandt Harmensz. van Rijn, Adam and Eve, etching with touches of drypoint, 1638, second (final) state, 164 x 117mm. (Christie's) $10,648

Hiroshige (1797-1858), from the Meisho Edo Hyakkei, Hundred Views of Edo, Ohashi atake no yudachi, 36 x 24cm. (Christie's) $11,880

Edvard Munch, 'Madchen auf der Brucke', woodcut and lithograph printed in five colors, signed in pencil, generally in very good condition, 664 x 570mm.(Christie's) $151,360

After Sir William Russell Flint, R.A., 'A question of attribution', reproduction in colors, signed in pencil, 21½ x 16in. (Christie's) $1,234

Louis Icart, 'Fumee', drypoint part printed in colors, finished by hand, 1926, published by Graveurs Modernes, Paris, 380 x 514mm.(Christie's) $3,784

Conrad Felixmuller, 'Die Sohne des Malers', woodcut, 1924, on wove paper, a fine fresh impression, signed, dated and titled in pencil, 622 x 538mm. (Christie's) $1,892

PRINTS

Louis Icart, 'L'Heure de la Melodie', drypoint with aquatint printed in colors finished by hand, 1934, on wove paper, signed in pencil, published by Icart, New York, 475 x 596mm. (Christie's) $5,298

Tsuguji Foujita, 'Jeune Fille a la Pelerine', etching with roulette work, on wove paper, signed in pencil, 160 x 111mm. (Christie's) $6,054

Graham Sutherland, O.M., R.A., St Marys Hatch, etching 1926, on wove paper, watermark indistinct initials with date 1849, 132 x 185mm.(Christie's) $1,548

Andy Warhol, 'Mick Jagger', screenprint in colors, 1975, on firm D'Arches wove paper, from the set of ten, signed in pencil or orange fibre-tip pen by artist and sitter, published by Seabird Editions, London, 985 x 735mm. (Christie's) $4,919

'Attic Room', by Louis Icart, etching and drypoint, printed in colors, signed lower right, 36.2 x 42.1cm. (Christie's) $8,324

Emil Orlik, 'Ferdinand Hodler', woodcut, 1904, on gray Japan, signed and dated in pencil,and seven others. (Christie's)
Eight $1,135

Anders Leonard Zorn, 'Dagmar', etching, signed in pencil, 10 x 7in.(Christie's) $740

Albrecht Durer, Nemesis, engraving, 1502, a Meder II impression watermark City Gate, generally in good condition, 336 x 232mm. (Christie's) $5,033

An early cricketing print showing Miss Wicket and Miss Trigger, printed for and sold by Carington Bowles, 'published as the act directs 1778', 25 x 35cm. (Phillips) $1,800

PRINTS

After Sidney R. Wombill, 'The finish for the Derby, 1885', by C. R. Stock, colored aquatint, 16 x 23in. (Christie's) $190

Edvard Munch, 'Das Weib', drypoint with aquatint, 1895, on firm, cream wove paper, fifth state, signed and dated '1913' in pencil, 297 x 348mm. (Christie's) $34,056

T. Hollins, 'View of the High Street, Birmingham, in July 1812', by J. C. Lailler, colored aquatint, 51 x 76cm. (Christie's) $720

Rembrandt Harmensz. van Rijn, Self Portrait with Saskia, etching, third (final) state, with margins, 104 x 95mm. (Christie's) $3,678

Edouard Manet, 'Polichinelle', lithograph printed in colors, with extensive white gouache highlighting, 1876, on wove paper, a trial proof in the extremely rare second state, 626 x 449mm. (Christie's) $18,920

Edgar Chahine, Lily Arena assise, drypoint, 1907, on Japan, signed in pencil, an artist's proof aside from the full numbered edition of 90, 548 x 440mm. (Christie's) $813

Hiroshige II (1826-69), from Shokoku meisho hyakkei, The Hundred Views of various provinces, Taishu kaigan, a three-masted European ship off the coast of Tsushima, 35.5 x 23.6cm. (Christie's) $1,386

Spanish Nights, by Louis Icart, etching and drypoint, signed lower right, numbered 63, Copyright 1926, by Byles Gravures Modernes, 194 Rue de Rivoli, Paris, 52.4 x 33cm. (Christie's) $2,230

Goyo (1880-1921), a girl combing her long hair, signed Goyo ga, sealed Hashiguchi Goyo, 44.5 x 34.7cm. (Christie's) $6,336

Herbert Dicksee, 'Two terriers', etching, signed in pencil, 11 x 16¼in. (Christie's) $228

Andy Warhol, 'Marilyn', screenprint in colors 1967, on wove paper, signed in pencil on the reverse, published by Factory Additions, New York, 915 x 915mm. (Christie's) $15,136

Henry Moore, O.M., C.H., 'Sheep in stormy landscape', lithograph printed in colors, 1974, on T. H. Saunders wove paper, signed in pencil, published by Raymond Spencer Ltd., 190 x 277mm.(Christie's) $4,352

Utamaro (1754-1806) — oban tate-e, 38.5 x 25.5cm., okubi-e from the set Tosei onna fuzoku tsu, 'Women's fashions of the day', signed Utamaro hitsu, published by Murataya Jirobei. (Christie's) $15,664

Shinsui (1898-1972), okubi-e of a beauty applying a rouge with her finger, dated Taisho II jugatsu, signed Shinsui ga, 43 x 26.1cm. (Christie's) $4,356

Kunisada (1786-1864), the courtesan Ohatsu of Tenmaya seated with a tooth pick in her mouth and one hand inside her kimono collar, 37.8 x 25.9cm. (Christie's) $1,386

Gerald Leslie Brockhurst, A.R.A., Adolescence, etching, 1932, on wove paper, fifth (final) state, a fine, strong impression, signed in pencil, 368 x 265mm. (Christie's) $16,456

Paul Nash, German Double Pill-box, Gheluvelt, lithograph, 1918, on laid paper, watermark Antique del Luxe, signed and dated Feb 1918, 455 x 358mm. (Christie's) $871

Gerald Leslie Brockhurst, A.R.A., Dorette, etching, 1932, on J. Whatman wove paper, sixth (final) state, a good impression, signed in pencil, 283 x 185mm. (Christie's) $1,645

PRINTS

Sofa, by Louis Icart, etching and drypoint, signed lower right, with artist's blindstamp, full mint uncirculated, Copyright 1937, 42.5 x 64.5cm. (Christie's) $7,436

A 17th century stumpwork picture, designed with a lady and gentleman amidst animals, birds, insects, trees and flowers, 23cm. x 34cm. (Phillips) $8,228

English School, late 18th century: 'Grand Cricket Match for One Thousand Guineas', an interesting watercolor, 8 x 12cm. (Phillips) $990

Hiroshige (1797-1858) — oban tate-e, 34.7 x 23.1cm., from Meisho Edo Hyakkei, Meguro Taiko-bashi Yuhi no zu, Evening at Drum Bridge at Meguro, signed Hiroshige ga. (Christie's) $3,133

Sketches of the Surrey Cricketers: a hand colored tinted lithograph of four cricketers on a pitch, pub. 16th July, 1852, 38 x 35cm. (Phillips) $2,160

Utamaro (1754-1806) — oban tate-e, approx. 37.8 x 25cm., a bust portrait of two women and a baby, signed Utamaro hitsu. (Christie's) $3,133

Jeanne d'Arc, by Louis Icart, dry-point with aquatint printed in colors, signed in pencil (1929), 54 x 37cm. (Christie's) $966

Gakutei (1786?-1868) — surimono, 21.2 x 19.7cm., a carp among aquatic plants, three kyoka poems above, signed Gakutei, sealed Yashima. (Christie's) $3,720

Toraji Ishikawa (1875-1964) — dai oban-tate, 48.5 x 36.7cm., a back view of a nude dancer, signed Ishikawa, sealed Tora. (Christie's) $1,273

PURSES

A drawstring purse of ivory colored silk, embroidered with a basket of naturalistic flowers, 7in. deep x 5in., circa 1830. (Christie's) $598

An ivory silk purse, painted with rural scenes, the back with a shepherdess and her flock by a river, 4 x 6in., circa 1780. (Christie's) $299

A beadwork purse, the four shield shaped panels worked with putti holding coronets, 3½in. high, French 17th century. (Christie's) $2,702

A Wiener Werkstatte beaded purse, attributed to Maria Likarz, of oval shape with a draw-string, 20.5cm. long. (Phillips) $633

A sable purse, worked in colored beads, with four shield shaped panels, 5in. deep, 17th century. (Christie's) $1,386

A 19th century Japanese purse embroidered mainly in purple and gray silks with French knot. (Phillips) $280

A shield shaped purse of ivory colored silk, embroidered in gilt thread, 18th century. (Christie's) $355

A mid-17th century German hunting bag of stencilled and cut crimson velvet. (Phillips) $448

An embroidered purse worked with silver gilt thread with a large stylized plant with flowers on coiling stems, 4in. square, 17th century. (Christie's) $1,732

A pieced wool quilted coverlet, Lancaster County, Pennsylvania, 1900-1910, worked in the Bars pattern in alternating light and dark brown surrounded by a red inner border with purple corners and grape and oak leaf stitching, 75 x 75in. (Christie's) $8,250

An Amish pieced wool quilted coverlet, Lancaster County, Pennsylvania, circa 1920, worked in the Diamond-in-the-Square pattern with mulberry and slate fabrics framed in deep pink and with a mulberry border and slate blue binding, 76 x 76in. (Christie's) $10,450

A pieced and embroidered silk and velvet coverlet, Lexington, Kentucky, 1880-1900, the contained Crazy Quilt pattern worked in various jewel-tone velvet fabrics and herringbone embroidery stitches with four center blocks of eight-point stars enclosed by five concentric borders, 89 x 89in. (Christie's) $8,250

A pieced and embroidered wool coverlet, by Mary T. H. Willard, Evanston, Illinois, 1889, worked in a Crazy Quilt pattern in three vertical panels, each with polychrome fabrics embroidered with floral motifs and sentimental cross-stitch inscriptions of Biblical quotations, 67 x 85in.(Christie's) $12,100

An Amish pieced cotton quilted coverlet, Midwestern, 1900-1925, worked in thirty blocks of Jacob's Ladder pattern with deep blue, purple, black, gray and brown fabrics, 76 x 89in. (Christie's) $2,090

A pieced silk quilted coverlet, probably Philadelphia, 1880-1900, centering a Rising Star in reds, green, white, purple and blue on a gray ground, 80 x 80in. (Christie's) $8,800

QUILTS

An Amish pieced cotton quilted coverlet, probably Indiana, circa 1930, the sixteen blocks each in the Broken Star pattern in blue, pink, purple and green on a black ground, 86 x 86in. (Christie's) $2,640

A pieced and embroidered silk and velvet quilted coverlet, American, 1880-1890, with 169 blocks, worked in the Log Cabin pattern. (Christie's) $4,400

A Mennonite pieced cotton quilted coverlet, made by Fanny Snyder of Manheim, Pennsylvania, circa 1890, in the Joseph's-Coat-of-Many-Colours pattern, worked in the spectrum of primary colors, with fine feather and diaper stitching, 75 x 80in. (Christie's) $5,280

An appliqued cotton quilted coverlet, American, 1840-1860, worked in eight blocks of Oak Leaf variation interspersed with twelve blocks of assorted appliqued designs, including hearts and hands and birds in trees, each in red, green, yellow and pink calicos on natural ground, 68 x 86in. (Christie's) $1,980

An appliqued quilted cotton coverlet, probably New York, 1820-1830, centering a square reserve with red calico sawtooth border and enclosing a diamond reserve with red and yellow calico sawtooth border with a brown broderie perse floral spray, 105 x 105in. (Christie's) $3,080

An Amish pieced cotton quilted coverlet, Midwestern, 1900-1925, with sixteen blocks of Birds in Flight variation within a nine patch pattern worked in deep-tone fabrics, alternating with blocks of slate blue fabric, 72 x 72in. (Christie's) $9,350

An Amish pieced cotton quilted coverlet, Midwestern, 1900-1925, worked in the Ocean Waves pattern with royal blue, slate green, brown, tan and mulberry fabric, 75 x 75in. (Christie's) $3,520

A fine white-on-white stuffed cotton quilt, signed Mary Young, August 23, 1821, centering a large Federal urn with floral swags and on a patterned pedestal surrounded by be-ribboned sheaves of wheat and an inner border of meandering vines, 100 x 100in. (Christie's) $13,200

An unusual appliqued and embroidered cotton pictorial quilted coverlet, by Jennie C. Trein, Nazareth, Pennsylvania, 1932, centering a scene depicting a family Sunday picnic with gathering guests, a house in the background, boats in the water, and the family graveyard surrounded by an inner border with "Sunbonnet Sue" figures, 84 x 82in. (Christie's) $41,800

An Amish pieced wool quilted coverlet, Lancaster County, Pennsylvania, circa 1900, worked in the Diamond-in-the-Square pattern, the cranberry diamond stitched with an 8-point star enclosed by a feathered wreath, on a turquoise ground framed in deep pink, 78 x 78in. (Christie's) $7,150

A Mennonite pieced wool quilted coverlet, Cumberland County, Pennsylvania, circa 1900, worked in the Barn Raising pattern, each block centering a red square with maroon inner border, 90 x 90in. (Christie's) $2,640

An Amish pieced and embroidered quilted wool coverlet monogrammed "K.F.", Lancaster County, Pennsylvania, dated 1922, worked in 16 blocks of contained Crazy Quilt pattern, 82 x 82in. (Christie's) $8,800

A fine pieced and appliqued cotton quilted coverlet, Palama Mission, Hawaii, 1899, centering a square reserve depicting the crest of the Hawaiian monarchy and inscribed "Ku'u Hae Aloha" surrounded by four Hawaiian flags and a yellow binding, 84 x 88in. (Christie's) $44,000

An Amish pieced cotton quilted coverlet, Lancaster County, Pennsylvania, 1920-1940, worked in the Sunshine-and-Shadow pattern, with a spectrum of green, purple and pink blocks, surrounded by a wide slate blue border, 84 x 88in. (Christie's) $3,850

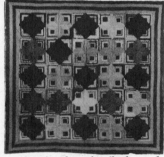

A Mennonite pieced wool quilted coverlet, Lancaster County, Pennsylvania, 1900-1925, worked in 100 blocks of Log Cabin pattern, each centering a green square surrounded by a quadruple border of alternating green and orange bands, 96 x 96in. (Christie's) $2,200

An appliqued and stuffed cotton coverlet, by Mary Clapper, Boonesboro, Maryland, 1830-1850, with three concentric rings of star-filled hexagons in the Grandmother's Garden pattern, alternating with elaborately quilted bands of flower baskets, 104 x 96in.(Christie's) $3,520

An appliqued cotton quilted coverlet, American, 1820-1830, centering a broderie perse floral urn with two square printed borders enclosing a zigzag printed border, surrounded by a border of appliqued eight-pointed stars in red, yellow and blue, 92 x 92in. (Christie's) $5,500

A fine stencilled cotton quilted coverlet, Vermont 1835-1840, with fifteen blocks stencilled with an eight pointed star in red, green and blue alternating with quilted blocks of white, 82 x 84in. (Christie's) $8,800

A page from an autograph book signed by Buddy Holly, Jerry Allison and Joe Mauldin, and inscribed in a separate hand 'Tues. March 4th 1958, Sheffield City Hall'. (Christie's) $1,301

An autographed black leather 'Harley Davidson Motor Cycles' hat, signed and inscribed 'To Hells Angels, Keith Moon'. (Christie's) $743

An illustrated souvenir programme for The Jacksons tour, February 1979, the center page signed by Randy, Tito, Jackie, Marlon and Michael Jackson. (Christie's) $241

A concert advertising bill for 'The Beatles Christmas Show' at Finsbury Park, Astoria, 24th December to 11 January 1964. (Christie's)$2,044

An exotic stage suit of two-tone electric blue and scarlet, lined with scarlet 'silk', signed and inscribed 'Smokey Robinson 7-1984'. (Christie's) $1,859

One of a rare set of five previously unpublished portrait photographs by Michael Randolph, circa 1968, subjects include Mick Jagger, John Lennon, Robert Plant, Tiny Tim and Barry Gibb. (Christie's)$3,718

A single cover, 'You'll think of me/Suspicious Minds', RCA Victor, signed and inscribed 'Sincerely Elvis Presley'. (Christie's) $946

Two posters, one of a concert advertising poster for 'T. Rex, May 1971 in concert', Monday 24th May, Colston Hall, Bristol, the other a promotional poster for four T. Rex albums. (Christie's) $1,301

An album cover 'Something New', Capital Records, signed by each member of the group and inscribed 'Beatles' in Ringo Starr's hand.(Christie's) $2,044

A page taken from the Glasgow Apollo Theatre visitors' book inscribed '16/17th May '81, Bruce Springsteen & The E Street Band', signed by Bruce Springsteen and six members of the band. (Christie's) $464

An album cover, 'Who's Next', signed by Keith Moon, Pete Townshend, Roger Daltry and John Entwistle.(Christie's) $1,394

An album cover 'Born In The U.S.A.', Columbia, 1984, signed in black felt pen, with a red printed cotton scarf signed 'Bruce Springsteen' in black felt pen. (Christie's) $408

A 1970's elaborate 'Stars and Stripes' stage suit designed by Bob Mackie, with maker's label 'Cotroneo, Mr Elton John' stitched to inside pocket, and matching top hat with maker's label 'Bob Mackie' stitched inside. (Christie's)$1,859

Elton John — an extremely rare album, 'The Bread and Beer Band', with ten tracks produced by Chris Thomas and Tony King on hand-written 'Rubbish Records' label, features 'Reg Dwight' on keyboards, 'Roger Pope' on drums and 'Caleb Quaye' guitar. (Christie's) $3,160

The Sex Pistols — an early promotional handbill featuring Johnny Rotten, Steve Jones and Glen Matlock, lithographed in two colors, circa 1975. (Christie's) $669

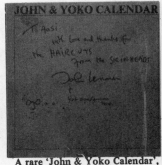

A 'Travelling Wilburys' 45 r.p.m. picture sleeve signed by Roy Orbison in gold felt pen, 7x7in. (Christie's) $316

A shimmering stage jacket of turquoise lurex, lined in brown, with two stills of Elvis Costello and the Attractions. (Christie's) $743

A rare 'John & Yoko Calendar', the cover signed and inscribed in John Lennon's handwriting 'To Aasi with love and thanks for the haircuts from the skinheads, John Lennon'. (Christie's) $1,673

An Angus McBean portrait of The Beatles 1970, signed and dated by photographer on mount, 12 x 9in.(Christie's) $1,115

An 'Old England' Apple wristwatch, unused with original box and packaging. (Phillips) $519

A rare 35mm. motion picture print of a screen test for Mick Jagger in the role of Antonin Artaud in the Silver Screen film 'Wings of Ash', 1978. (Christie's) $1,673

A machine print group photograph signed and inscribed 'To Leslie love from the Beatles, John Lennon xxx' and 'Love from George Harrison xxx', 'Paul McCartney xxx' and 'Love Ringo Starr xxx', 8¼ x 10¼in. (Christie's) $1,208

A colored magazine cover illustrating the four Beatles, 1964, signed and inscribed 'Love from The Beatles, Paul McCartney xxx', 'George Harrison xxx', 'John Lennon xxx', and 'Ringo Starr xxx'. (Christie's) $1,673

Derek and the Dominoes — a presentation 'Gold' disc, 'Layla', inscribed 'Presented to Eric Clapton to recognise sales in the United Kingdom of more than 500,000 copies of the Polydor single "Layla" 1982'. (Christie's) $5,577

A presentation 'Silver' disc, inscribed 'Presented to Virgin Retail Ltd. in recognition of helping to achieve sales in excess of 300,000 copies Mike Oldfield "Tubular Bells" '. (Christie's) $650

The Sex Pistols — a printed inner sleeve decorated with photomechanical portraits of Paul Cook, Steve Jones , Johnny Rotten and Sid Vicious, signed and inscribed 'Love from Sid Vicious xxx'. (Christie's) $1,208

Prince — a presentation 'Gold' disc, 'When doves cry', the single mounted above a plaque, 16¾ x 12¾in., framed and glazed. (Christie's) $2,619

One of a set of seven previously unpublished photographs by Michael Randolph, each taken during the filming of the 'Rolling Stones Rock 'n' Roll Circus Show', 1968.(Christie's) $4,833

An original artist's proof for the album cover 'Never Mind The Bollocks Here's The Sex Pistols', 1977. (Christie's) $557

An 18in. cymbal signed by all four members of The Who, Roger Daltrey, Pete Townshend, John Entwistle and Keith Moon. (Christie's) $1,580

The Beatles — an album cover for the soundtrack of 'A Hard Day's Night', signed and inscribed by each member of the group in blue and black biro, 12 x 12in. (Christie's) $2,230

Sting's Fender Stratocaster guitar, with rosewood neck and cream/ivory finish, serial number E471849, signed. (Phillips) $5,160

Fleetwood Mac — a presentation 'Platinum' disc, inscribed 'Presented to Mick Fleetwood to recognise the sale in the United Kingdom of more than £1,000,000 worth of the Warner Bros. long playing Album "Rumours" 1977'. (Christie's) $2,028

Phil Collins — an autographed drum skin, signed and inscribed 'Thank you for all your help! Cheers, Phil Collins, this was used on my 16in. Floor Tom Tom throughout the early Genesis albums'. (Christie's) $2,788

Elvis Presley — a casual short-sleeved shirt of white jersey decorated with black 'domino' squares and a pair of navy and white patent leather shoes by Johnston & Murphy.(Christie's) $1,208

A good souvenir programme for The Beatles in concert with Roy Orbison 1963, signed by The Beatles, Roy Orbison, Gerry and The Pacemakers and David Macbeth.(Christie's) $1,673

The Beatles — A polychrome film poster for 'Help', United Artists, 1969, 28 x 39in.; with a polychrome film poster for 'A Hard Day's Night', United Artists, 1964. (Christie's) $464

An autographed single 'I am the Walrus', Capital Records, 45 r.p.m., Lennon's annotations on the label including underlining his own name.(Christie's) $3,718

Two handwritten verses of a poem illustrated with a cartoon caricature of a 'Humbled fat man' seated beneath a tree, signed and inscribed, 'To Leslie . . . love, John Lennon xxx', 8¾ x 7¾in. (Christie's) $5,948

Wings — a duplicate copy presentation 'Platinum' disc, 'Back to the Egg', bearing the R.I.A.A. Certificate Sales Award, and inscribed, 'Presented to Linda McCartney'. (Christie's) $1,022

Two pages from an autograph book, one signed by Jimi Hendrix and Mitch Mitchell, the other by Noel Redding. (Christie's) $836

The Beatles/John Lennon — a presentation 'Gold' disc, for 'Something', the single mounted above a plaque bearing R.I.A.A. Certified Sales Award, and inscribed 'Presented to John Ono Lennon'. (Christie's) $7,436

Eric Broadbelt, 'Jimi Hendrix', watercolor heightened with white, initialled and dated 'EB '67', signed and inscribed, 11¾ x 9in. (Christie's) $464

A presentation 'Gold' disc, 'The Beatles 1967-1970', the album mounted above a plaque bearing R.I.A.A. Certified Sales Award and inscribed 'Presented to George Harrison'. (Christie's) $3,532

A polychrome tour poster for 'Jimi Hendrix Experience, presented by Lippmann and Rau', 47 x 33in.(Christie's) $464

1970 Mercedes-Benz 600 Pullman four door limousine, ordered by John Lennon, built to his specifications and delivered to him of February 19th 1970. (Christie's) $232,375

A mirrored heart shaped 'bracelet', 3½ x 5in., signed and inscribed 'Love God P '88 x', reputedly worn by Prince on his recent 'Love Sexy '88' tour. (Christie's) $304

A Dezo Hoffmann portrait photograph of The Beatles at EMI's Abbey Road studio during transmission of the world-wide television show 'Our World' June 1967. (Christie's) $353

A presentation 'Gold' disc, inscribed 'Presented to Al Green to commemorate the sale of more than 500,000 copies of the Hi Records album and cassette "Call Me". (Christie's) $1,580

A page from an autograph book signed and inscribed 'Best Wishes, Elvis Presley', 2¾ x 4½in., in common mount with a head and shoulders color machine print photograph. (Christie's) $408

The Police — a presentation 'Platinum' disc 'Zenyatta Mondatta', the LP mounted above a plaque. (Christie's) $408

The Beatles — a presentation 'Gold' disc, 'Abbey Road', the LP mounted above a reduction of the album cover, framed and glazed. (Christie's) $5,948

A copy of the Marriage Certificate of James Paul McCartney and Linda Eastman solemnized at the St Marylebone Register Office in the City of Westminster on 12th. March, 1969. (Christie's) $371

A presentation 'Gold' disc, inscribed 'Presented to The Jacksons to commemorate the sale of more than 500,000 copies of the Epic Records album and cassette "Victory" '. (Christie's) $1,487

A rare autographed 'Abbey Road' LP sleeve, signed by each member. (Phillips) $2,236

A good set of autographs on black and white picture, circa 1964, signed by all four Beatles. (Phillips)$1,462

The Beatles, one of a collection of twelve 2¼in. and 35mm. color transparencies, circa 1964. (Phillips)$1,376

An 8 x 10in. black and white Apple publicity photograph of The Beatles, signed in full by all four, circa 1969. (Phillips) $1,462

A rare silkscreen printed poster from The Kaiserkeller-Hamburg, presenting 'Original Rock 'n' Roll bands — Rory Storm and his Hurican und The Beatles', 76 x 52cm., circa 1960. (Phillips) $5,504

A rare, early black and white promotional German postcard, signed by Elvis Presley on the front in black ink, circa 1959. (Phillips) $550

One of four good 2¼in. unpublished black and white negatives of Cliff Richard, circa early 1960's, with full coypright release. (Phillips) $223

A rare, late, signed promotional photograph of The Beatles, circa 1969/70, the photograph signed on the reverse by all four Beatles in different inks. (Phillips) $481

Twelve excellent unpublished negatives of The Rolling Stones, circa 1964, showing seven group shots, with full copyright release. (Phillips) $447

'Love Me Do/P.S. I Love You' Parlophone 45 — R4949, demonstration record, white label with red 'A' and misspelling of McCartney.(Phillips) $1,290

A set of Beatles autographs on an album page in blue ball-point pen, mounted with Brian Epstein's signature on a piece of paper, all in a common mount with two pictures of The Beatles measuring 33 x 41cm. (Phillips) $997

One of nine 2¼ in. black and white unpublished negatives of The Beatles outside and inside a small aeroplane, circa 1964. (Phillips) $602

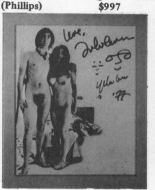

One of three rare Beatles 'pencil by number' coloring sets, each includes five numbered ready to color portraits of the Beatles, unused.(Phillips) $1,410

A signed 'Two Virgins' picture showing full frontal nude shot of John and Yoko signed 'love John Lennon, Yoko Ono '77', 24 x 19cm. (Phillips)$894

A good clearly signed Beatles concert programme from The Beatles 1964 UK Tour. (Phillips) $1,548

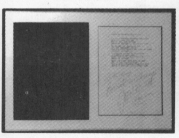

Gene Vincent, a good signed color picture, circa 1956, signed 'To Toni Regards Gene Vincent', 24 x 20cm.(Phillips) $189

The Doors, a signed typed lyric sheet 'Break on Through', the lyrics typed on a sheet of note paper, 22 x 15cm., signed. (Phillips) $1,032

Prince presentation R.I.A.A. platinum record for '1999', framed and glazed, 53x43cm. (Phillips) $1,032

A promotional photographic handbill 'The Beatles for their fans — an evening with John, Paul, George and Pete' at the Cavern, Thursday 5th April 1962. (Phillips) $2,064

'All you need . . . ' a very limited edition poster by Martin Sharp, silk screen on acetate. One of a series of seven Beatles songs published by Big O Posters in 1967. (Phillips) $447

An excellent original cartoon celluloid from 'Yellow Submarine' showing John, Paul and Ringo, 30 x 40cm. (Phillips) $894

A hardback copy of the book 'Thought in English Prose' by J. C. Dent, signed by Paul McCartney.(Phillips) $1,548

Elvis Presley - 'That's the Way It Is' a black cotton shirt printed in shades of brown as worn in the film c.1971. (Phillips) $10,150

A souvenir programme from the Albany Cinema, Maghull's 'Star Matinee in aid of The St Johns Ambulance Brigade,' Sunday October 15th 1961, performers included The Beatles and fifteen other acts. (Phillips) $653

An R.I.A.A. multi-platinum presentation disc 'Presented to Bill Medley to commemorate the sales of more than 6,000,000 copies of the RCA Records album and Cassette Dirty Dancing' c,1987. (Phillips) $2,595

A good John Lennon autograph on a sheet of 'Lennono' headed notepaper signed 'Love John Lennon' with two good facial caricatures of John and Yoko in black felt-tip pen, circa 1980. (Phillips) $1,238

John Lennon — 'Imagine' signed LP cover, signed on the front 'Love John Lennon' with a facial caricature in black felt tip pen. (Phillips)$1,892

Jimi Hendrix, a signed, typed lyric sheet for 'Are You Experienced', mounted with a reduction of the U.S. 'Are You Experienced' LP sleeve. (Phillips) $860

Madonna presentation R.I.A.A. platinum record for 'Like a Virgin', 'presented to Warner Bros. Records to commemorate the sale of more than 1,000,000 copies'. (Phillips) $1,032

Bill Haley and the Comets, a good signed 8 x 10in. black and white publicity photograph, circa 1955/6.(Phillips) $481

A postcard of the George V Hotel in Paris from Paul McCartney, 1964, reads 'Dear Jimmy and Gang, Having a lovely time here in Wales, but we don't understand what they're talking about — Ta Ta, Paul, John, George, Ringo'. (Phillips) $946

A maple wood finish Ludwig drum kit, circa 1971, belonging to Don Powell of Slade. (Phillips) $774

A page from the programme for the film 'Help!', signed in various inks by all four Beatles together with Brian Epstein, Cynthia Lennon, Pattie Boyd, Jane Asher, George Martin (and his wife Judy), Victor Spinetti, Roy Kinnear, Patrick Cargill, and Michael McGear. (Phillips) $3,979

A set of four colorful cardboard coat-hangers, one for each Beatle, unused, circa 1968, made by Henderson-Hoggand Inc. (Phillips) $344

A rare silkscreen printed concert poster from The Tower Ballroom — Merry-Go-land, New Brighton, which included The Beetles, 76 x 50.5cm. circa 1961. (Phillips) $3,784

Two facial caricatures of John and Yoko signed 'love from John Lennon and Yoko Ono', both on the same piece of paper in black ink. (Phillips)$1,032

Led Zeppelin, a set of eight concert tickets for a show at the Chicago Stadium on Wednesday November 12th 1980. (Phillips) $481

'Heartbreak Hotel' ten inch acetate with printed label 'Demonstration Record Not for Sale — The B.F. Wood Music Co., Mills House, London WC2'. (Phillips) $550

A signed, typed lyric sheet for the song 'Little Wing', signed beneath 'Love Jimi Hendrix', in black ballpoint pen, 31.5 x 42cm. (Phillips) $860

An original copy of 'Mersey Beat' January 4-18 1962, (Vol. 1 No.13), showing the headline 'Beatles Top Poll'. (Phillips) $4,128

Buddy Holly, The Lubbock High School 'Westerner' yearbook 1953, signed by Buddy Holly on his photograph. (Phillips) $5,160

The Clash, R.I.A.A. presentation platinum disc for 'Combat Rock', 'presented to Rick Carroll to commemorate the sale of more than 1,000,000 copies of the Clash record album 'Combat Rock'. (Phillips) $481

Sgt. Pepper's Lonely Hearts Club Band — signed on the inside cover by all four Beatles in black felt tip pen. (Phillips) $2,236

John Lennon, a signed copy of the LP 'Double Fantasy', signed clearly on the front cover in black felt tip pen. (Phillips) $1,548

George Harrison — presentation R.I.A.A. platinum disc 'presented to WDNG to commemorate the sale of more than 1,000,000 copies of the Dark House'. (Phillips) $1,376

'A Hard Days Night' original
UK film poster, circa 1964,
together with ten issues of
'The Beatles Monthly Book',
and a fan club card. (Phillips)
$447

Jimi Hendrix's 'Disc and Music
Echo — Valentine Pop Poll'
award for 1969, where he was
named 'best guitarist in the
world'. (Phillips) $3,784

A colorful promotional
concert poster for a show at
the ABC Theatre in Hudders-
field, 6th May (1964), in
excellent condition (folded),
76 x 112cm. (Phillips)
$447

A complete set of Beatles
Christmas flexi-discs (dating
from 1963-1969 inclusive), all
copies retain their original
picture sleeves. (Phillips)
$722

A programme from January
1964 entitled 'Group Scene
'64', with The Ronnettes
and Rolling Stones, signed
on the front cover. (Phillips)
$722

The Hollies — former bass
player Eric Haydock's Fender
Precision bass guitar, Sunburst,
manufactured October 1955.
(Phillips) $2,236

John Lennon and Yoko Ono's
Art Deco etched glass table
lamp, sold with a certificate
of authenticity, signed by
Yoko Ono. (Phillips)
$1,376

Derek and the Dominoes at
the Fairfield Hall, Croydon,
Sunday 20th September (1970),
concert poster, 76 x 102cm.
(Phillips) $412

A 10 x 8in. black and white
photograph of Elvis on stage
circa 1975, signed clearly on
the front 'Best Wishes, Elvis
Presley'. (Phillips) $481

A Hamadan rug, Northwest Persia, early 20th century, with a rust vine and boteh main border, 5ft. x 6ft.4in. (Robt. W. Skinner Inc.) $600

An East Caucasian prayer rug, late 19th century, the blue-black field with ivory mihrab and repeating ram's horn motifs, 5ft. x 3ft.6in. (Robt. W. Skinner Inc.) $500

A Kashan rug, the dark blue field woven with a floral and palmette trellis, the tendrils in pale blue, 6ft.6in. x 4ft.2in. (Lawrence Fine Arts) $3,384

An Erivan rug, the brick-red field with the classical Caucasian design of a stylized dragon and palmette lattice, 5ft.7in. x 4ft.1in. (Christie's) $925

A Karabagh prayer rug, South Caucasus, late 19th/early 20th century, the midnight blue mihrab with all-over "crab" motifs, 3ft.3in. x 5ft.5in. (Robt. W. Skinner Inc.) $425

An Azerbaijan area rug, Northwest Persia, South Caucasus, early 20th century, the stepped rust medallion inset with large palmettes and bird motifs, 5ft.6in. x 8ft.7in. (Robt. W. Skinner Inc.) $1,800

A Maslaghan rug, the rust field woven with florettes and a blue medallion, 6ft.8in. x 4ft.5in. (Lawrence Fine Arts) $676

An English School woollen carpet, the purple field with dark green floral pattern within a turquoise, red and salmon pink border of stylized flowerheads, 293.5cm x 407cm. (Christie's) $1,673

An Agra rug, the pale blue green field woven with scattered palmettes in cream, magenta and orange, 7ft x 4ft.1in. (Lawrence Fine Arts)$1,194

An antique Senneh rug, the serrated ivory field, with an allover stylized foliate pattern within a flame-red palmette, 6ft.8in. x 4ft.4in. (Phillips) $2,340

A pile carpet in the Savonnerie style woven in various colors, the center with a radiating flowerhead, late 18th century, 13ft. 9in. x 13ft. 1in. (Christie's) $32,164

An India hemp scatter rug, early 20th century, of Nile pattern, 5ft.11in. x 3ft. (Robt. W. Skinner Inc.) $1,100

An antique Agra carpet, the shaped ivory field with an allover symmetrical design of palmettes, 14ft.7in. x 11ft.8in. (Phillips) $7,920

A rare yarn sewn hearth rug, America, early 19th century, in shades of blue, green, gold, beige, brown and red, 58in. long. (Robt. W. Skinner Inc.) $13,000

A Scottish School woollen carpet, the design attributed to Charles Rennie Mackintosh, the green field with oval panel of lilac, green, puce and beige stylized flowers, 193 x 290cm. (Christie's) $1,496

A Persian rug, possibly Nain, the cream field woven with lotus palmette scrolls in pale blue, 7ft x 4ft.8in. (Lawrence Fine Arts) $1,114

A George II needlework carpet woven in well preserved colors with the arms of Palmer impaling Harpur and motto *Par Sit Fortuna Labori*, 10ft. 3in. x 8ft. 2in. (Christie's) $68,112

A Hamadan rug, Northwest Persia, early 20th century, with overall Mina Khani design, 6ft.6in. x 4ft.6in. (Robt. W. Skinner Inc.) $850

A Sennah rug, the off white field woven with an herati pattern, 6ft.4in. x 4ft.8in. (Lawrence Fine Arts) $1,692

A pictorial hooked cotton rug, American, late 19th/early 20th century, with central oval depicting a three masted ship, 30 x 43¼in. (Christie's) $550

A Peripedil rug, the rich dark blue field woven with ram's horn motifs, 6ft. x 4ft.5in. (Lawrence Fine Arts) $3,762

An Isphan rug, the cream field woven with lotus tendrils, centered by a rust lobed pole medallion, 7ft.2½in. x 4ft.11in. (Lawrence Fine Arts) $3,479

One of a pair of Kashan rugs, each with a midnight blue field, 7ft. x 4ft.3in. (Lawrence Fine Arts)
Two $1,598

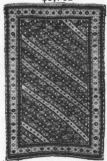

A Genje rug, the red, white, blue and yellow diagonal stripes woven with rows of hooked cubes, 6ft.3in. x 3ft.8in. (Lawrence Fine Arts) $1,354

A Kazak corridor carpet, the dark blue field woven with six hooked chamfered rectangular lozenges, 10ft.5in. x 4ft. (Lawrence Fine Arts) $1,279

A Qum rug, the brick field woven with a Shah Abbas design, 5ft.4in. x 3ft.7in. (Lawrence Fine Arts) $940

A Hammadan runner, the cream field woven with rows of small boteh, 15ft.8in. x 3ft.1in. (Lawrence Fine Arts) $526

SAMPLERS

An early 19th century needle-work sampler by Lehizo Maria Dolores Gomez, the linen ground embroidered in colored silks with a farmyard scene, 35x57cm. (Phillips) $661

A sampler by Ann Watkins, 1811, worked in colored silks with a verse, and a scene depicting Adam and Eve, 16 x 4in. (Christie's) $900

A needlework sampler, "Apphia Amanda Young's sampler wrought in the twelfth year of her age July 22 A.D. 1833", probably New Hampshire, 17in. wide. (Robt. W. Skinner Inc.) $1,200

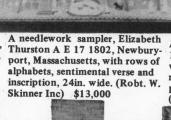

A long sampler worked in blue, purple, pink, yellow and green, by Mary Phippard 1685, 39 x 9½in., English 1685. (Christie's) $3,742

A needlework sampler, Elizabeth Thurston A E 17 1802, Newbury-port, Massachusetts, with rows of alphabets, sentimental verse and inscription, 24in. wide. (Robt. W. Skinner Inc) $13,000

A sampler by Alice Hester, 1651, worked in colored silks with rows of figures, Tudor roses and stylized flowering plants, 30 x 10in., 1651. (Christie's) $3,657

An early 18th century needle-work sampler by Hephzibah Tillsey finisht in the eleventh year of my age in the year 1728, 51cm. x 37cm. (Phillips) $1,122

A Queen Anne large strip sampler worked with cross and satin stitch with a verse and date 1710, 35in. x 10in. (David Lay) $995

An early 19th century needle-work sampler by Ann McGill, the canvas ground embroidered mainly in shades of green and brown colored silks, 52x45cm. (Phillips) $609

SAMPLERS

A sampler by ME, 1678, worked in colored silks, with a central wreath surrounding the letters, 15 x 11in. probably Dutch, 17th century. (Christie's) $2,150

A late 18th century Dutch needlework sampler by Maria Cornelia van der Bilde Oude 10 Iaar 1784, 46cm. x 44.5cm., lined. (Phillips) $448

A needlework sampler "Betsy Davis's sampler wrought at eight years of age, Providence October 22 1794", Balch School, Providence, Rhode Island, 11¾ x 8in. (Robt. W. Skinner Inc.) $1,700

A needlework sampler, Joanna Maxwell, Warren, Rhode Island, dated 1793, made by Joanna Maxwell, born May the 8 A D 1782 at Warren and further inscribed Wrought at Warren, September the 12 A D 1793. (Robt. W. Skinner Inc.) $40,000

An early 19th century needlework sampler by Sarah Mitton finish'd April 2nd in the year of our Lord 1825, 31cm. x 33cm. (Phillips) $598

A late 18th century needlework sampler by Jane Doughty, the linen ground embroidered in colored silks designed with Adam and Eve in the Garden of Eden, 62 x 53cm. (Phillips) $3,480

Needlework sampler "Polley Woodbery her sampler A 14 1787 Essex, Massachusetts', 10½ x 8in. (Robt. W. Skinner Inc.) $700

A sampler by Ann Diggle, Rochdale Free English School, 1820, worked in black silk with a verse "the interest of the poor", 18 x 17in. (Christie's) $598

A sampler by Charlott Webb, worked in brown silk with a verse "Happy the man", 16 x 12in., first half of 19th century. (Christie's) $411

A mid-18th century needle-work sampler by Ann Clowes, the linen ground embroidered in autumnal colored silks designed with a verse, 45 x 32cm. (Phillips) $1,218

An early 19th century needle-work sampler by Elizabeth Eady aged 10 years 1834, 31.5cm. x 29.5cm., framed and glazed. (Phillips) $673

A fine sampler, by Martha Mabe, 1837, worked in colored silks with a large house, caption and various spot motifs, 18 x 13in. (Christie's) $3,179

An early 18th century needle-work sampler by Suzannah Jeffery, the linen ground embroidered in mainly red, green, yellow and blue wools, 48 x 25cm. (Phillips) $730

An early Victorian needle-work sampler by Martha Bitterson, signed and in-scribed 'Martha Bitterson/ her work/Aged 9 years 1841', 16½in. by 17½in. (Bearne's) $782

A George III linen sampler worked in polychrome threads with a verse and "Mary Hand finished this work in December '15, Piddletown 1801", 18 x 12in. (Hy. Duke & Son) $388

A sampler by Ann Ariss, 1756, worked in colored silks with a central hexagonal border framing the Lord's Prayer, 15 x 12in. (Christie's) $411

A late 18th century darning sampler, by Maria Jesup 1799, the linen ground embroidered in mainly red, green and ochre silks, 45 x 42cm. (Phillips) $1,470

An early 19th century needle-work sampler by Ann Essex aged 10, born Sept 18 1800, Surfleet Lincolnshire, 42.5cm. x 31cm. (Phillips) $785

SHOES

A pair of ladies' shoes of grape colored leather, with sharply pointed toes and low wedge heels, circa 1790. (Christie's) $1,925

An unusual pair of shoes, probably for a young man, of netted string over pink cotton, circa 1810, possibly Colonial. (Christie's) $635

A pair of ladies' shoes of red morocco trimmed with bottle green silk ribbon and with bottle green kid heels, circa 1790. (Christie's) $1,346

A pair of black velvet shoes, the black velvet straps with eyelets with a black kid rand and a low wedge heel, circa 1790. (Christie's) $346

A pair of mule slippers of maroon velvet, embroidered with gold thread with three carnation-type flowers, with a maroon velvet sock, circa 1700. (Christie's) $19,250

A pair of ladies' shoes of pink kid and buff cotton, the pink kid toes slashed to reveal cotton and resemble sandals, circa 1795. (Christie's) $1,683

A pair of mid 19th century kid shoes with green satin uppers trimmed with lace and green ribbon rosettes, circa 1850's. (Phillips) $4,810

A pair of ladies' lace-up boots, the fronts of scarlet glace leather with red covered Louis heel 3½in. high, circa 1889. (Christie's) $1,028

A pair of ladies' clogs of white satin trimmed with silver lace, 7in. long, early 18th century. (Christie's) $935

A pair of Indian embroidered shoes with curled toes, embroidered with floral rosettes of gilt thread and sequins, 1857. (Christie's) $261

A lady's mule of yellow and brown silk brocade woven with abstract designs and cartouches, 2.5in. high, 10in. long, circa 1660. (Christie's) $25,025

A pair of clogs of black kid bound with morocco braid, with wide blue linen band across the toe cap, probably late 18th century. (Christie's) $311

A pair of gentlemen's heelless shoes of blue glace leather, edged with blue silk, circa 1810. (Christie's) $4,235

A pair of ladies' shoes of ivory damask with a white kid rand, circa 1750. (Christie's) $4,042

A fine pair of yellow satin shoes applied allover with narrow strips of yellow braid, circa 1730. (Christie's) $7,854

A pair of ladies' pink silk shoes with a 3in. high Italian heel lined with ivory kid, circa 1770. (Christie's) $1,951

A pair of ladies' white satin square toed boots, front fastening with three pairs of ribbon ties over a tongue, lined with white wool, circa 1820. (Christie's) $1,122

A pair of shoes of fine canvas worked in colored beads with sprays of poppies and other flowers, labelled N. G. Soderlund, Stockholm, circa 1840. (Christie's) $486

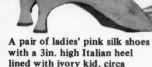

A pair of 1900's wedding shoes, the ivory silk uppers and cross bar embroidered with diamante and glass beads. (Phillips) $142

A pair of ladies' button boots, the front of gilt leather with a stitched scallopped edge, with a gilt painted Louis 4in. heel, 1880's. (Christie's) $6,545

A pair of pink silk shoes, the toes embroidered with metal sequins and coiled metal braid with a floral spray design, circa 1760. (Christie's) $6,545

A pair of gentleman's slippers with a square domed toe, the ivory suede upper covered with pink damask, 1720's. (Christie's) $1,828

A pair of ladies' shoes of purple silk the latchets and heel covered with sky blue silk, 2in. high wedge heel, circa 1775-85. (Christie's) $2,021

A pair of ladies' black cotton shoes with a low wedge heel and pointed toe, circa 1790. (Christie's) $3,850

A massive Victorian oval basket, with cast scroll and acanthus handles, bearing plaques recording the 90th birthday of the Earl of Stradbroke, London 1878, 29in. long, 270oz. (Prudential) $58,140

A late Victorian pierced molded oval fruit basket chased with rococo floral and foliate swags, Charles Stuart Harris, London 1875, 13in., 31.75oz.(Christie's) $1,732

A George III oval pierced cake basket, by Wakelin and Garrard, London 1794, 15in. long, 39½oz. (Prudential) $4,446

A good George IV fruit basket of rectangular shape with ribbed handle. (David Lay) $253

An oval silver gilt cake basket, with swing handle decorated en suite, by Nichols & Plincke, St. Petersburg, 1871, 23.3cm. long, 476.2gr. (Christie's) $929

A foliate pierced and fluted oval fruit basket, applied with rococo floral and foliate handles and with a scroll rim, London 1915, 8¾in., 22.50oz. (Christie's) $924

A fine George II shaped oval bread basket, with a reed-and-tie band and shell and scroll ornament, by Christian Hillan, 1741, 13½in. long, 68ozs. (Christie's) $47,300

An attractive George III swing handled cake basket of shaped oval form, the open wired sides applied with fruiting vines, by Emick Romer, 1766-32ozs. (Phillips) $4,498

An early George III swing handle fruit basket, by Richard Mills, probably 1770, 37oz. (Phillips) $3,740

BASKETS

An oval silver trompe-l'oeil basket, with twisted ropework handles, on four pierced feet, possibly by Piotr Loskutov, Moscow, 1882, 40cm. long, 723gr. (Christie's)
$2,230

A George II oval cake basket, the center engraved with arms within a foliate mantling, 1755 by Edward Aldridge and John Stamper, 27.6oz.
(Lawrence Fine Arts)
$4,042

An 18th century Dutch shaped oval basket, with bead borders and pierced sides, on beaded cushion feet, by Jan Hendrick Middelhuysen, Amsterdam, 1784, 42.8cm. long, 32.25ozs.
(Phillips) $5.536

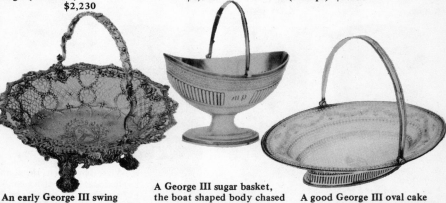

An early George III swing handled fruit or cake basket, with an applied cast border of gadrooning, 38cm long, by S.Herbert & Co.,1767, 48½ozs. (Phillips)
$6,300

A George III sugar basket, the boat shaped body chased with vertical lobes below a vermiculated band. 1795 by Robert and David Hennell, 17cm. overall height, 8.2oz.
(Lawrence Fine Arts)
$799

A good George III oval cake basket, 1783 maker's mark of James Sutton and James Bult over-striking that of another, 35.3cm., 25.2oz. (Lawrence Fine Arts) $4,114

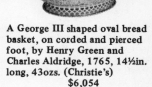

An important George II shaped oval bread basket, on four cast panther-head feet, by Paul De Lamerie, 1740, 14½in. long, 66ozs. (Christie's)
$350,020

A Victorian swing handled circular cake basket with trailing wheatsheaf rim, by Harrison Bros & Howson, Sheffield, 1857, 44.5oz.
(Phillips) $3,740

A George III shaped oval bread basket, on corded and pierced foot, by Henry Green and Charles Aldridge, 1765, 14½in. long, 43ozs. (Christie's)
$6,054

BEAKERS

A late 17th century Danish beaker, with broad stippled band to body and engraved armorial within oval cartouche, circa 1680, 4¼in. high. (Bonhams) $787

A German parcel gilt beaker and cover, on three ball feet, circa 1710, maker's mark S.W.P., presumably for Sigmund Wolfgang Preuss, 6½in. high. (Christie's) $4,026

A Danish tapering cylindrical beaker, on three ball feet, by Giert Reber, Viborg, circa 1750, 3¼in. high, 114grs. (Christie's) $1,097

A German silver gilt tapering cylindrical beaker, punched with a broad band of matting and with a molded rim, by Johann Seutter, Augsburg, circa 1680, 3¾in. high, 162gr. (Christie's) $2,616

A pair of plique-a-jour enamelled and gilt beakers, by P. Ovchinnikov with the Imperial warrant, Moscow, 1899-1908, 3¾in. high. (Christie's) $8,365

A Victorian beaker, the almost cylindrical body with a band of reciprocating pear shape lobes, 1862 by George Angell, 12.8cm. (Lawrence Fine Arts) $287

A late 17th century German beaker of tapering shape, embossed with large flowers and swirling foliage, by Johann Hoffler, 9.2cm. high, 5.5ozs. (Phillips) $1,903

A late 17th century German parcel gilt beaker of usual tapering form, probably by Johann Hoffler, Nuremburg, circa 1685, 8.9cm. high, 3.5oz. (Phillips) $1,963

A rare silver beaker by Samuel Kirk, Baltimore, circa 1840, deeply repousse and chased with buildings surrounded by flowers and trees, 3½in. high, 4½oz. (Christie's) $1,485

BOWLS

An Edwardian punch bowl, the hemispherical body with narrow vari-height flutes. Sheffield 1901 by Fenton Brothers Ltd. 27.5cm. diameter. 37.7oz. (Lawrence Fine Arts) $1,617

A Hukin and Heath electroplated two handled bowl with hinged cover decorated with four engraved roundels of stylized floral motifs, designed by Dr C. Dresser and date code for 26th March 1879, 19.1cm. high. (Christie's) $16,830

A late Victorian punch bowl, the lower part of the hemispherical body with swirl flutes, 1895, by Job Frank Hall of Sibray, Hall and Co, 28.8cm. diam., 31.5oz. (Lawrence Fine Arts) $662

A heavy Celtic Revival bowl, the almost hemispherical body with a lightly hammered finish, 1937 by the Goldsmiths and Silversmiths Company Ltd., 17.5cm. across handles, 13.3oz. (Lawrence Fine Arts) $228

A good Japanese rose bowl, of quatrefoil form, by Kunn & Komor, circa 1900 (base inscribed), 21.9cm. diam. (Phillips) $2,187

A Georg Jensen footed bowl, hemispherical form with inverted rim, supported by eight foliate brackets on concave circular base, London import marks for 1930, 11.5cm. high, 505 grams. (Christie's) $1,084

A footed bowl by John and John B. Jones, Boston, circa 1820, on a stepped circular foot, the everted rim with a gadrooned border, 5½in. high, 17oz. (Christie's) $330

A fine George III bowl, of hemispherical shape, the rim with laurel leaf and bead swags, the sides applied with similar motifs and rosettes by James Young,1773, 11½cm. high, 18cm. diam., 24½ozs. (Phillips) $8,050

A Georg Jensen silver bowl, supported on leaves and berried stems above a spreading circular foot, 17.2cm. high. (Phillips) $2,024

BOXES

A German decorative casket of rectangular bombe form, die stamped with masks within wreaths, import marks for 1897, psuedo 18th century Augsburg marks. (Lawrence Fine Arts) $962

An attractive late 19th century French enamel and silver gilt box depicting courting couples in 18th century costume, circa 1890, 5.2cm. long. (Phillips) $560

An A. E. Jones Arts and Crafts silver and copper jewellery casket, with a turquoise enamelled disc and pierced heart-shaped hinge, Birmingham hallmarks for 1929, 13.6cm. long. (Christie's) $1,115

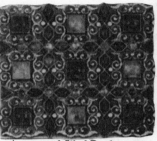

A Victorian Aesthetic Movement swing handled biscuit box, the curved body with twin fan shaped covers engraved with birds, circa 1880. (Phillips) $735

An unusual late 19th century German parcel gilt charity box, the hexagonal body modelled as a synagogue, circa 1880, 10cm. high, 2ozs. (Phillips) $787

An unusual Sibyl Dunlop gemset rectangular silver box, embellished with scrollwork in relief, punctuated by square cabochons of rose quartz, 7.3cm. x 6.5cm., 1929. (Phillips) $1,118

A John Paul Cooper shagreen circular box and cover, with finely worked silver bands, having wooden interior, 7.5cm. diam. (Phillips) $561

An Old Sheffield plate box of circular shape, chased on cover with a cloaked figure holding a spear, circa 1765, 5.6cm. diam. (Phillips) $87

A German oval toilet box and cover, the sides chased with flowers and acanthus foliage, by Daniel Michael II, Augsburg, circa 1675, 5¼in. long, 170grs. (Christie's) $2,081

BOXES

A cigarette box, by Ramsden and Carr, the bowed hand-hammered sides with applied entrelac band, London, 1908, 3¾ x 3¼ in. (Bonhams) $1,202

An interesting theatrical presentation cigar box of plain rectangular form, the cover engraved with an inscription and along with the four sides numerous facsimile signatures. (Lawrence Fine Arts) $1,251

A Victorian oblong box, the cover chased in low relief with a pastural scene, cows grazing and rabbits in the foreground, by F.B. Thomas, 1879, 18.4cm. x 13.3cm., 20ozs. (Phillips) $1,365

An 18th century Dutch tobacco box of square form with curved corners, Amsterdam marks, 6½in. high, 22½oz. (Prudential) $9,234

A rare stone set silver box with key by Tiffany & Company, New York, the hinged cover set with seven carved and polished amber stones, 3¼in. high, gross weight 22½oz. (Christie's) $7,700

A circular niello and silver gilt box, the lift-off cover with a courting couple, unmarked, Moscow, circa 1770, 6cm. diam. 110.9gr. (Christie's) $2,416

BUCKLES

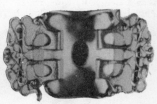

A Liberty hammered silver and enamelled belt buckle, the pierced floral decoration enamelled in blue and green, Birmingham hall marks for 1910. 7.5cm. long. (Christie's) $935

A pair of Regency paste buckles, in original fish skin case. (Prudential) $650

A Liberty & Co. 'Cymric' silver belt buckle, set with an oval cabochon lapis lazuli, stamped 'Cymric', L & Co and Birmingham hallmarks for 1900, 11cm. long. (Christie's) $557

A George III caddy spoon, the deep shell shaped bowl with scalloped edge, by Joseph Taylor, Birmingham, 1804. (Phillips) $281

A rare Victorian novelty caddy spoon modelled as a broom or besom with simulated wood handle, by George Fox, 1867, 16.6cm. (Phillips) $1,196

A George III caddy spoon with acorn bowl, engraved with prick-dot diaperwork maker's mark an incuse G.D. (untraced), Birmingham,1804. (Phillips) $281

An unusual, early Victorian caddy spoon the bowl of holly leaf shape, by Taylor and Perry, Birmingham, 1837. (Phillips) $448

A George III leaf caddy spoon, engraved veins with a wired twig handle, no maker's mark, Birmingham 1807. (Phillips) $121

A George III right hand caddy spoon, with bright engraved initialled, trefoil handle, by Joseph Taylor, Birmingham, 1806. (Phillips) $422

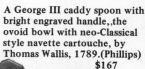

A George III caddy spoon with bright engraved oval bowl and zigzag borders to handle, by Alice & George Burrows, 1802. (Phillips) $149

A George III eagle's wing caddy spoon, the chased feathered bowl with a wired ring handle, by J. Wilmore, Birmingham, 1806. (Phillips) $168

A George III caddy spoon with bright engraved handle, the ovoid bowl with neo-Classical style navette cartouche, by Thomas Wallis, 1789.(Phillips) $167

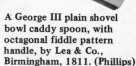

A George III caddy spoon, the oval bowl pierced with a border of arrowhead motifs, by George Brasier, 1796. (Phillips) $211

A good George III caddy spoon with flat rounded handle engraved with script initials, by Thomas Tookey, circa 1780. (Phillips) $387

A George III plain shovel bowl caddy spoon, with octagonal fiddle pattern handle, by Lea & Co., Birmingham, 1811. (Phillips) $96

A massive Victorian oak tree seven light candelabrum applied with acorns and oak leaves, Elkington & Co., Birmingham, 29¾in. overall. (Christie's) $1, 347

A very attractive pair of Old Sheffield Plate candlesticks with accompanying branches, 16½in. high, circa 1780. (Bonhams)
Two $1,416

An early 19th century Sheffield plate candelabrum with four curved branches supporting candleholders, 30in. high. (Prudential)
$1,539

A pair of late Victorian silver three light candelabra, London 1896, maker's mark Thomas Bradbury of Sheffield, 46cm. high, weight of branches 64¾oz. (Geering & Colyer)
$2,450

A Victorian four light candelabrum, with double scroll branches and shaped circular drip pans, 1860 by Robert Hennell, 54.5cm., 104.3oz. (Lawrence Fine Arts) $4,114

A pair of Art Nouveau plated metal figural candlesticks, designed by C. Bonnefond, each modelled as a girl with long hair, 36.5cm. high. (Phillips)
$2,197

A pair of early Elkington electro-plated three light candelabra, the shaped circular bases with vertical matted leafage, 59.5cm. overall height. (Lawrence Fine Arts)
$1,475

A Hagenauer chromium plated four branch candelabra, the forked tubular branches on knopped stem, 50.7cm. high. (Christie's) $4,089

One of a George IV magnificent matching pair of five light candelabra, of heavy gauge, by Charles and John Fry II, 1824/1825, 541oz. (Phillips) $67,320

A pair of candlesticks, each on shaped square base, by Elkington and Co., Sheffield, 1911, 11¾in. high. (Christie's)
$1,135

A Queen Anne taper stick, with spool nozzle, by John Fawdery, London 1707, 4in. high, 3½oz. (Prudential)
$5,130

A pair of late Victorian candlesticks, each on shaped square base, by William Hutton and Son Ltd., 1900, 11½in. high. (Christie's) $1,229

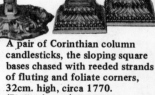

A rare pair of paktong candlesticks of Corinthian column design, late 18th century, 18in. (Lawrence Fine Arts)
$5,698

A set of four George II candlesticks of rococo design, possibly by John Edwards II, London 1748, 8½in. high, 61oz. (Prudential) $10,260

A pair of Corinthian column candlesticks, the sloping square bases chased with reeded strands of fluting and foliate corners, 32cm. high, circa 1770. (Phillips) $735

A pair of George III large table candlesticks, the circular bases with bands of wrapped pellets. Sheffield 1802 by John Green and Co. 32.7cm, loaded. (Lawrence Fine Arts) $1,427

A pair of Victorian novelty bedroom candlesticks, each modelled as three grotesque faces; one sleeping, one yawning and one smiling; 21cm. high, by Henry William Dee, 1878, 19½ozs. (Phillips)
$7,700

A pair of fine George II plain case candlesticks, each on shaped square base with sunken center, by Paul de Lamerie, 1739, 7¼in. high, 26ozs. (Christie's)
$34,056

CASTERS

An 18th century Dutch sugar dredger of octagonal form, the Hague, circa 1745, 15.5cm. high, 6oz. (Phillips) $1,683

A set of three George I plain octagonal pear shaped casters, 1724, maker's mark S.W. for Samuel Welder or Starling Wilford, 6in. and 7in. high, 19ozs. (Christie's) $5,297

A George II caster, the plain cup shape body with a molded girdle and rising neck, 1736 by Samuel Wood, 21cm., 21.1oz. (Lawrence Fine Arts) $1,040

Silver pepper box, by Thomas Coverly, Newburyport, Massachusetts, circa 1760, with knob finial and domed cover above the straight sided octagonal body, 3 troy oz. (Robt. W. Skinner Inc.) $4,800

A pair of embossed baluster muffineers with engraved armorials in cartouche, London, 1772, 10oz. (Tennants) $1,050

An Edwardian hammered baluster sugar caster by Ramsden & Carr with buntop, 1907, 17.5cm. high, 8ozs. (Phillips) $1,006

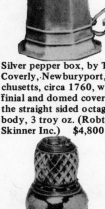

An Omar Ramsden hammered silver sugar caster, the elaborately pierced cover with beaded rim and Galleon plaque, London hallmarks for 1936, 15.3cm. high, 250 grams. (Christie's) $2,416

A set of three George I octagonal vase shaped casters, by Glover Johnson, 1720, 6¼in. and 7¼in. high, 18ozs. (Christie's) $8,514

A large inverted pear shaped sugar caster, the body decorated with two friezes of flowers and foliage, Arthur and Frank Parsons, London 1927, 9½in., 14.75oz. (Christie's) $673

CENTREPIECES

SILVER

A German white metal Art Nouveau centerpiece, decorated with pierced floral and scrolling decoration, on four pierced cabriole legs, 26.7cm. long, 250 grams without liner. (Christie's) $483

An unusual Victorian oval centerpiece with cut glass bowl with shaped rim, with several diamond registration marks for the 29th March 1876, overall height 9½in. (Christie's) $1,347

A Victorian three light beaded and gadrooned centerpiece supported by three recumbent camels on a shaped base, and a pair of dessert stands with glass bowls, en suite, (Christie's) $1,925

CHAMBERSTICKS

A George III gadrooned circular chamber candlestick with leaf-capped rising handle, Jonathan Alleine, London 1772, 7in., 12.25oz. (Christie's) $1,251

A Tiffany & Co unusual late 19th century American Aesthetic Movement parcel gilt chamberstick, with incurved sides, circa 1880, 11ozs. (Phillips) $10,500

A George III chamber candlestick, with circular dished base of plain form, engraved with crest within a tasselled cartouche, London 1787, 12oz., maker, John Scofield. (Henry Spencer) $1,253

CHOCOLATE POTS

A German hot water or chocolate pot, the baluster body divided into swirl lobes, Augsburg 1763-65 maker's mark probably that of Johann Christian Girschner, 26.5cm., 627g. (Lawrence Fine Arts) $4,919

A George III plain pear shaped chocolate pot, on spreading circular base and with fluted curved spout, by Francis Stamp 1780, 12in.high, 31ozs gross. (Christie's) $4,629

A silver chocolate pot by Tiffany & Company, New York, tapering cylindrical and partly reeded, on a molded circular foot, marked, 9¼in. high, gross weight 31oz. (Christie's) $3,300

CIGARETTE CASES

A French Art Deco lacquered and eggshell cigarette case, with broad band of crushed eggshell reserved against a black background, 10.3cm. (Phillips) $352

A cigarette case, sunburst pattern, yellow metal, St. Petersburg, 1908-1917, with unrecorded maker's initial LK, 10cm. long, 163.9gr. (Christie's) $2,416

An Austrian silver cigarette case, designed in the manner of Koloman Moser, set with a green-stained chalcedony cabochon, 8.5cm., 1902. (Phillips) $387

A Samorodok cigarette case, with cabochon sapphire gold mounted thumbpiece, white metal, by Ivan Arkharov, St. Petersburg, 1898-1903, 9.5cm. 172.8gr. gross. (Christie's) $483

A Soviet propaganda cigarette case, the foreground with crossed banners and Red Star, white metal, Moscow, 1927, 4½in. long, 162.8gr. gross. (Christie's) $1,394

A cigarette case, the cover cast with Napoleon mounted on a rearing horse, white metal, by Konstantin Skvortsov, Moscow, 1908-1917, 4½in. long, 204.6gr. (Christie's) $743

A stylish Art Deco cigarette case, formed by geometric segments of black, brown, brick-red and silver colored metal, 10.7cm. (Phillips) $264

An Art Nouveau hammered silver cigarette box, decorated in relief with an Art Nouveau maiden within a keyhole reserve, with Chester hallmarks for 1902, 12.5cm. long. (Christie's) $483

A French Art Deco cigarette case, with black lacquered background, punctuated with random squares of golden colored metal, 11.5cm. (Phillips) $158

CLARET JUGS

A Victorian 'Cellini' pattern claret jug, the ovoid body cast with masks in beaded cartouches, Birmingham 1872, by Frederick Elkington, 33.1oz. (Lawrence Fine Arts) $1,578

A Victorian novelty clear glass claret jug, formed as a seal, the hinged silver head and neck realistically chased with fur and inset with glass eyes, by William Leuchars, 1881, 12½in. long. (Christie's) $4,235

A Hukin & Heath claret jug designed by Dr Christopher Dresser, the tapering cylindrical clear glass body surmounted with white metal section, 9½in. high. (Christie's) $1,645

A Victorian silver and etched glass claret jug, by George Fox, London, 1895, with repousse and chased silver spout, 12½in. high. (Robt. W. Skinner Inc.) $600

A Hukin and Heath silver and glass claret jug, designed by Christopher Dresser, marked JWH/JTH for London 1879, 22.2cm. high. (Phillips) $1,936

An Elkington & Co. plated claret jug, designed by Christopher Dresser, date letter for 1885, 24.4cm. high. (Phillips) $44,000

A Victorian vase shaped claret jug, on molded shaped circular foot with scroll border, engraved with a coat-of-arms and crest, 1846, maker's mark T.H.H., 13¾in. high. (gross 41ozs.) (Christie's) $2,838

A mounted cut glass claret jug, engraved with the initial Z, white metal, marked Faberge, with Imperial warrant, Moscow, 1899-1908, 9in. high. (Christie's) $1,580

A good Victorian claret jug, the slender baluster body on a spreading foot. 1870 by John Edward, Walter and John Barnard. 36.5cm. 31.9oz. (Lawrence Fine Arts) $2,664

CLARET JUGS

A Victorian claret jug, the ovoid body chased with fruit and foliage within scroll panels, 1864 by Edward and John Barnard, 20.6oz. (Lawrence Fine Arts) $1222

A late Victorian claret jug, the oval diamond cut glass body etched with a golfer in full swing, circa 1880, 25.5cm. high. (Phillips) $1,522

A rare, mounted glass, ovoid shaped claret jug on circular foot with coronet pierced gallery collar, 34.5cm. high, 1922. (Phillips)$11,220

A Victorian claret jug, on spreading circular foot and with applied snake forming the handle, by E. and J. Barnard, 1866, 13in. high. (27ozs.) (Christie's) $3,027

A pair of silver-mounted cut-glass claret jugs, each of elongated baluster form on spreading chased silver foot, St. Petersburg, circa 1890, 15½in. high. (Christie's) $9,295

A Victorian pear-shaped claret jug, on domed foot, by Richard Martin and Ebenezer Hall, 1877, 14in. high. (gross 44ozs.) (Christie's) $2,459

A Victorian silver gilt mounted claret jug, the spherical glass body and rising neck etched with stars, Sheffield 1875 by William and George Sissons, 25.7cm. (Lawrence Fine Arts) $1,617

A good Victorian claret jug, the ovoid body with an electro-type band of a Bacchanalian orgy, 1874 by Henry William Curry, 32.2cm., 24.7oz. (Lawrence Fine Arts) $3,085

A mounted cut-glass claret jug, the tapering cylindrical glass body with stellar motif, white metal, marked Khlebnikov, with Imperial warrant, St. Petersburg, 1908-1917, 11¾in. high, 1263.8gr. gross. (Christie's) $2,602

COASTERS

A pair of Victorian Sheffield plate wine coasters, each circular with foliate and scroll embossed border. (Hobbs and Chambers) $312

A good coaster with slightly bevelled sides, the surface hammered and applied with a frieze of stylized leaf motifs, 1926, 5.2cm. high, 11.5cm. diam. (Phillips) $1,402

A fine pair of George IV silver wine coasters, having fluted bodies and beaded edges, Sheffield, circa 1826. (G. A. Key) $962

A pair of early Victorian Sheffield plate coasters, the panelled sides with grape vine borders. (Woolley & Wallis) $635

A George V two handled bottle holder of cylindrical form pierced and cast with stylized flower heads, London 1910, 535 grammes, 16.5cm. high. (Henry Spencer) $581

A pair of George IV circular wine coasters, the bases engraved with a band of foliage, by S.C. Younge & Co., Sheffield, 1827. (Christie's) $2,310

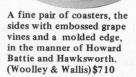

One of four George IV wine coasters, two by Rebecca Emes and Edward Barnard, 1820 and 1826. (Christie's)
Four $7,568

A fine pair of coasters, the sides with embossed grape vines and a molded edge, in the manner of Howard Battie and Hawksworth. (Woolley & Wallis)$710

A George III silver gilt wine coaster, the sides cast and pierced with bacchantes, lions and trailing vines, 5¾in. diam. (Christie's) $13,475

A George II coffee pot of baluster form cast in high relief, by Thomas England, London 1741, 9½in. high. 43oz all in. (Prudential) $10,260

A good early Victorian Scottish coffee pot, with a foliate knop finial and corkscrew thumbpiece, Edinburgh 1840 by J. McKay, 22cm., 31.9oz. (Lawrence Fine Arts) $2,159

A George II small coffee pot, the tapering body engraved with a shield of arms, date letter and maker's mark worn, 1739-1755, 20.5cm. high, 17.3oz. all in. (Lawrence Fine Arts) $1,324

A George III pedestal coffee pot, the lower part of the ogee baluster body chased with swirl beaded lobes, 1764 by William Shaw II, 30.7cm. 35.8oz all in. (Lawrence Fine Arts) $3,235

A George IV coffee pot, the baluster body chased with two scroll leaf cartouches engraved with a crest below vertical flutes. 1823 by John Bridge. 24.5cm. high, 28.6oz. (Lawrence Fine Arts) $875

A George III pedestal coffee pot, the high domed cover with a beaded rim, 1775 maker's mark I * M possibly an unregistered mark of Jacob Marsh, 32cm. high, 33oz. all in. (Lawrence Fine Arts) $4,114

A silver Martele coffee pot by Gorham Manufacturing Company, Providence, 1899, of baluster form, 10¼in. high, 32oz. (Christie's) $3,850

A George II tapering cylindrical coffee pot, with curved spout, hinged domed cover and bell shaped finial, by Ayme Videau, 1741, 8½in. high, gross 26ozs. (Christie's) $6,054

A George II Irish coffee pot, the tapering cylindrical body with contemporary bands of flat chased and engraved scroll foliage, Dublin 1734, mark probably David King, 23.8cm., 30oz. all in. (Lawrence Fine Arts) $5,965

CREAM JUGS

Dutch hallmarked figural creamer, circa 1900, of cow form, with hinged lid, 5½ troy oz. (Robt. W. Skinner Inc.) $550

A Victorian wirework swing-handled cream pail in the 18th century taste, with a blue glass liner, London 1857, 5¼in. overall. (Christie's) $423

A fine George II silver gilt cow creamer with textured body, by John Schuppe, 1756, 5oz. (Phillips) $24,310

An Irish helmet cream jug on lion mask and paw feet, sides chased with flowers and fish scale decoration, an unrecorded mark of George Moore of Limerick, circa 1765, 6ozs. (Phillips) $1,085

A Victorian novelty cream jug, modelled as a Chinaman, the handle his plaited hair, maker Thomas Smiley, London 1882, 2.5oz. (Woolley & Wallis) $756

A Georg Jensen silver cream jug, supported on three foliate feet and having a leaf and magnolia bloom handle, 7.5cm. high. (Phillips) $378

A cream jug by Ephraim Brasher, New York, 1775-1785, with a beaded rim and a twisted scroll handle, 5¼in. high, 4oz. (Christie's) $2,200

A George III cream pail, the cylindrical body pierced with an eagle, a leaping dog and a bird in flight, by Francis Spilsbury II, 1768, 3oz. (Phillips) $2,244

A George IV pear shaped cream jug, on three foliate scroll feet, by Paul Storr, 1821, 5in. high, 9ozs. (Christie's) $2,081

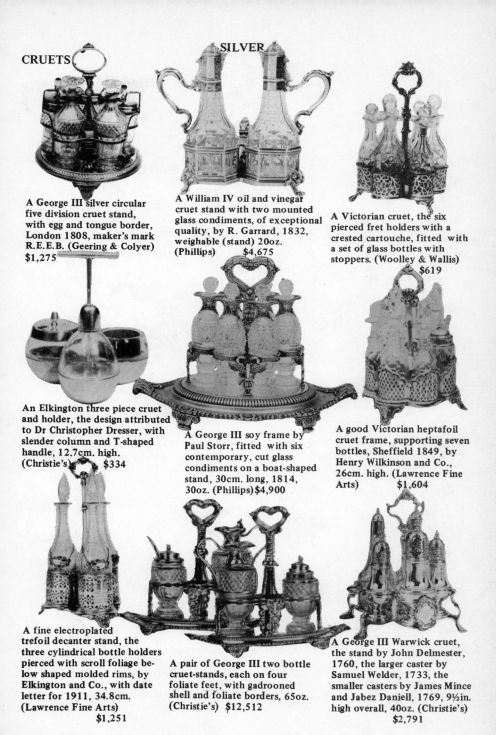

A George III silver circular five division cruet stand, with egg and tongue border, London 1808, maker's mark R.E.E.B. (Geering & Colyer) $1,275.

A William IV oil and vinegar cruet stand with two mounted glass condiments, of exceptional quality, by R. Garrard, 1832, weighable (stand) 20oz. (Phillips) $4,675

A Victorian cruet, the six pierced fret holders with a crested cartouche, fitted with a set of glass bottles with stoppers. (Woolley & Wallis) $619

An Elkington three piece cruet and holder, the design attributed to Dr Christopher Dresser, with slender column and T-shaped handle, 12.7cm. high. (Christie's) $334

A George III soy frame by Paul Storr, fitted with six contemporary, cut glass condiments on a boat-shaped stand, 30cm. long, 1814, 30oz. (Phillips) $4,900

A good Victorian heptafoil cruet frame, supporting seven bottles, Sheffield 1849, by Henry Wilkinson and Co., 26cm. high. (Lawrence Fine Arts) $1,604

A fine electroplated trefoil decanter stand, the three cylindrical bottle holders pierced with scroll foliage below shaped molded rims, by Elkington and Co., with date letter for 1911, 34.8cm. (Lawrence Fine Arts) $1,251

A pair of George III two bottle cruet-stands, each on four foliate feet, with gadrooned shell and foliate borders, 65oz. (Christie's) $12,512

A George III Warwick cruet, the stand by John Delmester, 1760, the larger caster by Samuel Welder, 1733, the smaller casters by James Mince and Jabez Daniell, 1769, 9½in. high overall, 40oz. (Christie's) $2,791

CUPS

A German wine cup, on circular foot, by Rabanus Raab I, Kalkar, 1697, 7in. high, 180gms. (Christie's) $2,270

A silver stirrup cup in the form of a stag's head, by Samuel Arnd, St. Petersburg, 1863, 8cm. high, 134.5gr. gross. (Christie's) $2,974

An interesting George III Irish two-handled cup, inscribed with motto 'Death or Glory', by Charles Townsend, Dublin, 1774, 14cm. high, 14.25oz. (Phillips)) $1,349

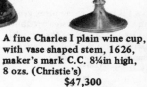

A Georg Jensen hammered silver and amethyst cup and cover, Copenhagen mark and London import marks for 1926, 19.9cm. high. (Christie's) $7,436

A pair of George II Irish two handle cups, the baluster bodies and pedestal feet chased with spiral and scaled fluting, 16cm. high, probably by John Gumley, Dublin, circa 1745, 30oz. (Phillips) $1,575

A fine Charles I plain wine cup, with vase shaped stem, 1626, maker's mark C.C. 8¼in high, 8 ozs. (Christie's) $47,300

A Dutch stirrup cup, the base naturalistically formed as a fox mask, apparently unmarked, silver colored metal, 12.6cm. (Lawrence Fine Arts) $794

A Channel Islands two handled christening cup, on slightly spreading foot, with everted rim and beaded scroll handles, circa 1784, 7.3cm. high, 108gr. (Christie's) $3,405

A German silver gilt mounted ivory cup and cover, by Hans Jakob Mair, Augsburg, circa 1680, the ivory split, 10½in. high. (Christie's) $18,920

A George I two handled plain baluster cup and cover, on circular foot with molded girdle, by Abraham Buteux, 1727, 98oz. (Phillips) $8,228

A late Victorian stirrup cup modelled as a fox's head, with circular cartouche, by Elkington & Co., Birmingham, 1897, 7.25oz. (Phillips) $1,828

A William IV two handled silver gilt cup and cover, chased with a band of oak foliage, by Barnard Bros., 1836, 10½in. high. (47ozs.) (Christie's) $3,784

A rare George I stirrup or tot cup of plain circular shape on cast spreading circular foot, by John Chartier, 1717, 3oz. (Phillips) $3,366

A covered silver mounted coconut cup, carved with medallions enclosing the portrait profiles of Peter the Great, Catherine I and Catherine II, Moscow, 1763, 10in. high. (Christie's) $1,673

A William IV silver gilt two handled cup, on a pedestal foot, the campana shaped body partly plain and with a flared rim, 29cm high, by E.,E. & J. Barnard, 1834, 60oz. (Phillips) $4,152

A two handled cup applied with Celtic style frieze and boss decoration incorporating various gem stones, height without plinth, 7in., 40.25oz. (Christie's) $1,540

The Doncaster Race Cup, 1798, a fine George III silver gilt two handled cup and cover, by Paul Storr, 1798, 25in., 203ozs. (Christie's) $79,464

A coconut cup, with plain rim, tubular stem and circular spreading base with reeded border, London 1803, 6in. high. (Bonhams) $332

DISHES

An Omar Ramsden hammered silver tazza, the shallow circular bowl with inverted rim and scalloped sides, with maker's marks and London hallmarks for 1925, 22.3cm. diam. 927 grams. (Christie's)
$2,805

A fine mid 17th century German oval rosewater dish, silver gilt, maker's mark crossed staves, Augsburg, circa 1640, 24in. x 19½in., 88½oz. (Prudential)
$30,780

One of a pair of George IV circular muffin dishes and covers, with detachable acorn, oak-leaf and simulated bark handles, by Paul Storr, 1825, 8in. wide, (62ozs.). (Christie's)
Two $17,974

A pair of entree dishes and covers, rounded rectangular with gadrooned borders and domed pull-off covers, 11in. wide, London, 1938, 97oz. (Bonhams) $2,220

A Hukin and Heath silver sugar basin designed by Dr Christopher Dresser, with hinged loop handle, the hemispherical bowl with raised double-rib decoration, with stamped maker's marks and London hallmarks for 1879, 12.5cm. diam. 182 grams. (Christie's) $6,732

A good pair of plated entree dishes and covers, engraved with floral rosettes with two side handles, on four ball-and-claw feet, circa 1880. (Bonhams) $700

A William IV plaque or sideboard dish, by Charles Fox II, pleated and chased with foliate scrolls, 1836, 68oz. (Phillips) $2,431

A pair of gadrooned edge rectangular entree dishes and covers, with foliate capped stylised loop handles, on leaf capped paw feet, circa 1820. (Phillips) $1,720

A pair of Old Sheffield Plate shaped-oval, tree and well venison dishes, each on four lion's paw and foliage feet, by Waterhouse and Co., circa 1835, 23in. and 22in. long. (Christie's)
Two $2,365

DISHES

A Spanish shaving dish, with sunken center and the wide flat rim, Barcelona, late 18th century, maker's mark F.PNO., 32.2cm., 19.3oz. (Lawrence Fine Arts) $1,851

A scarce George III toasted cheese dish and cover, the base of plain shallow rectangular form, by James Sutton and James Bult, 1782. 21.7cm. 16oz. (Lawrence Fine Arts) $856

A Queen Anne circular strawberry dish, probably by David Willaume, scratch mark under base '1712J', marks rubbed, 9in. diameter. (Prudential) $1,966

An Iberian parcel gilt circular dish, the molded border chased with stylized quatrefoils, unmarked, probably 19th century, 7¼in. diam., 304grs. (Christie's) $1,324

A late Victorian part gilt tazza, by George Fox, in the Renaissance manner, 16.5cm. high, 1872, 19oz. (Phillips) $1,215

An Elizabeth Petrovna parcel gilt Imperial kovsh, the silver center of the bowl repousse in high relief with the Russian double-headed eagle, marked with unrecorded initials, G.I., Moscow, 1751, 12½in. long, 645.8gr. (Christie's) $18,590

FLASKS

A French silver gilt mounted spirit flask, the glass body etched with scroll foliage, late 19th/early 20th century, 13.6cm. (Lawrence Fine Arts) $264

A silver flask by Whiting Manufacturing Company, circa 1885, the front repousse and chased with a seahorse, 6in. long, 7½oz. (Christie's) $2,860

A Chinese Export spirit flask, the body applied with a Chinaman playing a stringed instrument below an oak branch, silver colored metal, 16.4cm. (Lawrence Fine Arts) $283

FLATWARE

A George III Old English pattern table service, by Eley and Fearn, 1804, the table forks 1805, comprising: 60 pieces, 78 ozs. (Christie's) $6,054

A silver fish slice and serving fork by Whiting Manufacturing Company, probably Newark, circa 1885, each applied with a seahorse and seaweed, slice 14½in. long, fork 10¼in. long, 12oz. (Christie's) $3,080

A James I seal top spoon, of good gauge, the pear shaped bowl curved and with a thick tapering hexagonal stem, by Daniel Cary, 1619. (Christie's) $525

A spoon with decorative fruiting vine stem and hammered egg shaped bowl, 1925, 16.2cm. long, 1.5oz. (Phillips) $210

A Victorian pierced vine pattern dessert-service, by Robert Roskell, Allan Roskell and John Hunt, 1882 and 1883, comprising. 91 pieces, 115ozs. (Christie's) $8,514

A New Zealand gilt tea equipage with nephrite handles comprising twelve teaspoons, a butterknife, a jam spoon and a sugar sifter, by A. Kohn of Auckland. (Phillips) $2,795

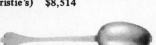

A William III trefid spoon, maker's mark IP crescent above and below in a shaped shield, 1696. (Phillips) $411

A 17th century Provincial seal top spoon with fig shaped bowl, RA IA 1676, 17.5cm. (Lawrence Fine Arts) $454

A spoon with leaf wrapped stem, hammered bowl and leaf embellished onion knop finial, 1931, 20cm. long, 3oz. (Phillips) $560

A Charles I seal top spoon, by Richard Crosse, 1636. (Christie's) $908

A Victorian pair of fish carvers, each engraved with an inset silver gilt fish, by George Adams, 1868(Phillips)
$1,159

An ice or ice-cream silver serving spoon by Gorham Manufacturing Company, Providence, circa 1870, in the "Alaskan" style, the handle in the form of two crossed harpoons, 11in. long, 3oz. (Christie's)
$1,650

A Charles I apostle spoon, Saint Jude, the tapering hexagonal stem, later inscribed St Jude 1634, surmounted by a cast parcel gilt figure, 18cm. long, 1634. (Phillips)
$1,589

A fine silver soup ladle by Myer Myers, New York, circa 1785, the circular bowl with wavy fluting, marked Myers twice on back of handle, 13½in. long, 4½oz. (Christie's)
$7,150

An Edwardian service of cutlery for twenty-four place settings, threaded shaped terminal pattern engraved with an initial, Sheffield 1908 by Harry Atkin of Atkin Brothers, 197.8oz. of weighable silver. (Lawrence Fine Arts)
$4,812

A set of six Liberty silver and enamel coffee spoons, the terminal of each decorated with stylized buds on a torquoise ground, stamped maker's mark L & Co and Birmingham hall marks for 1930, 11.1cm. long. (Christie's)
$748

A Victorian part gilt seal top spoon by George Fox, the oval bowl plain with winged surround to the shoulders, 18cm. long, 1873. (Phillips)
$227

An early Charles I slip top spoon, the curved pear shaped bowl with a tapering thick hexagonal stem, maker's mark 'D' enclosing 'C' for Daniel Cary, London, 1627, length 18cm. (Phillips) $1,050

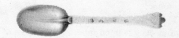

A William III trefid spoon, plain, of good gauge, the egg shaped bowl with a beaded rat tail, by Jonathan Bradley, 1696. (Phillips)
$841

GOBLETS

A China Trades gilt lined goblet chased with flowering prunus on a crackled ground, Wang Hing, 6in. high. (Christie's) $385

A replica of a late 17th century goblet and cover with an inscription to the rim dated 1653, 18.5 in. tall. (Christie's) $673

A George III gilt lined large goblet on a reeded rising circular foot, Henry Nutting, London 1803, 6in., 9¼oz. (Christie's) $577

A China Trades gilt lines goblet chased with bamboo on a textured ground, with presentation inscription dated 1864, bearing maker's initials only, L.C., 7½in. (Christie's) $385

An Arts and Crafts silver two handled goblet by Skinner & Co., the flared bowl with knopped base, with London hallmarks for 1907, 14.5cm. high, 309 grams. (Christie's) $411

A Charles II wine goblet, the bucket bowl engraved with a later boar's head crest, possibly for Abercorne, London 1661, 231 grammes. (Henry Spencer) $845

A George III gilt lined tapering goblet on a reeded rising circular foot, Robert and Samuel Hennell, London 1807, 7¼in., 12.75oz. (Christie's) $423

A pair of George III goblets, each on hexagonal foot, engraved with a band of bright-cut ornament within reeded borders, by D. Urquhart and N. Hart, 1791, 16.8cm. high, 14oz. (Christie's) $3,216

A plated trophy goblet by Pairpoint, New Bedford, last quarter 19th century, the interior gilt, marked, 12in. high. (Christie's) $935

A Regency Premiere Partie boulle inkstand, the rectangular top with a pair of cut glass wells, 16in. wide. (Christie's) $2,776

A rare Mexican shaped oval inkstand, circa 1770, with the assay master's mark of Jose Antonio Lince y Gonzalez, 11¾in. long, 1437grs. (Christie's) $6,622

An attractive silver and tortoiseshell inkstand, inlaid with rosettes and floral swags, London 1910, by William Comyns. (Bonhams) $1,309

A mounted emu egg inkwell, enclosed by leaves and ferns upon an oval stand applied with an Aborigine throwing a boomerang. (Phillips) $692

A large Victorian presentation inkstand, with glass bottles, with silver caps and two pen trays, 1891 by Turner Bradbury, 31.9cm. (Lawrence Fine Arts) $2,262

A Victorian presentation ink stand, the glass ink bottle with a conforming silver cover, Sheffield 1865, by Richard Martin and Ebenezer Hall, 4.9oz. of weighable silver. (Christie's) $885

An Edwardian silver and tortoiseshell tapering square inkstand on bracket feet, by Goldsmiths & Silversmiths Company Ltd., London 1902, 4¾in. (Christie's) $1,116

A late Victorian rectangular inkstand, the three quarter gallery pierced with scroll foliage, 1895 by William Hutton and Sons Ltd., 29.7cm. across, 26oz. weighable silver. (Lawrence Fine Arts) $1,608

An oblong inkstand with pierced gallery and gadroon borders, London 1902, weighable silver 30oz., 12in. long. (Tennants) $2,012

A Victorian beaded and spiral fluted hot water jug, with a foliate decorated spout, by George Lambert, London 1880, 11in., 21oz. gross. (Christie's) $731

A silver water jug, the bulbous form decorated with a frieze of repousse laurel leaves, the handle in the shape of a rampant leopard, with London import marks for 1973, 23cm. high, 2,090 grams. (Christie's) $1,122

A fine quality George IV silver wine jug of baluster form, plain domed cover with shell shaped thumbpiece, gilt interior, 10in., London 1825, maker probably William Bell, 29½oz. (Prudential) $2,332

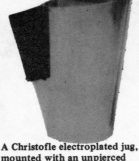

A massive Victorian covered jug of baluster form, by George Fox, London 1861, 16in. high, 124oz. (Prudential) $8,892

A Christofle electroplated jug, mounted with an unpierced wooden handle, the base stamped with marks and Gallia, prod. Christofle, Italy, 22.5cm. high. (Christie's) $411

A water pitcher, American, circa 1815, with a squared handle and a broadly reeded body, unmarked, 8¼in. high, 26oz. (Christie's) $990

A Continental fluted inverted pear-shaped jug, deeply chased with shells, baskets of flowers and with an elaborate cast scroll handle, 9½in. (Christie's) $962

A 19th century Russian parcel gilt 'trompe l'oeil' jug of basketwork design, by Pavel Sasikov, St Petersburg, 1862, 14.5cm. high, 13.25oz. (Phillips) $1,215

A silver ewer by Edwin Stebbins & Company, New York, 1850-1856, with a scroll handle cast in the form of a branch, 15in. high, 30oz. (Christie's) $1,210

SILVER

A George III Scottish hot water jug and stand, on three reeded and lion's paw feet, by G McHattie, 1813, with detachable electro plated burner, 11¾in. high, 44oz.gross. (Christie's) $2,648

A plain oval silver milk jug, marked Fáberge, with Imperial warrant, St. Petersburg, circa 1880, 2¾in. high, 168.9gr. (Christie's) $706

A silver covered water pitcher by S. Kirk & Son Co., Baltimore, circa 1920, the flat hinged cover with a pierced thumbpiece, 9in. high, overall, 52oz. (Christie's) $3,850

A large pear shaped silver water jug, the body repousse and chased with rococo cartouche enriched with flowering blossoms, marked Faberge, with Imperial warrant, Moscow, 1891, 11in. high, 2208.4gr. (Christie's) $6,506

Two mid-Victorian covered wine or claret ewers, by Charles Thomas and George Fox, cast and decorated in the Chinese manner, 1855, 60oz. (Phillips) $5,610

A mid-Victorian presentation wine jug, of slender form, with high loop handle, London 1866, maker's mark CH, 1032 grammes, 36cm. high. (Henry Spencer) $1,026

A Victorian large cylindrical jug, on waisted circular base, chased in high relief, by Robert Hennell, 1863, 16in. high. (104ozs.) (Christie's) $5,486

A silver water pitcher, attributed to Dominick & Haff, New York, circa 1880, with an everted brim and a scroll handle, marked Sterling on base, 6¾in. high. (Christie's) $1,650

An early 19th century Portuguese jug, of baluster form, the scroll handle issuing from fantastical mask, Lisbon circa 1820, 38.5oz., 23.5cm. (Osmond Tricks) $1,332

MISCELLANEOUS

A parcel gilt punch service, with repousse and chased view of the Kremlin, by Antip Kuzmichev, Moscow, 1882, the tray 12½in. wide, 3486.4gr. (Christie's) $6,506

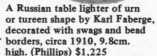

A Russian table lighter of urn or tureen shape by Karl Faberge, decorated with swags and bead borders, circa 1910, 9.8cm. high. (Phillips) $1,225

A George II pap boat of conventional single lipped oval form, 1751 by William Justis, 10.2cm. (Lawrence Fine Arts) $699

A silver, onyx and coral paper knife and book mark, signed Cartier, London, 1934, 14cm. (Lawrence Fine Arts) $370

Two Victorian model figures of Mr Punch, by Charles and George Fox, 1844 and 1845, 7¾in high overall, gross 19ozs. (Christie's) $3,216

A silver model of a bogatyr's boot, engraved with strapwork simulating embroidery, Moscow, circa 1860, 18cm. high, 200.8gr. (Christie's) $2,789

A William IV hollow, heart-shaped badge chased on either side with two Biblical shepherds and their flocks, by James Dixon & Son, Sheffield, 1830. (Phillips) $245

A napkin ring, repousse and chased with two bogatyrs, dated 1911, white metal, by Mikhail Tarasov, Moscow, 1908-1917, 38.3gr. (Christie's) $371

A good Continental silver-gilt and enamel aide-de-memoire, enamelled with a rower in student's cap, probably German, circa 1895. (Phillips) $1,015

A George III orange or lemon strainer, the pierced shallow circular body, 1799 by Henry Nutting. 19.7cm. across handles. (Lawrence Fine Arts) $475

An unusual cased pair of silver gilt ear trumpets with ivory earpieces, the trumpets engraved F. C. Rein & Son, London, in leather covered case with velvet lining, case 4¾in. wide. (Lawrence Fine Arts) $671

An Edwardian crouching rabbit pin cushion, by Adie & Lovekin Ltd., Birmingham, 1907. (Phillips) $245

A William IV table bell, the slender baluster handle engraved with scroll foliage. 1832 maker's mark rubbed but probably that of Edward, Edward Jn., John and W. Barnard. 11.5cm. (Lawrence Fine Arts) $951

A rare 18th century German Hannukah lamp, of small size, the rectangular body with foliate chased cover opening to reveal eight oil compartments, by Rotger Herfurth, Frankfurt-on-Main, circa 1765, 13cm. long, 9oz. (Phillips) $10,150

A George III Irish swing handle cream pail, the tapering circular body attractively chased and pierced in the traditional manner, maker's mark RM not recorded, Dublin, circa 1785. (Phillips) $385

A silver tea glass holder, with applied troika horse heads, by V. Akimov, Moscow, circa 1900, overall 4¾in. high, with glass liner, 206.9gr. (Christie's) $836

A George II Provincial brandy warmer of plain compressed baluster form, maker's mark IP, circa 1730, 6cm. height of bowl. (Lawrence Fine Art) $3,027

A pair of silver gilt and rock crystal obelisks, supported on four reclining cherubs, 17¼in. high. (Christie's) $7,858

MISCELLANEOUS

An unusual Victorian silver mounted table lighter in the form of a fish with cow horn body, 1883 by George Havell, 39cm. long. (Lawrence Fine Arts) $2,057

A Continental model of a cow, naturalistically formed, the head hinged, silver colored metal, 8.8cm. (Lawrence Fine Arts) $208

A German two handled circular ecuelle and cover, by Johann Heuss, Augsburg, 1722-1726, diam. of bowl 5¾in., 378grs. (Christie's) $6,243

A George III plain cylindrical argyle with gadroon border and cane handle, by Andrew Fogelberg, London 1773, 12oz all in. (Prudential) $2,394

A Hukin and Heath electro-plated letter stand designed by Dr Christopher Dresser, the convex base on four bun feet, the middle support raised to a handle, registration mark for 9 May 1881, 12.5cm. high. (Christie's) $710

A William Hutton & Sons silver and enamelled picture frame, embellished with tendrils and blue and green enamelling, 9cm. high, London 1904. (Phillips) $550

A Victorian boulle dressing case with silver gilt fittings, with maker's name F. L. Hausburg, Liverpool, and the silver gilt mounts 1843, 32.3cm. wide. (Lawrence Fine Arts) $1,851

An unusual German silver cas-ket, the front with two doors pierced with figures, import marks for 1892, sponsor's mark of Joseph Morpurgo, 14.7cm. high. (Lawrence Fine Arts) $781

A silver mounted and tortoise-shell pique desk timepiece, with a domed top, pique worked with foliage pendant from rib-bon ties, 1908 by Harris Adel-stein, 9.5cm. (Lawrence Fine Arts) $946

A George II Scottish brandy warmer, the plain baluster body with a turned wood handle. Edinburgh 1746 by James Weems. 7.8cm. high. 10oz all in. (Lawrence Fine Arts) $3,235

A German decorative silver carriage, import marks for 1901, sponsor's mark of John George Piddington, 12.7cm. (Lawrence Fine Arts) $534

A George III two handled oval verriere, with applied ram's mask, by John Wakelin and William Taylor, 1790, 13½in. long, overall, 49ozs. (Christie's) $16,082

A Georg Jensen small tazza, the shallow bowl form supported on tendrils with pendant grapes above a spiralling stem, 13cm. high. (Phillips) $598

A George III honey pot on stand modelled as a skep, 1803 by Paul Storr, marked on the base, 10cm. high, 13.8oz. (Lawrence Fine Arts) $17,507

The Royal Hunt Cup 1845 - A Victorian Racing Trophy, by John S. Hunt of Hunt and Roskell, London 1844, on wood plinth applied with gothic lettering, 24in. high overall. (Prudential) $30,780

A Victorian model of a knight in armour, by John Samuel Hunt, 1841, height overall 15in., 42ozs. (Christie's) $3,216

A William Hutton & Sons silver and enamel picture frame, with repousse decoration and entrelac motif, London hallmarks for 1903, 20.4cm. high. (Christie's) $1,673

Miniature silver tripod table, the circular top with Chippendale border, 3¾in. high, London assay, 3oz. (Hobbs and Chambers) $126

MISCELLANEOUS

A Queen Anne torah mount, with fluted stem and partly fluted finial, circa 1710, the stand 5¼in. high. (Christie's) $4,919

A George IV nipple shield, plain, of usual form, by T. & I. Phipps, 1821.(Phillips) $486

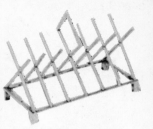

A Hukin & Heath plated toastrack, attributed to Christopher Dresser with open rectangular base supported on block feet, 11.5cm. high. (Phillips) $963

A silver parcel gilt pomander formed as a human skull, hinged at the jaw bone, 1¼in. high. (Christie's) $756

A rare James Dixon & Sons electroplated toastrack designed by Dr Christopher Dresser, the rectangular frame with seven triangular supports, each with angular wire decoration, on four spike feet and with a raised vertical handle, stamped with maker's marks and facsimile signature Chr. Dresser, 16.4cm. high. (Christie's) $24,167

A silver mounted walking stick watch, the movement with cylinder escapement, signed Ludvig Holuska, the white enamel dial with Roman numerals, 1899, 35½in. (Lawrence Fine Arts) $1,668

A Hukin & Heath plated toastrack designed by Christopher Dresser with rectangular base, having seven sets of rod divisions, 13.7cm. high. (Phillips) $5,504

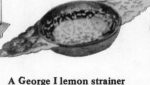

A George I lemon strainer with two pierced flat triangular handles, London marks indistinct, 8in. long, 4oz. (Prudential) $1,795

A 17th century Continental parcel gilt pomander of segmented apple form, the eight spice compartments with sliding lids. (Phillips) $3,806

A Victorian gilt lined cylindrical christening mug on a rising circular foot decorated with an egg and dart frieze, I.H., Sheffield 1859, 3¼in. (Christie's)   **$365**

A Victorian gilt lined christening mug on a chased rising shaped circular foot, London 1857, 4¼in., 6.75oz.(Christie's)   **$539**

A Victorian gilt lined tapering christening mug on mask and scroll feet, William Ker Reid, London 1851, 4in. high. (Christie's)   **$404**

A George III baluster mug, the plain body on spreading foot rim, 1769 by James Stamp and John Baker I, 10cm. (Lawrence Fine Arts)   **$681**

A George III mug, the tapering cylindrical body with two reeded bands, 1803 by Thomas Wallis II, 14.6cm. 22.9oz. (Lawrence Fine Arts)   **$1,141**

A Victorian christening mug, on a molded foot rim scroll handle, 1851 by Samuel Whitford, 7.9cm. (Lawrence Fine Arts)   **$329**

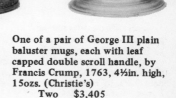

A George III small silver mug, with two reeded bands, Newcastle 1784 by Langlands and Robertson, 6.7cm. (Lawrence Fine Arts)   **$267**

A pair of cast 19th century Chinese Export mugs with dragon handles, chased in traditional style with market and dockside scenes, circa 1850, 22oz. (Phillips)   **$2,805**

One of a pair of George III plain baluster mugs, each with leaf capped double scroll handle, by Francis Crump, 1763, 4½in. high, 15ozs. (Christie's)   Two   **$3,405**

MUSTARDS

A late Victorian mustard pot, by George Fox, of shallow circular baluster form, on three ball feet, and a small foreign salt spoon with windmill finial, 2cm. high, 1874, 5oz.(Phillips) $152

A rare example of a Bates improved mustard pot, the plain cylindrical body with spread base, by Arnold Neale Baily and Thomas House Bates, 1914, gross weight 2.5oz. (Phillips) $1,075

A mixed metal mustard pot by Dominick & Haff, New York, 1880, the surface engraved in an all over blossom pattern, 6.04cm. high, gross weight 3oz. (Christie's) $990

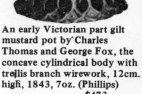

An early Victorian mustard pot by Charles Thomas and George Fox, the drum shaped body with scroll pierced decoration, 12cm. high, 1841, 9.5oz. (Phillips) $709

A Liberty and Co. Cymric hammered silver condiment set, comprising two bombe sided salts, similarly decorated mustard pot stamped with maker's marks and London hallmarks for 1897, height of mustard pot 7.8cm. (Christie's) $1,309

An early Victorian part gilt mustard pot by Charles Thomas and George Fox, the concave cylindrical body with trellis branch wirework, 12cm. high, 1843, 7oz. (Phillips) $473

A George IV unusual mustard pot, the squat bellied circular body cast and raised with intervals of lion masks and floral and foliate festooning, 8cm. high, by Rebecca Emes & Edward Barnard, 1824, 12½oz. (Phillips) $525

A French Empire style mustard pot, the vase shape body with a band of bar piercing, clear glass liner, Paris 1798-1809, 15.3cm. (Lawrence Fine Arts) $321

A mid Victorian mustard pot by George Fox, the shaped cylindrical body finely pierced with foliate scrolls and intervals of lion mask and drop-ring bosses, 1862, 5.75oz. (Phillips) $304

SILVER

A William and Mary part spiral-fluted porringer decorated with stamped stylized foliage, William Andrews, London 1701, 5¾in. overall, 5oz. (Christie's) $866

A Guild of Handicrafts silver loop handled porringer, designed by C. R. Ashbee, London hallmarks for 1902, 17.6cm. wide, 136 grams. (Christie's) $1,580

A William and Mary porringer, of slightly tapering cylindrical form, raised upon a short foot, London 1689, by Timothy Ley, 172 grammes, 7.5cm. high. (Henry Spencer) $534

A silver porringer, by Benjamin Burt, Boston, 1750-1800, with a pierced keyhole handle, 5¼in. diam. 8oz. (Christie's) $1,980

A Queen Anne small silver bleeding bowl or porringer, Britannia standard 1706 , maker's mark rubbed, 7.4cm. (Lawrence Fine Arts) $946

A silver porringer by Thomas Edwards, Boston, circa 1750, with a pierced keyhole handle engraved with script initials, 5¼in. diam. 9½oz. with cover. (Christie's) $3,080

A very fine early Restoration two handled porringer and cover, the bulbous body repousse with flowering stems, and engraved with coats of arms, 1664, WC., 28oz., overall height 18cm. (Henry Spencer) $8,950

A George II porringer with moulded circular bowl, Issac Cookson, Newcastle, probably 1731, 6¾in. overall, 4.50oz. (Christie's) $1,155

A Charles II two handled porringer, the waisted sides chased with a stag and hound within a border of stylized leaves and foliage, 1672, maker's mark C.K., 4½in. high, 10ozs. (Christie's) $4,831

SALTS & PEPPERS

A pair of Queen Anne compressed circular trencher salts, probably by George Havers, 1707, 3.25oz. (Phillips) $692

A pair of electroplated salt cellars, each cast as a dog, one standing, the other sitting, marked Orfevrerie Gallia. (Christie's) $1,487

Two of a set of four Victorian salts, the cauldron shaped bodies of open pierced scroll design, by J. C. Eddington, 1849, 12oz. (Phillips) Four $486

Two of a set of four George III two handled boat shaped salts on oval pedestal bases, by William Fountain, 1778, 17.5oz. (Phillips) Four $1,346

A set of four Victorian silver gilt standing figure salt cellars, each on circular base cast and chased with simulated rockwork, by C.F. Hancock, 1859, 6½in. to 7½in. high, 54ozs. (Christie's) $34,650

A set of four salts by Daniel Fueter, New York, 1786-1806, on a spreading oval stem on a rectangular foot, 5.4cm. high, 12½oz. (Christie's) $3,520

Four George II shell shaped salt cellars, each on simulated wave and rockwork base, engraved with a crest, circa 1750, 3¾in. wide, 23ozs. (Christie's) $5,005

A pair of Victorian novelty pepperettes, one formed as a Harlequin, the other as a court jester, by James Barclay Hennell, 1877, the court jester's hat by Robert Hennell, 1867, 5¼in. high, 11ozs. (Christie's) $1,513

A good George III set of four two handled oval salts, by Matthew Boulton and John Fothergill. 13cm. long, Birmingham, 1776-19.5ozs. (Phillips) $7,612

SAUCE BOATS

One of a pair of George II large plain shaped oval sauceboats, by John Jacobs, 1753, 8¾in. long, 35ozs. (Christie's)
Two $5,676

A good quality silver sauce-boat, with leaf capped double scroll handle, London 1901, by the Barnards, 8½in. long, 15oz. (Bonhams)
$424

A George II shaped oval sauce-boat, on four cast lion's paw feet, by Paul de Lamerie, 1737, 7½in. long, 12ozs. (Christie's)
$11,352

A pair of George III sauceboats, engraved with crest, by Robert Hennell II, 1816, 33oz.(Phillips)
$3,740

A pair of 18th century style gadrooned sauce boats on shell feet, Goldsmiths and Silver-smiths Co. Ltd., London 1913, 7½in., 20oz. (Christie's)
$673

A good pair of early George III sauceboats, of good gauge, the oval and curved bodies with concave spiral fluting in scallop fashion, possibly by William Turner?, 1761(?), 32oz. (Phillips) $2,244

A pair of gadrooned sauce boats in the 18th century taste, each on shell and hoof feet, Roberts & Belk, 8¼in., 26oz. (Christie's)$1,155

A George III sauceboat on shell and hoof feet, with a shaped rim and leaf capped double scroll handle, maker's mark probably W.S., London 1764, 6½in., 7.25oz.(Christie's)
$423

A pair of George III cast sauceboats, of exceptional quality, by John Parker & Edward Wakelin, 1769, 47.5oz. (Phillips)
$12,155

SNUFF BOXES

A George I silver parcel gilt and tortoiseshell oval snuff box, circa 1715, maker's mark GA or EA, a mitre above, 3¼in. long. (Christie's) **$1,702**

An interesting William IV oblong snuff box, the cover engraved with a live pigeon trap shooting contest, by Thomas Shaw, Birmingham, 1833, 7.5cm. long. (Phillips) **$1,234**

A Russian niello snuff box of oval form, the cover decorated with a street scene with a border of trellis pattern, the base with further trellis decoration. Moscow 1872 maker's mark Ae, 84 zolotniki marks. 10.5cm. (Lawrence Fine Arts)**$731**

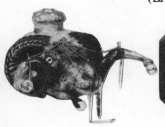

A Chinese export silver gilt cartouche-shaped filigree snuff box, second half of 18th century, 9.2cm. wide. (Christie's) **$4,351**

A Victorian Scottish silver mounted ram's head snuff mull, on three castors, with various attachments, Edinburgh, 1881, height overall 12in. (Christie's) **$3,027**

A silver parcel gilt and enamel snuff box, the cover and base painted with portraits of Louis XIV and Marie Therese, German, circa 1760, 2½in. long. (Christie's) **$3,027**

A Russian niello snuff box of slightly curved rectangular form, the cover decorated with a battle scene, Moscow 1829 Assay Master N. Dubrovin, 7.6cm. (Lawrence Fine Arts) **$756**

A rectangular niello silver gilt snuff box, the cover depicting a monarch examining cloth, by Dimitri Kolesnikov, Moscow, circa 1821, 3¼in. long, 107gr. (Christie's)   **$1,264**

A Victorian presentation snuff box of the Order of Odd Fellows Manchester Unity, by John Tongue, Birmingham, 1839, 7.8cm. long. (Phillips) **$1,028**

A Scandinavian small tankard, on three pomegranate feet, bearing marks for Copenhagen, 1754, 5½in. high, 378grs. (Christie's) $3,405

A William IV large baluster tankard, the body chased with a gentleman and two greyhounds, by Barnard Bros., 1835, 9¼in. high. (39ozs.) (Christie's) $3,027

A Danish cylindrical peg tankard, on three claw and ball feet, by Frands Bang, Naestred, circa 1800, 8in. high, 975grs. (Christie's) $4,351

A George I tapering cylindrical tankard the domed cover with molded thumbpiece, by Humphrey Payne, London 1722, 6½in high, 19oz. (Prudential) $4,446

A good Charles II tankard, the tapering cylindrical body engraved with the arms of the Grocers' Company of the City of London. 1680 maker's mark IS. 17cm. high. 26.4oz. (Lawrence Fine Arts) $9,515

A William III tankard, the tapering cylindrical body engraved at a later date, 1697 by Thomas Parr, I., 18.6cm., 25.3oz. (Lawrence Fine Arts) $3,027

A Queen Anne tankard, the slight spread base reeded, the cover domed and with wide flat rim overlapping, 19cm. high overall, by Robert Timbrell & Joseph Bell I, 1710 - 23½ozs. (Phillips) $4,375

A late 17th century Norwegian peg tankard, parcel gilt, on three claw and ball feet, with cast lion and ball thumbpiece, 8½in. high, 32oz. (Prudential) $25,650

A rare 17th century Norwegian cylindrical tankard, on four cast reeded pomegranate feet, by Jon Jorgensen Fieff, Stavanger, 1671, 38.75oz. (Phillips) $13,090

TEA & COFFEE SETS

A five piece silver tea and coffee service by Thomas Whartenby, Philadelphia, circa 1825, on spreading cylindrical feet with square bases, each marked, except teapot, coffee pot 10¾in. high, gross weight 129oz. (Christie's) $4,180

A four piece oval section conical tea and coffee service engraved in the manner of The Aesthetic Movement. (David Lay) $298

A composite three piece Irish teaset, the teapot with cast floral finial to hinged cover, Dublin 1844, the sugar bowl and cream jug, Dublin 1839, all by Richard Sawyer, 63oz. (Bonhams) $1,327

Victorian four piece Elkington and Company tea and coffee service , with melon finials. (Hobbs & Chambers) $169

TEA & COFFEE SETS

A four piece silver tea service, comprising a shaped covered water jug, a teapot, a two handled covered sugar bowl and a milk jug, by Matvei Grechushnikov, Moscow, 1823, 2039 gr. gross. (Christie's) $3,903

A Grant & Son Art Deco five piece tea and coffee service, with ivory finials and handles, on stepped cone shaped bases, with incised signature Grant & Son, Carlisle and London hallmarks for 1936, 2,267 grams gross. (Christie's) $2,431

A Charles Boyton silver three piece tea service, comprising a teapot, a milk jug and a sugar basin, with stamped London hallmarks for 1931, signed Charles Boyton, 562 grams gross. (Christie's) $1,776

A silver three piece tea service by I. W. & C. Forbes, New York, circa 1815, on four lion's paw and ball feet with acanthus leaf joins, each marked, 8¼in. high, gross weight 52½oz. (Christie's) $1,760

TEA CADDIES

A pair of George III tea caddies and sugar casket, by Emick Romer, London 1768, 26½oz all in. (Prudential)
$11,970

A Continental late 19th century oblong tea caddy in the George II taste, chased with a vignette of a woman picking tea leaves, import marks for Sheffield 1896, 5¾in., 12oz. (Christie's) $866

A George II plain oblong tea caddy and sugar box, by Pierre Gillois, 1759, contained in a brass bound shagreen casket, height of sugar box 5in., 17oz. gross. (Christie's)
$3,594

A George III shaped oval tea caddy, the domed cover with a later disc finial, 1798 by James Mince, 15.4cm. across, 17.2oz. (Lawrence Fine Arts)
$2,262

An early 19th century Swedish caddy of oval, half fluted form with floral rosettes either side of the keyhole, by Olof Hellbom, Stockholm, 1818, 26oz. (Phillips) $2,711

A George III octagonal tea caddy, with waved border, the domed cover with ivory finial, by Robert Hennell, 1789, 13oz. gross. (Christie's)
$4,540

A George III shaped oval tea caddy, the straight sided body engraved with foliate swags. 1785 by William Abdy. 13.7cm. 13oz. (Lawrence Fine Arts) $2,854

A German 19th century gilt lined moulded shaped oblong tea caddy on scrolling foliate feet, Hamburg, 5¾in., 15oz. (Christie's) $770

A George III tea caddy, the oval body attractively engraved with intertwined foliate festooning, 13cm high overall, by R.Hennell, 1782, 12.5oz. (Phillips)
$2,941

TEA KETTLES

A Victorian tea kettle, inscribed *'Ashdown Park, February 1841. Won by the Earl of Stradbroke's 'Mosquito',* maker's mark 'I W' over 'W M', London 1839, 78oz. all in. (Prudential)$4,446

A Continental fluted pear shaped swing handled tea kettle chased with flowers and foliage, 8¾in. overall. (Christie's) $327

Fine Victorian silver spirit kettle and stand of melon form with engraved cartouche panels, Sheffield 1866, by Martin Hall & Co., 68oz. (G. A. Key) $1,750

A late Victorian part fluted and gadrooned molded oblong tea kettle with rising curved spout, W.S. & C.S., Sheffield 1900, 14¾in. overall, 54oz. gross. (Christie's) $1,135

A George II circular kettle, stand and lamp on triangular stand, the kettle, spirit stand lamp by George Wickes, 1738, the triangular stand by Robert Abercrombie, 1738, 90oz. gross. (Christie's) $11,071

A Victorian silver tea kettle, stand and burner, the kettle of oval lobed form with part fluting, Sheffield 1895, makers Mappin Brothers, 38½oz. (Prudential) $996

A Victorian rococo plated kettle on stand, the inverted pear shape body embossed with scrolls and flowers, made by Martin Hall & Co., circa 1860. (Woolley & Wallis) $822

A William IV inverted pear shaped tea kettle chased with arabesques incorporating scroll cartouches, by Mary and Richard Sibley, London 1835, overall height 14in., 97.25oz. gross. (Christie's)$2,887

A moulded shaped oblong tea kettle with panelled rising curved spout and ebonized wood handle, by Charles Stuart Harris & Son, London 1911, 13in., 42.25oz. gross. (Christie's) $886

A George III circular teapot, on rim foot, the short curved spout applied with shells, by Paul Storr, 1816, 4¾in. high, (gross 21ozs.) (Christie's) $1,892

A Dutch 19th century melon fluted compressed teapot on a rising octafoil foot, with a rising curved spout, 5¼in., 12.50oz. (Christie's) $577

A reeded fluted oval teapot in the George III taste, with a fluted rising curved spout, Elkington and Co., Birmingham 1916, 5¾in., 16oz. gross. (Christie's) $481

A George III Irish reeded and molded oval teapot, with a rising curved spout, Dublin circa 1810, 6¾in., 19.75oz. (Christie's) $860

An unusual part fluted tapering teapot with rising curved spout, the base engraved: "Patent Trade S.Y.P. Mark Teapot", James Dixon & Son, Sheffield 1912, 9¼in., 42oz. gross. (Christie's) $939

A Dutch 19th century spiral fluted miniature teapot on a flaring foot, with a floral and foliate chased rising curved spout, 4¼in., 9oz. gross. (Christie's) $462

An early Victorian compressed afternoon teapot chased with a frieze of arabesques incorporating two scroll cartouches, E. & J. Barnard, London 1861, 4in., 9.75oz. (Christie's) $539

A silver pear shaped teapot, fluted, on four foliate capped scroll feet, by Sazikov, Moscow, circa 1890, 4¼in., 280.5gr. (Christie's) $1,078

A George III teapot with oval beaded borders, angled spout and ivory scroll handle, London 1782, by William Potter, 5in. high, 15oz. (Bonhams) $1,015

A Regency teapot, the rectangular curved body with a
gadrooned edge, part fluted, on
ball feet, London 1814,
24.5oz. (Woolley & Wallis)
$635

An attractive George IV
teapot, of flattened globular
melon fluted form, London
1825, by Charles Fox,
769 grammes gross. (Henry
Spencer) $676

A William IV teapot of compressed globular form, with
half lobe decoration, London
1832, by Richard Sibley,
25.5oz., length 26cm.
(Osmond Tricks)
$647

A Victorian floral and foliate
chased pear shaped teapot on
scrolling foliate feet, with
chased rising curved spout,
C.B., London 1872, 7¼in.
(Christie's) $836

A Victorian beaded tapering
teapot with rising curved spout,
scroll handle and domed hinged
cover, Joseph and Edward
Barnard, London 1867, 7¼in.,
23.75oz. (Christie's)$924

A George III beaded slightly
tapering drum teapot with
tapering angular spout, Daniel
Smith and Robert Sharp,
London 1775, 4½in., 13.25oz.
gross. (Christie's)$1,001

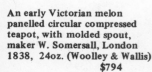

An early Victorian melon
panelled circular compressed
teapot, with molded spout,
maker W. Somersall, London
1838, 24oz. (Woolley & Wallis)
$794

A Portuguese early 19th century
compressed inverted pear-
shaped teapot on shell and
pad feet, 7½in., 32oz. gross.
(Christie's) $2,117

George III silver teapot,
London mark 1799, gross
weight 15oz. (Brogden & Co.)
$717

TRAYS & SALVERS

A George II salver with acanthus molded and piecrust border, by William Hunter, London 1750, 24½in. diameter, 150oz. (Prudential) $7,182

A silver smoking tray, by Tiffany & Company, New York, circa 1900, the hammer faceted tray with three rectangular wells for cigars and cigarettes, 10¼in. wide, 30oz. (Christie's) $1,320

A fine Old Sheffield Plate two-handled shaped rectangular tray, with shell and foliage scroll handles, circa 1815, 29in. long. (Christie's) $2,648

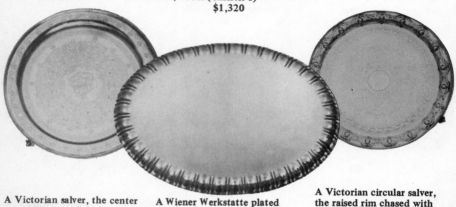

A Victorian salver, the center engraved with arms above a motto, on four ball and claw supports, 1873, by Joseph and Edward Bradbury, 30.6oz. (Phillips) $1,251

A Wiener Werkstatte plated oval tray, designed by Josef Hoffmann, embellished with vertical lobes and fluting, 34cm. wide. (Phillips) $1,408

A Victorian circular salver, the raised rim chased with raised roundels on a matted and strapwork ground. Sheffield 1865 by Richard Martin and Ebenzer Hall, 31.3cm. 27.2oz. (Lawrence Fine Arts) $913

A George II shaped circular salver, on four scroll vine tendril feet, by Philips Garden, 1752, 13in. diam., 45ozs. (Christie's) $4,540

Victorian silver salver, circular with embossed scroll and shell border, 12½in. diameter, London 1850, 25oz. (Hobbs and Chambers) $794

A George III shaped circular salver, on three claw and ball feet, by Ebenezer Coker, 1764, 13¼in. diam., 35ozs. (Christie's) $3,594

TRAYS & SALVERS

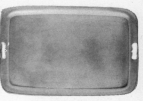

A George III oval salver, on four fluted and beaded bracket feet, by John Scofield, 1781, 18¼in. long, 62ozs. (Christie's) $4,351

A Japanese Export silver tray, 19th century, with cut corners, the convex rim applied with dragons in high relief, 26in. long, approximate weight 114 troy oz. (Robt. W. Skinner Inc.) $4,000

A rare silver tray by Joel Sayre, New York, 1802-1818, with a reeded border and a flaring brim, 20½in. long, 69½oz. (Christie's) $4,950

A large shaped circular presentation salver, the raised molded rim with scroll leafage, 1912 by Edward Barnard and Sons, 51cm. diam. (Lawrence Fine Arts) $1,398

A George III oval tea tray, with a beaded edge and two similar handles springing from leafage, 1804 by Richard Sibley I, 69cm. across handles, 97.7oz. (Lawrence Fine Arts) $3,394

A Victorian salver of shaped circular form with stylised scroll and matt borders, 50cm. diam., by Daniel and Charles Houle, 1854, 89ozs. (Phillips) $7,350

A George III shaped circular salver, on four claw and ball feet, by Ebenezer Coker, 1769, 15½in. wide, 52ozs. (Christie's) $3,973

A George III circular salver, on four fluted and scroll feet, by John Scofield, 1780, 16in. diam, 58ozs. (Christie's) $4,162

A George II shaped circular salver, on three scroll hoof supports, by Robert Abercromby, 1744, 27cm., 22oz. (Lawrence Fine Arts) $1,439

TUREENS

A rare turtle soup tureen, life size, finely modelled, the hinged shell back forming the cover, circa 1800. (Phillips) $12,456

A Georg Jensen tureen designed by Henning Koppel, the hand raised and sculpted slender boat shaped body with narrow everted lips forming handles, 72cm. long, 3,484 grams. (Christie's) $31,790

One of a pair of George III plain two handled oval sauce tureens and covers, each on a spreading foot, by John Robins, 1789, 5½in. high, 34ozs. (Christie's)
Two $5,108

One of a set of four Old Sheffield Plate two handled shaped-oval sauce tureens and covers, by T. and J. Creswick, circa 1820, 8¾in. long overall. (Christie's)
Four $4,919

A George IV two handled soup-tureen and cover, with foliage scroll handles and gadrooned border, by R. Emes and E. Barnard, 1827, 10¾in. diam. (88ozs.) (Christie's) $5,298

A Victorian melon fluted shaped oval soup tureen and cover on elaborate scrolling foliate feet, 16in. overall. (Christie's) $1,443

A George III two handled oval soup tureen and cover, with fluted and beaded rim and domed cover, by Paul Storr, 1807, 11½in. high, 144ozs. (Christie's)
$16,082

A pair of Victorian sauce tureens and covers of oval shape with side reeded handles, Birmingham 1867, 43oz. (Tennants) $4,550

A plated soup tureen by Meriden Britannia Company, Meriden, 1875-1885, in the Japanese taste, with a flaring brim, together with a plated ladle by Rogers Brothers, tureen 17in. wide. (Christie's)
$880

URNS

A George III two handled tea urn of ovoid form, by Francis Butty and Nicholas Dumee, London 1769, 20½in. high, 90oz. (Prudential) $7,524

An Old Sheffield Plate spherical tea urn engraved with floral swags and friezes of foliage, fitted with a brass and ivory tap, 18in. overall. (Christie's) $1,251

A fine sugar urn by Robert Swan, Philadelphia, circa 1800, with a pierced gallery at the rim, a conical cover with an urn finial, 11in. high, 16¼oz. (Christie's) $4,180

A Regency scarlet tole and silver plate tea urn, the concave sided platform with a turned knob and bun feet, 16½in. high. (Christie's) $2,262

A rare Old Sheffield Plate tea and coffee machine, on shaped base and ball feet, comprising a large water urn, with two smaller tea and coffee urns, circa 1800, 24¼in. high. (Christie's) $9,240

A good quality George III tea urn, of vase form, engraved with an armorial to side and a crest to the cover, London 1788, by Henry Couper, 21½in. high, 98oz. (Bonhams) $4,025

A George III neo-Classical tea urn of vase shape, embossed with draped swags and ribbons, by Richard Carter, Daniel Smith & Robert Sharp, 1778, 52.5cm. high, 103.5oz. (Phillips) $6,358

A rare silver tea urn by Stephen Richard, New York, circa 1812, with a domed rectangular cover, a knop finial, a curved spigot and two cylindrical open handles, 14¾in. high, 104oz. (Christie's) $38,500

A French two handled fluted pear shaped coffee urn and stand, the tap formed as the mask of Bacchus with shell terminal, circa 1880, maker's mark G.F., 18½in.high. 2.13gr. gross. (Christie's)$2,406

VASES

A 19th century Turkish parcel-gilt vase of fluted, campana shape with applied surround of birds, flowers and leaves, 13.5cm high, 12oz. (Phillips) $692

Goldsmiths and Silversmiths Company: Replica of the Warwick Vase, 8in. high, on square base, London, 1912, 65oz. (Bonhams) $3,330

A large Eastern vase on a lobed hexafoil base with applied floral and shell feet, 20½in. high. (Christie's) $808

A tapering cylindrical vase, with a roundel enclosing a collie's head in relief, by I. Marshak, St Petersburg, 1908-1917, 7½in. high, 424.1gr. (Christie's) $1,766

A Continental suite of three gadrooned tapering vases pierced and chased with rococo flowers and scrolling foliage, 10¾in. and 6½in. (Christie's) $1,925

A Liberty & Co. 'Cymric' silver and enamel vase, the body decorated with a band of blue and orange enamelled stylized fruit branches, Birmingham hallmarks for 1905, 19.2cm. high. (Christie's) $1,673

A Sterling silver vase with Celtic style motif, Towle Co., Newburyport, Massachusetts, circa 1900, approximately 30 troy oz., 9¾in. high. (Robt. W. Skinner Inc.) $550

A pair of late 19th century Turkish vases, one for burning incence, the other for rose-water, 25cm. high - 50.5ozs. (Phillips) $3,287

An Edwardian Irish spot-hammered flaring vase applied with foliate decorated scroll handles, Goldsmiths & Silversmiths Co. Ltd., Dublin 1903, 8¼in., 28.75 oz. (Christie's) $1,001

VESTA CASES

A Victorian book vesta case, the cover enamelled 'en grisaille' with the cover of Punch magazine No. 2375, by Hubert Thornhill, 1887, 3.6cm. long. (Phillips) $770

An Edwardian circular vesta case, the front chased with a Victorian Rifle Volunteers shooting competition, Birmingham, 1906. (Phillips) $343

A Victorian combined vesta case and cachou box, engraved all over with leafage, 'Cachous', Birmingham, 1887. (Phillips) $227

VINAIGRETTES

A very attractive William IV silver gilt oblong vinaigrette, engine-turned and with floral borders, by Thomas Edwards, 1832. (Phillips) $2,275

A Victorian silver gilt railwayman's lantern vinaigrette with fluted top and hinged cover, by Henry William Dee, 1870. (Phillips) $840

A very rare early Victorian silver gilt cat vinaigrette, the oblong body engraved with peacocks and foliate scrolls, by James Beebe, 1837. (Phillips) $4,550

A Victorian novelty vinaigrette by Sampson Mordan & Co. modelled as a walnut, the grille pierced and engraved with a flower within a circle, circa 1880. (Phillips) $490

A Victorian shaped rectangular vinaigrette, engraved with view of Magdalen College, Oxford, by Nathaniel Mills, Birmingham 1846. (Phillips) $270

A Victorian oval vinaigrette, cover applied with the Scott Memorial within a surround of thistles and scrolls, by William & Edward Turnpenny, Birmingham, 1845. (Phillips) $1,050

WINE COOLERS

A George IV two handled baluster wine cooler, the spreading shaped circular foot cast and chased with dolphin's, lion's and dragon's masks, by George Clements, 1825, 10¼in. high, 185oz. (Christie's) $7,189

A pair of Regency Sheffield plate wine coolers with plain cylindrical bodies, 7in. high. (Prudential) $4,788

One of a pair of Old Sheffield Plate two handled wine coolers, each on circular base and chased with a band of flutes, circa 1810, 9½in. high. (Christie's) $2,648

A pair of Old Sheffield Plate two-handled partly fluted wine coolers, each on circular gadrooned foot, circa 1825, 9½in. high. (Christie's) $4,620

One of a pair of William IV two handled campana shaped wine coolers, each on circular foot, with applied vine borders and tendril and vine handles, by Howard & Hawksworth, Sheffield, 1832, 10¼in. high, 127ozs. (Christies) $17,325

A fine pair of George IV wine coolers by John Bridge, with leaf and berry borders, fully hallmarked, London 1826, 9in. high, 165oz. (Bonhams) $19,250

WINE FUNNELS

A good George III silver gilt wine funnel, the spout half fluted, by Michael Plummer, 1792, 8.75oz. (Phillips) $3,287

A rare George III magnum wine funnel, by Paul Storr, with fluted body and frieze of shells, 1816, 30cm. high, 13.25ozs. (Phillips) $21,625

A George III campana shaped wine funnel, the upper part fluted, with tongue and dart border, by Chrispin Fuller, 1811 5.5ozs. (Phillips) $865

WINE LABELS

A George IV Scottish stamped out wine label chased with satyr's mask, incised and filled 'Hollands', probably by William Russell, Glasgow, 1827. (Phillips) $205

An unusual pair of George III wine labels, probably Irish, of curved rectangular form with incurved sides and bright engraved borders, probably by Samuel Teare of Dublin, circa 1790. (Phillips) $315

A good and rare crescent wine label with laurel leaf border and neo-Classical urn surmount, incised 'White Wine', circa 1780. (Phillips) $177

Two of a rare set of four stylised 'batswing' wine labels stamped with fruiting vines and incised 'Whisky', 'Brandy' 'Rum' and 'Bitters', after designs by Matthew Boulton, circa 1780. (Phillips) Four $729

A pair of George IV wine labels of bacchanalian mask, scroll and fruiting vine design, pierced 'Sherry' and 'Madeira', by Charles Rawlings, 1818. (Phillips) $297

À pair of George III wine labels of lion mask, shell, scroll and fruiting vine design, engraved with pierced titles 'Hock' and 'Claret', by Daniel Hockley, 1816. (Phillips) $350

A George III shaped wine label of twin lion masks, shell, fruiting vine, thistle, rose and shamrock design, by Joseph Angell, 1819. (Phillips) $227

An unusual late 19th century American stamped out wine label by Tiffany & Co., of boat shape terminating at either end in swan's head. (Phillips) $420

A George IV wine label of pierced fruiting vine and tendril design, incised 'Bronte', by Joseph Willmore, Birmingham, 1827. (Phillips) $227

A glass overlay snuff bottle, mid Qing Dynasty, the semi-opaque milky ground with ruby-red glass overlay carved to one face with a chilong confronted with a kui dragon. (Christie's) $987

A fine Imperial green jadeite globular snuff bottle, 18th century or later well hollowed, flattened at the base and slightly waisted at the short cylindrical neck. (Christie's) $98,717

A shadow agate bottle, early 19th century, of rounded square form carved to the front with the dancing Liuhai swinging his string of cash over his head. (Christie's) $1,339

A fine jadeite snuff bottle, of rounded rectangular shape, the plain sides ranging from light to rich mottled apple-green tones. (Christie's) $11,282

A glass overlay snuff bottle, 19th century, of flattened globular form, the snowstream (hefengdi) ground with red glass overlay. (Christie's) $846

A moss agate bottle, the rounded rectangular body uncarved, with light and dark green inclusions to both sides. (Christie's) $846

A shadow agate snuff bottle, 19th century, of rounded rectangular form, the agate of opaque milky tones with very attractive abstract amber and dark brown inclusions to each face. (Christie's) $1,128

A yellow glass snuff bottle, 19th century, of rounded rectangular shape, the opaque glass of rich golden-yellow tone, the interior well hollowed. (Christie's) $1,833

A jasper agate snuff bottle, Qing Dynasty, of flattened ovoid form, the stone of rich caramel tones with swirling mottled inclusions. (Christie's) $564

A red glass snuff bottle, 19th century, of flattened spherical form, carved to each face with a large stylized flowerhead, the sides with lion-mask ring handles. (Christie's) $916

A white jade bottle, 18th century, with a fruiting melon on a curled stem issuing smaller fruits and tendrils, a butterfly to one side. (Christie's) $987

An apple-green and lavender jadeite snuff bottle, Qing Dynasty, of wide baluster form, carved to one face with flowering pansy, the other with daisy. (Christie's) $1,269

An amber snuff bottle, 19th century, of rounded rectangular shape, the unpolished interior well hollowed and with frosted texture. (Christie's) $1,551

A white jade bottle, 19th century, of flattened pear shape carved with two stylized cicadas back to back, the wings lightly incised. (Christie's) $987

A caramel agate snuff bottle, 19th century, of rounded square form, carved to the front with an equestrian bannerman. (Christie's) $1,692

A Beijing glass blue overlay bottle, 19th century, of flattened pear shape the translucent glass with blue glass overlay. (Christie's) $494

A shadow agate bottle, 19th century, of rounded square form, with dark inclusions to one side carved as a bird perched on rockwork. (Christie's) $507

An inside-painted glass snuff bottle, of rounded rectangular form, painted to one face with dragonfly and praying mantis, the other with other insects, signed by Ye Zhongsan. (Christie's) $1,410

A Flemish tapestry woven with a seated King and attendants with noblemen and foot soldiers beyond, 17th century, possibly Arras, 16ft.8in. x 7ft.10in. (Christie's)
$15,752

A tapestry panel woven in many colors, with figures by a carriage in a formal garden, 25 x 38in., 17th century. (Christie's)
$1,540

A fragment of Flemish tapestry with travellers in a boat, the foreground with stylized foliage and tree stump, 6ft.8in x 5ft.8in. (Christie's) $6,891

A Brussels tapestry woven in silks and wools with Alexander The Great on horseback in the midst of a fierce battle, 17th century, 9ft.4in. x 9ft.8in. (Christie's) $16,280

A Flemish tapestry woven in silks and wools with two allegorical figures in rich costume beneath alcoves by a balcony, the tapestry late 16th century, 10ft.9in. x 10ft.1in. (Christie's) $11,193

A fragment of Brussels verdure tapestry woven with two figures in a landscape, one with blue helmet, 6ft.5in. x 4ft.1in. (Christie's) $3,150

A Flemish tapestry woven in silks and wools with a lady seated upon a throne beneath a baldachino with attendants to her left and a bearded councillor to her right, 17th century, 13ft.2in. x 9ft.5in. (Christie's)
$10,829

'Fete Champetre', by Eugene Grasset, a tapestry depicted in shades of gold and brown, signed with monogram E.G., 177.5 x 213cm. (Christie's) $4,089

A Brussels tapestry woven in silks and wools with an episode from the Trojan wars, perhaps with Achilles in the foreground, late 16th century, 11ft.7in. x 7ft.5in. (Christie's)
$7,123

A Brussels tapestry woven with Alexander The Great on horseback and the dying Emperor Darius supported by soldiers, 17th century, 9ft.7in. x 8ft.5in. (Christie's)
$13,228

A fine 17th century Beauvais Verdure tapestry depicting in the foreground tropical and game birds among trees, 11ft.9½in. x 9ft.7½in. (Phillips) $50,400

A fragment of Flemish tapestry woven with dignitaries in associated borders, early 17th century and later, 15ft. x 5ft.2in. (Christie's)
$3,051

A cinnamon plush covered teddy bear, with boot button eyes, 24in. high, probably Steiff, circa 1908. (Christie's) $2,664

German gold plush teddy bear with stitched pointed snout, hump, black shoe button eyes, circa 1910, 21in. high. (Hobbs & Chambers) $374

An early golden plush covered teddy bear with boot button eyes, Steiff button in ear, 8½in. high. (Christie's) $1,107

A dark gold plush covered teddy bear with brown glass eyes, 19½in. high with Steiff button, circa 1920. (Christie's) $489

A blonde plush covered teddy bear, with Gebruder Bing button on side, Nuremberg, circa 1910, 11½in. high. (Christie's) $905

A blonde plush covered teddy bear with boot button eyes, wide apart ears, 13in. high, Steiff button in ear. (Christie's) $1,075

A Steiff pale plush teddy bear with rounded wide-apart ears, black button eyes and large felt pads. (Phillips) $540

An early gold plush teddy bear, with protruding black stitched snout, glass eyes, rounded ears and back hump, 15in. high. (Lawrence Fine Arts) $677

A strawberry blonde plush covered teddy bear with boot button eyes, 12in. high, with plain Steiff button in ear, circa 1903/1904. (Christie's) $913

A golden plush covered teddy bear with hump and Steiff button in ear, 14in. high. (Christie's) $644

A honey plush covered teddy bear with boot button eyes, 14in. high, Steiff button in ear, circa 1903. (Christie's) $1,336

An early 20th century blonde plush, straw filled teddy bear with black and orange glass eyes, 50cm. high. (Henry Spencer) $371

A blonde plush covered teddy bear, with boot button eyes, long arms and felt pads, 10½in. high, circa 1910. (Christie's) $520

Alfonzo — a very rare short red plush teddy bear, with button eyes, excelsior stuffing and felt pads, dressed as a Russian, 13in. high, with Steiff button. (Christie's) $19,600

A golden plush covered teddy bear with boot button eyes, wide apart ears, and Steiff button in ear, 16in. high. (Christie's) $2,214

A cinammon plush covered bear with large black boot button eyes, 29in. long, Steiff button in ear, circa 1904. (Christie's) $3,048

A blonde plush covered teddy bear with boot button eyes, 17in. high with Steiff button in ear. (Christie's)$761

A light brown plush covered teddy bear with boot button eyes, 21in. high, by Steiff, circa 1905. (Christie's) $489

"The dance of death", a printed
handkerchief with a series of
scenes depicting the triumph
of death, 19 x 23in., first
quarter of 19th century.
(Christie's) $748

A 17th century oval
embroidered picture finely
worked in brightly colored
silks with ladies and gentlemen
en fete, 30 x 35.5cm., circa
1660's. (Phillips)$3,114

An early 19th century silkwork picture embroidered
with a central rectangular panel
of a girl on a path, 23 x 29.5cm.
(Phillips) $519

An embroidered picture,
worked in colored silks and
chenille threads, depicting a
mythological scene with two
Roman soldiers greeting a
foreign prince, 20in. square,
circa 1820. (Christie's)
          $1,271

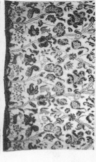

A pair of crewelwork curtains,
embroidered in colored wools
with a pattern of flowering
trees with large leaves, 66x78in.
early 18th century. (Christie's)
          $3,927

A Victorian woolwork pic-
ture of H.M.S. Warrior, the
three-masted steam assisted
vessel depicted under reduced sail in a heavy sea,
16in. by 19in. (Bearne's)
          $873

A needlework single pocketbook, signed Ann Pitman,
Rhode Island, and dated 1793,
worked in Queen's stitch, 4¼in.
high. (Christie's)
          $440

A Victorian wool and beaded
panel of an exotic bird, worked
in low relief. (David Lay)
          $388

A small fragment woven in
silk, linen and gold, Venetian,
late 13th/early 14th century.
(Christie's) $1,683

A fine and rare pictorial needlework single pocketbook, probably Rhode Island, third quarter 18th century, worked in wool tent stitch, 5in. high. (Christie's) $18,700

An embroidered picture, worked in colored silks and silver gilt thread, depicting a princess meeting a hero outside a castle, 11 x 16in., English, second half of 17th century. (Christie's) $2,431

A 17th century mirror frame embroidery depicting the Four Parts of the World finely worked in brightly colored silks, 46 x 57cm., circa 1660's. (Phillips) $4,498

The Great Exhibition "Wot is to be", a comic commemorative handkerchief, 16 x 20in., 1851. (Christie's) $935

A fragment of lampas with a pattern of foliage and flowers, 9 x 3in., possibly Spanish, 14th/15th century. (Christie's) $1,683

An Egyptian applique wall hanging, the sand ground designed with figures, hieroglyphs, sphinx and foliage 90 x 200cm. (Phillips) $178

An embroidered and drawn threadwork show towel, signed Frei Frick, Lancaster County, Pennsylvania, 1835, worked in blue and pink threads, 62in. long. (Christie's) $1,430

A mid 19th century lawn handkerchief with Honiton lace surround, decorated with roses, thistles, shamrock and other leaves, dated 1868. (Phillips) $207

A pair of needlework cushions, embroidered in colored wools and silks, each with a central figure, 16in. square, 18th century. (Christie's) $598

A tapestry cushion, woven in many colors with a parrot sitting on a branch, 12 x 17in., the tapestry 17th century. (Christie's) $1,540

A beadwork lace box, worked in colored beads, the lid with a medallion of the bust of a lady surrounded by branches of fruit and flowers, 16 x 11in., mid 17th century. (Christie's) $2,310

A beadwork tea cosy, worked in grisaille beads with a spray of oak leaves and acorns, 10 x 12in., 19th century. (Christie's) $56

A late 19th century Japanese wall hanging, designed with an eagle and a dragon amongst clouds and leaves, 4.6m. x 2.97m. (Phillips) $5,049

A crewelwork panel, England, 18th century, intertwining trees and floral vines over hillock with berries, squirrel, deer, rabbit and dog, 80 x 100in. (Robt. W. Skinner Inc.) $1,400

A late 18th century en grisaille pastoral silkwork picture depicting a shepherdess in a rural landscape, 24cm. (Phillips) $522

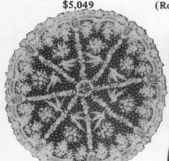

A parasol cover of black net trimmed with applied Brussels motifs including exotic birds and sprays of flowers. (Christie's) $317

A fragment with a delicate repeated pattern of leaves and birds, 4½ x 3½in., Italian, 14th century. (Christie's) $710

An 18th century needlework coverlet, the central Florentine stitch square enclosed by panels of flowers, 41 x 41cm. (Phillips) $1,044

'Autobus', a printed and painted tinplate open 'Berlin' type double deck omnibus, by Lehmann, circa 1912, 8in. long. (Christie's)$1,255

A rare printed and painted tinplate high-wing, cabin monoplane, with two blade propeller and helicopter blades, 8½in. long, German, circa 1920. (Christie's) $304

'The Performing Sea-Lion', a painted tinplate sea-lion with clockwork mechanism, by Lehmann, circa 1910, 7½in. long. (Christie's) $372

A Meccano No. 1 Aeroplane Constructor Outfit, with instructions, in original box, circa 1937. (Christie's) $391

A painted wooden toy stable with stalls and alcoves above, with fretted decorations, 18in. high, French. (Christie's) $260

A painted wooden dolls' house of four bays and three storeys, 50in. high x 46in. wide on stand, circa 1840. (Christie's) $9,058

Dinky Supertoys Foden 'Mobilgas' tanker, fair condition. (Lawrence Fine Arts) $94

Nomura Toys, battery operated tinplate Robbie the Robot, 32.5cm., 1956. (Phillips) $1,436

A printed and painted tinplate motorcycle and sidecar, lithographed gentleman rider and lady passenger, 4½in. long, German, 1920's. (Christie's) $706

A 1930's Lines Bros. pedal car with wooden body and chassis, mock honeycomb radiator grill, and pneumatic tyres 47in. long. (Andrew Hartley) $1,379

A rare and early hand enamelled tinplate woman pushing a cart, with caged goose, probably by Gunthermann, circa 1903, 7½in. long. (Christie's) $864

A Marx clockwork Rookie Pilot, boxed. (Phillips) $155

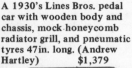

A painted wooden dolls' house of two separated storeys, with original wall and some floor coverings. (Christie's) $529

A good metal miniature toy zoetrope on ornate metal base with a quantity of picture strips, marked 'Made in Germany'. (Christie's) $372

A Meccano No. 2 Electrical Experiments Set, in original box, 1930's. (Christie's) $352

'Caravan Novelty', a lithographed tinplate gypsy caravan, by Chad Valley for Jacobs, circa 1937, 6¼in. long. (Christie's) $293

A painted wooden dolls' house, simulating stone with red roof and bay windows flanking the marbelized porch, 43in. high. (Christie's) $1,208

A Dinky 917 Guy van, advertising 'Spratt's', in original paintwork, fair condition, unboxed. (Lawrence Fine Arts) $225

A Carette lithographed tinplate clockwork model of a four seater tonneau, with rubber tyred spoked wheels, handbrake, and side lamps, 33cm. long. (Henry Spencer)$3,211

A rare humorous composition toy, modelled as a red faced man with startled eyes hanging on to a runaway donkey, 6½in. long, mid 19th century, German. (Christie's) $1,157

A short plush covered nodding Boston terrier, with pull growl and lower jaw movement, 22in. long, circa 1910, French. (Christie's) $557

A fine late 19th century dolls' house, the front removable to reveal a six roomed interior with original papers, 41½in. wide. (Phillips) $1,267

An early Japanese lithographed tinplate travelling boy, with clockwork mechanism, 1930's, 8in. high. (Christie's) $783

A mahogany dolls' house of two bays and two storeys with castellated bow window, 47in. high, late 19th century. (Christie's) $2,616

An early hand painted maid, standing at an ironing board, holding an iron and a winged collar, 8in. high, probably by Gunthermann, circa 1903. (Christie's) $929

French Dinky Supertoys, Set No. 60, Coffret Cadeau Avions, in original box. (Christie's) $464

A late nineteenth century painted wood and composition rocking horse, with jockey rider, 10½in. long, German. (Christie's) $1,236

Dinky Supertoys, 923 Big Bedford Van, advertising 'Heinz 57 Varieties', with Baked Bean tin on sides, in original paintwork. (Christie's) $288

A model of a Georgian house with portico entrance and large bay, two storeys with basement, the case 19in. wide. (Christie's) $1,143

A Kingsbury Sunbeam racer, tinplate clockwork model complete with driver, steering wheel and original box. (David Lay) $929

A short golden plush covered standing clockwork bear, with broom handle attached to his right paw, 8in. high, circa 1933. (Christie's) $723

Dinky pre-war Set No. 60 Aeroplanes (2nd Issue), including Imperial Airway Liner, D. H. Leopard Moth, Percival Gull, Low Wing Monoplane, General 'Monospar' and Cierva Autogiro, in original box, circa 1934. (Christie's) $7,816

A skin covered horse on wheels with leather saddle and bridle, 16in. high, circa 1890. (Christie's) $489

Britains full band of the Coldstream Guards, 22 pieces in all, in 'Armies of the World' box, no. 37. (Lawrence Fine Arts) $438

Britains rare set 1431 Army Co-operation Autogiro with pilot, in original box, 1937. (Phillips) $3,969

Dinky Lyons 'Swiss Rolls' Guy van No.514, boxed. (Hobbs & Chambers) $598

TOYS

Dinky Supertoys 514 Guy Van, advertising 'Slumberland', in original paintwork, with box. (Christie's) $329

'Mac 700', a printed and painted tinplate motorbike and rider, with clockwork mechanism, by Arnold, W. Germany, circa 1955 (one arm damaged, slightly worn), 7½in. long. (Christie's) $247

Dinky Supertoys, 919 Guy van, advertising 'Golden Shred', in original paintwork, unboxed, slightly chipped. (Lawrence Fine Arts) $139

A rubber inflatable Mickey Mouse 41cm. high. (Phillips) $48

Dinky rare pre-war French Set No. 60 Avions, including Arc-en-ciel, Potez Type 58, Hanriot Type 180T, Dewoitine Type 500, Breguet Type Corsaire and Autogire, in original box, circa 1937. (Christie's) $10,285

A very fine French tinplate dolls' pram, the body with blue and gold lithograph paintwork, 23cm. (Phillips) $2,992

Scamold clockwork die-cast Grand Prix racing cars, including ERA, Maserati and Alta, in original boxes. (Christie's)
Three $782

Lineol made 5/32, Wehrmacht standard bearer, tin color one shoulder, 1938. (Phillips) $113

Britains set 1321, large armored car with swivelling gun, khaki finish with white rubber treaded tyres in original box (E-G, box G)1937. (Phillips) $529

"Zulu", EPL 721, a painted and lithographed tinplate ostrich pulling a two wheel mail cart, by Lehmann, circa 1920, 7½in. long. (Christie's) **$1,131**

Marx, clockwork Dagwoods aeroplane boxed. (Phillips) **$311**

Britains rare individual United States cavalry figures in steel helmets, probably exported to USA without set boxes, circa 1940. (Phillips) **$1,228**

Lesney Model No.12. A horse bus. (David Lay) **$81**

Dinky Supertoys 918 Guy Van, advertising 'Ever Ready', in original paintwork, with box. (Christie's) **$288**

A Meccano No. 1 Motor Car Constructor Outfit, assembled as a Grand Prix racing car, with clockwork mechanism, circa 1934, (Christie's) **$658**

Dinky Supertoys 514 Guy Van, advertising 'Slumberland', in original paintwork, with box. (Christie's) **$309**

A Spot On Ford Zodiac No.100, original factory box. (Hobbs & Chambers) **$95**

A rare painted and lithographed tinplate hansom cab, with brown galloping horse on a metal wheel, driver and passenger, in original paintwork, probably by Gunthermann, circa 1908, 8½in. long. (Christie's) $1,954

A Dinky 920 Guy Warrior Van 'Heinz' Tomato Ketchup, boxed. (Phillips) $1,496

Chad Valley 10005 blue and cream passenger coach, 30cm. (Phillips) $294

Gama "Cadillac 300", a printed and painted tinplate car, with friction-drive mechanism, adjustable front wheel, W. Germany, circa 1954, 12in. long. (Christie's) $925

Marx-Sparkling fighter rocket ship, 30cm. long. (Phillips) $224

Dinky Supertoys 923 Big Bedford Van, advertising 'Heinz 57 Varieties', with Baked Beans tins on sides, in original box. (Christie's) $309

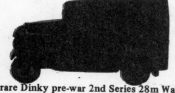

A rare Dinky pre-war 2nd Series 28m Wakefield's Castrol Oil Van, with metal wheels, tinplate radiator, finished in green and inscribed in red. (Christie's) $1,234

A Dinky DY-1 1968 E Type Jaguar, this is the prototype of the first Dinky model produced commercially by Matchbox Toys Limited in November 1968, 10.3cm. (Phillips) $636

A Meccano motor car
Constructor, no. 2, assembled
as a Grand Prix racing car,
circa 1934. (Lawrence Fine
Arts) $1,222

Marx spring action two door
saloon finished in red, black
and brown, 19.5cm. (Phillips)
          $86

A printed and painted tinplate
"Carter Paterson" delivery
van, with clockwork mechanism, 9¾in. long, by Tipp, circa
1930. (Christie's)$1,522

'Echo', EPL No. 725, a rare
printed and painted tinplate
motor cyclist, with clockwork
mechanism, 8¾in. long, by
Lehmann, circa 1910.
(Christie's) $3,235

A carpenter made wooden
dolls' house with white painted
gothic details and brass pediment, 23in. high. (Christie's)
          $1,580

'Dux-Astroman', No. 150, a
plastic robot, with battery
operated remote control, by
Dux, W. Germany, 1950's,
12in. high. (Christie's)
          $304

A tinplate pool player, at a
printed and painted tinplate
pool table, with clockwork
mechanism, 7¼in. long,
stamped P.W., German, circa
1912. (Christie's) $660

Britains Hunting Display Set
No. 235, "Full Cry", in
original green illustrated box,
circa 1939. (Christie's)
          $446

Lineol made model of Goering
standing, Luftwaffe uniform,
holding Marshal's baton, 1939.
(Phillips) $170

Greppert and Kelch, spring action lithographed tipper lorry finished in orange and black, 21cm. long. (Phillips) $405

'Sparkling Rocket Fighter Ship', a printed and painted tinplate rocket fighter, by Marx, American, 1950's, 12in. long. (Christie's) $361

Distler, open top bus 'Health Virol Strength/Bovril' advertisement, with moving bus conductor, 22.5cm., circa 1929. (Phillips) $709

'Answer-Game', a lithographed and painted tinplate Robot, battery operated, computes simple mathematics, by Ichida, Japan, 1960's, 36.5cm. high. (Christie's) $537

A Meccano No. 1 Aeroplane Constructor Outfit, assembled as a light biplane, silver plates, R.A.F. roundels, circa 1931. (Chrsitie's) $293

A Wilhelm Krauss spring action lithographed AA Road Services motorcyclist and sidecar, 18cm. long. (Phillips) $845

A Wells printed and painted tinplate Rolls-Royce 'Coupe de Ville' limousine, with clock-work mechanism, 8¾ in. long British, circa 1950. (Christie's) $297

A Dinky 918 Guy van, advertising 'Ever Ready', in original paintwork. (Lawrence Fine Arts) $188

A printed and painted tinplate elephant and Indian native boy rider, 7in. high, probably German, circa 1925. (Christie's) $464

1955 Daimler DK 400 Regina limousine,
coachwork by Hooper, engine: six-cylinder,
overhead valve, 4,617cc., 130bhp.; gearbox:
four-speed, pre-selective with fluid flywheel;
brakes: vacuum servo-assisted hydraulic drum.
(Christie's) $11,088

1947 Daimler DE36 5.5 litre Straight Eight
touring limousine, coachwork by Hooper,
engine: eight cylinders in line, overhead
valves, 5,460cc., 36hp.; gearbox: four-speed
preselective with fluid flywheel. (Christie's)
                                      $12,012

1949 Healey Silverstone Alpine two seater,
engine: Riley four-cylinder, overhead valve,
2,443cc.; gearbox: four-speed synchromesh;
brakes: four-wheel hydraulic drum.
(Christie's) $96,096

1952 Bentley MkVI four door sports saloon,
coachwork by Freestone & Webb, engine:
six-cylinder, overhead inlet side exhaust
valve, 4,566cc., 33.7hp.; gearbox. four-speed
synchromesh. (Christie's) $19,404

1975 Ferrari 312T Grand Prix single seater,
Chassis No. 018. (Christie's)
                    $450,044

1961 Jaguar 3.8 Mk2 four door sports
saloon,engine: six-cylinder, twin overhead
camshaft, 3,781cc., 220 bhp.; gearbox: three-
speed automatic; brakes: four-wheel hydraulic servo disc. (Christie's) $12,474

1968 Jaguar E-type 4.2litre two seater fixed
head coupe, engine six-cylinder, twin overhead camshaft, triple SU carburettors,
4,235cc., 265bhp.; gearbox: four-speed
synchromesh. (Christie's) $37,884

A 1955 Daimler Conquest Century saloon
with automatic transmission, sold with
owner's handbook and old style log book.
(Bearne's) $1,496

1969 Jensen FF 6.3 litre Grand Touring four seater, engine: Chrysler vee-eight, overhead valve, 6,276cc., 330bhp.; gearbox: Torque-flite three-speed automatic. (Christie's)
$17,556

1932 Morris Cowley four door saloon, engine: four-cylinder, side valve, 1,548cc., 11.9hp.; gearbox: three-speed sliding mesh; brakes: four-wheel hydraulic. (Christie's)
$10,718

1935-36 3.8 litre Alfa Romeo 8C-35 Grand Prix single seater, Chassis No. 50013, Scuderia Ferrari number: 65. (Christie's)
$2,837,247

1929 Rolls-Royce Phantom II replica bodied open tourer, engine: six-cylinder, overhead valve, 7,668cc., 40/50hp.; gearbox: four-speed sliding mesh. (Christie's)
$68,376

An American International 50cwt. model SL 34, 22.5hp., four cylinder speed truck, registration number TH 1451, first registered in May 1934, manufactured by the International Harvester Company, Chicago. (John Francis) $7,875

1937 Ford Model 78 V8 'Woody' shooting brake, engine: vee-eight, side valve, 3,622cc., 30hp.; geargox: three-speed synchromesh; brakes: four-wheel mechanical. (Christie's)
$12,936

1933 Austin Seven four seat tourer, engine: four-cylinder, side valve, 474cc., 7.8hp.; gearbox: sliding mesh; brakes: four-wheel mechanical. (Christie's) $5,913

1955 MG TF1500 sports two seater, engine: four-cylinder, overhead valve, 1,496cc., 63bhp.; gearbox: four-speed synchromesh; brakes: four-wheel drum hydraulic; suspension: independent front, semi-elliptic rear. (Christie's)
$20,328

1977 Ferrari 308GTB, engine: vee-eight, double overhead camshafts per bank, 2,962cc., 250bhp.; gearbox: five-speed synchromesh; brakes: four-wheel disc. (Christie's) $75,768

1973 Ferrari 365 GT4 Grand Touring 2-2, coachwork by Pininfarina, engine: vee-twelve, double overhead camshafts per bank, 4,390cc., 320bhp.; gearbox: five-speed synchromesh; brakes: four-wheel servo disc. (Christie's) $55,440

1962 Chevrolet Corvette two seat roadster, engine: vee-eight, overhead valve, 5,360cc., 300 bhp.; gearbox: four-speed synchromesh; brakes: four-wheel servo-assisted drum. (Christie's) $25,872

1937 Morris Eight Series II four door saloon, engine: four-cylinder, side valve, 918cc., 8hp.; gearbox: three-speed synchromesh, brakes: four-wheel hydraulic. (Christie's) $2,587

1935 MG NB Magnette four seat tourer, engine: six-cylinder, overhead camshaft, 1,271cc., 57bhp.; gearbox: four-speed sliding mesh; brakes: four-wheel mechanical.(Christie's) $42,304

1925/6 Genestin G6 four door tourer engine: four-cylinder, 1,200cc., 7CV/10hp., RAC rating; gearbox: three-speed sliding mesh; suspension: leaf spring; brakes: four-wheel mechanical, right-hand drive. (Christie's) $14,784

1968 Aston Martin DBS grand touring four seater, engine: six-cylinder, twin overhead camshaft, four-litres, 282bhp.; gearbox: Borg Warner automatic; brakes: four-wheel servo disc. (Christie's) $31,416

1929 Rolls-Royce Phantom II Dual Cowl Phaeton, replica coachwork by Jarvis and Brockman, engine: six-cylinder, overhead valve, 7,668cc.; 40/50hp. (Christie's) $73,920

1972 4.4 litre Ferrari 365GTS/4 Daytona Spyder, Chassis no. 14737. (Christie's) $587,015

1937 Cord 812 Beverly four door sedan, engine: Lycoming vee-eight. side valve. 4,729cc.; gearbox: four-speed with electro-vacuum pre-selector shift and front wheel drive; brakes: four-wheel hydraulic. (Christie's) $57,288

A Triumph model 'H' 550cc. motorbike combination, first registered in 1923, registration number DE 3583, engine no. 86108, with log book. (John Francis) $2,100

1937 1.5 litre Supercharged Maserati 6CM 'Vetturetta', Chassis No. 1542, Engine No. 1542. (Christie's) $371,776

1912, Wall Wallcycar, engine: precision single-cylinder, air-cooled, four-stroke, 500cc., 4¼hp.; gearbox: two-speed epicyclic with shaft final drive, brakes: on rear wheel. (Christie's) $112,728

1911 Studebaker Flanders 20 two seat roadster, engine: four-cylinder, side valve, 2,554cc., 15/20hp.; gearbox: three-speed sliding mesh in unit with rear axle; brakes: rear wheel mechanical. (Christie's) $16,632

1906 Rolls-Royce Light Twenty two seater, engine: four-cylinder, overhead inlet valves, side exhaust valves. (Christie's) $554,400

1971 Citroen SM two door sports saloon, engine: Maserati vee-six cylinder, twin over-head camshafts, per bank, 2,670cc., 180bhp.. gearbox: five-speed synchromesh, front-wheel drive. (Christie's) $11,088

A molded copper cow weathervane, probably Cushing & White, Waltham, Massachusetts, late 19th century, flattened full bodied figure of standing cow, 25in. long. (Robt. W. Skinner Inc.) $3,250

A copper and zinc horse and sulky weathervane, attributed to W. A. Snow, Boston, Massachusetts, late 19th century, 37in. wide. (Robt. W. Skinner Inc.) $8,000

A cast iron prancing horse weathervane, Rochester Iron Works, third quarter 19th century, the prancing horse with raised foreleg and wavy sheet metal tail, 27¾ x 36¼in. (Christie's) $4,950

A fine and rare molded and gilt copper weathervane, American, 19th century, modelled in the form of a centaur with bow and arrow, retaining traces of original gilding, 32in. high, 40in. long. (Christie's) $71,500

Cast zinc and copper weathervane, by J. Howard & Company, West Bridgewater, Massachusetts, circa 1875, 24¾in. wide. (Robt. W. Skinner Inc.) $3,000

A painted zinc horse weathervane, America, 19th century, flattened, full bodied figure of standing horse, with applied ears and glass eyes, approx. 29in. long. (Robt. W. Skinner Inc.) $2,700

A cast iron horse weathervane, American, 19th century, of a full bodied figure of a horse with raised foreleg, 35in. wide. (Christie's) $8,250

A molded copper trotting horse weathervane, America, 19th century, flattened full bodied figure of Black Hawk, 16in. high. (Robt. W. Skinner Inc.) $3,100

Large molded zinc and copper horse weathervane, America, 19th century, flattened full bodied figure of 'Colonel Patchen' (bullet holes). (Robt. W. Skinner Inc.) $3,000

A copper and zinc cow weathervane, America, late 19th century, the full bodied copper figure of standing cow, 43in. long. (Robt. W. Skinner Inc.) $1,800

Sheet copper weathervane, America, 19th century, the finial in the form of a sunflower molded in the full round, above a square banneret, 37in. wide (Robt. W Skinner Inc.) $550

A molded sheet iron weathervane, American, late 18th/early 19th century, molded in the form of a swell bodied rooster, 54.3cm. high. (Christie's) $132

A copper and zinc horse weathervane, attributed to A. L. Jewell & Co., Waltham, Massachusetts, 19th century, 29in. long. (Robt. W. Skinner Inc.) $4,000

A molded and gilt copper weathervane, American, molded as a standing rooster with a sheet iron tail on a feathered arrow, 25in. high, 32in. long. (Christie's) $1,210

Moulded gilt copper weathervane, America, 19th century, figure of an eagle with outspread wings perched above a sphere, 19in. high. (Robt. W. Skinner Inc.) $2,600

A copper and zinc banneret weathervane, America, 19th century, surmounted by cast lightning bolt and ball finial, regilded, 72in. high, 66in. wide. (Robt. W. Skinner Inc.) $1,600

WOOD

An Indian ebony watch and ink stand, decorated with five elephants and with a quill rest, 8in. high. (Phillips) $185

An inlaid wood trying plane, America, 19th century, the stock and wedge of plane inlaid with contrasting woods and bone in variety of Masonic symbols, 23in. long. (Robt. W. Skinner Inc.) $900

A crow decoy, attributed to Gus Wilson, Maine, first half 20th century, with carved wings and tail, 9½in. high. (Robt. W. Skinner Inc.) $550

A 19th century English mahogany bust of the young Queen Victoria, 47.5cm. high. (Christie's) $1,240

A George III giltwood wall bracket, with pierced zoomorphic mask flanked by scrolling foliage, 15½in. high. (Christie's) $14,190

An unusual mid 19th century boxwood 'buxer dog' head inkwell, the well modelled head with glass eyes and bone teeth, 11cm. (Phillips) $898

A carved and painted blue jay, carved by A. Elmer Crowell, East Harwich, Massachusetts, early 20th century, life-size figure, 23.1cm. high. (Robt. W. Skinner Inc.)$1,100

A lacquered rosewood and gilt panel by N. Brunet, deeply carved in intaglio with two pumas by a lakeside, mounted on giltwood frame, 50.7cm. x 99.5cm. (Christie's) $4,675

A 19th century carved and painted hardwood Indian tobacco figure, 72cm. high. (Phillips) $1,346

WOOD

A George II carved giltwood picture frame with sanded and beaded slip, 79 x 90in. overall. (Christie's) $3,496

A 19th century carved wood ship's figurehead, in the form of a semi-clad blonde maiden rising from acanthus scrolls, 93cm. (Osmond Tricks) $543

A painted wooden scale tray, late 19th/early 20th century, depicting a farm scene, 8¼in. wide. (Christie's) $66

An Anglo-Dutch mahogany and wire birdcage with a central dome surmounted by a finial, early 19th century, 38in. high. (Christie's) $5,676

A Norwegian birchwood tankard of plain cylindrical form with slightly domed lid, 7¾in. high, 18th century (lacks thumbpiece). (Bearne's) $616

A carved and painted pine rooster by William Schimmel, Cumberland Valley, Pennsylvania, 1865-1890, painted yellow with carved red comb, 3¾in. long. (Christie's) $4,400

One of a pair of Regency gilt wood wall brackets, the D-shaped shelves with entrelac edges, 13in. high. (Christie's) Two $13,244

A carved wooden butter stamp, Pennsylvania, 19th century, depicting a stylized tulip, 4in. diam. (Christie's) $418

A carved and painted wood male figure by Henry Boehm, Allentown, Pennsylvania, circa 1920, modelled in the form of a man with a pipe, 12½in. high. (Christie's) $495

WOOD

An eider decoy, Monhegan Island, Maine, late 19th century, hollow carved with inletted head, (age cracks, paint and wood loss), 11in. high, 21in. long. (Robt. W. Skinner Inc.) $19,000

A pair of oak panels of Roman type with portraits in profile of a man and woman, early 17th century, 15 x 18in. high. (Lawrence Fine Arts) $743

One of a pair of German carved walnut hunting trophies, circa 1880, depicting captured game, 31in. high. (Robt. W. Skinner Inc.)
Two $750

A Baule male figure, standing with the arms carved in relief, coiffure drawn towards the top of the head, 39cm. high. (Phillips) $309

A George II pine chimney-piece, the later overmantel with a broken pediment and patera-carved frieze, 85in. wide, 140in. high. (Christie's) $13,244

Carved and painted parrot, probably Pennsylvania, late 19th/early 20th century, on a turned wooden base, 8¾in. high. (Robt. W. Skinner Inc.) $1,300

A carved wooden slaw cutter, American, 19th century, with medial blade, 35.9cm. long. (Christie's) $55

A carved wooden slaw cutter, Pennsylvania, Lebanon County, mid 19th century, the shaped handle pierced with six-pointed star, 58.7cm. long. (Christie's) $132

A Congo female fetish figure standing with legs flexed astride, on rounded base, the arms pressed to the side of the body, 35cm. high. (Phillips) $10,320

A carved and painted pine counter top figure of a fireman, signed by Lewis E. Tallier, Roxbury, Massachusetts, circa 1915, 27½in. high. (Christie's) $13,200

A carved pine standing leopard, attributed to Aaron Mountz, Carlisle, Pennsylvania, circa 1875, with carved spots and ears, 10¼in. long. (Christie's) $352

A female Ibeji with aquiline features and a line of worn lentoid scarifications on each cheek, 24.5cm. high. (Phillips) $395

A Yoruba wood headdress, for the Egungun society, Egungun slode, the head craning forwards on the slender neck, 28cm. high, from the Adugbologe carving house at Abeokuta. (Phillips) $309

An oak statuette carved as a female saint, wearing a crown, possibly Catherine of Alexandria, 60cm. high. (Osmond Tricks) $724

An Italian carved giltwood and white painted tondo depicting a Classical warrior, 34in. diam. (Christie's) $1,323

A Congo female fetish figure, crouching on an octagonal stand with layers of material bound between the legs, 22cm. high. (Phillips) $4,300

A cream painted carved wood and plaster rectangular plaque of Louis XVI style, 26½ x 47in. (Christie's) $2,849

'Polska Zakopane Szola', a carved wooden figure by Kut Wladyslaw, the woman standing holding a basket of fruit in front of her, 55.5cm. high. (Christie's) $561

WOOD

Camel carousel figure, possibly New York State, 19th century, the stylized carved and painted figure of a camel with hemp tail and fringed leather and canvas saddle, 48in. wide. (Robt. W. Skinner Inc.) $10,000

Carved spoon rack, America, 19th century, the tombstone shaped crest above a chip carved back mounted with two racks for spoons, 18in. high. (Robt. W. Skinner Inc.) $7,500

Carved and gilded wall bracket of cherub design in the style of Grinling Gibbons. (G. A. Key) $1,662

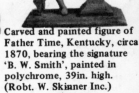

A decorative carved and painted preening yellowleg, A. Elmer Crowell, East Harwich, Massachusetts, 1862-1952, 14in. high. (Christie's) $8,800

A carved pine chimneypiece with molded serpentine shelf, the shaped frieze with a cartouche flanked by cherubs and flowers, 81½in. wide. (Christie's) $5,346

Carved and painted figure of Father Time, Kentucky, circa 1870, bearing the signature 'B. W. Smith', painted in polychrome, 39in. high. (Robt. W. Skinner Inc.) $69,000

Carved and painted counter figure, probably New York City, late 19th century, the stylized head of a bearded Turk wearing a turban, 19½in. high. (Robt. W. Skinner Inc.) $2,500

One of a pair of oak jardinieres, each with open top, the sides carved with scrolling foliate angles, 7½in. high. (Christie's) Two $1,526

One of a pair of Venetian scarlet painted and parcel gilt lanterns, each with three shaped glazed panels, 19th century, 36in. high, excluding poles. (Christie's) Two $4,477

INDEX

INDEX

INDEX

INDEX

INDEX

INDEX

INDEX

INDEX

INDEX